THE WORLD BOOK
ATLAS

World Book, Inc.
a Scott Fetzer company
Chicago

THE WORLD BOOK ATLAS

The World Book Atlas
Published in 2004 by World Book, Inc.

World Book, Inc.
233 N. Michigan Avenue
Chicago, IL 60601

© 2004 by Rand McNally and Company

WORLD BOOK and the GLOBE DEVICE are registered trademarks or
trademarks of World Book, Inc.

ISBN: 0-7166-2653-5
LC: 2003113610

1 2 3 4 5 06 05 04

For information about other World Book publications, visit our Web site at
http://www.worldbook.com, or call **1-800-WORLDBK (967-5325)**. For sales to
schools and libraries call **1-800-975-3250 (United States)**; **1-800-837-5365 (Canada)**.

This Atlas is also published under the title **The World Atlas**
© 2004 Rand McNally and Company.

Cover photo credits:
Jacques Descloitres, MODIS Land Rapid
Response Team/NASA/GSF; © Art Wolfe,
Getty Images; NASA/GSFC and U.S.
Japan ASTER Science Team

Cover design:
Norman Baugher

About the cover
 The large photograph on the cover of The World Book Atlas features one of Earth's most identifiable shapes—the boot-shaped peninsula occupied by Italy. This peninsula extends into the Mediterranean Sea from southern Europe.
 Italy also includes two large islands, Sicily and Sardinia. Sicily, which lies to the west of the boot's tip, is home to Mount Etna, one of the most famous volcanoes in the world. Etna rises on the eastern coast of the island. The volcano's eruptions, which have occurred periodically for thousands of years, are spectacular sights. As seen in the center inset photo, huge fiery clouds rise over the mountain, and glowing rivers of lava flow down its sides.
 The inset photo on the bottom right is an ASTER (Advanced Spaceborne Thermal Emission and Reflection Radiometer) image of a sulfur dioxide plume that originated from Etna's summit. The plume, shown in reddish-purple in this view from space, drifts over the city of Catania and continues over the Ionian Sea.

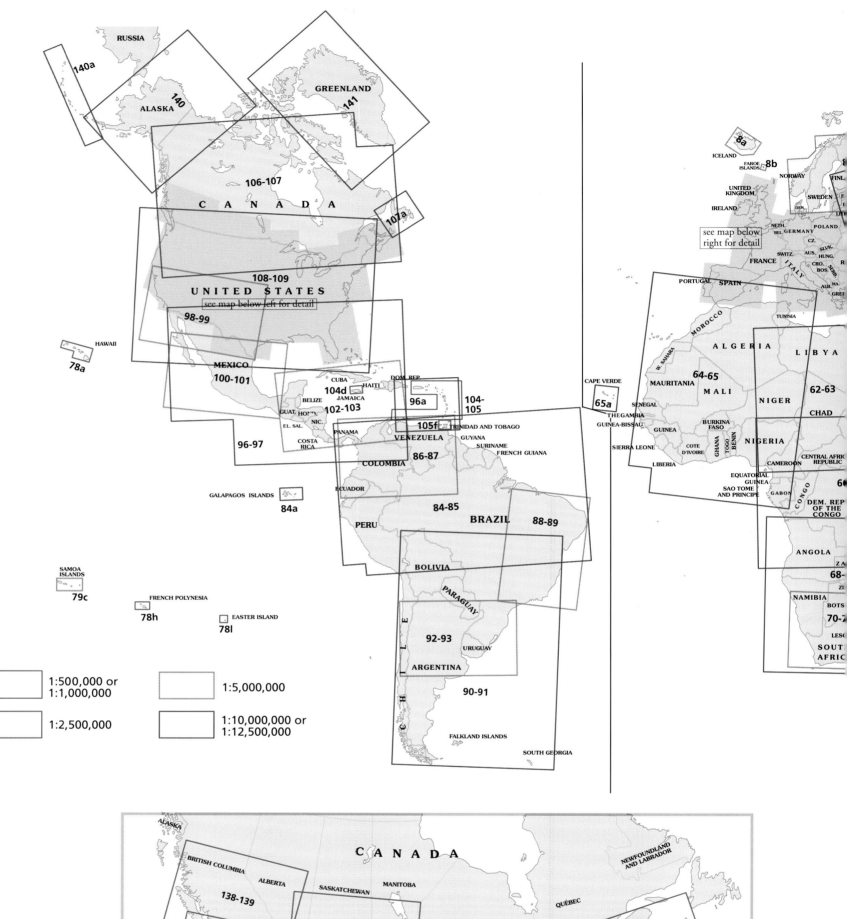
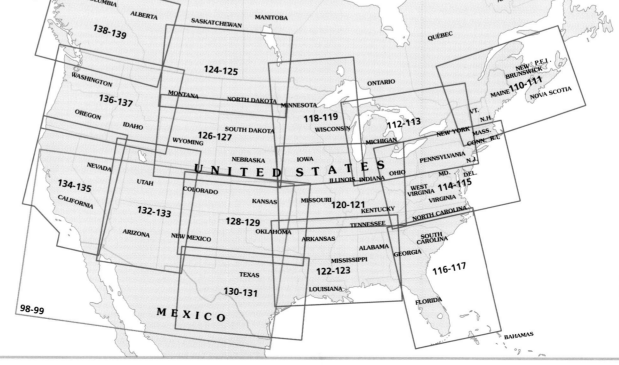

between São Paulo and Rio de Janeiro, Brazil, for example, follow these steps:

figure 7

1) Lay a piece of paper on the right-hand page of the "Eastern Brazil" map found on pages 88-89, lining up its edge with the city dots for São Paulo and Rio de Janeiro. Make a mark on the paper next to each dot (figure 7).

2) Place the paper along the scale bar found below the map, and position the first mark at 0. The second mark falls about a quarter of the way between the 200-mile tick and the 300-mile tick, indicating that the distance separating the two cities is approximately 225 miles (figure 8).

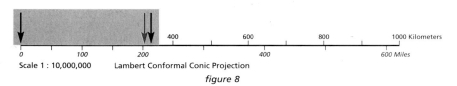

figure 8

3) To confirm this measurement, make a third pencil mark (shown in red in figure 8) at the 200-mile tick. Slide the paper to the left so that this mark lines up with 0. The Rio de Janeiro mark now falls about halfway between the 0 tick and the 50-mile tick. Thus, São Paulo and Rio de Janeiro are indeed approximately 225 (200 + 25) miles apart.

Using the Index to Find Places

One of the most important purposes of an atlas is to help the reader locate cities, towns, and geographic features such as rivers, lakes, and mountains. This atlas uses a "bingo key" indexing system. In the index, found on pages I•1 through I•64, every entry is assigned an alpha-numeric code that consists of a letter and a number. This code relates to the red letters and numbers that run along the perimeter of each map. To locate places or features, follow the steps outlined in this example for the city of Bratsk, Russia.

1) Look up Bratsk in the index. The entry (figure 9) contains the following information: the place name (Bratsk), the name of the country (Russia) in which Bratsk is located, the map reference key (C18) that corresponds to Bratsk's location on the map, and the page number (32) of the map on which Bratsk can be found.

figure 9

2) Turn to the Northwestern Asia map on pages 32-33. Look along either the

left- or right-hand margin for the red letter "C"—the letter code given for Bratsk. The "C" denotes a band that arcs horizontally across the map, between the grid lines representing 55° and 60° North latitude. Then, look along either the top or bottom margin for the red number "18"—the numerical part of the code given for Bratsk. The "18" denotes a widening vertical band, between the grid lines representing 100° and 105° East longitude, which angles from the top center of the map to right-hand edge.

3) Using your finger, follow the horizontal "C" band and the vertical "18" band to the area where they overlap. Bratsk lies within this overlap area.

Physical Maps and Political Maps

Most of the maps in the atlas are physical maps (figure 10) emphasizing terrain, landforms, and elevation. Political maps, as in figure 11, emphasize countries and other political units over topography. The atlas includes political maps of the world and each of the continents except Antarctica.

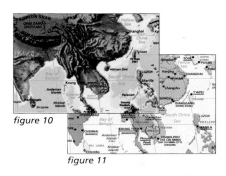

figure 10

figure 11

How Maps Show Topography

The physical maps in this atlas use two techniques to depict Earth's topography. Variations in elevation are shown through a series of colors called hypsometric tints. Areas below sea level appear as a dark green; as the elevation rises, the tints move successively through lighter green, yellow, and orange. Similarly, variations in ocean depth are represented by bathymetric tints. The shallowest areas appear as light blue; darker tints of blue indicate greater depths. The hypsometric/bathymetric scale that accompanies each map identifies, in feet and meters, all of the elevation and depth categories that appear on the map. Principal landforms, such as mountain ranges and valleys, are rendered

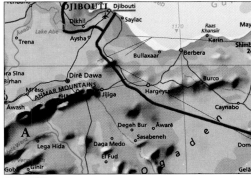

Hypsometric tints

Shaded relief

figure 12

in shades of gray, a technique known as shaded relief. The combination of hypsometric tints and shaded relief provides the map reader with a three-dimensional picture of Earth's surface (figure 12).

Time Zone Map

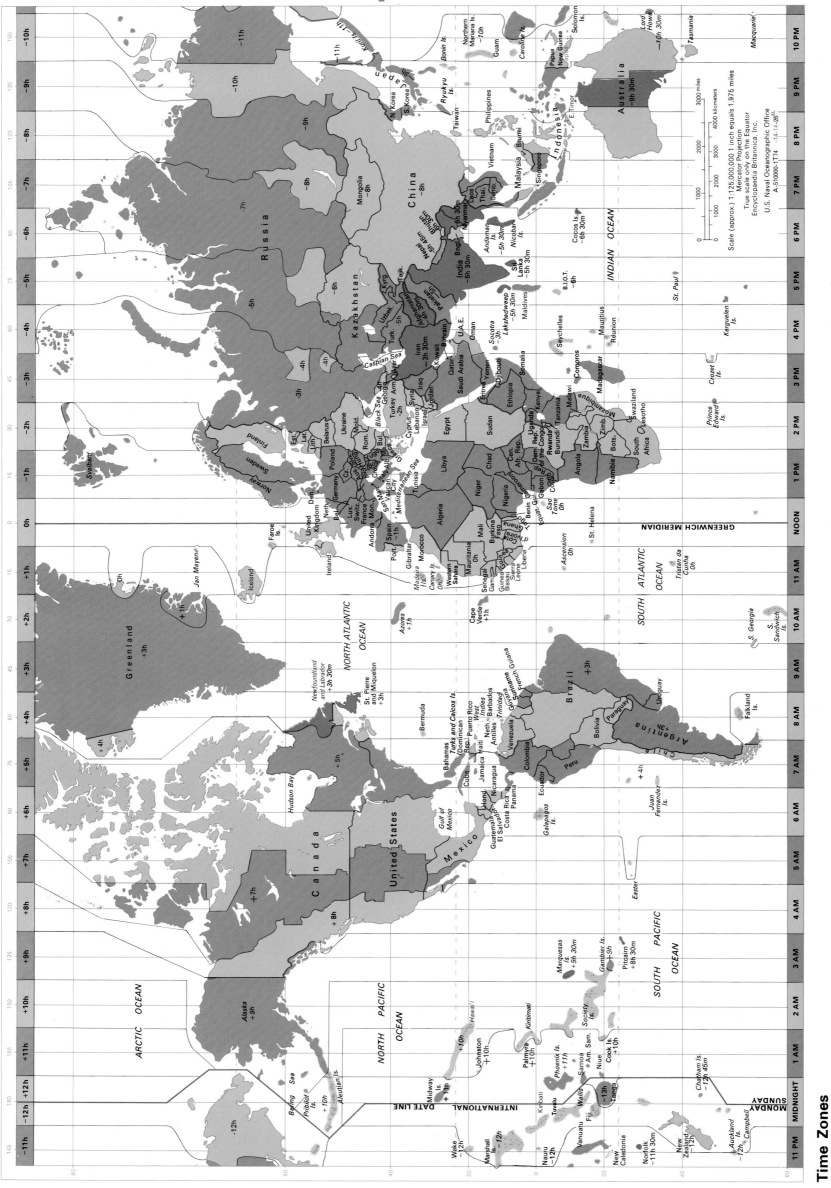

Time Zones

■ Standard time zone of even-numbered hours from Greenwich time

■ Standard time zone of odd-numbered hours from Greenwich time

■ Time varies from the standard time zone by half an hour

■ Time varies from the standard time zone by other than half an hour

h m hours, minutes

The standard time zone system, fixed by international agreement and by law in each country, is based on a theoretical division of the globe into 24 zones of 15° longitude each. The mid-meridian of each zone fixes the hour for the entire zone. The zero time zone extends 7½° east and 7½° west of the Greenwich meridian, 0° longitude. Since the earth rotates toward the east, time zones to the west of Greenwich are earlier, to the east, later. Plus and minus hours at the top of the map are added to or subtracted from local time to find Greenwich time. Local standard time can be determined for any area in the world by adding one hour for each time zone counted in an easterly direction from one's own, or by subtracting one hour for each zone counted in a westerly direction. To separate one day from the next, the 180th meridian has been designated as the international date line. On both sides of the line the time of day is the same, but west of the line it is one day later than it is to the east. Countries that adhere to the international zone system adopt the zone applicable to their location. Some countries, however, establish time zones based on political boundaries, or adopt the time zone of a neighboring unit. For all or part of the year some countries also advance their time by one hour, thereby utilizing more daylight hours each day.

Legend

Hydrographic Features

Perennial river

Seasonal river

Aswan High Dam — Dam

— Falls
Salto Ángel

Los Ángeles Aqueduct — Aqueduct

Lake, reservoir

Seasonal lake

Salt lake

Seasonal salt lake

Dry lake

395 — Lake surface elevation

Swamp, marsh

Reef

Glacier/ice sheet

Topographic Features

764 ▽ — Depth of water

2278 ▲ — Elevation above sea level

1700 ▼ — Elevation below sea level

✕ — Mountain pass

Huo Shan 1774 — Mountain peak/elevation

The highest elevation on each continent is underlined.

The highest elevation in each country is shown in boldface.

Transportation Features

Motorway/Special Highway

Major road

Other road

Trail

Major railway

Other railway

Navigable canal

Tunnel

Ferry

✈ International airport

✦ Other airport

Political Features

International boundaries (First-order political unit)

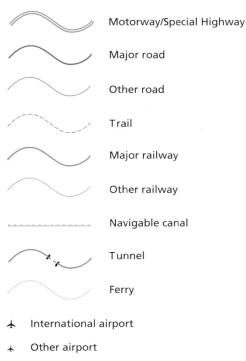

Demarcated

Disputed (de facto)

Disputed (de jure)

Indefinite/undefined

Demarcation line

Internal boundaries

State/province

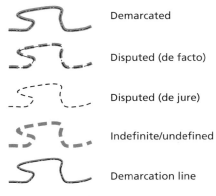

Third-order (counties, oblasts, etc.)

NORMANDIE — Cultural/historic region
(Denmark) — Administering country

Cities and Towns

The size of symbol and type indicates the relative importance of the locality

■ **LONDON**

▣ **CHICAGO**

◉ **Milwaukee**

◎ Tacna

⊙ Iquitos

○ Old Crow

∘ Mettawa

Urban area

Capitals

MEXICO CITY
Bratislava — Country, dependency

RIO DE JANEIRO
Perth — State, province

MANCHESTER
Chester — County

Cultural Features

⬚ or ▪ National park, reservation

▪ Point of interest

Wall

∴ Ruins

Military installation

• Polar research station

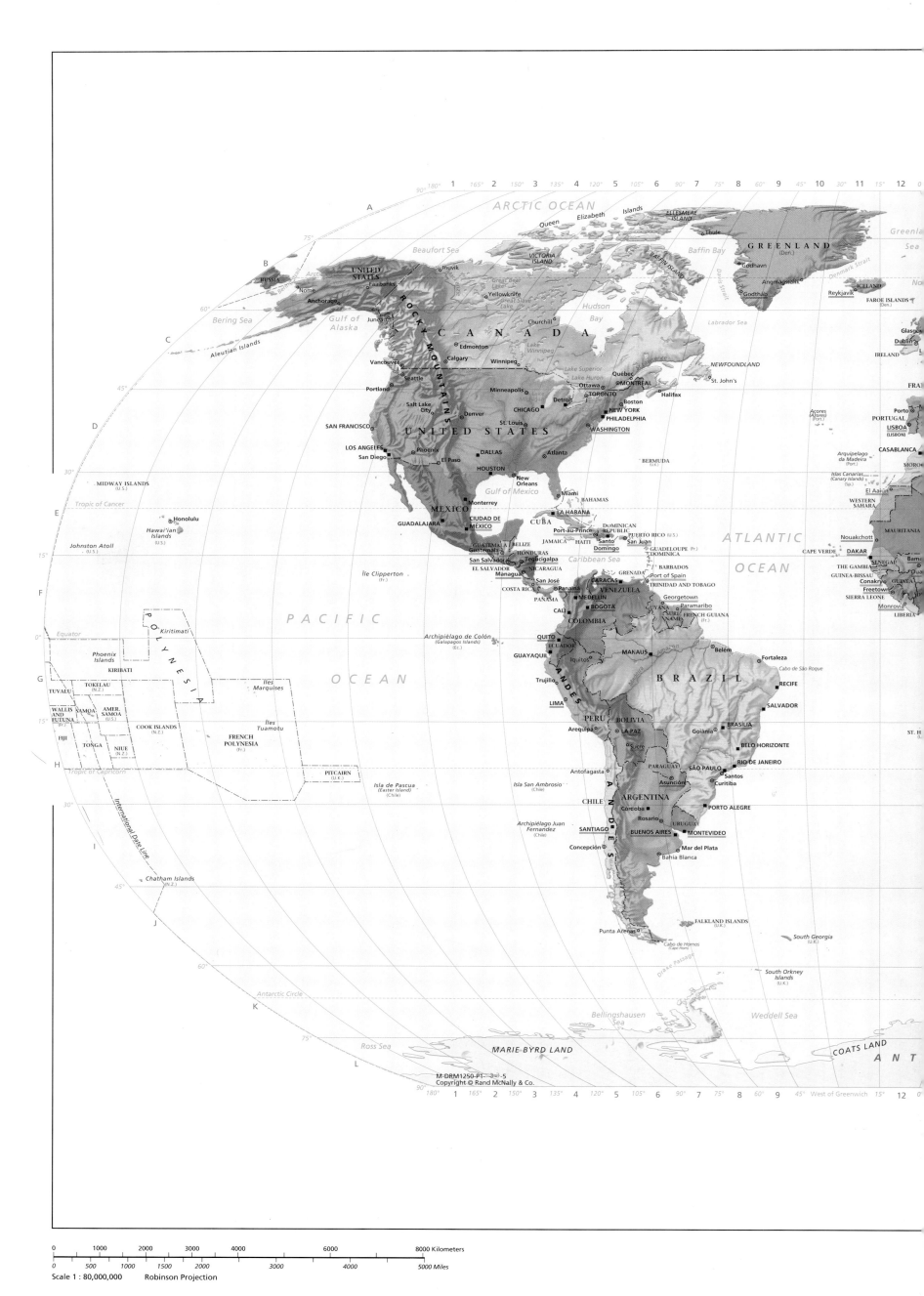

Scale 1 : 80,000,000   Robinson Projection

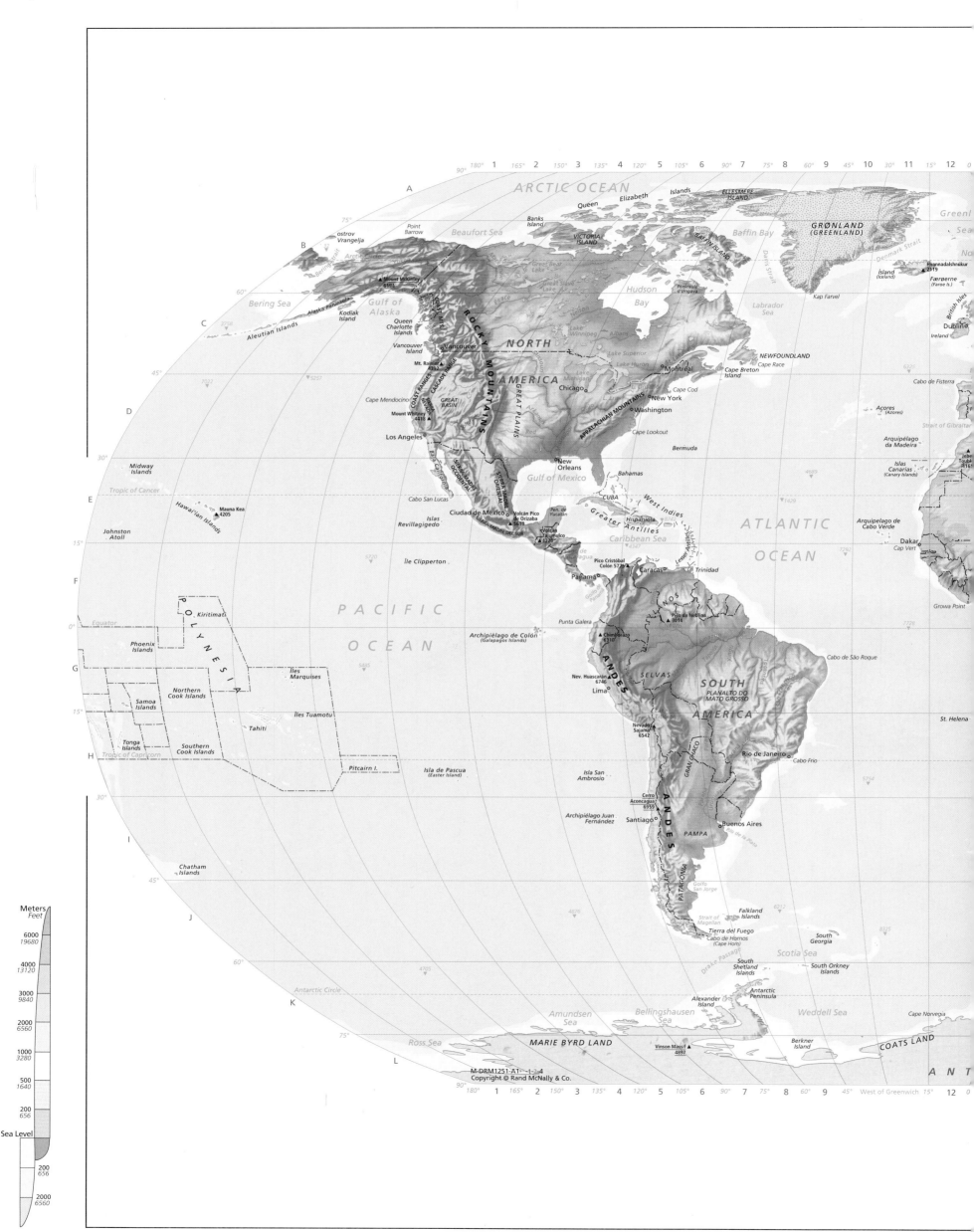

Meters
Feet

6000
19680

4000
13120

3000
9840

2000
6560

1000
3280

500
1640

200
656

Sea Level

200
656

2000
6560

0   1000   2000   3000   4000   6000   8000 Kilometers

0   500   1000   1500   2000   3000   4000   5000 Miles

Scale 1 : 80,000,000   Robinson Projection

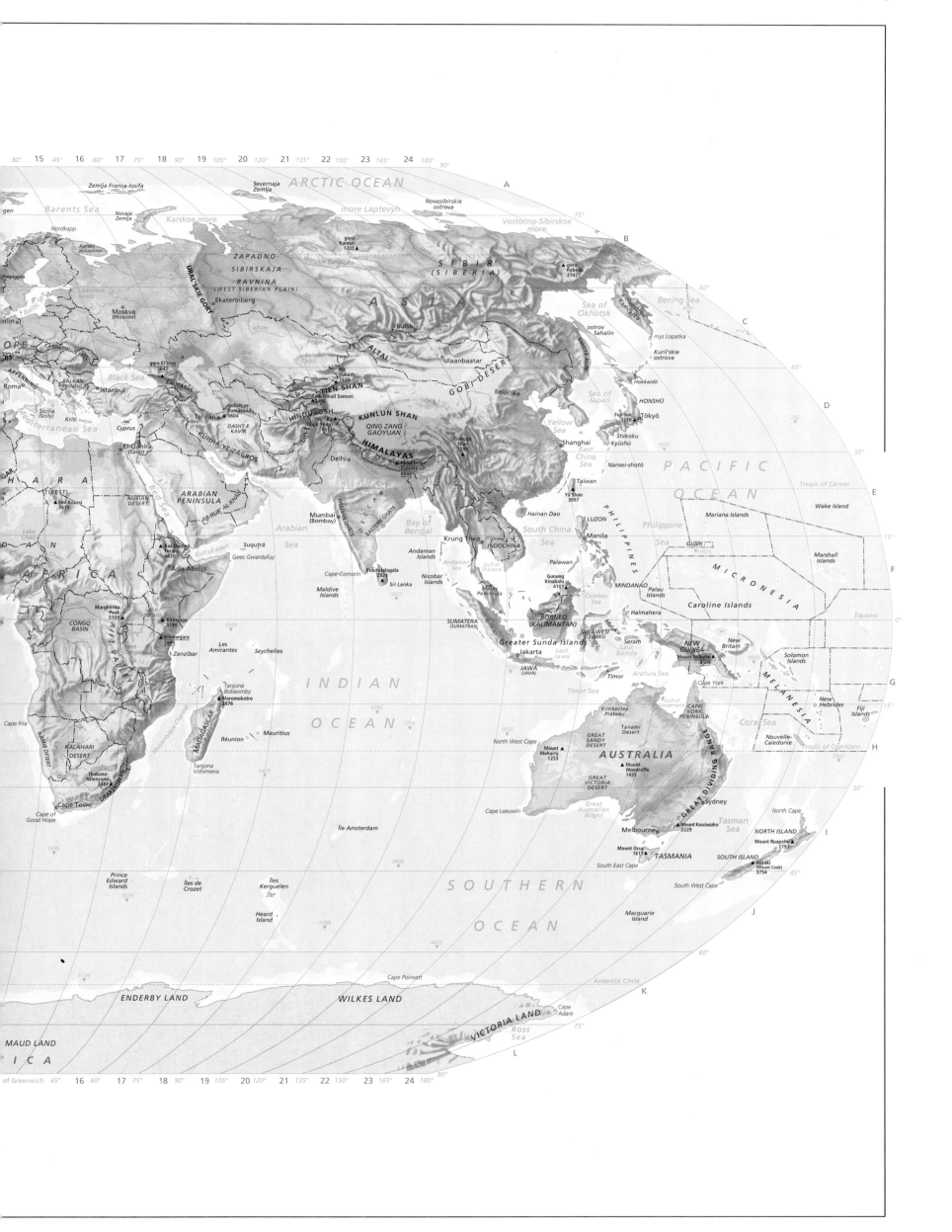

15 30° 16 45° 17 60° 18 75° 19 90° 20 105° 21 120° 22 135° 23 150° 24 165° 180° 90°

Zemlja Franca-Iosifa
Severnaja
Zemlja
ARCTIC OCEAN
A
Barents Sea
Novaja
Zemlja
Novosibirskie
ostrova
Nordkapp
Vostočno-Sibirskoe
more
more Laptevyh
75°
gora
Kamen
1701
B
Koryakskoe
poluostrov
gora
Pobeda
3147
ZAPADNO-
SIBIRSKAJA
RAVNINA
(WEST SIBERIAN PLAIN)
SIBIR'
(SIBERIA)
Severnaja Kamčatka
60°
Bering Sea
Nižnjaja Tunguska
Kr
U
R
A
L
S
K
I
E
G
O
R
Y
Ekaterinberg
A
S
I
A
Sea of
Okhotsk
C
Irkutsk
ostrov
Sahalin
mys Lopatka
45°
Moskva
(Moscow)
Ladožskoe
Balkaš
Irtyš
ALTAI
Ulaanbaatar
Kuril'skie
ostrova
Hokkaido
Ob'
Ishim
Aral
gora El'brus
5642
pik
Pobedy
7439
Beijing
Sea of
Japan
HONSHŪ
D
Black Sea
CAUCASUS
TIEN SHAN
GOBI DESERT
Fuji-san
3776
Tōkyō
Roma
BALKAN
PENINSULA
Istanbul
pik Ismail Samani
7495
HINDUKUSH
KUNLUN SHAN
SHIKOKU
Kyūshū
30°
Sicilia
(Sicily)
Kriti
Golleh-ye
Damavand
5604
Tehran
QING ZANG
GAOYUAN
Yellow
Sea
Nansei-shotō
Cyprus
DASHT-E
KAVIR
Qogir Feng
8611
HIMALAYAS
Gongga
Shan
7590
Shanghai
Mediterranean Sea
El-Qahira
(Cairo)
KUHHĀ-YE ZAGROS
Delhio
Mount
Everest
8846
East
China
Sea
PACIFIC
OCEAN
Tropic of Cancer
E
SAHARA
TIBESTI
Emi Koussi
3415
ARABIAN
PENINSULA
AR-RUB' AL-KHALI
Godavari
Mumbai
(Bombay)
DECCAN
Hainan Dao
South China
LUZON
Wake Island
15°
NUBIAN
DESERT
Arabian
Krung Thep
Sea
Manila
Mariana Islands
Red Sea
Gulf of Aden
Gulf of Oman
Persian Gulf
Andaman
Islands
INDOCHINA
Philippine
Sea
Guam
Lake
Chad
Ras Dashen
Terara
4620
Suquṭrā
Gees Gwardafuy
Andaman
Sea
Gulf of
Thailand
Palawan
Marshall
Islands
F
SUDAN
'Adis Abeba
EASTERN GHATS
WESTERN GHATS
Cape Comorin
Pidurutalagala
2524
Sri Lanka
Nicobar
Islands
Malay
Peninsula
Gunong
Kinabalu
4101
MINDANAO
Palau
Islands
M
I
C
R
O
N
E
S
I
A
AFRICA
Maldive
Islands
Celebes
Sea
Caroline Islands
Equator
0°
CONGO
BASIN
Margherita
Peak
5109
Kirimaya
5199
RIFT VALLEY
Les
Amirantes
Seychelles
SUMATERA
(SUMATRA)
BORNEO
(KALIMANTAN)
SULAWESI
(CELEBES)
MOLUK
Seram
Halmahera
NEW
GUINEA
Mount Wilhelm
4509
New
Britain
G
Kilimanjaro
5895
Zanzibar
Lake Tanganyika
Greater Sunda Islands
Jakarta
Laut
Jawa
Laut
Banda
Solomon
Islands
MELANESIA
Cape Fria
Tanjona
Bobaomby
Maromokotro
2876
INDIAN
JAWA
(JAVA)
Timor
Arafura Sea
Cape York
New
Hebrides
Fiji
Islands
15°
NAMIB DESERT
KALAHARI
DESERT
MADAGASCAR
Réunion
Mauritius
OCEAN
Timor Sea
Kimberley
Plateau
Tanami
Desert
CAPE
YORK
PENINSULA
GREAT DIVIDING RANGE
Nouvelle-
Calédonie
Coral
Sea
H
Thabana-
Ntlenyana
3482
DRAKENSBERG
Orange
Tanjona
Vohimena
North West Cape
GREAT
SANDY
DESERT
Mount
Meharry
1253
AUSTRALIA
Mount
Woodroffe
1435
Tropic of Capricorn
Cape Town
Cape of
Good Hope
Île Amsterdam
Cape Leeuwin
GREAT
VICTORIA
DESERT
Great
Australian
Bight
Sydney
North Cape
30°
Melbourne
Mount Kosciuszko
2229
Tasman
Sea
NORTH ISLAND
Mount Ruapehu
2797
I
Mount Ossa
1617
TASMANIA
SOUTH ISLAND
Aoraki
(Mount Cook)
3754
Prince
Edward
Islands
Îles de
Crozet
Îles
Kerguélen
SOUTHERN
South East Cape
South West Cape
45°
Heard
Island
J
OCEAN
Macquarie
Island
60°
Cape Poinsett
Antarctic Circle
K
ENDERBY LAND
WILKES LAND
VICTORIA LAND
Cape
Adare
75°
MAUD LAND
ANTARCTICA
Ross
Sea
L
of Greenwich 45° 16 60° 17 75° 18 90° 19 105° 20 120° 21 135° 22 150° 23 165° 24 180° 90°

0		200		400			800		1200 Kilometers

0	100	200	400	600	800 Miles

Scale 1 : 12,500,000   Conic Equidistant Projection

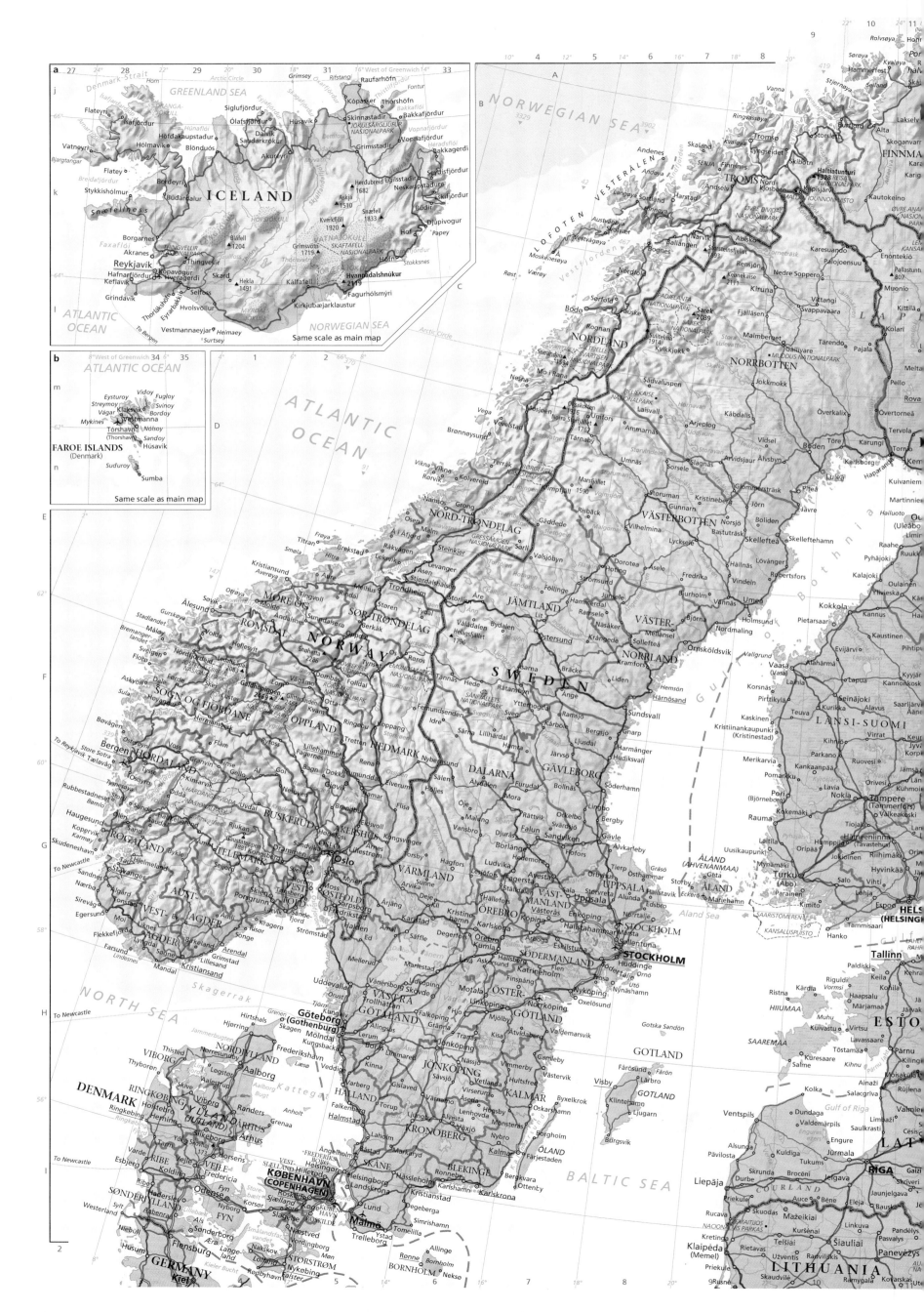

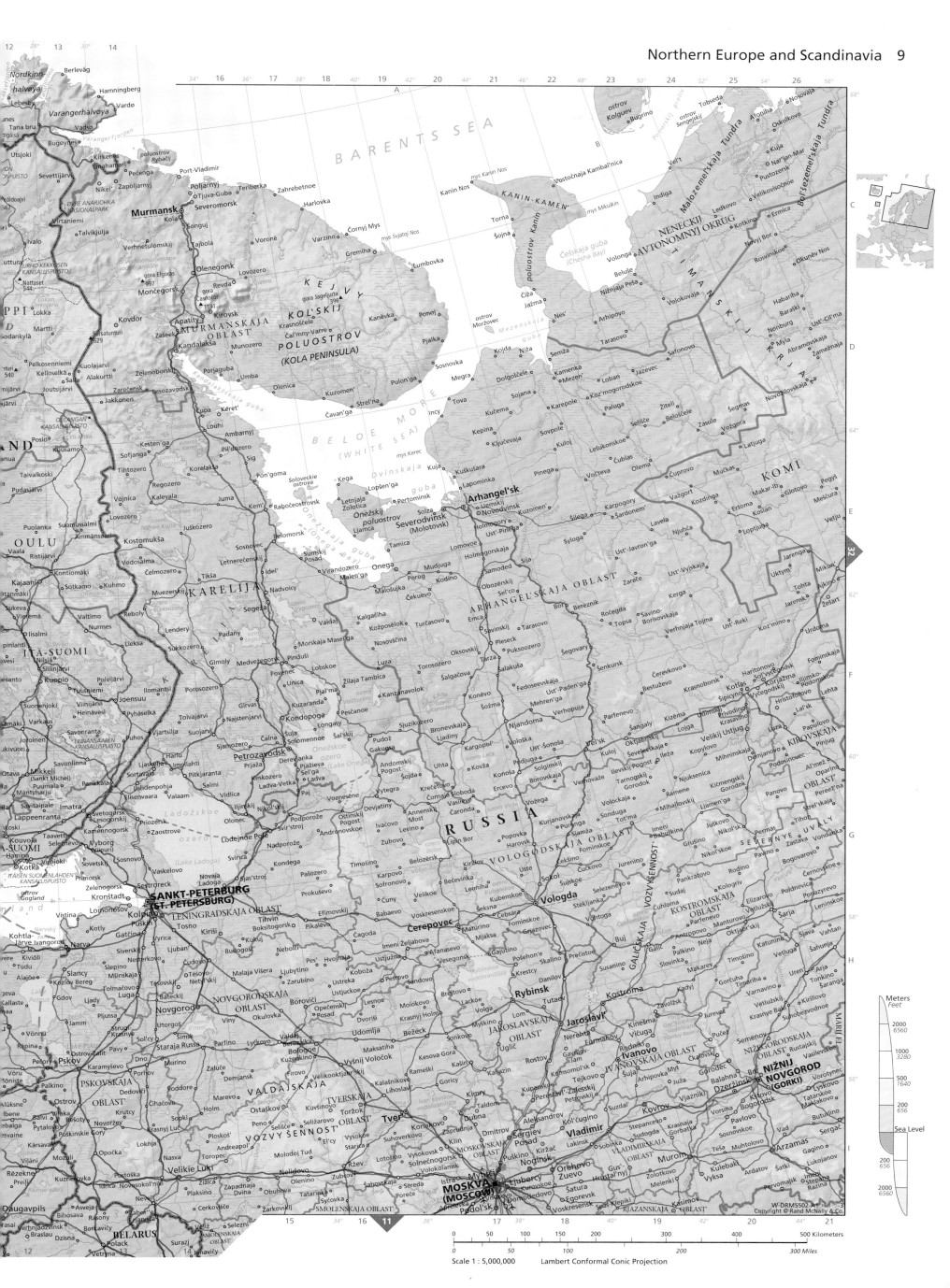

BARENTS SEA

KANIN-KAMEN'

NENECKIJ AVTONOMNYJ OKRUG

TIMANSKIJ KRJAZ

Murmansk

KOL'SKIJ POLUOSTROV
(KOLA PENINSULA)

KEJVY

Mezenskaja guba

KOMI

BELOE MORE
(WHITE SEA)

Čё̆sskaja guba
(Chesha Bay)

Arhangel'sk

Severodvinsk
(Molotovsk)

ARHANGEL'SKAJA OBLAST

OULU

ITÄ-SUOMI

KARELIJA

KIROVSKAJA OBLAST

Petrozavodsk

RUSSIA

VOLOGODSKAJA OBLAST

SEVERNYE UVALY

SANKT-PETERBURG
(ST. PETERSBURG)

Vologda

KOSTROMSKAJA OBLAST

LENINGRADSKAJA OBLAST

Čerepovec

Rybinsk

GALIČSKAJA OBLAST

NOVGORODSKAJA OBLAST

Jaroslavl'

JAROSLAVSKAJA OBLAST

PSKOVSKAJA OBLAST

Novgorod

IVANOVSKAJA OBLAST

Ivanovo

NIŽNIJ NOVGOROD
(GORKI)

NIŽEGORODSKAJA OBLAST

VALDAJSKAJA

TVERSKAJA OBLAST

Tver'

Vladimir

VLADIMIRSKAJA OBLAST

VOZVYŠENNOST'

MOSKVA
(MOSCOW)

Murom

Arzamas

SMOLENSKAJA OBLAST

MOSKOVSKAJA OBLAST

RJAZANSKAJA OBLAST

W-DRM5502-A1
Copyright © Rand McNally & Co.

BELARUS

Meters
Feet
2000
6560
1000
3280
500
1640
200
656
Sea Level
200
656
2000
6560

0   50   100   150   200   300   400   500 Kilometers
0   50   100   200   300 Miles

Scale 1 : 5,000,000   Lambert Conformal Conic Projection

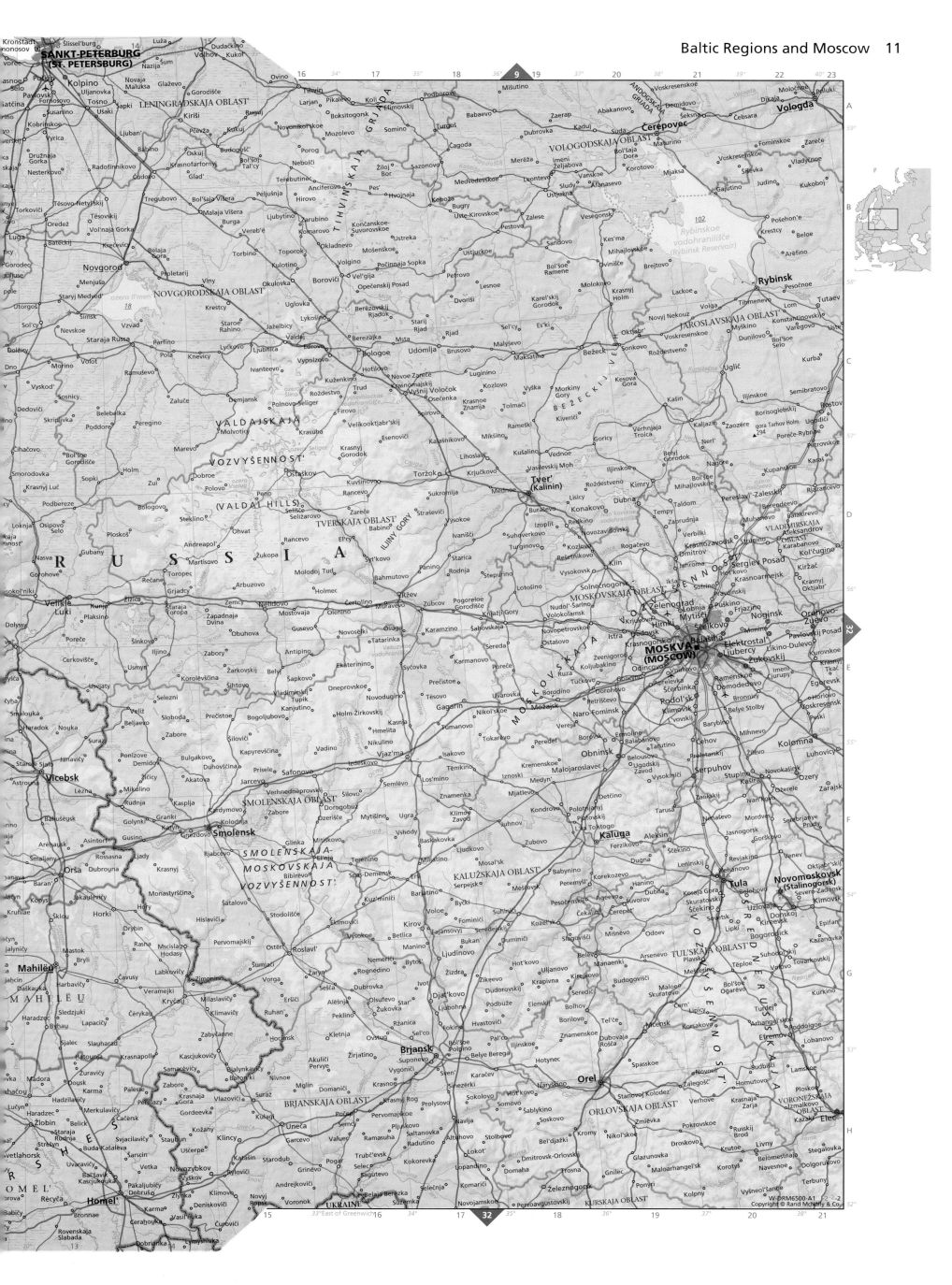

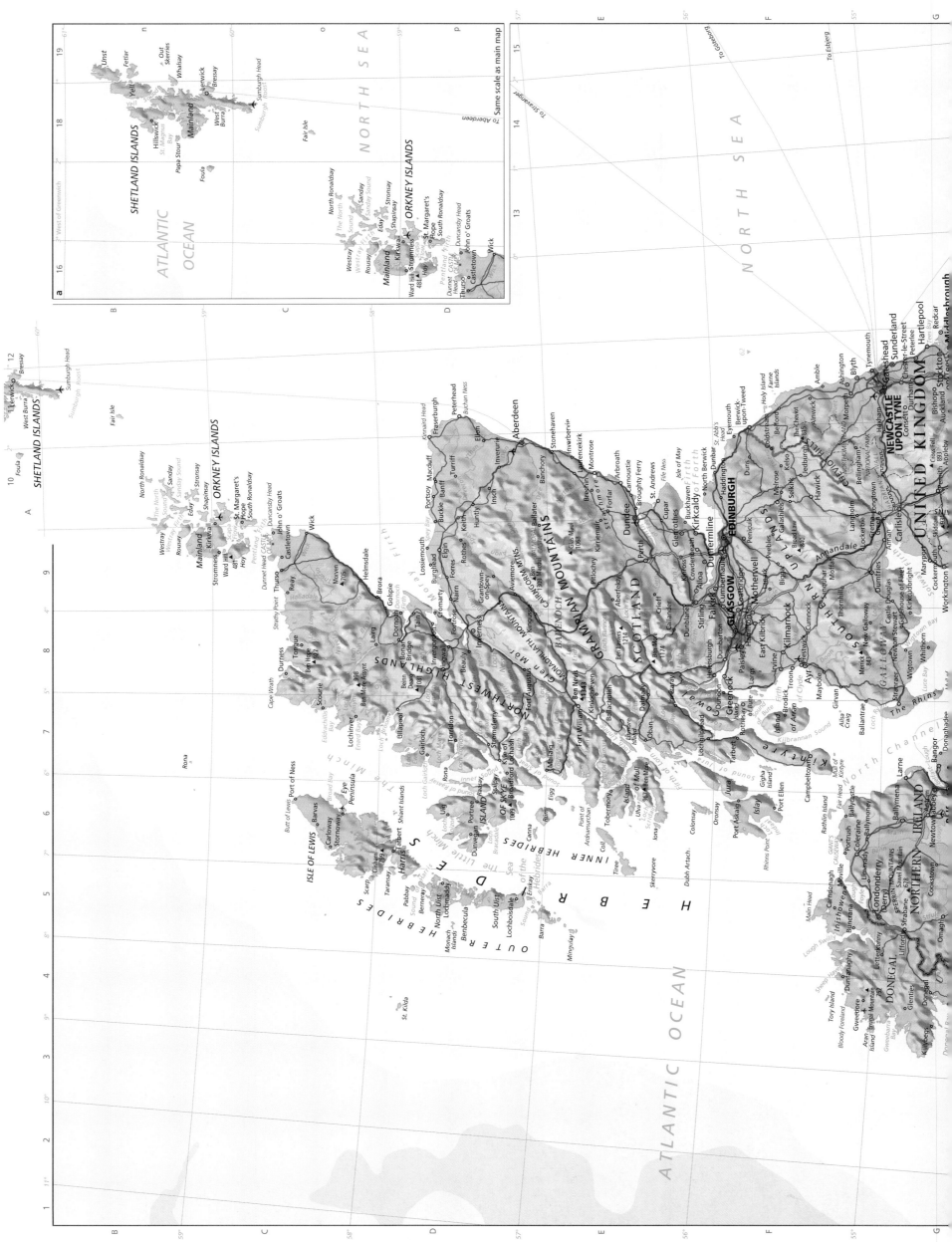

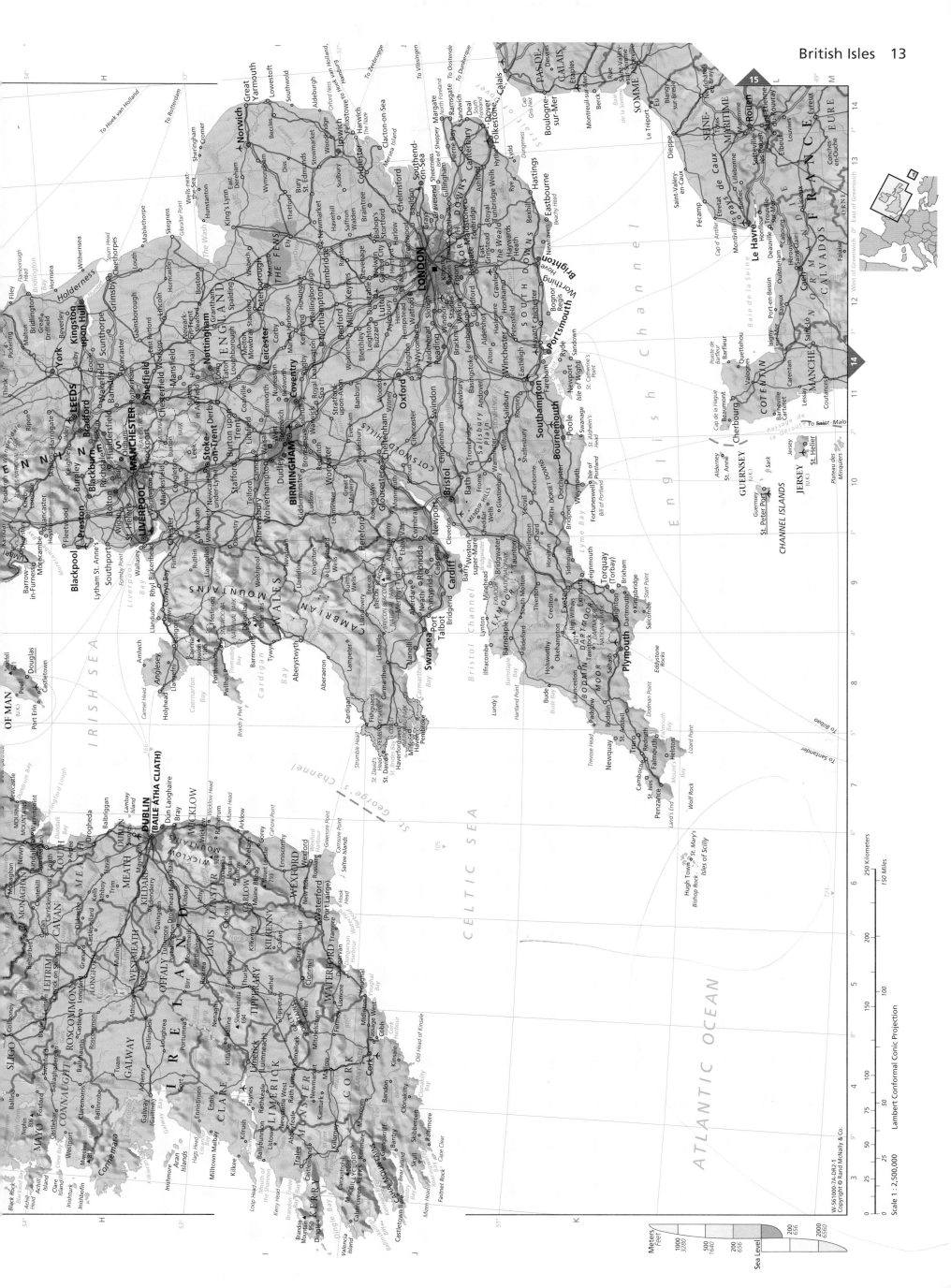

Scale 1 : 2,500,000

Lambert Conformal Conic Projection

W-561000-7A-DR2-1
Copyright © Rand McNally & Co.

Meters	Feet	
2000	6560	
1000	3280	
500	1640	
200	656	
Sea Level		
200	656	

14

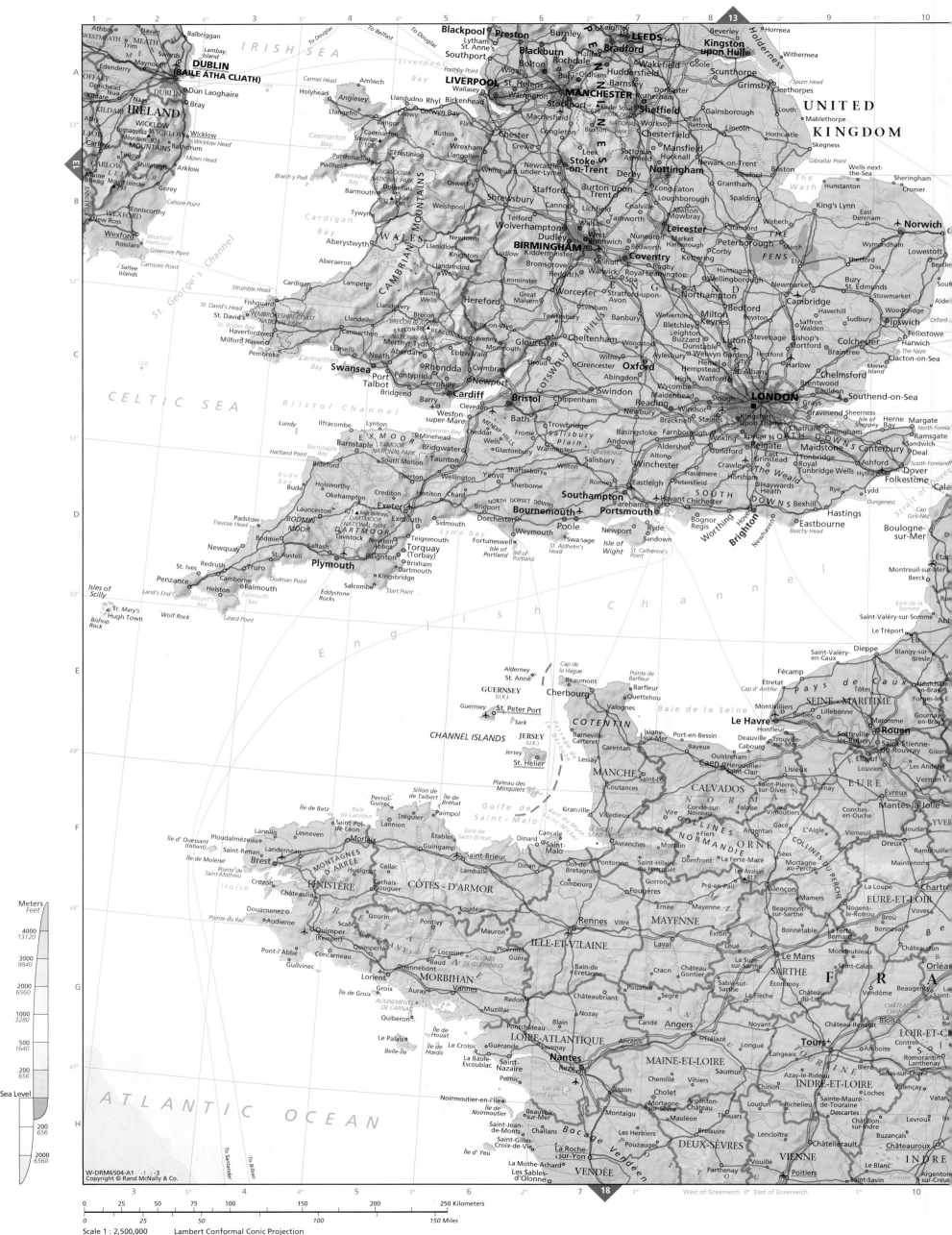

Scale 1 : 2,500,000   Lambert Conformal Conic Projection

250 Kilometers

150 Miles

Meters / Feet
4000 / 13120
3000 / 9840
2000 / 6560
1000 / 3280
500 / 1640
200 / 656
Sea Level
200 / 656
2000 / 6560

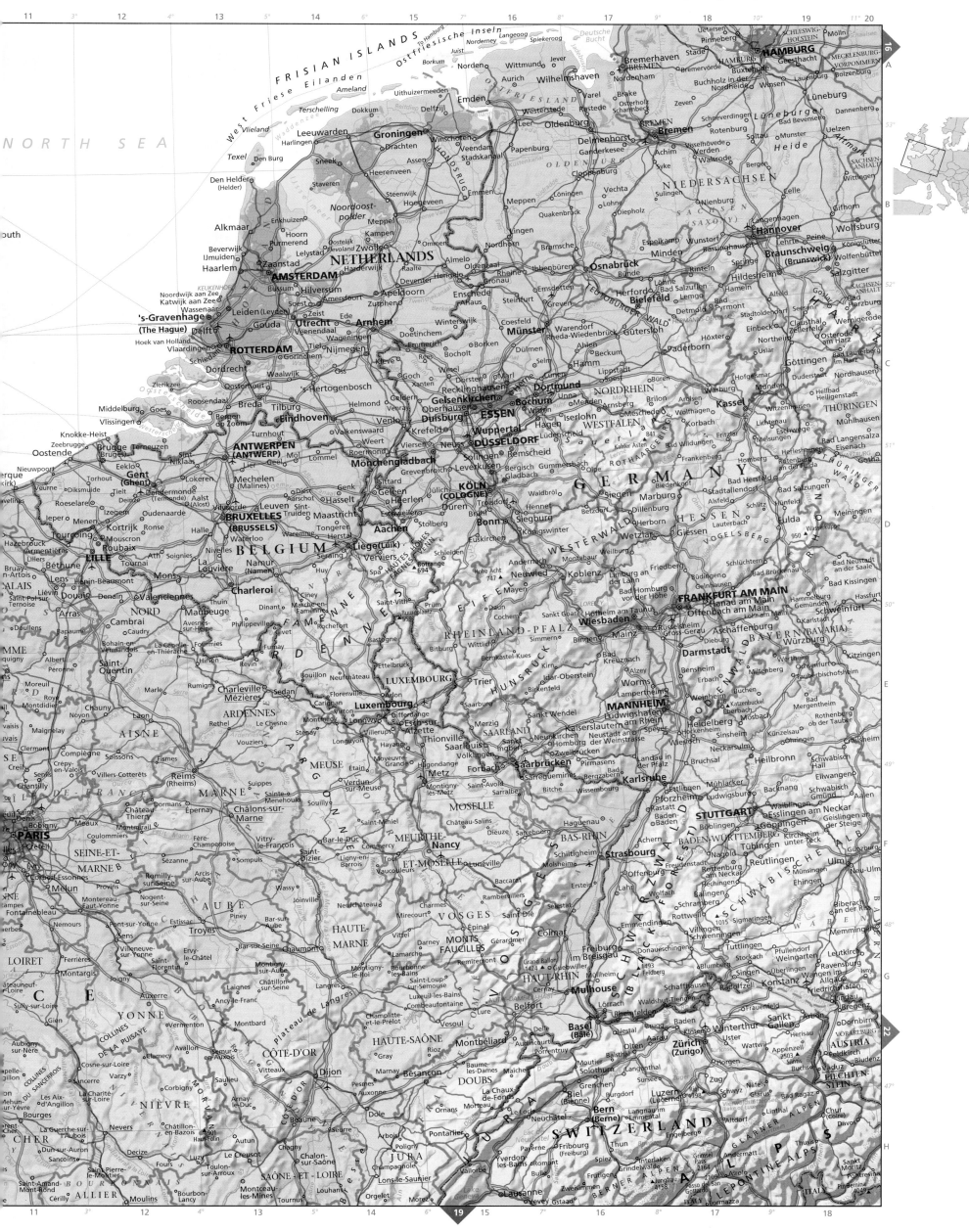

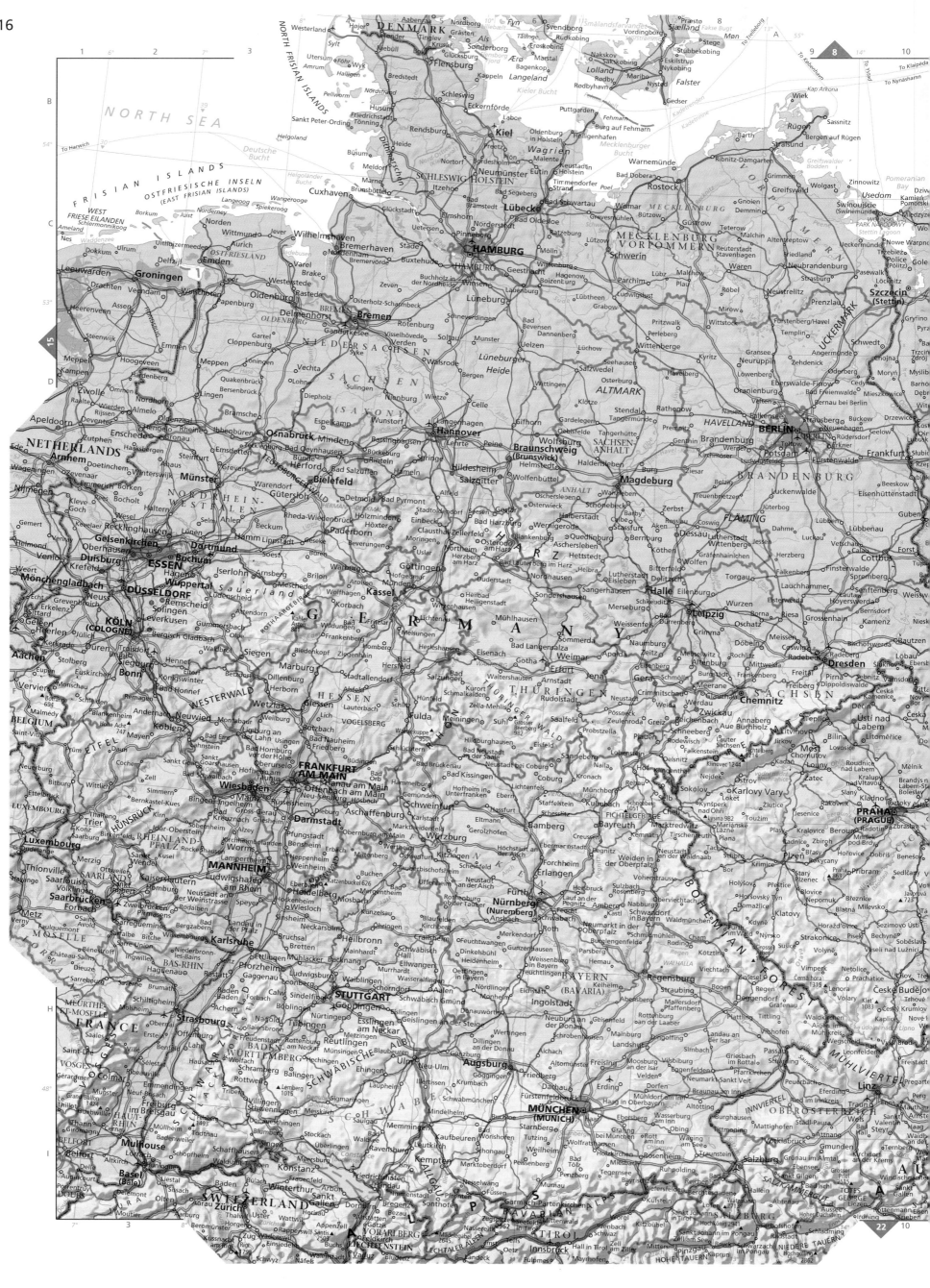

Scale 1 : 2,500,000   Lambert Conformal Conic Projection

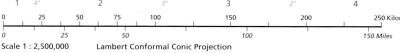

Scale 1 : 2 500 000   Lambert Conformal Conic Projection

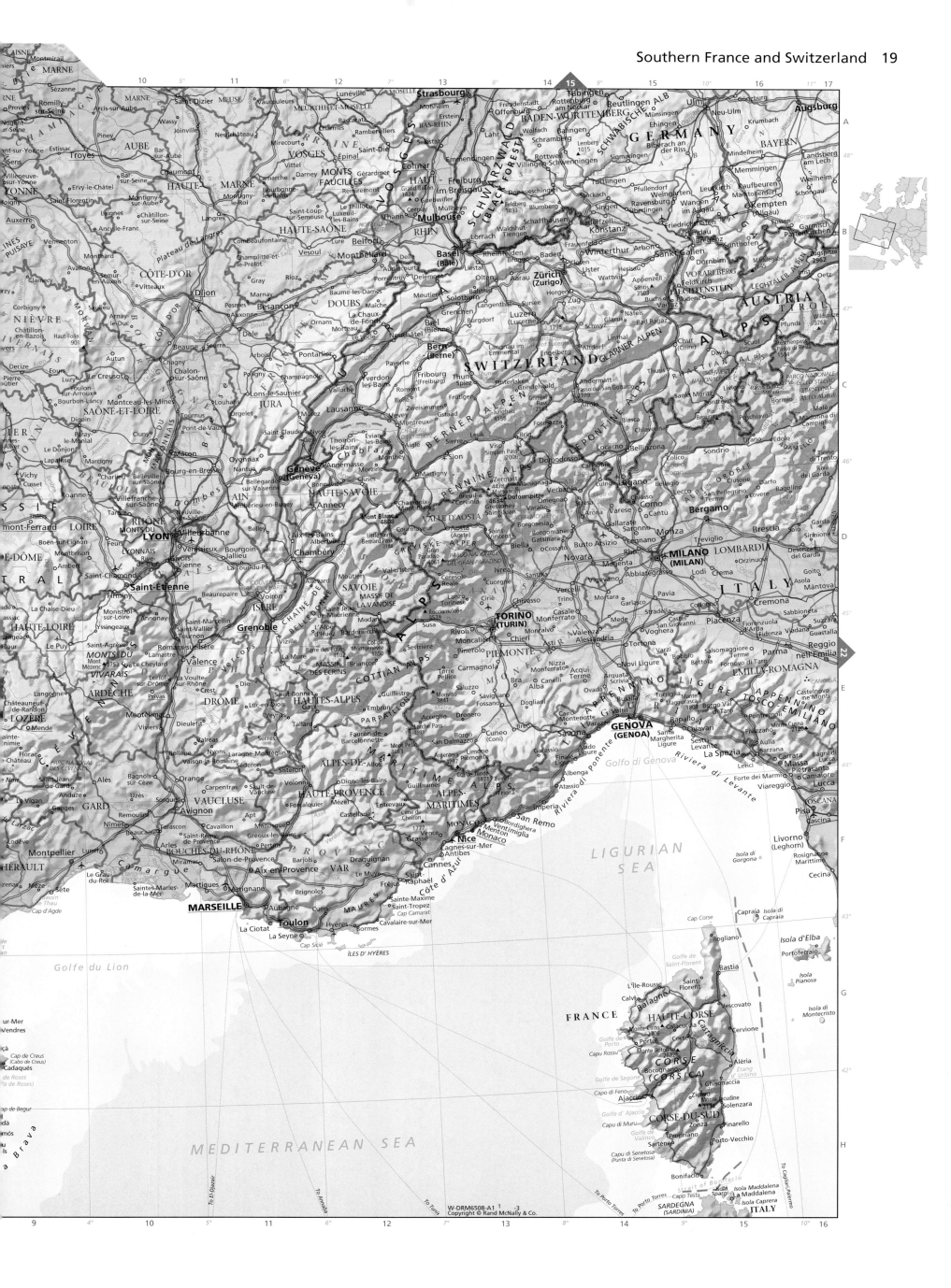

Meters
Feet

4000
13120

3000
9840

2000
6560

1000
3280

500
1640

200
656

Sea Level

200
656

2000
6560

0   25   50   75   100   150 Kilometers
0   25   50   100 Miles
Scale 1 : 2,500,000   Lambert Conformal Conic Projection

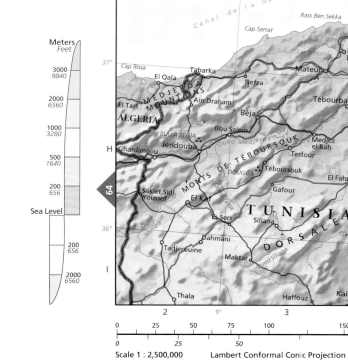

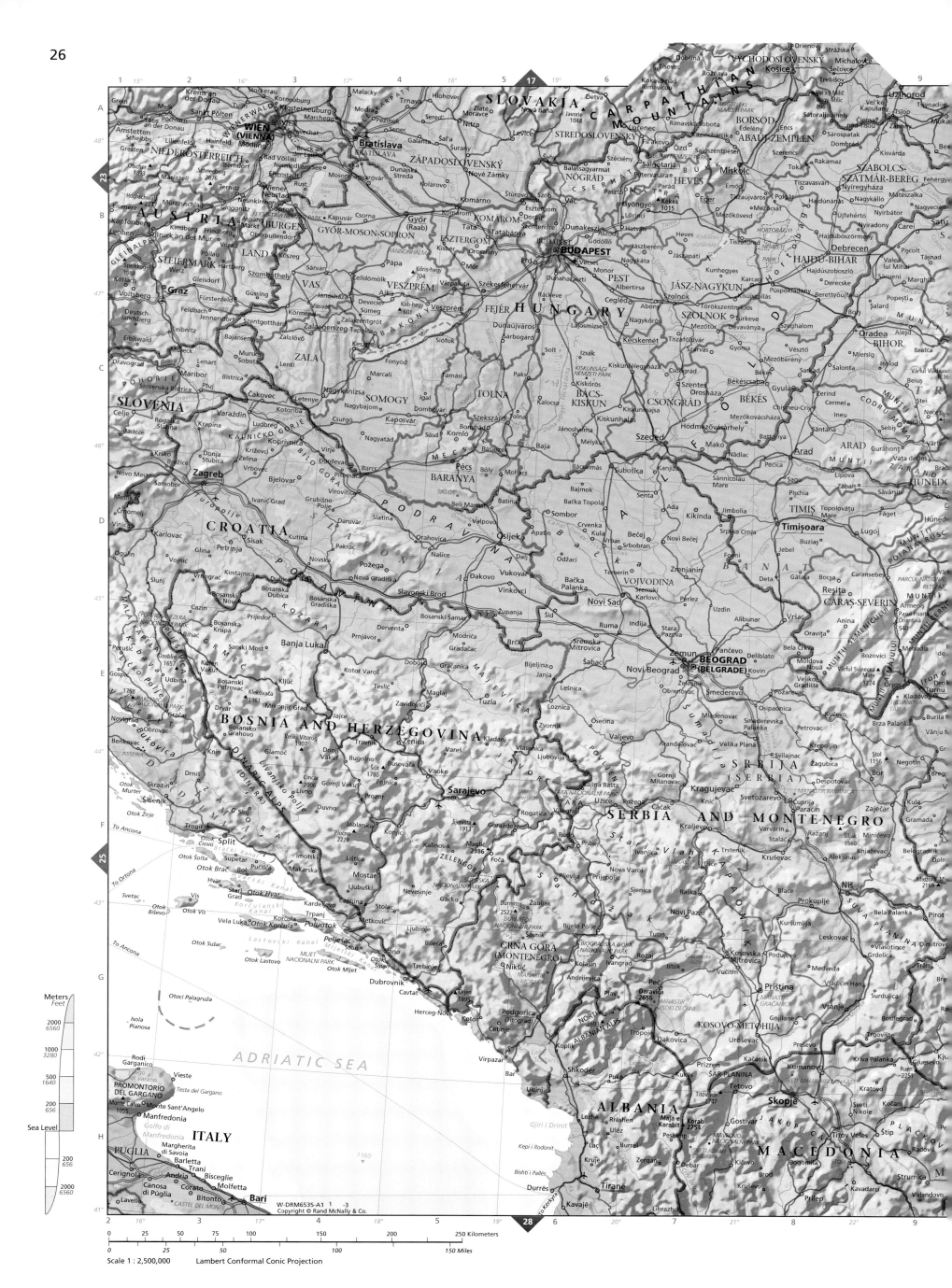

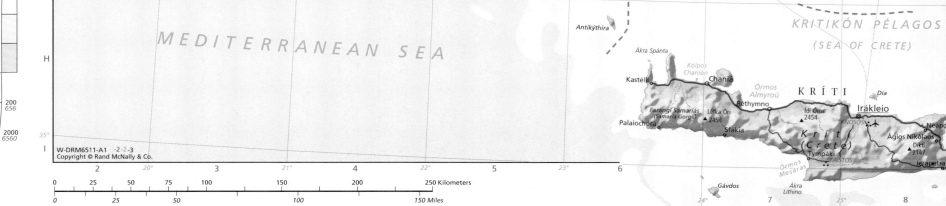

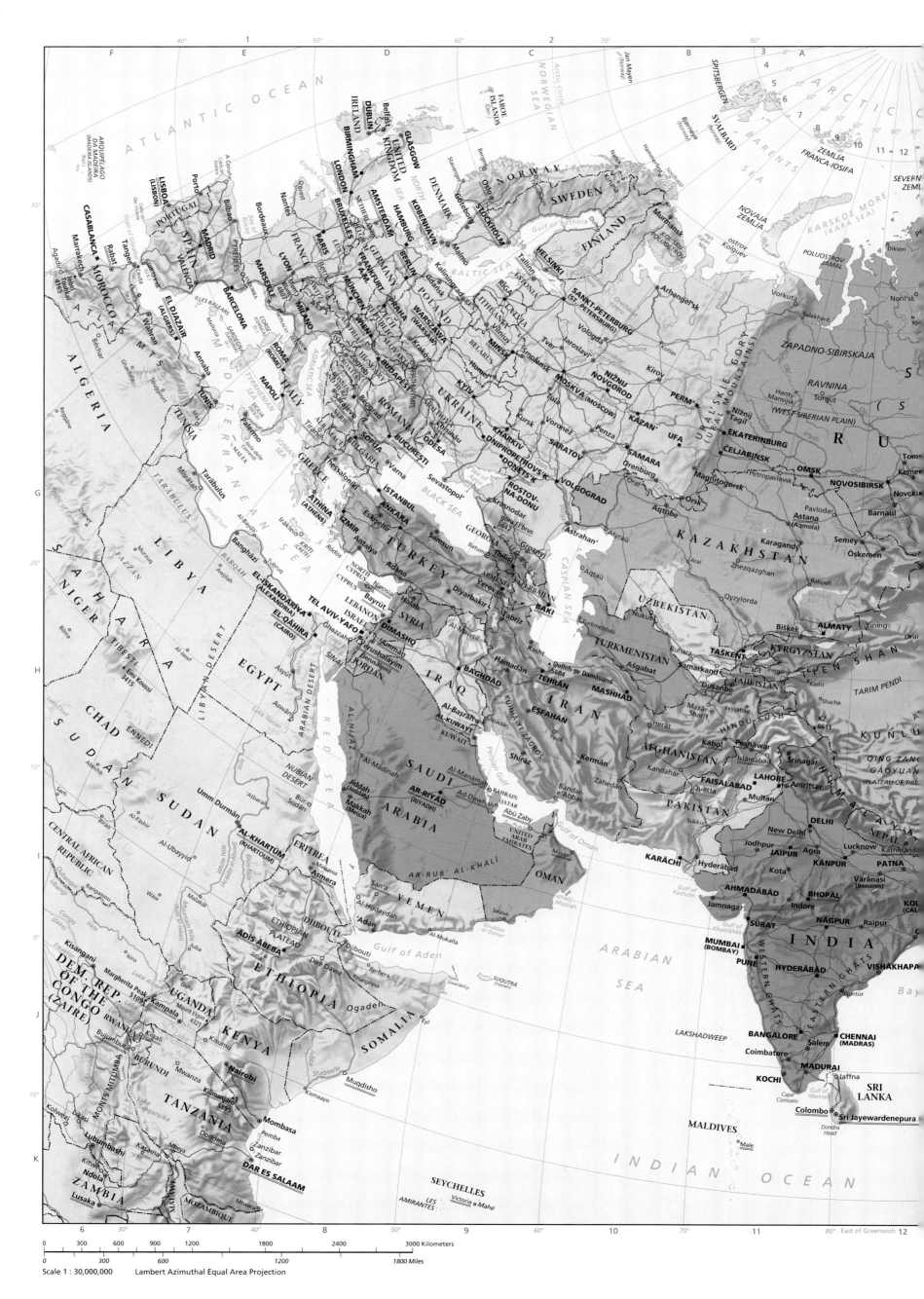

0   300   600   900   1200   1800   2400   3000 Kilometers

0   300   600   1200   1800 Miles

Scale 1 : 30,000,000   Lambert Azimuthal Equal Area Projection

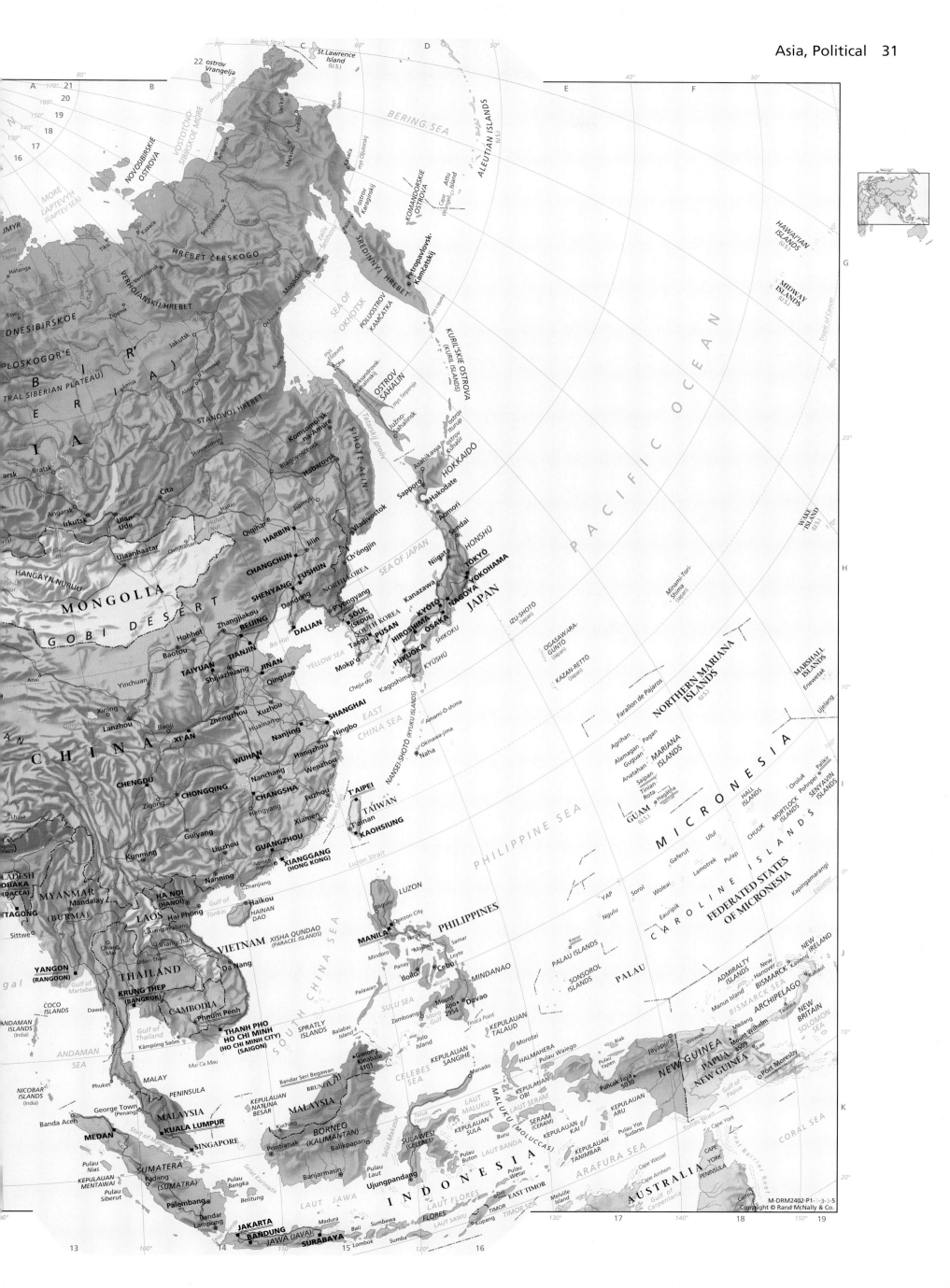

A   170° 21   80°
20
150° 19
140° 18
130° 17
16

JMYR

ozero Tajmyr
MORE
LAPTEVYH
(LAPTEV SEA)

Hatanga

PLOSKOGOR'E
TRAL SIBERIAN PLATEAU)
SIBERIA
R')

DNESIBIRSKOE

Essej

Tura

Bratsk

arsk

Angarsk

Irkutsk

Ulan-
Ude

HANGAYN NURUU

MONGOLIA

Ulaanbaatar

GOBI DESERT

Hohhot

Baotou

Yinchuan

Anxi

Xining

Lanzhou

Baoji

Anxi

CHINA

Lhasa

AN
LADESH
DHAKA
(DACCA)
TAGONG
(CHITTAGONG)

MYANMAR
Mandalay
(BURMA)

Sittwe

YANGON
(RANGOON)

COCO
ISLANDS

THAILAND

Dawei

ANDAMAN
ISLANDS
(India)

KRUNG THEP
(BANGKOK)

CAMBODIA

Phnum Pénh

THANH PHO
HO CHI MINH
(HO CHI MINH CITY)
(SAIGON)

Kâmpóng Saôm

Mui Ca Mau

MALAY

NICOBAR
ISLANDS
(India)

Phuket

PENINSULA

George Town
(Penang)

MALAYSIA

Banda Aceh

MEDAN

Pulau
Nias

KEPULAUAN
MENTAWAI

Pulau
Siberut

SUMATERA
(SUMATRA)

Padang

Palembang

Bandar
Lampung

JAKARTA

BANDUNG

KUALA LUMPUR

SINGAPORE

Pontianak

BORNEO
(KALIMANTAN)

Balikpapan

Banjarmasin

Pulau
Laut

Pulau
Bangka

Belitung

Madura

JAWA (JAVA)

SURABAYA

Ujungpandang

INDONESIA

Bandar Seri Begawan

BRUNEI

MALAYSIA

Kuching

Gunong
Kinabalu
4101

C   St.Lawrence
Island
(U.S.)

ostrov
Vrangelja

proliv Longa

VOSTOČNO-
SIBIRSKOE MORE

Kazače

ALEUTIAN ISLANDS
(U.S.)

Attu
Island

Attu
Island

KOMANDORSKIE
OSTROVA

SREDINNYJ HREBET

Petropavlovsk-
Kamčatskij

POLUOSTROV
KAMČATKA

SEA OF
OKHOTSK

KURIL'SKIE OSTROVA
(KURIL ISLANDS)

OSTROV
SAHALIN

Južno-
Sahalinsk

ostrov
Iturup

ostrov
Kunašir

Aŝikawa

HOKKAIDO

Sapporo

Hakodate

Aomori

Sendai

HONSHŪ

Niigata

Kanazawa

TŌKYO

YOKOHAMA

KYŌTO

NAGOYA

OSAKA

JAPAN

SHIKOKU

HIROSHIMA

FUKUOKA

KYŪSHŪ

Kagoshima

Amami-Ō-shima

NANSEI-SHOTŌ (RYUKYU ISLANDS)

Okinawa-jima

Naha

BERING SEA

BERING STRAIT

PACIFIC OCEAN

HAWAIIAN
ISLANDS
(U.S.)

MIDWAY
ISLANDS
(U.S.)

Tropic of Cancer

WAKE
ISLAND
(U.S.)

Minami-Tori-
Shima
(Japan)

OGASAWARA-
GUNTO
(Japan)

KAZAN-RETTŌ
(Japan)

Farallon de Pajaros

NORTHERN MARIANA
ISLANDS
(U.S.)

MARSHALL
ISLANDS

Enewetak

Ujelang

Agrihan

Alamagan
Guguan

Anatahan

Saipan
Tinian
Rota

MARIANA
ISLANDS

Aganña

GUAM
(U.S.)

M I C R O N E S I A

PHILIPPINE SEA

Gaferut

Lamotrek

Pulap

Ulul

CHUUK

HALL
ISLANDS

MORTLOCK
ISLANDS

Oroluk

Pohnpei

Pakin

SENYAVIN
ISLANDS

C A R O L I N E   I S L A N D S

YAP

Sorol

Woleai

Eauripik

FEDERATED STATES
OF MICRONESIA

Kapingamarangi

Ngulu

Ulithi

Equator

PALAU ISLANDS

Koror

SONSOROL
ISLANDS

PALAU

ADMIRALTY
ISLANDS

New
Hanover

NEW
IRELAND

BISMARCK

BISMARCK
ARCHIPELAGO

Manus Island

Kavieng

Rabaul

NEW
BRITAIN

SOLOMON
SEA

Madang

Talasea

Mount Wilhelm
4509

NEW GUINEA

Jayapura

Wewak

Lae

PAPUA
NEW GUINEA

Port Moresby

Gulf
of Papua

Puncak Jaya
5030

Biak

Pulau
Yapen

Pulau Waigeo

HALMAHERA

Manado

Morotai

KEPULAUAN
SANGIHE

KEPULAUAN
TALAUD

CELEBES
SEA

SULU SEA

Zamboanga

Jolo
Island

Balabac
Island

SPRATLY
ISLANDS

Palawan

Mindoro

MANILA

Quezon City

LUZON

Baguio

Naga

Panay

Iloilo

Cebu

Leyte

Samar

Mactan

PHILIPPINES

MINDANAO

Davao

Mount
Apo
2954

Moro
Gulf

Tinaca Point

KEPULAUAN
TALAUD

SULAWESI
(CELEBES)

Teluk
Tomini

Pulau
Buton

Pulau
Muna

KEPULAUAN
SULA

Buru

SERAM
(CERAM)

Pulau
Obi

LAUT MALUKU

KEPULAUAN
OBI

LAUT SERAM

MALUKU (MOLUCCAS)

LAUT BANDA

KEPULAUAN
KAI

KEPULAUAN
ARU

KEPULAUAN
TANIMBAR

Pulau Yos
Sudarso

ARAFURA SEA

Cape Arnhem

Cape Wessel

Gulf
of
Carpentaria

AUSTRALIA

CAPE
YORK
PENINSULA

Cape York

Torres Strait

CORAL SEA

Great Barrier Reef

Melville
Island

Dili

EAST TIMOR

TIMOR SEA

Kupang

TIMOR

Sumba

Sumbawa

FLORES

LAUT FLORES

LAUT SAWU

Bali

Lombok

RUSSIA

Jakutsk

Lensk

Aldan

Tommot

Kirensk

Čita

Ulan-Ude

Chojbalsan

HREBET ČERSKOGO

VERHOJANSKIJ HREBET

STANOVOJ HREBET

SIHOTE-ALIN'

Blagoveščensk

Habarovsk

Komsomol'sk-
na-Amure

Vladivostok

HARBIN

CHANGCHUN

Qiqihar

Jilin

FUSHUN

SHENYANG

Dandong

NORTH KOREA

P'yŏngyang

SOUL
(SEOUL)

SOUTH KOREA

Taegu

PUSAN

Mokp'o

Kwangju

Taejŏn

Inch'ŏn

Cheju-do

Ch'ŏngjin

SEA OF JAPAN

BEIJING

Zhangjiakou

TIANJIN

TAIYUAN

Shijiazhuang

JINAN

Qingdao

Bo Hai

YELLOW SEA

Bo Hai

SHANGHAI

Zhengzhou

Xuzhou

Huainan

Nanjing

Hangzhou

Ningbo

EAST
CHINA SEA

XI'AN

WUHAN

Nanchang

Wenzhou

CHENGDU

CHONGQING

CHANGSHA

Hengyang

Zigong

Guiyang

Liuzhou

GUANGZHOU

Nanning

Kunming

Fuzhou

Xiamen

T'AIPEI

TAIWAN

Tainan

KAOHSIUNG

XIANGGANG
(HONG KONG)

Zhanjiang

Haikou

HAINAN
DAO

Gulf of
Tonkin

HA NOI
(HANOI)

Hai Phong

LAOS

Viangchan

VIETNAM

Da Nang

XISHA QUNDAO
(PARACEL ISLANDS)

SOUTH CHINA SEA

Udon Thani

Chiang
Mai

NATUNA
BESAR

KEPULAUAN
NATUNA
BESAR

13   100°   14   110°   15   120°   16   130°   17   140°   18   150°   19

ANDAMAN
SEA

Gulf of
Martaban

Gulf of
Thailand

M-DRM2402-P1- -3-2-5
Copyright © Rand McNally & Co.

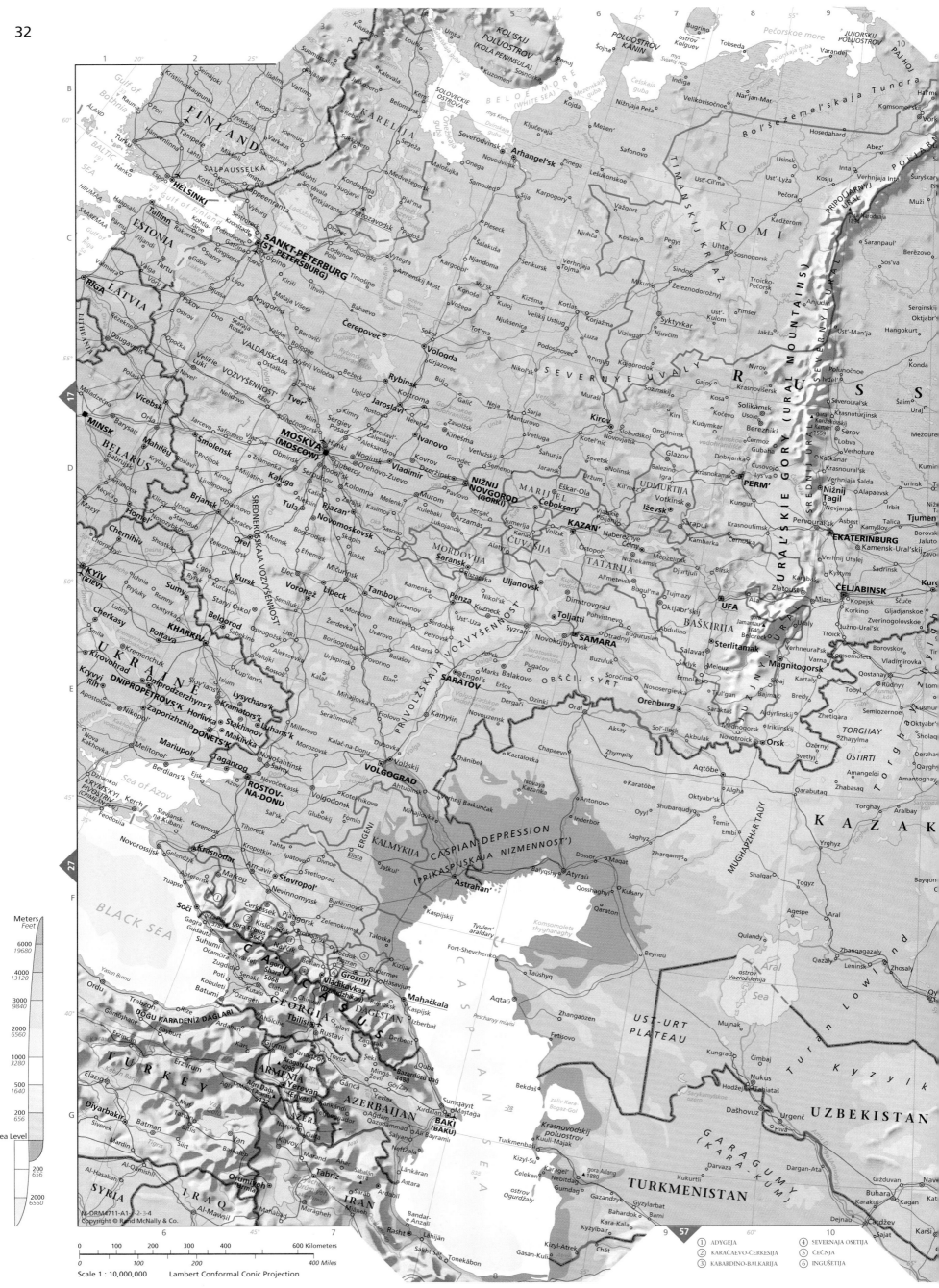

Meters / Feet

6000 / 19680
4000 / 13120
3000 / 9840
2000 / 6560
1000 / 3280
500 / 1640
200 / 656

Sea Level

200 / 656
2000 / 6560

NL-DRM4711-A1--2-3-4
Copyright © Rand McNally & Co.

0 100 200 300 400 600 Kilometers
0 100 200 400 Miles

Scale 1 : 10,000,000   Lambert Conformal Conic Projection

57

① ADYGEJA   ④ SEVERNAJA OSETIJA
② KARAČAEVO-ČERKESIJA   ⑤ ČEČNJA
③ KABARDINO-BALKARIJA   ⑥ INGUŠETIJA

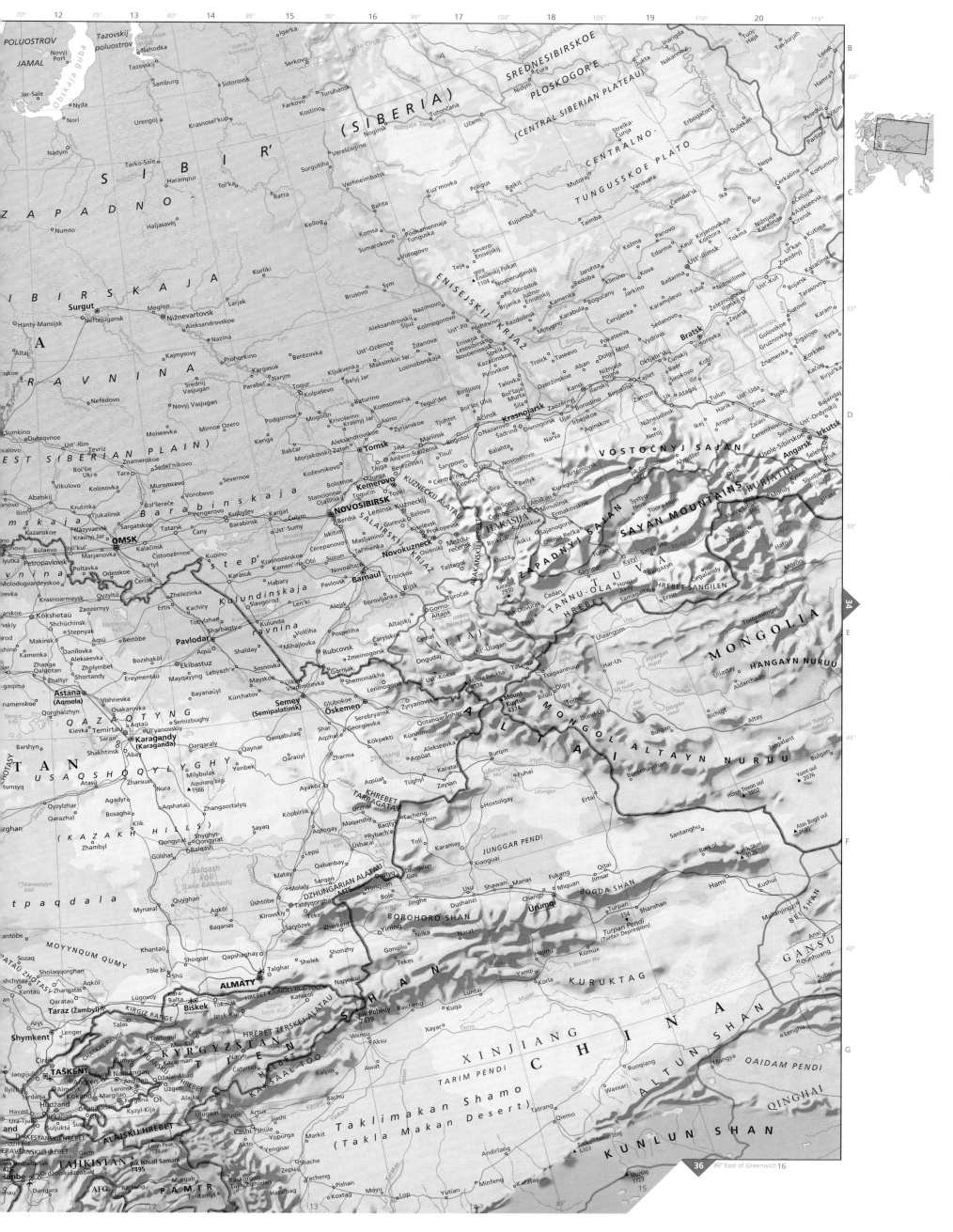

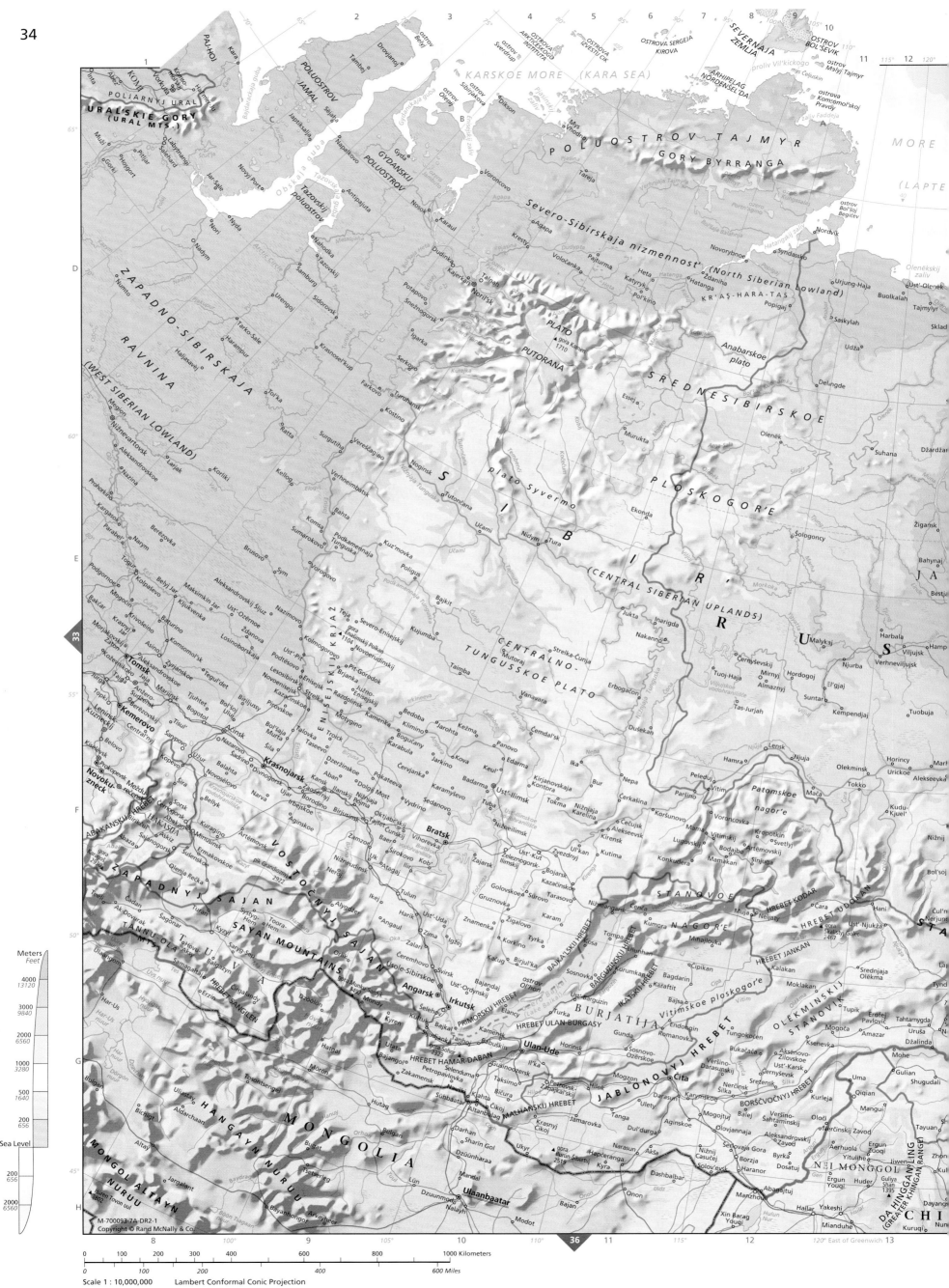

Meters
Feet

4000
13120

3000
9840

2000
6560

1000
3280

500
1640

200
656

Sea Level

200
656

2000
6560

M-700093-7A-DR2-1
Copyright © Rand McNally & Co.

Scale 1 : 10,000,000   Lambert Conformal Conic Projection

0   100   200   300   400   600   800   1000 Kilometers

0   100   200   400   600 Miles

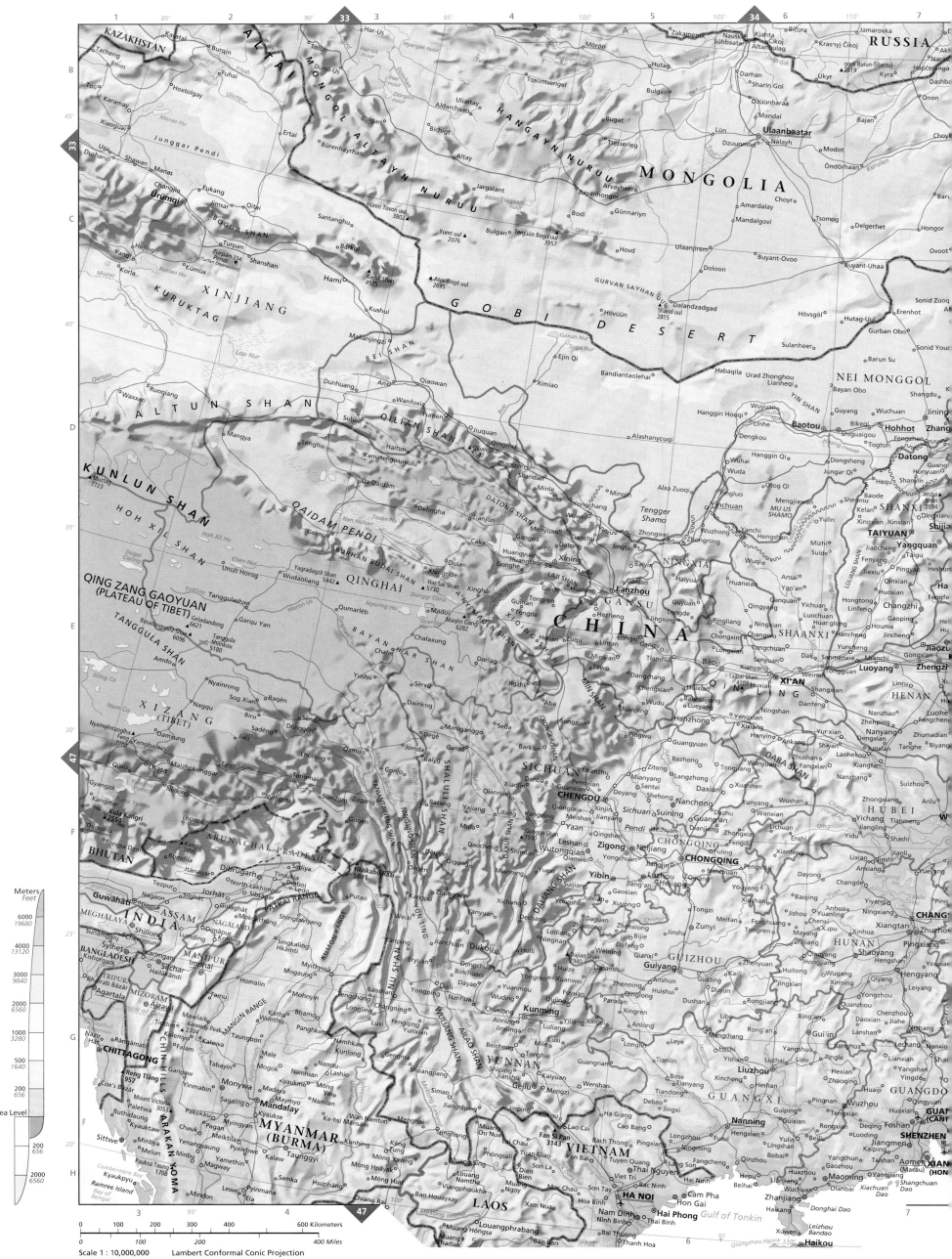

Meters / Feet

6000 / 19680

4000 / 13120

3000 / 9840

2000 / 6560

1000 / 3280

500 / 1640

200 / 656

Sea Level

200 / 656

2000 / 6560

Scale 1 : 10,000,000   Lambert Conformal Conic Projection

0   100   200   300   400   600 Kilometers

0   100   200   400 Miles

Meters
Feet

3000
9840

2000
6560

1000
3280

500
1640

200
656

Sea Level

200
656

2000
6560

0   50   100   150   200   300   400   500 Kilometers
0   50   100   200   300 Miles

Scale 1 : 5,000,000   Lambert Conformal Conic Projection

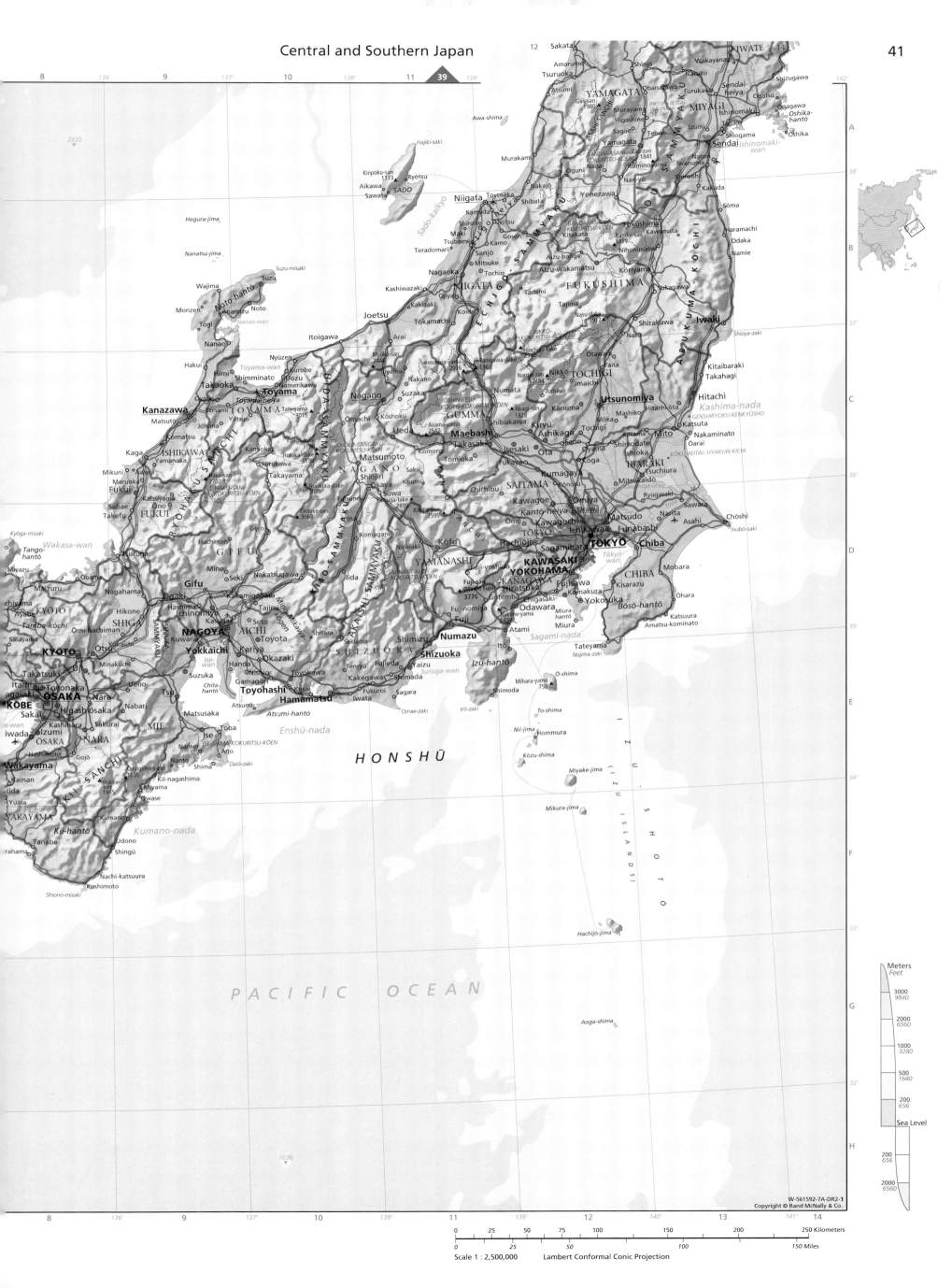

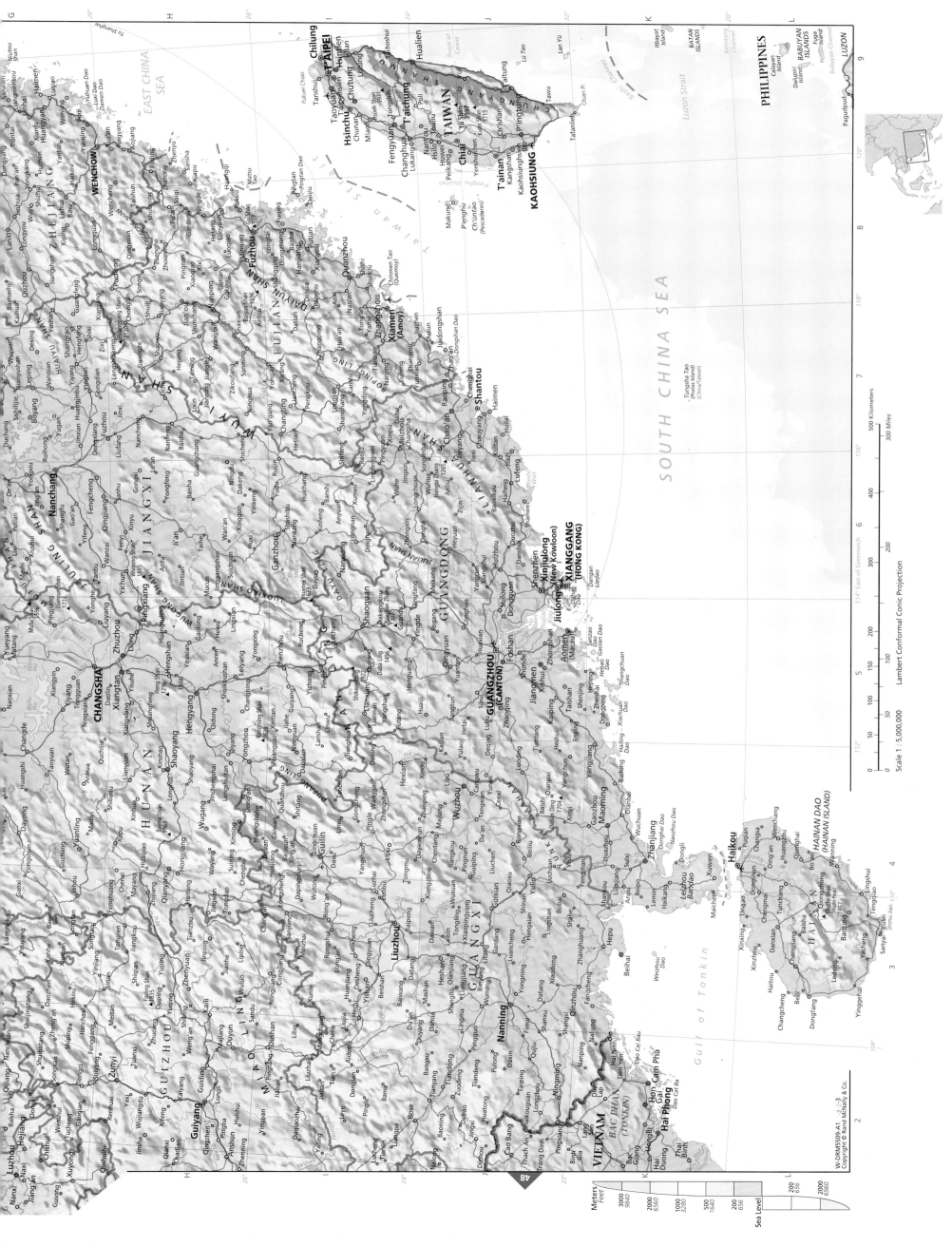

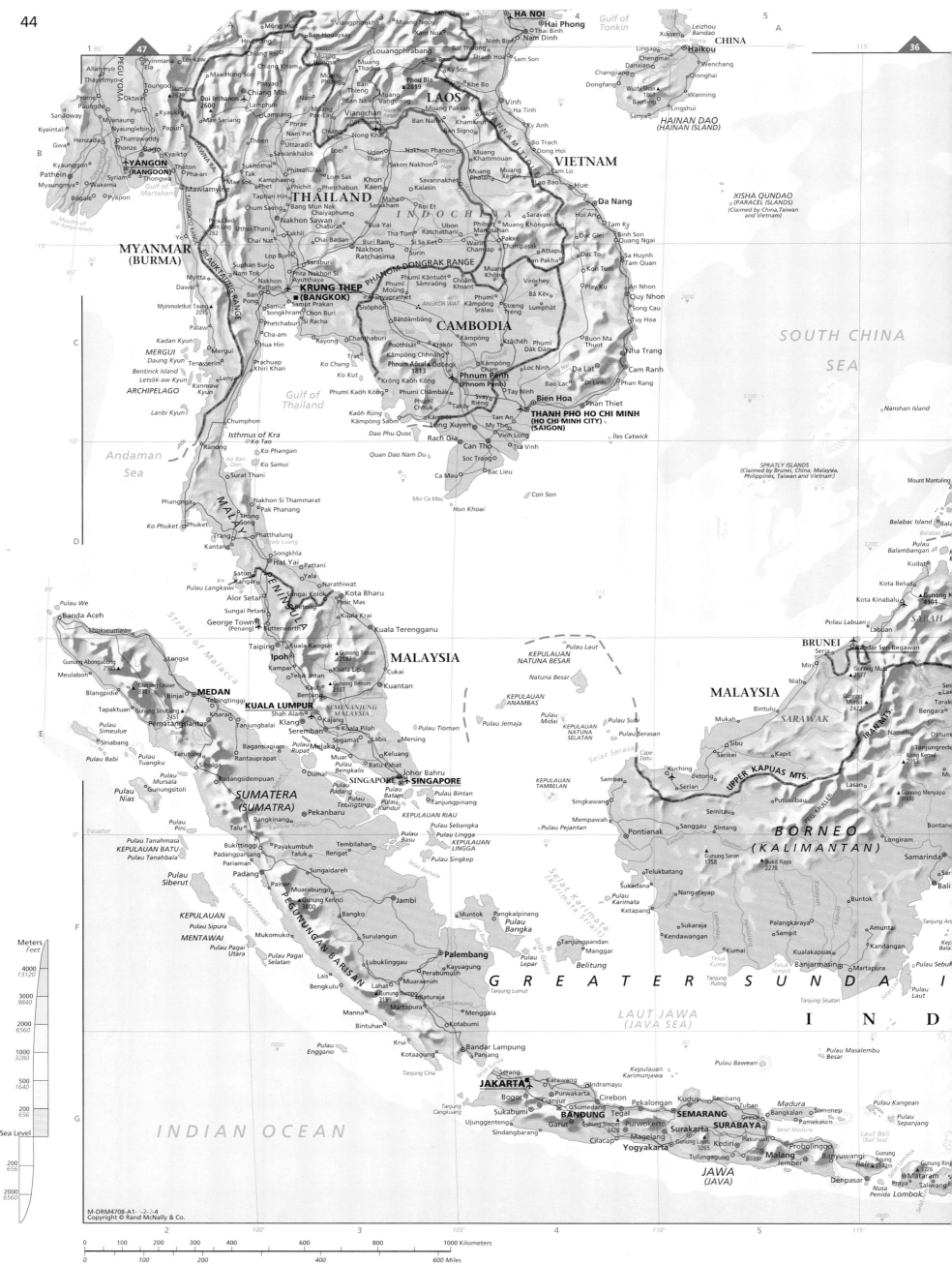

CHINA

HA NOI
Hai Phong
Nam Dinh
Gulf of Tonkin

HAINAN DAO
(HAINAN ISLAND)
Haikou

LAOS

VIETNAM

THAILAND

INDOCHINA

Da Nang

MYANMAR
(BURMA)

YANGON
(RANGOON)

XISHA QUNDAO
(PARACEL ISLANDS)
(Claimed by China, Taiwan
and Vietnam)

KRUNG THEP
(BANGKOK)

CAMBODIA

SOUTH CHINA
SEA

ANGKOR WAT

Phnum Pénh
(Phnom Penh)

THANH PHO HO CHI MINH
(HO CHI MINH CITY)
(SAIGON)

Gulf of
Thailand

Isthmus of Kra

SPRATLY ISLANDS
(Claimed by Brunei, China, Malaysia,
Philippines, Taiwan and Vietnam)

Andaman
Sea

Ko Phuket

MALAY

PENINSULA

Hat Yai

George Town
(Penang)

KEPULAUAN
NATUNA BESAR

Natuna Besar

BRUNEI
Bandar Seri Begawan

MALAYSIA

SABAH

Kota Kinabalu

MALAYSIA

Strait of Malacca

MEDAN

KUALA LUMPUR

SEMENANJUNG
MALAYSIA

KEPULAUAN
ANAMBAS

KEPULAUAN
NATUNA
SELATAN

SARAWAK

IRAN MTS.

KEPULAUAN
RIAU

SINGAPORE

KEPULAUAN
TAMBELAN

UPPER KAPUAS MTS.

SUMATERA
(SUMATRA)

BORNEO
(KALIMANTAN)

Equator

KEPULAUAN
LINGGA

KEPULAUAN
BATU

Palembang

KEPULAUAN
MENTAWAI

PEGUNUNGAN BARISAN

GREATER SUNDA

IND

LAUT JAWA
(JAVA SEA)

INDIAN OCEAN

JAKARTA

BANDUNG

SEMARANG
SURABAYA

SURAKARTA

Yogyakarta

MALANG

JAWA
(JAVA)

Denpasar

BALI

LOMBOK

M-DRM4708-A1- -2- -4
Copyright © Rand McNally & Co.

Meters
Feet
4000
13120
3000
9840
2000
6560
1000
3280
500
1640
200
656
Sea Level
200
656
2000
6560

0   100   200   300   400   600   800   1000 Kilometers
0   100   200   400   600 Miles
Scale 1 : 10,000,000   Sinusoidal Projection

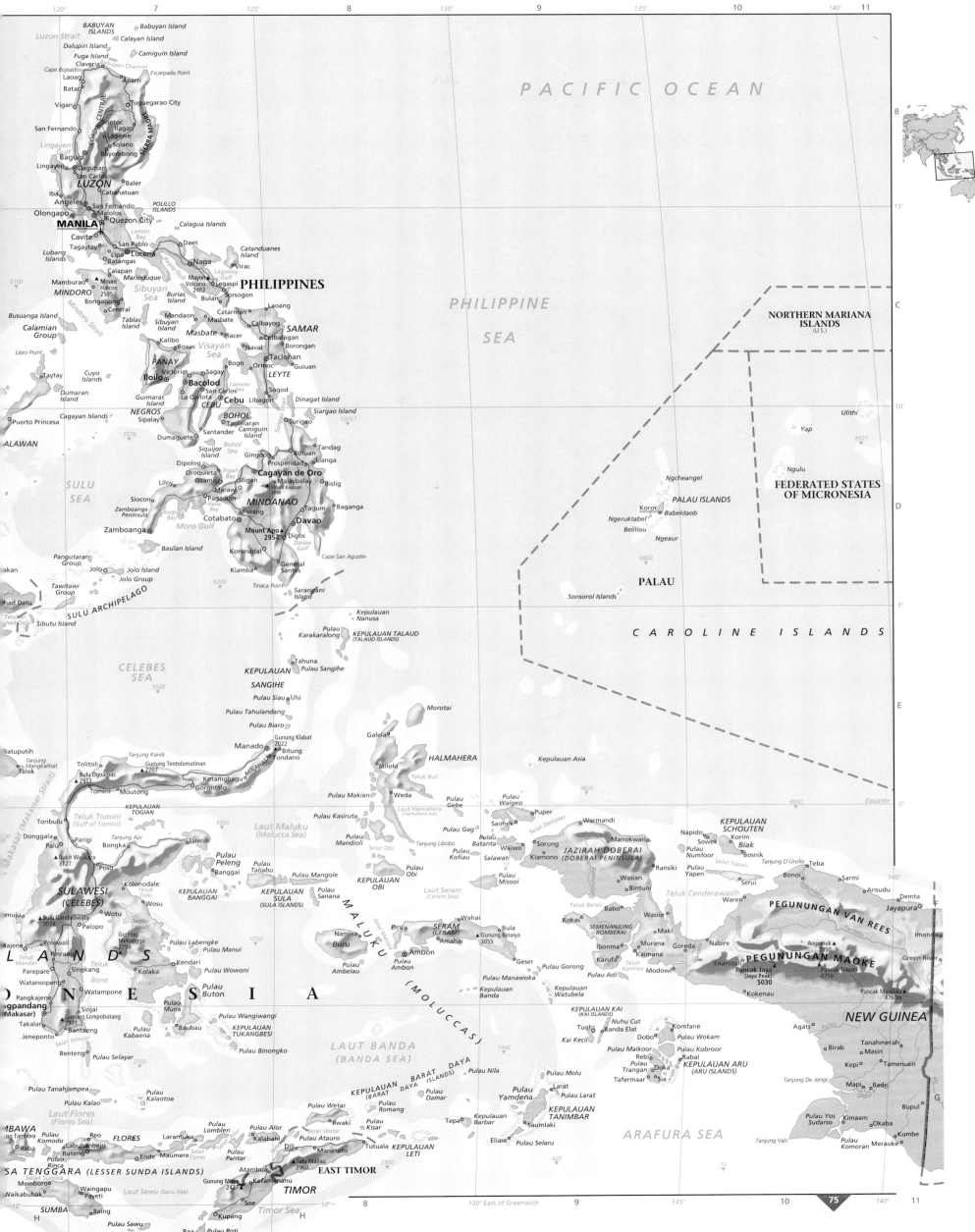

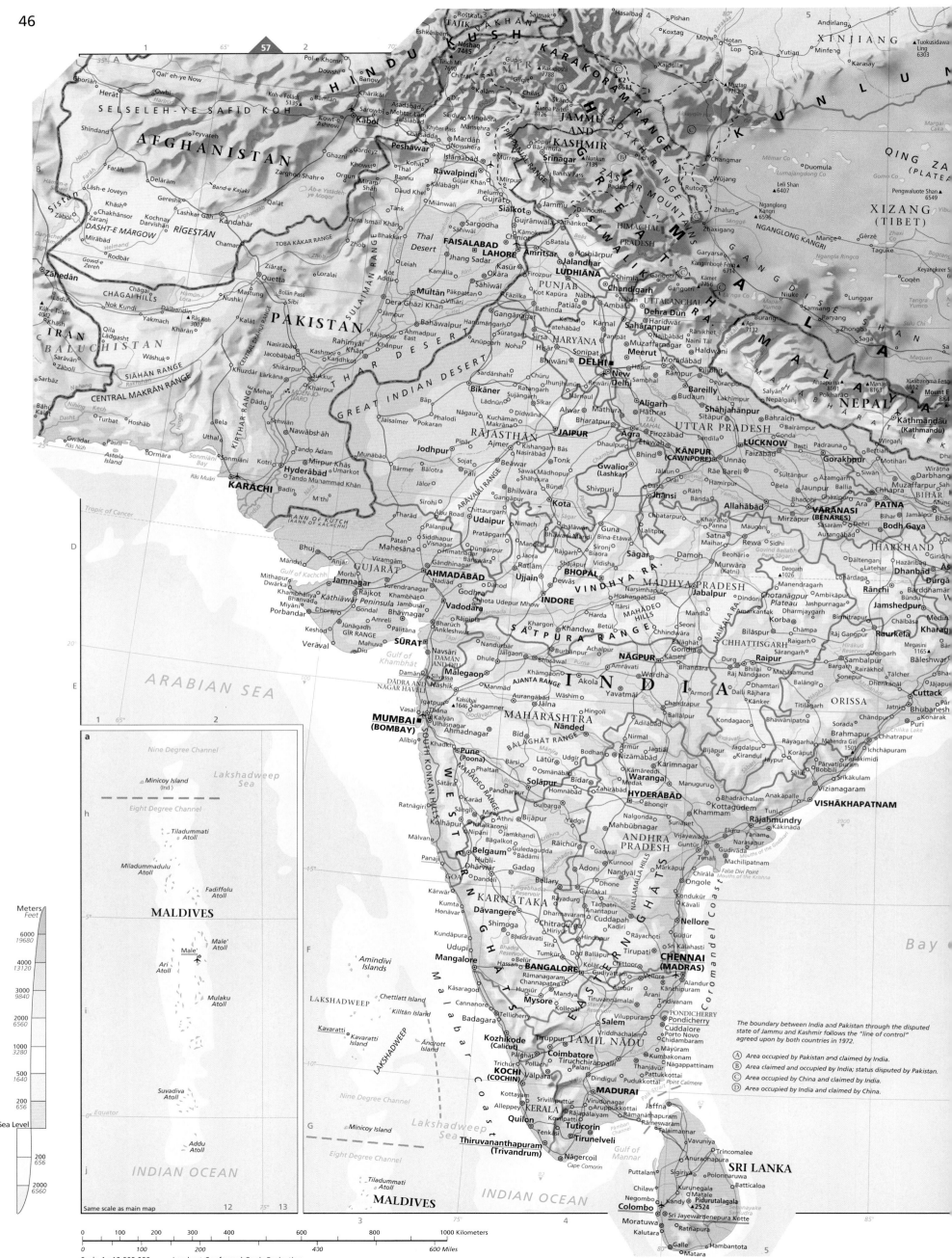

The boundary between India and Pakistan through the disputed state of Jammu and Kashmir follows the "line of control" agreed upon by both countries in 1972.

Ⓐ Area occupied by Pakistan and claimed by India.
Ⓑ Area claimed and occupied by India; status disputed by Pakistan.
Ⓒ Area occupied by China and claimed by India.
Ⓓ Area occupied by India and claimed by China.

Scale 1 : 10,000,000   Lambert Conformal Conic Projection

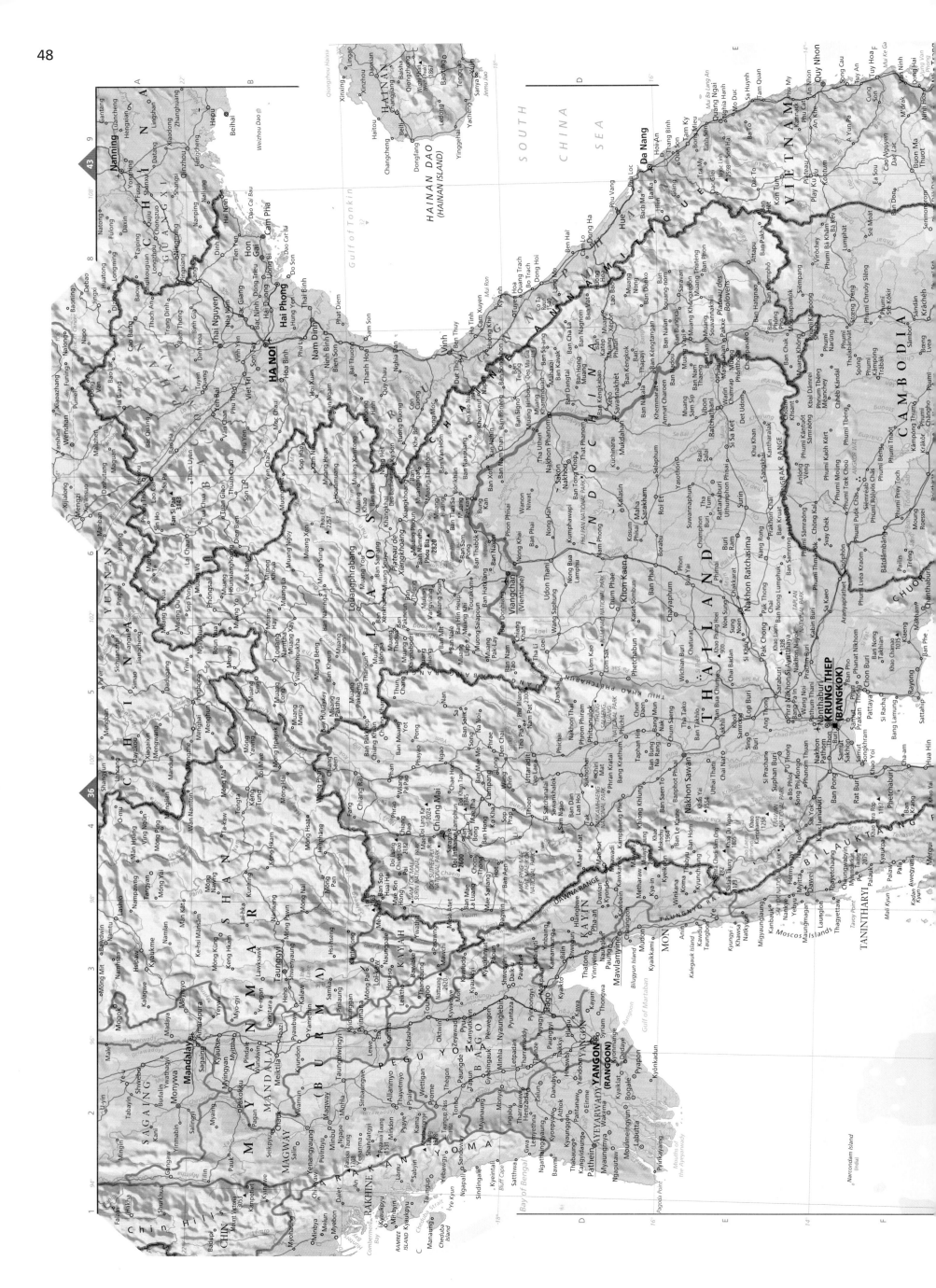

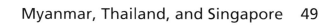

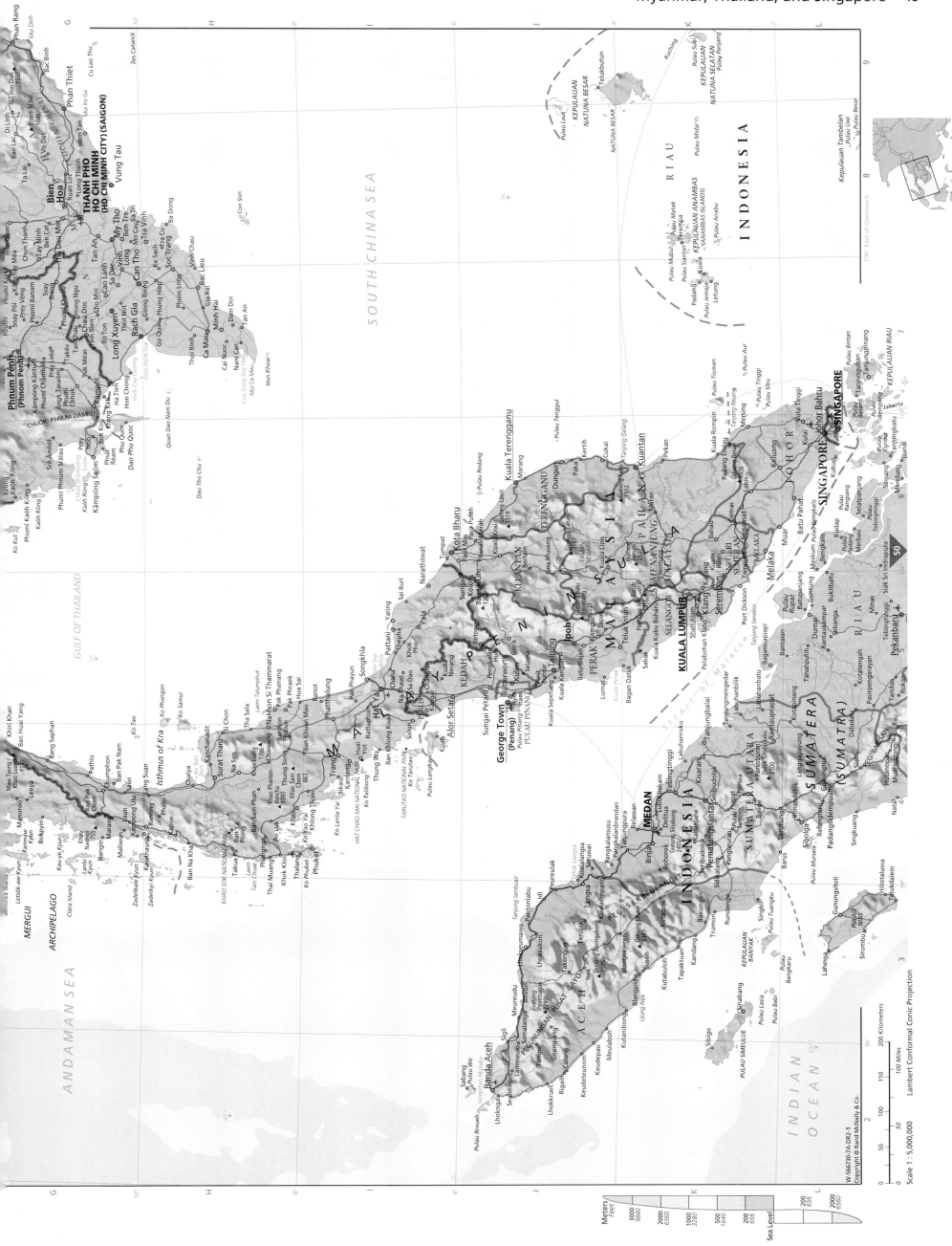

Scale 1 : 5,000,000

Lambert Conformal Conic Projection

W-566730-7A-DR2-1
Copyright © Rand McNally & Co.

Scale 1 : 5,000,000   Sinusoidal Projection

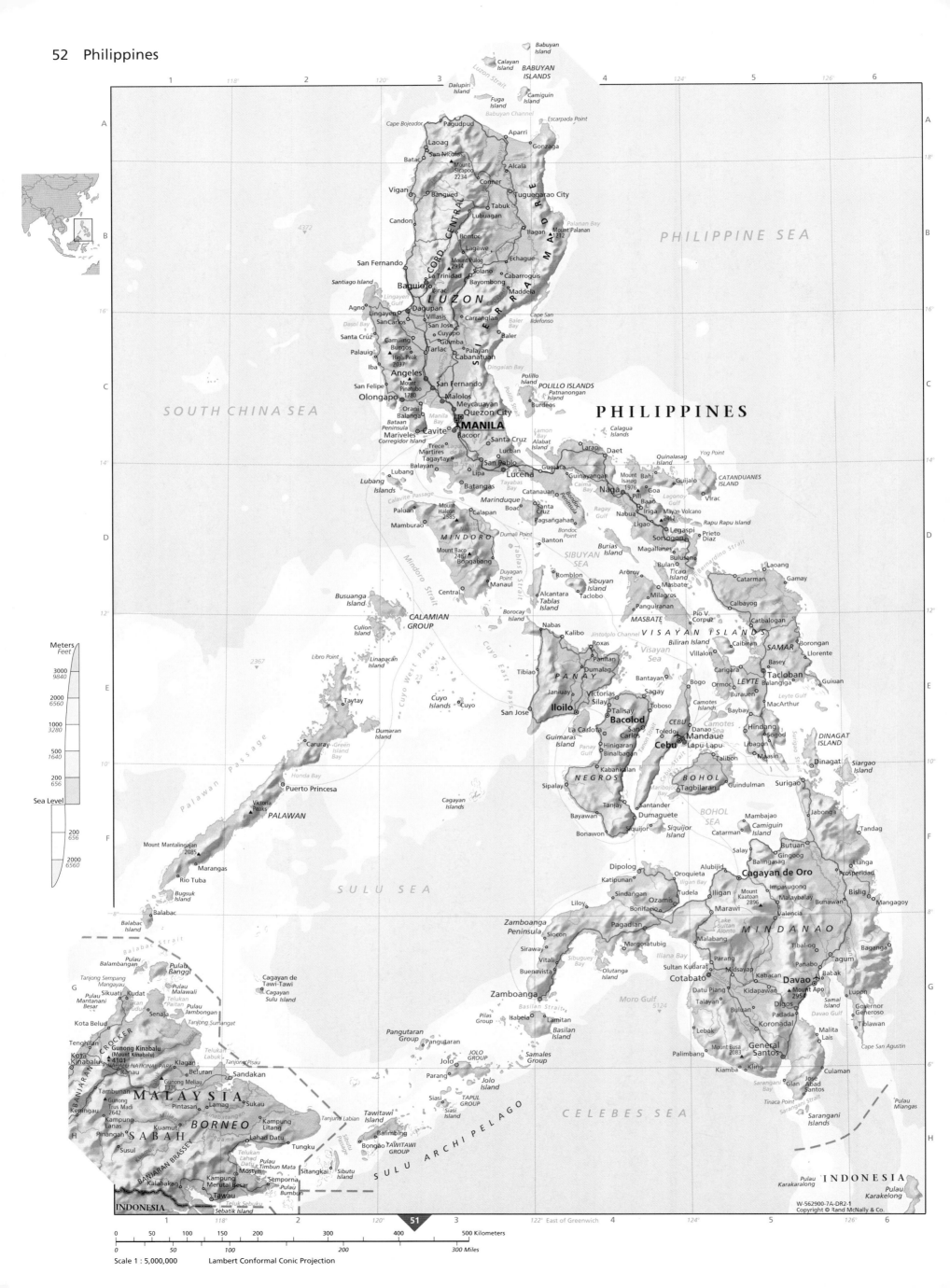

PHILIPPINE SEA

SOUTH CHINA SEA

SULU SEA

CELEBES SEA

Meters
Feet

3000
9840

2000
6560

1000
3280

500
1640

200
656

Sea Level

200
656

2000
6560

LUZON

MINDORO

PALAWAN

NEGROS

PANAY

SAMAR

LEYTE

CEBU

BOHOL

MINDANAO

MALAYSIA

BORNEO

SABAH

INDONESIA

MANILA

W-562900-7A-DR2-1
Copyright © Rand McNally & Co.

0   50   100   150   200   300   500 Kilometers
0   50   100   200   300 Miles

Scale 1 : 5,000,000   Lambert Conformal Conic Projection

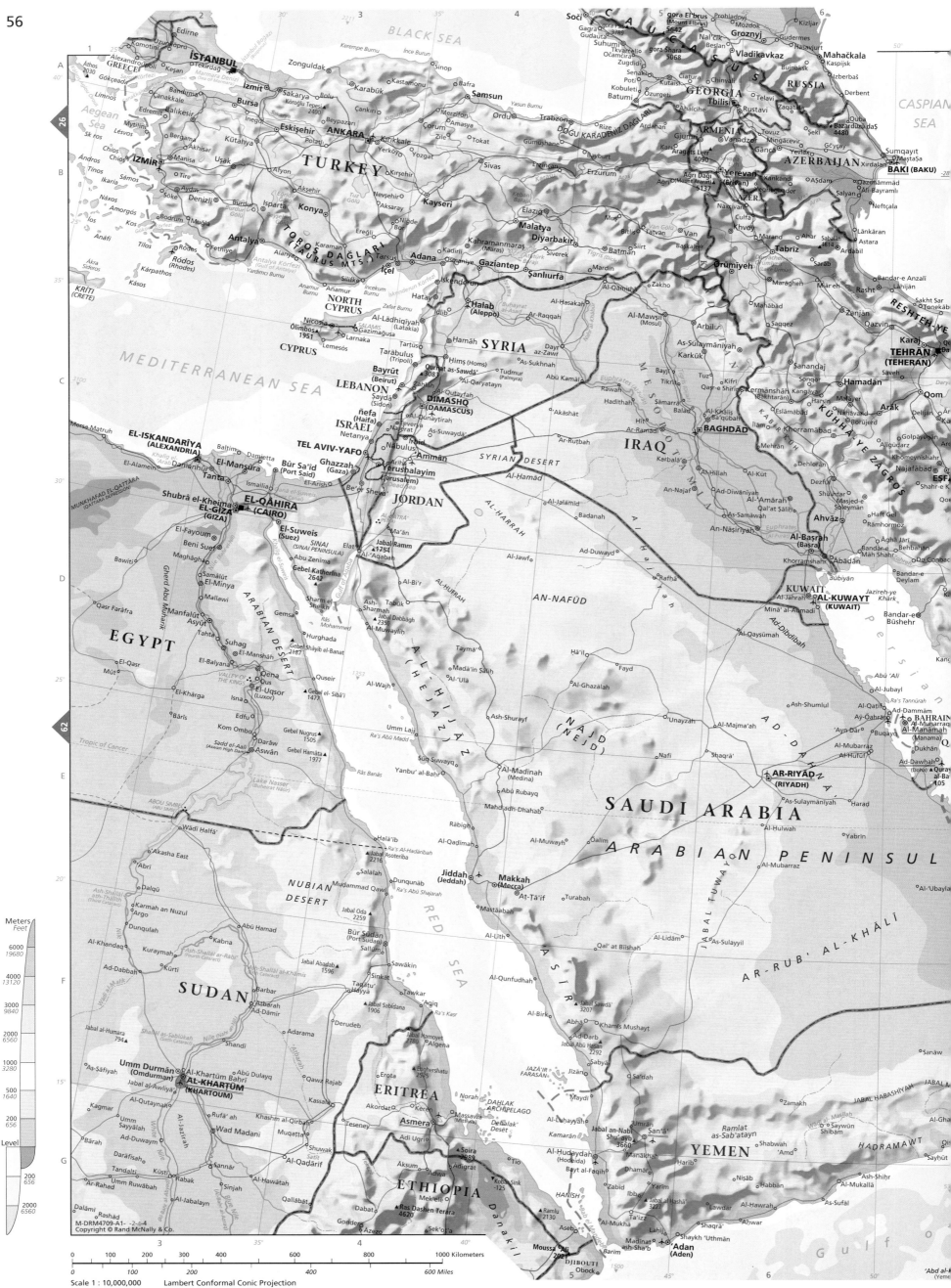

BLACK SEA

GREECE
İSTANBUL
Tekirdağ
Edirne
Komotini
Alexandroúpoli
Gökçeada
Áthos 2030
Keşan
İzmit
Zonguldak
Kastamonu
Sinop
İnce Burun
Kerempe Burnu
Bafra
Samsun
Ordu

CAUCASUS
Soči
gora El'brus (Mount Elbrus) 5642
gora Shara 5068
Prohladnyj
Mozdok
Nal'čik
Groznyj
Gudermes
Kizljar

Vladikavkaz
Mahačkala
Kaspijsk
Izberbaš
Derbent

RUSSIA

Mytilíni
Aegean Sea
Límnos
Bergama
Akhisar
Balıkesir
Bursa
Eskişehir
ANKARA
Kırıkkale
Yozgat
Sivas
Erzincan
Erzurum

TURKEY

GEORGIA
Tbilisi
ARMENIA
Yerevan (Erivan)
Ağrı Dağı (Mount Ararat) 5137

AZERBAIJAN
BAKI (BAKU)

CASPIAN SEA

MEDITERRANEAN SEA

NORTH CYPRUS
CYPRUS

SYRIA
Halab (Aleppo)
DIMASHQ (DAMASCUS)

LEBANON
Bayrūt (Beirut)

ISRAEL
TEL AVIV-YAFO
Yerushalayim (Jerusalem)

JORDAN

IRAQ
BAGHDĀD

MESOPOTAMIA

SYRIAN DESERT

KUWAIT
AL-KUWAYT (KUWAIT)

EGYPT

EL-QÂHIRA (CAIRO)
EL-GIZA (GIZA)

ARABIAN DESERT

SINAI (SINAI PENINSULA)

AN-NAFŪD

NAJD (NEJD)

AD-DAHNĀ'

BAHRAIN
Al-Manāmah (Manama)

SAUDI ARABIA

AR-RIYĀD (RIYADH)

ARABIAN PENINSULA

SUDAN

NUBIAN DESERT

RED SEA

AR-RUB' AL-KHĀLĪ

Tropic of Cancer

Umm Durman (Omdurman)
AL-KHARṬŪM (KHARTOUM)
Al-Khartūm Bahri

ERITREA
Asmera

ETHIOPIA

YEMEN

Adan (Aden)

DJIBOUTI

Meters / Feet
6000 / 19680
4000 / 13120
3000 / 9840
2000 / 6560
1000 / 3280
500 / 1640
200 / 656
Sea Level
200 / 656
2000 / 6560

0   100 200 300 400 500 600 800 1000 Kilometers
0   100 200 300 400 600 Miles
Scale 1 : 10,000,000   Lambert Conformal Conic Projection

M-DRM4709-A1— -2-s-4
Copyright © Rand McNally & Co.

The boundary between India and Pakistan through the disputed
state of Jammu and Kashmir follows the "line of control"
agreed upon by both countries in 1972.

Ⓐ Area occupied by Pakistan and claimed by India.

Ⓑ Area claimed and occupied by India; status disputed by Pakistan.

Ⓒ Area occupied by China and claimed by India.

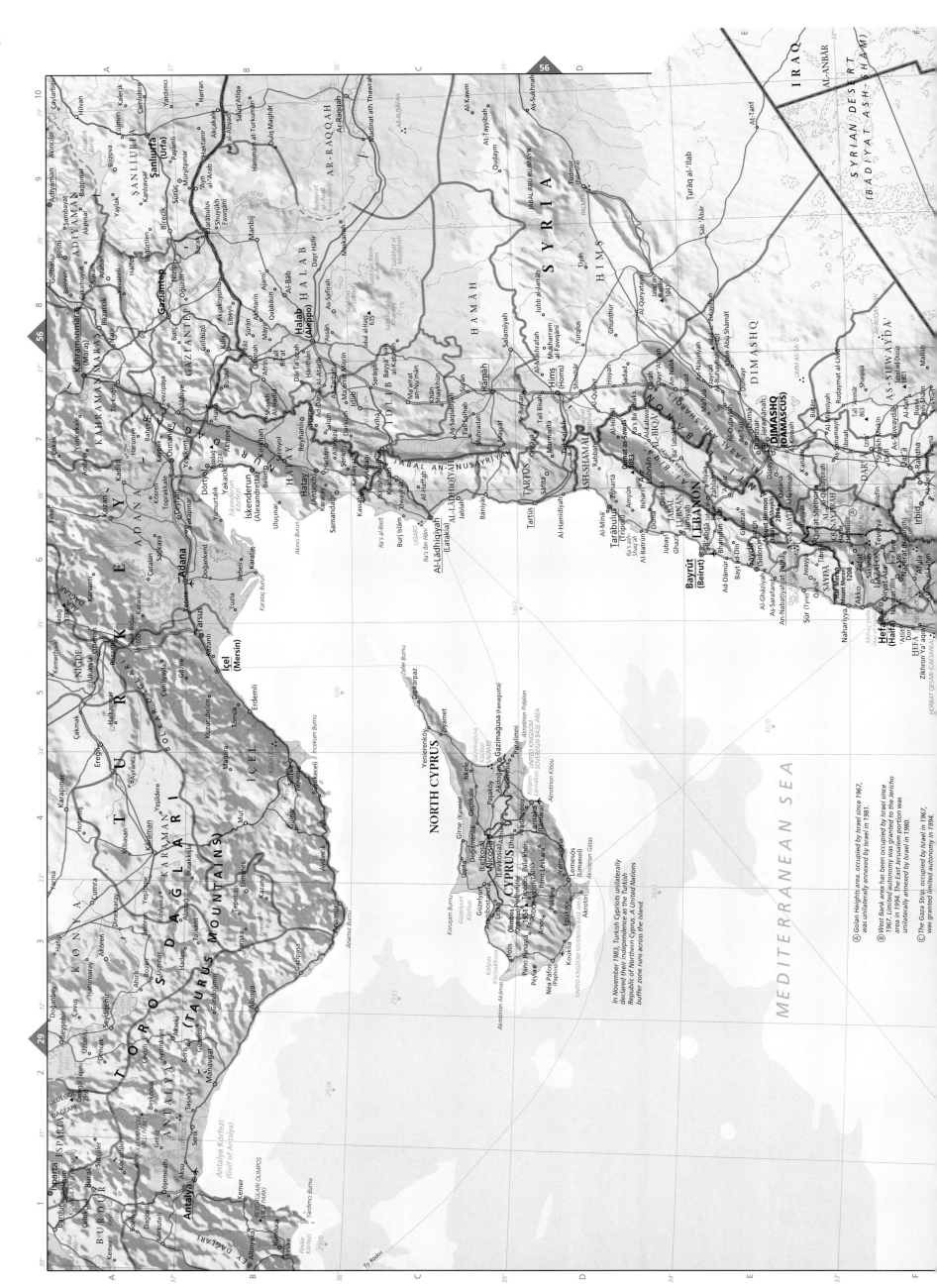

MEDITERRANEAN SEA

SYRIA

IRAQ

AL-ANBAR

SYRIAN DESERT
(BADIYAT ASH-SHAM)

AR-RAQQAH

HALAB

HAMAH

HIMS

DIMASHQ

AS-SUWAYDA'

LEBANON

NORTH CYPRUS

CYPRUS

TURKEY

TOROS DAĞLARI (TAURUS MOUNTAINS)

KONYA

ADANA

İÇEL

ANTALYA

BURDUR

ISPARTA

NIĞDE

KARAMAN DAĞLARI

HATAY

GAZIANTEP

ŞANLIURFA

ADIYAMAN

KAHRAMANMARAŞ

Ⓐ Golan Heights area, occupied by Israel since 1967, was unilaterally annexed by Israel in 1981.

Ⓑ West Bank area has been occupied by Israel since 1967. Limited autonomy was granted to the Jericho area in 1994. The East Jerusalem portion was unilaterally annexed by Israel in 1980.

Ⓒ The Gaza Strip, occupied by Israel in 1967, was granted limited autonomy in 1994.

In November 1983, Turkish Cypriots unilaterally declared their independence as the Turkish Republic of Northern Cyprus. A United Nations buffer zone runs across the island.

Scale 1 : 2,500,000

Lambert Conformal Conic Projection

Meters
Feet
3000 / 9840
2000 / 6560
1000 / 3280
500 / 1640
200 / 656
Sea Level
200 / 656
2000 / 6560

0   25   50   75   100   150   200   250 Kilometers
0   25   50   75   100   150 Miles

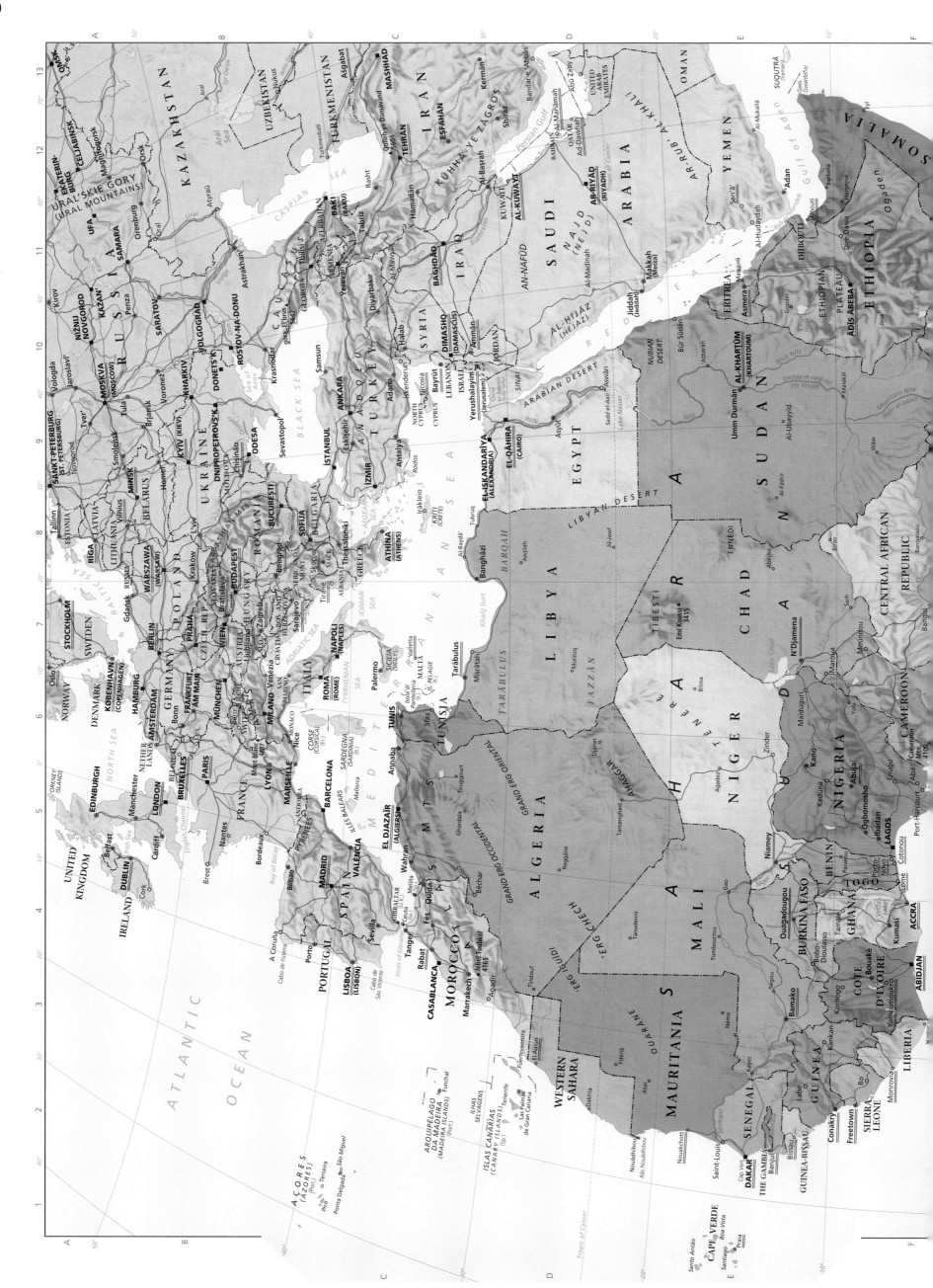

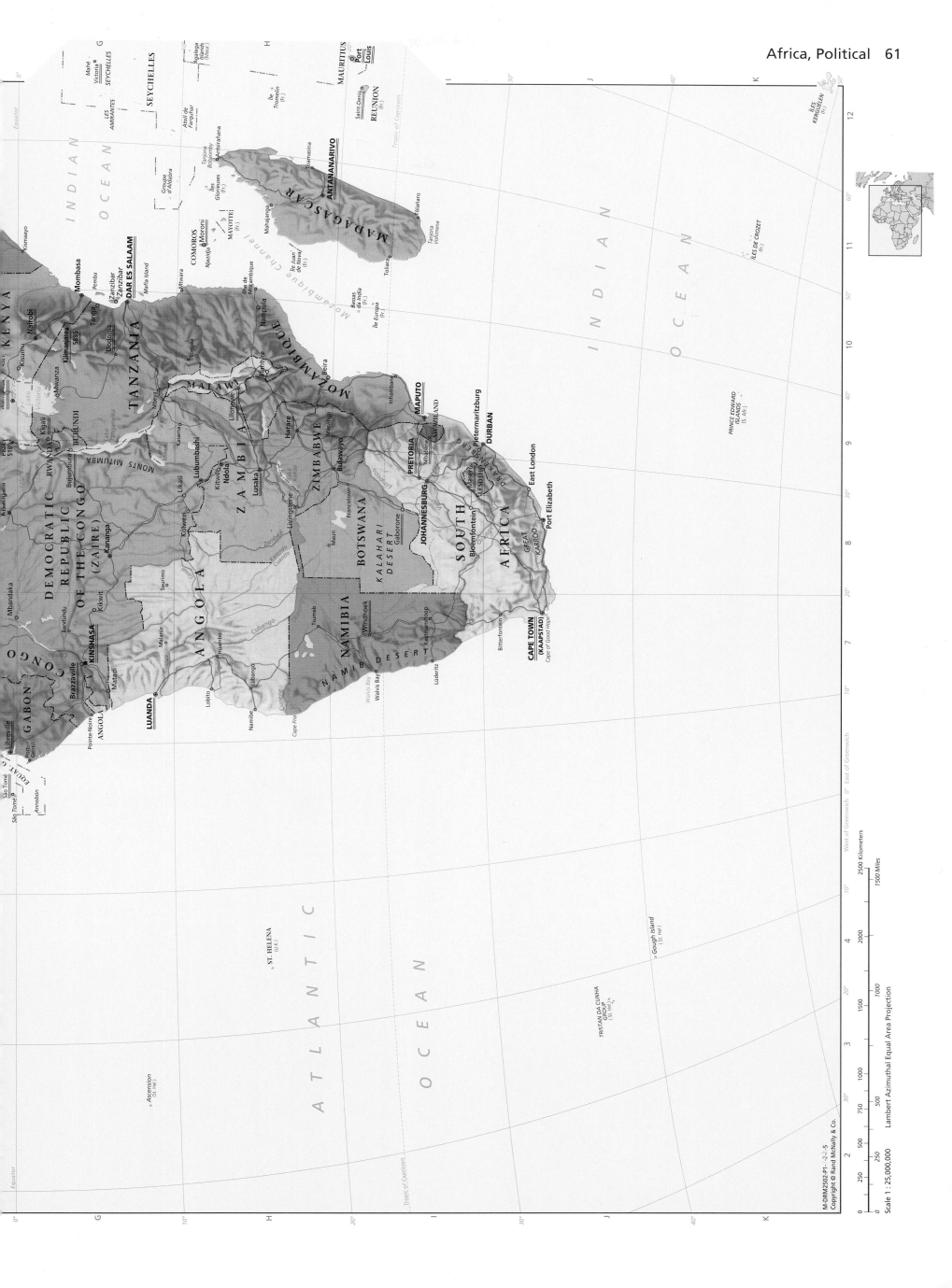

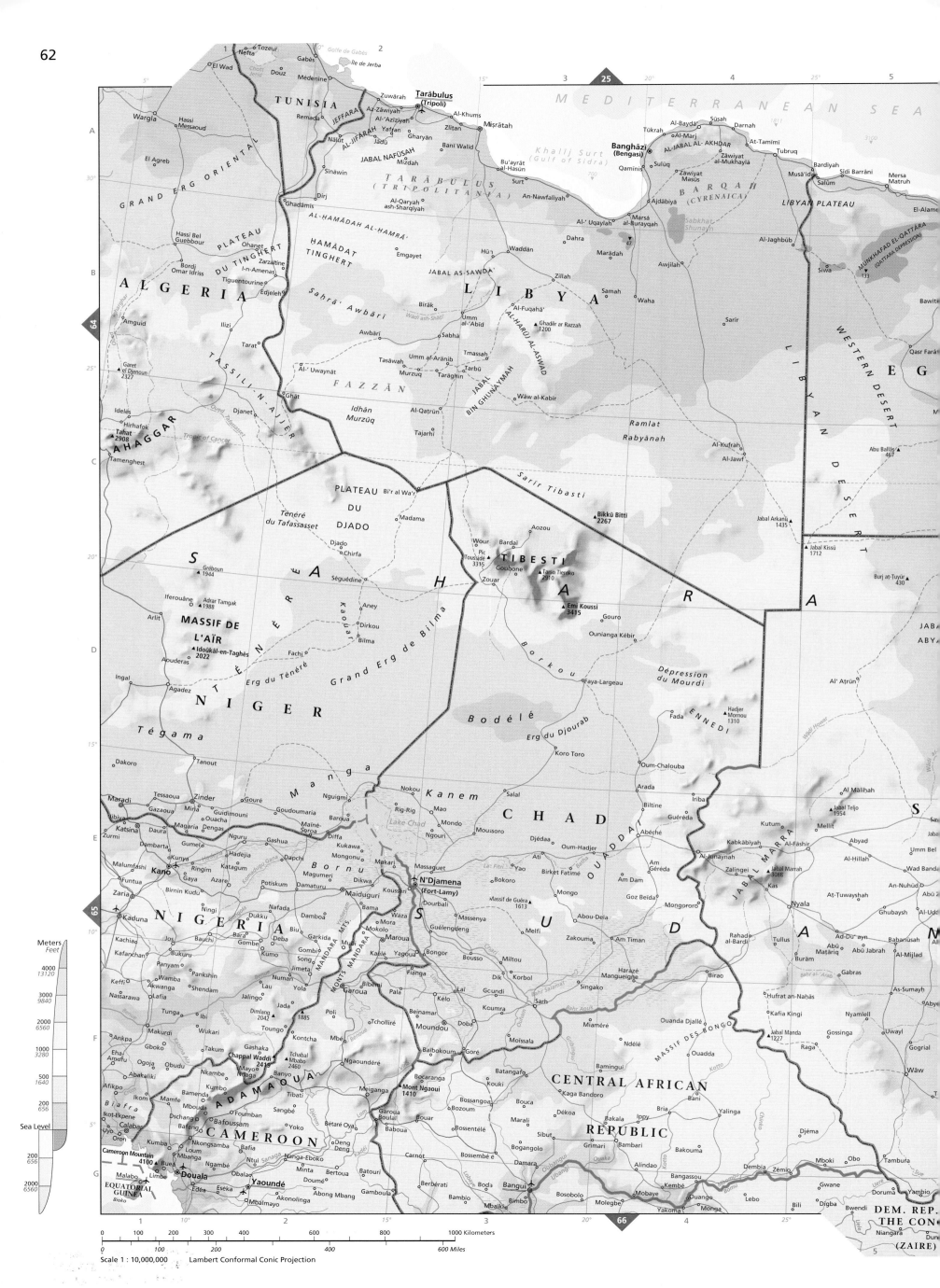

1 | 2 | 3 | **25** | 20° | 4 | 25° | 5

Golfe de Gabès
Île de Jerba

M E D I T E R R A N E A N   S E A

o Tozeur
o Nefta
Gabès o
El Wad o
Douz o
Médenine o

TUNISIA

Zuwārah o
Tarābulus
(Tripoli)
Al-Khums o
Zlitan o
Misrātah o

Tükrah o
Al-Baydā o
Sūsah o Darnah o
Al-Marj o
Banghāzī
(Bengasi)
At-Tamīmī o
Tubruq o
Bardīyah o
Sidi Barrānī o

A

Wargla o
Hassi
Messaoud o

Remada o
Nālūt o
Al-'Azīzīyah o
Yaffan o
Gharyān o
Banī Walid o

Az-Zāwiyah o
Bu'ayrāt
al-Hasūn o
Surt o

Marsa
Matrūh o
El Alamei

El Agreb o

JEFFARA
AL-JIFĀRAH

Sīnāwin o
Dirj o

T A R Ā B U L U S
(T R I P O L I T A N I A)

Khalīj Surt
(Gulf of Sidra)

Qamīnis o
Sulūq o
Ajdābiyā o

B A R Q A H
(CYRENAICA)

Zāwiyat
Masūs o
Zāwiyat
al-Mukhaylā o

Salūm o

LIBYAN PLATEAU

30°

Hassi Bel
Guebbour o

PLATEAU
DU TINGHERT

Ghadāmis o

AL-HAMĀDAH AL-HAMRĀ'

An-Nawfalīyah o
Al-'Uqaylah o
Al-Burayqah o

Dahra o

Marādah o

Sabkhat
Shunayn

Al-Jaghbūb o

Siwa o

MUNKHAFAD EL-QATTĀRA
(QATTĀRA DEPRESSION)
133

B

Ohanet o
Bordj
Omar Idriss o

HAMĀDAT
TINGHERT

Emgayet o

JABAL AS-SAWDA'

Hū o
Waddān o

Zillah o

Samah o
Waha o

Awjilah o

Qasr Farāfi

Zarzaïtine o
I-n-Amenas o
Tiguentourine o
Edjeleh o

Sahrā' Awbārī

Birāk o

JABAL AS-SAWDA'
Umm
al-'Abīd o

Sarir o

Bawīti

64

Amguid o

Ilizi o

Tarat o

Awbārī o

Sabhā o
Umm al-Arānib o
Murzuq o
Tarāghin o

JABAL
BIN GHUNAYMAH

Waha o

Qasr Farāfi

25°

ALGERIA

L I B Y A

Al-'Uwaynāt o

Tasāwah o
Tmassah o
Tarbū o

Wāw al-Kabīr o

Ramlat
Rabyānah

W E S T E R N   E G
D E S E R T

C

Garet
el Djenoun
2327

TASSILI-N-AJJER
Ghat o

Al-Qatrūn o

Tajarhī o

Al-Kufrah o
Al-Jawf o

Idelès o
Hirhafok o

AHAGGAR
Tahat
2908

F A Z Z Ā N

Idhān
Murzūq

Abu Ballās o
467

Tamenghest o

Djanet o

Sarīr Tibasti

Jabal Arkanū
1435

Tropic of Cancer

Jabal Kissū
1712

Burj at-Tuyūr
430

20°

PLATEAU
DU
DJADO
Bi'r al Wa'r o

Bikkū Bittī
2267

Aozou o

Madama o

Ténéré
du Tafassasset

Djado o
Chirfa o

Séguédine o

Wour o
Pic
Toussidé
3315
Bardaï o
Goubone o

TIBESTI

Tarso Tieroko
2910

Grébourn
1944

D

Iferouâne o
Adrar Tamgak
1988

Aney o

Dirkou o
Bilma o

Zouar o

Emi Koussi
3415

Gouro o

Arlit o

MASSIF DE
L'AÏR
Idoûkâl-en-Taghès
2022

Fachi o

Kaouar

Ounianga Kébir o

JAB
ABY

Aouderas o

Erg du Ténéré

Grand Erg de Bilma

Ingal o

B o r k o u

Faya-Largeau o

Dépression
du Mourdi

Al' Atrūn o

Agadez o

N   I   G   E   R

S
A
H
A
R
A

Hadjer
Mornou
1310

Fada o

E N N E D I

Tégama

T   É   N   É   R   É

Dakoro o
Tanout o

M a n g a

Bodélé

Erg du Djourab

Koro Toro o

Oum-Chalouba o

15°

E

Maradi o
Tessaoua o
Zinder o
Gazaoua o
Mirria o

Guidimouni o
Ouacha o
Goudoumaria o
Maïné-
Soroa o

Nguigmi o

Nokou o
Mao o

K a n e m

Salal o

Arada o

Al Māliḥah o

Libiya o
Katsina o
Daura o

Magaria o
Dengas o
Nguru o
Gashua o

Diffa o
Kukawa o

Mondo o
Ngouri o

Moussoro o

Biltine o
Guéréda o

Iriba o

Kutum o
Mellit o

Jabal Teljo
1954

Sa

Zurmi o
Dembarta o
Gumel o
Hadejia o
Katagum o
Dapchi o

Magumeri o

Makari o

Mongonu o

Massaguet o

Djédaa o
Ati o
Oum-Hadjer o
Birket Fatimé o
Yao o

Am
Géréda o

Abéché o

O U A D D A Ï

Kabkābīyah o
Al-Junaynah o
Al-Fāshir o

Abyad o

Umm Bel o

Kano ✈

Ringim o
Azare o

Damaturu o
Dikwa o

Bama o

Maiduguri o
Kousséri o

Makari o

La: Fitri

Am Dam o
Mongo o

Zalingei o

Jabal Marrah
3088

Kas o

An-Nuhūd o
Abū 2

65

Malumfashi o
Funtua o
Zaria o

aKunya o
Gaya o
Birnin Kudu o

Dukku o
Nafada o
Potiskum o
Damboa o

Mora o
Waza o

N'Djamena
(Fort-Lamy)

Bokoro o

Massenya o

Goz Beïda o

Mongororo o

Nyala o
Ghubaysh o
Al-Ud

10°

F

Kaduna o

N I G E R I A

Kachia o
Kafanchan o

Jos o
Bauchi o
Gombe o

Garkida o
Mubi o

Mokolo o
Maroua o

Dourbali o

Abou-Deïa o

Melfi o
Am Timan o

Zakouma o

Rahad
al-Bardi o
Tullus o

Ad-Du'ayn o

Abū
Matāriq o
Buram o
Abū Jabrah o
Al-Mijlad o

Birao o

As-Sumayh o
Abyei

Keffi o
Wamba o
Shendam o

Panyam o
Pankshin o

MANDARA MTS.
MTS MANDARA

Kaélé o
Yagoua o

Bongor o
Bousso o

Dik o
Korbol o

Miltou o
Fianga o

Harazé
Mangueigne o

Hufrat an-Nahās o

Kafia Kingi o

Nyamlell o
Uwayl o

Nassarawa o
Lafia o

Numan o
Jimeta o
Song o

Lau o

Laï o

Dimlang
2042

Jada o
Yola o
Poli o

Garoua o

Beinamar o

Gcundi o

Singako o
Miaméré o

Gossinga o
Gogrial o

Tunga o
Ibi o
Wukari o

Jalingo o

Toungo o
Tcholliré o

Moundou o

Doba o

Ouanda Djallé o
Ouadda o

Jabal Manda
1227

Raga o

Ankpa o
Makurdi o

1885

Kontcha o

Baïbokoum o

Goré o

Moissala o

Ndélé o

Bamingui o
Mayo o
Wâw o

5°

G

Gboko o
Takum o
Gashaka o

Chappal Waddi
2419

Tchabal
Mbabo
2460

Ngaoundéré o

Batangafo o
Kaga Bandoro o

Bria o
Bani o
Yalinga o

CENTRAL AFRICAN

Eha-
Amufu o
Obudu o

Nkambe o
Bamenda o
Mbouda o
Foumban o

Banyo o
Tibati o

Meiganga o

Mont Ngaoui
1410

Bossangoa o

Kouki o

Bouca o

Dékoa o

Ippy o
Grimari o

Bakala o

Kouango o

Bambari o

Bakouma o

Afikpo o
Ikom o
Mamfe o

ADAMAOUA

Tignère o
Ngao o

Sangbé o

Garoua
Boulaï o

Bocaranga o

Bozoum o

Bossembélé o

Bouar o
Baboua o

Marali o

Sibut o
Bogangolo o

REPUBLIC

Djéma o

Calabar o
Uyo o
Oron o

Kumba o
Mamfe o
Nkongsamba o
Bafia o

Bafoussam o
Dschang o

Yoko o

Deng
Deng o

Bétaré Oya o

Bangassou o
Kembé o
Dembia o
Zémio o
Gwane o

EQUATORIAL
GUINEA

Cameroon Mountain
4100
Buea o

Limbe o
Douala

Mbanga o
Loum o

Ngambé o
Obala o

Ntui o
Minta o
Doumé o
Batouri o

Berbérati o

Boda o

Bozo o

Bakouma o

Mobaye o
Ouango o
Monga o

Bili o
Dïgba o

DEM. REP.
THE CON

Malabo o
Bioko

Yaoundé
Eséka o
Edéa o
Mbalmayo o

Abong Mbang o

Gamboula o
Bambio o

Bimbo o
Bangui

Bosobolo o
Yakoma o
Monga o

Bwendi o
Yambio o
Dun

(ZAIRE)

5

66
20° | 25°

Meters
Feet

4000
13120

3000
9840

2000
6560

1000
3280

500
1640

200
656

Sea Level

200
656

2000
6560

0   100   200   300   400   500   600   700   800   900   1000 Kilometers

0   100   200   300   400   500   600 Miles

Scale 1 : 10,000,000   Lambert Conformal Conic Projection

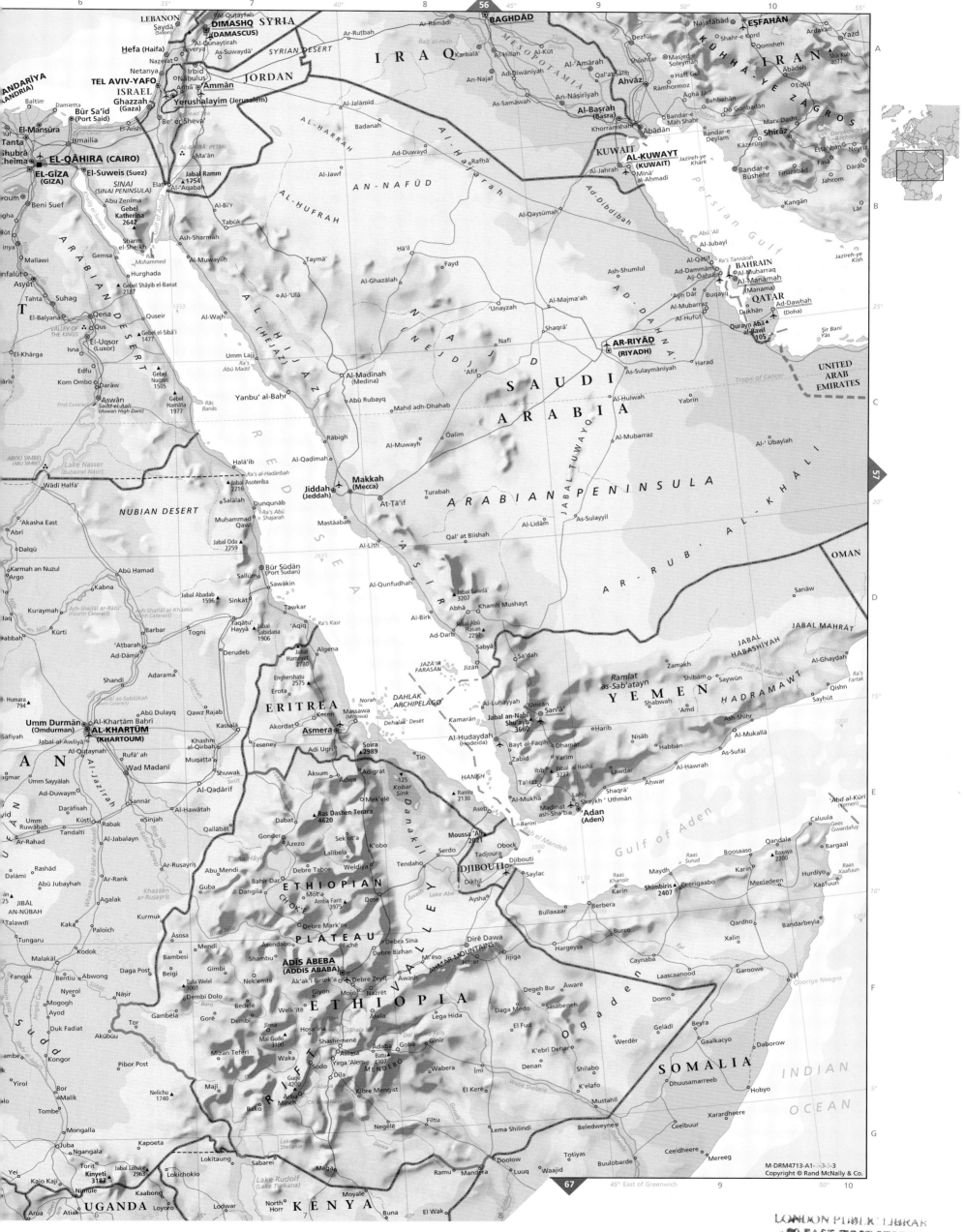

M-DRM4713-A1- -3-3-3
Copyright © Rand McNally & Co.

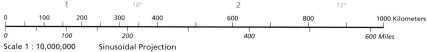

M-DRM4712-A1- -2- -2
Copyright © Rand McNally & Co.

Scale 1 : 10,000,000   Sinusoidal Projection

A

CONGO

Pointe-Noire
Làndana
Cabinda
ANGOLA
Muanda
Cabinda
Soyo
Boma
Nóqui
Quimaria
N'zeto
Nova Caipemba

LUANDA
Ponta das Palmeirinhas
Barra do Cuanza

Porto Amboim

Sumbe

Lobito
Baía Farta
Benguela
Ponta das Salinas

Cabo de
Santa Maria
Cabo de
Santa Marta
Lucira

Namibe
Ponta
Albina Tombua

Ponta
de Marca
Foz do
Cunene

Cape Fria

2   66

DEMOCRATIC
REPUBLIC
OF THE CONGO
(ZAIRE)

ANGOLA

ZAMBIA

OVAMBOLAND

KAOKOVELD
NAMIB

DAMARALAND
Windhoek

Swakopmund
Walvis Bay
Walvis Bay

NAMIBIA

BOTSWANA

KALAHARI

DESERT

Tropic of Capricorn

Conception Bay

GREAT NAMAQUALAND

DESERT

LITTLE
NAMAQUALAND
BUSHMAN LAND

ATLANTIC   OCEAN

SOUTH AFRICA

JOHANNESBURG

PRETORIA

LESOTHO

GREAT KARROO

LITTLE KARROO

CAPE TOWN
(KAAPSTAD)

Cape of Good Hope

Port Elizabeth

Meters
Feet

3000
9840

2000
6560

1000
3280

500
1640

200
656

Sea Level

200
656

2000
6560

M-800092-7A-DR2-1
Copyright © Rand McNally & Co.

0   100   200   300   400   600   800   1000 Kilometers

0   100   200   400   600 Miles

Scale 1 : 10,000,000   Lambert Conformal Conic Projection

INDIAN OCEAN

SEYCHELLES

Groupe d'Aldabra
Assomption   Atoll de Cosmoledo   St. Pierre   Atoll de Providence
Astove

Atoll oe Farquhar

COMOROS
Njazidja   Moroni   Kartala 2361
Mwali   Nzwani   Mutsamudu
Fomboni   Antsiranana
Dzaoudzi
MAYOTTE (Fr.)

ARCHIPEL DES COMORES

Iles Glorieuses (Fr.)

Uruwira   Inyonga   Kitunda   Dodoma   Mpwapwa   Zanzibar
Karema   Kipembawe   Kilosa   Morogoro   Zanzibar
Lake Tanganyika   Rungwa   Mikumi   DAR ES SALAAM
Kipili   Rungwa   Great Ruaha   Kisiju
Namanyere   Sumbawanga   Iringa   Kidatu   Mafia Island
Kasanga   Makongolosi   Sao Hill   Ifakara   Kilindoni
lungu   Chunya   Utete   Kilwa Kivinje
Mbala   Mbeya   TANZANIA   Kilwa Masoko
koso   Nakonde   KIPENGERE RANGE   Mdandu   Zinga Mulike
Kasama   Isoka   Chitipa   Karonga   Njombe   Liwale
Chinsali   Nyika Plateau 2606   Nyamtumbo   Lindi
Chitambo   Rumphi   Chilumba   Nachingwea   Mtama   Mtwara
Mpika   Mzuzu   474   Songea   Mikindani
Lundazi   Nkhata Bay   Mbamba Bay   Tunduru   Ntwara   Cabo Delgado
Mzimba   Olivenca   Masasi   Newala   Palma
Chitambo   Cobue   Diaca   Revuma
Metangula   Mueda   Quiterajo
MALAWI   Lichinga   Mecula   Macomia
Chipata   Mchinji   Nantulo   Quissanga
Katete   Salima   Niassa   Marrupa   Montepuez   Ancuabe   Pemba
Vila Gamito   Lilongwe   Catur   Balama
Furancungo   Mandimba   Lurio   Namapa
Kazula   Ulongue   Cuamba   Muite   Memba   Nampa
Zambue   Fingoe   Belem   Malema   Ribaue   Mecuburi   Nacala-a-Velha
Albufeira Cahora Bassa   Liwonde   Serra Namuli 2419   Murrupula   Monapo   Nacala
Tete   Blantyre   Zomba   Namarroi   Alto Molocue   Ilha de Mocambique
Moatize   Sapitwa 2002   Milange   Errego   Lumbo
Chioco   Thyolo   Chiromo   Lugela   Nametil
RPMENT   Tambara   Doa   Chiperone 2054   Mulevala   Mogincual
MAVURADONHA   Shamva   Changara   Nsanje   Mocuba   Mocubela   Angoche
MTS.   Bindura   Chemba   Morrumbala   Larde
Mutoko   Vila de Sena   Namacurra   Moma
Murewa   Inhaminga   Mopeia   Quelimane
ungwiza   Marondera   Vila Fontes   Marromeu
WE   Rusape   Manica   Serra da Gorongosa 1856   Chinde
Mutare   Inyangani 2592   993
Chivhu   Chimoio   Dondo   Beira
Machez   Monte Binga 2437   Chibabava   Sofala
Chipinge   Espungabera   Nova Mambone
Mwenezi   Chibuto   Vilankulo   Ilha do Bazaruto
ge   Massangena   Mabote   Ponta Sao Sebastiao
Malvernia   Mapinhane
unda   Pafuri   Chigubo   Funhalouro   Massinga
Milia   Morrumbene
Phalaborwa   Chokwe   Mabalane   Maxixe   Inhambane
Xinavane   Panda   Ponta da Barra
enburg   Komatipoort   Macia   Inharrime
pruit   Barberton   Xai-Xai   Quissico
mba   Mbabane   MAPUTO   Chidenguele
Manzini   Ilha da Inhaca
AZILAND   Bela Vista
Retief   Zitundo
Vryheid   Lavumisa   Baia de Maputo
Nongoma   Lake St. Lucia
Ulundi   Cape St. Lucia
Empangeni   Mtubatuba
town   Richard's Bay
termaritzburg   Pinetown
DURBAN
mzinto
urg

INDIAN
OCEAN

MADAGASCAR

Tanjona Bobaomby
Nosy Mitsio   Antsiranana
Nosy Be   Ambilobe   Iharana
Andoany   Ambanja   Antohira 1475
Maromandia   Maromokotro 2876   Sambava
Analalava   TSARATANANA   Andapa
Bealanana   Antsohihy   Antalaha
Mahajanga   Mandritsara   Rantabe   Maroantsetra
Soalala   Marovoay   Mampikony   Tanjona Masoala
Besalampy   Madirovalo   Tsaratanana   Andilamena   Nosy Sainte Marie
Bekodoka   Maevatanana   Ambatondrazaka   Ambodifototra
Maintirano   Morafenobe   Kandreho   Andriamena   Farihy Alaotra   Fenoarivo Atsinanana
Nosy Barren   Antsalova   Ankazobe   ANTANANARIVO   Toamasina
Ankavandra   Arivonimamo   Moramanga   Ampasimanolotra
Belo-Tsiribihina   Miandrivazo   Soavinandriana   Vatomandry
Morondava   Mahabo   Tsiafajavona 2642   Ambatolampy   Ambositra
Belo-sur-Mer   Malaimbandy   Antsirabe
Andranopasy   Mandabe   Ambatofinandrahana   Nosy-Varika
Morombe   Manja   Ambohimahasoa
Tanjona Ankaboa   Fianarantsoa   Ifanadiana
Mangoky   Beroroha   Ambalavao   Manakara
Ankazoabe   Ihosy   Ibity 2658   Vohipeno
Manombo Atsimo   Sakaraha   Ranohira   Ivolibe   Farafangana
Toliara   Bezaha   Betroka   Vondrozo   Vangaindrano
Ejeda   Bekily   Beraketa   Manantenina
Itampolo   Ampanihy   Amboasary
Androka   Midongy Atsimo
Tsiombe   Ambovombe
Tanjona Vohimena

Tropic of Capricorn

INDIAN   OCEAN

SEYCHELLES
Praslin   La Digue
Silhouette   Victoria   Mahe
SEYCHELLES
Poivre Atoll   Desroches   Ile Plate
LES AMIRANTES
Alphonse   Coetivy

a Same scale as main map
INDIAN OCEAN
Port Louis   MAURITIUS
Piton de la Petite   Curepipe
Riviere Noire   Mahebourg
828
Saint-Denis   Piton des Neiges
Saint-Paul   3070
Saint-Pierre   REUNION (Fr.)
MASCARENE ISLANDS
55° East of Greenwich   10

b Same scale as main map
INDIAN OCEAN
SEYCHELLES
Groupe d'Aldabra   St. Pierre   Atoll de Providence
Assomption   Atoll de Cosmoledo
Astove   Atoll de Farquhar   Agalega Islands (Maur.)
50° East of Greenwich

68

Meters
Feet
3000
9840

2000
6560

1000
3280

500
1640

200
656

Sea Level

200
656

2000
6560

0   100   200   300   400   600   800   1000 Kilometer

0   100   200   300   400   600 Miles

Scale 1 : 5,000,000   Lambert Conformal Conic Projection

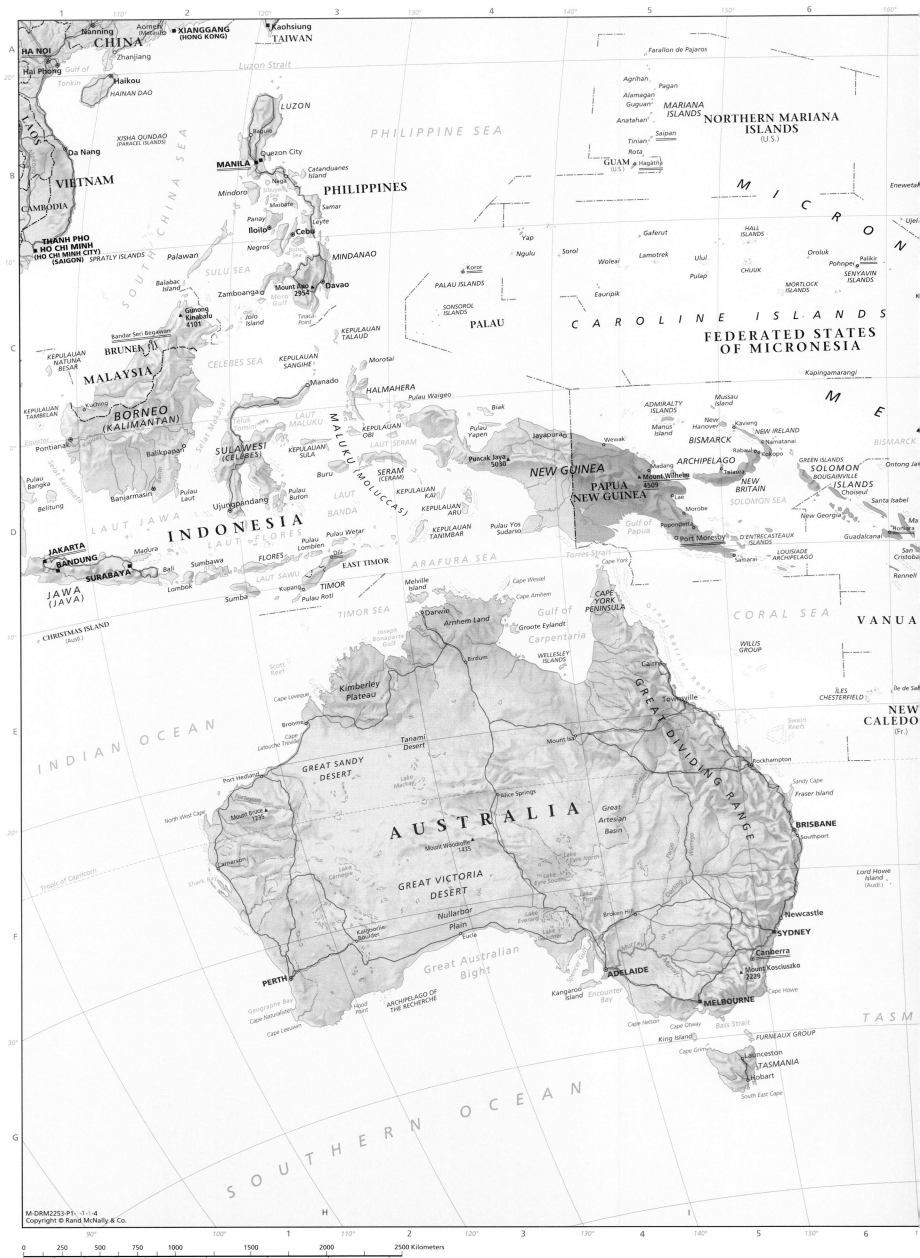

0   250   500   750   1000   1500   2000   2500 Kilometers

0   250   500   1000   1500 Miles

Scale 1 : 25,000,000   Lambert Azimuthal Equal Area Projection

WAKE ISLAND
(U.S.)

Taongi

RSHALL ISLANDS

Bikar

Rongelap

Utrik

Kwajalein   RATAK
                 CHAIN
         Maloelap
RALIK
CHAIN
Ailinglaplap   Majuro   Arno

Jaluit   Mili

Ebon

Butaritari

Tarawa Bairiki
Kuria Abemama
GILBERT ISLAND
NAURU   Banaba   Nonouti

Nikunau

Onotoa

Arorae

KIRIBATI

Kanton

Rawaki

Orona   Manra
Nikumaroro
PHOENIX ISLANDS

Nanumea
Niutao

Nui

TUVALU   Funafuti

Niulakita

Rotumā

WALLIS AND FUTUNA
(Fr.)
ÎLES WALLIS   Matā'utu
Île Futuna
Île Alofi

FIJI   VANUA
        LEVU

VITI
LEVU   Suva
        KORO SEA

LAU
GROUP

Vava'u

TONGA

Tongatapu   Nuku' alofa
          'Eua

'Ata

NORFOLK ISLAND
(Austl.)

Raoul
Island
KERMADEC ISLANDS
(N. Z.)
Curtis
Island

THREE KINGS
ISLANDS   North
             Cape
          Great Barrier
          Island
Auckland
          Bay of
NORTH ISLAND Plenty
              East Cape
New Plymouth
Cape Egmont Mount Ruapehu
             2797 Napier
             Hawke Bay
NEW
ZEALAND   Wellington
SOUTH ISLAND   Cook Strait

Aoraki
(Mount Cook) Christchurch
3754
       Canterbury
       Bight
    Dunedin
art Island Invercargill
South West Cape

CHATHAM
ISLANDS
(N. Z.)

AUCKLAND ISLANDS
(N. Z.)

ANTIPODES ISLANDS
(N. Z.)

Campbell Island
(N. Z.)

BOUNTY ISLANDS
(N. Z.)

PACIFIC

OCEAN

Kauai
Ni'ihau   O'ahu
       Honolulu Molokai
                 Maui
HAWAI'IAN
ISLANDS   Mauna Kea Hilo
(U.S.)   4205
       Kalae   HAWAI'I

Johnston Atoll
(U.S.)

Kingman Reef
(U.S.)
Palmyra Atoll
(U.S.)
       Teraina
    Tabuaeran

Howland Island
(U.S.)
Baker Island (U.S.)

KiritImati
(Christmas Island)

Jarvis
Island
(U.S.)

Equator

Malden

Starbuck

LINE ISLANDS

POLYNESIA

TOKELAU
(N. Z.)

SAMOA   Swains   AMERICAN
        Island   SAMOA
        SAMOA (U.S.)
        ISLANDS
Savai'i
Apia
Upolu Tutuila
       Pago Pago

Tafahi

Nassau Island   Manihiki

NORTHERN COOK
ISLANDS

'Suwarrow

Palmerston

COOK ISLANDS
(N. Z.)

SOUTHERN
COOK   Aitutaki
ISLANDS   Manuae
        Takutea
Rarotonga Atiu
   Avarua

ÎLES MARIA
Rurutu
     ÎLES AUSTRALES
Rimatara
Tubuai
Ralvavae

Eiao
ÎLES
MARQUISES

Hiva Oa

Fatu Hiva

Vostok

Flint

Caroline

ÎLES DU
ROI GEORGES
Mataiva
Manuae   Bora-Bora   Raraka
Maupihaa
        ARCHIPEL DE LA SOCIÉTÉ   Anaa
        (SOCIETY ISLANDS) Tahiti
                Papeete
          Maua Mataiva

FRENCH POLYNESIA
(Fr.)

Tematangi Tureia
Mururoa   Marutea
        Tropic of Capricorn

Rapa

ÎLES STUAMOTU

ÎLES DU
DÉSAPPOINTEMENT

Marutea

Ahunui   Pukaruha
         Reao

ÎLES
GAMBIER

PITCAIRN
(U.K.)
       Adamstown

Ernest Legouvé
Reef

Maria Teresa
Reef

PACIFIC OCEAN

International Date Line

SOLOMON
ISLANDS

SANTA CRUZ
ISLANDS
Vanikolo

ÎLES BANKS
Vanua Lava
Espiritu
Santo   NEW
        Pentecôte
Malakula Ambrym
HEBRIDES
Port Vila Éfaté
Erromango
Tanna
NOUVELLE-
CALÉDONIE
Lifou
ÎLES LOYAUTÉ
Nouméa Maré
   Île des
   Pins

Anatom

Kaduvu

Meters
Feet

2000
6560

1000
3280

500
1640

200
656

Sea Level

200
656

2000
6560

0 100 200 300 400 600 800 1000 Kilometers

0   100   200   400   600 Miles

Scale 1 : 10,000,000   Lambert Conformal Conic Projection

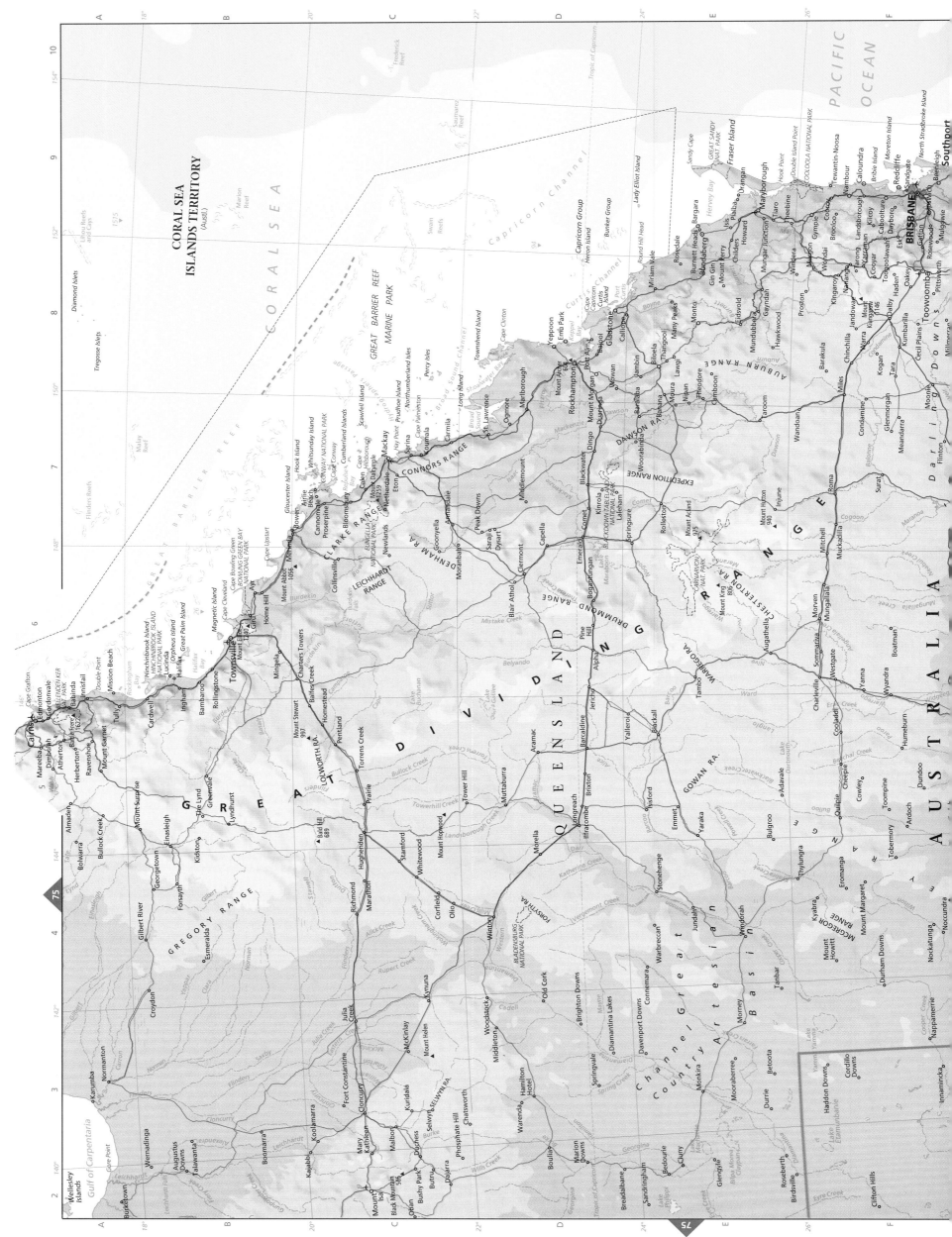

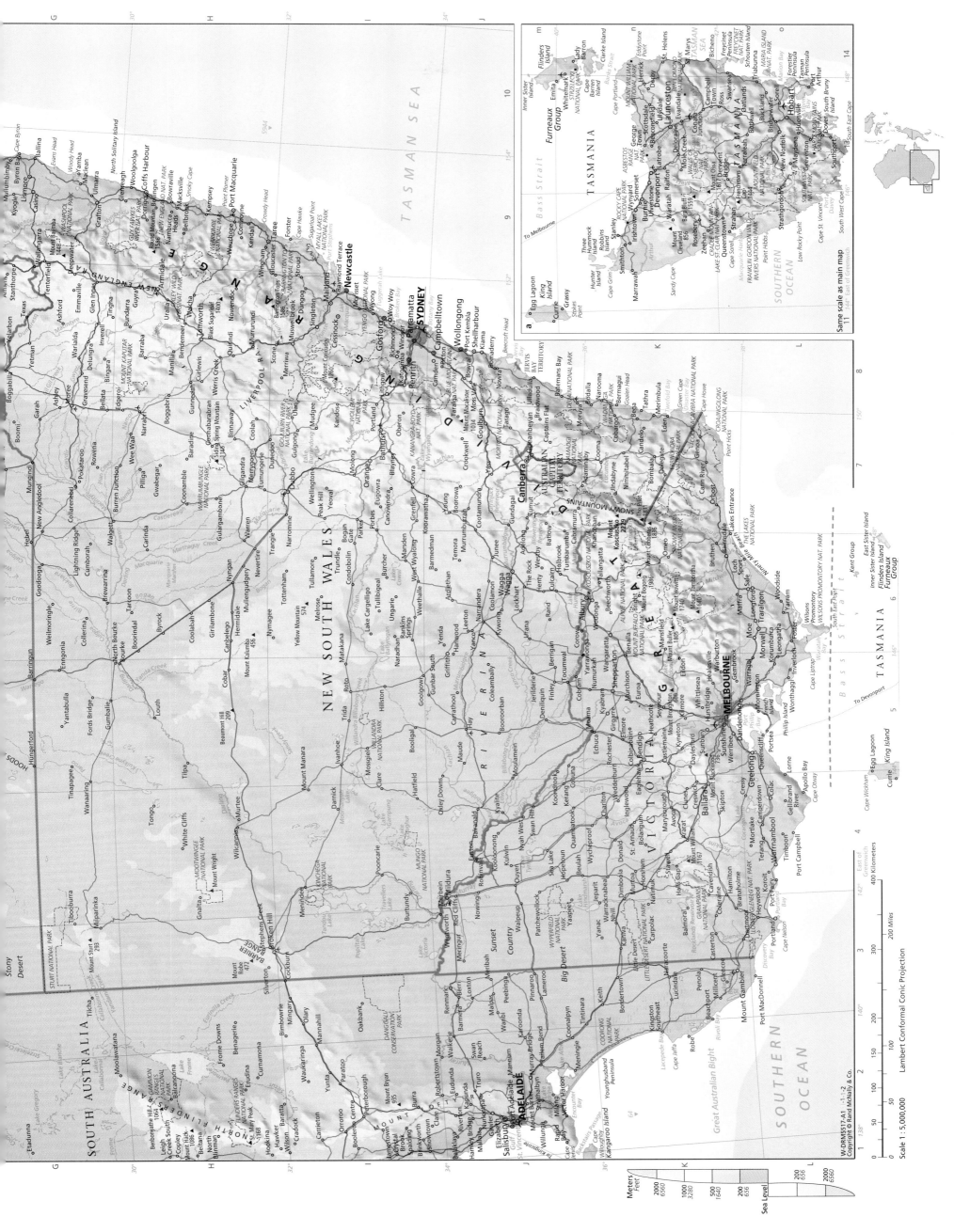

TASMAN SEA

TASMANIA

Same scale as main map

Bass Strait

Furneaux Group

SOUTHERN OCEAN

QUEENSLAND

NEW SOUTH WALES

SYDNEY
Newcastle
Wollongong

Canberra
AUSTRALIAN CAPITAL TERRITORY

SOUTH AUSTRALIA

ADELAIDE

VICTORIA

MELBOURNE

TASMANIA

Bass Strait

SOUTHERN OCEAN

Great Australian Bight

Stony Desert

GREAT DIVIDING RANGE

RIVERINA

Scale 1 : 5,000,000

Lambert Conformal Conic Projection

Meters Feet
2000 6560
1000 3280
500 1640
200 656
Sea Level
200 656
2000 6560

0   50   100   150   200   300   400 Kilometers
0   50   100   200 Miles

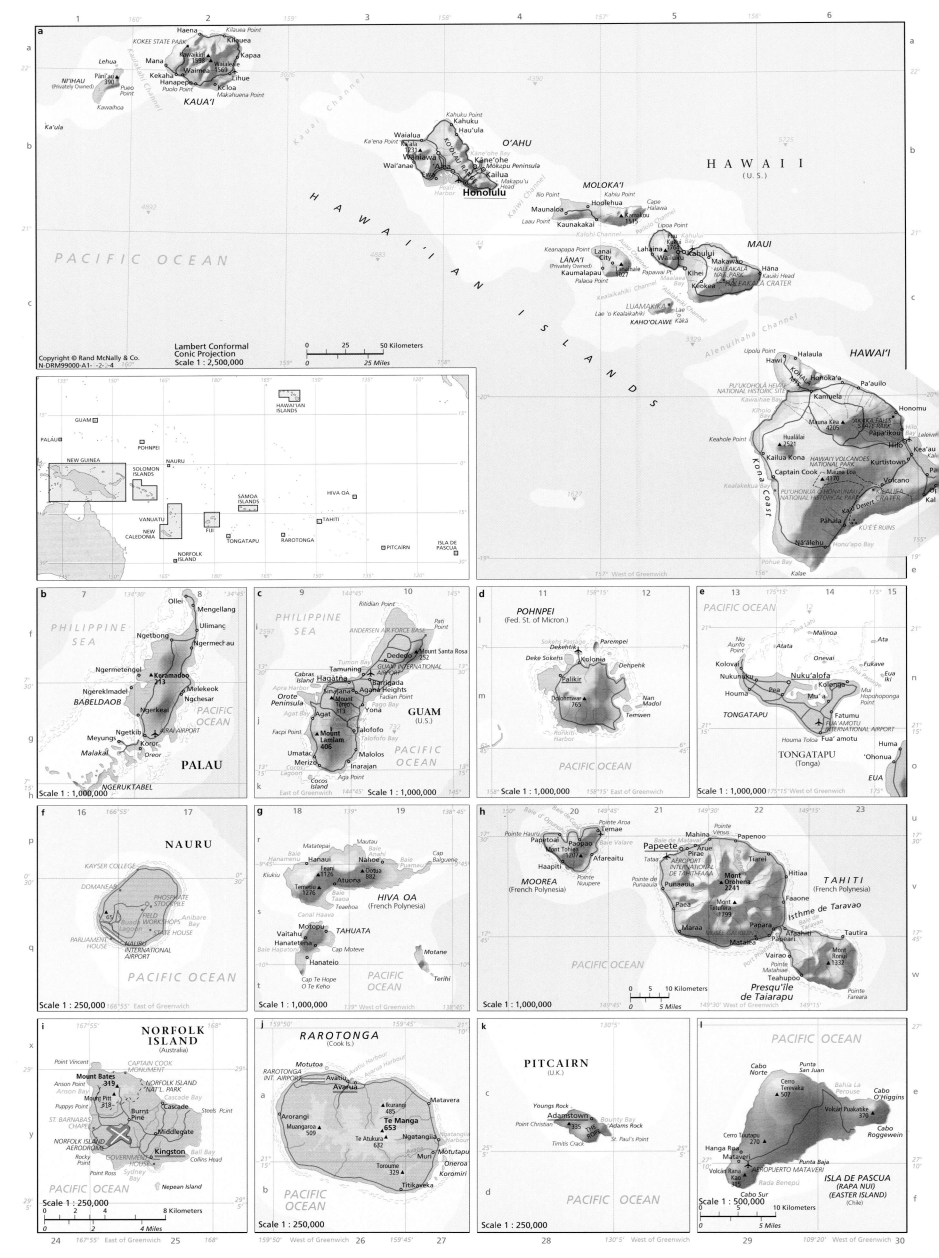

a

Haena • Kilauea Point
KOKEE STATE PARK • Kilauea
Lehua • Kawaikini • Kapaa
1598 ▲ • Waialeale
Mana • Waialeale
NI'IHAU • Pāni'au • Waimea 1563 ▲
(Privately Owned) 390 ▲
Kekaha • Hanapepe • Lihue
Pueo • Puolo Point • Koloa
Point • Makahuena Point
Ka'ula • **KAUA'I**

Kawaihoa

HAWAII
(U. S.)

Kahuku Point
Waialua • Kahuku
Ka'ena Point • Hau'ula
Wahiawa • **O'AHU**
Wai'anae • Kane'ohe • Mokapu Peninsula
Kailua • Makapu'u Head

Honolulu • Pearl Harbor

Ilio Point • **MOLOKA'I** • Kahiu Point
Maunaloa • Hoolehua • Cape Halawa
Kaunakakai • Kamakou 1515 ▲
Laau Point • Lipoa Point

Kahului Bay • Pu'u Kahului • Kahului
LĀNA'I • Lahaina • Wailuku • Kahului **MAUI**
Lanai City • Makawao
Kaumalapau • Lanaihale • Papawai Pt • HALEAKALA NAT'L PARK
Palaoa Point • Kihei • Kauiki Head
Keokea • HALEAKALA CRATER
LUAMAKIKA
Lae 'o Kealaikahiki • Lae
KAHO'OLAWE • Kākā

PACIFIC OCEAN

Alenuihaha Channel

Upolu Point • Halaula • **HAWAI'I**
Hawi • Honoka'a • Pa'auilo
PU'UKOHOLA HEIAU NATIONAL HISTORIC SITE
Kawaihae Bay • Kamuela • Honomu
Mauna Kea 4205 ▲ • Papa'ikou
Keahole Point • Hualalai 2521 ▲ • Hilo • Kea'au
Kailua Kona • HAWAI'I VOLCANOES NATIONAL PARK • Kurtistown
Captain Cook • Mauna Loa 4170 ▲ • Volcano
Kealakekua Bay • PU'UHONUA O HONAUNAU NATIONAL HISTORICAL PARK • Papeari
Kona Coast • KILAUEA CRATER
Nā'ālehu • Pahala • KŪ'Ē'Ē RUINS
Pōhue Bay • Honu'apo Bay
Kalae

Copyright © Rand McNally & Co.
N-DRM99000-A1- -2- -4
Lambert Conformal Conic Projection
Scale 1 : 2,500,000

0 25 50 Kilometers
0 25 Miles

b Ollei
PHILIPPINE SEA • Mengellang
Ulimang
Ngetbong • Ngermechau
Ngermetengel • **Keramadoo** 213 ▲
Ngereklmadel • Melekeok
BABELDAOB • Ngchesar
Ngerkeai • **PACIFIC OCEAN**
Meyungs • Ngetkib
Malakal • Koror • Oreor
PALAU
NGERUKTABEL
Scale 1 : 1,000,000

c Ritidian Point
PHILIPPINE SEA
ANDERSEN AIR FORCE BASE • Pati Point
Dededo • Mount Santa Rosa 252 ▲
Tumon Bay • GUAM INTERNATIONAL AIRPORT
Cabras Island • Tamuning
Apra Harbor • **Hagåtña** • Barrigada
Orote Peninsula • Sinajana • Agana Heights • Fadian Point
Agat • Mount Tenjo • Yona • Pago Bay
Facpi Point • Talofofo 732 ▲ • **GUAM** (U.S.)
Mount Lamlam 406 ▲ • Talofofo Bay
Umatac • Malolos • **PACIFIC OCEAN**
Merizo • Inarajan
Cocos Lagoon • Aga Point
Cocos Island
Scale 1 : 1,000,000

d **POHNPEI** (Fed. St. of Micron.)
Sokehs Passage • Parempei
Dekehtik • Deke Sokehs • Kolonia
Palikir • Dehpehk
Dolohnmwar 765 ▲ • Nan Madol
Roñkiti Harbor • Temwen
PACIFIC OCEAN
Scale 1 : 1,000,000

e **PACIFIC OCEAN**
Aiva Lahi
Niu • Malinoa • Ata
Aunfo Point • Atata • Onevai • Fukave
Koloval • Nukunuku • **Nuku'alofa** • Eua Iki
Houma • Pea • Kolonga • Mui Hopohoponga Point
TONGATAPU • Mu'a • Fatumu • FUA'AMOTU INTERNATIONAL AIRPORT
Houma Toloa • Fua' amotu • Huma • 'Ohonua
TONGATAPU (Tonga) • **EUA**
Scale 1 : 1,000,000

f **NAURU**
KAYSER COLLEGE
DOMANEAB • Anibare Bay
PHOSPHATE STOCKPILE
FIELD WORKSHOPS • STATE HOUSE
Buada Lagoon 65 ▲
PARLIAMENT HOUSE
NAURU INTERNATIONAL AIRPORT
PACIFIC OCEAN
Scale 1 : 250,000

g Baie Matatepai • Mautau • Baie Anahi
Baie Hanamenu • Hanaui • Nahoe • Cap Balguerie
Kiukiu • Feani 1126 ▲ • Baie Puamau
Temetiu 1276 ▲ • **Ootua** 882 ▲
Atuona • **HIVA OA** (French Polynesia)
Baie Taaoa • Teaehoa
Motopu • **TAHUATA**
Vaitahu • Canal Haava
Hanatetena • Motane
Baie Hapatoni • Cap Moteve • Terihi
Cap Te Hope • Hanateio • **PACIFIC OCEAN**
O Te Keho
Scale 1 : 1,000,000

h Baie d'Opunohu • Pointe Aroa • Pointe Venus • Papenoo
Pointe Hauru • Temae • Mahina
Papetoai • Paopao • **Papeete** • Arue • Tiarei
Mont Tohiea 1207 ▲ • Pirae
Haapiti • Afareaitu • Hitiaa
MOOREA (French Polynesia) • AEROPORT INTERNATIONAL DE TAHITI-FAAA
Pointe Nuupere • Tataa • Punaauia • Mont Orohena 2241 ▲
Pointe de Punaauia • Paea • Faaone
Maraa • Mont Teufaiva 1799 ▲ • Faaone
Papara • Afaahiti • **TAHITI** (French Polynesia)
PACIFIC OCEAN • Vairao • Tautira
Matalea • Pointe Matahiae • Mont Ronui 1332 ▲
Teahupoo • Papeari • Isthme de Taravao
Presqu'île de Taiarapu • Port Phaeton
Pointe Fareara

0 5 10 Kilometers
0 5 Miles
Scale 1 : 1,000,000

i **NORFOLK ISLAND** (Australia)
CAPTAIN COOK MONUMENT
Point Vincent • NORFOLK ISLAND NAT'L PARK • Cascade Bay
Mount Bates 319 ▲
Anson Bay • Mount Pitt 318 ▲ • Cascade
Puppys Point • Burnt Pine • Steels Point
ST. BARNABAS CHAPEL • Middlegate
NORFOLK ISLAND AERODROME • **Kingston**
Rocky Point • GOVERNMENT HOUSE • Collins Head
Point Ross • Sydney Bay • Ball Bay
Nepean Island
PACIFIC OCEAN
Scale 1 : 250,000
0 2 4 8 Kilometers
0 2 4 Miles

j **RAROTONGA** (Cook Is.)
Motutoa • Avatiu Harbour • Avana Harbour
RAROTONGA INT. AIRPORT • Avarua
Arorangi • Ikurangi 485 ▲ • Matavera
Muangaroa 509 ▲ • **Te Manga** 653 ▲ • Ngatangiia Harbour
Te Atukura 632 ▲ • Muri • Motutapu
Toroume 329 ▲ • Oneroa • Koromiri
PACIFIC OCEAN • Titikaveka
Scale 1 : 250,000

k **PITCAIRN** (U.K.)
Youngs Rock • Bounty Bay
Adamstown 335 ▲ • THE ROPE • Adams Rock
Point Christian • St. Paul's Point
Timitis Crack
PACIFIC OCEAN
Scale 1 : 250,000

l **PACIFIC OCEAN**
Cabo Norte • Punta San Juan
Cerro Terevaka 507 ▲ • Bahia La Perouse
Cabo O'Higgins
Volcán Puakatike 370 ▲
Cerro Tautapu 270 ▲ • Cabo Roggewein
Hanga Roa • Mataveri
Punta Baja • AEROPUERTO MATAVERI
Volcán Rana Kau 345 ▲
Cabo Sur • Rada Benepú
ISLA DE PASCUA (RAPA NUI) (EASTER ISLAND) (Chile)
Scale 1 : 500,000
0 5 10 Kilometers
0 5 Miles

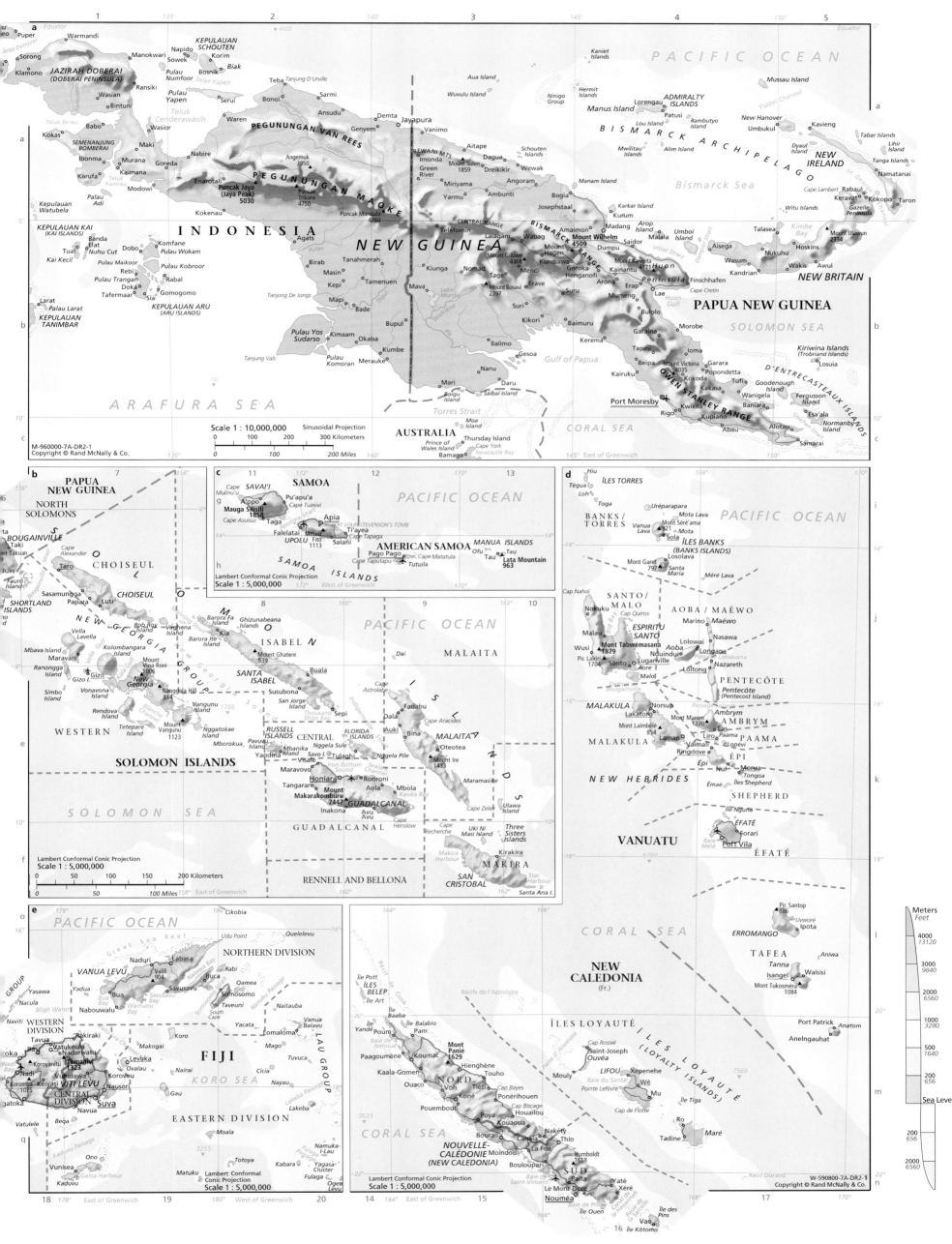

a

Equator

PACIFIC OCEAN

Puper
Warmandi
Sorong
Manokwari
KEPULAUAN SCHOUTEN
Napido
Korim
JAZIRAH DOBERAI
(DOBERAI PENINSULA)
Klamono
Sowek
Pulau Numfoor
Biak
Selat Yapen
Teba
Tanjung D'Urville
Kaniet Islands
Mussau Island
Bosnik
Ransiki
Pulau Yapen
Serui
Sarmi
Wuvulu Island
Aua Island
Hermit Islands
Lorengau
ADMIRALTY ISLANDS
Patusi
Manus Island
Lou Island
Rambutyo Island
New Hanover
Dyaul Island
Umbukul
Kavieng
Tabar Islands
Wasian
Bintuni
Waren
Wasior
Demta
Jayapura
BISMARCK ARCHIPELAGO
NEW IRELAND
Lihir Island
Kokas
Babo
PEGUNUNGAN VAN REES
Genyem
Vanimo
Aitape
Schouten Islands
Wewak
Bogia
Karkar Island
Mwililai
Alim Island
Witu Islands
Cape Lambert
Rabaul
Keravat
Kokopo
Taron
Namatanai

INDONESIA
NEW GUINEA
PAPUA NEW GUINEA

ARAFURA SEA
CORAL SEA
AUSTRALIA

b

PAPUA NEW GUINEA
NORTH SOLOMONS
BOUGAINVILLE
CHOISEUL
NEW GEORGIA GROUP
SHORTLAND ISLANDS
ISABEL
SANTA ISABEL
MALAITA
WESTERN
SOLOMON ISLANDS
CENTRAL
RUSSELL ISLANDS
FLORIDA ISLANDS
Honiara
GUADALCANAL
Mount Makarakomburu 2447
SOLOMON SEA
MAKIRA
RENNELL AND BELLONA
SAN CRISTOBAL

c

SAMOA
PACIFIC OCEAN
SAVAI'I
Apia
UPOLU
AMERICAN SAMOA
MANUA ISLANDS
Pago Pago
Lata Mountain 963
SAMOA ISLANDS

d

ÎLES TORRES
BANKS / TORRES
ÎLES BANKS (BANKS ISLANDS)
PACIFIC OCEAN
SANTO / MALO
ESPIRITU SANTO
Mont Tabwémasana 1879
AOBA / MAÉWO
PENTECÔTE
Pentecôte (Pentecost Island)
MALAKULA
AMBRYM
PAAMA
ÉPI
NEW HEBRIDES
SHEPHERD
VANUATU
ÉFATÉ
Port Vila

e

PACIFIC OCEAN
VANUA LEVU
NORTHERN DIVISION
Labasa
FIJI
WESTERN DIVISION
VITI LEVU
Suva
CENTRAL DIVISION
EASTERN DIVISION
LAU GROUP
KORO SEA
CORAL SEA

NEW CALEDONIA (Fr.)
ERROMANGO
TAFEA
Tanna
ÎLES BELEP
NORD
Mont Panié 1629
ÎLES LOYAUTÉ (LOYALTY ISLANDS)
LIFOU
SUD
NOUVELLE-CALÉDONIE (NEW CALEDONIA)
Nouméa
CORAL SEA

Meters
Feet
4000 / 13120
3000 / 9840
2000 / 6560
1000 / 3280
500 / 1640
200 / 656
Sea Level
200 / 656
2000 / 6560

PACIFIC OCEAN

TASMAN SEA

NORTH ISLAND

Three Kings Islands

Cape Reinga
North Cape
Rangaunu Bay
Doubtless Bay
Ahipara Bay
Cape Brett
Taurca Point
Okaihau
Opua
Whangarei

Dargaville
Wellsford
Bream Bay
Great Barrier Island
Kaipara Harbour
Mercury Islands
Hauraki Gulf
Auckland
North Shore City
Coromandel Peninsula
Waitemata
Manukau
Manukau Harbour
Thames
Mayor Island
Pukekohe
Waiuku
Waihi
Bay of Plenty
White Island
Cape Runaway
East Cape
Huntly
Morrinsville
Tauranga
Hamilton
Cambridge
Te Awamutu
Whakatane
Opotiki
Hikurangi 1752
Kawhia Harbour
Te Kuiti
Rotorua
Murupara
UREWERA NATIONAL PARK
RAUKUMARA RA.
Taumarunui
TONGARIRO NATIONAL PARK
Taupo
Lake Taupo
Gisborne
Waitara
New Plymouth
Mount Taranaki (Mount Egmont)
EGMONT NATIONAL PARK
Cape Egmont 2518
Stratford
Tarawera
Wairoa
Mahia Peninsula
Opunake
Hawera
Mount Ruapehu 2797
Raetihi
Napier
South Taranaki Bight
Patea
Taihape
Hastings
Cape Kidnappers
Hawke Bay
Waitotara
Wanganui
Waipukurau
Dannevirke
Palmerston North
Woodville
Levin
Otaki
Masterton
RUAHINE RANGE
TARARUA RA.
Lower Hutt
Wellington
Cape Palliser
Cape Farewell
Golden Bay
D'Urville Island
Takaka
Tasman Bay
ABEL TASMAN NATIONAL PARK
Motueka
Nelson
Richmond
Picton
Blenheim
Karamea Bight
Seddonville
Mount Owen 1875
NELSON LAKES NATIONAL PARK
Cape Foulwind
Westport
Cape Campbell
Mount Uriah 1925
Mount Travers 2338
Tapuae-o-Uenuku 2885
Reefton
SPENSER MTS.
Manakau 2610
Runanga
Greymouth
Kaikoura
Hokitika
ARTHUR'S PASS NATIONAL PARK
Wiau
Ross
Culverden
Mount Murchison 2400
Waipara
Whataroa
Oxford
Pegasus Bay
Sheffield
Kaiapoi
SOUTHERN ALPS
MOUNT COOK NATIONAL PARK
Christchurch
WESTLAND NATIONAL PARK
Aoraki (Mount Cook) 3754
Methven
Little River
Banks Peninsula
Mount Somers
Lake Tekapo
Southbridge
Haast
Ashburton
Canterbury Plains
Cascade Point
MOUNT ASPIRING NATIONAL PARK
Fairlie
Canterbury Bight
Mount Aspiring 3030
Lake Hawea
Milford Sound
Timaru
LIVINGSTONE MTS.
Mount Tutoko 2746
Mount Aspiring
Omarama
Mount St. Bathans 2088
Wanaka
Kurow
Waimate
FIORDLAND NATIONAL PARK
Lake Wakatipu
Queenstown
Cromwell
Ranfurly
Oamaru
Doubtful Sound
Kingston
Alexandra
Resolution Island
Te Anau
Roxburgh
Palmerston
West Cape
Mossburn
Edievale
Beaumont
Port Chalmers
Cape Providence
Nightcaps
Dunedin
Otautau
Winton
Gore
Milton
Te Waewae Bay
Riverton
Invercargill
Kaitangata
Tahakopa
Bluff
Tokanui
Mount Anglem 980
Ruapuke Island
Foveaux Strait
South West Cape
STEWART ISLAND
Snares Islands
Bounty Islands

NEW ZEALAND

PACIFIC OCEAN

SOUTH ISLAND

Cook Strait

Meters / Feet
3000 / 9840
2000 / 6560
1000 / 3280
500 / 1640
200 / 656
Sea Level
200 / 656
2000 / 6560

0 50 100 150 200 300 400 500 Kilometers
0 50 100 200 300 Miles
Scale 1 : 5,000,000　Lambert Conformal Conic Projection

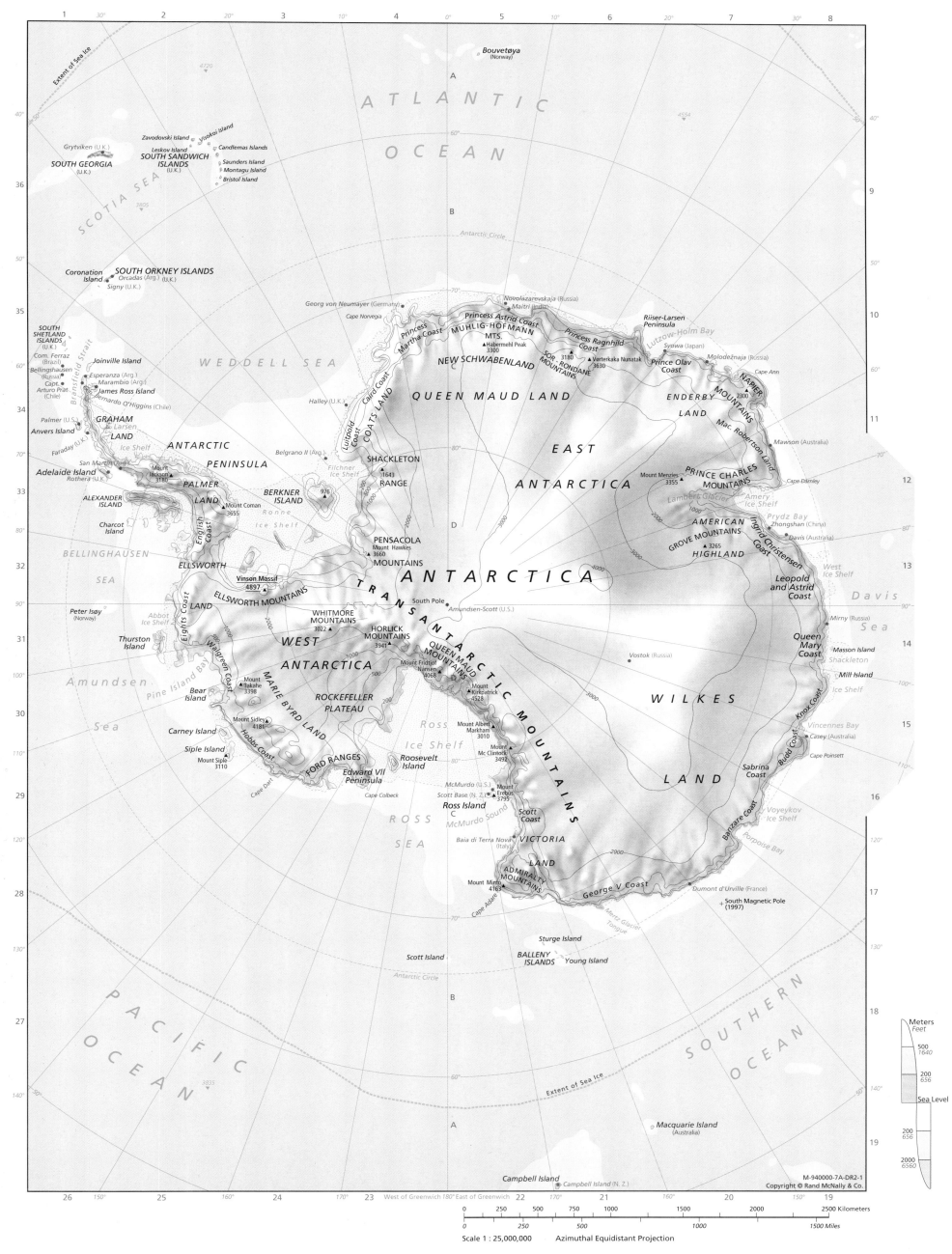

ATLANTIC

OCEAN

Bouvetøya
(Norway)

SCOTIA SEA

Grytviken (U.K.)
SOUTH GEORGIA
(U.K.)

Zavodovski Island
Visokoi Island
Leskov Island
SOUTH SANDWICH
ISLANDS
(U.K.)

Candlemas Islands

Saunders Island
Montagu Island
Bristol Island

Antarctic Circle

Georg von Neumayer (Germany)
Novolazarevskaja (Russia)
Maitri (India)

Cape Norvegia

Coronation
Island
SOUTH ORKNEY ISLANDS
Orcadas (Arg.) (U.K.)
Signy (U.K.)

SOUTH
SHETLAND
ISLANDS
(U.K.)
Com. Ferraz
(Brazil)
Bellingshausen
(Russia)
Capt.
Arturo Prat
(Chile)
Joinville Island
Esperanza (Arg.)
Marambio (Arg.)
James Ross Island
Bernardo O'Higgins (Chile)

WEDDELL SEA

Princess
Martha Coast
Princess Astrid Coast
MÜHLIG-HOFMANN
MTS.
NEW SCHWABENLAND
Habermehl Peak
3300

Princess Ragnhild
Coast
SØR RONDANE
MOUNTAINS
3180
3630
Varterkaka Nunatak

Riiser-Larsen
Peninsula
Lützow-Holm Bay
Syowa (Japan)
Molodežnaja (Russia)

Prince Olav
Coast
NAPIER
2300
Cape Ann

Halley (U.K.)

Caird Coast

COATS LAND

QUEEN MAUD LAND

ENDERBY
LAND

MOUNTAINS
Mac. Robertson Land

Palmer (U.S.)
GRAHAM
LAND
Larsen
Ice Shelf

ANTARCTIC
PENINSULA

Luitpold Coast

Belgrano II (Arg.)
Filchner
Ice Shelf

SHACKLETON
1643
RANGE

EAST
ANTARCTICA

Mawson (Australia)

PRINCE CHARLES
MOUNTAINS
Mount Menzies
3355

Anvers Island
Faraday (U.K.)
San Martín (Arg.)
Adelaide Island
Rothera (U.K.)
Mount
Jackson
3180

PALMER
LAND

ALEXANDER
ISLAND

Charcot Island

BELLINGHAUSEN

SEA

Berkner
Island
976

Mount Coman
3655

Ronne
Ice Shelf

PENSACOLA
Mount Hawkes
3660
MOUNTAINS

Cape Darnley
Lambert Glacier
Amery
Ice Shelf

AMERICAN
HIGHLAND
GROVE MOUNTAINS
3265

Prydz Bay
Zhongshan (China)
Davis (Australia)

West
Ice Shelf

English
Coast

ELLSWORTH

ANTARCTICA

Leopold
and Astrid
Coast

Davis

Sea

Peter Isøy
(Norway)

Vinson Massif
4897
ELLSWORTH MOUNTAINS

TRANSANTARCTIC MOUNTAINS

South Pole
Amundsen-Scott (U.S.)

Ingrid Christensen Coast

Queen
Mary
Coast

Mirny (Russia)

Abbot
Ice Shelf

WHITMORE
MOUNTAINS
3022

HORLICK
MOUNTAINS
3941

WEST
ANTARCTICA

Eights Coast

Thurston
Island

Walgreen Coast

QUEEN MAUD
MOUNTAINS

Vostok (Russia)

Masson Island
Shackleton
Mill Island
Ice Shelf

WILKES

LAND

Amundsen

Sea

Pine Island Bay

Bear
Island
Mount
Takahe
3398

MARIE BYRD LAND

ROCKEFELLER
PLATEAU

Mount Fridtjof
Nansen
4068

Mount
Kirkpatrick
4528

Mount Albert
Markham
3010

Knox Coast

Vincennes Bay
Casey (Australia)

Cape Poinsett

Carney Island

Siple Island
Mount Siple
3110

Mount Sidley
4181

Hobbs Coast

FORD RANGES

Roosevelt
Island

Ross
Ice Shelf

Mount
Mc Clintock
3492

Sabrina
Coast

Budd Coast

Banzare Coast

Cape Dart

Edward VII
Peninsula

Cape Colbeck

McMurdo (U.S.)
Scott Base (N. Z.)
Ross Island

Mount
Erebus
3795

Scott
Coast

Voyeykov
Ice Shelf

Porpoise Bay

ROSS

SEA

McMurdo Sound

Baia di Terra Nova (Italy)

VICTORIA

LAND

George V Coast

Dumont d'Urville (France)

South Magnetic Pole
(1997)

Mount Minto
4163
ADMIRALTY
MOUNTAINS

Cape Adare

Mertz Glacier
Tongue

Sturge Island

Scott Island

BALLENY
ISLANDS
Young Island

Antarctic Circle

PACIFIC

OCEAN

SOUTHERN

OCEAN

Macquarie Island
(Australia)

Campbell Island
Campbell Island (N. Z.)

West of Greenwich 180° East of Greenwich

0   250   500   750   1000   1500   2000   2500 Kilometers

0   250   500   1000   1500 Miles

Scale 1 : 25,000,000   Azimuthal Equidistant Projection

Meters
Feet

500
1640

200
656

Sea Level

200
656

2000
6560

Extent of Sea Ice

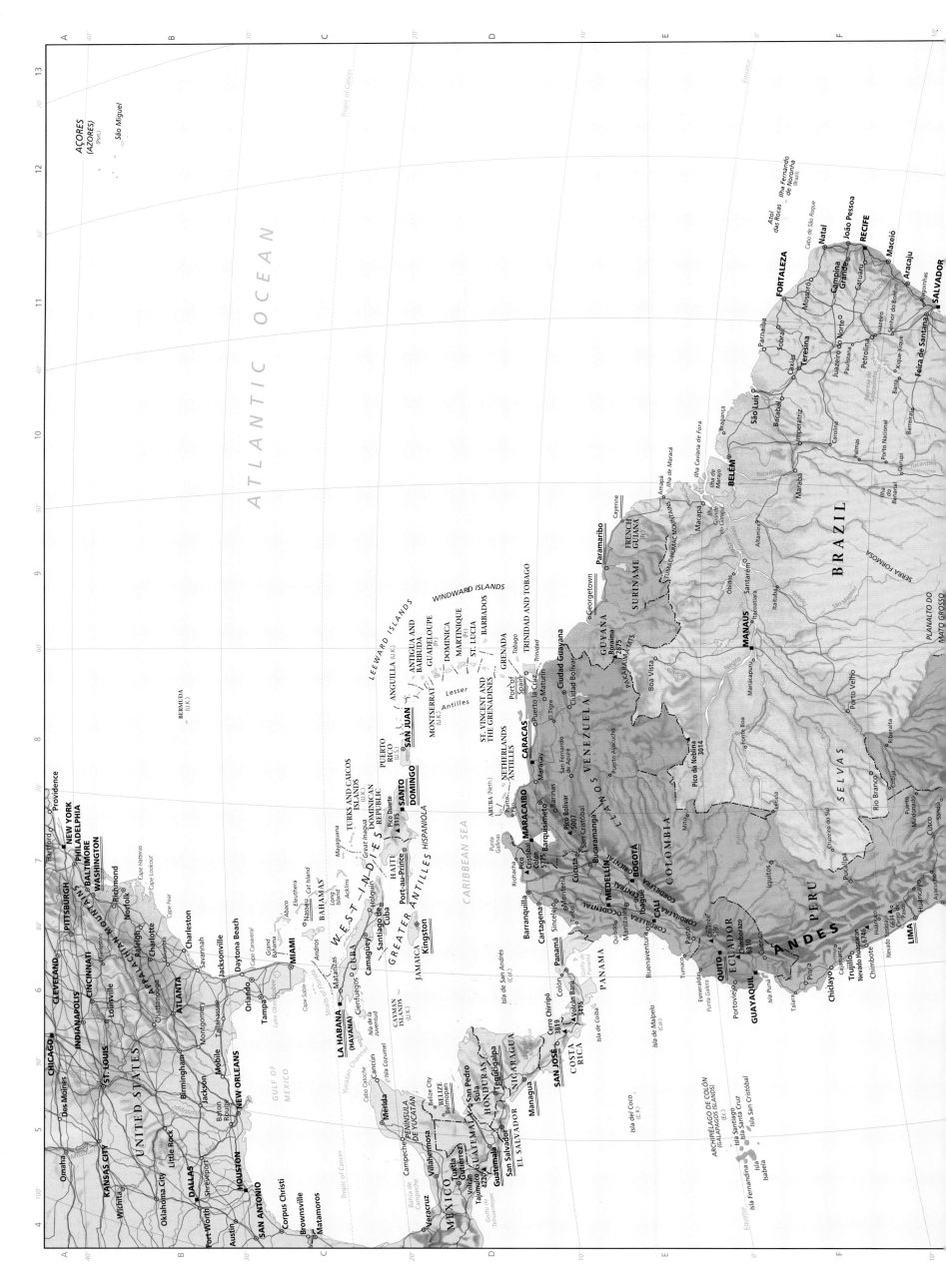

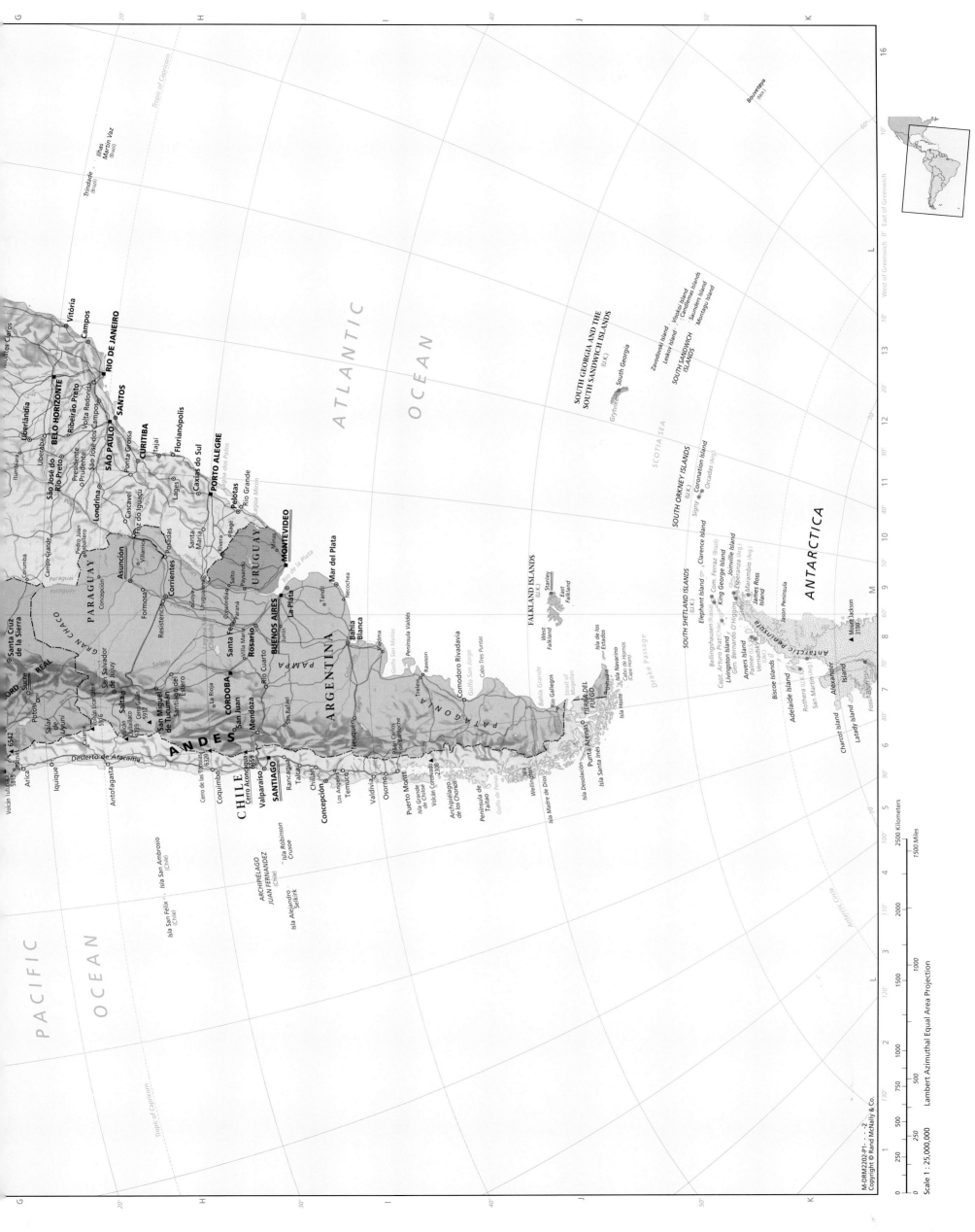

PACIFIC

OCEAN

ATLANTIC

OCEAN

ANDES

ARGENTINA

PARAGUAY

URUGUAY

CHILE

PAMPA

GRAN CHACO

PATAGONIA

ANTARCTICA

SCOTIA SEA

Tropic of Capricorn

Antarctic Circle

Drake Passage

RIO DE JANEIRO

SÃO PAULO

BELO HORIZONTE

CURITIBA

PORTO ALEGRE

SANTOS

Vitória

Campos

Ribeirão Preto

Volta Redonda

Londrina

Florianopolis

Caxias do Sul

Pelotas

Rio Grande

MONTEVIDEO

BUENOS AIRES

La Plata

Mar del Plata

Necochea

Bahía Blanca

CÓRDOBA

Rosario

Santa Fe

Mendoza

San Juan

SANTIAGO

Valparaíso

Concepción

Temuco

Valdivia

Osorno

Puerto Montt

Comodoro Rivadavia

Río Gallegos

Punta Arenas

Ushuaia

TIERRA DEL FUEGO

Cabo de Hornos
(Cape Horn)

FALKLAND ISLANDS
(U.K.)

Stanley

East
Falkland

West
Falkland

SOUTH GEORGIA AND THE
SOUTH SANDWICH ISLANDS

South Georgia

SOUTH SANDWICH
ISLANDS

SOUTH ORKNEY ISLANDS
(U.K.)

Coronation Island

SOUTH SHETLAND ISLANDS
(U.K.)

King George Island

Antarctic Peninsula

Bouvetøya
(Nor.)

ARCHIPIÉLAGO
JUAN FERNÁNDEZ
(Chile)

Isla Robinson
Crusoe

Isla Alejandro
Selkirk

Desierto de Atacama

Scale 1 : 25,000,000

Lambert Azimuthal Equal Area Projection

M-DRM2202-P1- - - -2
Copyright © Rand McNally & Co.

0   250   500   750   1000   1500   2000   2500 Kilometers

0   250   500   1000   1500 Miles

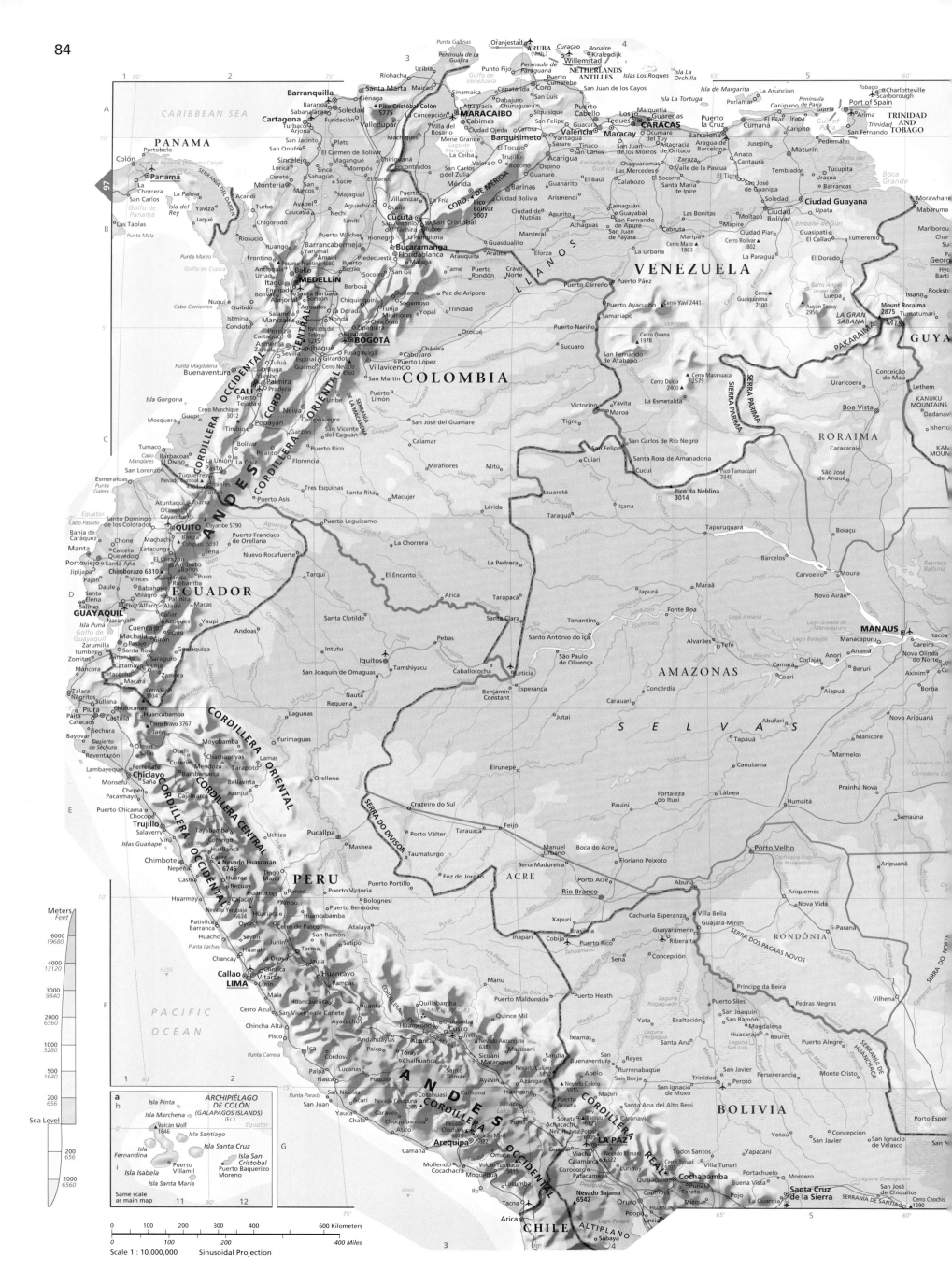

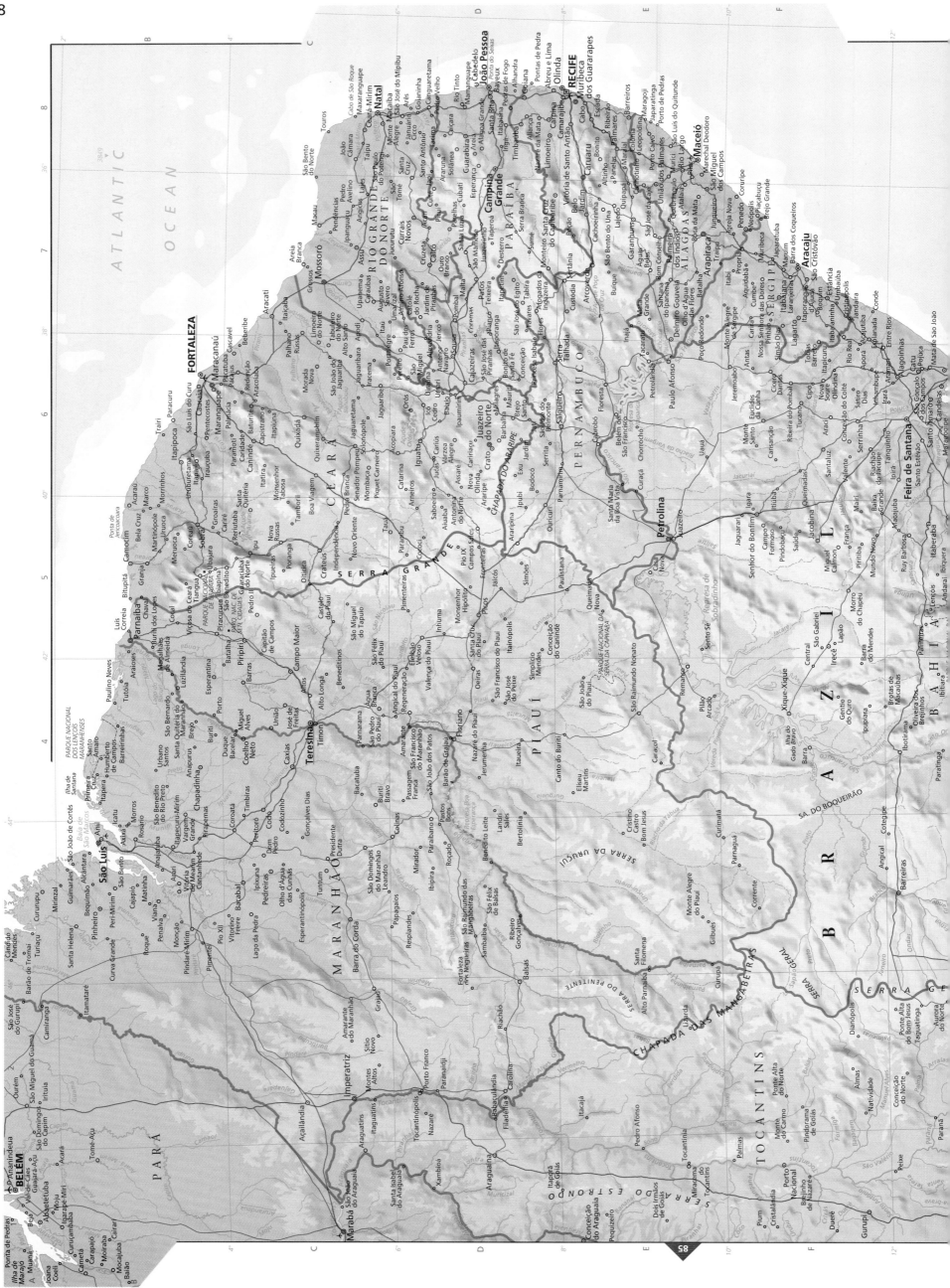

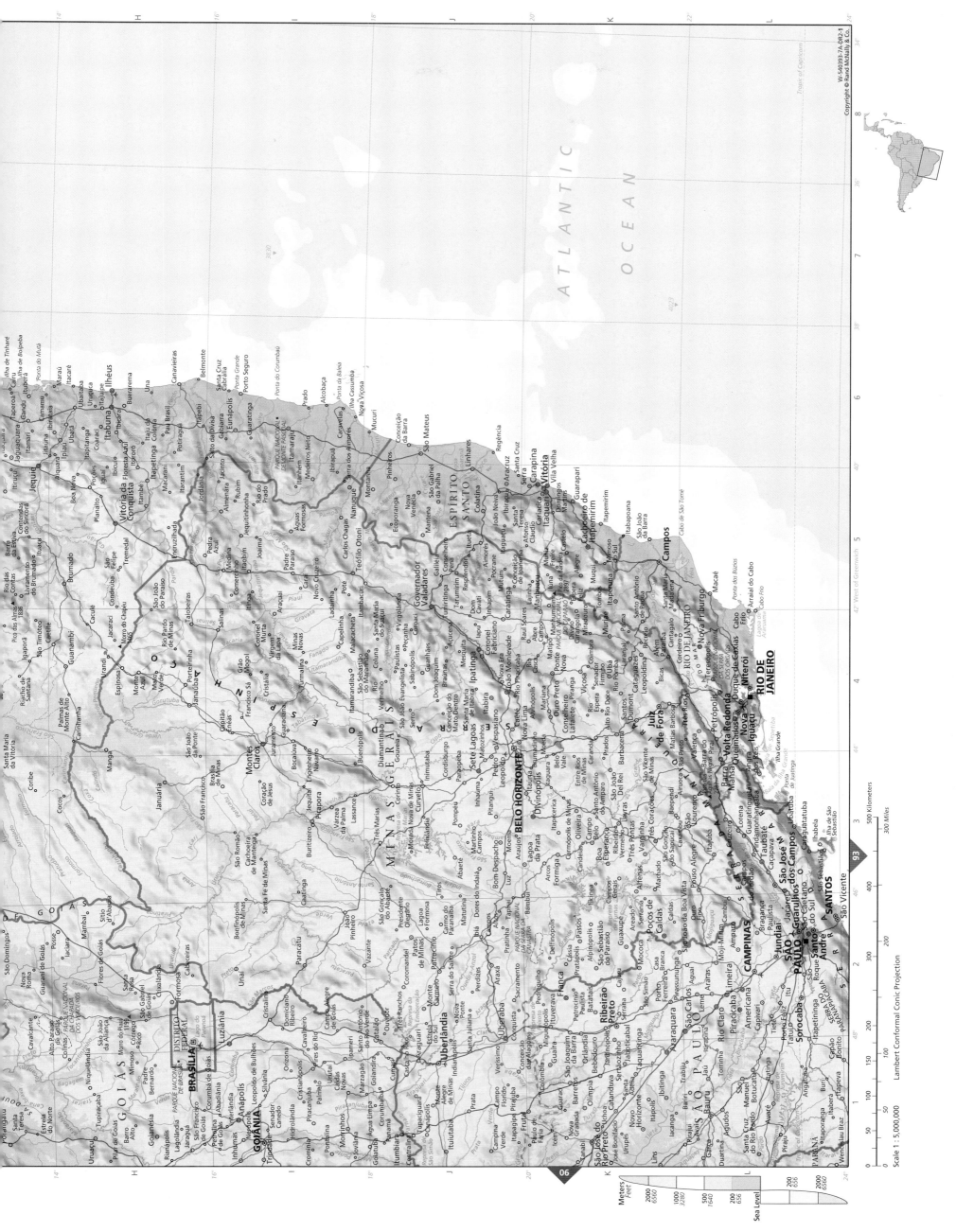

Scale 1 : 5,000,000   Lambert Conformal Conic Projection

Meters
Feet

2000	1000	500	200	Sea Level
6560	3280	1640	656	
200	2000			
656	6560			

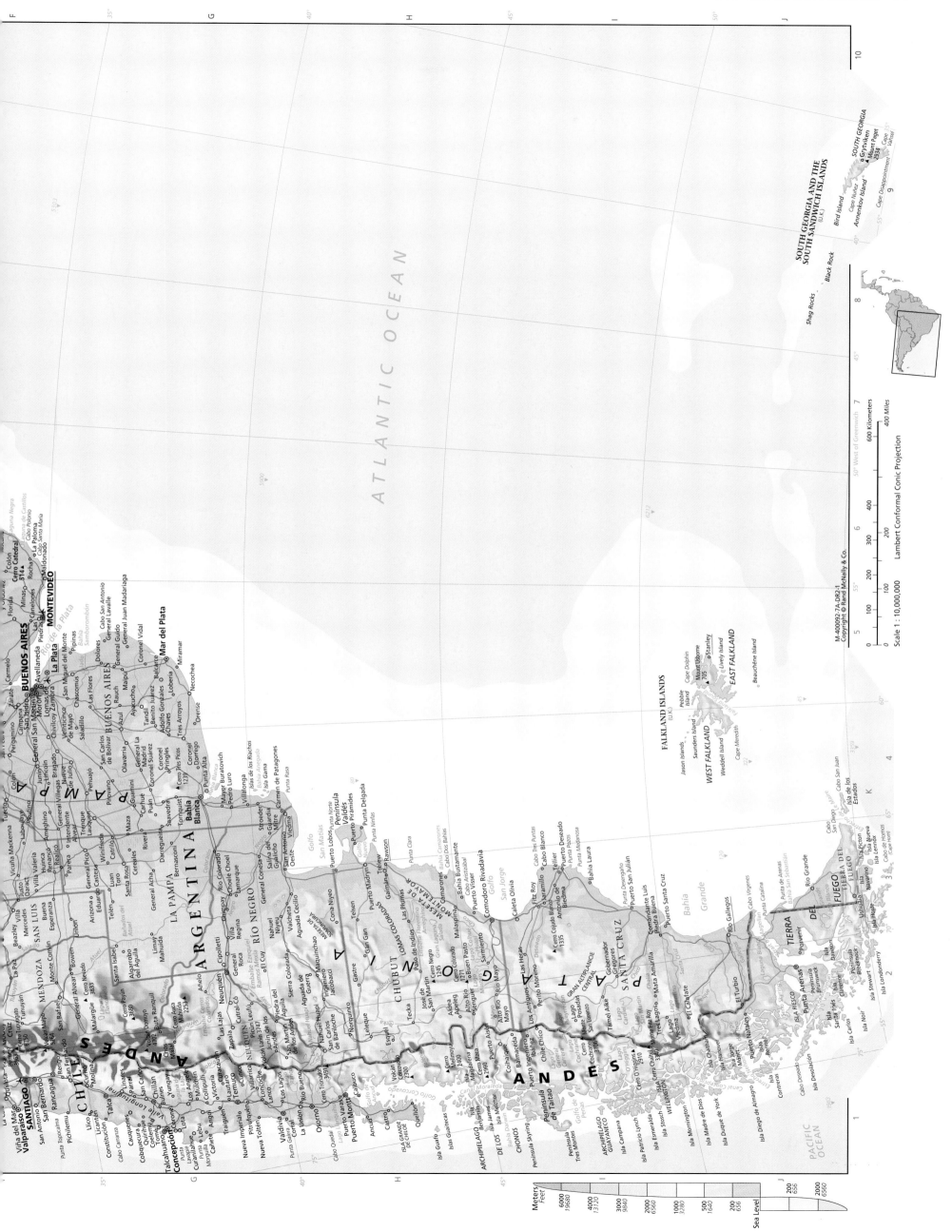

PACIFIC
OCEAN

ATLANTIC OCEAN

ARGENTINA

CHILE

ANDES

PAMPA

LA PAMPA

BUENOS AIRES

RIO NEGRO

NEUQUÉN

CHUBUT

SANTA CRUZ

MESETA DE
MONTEMAYOR

MESETA DE
LOS
LOMAS COLORADO

TIERRA
DEL
FUEGO

BUENOS AIRES
MONTEVIDEO
SANTIAGO
Valparaíso
Concepción
Mar del Plata
La Plata

FALKLAND ISLANDS
(U.K.)

WEST FALKLAND
EAST FALKLAND
Stanley

SOUTH GEORGIA AND THE
SOUTH SANDWICH ISLANDS
(U.K.)

SOUTH GEORGIA
Grytviken
Mount Paget
2934

ARCHIPIÉLAGO
DE LOS
CHONOS

ARCHIPIÉLAGO
DE GUAYANECO

ISLA GRANDE
DE CHILOÉ

WELLINGTON

Península
de Taitao

Meters
Feet
6000   19680
4000   13120
3000   9840
2000   6560
1000   3280
500   1640
200   656
Sea Level
200   656
2000   6560

0   100 200 300 400 500 600 Kilometers
0   100   200   300   400 Miles
Scale 1 : 10,000,000
Lambert Conformal Conic Projection
M-400092-7A-DR2-1
Copyright © Rand McNally & Co.

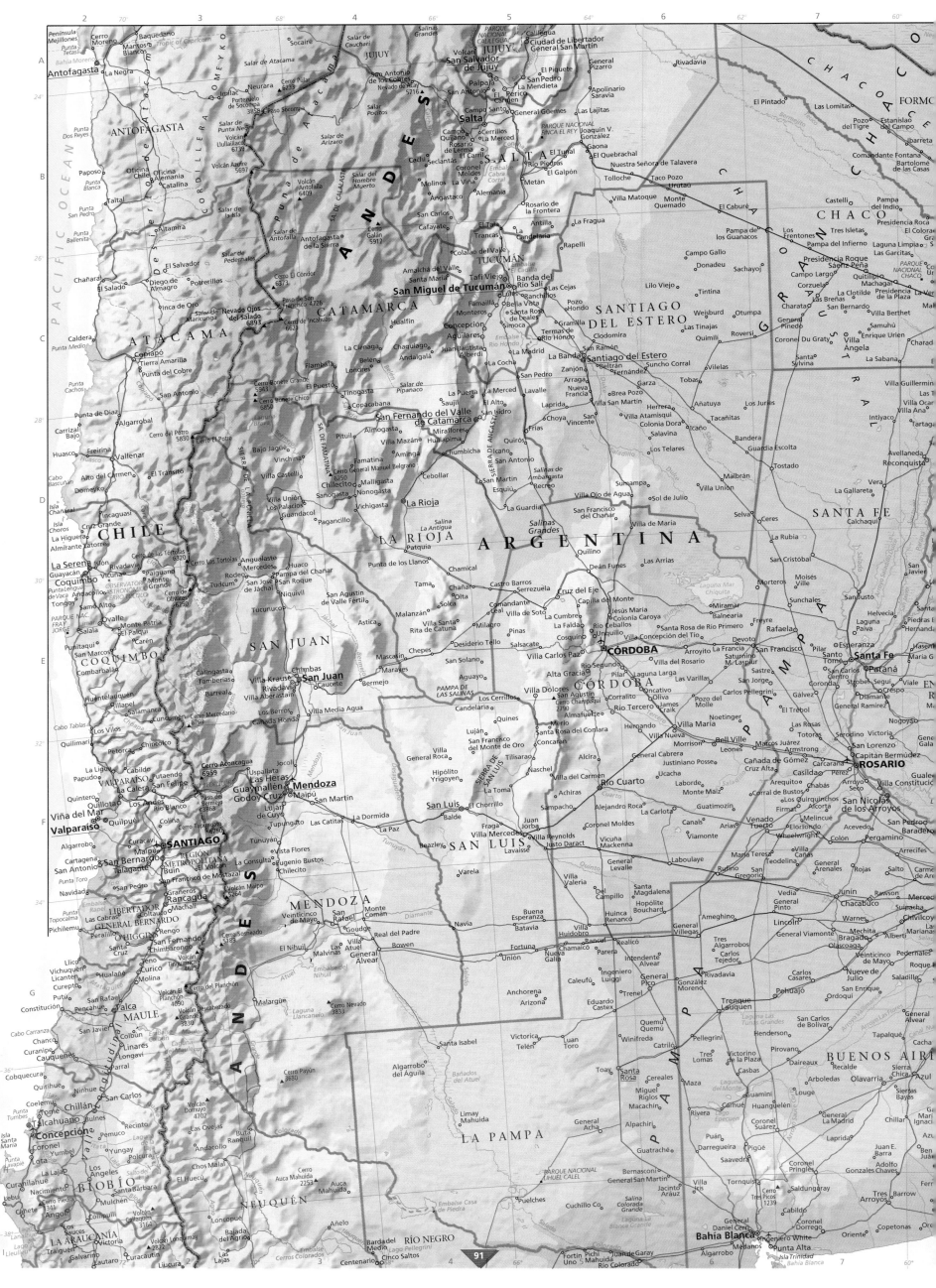

Scale 1 : 5,000,000   Lambert Conformal Conic Projection

W-540195-7A-DR2-1
Copyright © Rand McNally & Co.

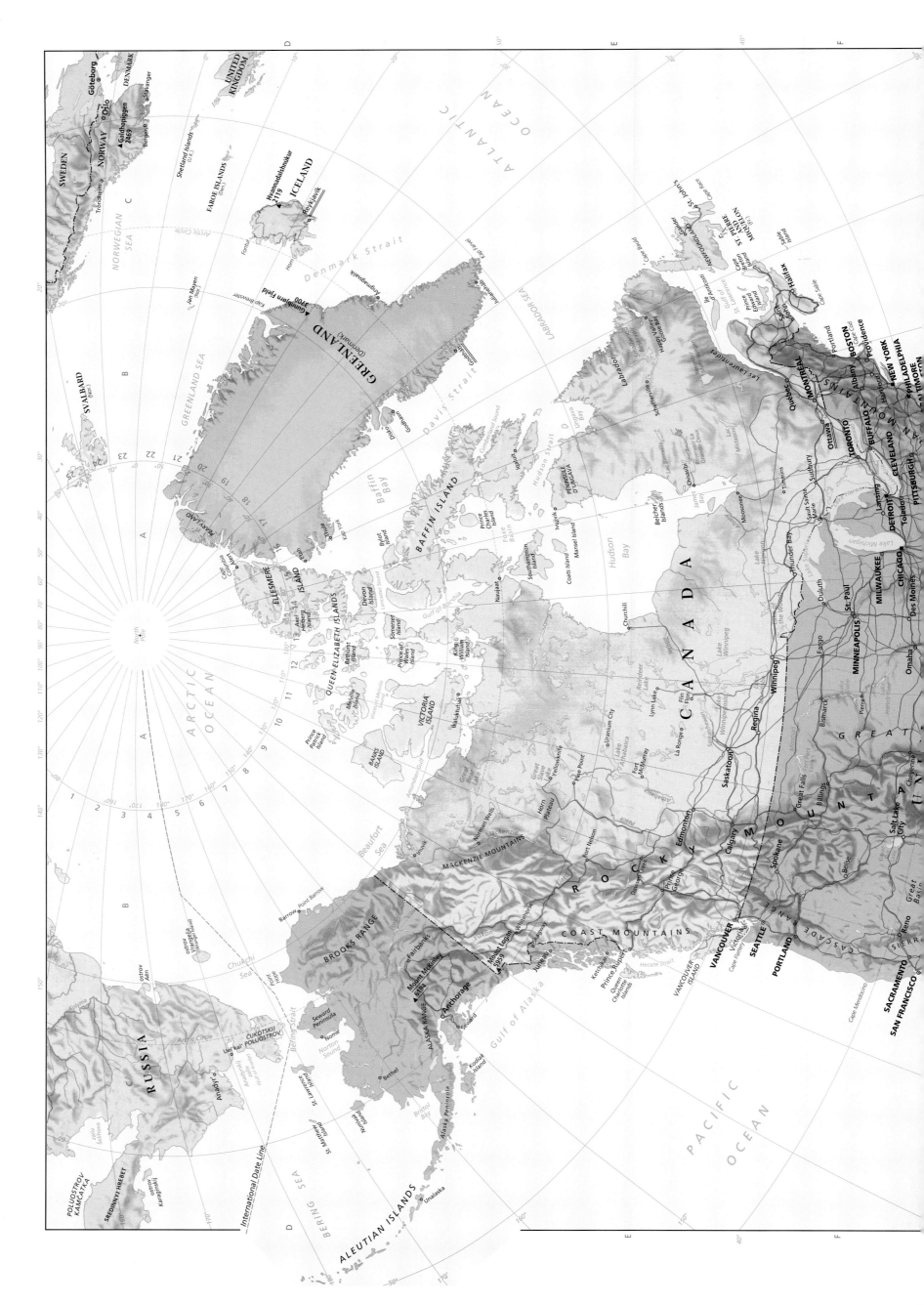

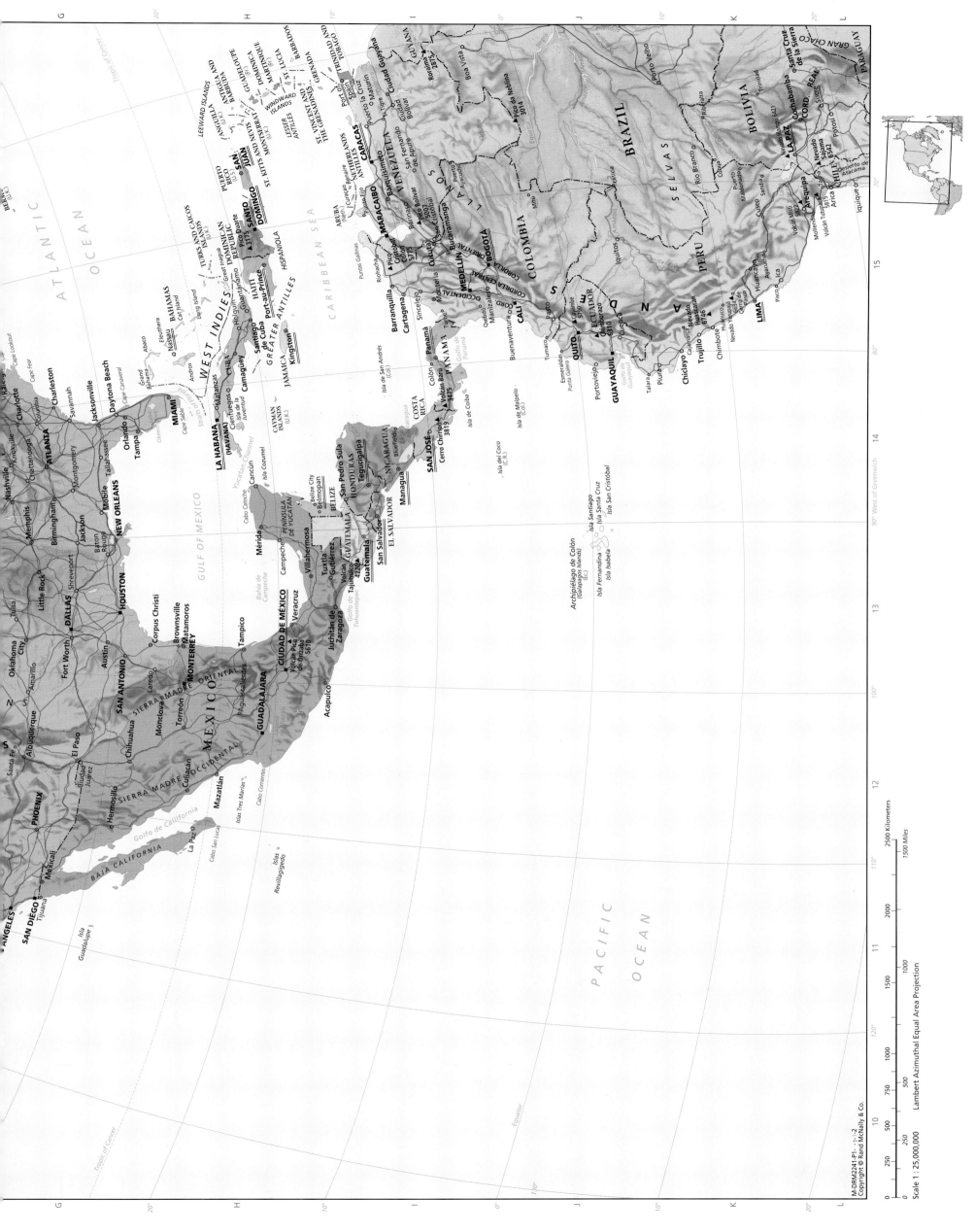

Meters
Feet

4000
13120

3000
9840

2000
6560

1000
3280

500
1640

200
656

Sea Level

200
656

2000
6560

Scale 1 : 10,000,000   Lambert Conformal Conic Projection

0   100   200   300   400   600   800   1000 Kilometers

0   100   200   400   600 Miles

M-DRM4703-A1-⌐-⌐-2
Copyright © Rand McNally & Co.

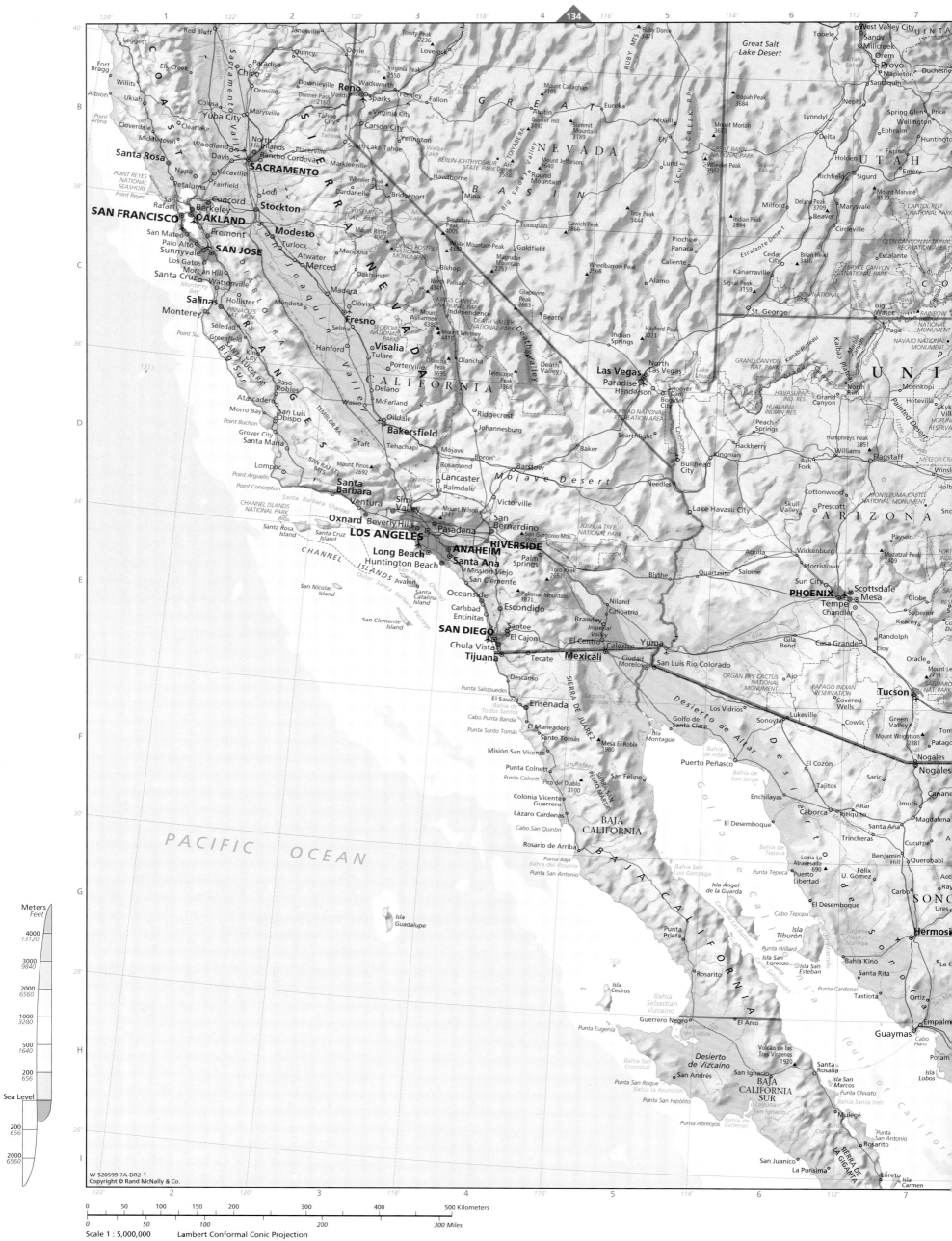

Scale 1 : 5,000,000   Lambert Conformal Conic Projection

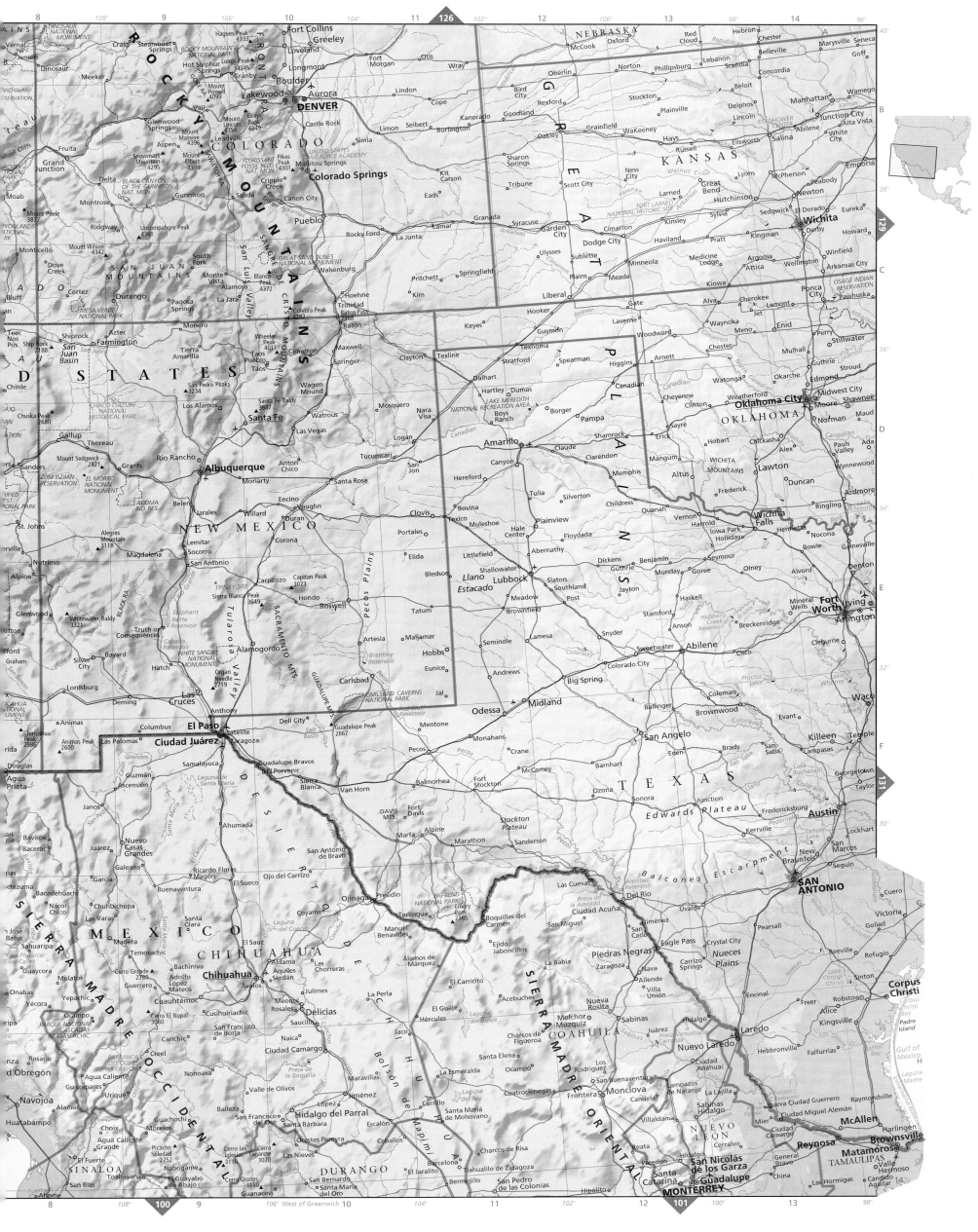

98

BAJA CALIFORNIA

Punta Prieta
Isla Ángel de la Guarda
Isla Tiburón
Rosar to
Isla San Esteban
Isla San Lorenzo
Punta Cardonal

Isla Cedros

BAJA CALIFORNIA

Bahía Sebastián Vizcaíno
Guerrero Negro
El Arco
Laguna Ojo de Liebre

Punta Eugenia

Desierto de Vizcaíno
Volcán de las Tres Vírgenes 1920

Bahía San Cristóbal
San Andrés
San Ignacio
Santa Rosalía
Isla San Marcos
Punta Chivato

Punta San Roque
Bahía la Asunción
Punta San Hipólito

Mulegé
Bahía Santa Inés
Bahía Concepción
Punta San Antonio

Punta Abreojos
Bahía de Ballenas

San Juanico
La Purísima
Loreto

BAJA CALIFORNIA SUR

La Poza Grande
Santo Domingo
Villa Insurgentes
Isla Carmen
Ligui
Isla Santa Catalina

Isla Santa Magdalena
Ciudad Constitución
Isla San José
Punta San Pasqual

Cabo San Lázaro
Bahía Magdalena
El Médano
Isla del Espíritu Santo

Isla Santa Margarita
Bahía Almejas
Isla de La Paz
Isla Cerralvo

La Paz

Punta Arena de la Ventana

El Triunfo
Punta Pescadores
Punta Arena
Las Casitas 2164
Todos Santos
Santiago
San Lucas
Villa Unión
San José del Cabo
Cabo San Lucas

Tropic of Cancer

SONORA

Punta Tiburón
Hermosillo
Bahía Kino
Santa Rita
La Colorada
Sahuaripa
Guaycora

San José de Batuc
Madera
Gómez Farías
Santa Clara

Onabas
Mulatos

Ortiz
Yécora
Yepachic

Empalme
Cumuripa
Ocampo

Guaymas
Cabo Haro
Presa Alvaro Obregón
PARQUE NACIONAL CASCADAS BASASEACHIC

Vícam
Potam
Esperanza
Rosario

Isla de Bácum
Ciudad Obregón

Villa Juárez
Pueblo Yaqui
Navojoa

Etchojoa
Álamos

Huatabampo
Yavaros

El Fuerte
San Blas

Higuera de Zaragoza
Ahome
Agua Caliente Grande

Los Mochis
General Juan José Ríos
El Palmar

Topolobampo
Corerepe
Guasave

Bahía de Ohuira
Guamúchil
Angostura

Isla San Ignacio
Badiraguato
Topia

Bahía Santa María
La Reforma
Jesús María
Canelas

Isla Altamura
Perical
Tamazula

Isla de Tachichilte
Culiacancito
Culiacán
Aguaruto

Navolato
Costa Rica

Ensenada del Pabellón
El Limón de Teachi
Coacoyole

Quilá
Ajoya
Tayoltita

Higuera de Abuya
Conitaca

Culiacán

SINALOA

Altata
San Miguel de Cruces
Canatlán

Higuera de Abuya
Antonio Amaro

CHIHUAHUA

Gómez Farías
Coyame
Presidio
Ojinaga
Terlingua

Temosachic
Cerro Grande 2780
Bachiniva
El Sauz
Aldama
Maclovio Herrera
Manuel Benavides

Guerrero
Adolfo López Mateos
Cuauhtémoc
Chihuahua
Aquiles Serdán
Las Chorreras

Creel
Carichi
Ávalos
Julimes
Meoqui
La Perla
Álamos de Márquez

Cerro El Nopal 3060
Cusihuiriachic
Delicias
Saucillo
Naica
Jaco
Hércules

San Francisco de Borja
Rosales
El Gua

Nonoava
Norogachi
Ciudad Camargo
Presa de la Boquilla
Valle de Zaragoza
Maravillas
La Esp

Guazárachi
López
Jiménez

Choix
Guachochi
San Francisco del Oro
Balleza
Hidalgo del Parral
Carrillo

Morelos
Picacho Soledad 2752
Santa Bárbara
Escalón
Ceballos
Santa de Me

Nabogame 3110
Cerro las Iglesias 3110
Otestes Pereyra
Las Nieves

Toahayana
Cerro Ocotes 3150
San Bernardo
El Jaralito
Tlahuálilo de Zaragoza

El Guayabo de Abajo
El Palmar de los Sepúlveda
Guanaceví
Tlahualilo
Berm

Tameapa
El Tecuán
General Escobedo
La Zarca
Mapimí
Gómez Palacio

Topia
Tepehuanes
Abasolo
Nazas
Pedriceña
Lerdo
Matan

Jesús María
San Pedro del Gallo
Rodeo
Cuenca
Cenice

DURANGO

Tejamén
Santiago Papasquiaro
San Juan del Río
Francisco I. Madero
Guadalupe Victoria

Canatlán
Cerro La Bandera 3230
Diez de Octubre

Durango
Nombre de Dios
Vicente Guerrero
Río El

Suchil
Sain

El Salto
La Ciudad
Mezquital
Cebollas
Jiménez de M

Concordia
Agua Caliente
Valparaíso
Mineral de Cucharas

Mazatlán

Escuinapa de Hidalgo
Rosario
Mineral de Cucharas

Teacapan
Acaponeta
Huazamota

NAYARIT

Tecuala
Rosamorada
Cerro Lechuguilla

Tuxpan
Ruiz
Santiago Ixcuintla

Isla San Juanito
Isla María Madre

Isla María Magdalena
San Blas

ISLAS TRES MARÍAS

Isla María Cleofas

Tepic
Teúl de González Ortega
Cerro el Vigía 2740

Compostela
Volcán Ceboruco 2280
Ixtlán del Río

Las Varas
Ahuacatlán

San Juan de Abajo

Punta de Mita
Cerro Peña Gorda 2560

JALISCO

Puerto Vallarta
Magdalena
GUADALA
Zapopan
Tlaquepa

Mascota
Ameca
Cocula
Aca

Bahía de Banderas
Cerro la Tetilla 2680
Atenguillo

Cabo Corrientes
Zacoalco de Torres

Ayutla
Unión de Tula

Tomatlán

Autlán de Navarro
PARQUE NACIONAL DEL NEVADO DE COLIMA
Nevado de Colima 4240

Purificación
Cuautitlán
Comala

COLIMA

Colima
Tecomán
Cerro 820

Manzanillo
Armería
Coalcom de Matan

Punta Tejupan

PACIFIC OCEAN

Isla San Benedicto
Isla Roca Partida

ISLAS REVILLAGIGEDO
Cerro Evermann 1050
Isla Socorro

SIERRA MADRE OCCIDENTAL

Scale

Meters / Feet
4000 / 13120
3000 / 9840
2000 / 6560
1000 / 3280
500 / 1640
200 / 656
Sea Level
200 / 656
2000 / 6560

0   50   100   150   200   300   400   500 Kilometers
0   50   100   200   300 Miles

Scale 1 : 5,000,000   Lambert Conformal Conic Projection

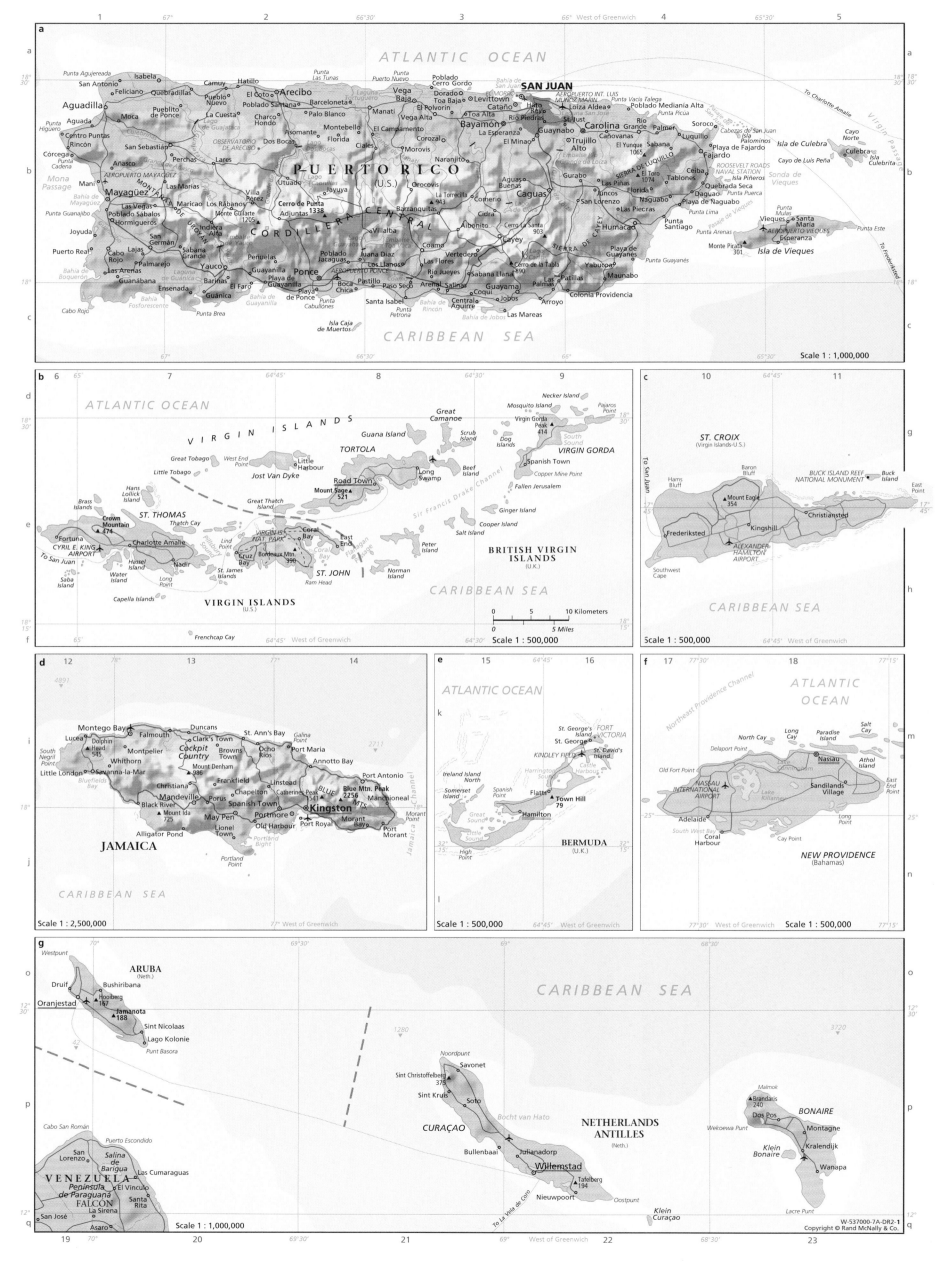

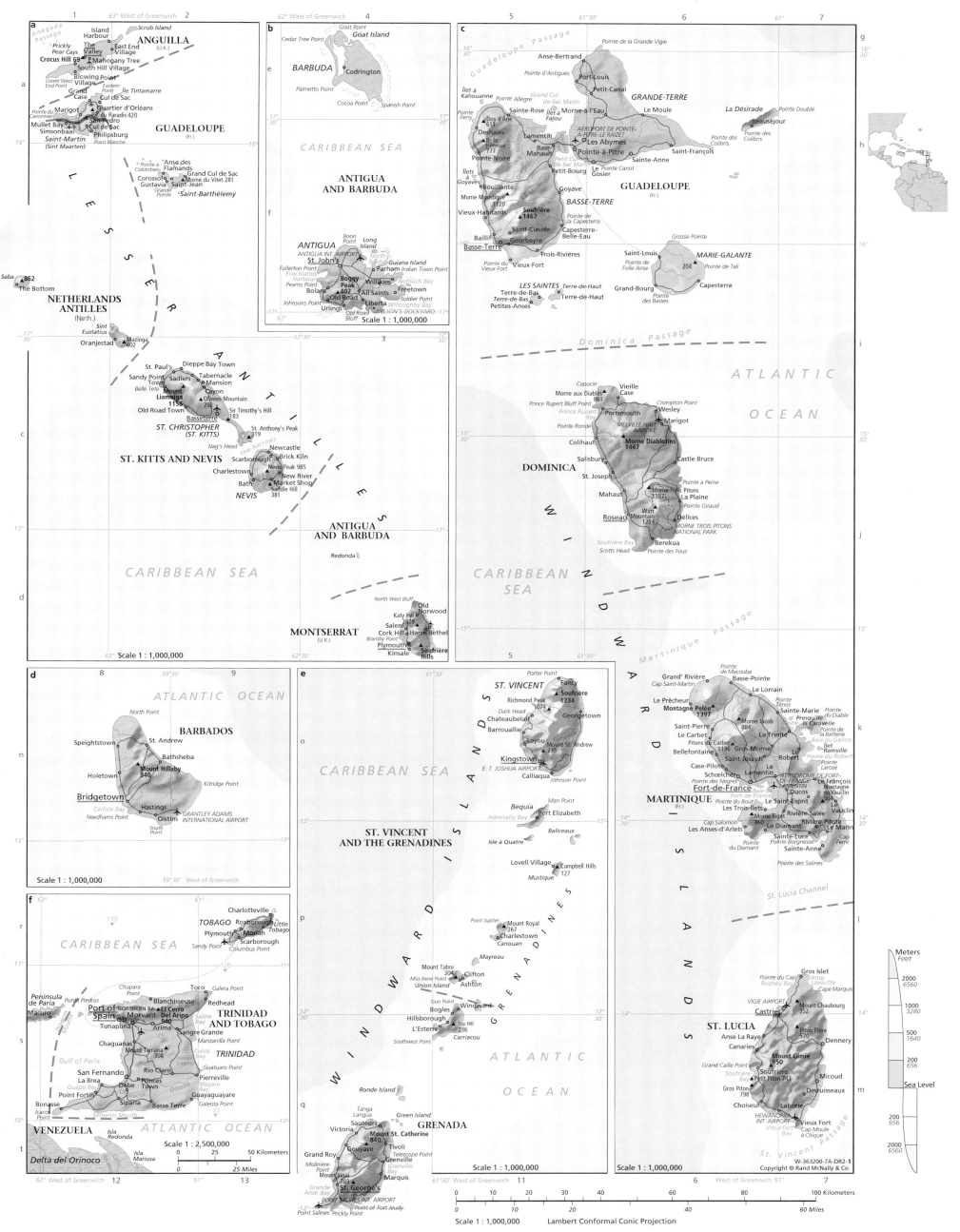

W-363200-7A-DR2-1
Copyright © Rand McNally & Co.

a

63° West of Greenwich

Scrub Island
Island Harbour
Prickly Pear Cays
The Valley
East End Village
ANGUILLA (U.K.)
Crocus Hill 69
South Hill Village
Mahogany Tree
Blowing Point
Lower West End Point
Grand Case
Cul de Sac
Quartier d'Orléans
Île Tintamarre
Pointe du Canonnier
Marigot
Pte du Paradis 420
San Pedro
GUADELOUPE (Fr.)
Mullet Bay
Simsonbaai
Cul de Sac
Saint-Martin (Sint Maarten)
Philipsburg
Point Blanche

Pointe à Colombier
Anse des Flamands
Grand Cul de Sac
Corossol
Morne du Vitet 281
Gustavia Saint-Jean
Grande Pointe
Saint-Barthélemy

Saba 862
The Bottom

NETHERLANDS ANTILLES (Neth.)

Sint Eustatius
Oranjestad
Mazinga 602

St. Paul's
Dieppe Bay Town
Sandy Point Town
Sadlers
Tabernacle
Mansion
Belle Tête
Mount Liamuiga 1156
Cayon
Olivees Mountain 790
Old Road Town
Basseterre
Sir Timothy's Hill 183
ST. CHRISTOPHER (ST. KITTS)
St. Anthony's Peak 319
Nag's Head
The Narrows
Newcastle
Brick Kiln
ST. KITTS AND NEVIS
Scarborough
Charlestown
Nevis Peak 985
New River
Market Shop
Bath
NEVIS
Saddle Hill 381

b

Goat Point
Goat Island
Cedar Tree Point
BARBUDA
Codrington
Palmetto Point
Cocoa Point
Spanish Point

CARIBBEAN SEA

ANTIGUA AND BARBUDA

Boon Point
Long Island
ANTIGUA
ANTIGUA INT. AIRPORT
St. John's
North Sound
Parham
Guiana Island
Indian Town Point
Fullerton Point
Five Islands Harbour
Willikies
Nonsuch Bay
Pearns Point
Bolans
Boggy Peak 402
Old Road
All Saints
Liberta
Freetown
Soldier Point
Willoughby Bay
Johnsons Point
Urlings
Old Road Bluff
NELSON'S DOCKYARD

Scale 1 : 1,000,000

c

Guadeloupe Passage
Pointe de la Grande Vigie
Anse-Bertrand
Pointe d'Antigues
Port-Louis
Petit-Canal
La Désirade
Pointe Doublé
Îlet à Kahouanne
Pointe Allègre
Grand Cul-de-Sac Marin
Îlet à Fajou
Morne-à-l'Eau
Le Moule
Beauséjour
Pointe Ferry
Sainte-Rose
GRANDE-TERRE
Pointe des Colibris
Dos d'Âne
Deshaies
Belle Hôtesse 777
Lamentin
AÉROPORT DE POINTE-À-PITRE-LE RAIZET
Pointe-Noire
Baie-Mahault
Pointe-à-Pitre
Sainte-Anne
Saint-François
Îlets à Goyaves
Petit-Bourg
Le Canot
Gosier
Bouillante
Goyave
GUADELOUPE (Fr.)
Morne Mustique
Soufrière 1467
BASSE-TERRE
Grosse Pointe
Vieux-Habitants
1120
Pointe de la Capesterre
Saint-Louis
MARIE-GALANTE
Saint-Claude
Capesterre-Belle-Eau
Pointe de Tali
Baillif
Gourbeyre
204
Basse-Terre
Trois-Rivières
Pointe de Folle Anse
Pointe du Vieux-Fort
Vieux-Fort
Grand-Bourg
Capesterre
LES SAINTES
Terre-de-Haut
Pointe des Basses
Terre-de-Bas
Terre-de-Haut
Petites-Anses

Dominica Passage

ATLANTIC OCEAN

Capucin
Vieille Case
Morne aux Diables 861
Crompton Point
Prince Rupert Bluff Point
Portsmouth
Wesley
Prince Rupert Bay
Marigot
Pointe Ronde
MELVILLE HALL AIRPORT
Colihaut
Morne Diablotins 1447
Castle Bruce
Salisbury
DOMINICA
St. Joseph
Pointe à Peine
Mahaut
Morne Trois Pitons 1387
La Plaine
Pointe Giraud
Roseau
Watt Mountain 1224
Délices
Berekua
MORNE TROIS PITONS NATIONAL PARK
Soufrière Bay
Scotts Head
Pointe des Fous

CARIBBEAN SEA

WINDWARD

Martinique Passage

d

ATLANTIC OCEAN

North Point
Speightstown
St. Andrew
BARBADOS
Bathsheba
Holetown
Mount Hillaby 340
Bridgetown
Kitridge Point
Carlisle Bay
Hastings
Needhams Point
Oistins
GRANTLEY ADAMS INTERNATIONAL AIRPORT
South Point

Scale 1 : 1,000,000

59°30' West of Greenwich

e

61°30'
Porter Point
ST. VINCENT
Fancy
Richmond Peak 1074
Soufrière 1234
Dark Head
Chateaubelair
Georgetown
Barrouallie
Mount St. Andrew 735
Layou
Kingstown
E. T. JOSHUA AIRPORT
Calliaqua
Johnson Point

CARIBBEAN SEA

Bequia
Man of War
Port Elizabeth
ST. VINCENT AND THE GRENADINES
Admiralty Bay
Baliceaux
Isle à Quatre

Lovell Village
Campbell Hills 127
Mustique

Point Jupiter
Mount Royal 267
Charlestown
Canouan

GRENADINES

Mayreau

Mount Taboi 304
Miss Irene Point
Clifton
Union Island
Ashton

Gun Point
Windward
Bogles
Hillsborough
Top Hill 236
L'Esterre
Carriacou
Southwest Point

WINDWARD ISLANDS

ATLANTIC OCEAN

Ronde Island

q

Tanga
Langua
Green Island
Victoria
Sauteurs
Tivoli
Grand Roy
Mount St. Catherine 840
Telescope Point
Gouyave
GRENADA
Grenville
Molinière
Mount Sinai 703
Grand Mal
Bay
Marquis
St. George's
Grande Anse Bay
POINT SALINES INT. AIRPORT
Point Salines
Point of Fort Jeudy
Prickly Point

f

62°
61°
Charlotteville
TOBAGO
Roxborough
Little Tobago
Plymouth
Moriah
Scarborough
Sandy Point
Columbus Point

CARIBBEAN SEA

Chupara Point
Toco
Galera Point
Peninsula de Paria
Punta Piedras
Blanchisseuse
Redhead
Macuro
Port of Spain
El Cerro Del Aripo 940
NORTHERN RA
Morvant
TRINIDAD AND TOBAGO
Tunapuna
Arima
Sangre Grande
Chaguanas
Manzanilla Point
Gulf of Paria
Mount Tamana 308
Cocos Bay
TRINIDAD
San Fernando
Rio Claro
Pierreville
La Brea
Guaratuaro Point
Princes Town
Mayaro Point
Point Fortin
Debe
Siparia
Mayaro Bay
Bonasse
Icacos Point
Basse Terre
Guayaguayare
Galeota Point
VENEZUELA
Serpents Mouth
Isla Redonda
Delta del Orinoco
Isla Mariusa

Scale 1 : 2,500,000
0   25   50 Kilometers
0   25 Miles

k / l / m — Martinique

Grand' Rivière
Pointe de Macouba
Basse-Pointe
Cap Saint-Martin
Le Lorrain
Le Prêcheur
Montagne Pelée 1397
Sainte-Marie
Pointe du Diable
Le Carbet
Morne Jacob 884
La Trinité
Pointe de la Batterie
Presqu'île la Caravelle
Saint-Pierre
Pitons du Carbet 1196
Gros-Morne
Ramville
Îlet
Bellefontaine
Saint-Joseph
Robert
Havre du Robert
Case-Pilote
Lamentin
AÉRODROME DE FORT-DE-FRANCE LAMENTIN
Pointe Larose
Schoelcher
Le François
Fort-de-France
Ducos
Montagne du Vauclin 504
MARTINIQUE (Fr.)
Le Saint-Esprit
Vauclin
Pointe du Bout
Les Trois-Îlets
Rivière-Salée
Le Marin
Cap Salomon
Morne Bigot 460
Rivière-Pilote
Les Anses-d'Arlets
Sainte-Luce
Pointe du Diamant
Le Diamant
Pointe Borgnesse
Sainte-Anne
Cap Ferré
Pointe des Salines

St. Lucia Channel

St. Lucia

Gros Islet
Pointe du Cap
Rodney Bay
Anse Lavoutte
Cape Marquis
VIGIE AIRPORT
Castries
Mount Chaubourg 352
ST. LUCIA
Anse La Raye
Canaries
Mount Gimie 950
Dennery
Soufrière
Petit Piton 743
Micoud
Choiseul
Grand Caille Point
Gros Piton 798
Laborie
HEWANORRA INT. AIRPORT
Vieux Fort
Cap Moule à Chique

St. Vincent Passage

Scale 1 : 1,000,000

Elevation legend (right side)

Meters / Feet
2000 / 6560
1000 / 3280
500 / 1640
200 / 656
Sea Level
200 / 656
2000 / 6560

Scale 1 : 1,000,000
0   10   20   30   40   50   60   70   80   90   100 Kilometers
0   10   20   30   40   50   60 Miles
Lambert Conformal Conic Projection

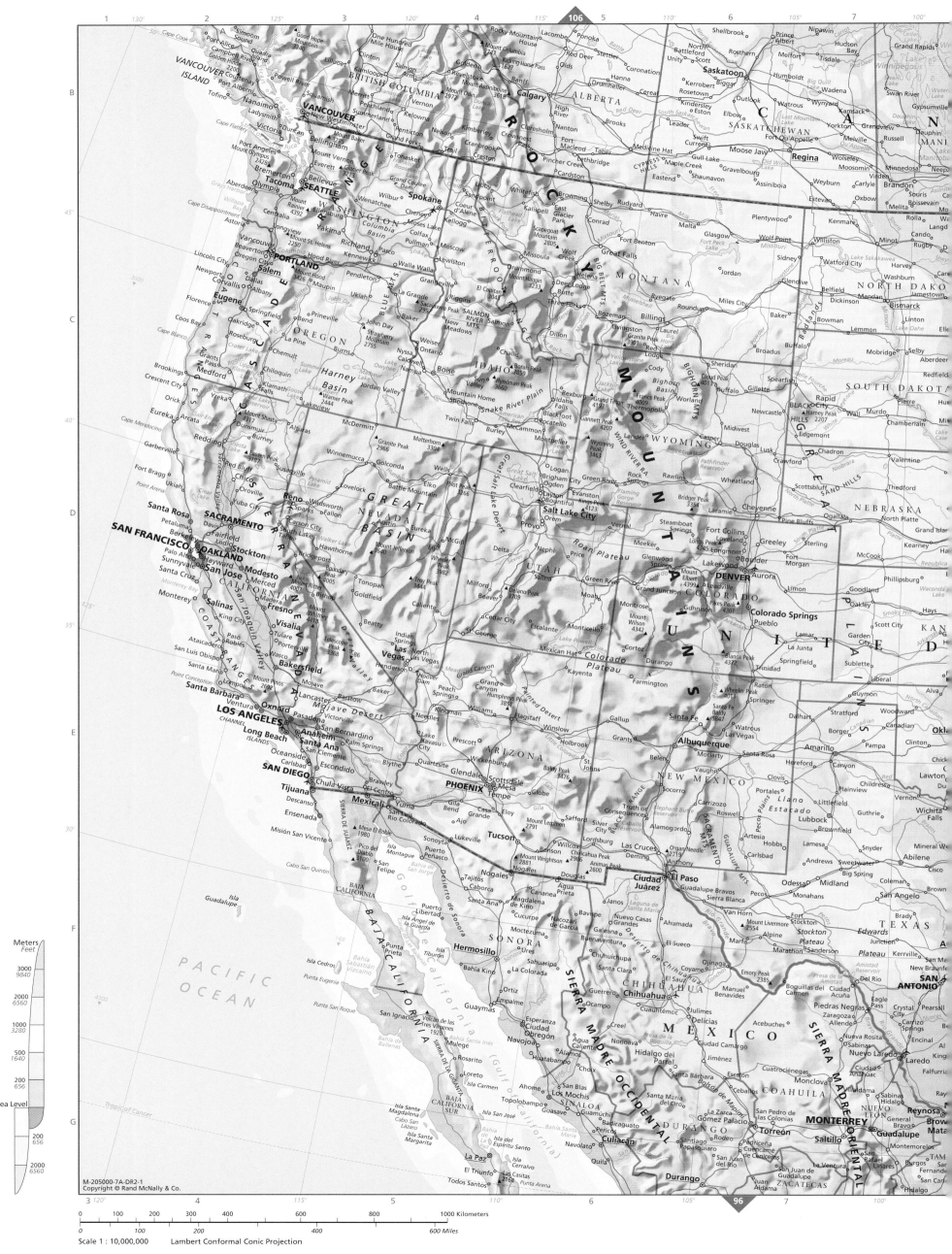

Meters
Feet

3000
9840

2000
6560

1000
3280

500
1640

200
656

Sea Level

200
656

2000
6560

M-205000-7A-DR2-1
Copyright © Rand McNally & Co.

0   100   200   400   600   800   1000 Kilometers

0   100   200   400   600 Miles

Scale 1 : 10,000,000   Lambert Conformal Conic Projection

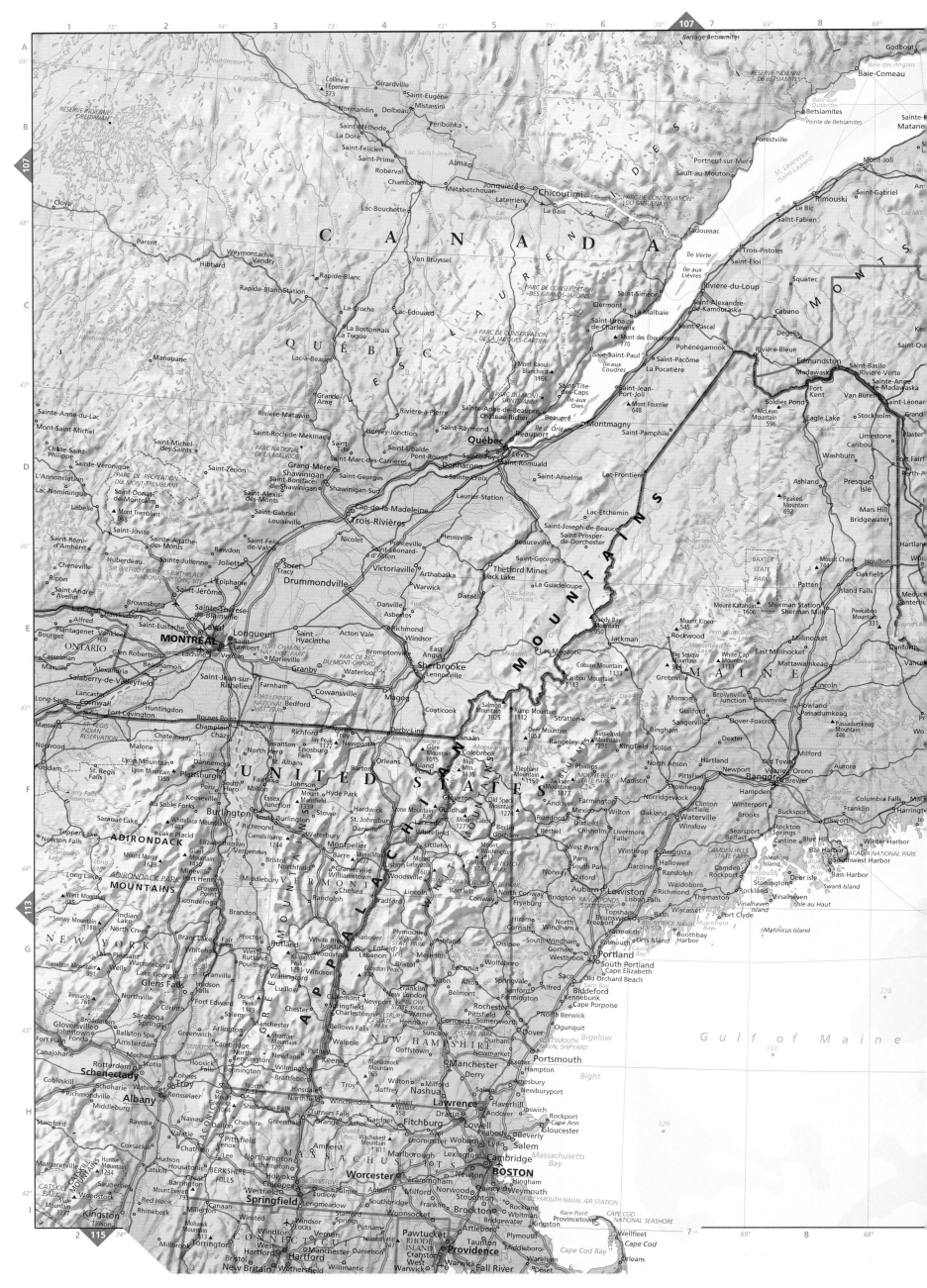

A

ÎLE D'ANTICOSTI

Pointe du Sud-Ouest
Rivière-de-la-Chaloupe
Pointe de l'Est
Pointe Heath

La Marte
Rivière-à-Claude
Madeleine-Centre
Saint-Yvon
Pointe-à-la-Frégate
354
Détroit d'Honguedo

Cap-Chat
Sainte-Anne-des-Monts
Mont Jacques-Cartier
Fontenelle
PARC NATIONAL DE FORILLON

Matane
PARC PROVINCIAL
DE LA GASPÉSIE
Gaspé
Cap Gaspé
Baie de Gaspé

Port au Port
Peninsula

Mont Blanc
1059
CHIC-CHOCS

Cape St. George

scal

MONTS
PÉNINSULE DE LA GASPÉSIE
(GASPE PENINSULA)
Saint-Gabriel-
de-Gaspé
La Malbaie
Percé
Île Bonaventure

B

NEWFOUNDLAND
AND LABRADOR

NOTRE-DAME

Grande-Rivière
Newport
Chandler

Gulf of St. Lawrence

NEWFOUNDLAND

48°

utherville
New Richmond
Pointe au Maquereau

Cape Anguille

Nouvelle
Caplan
Bonaventure
New Carlisle

Codroy
Doyle

Pointe-la-Garde
dia
Dalhousie
Chaleur
Bay
Miscou Point
Miscou Island

Île Brion
Tompkins
Table Mountain

Campbellton
Jacquet River
Miscou Centre

Cape Ray

Squaw Cap
Mountain
483
Lorne
Grande-Anse
Île Lamèque

La Grosse Île

C

Blue Mountain
528
Beresford
Caraquet
Lamèque

Grande-Entrée
Île de l' Est

Nepisiguit Bay
Saint-Isidore
Shippegan

ÎLES DE LA
MADELEINE
(Que.)

Cabot Strait

MOUNT CARLETON
PROVINCIAL PARK
Bathurst
Tracadie

60

Île du Cap
aux Meules
Cap-aux-Meules

St. Paul
Island

Mount Carleton
820
Haut Sheila
Brantville

Île du Havre Aubert
Baie de Plaisance

To Channel-Port-aux-Basques

Big Bald Mountain
672
Lavillette
Neguac

Havre-Aubert

47°

Miramichi
Bay

Cape St.
Lawrence
Cape North
Aspy
Bay
Long Point

Point Escuminac
Tignish
North Cape

Pleasant Bay
Dingwall

D

Newcastle
Chatham
Cape Kildare
Alberton

CAPE BRETON
HIGHLANDS
NATIONAL PARK
Ingonish

Renous
Chatham Head
Point
Sapin
Miscampec Bay

Grand-Étang
Cheticamp
Cape Smokey

KOUCHIBOUGUAC
NATIONAL PARK
Campbellton
Conway

Margaree Harbour
Margaree
Indian
Brook

Upper Blackville
Rogersville
Saint-Louis de Kent
Richibucto
O'Leary

53

Inverness
Strathlorne

Boularderie
Island
New Waterford

Doaktown
St.-Ignace
Rexton
West Point
Port Hill

PRINCE EDWARD
ISLAND NATIONAL PARK
Elmira

CAPE BRETON
ISLAND
Baddeck

Dominion

Boiestown
Bouctouche
Egmont
Bay
Wellington
Station
Kensington
North Rustico
Morell
St. Peters Bay

East Point
Mabou
North Sydney

Glace Bay
Port Morien

Stanley
Saint-Antoine
Cap-Pelé
Hunter River
Victoria
PRINCE EDWARD ISLAND
Mount Stewart
Souris

Iona
Sydney Mines
Sydney

NEW BRUNSWICK
Notre-Dame
Bonshaw
Charlottetown
Cardigan

Whycocomagh

Mira Bay
Scatarie
Island

Taymouth
Shediac
FORT AMHERST
NAT. HIST. PARK
Vernon
Georgetown

Judique
Louisbourg
LOUISBOURG
NAT. HIST. SITE

E

Minto
Chipman
Moncton
Lewisville
Port
Borden
Hillsborough
Cardigan Bay

Cape George
Pomquet
Mulgrave
L'Ardoise

Gabarus

Marysville
Rothwell
Dieppe
Murray
River
Montague

St. Georges
Bay
Port Hawkesbury
Arichat
Isle Madame

Fredericton
Oromocto
Turtle Creek
Memramcook
Mideic
Flat River
Murray Head
Murray Harbour

West Bay
Louisdale

Point Michaud

Geary
Gagetown
Petitcodiac
Dorchester
Sackville
Port Elgin
Wood Islands

Caribou
Lismore

St. Peters
Fourchu

CANADIAN FORCES
BASE GAGETOWN
Harvey
Joggins
FORT BEAUSEJOUR NAT'L
HISTORIC PARK
Amherst
Pugwash
Malagash
River John

Pictou
Island
Antigonish

Bras d'Or
Lake

Fredericton
Junction
Norton
Sussex
River Hebert
Oxford
Scotsburn

Pictou
New Glasgow

Guysborough

Canso

Nashwaaksis
Hampton
Springhill
Westchester Station
Westville
Stellarton

Goshen
Queensport

Mount
Pleasant
358
Welsford
COBEQUID MTS.
Londonderry
Nuttby Mountain
367
Sunnybrae

Goldboro
Larrys
River

F

St. Martins
Rothesay
Five
Islands
Bass River
Belmont
Truro
NOVA SCOTIA
Sherbrooke

Grand Bay
Alma
FUNDY
NATIONAL
PARK
Port Greville
Parrsboro
Cobequid Bay
Brookfield

45°

Saint John
Cape Chignecto
Advocate
Harbour
Greville
Bay
Maitland
North Stewiacke
Middle Stewiacke

en
ST. CROIX
IS. NAT'L MON.
Point Lepreau
Harbourville
Canning
Walton
Kennetcook
Stewiacke
Upper Musquodoboit

Mosers River
Ecum Secum

St. George
St. Andrews
Passamaquoddy Bay
Berwick
Gore
Milford Station
Middle Musquodoboit

Wilsons Beach
Deer Island
Kingston
Waterville
Wolfville
Hantsport
Windsor
Elmsdale

Sheet
Harbour

West Quoddy Head
ROOSEVELT
CAMPOBELLO
INTERNATIONAL PARK
Meaghers
Grant
Tangier

Grand Manan Island
Grand
Manan
Middleton
Three Mile Plains
Mount
Uniacke
New Road
Musquodoboit
Harbour

G

Bridgetown
Torbrook
CANADIAN
FORCES BASE
HALIFAX
Musquodoboit
Harbour

Digby
Neck
PORT ROYAL
NATIONAL
HISTORIC PARK
Annapolis Royal
Springfield
New
Ross
Hubbards
Halifax
Dartmouth
HALIFAX CITADEL NATIONAL HISTORIC PARK

Weymouth
Digby
Clementsport
Bear River
New Germany
Hemford
Western
Shore
Chester Basin
Hatchet Lake
Herring Cove
Terence Bay
Halifax Harbour

Long Island
Westport
Brier Island
Freeport
Meteghan
KEJIMKUJIK
NATIONAL PARK
Caledonia
South Brookfield
Mahone
Bay
Lunenburg
Pennant Point

44°

Cape St. Marys
Hectanooga
Bridgewater
Hell Point

162

Port Maitland
Brooklyn
Liverpool

18

Yarmouth
Liverpool
Port Mouton

Sable Island
(N.S.)

257

Chebogue Point
Wedgeport
Shelburne
Lockeport

G

Pubnico
Pubnico
ATLANTIC OCEAN

43°

Lower West Pubnico
Barrington
Clark's Harbour

Lower Woods Harbour
Cape Sable Island
Cape Sable

Seal
Island

H

Meters
Feet

1000
3280

500
1640

200
656

Sea Level

200
656

2000
6560

I

0   25   50   75   100   150   200   250 Kilometers
0   25   50   100   150 Miles

Scale 1 : 2,500,000   Lambert Conformal Conic Projection

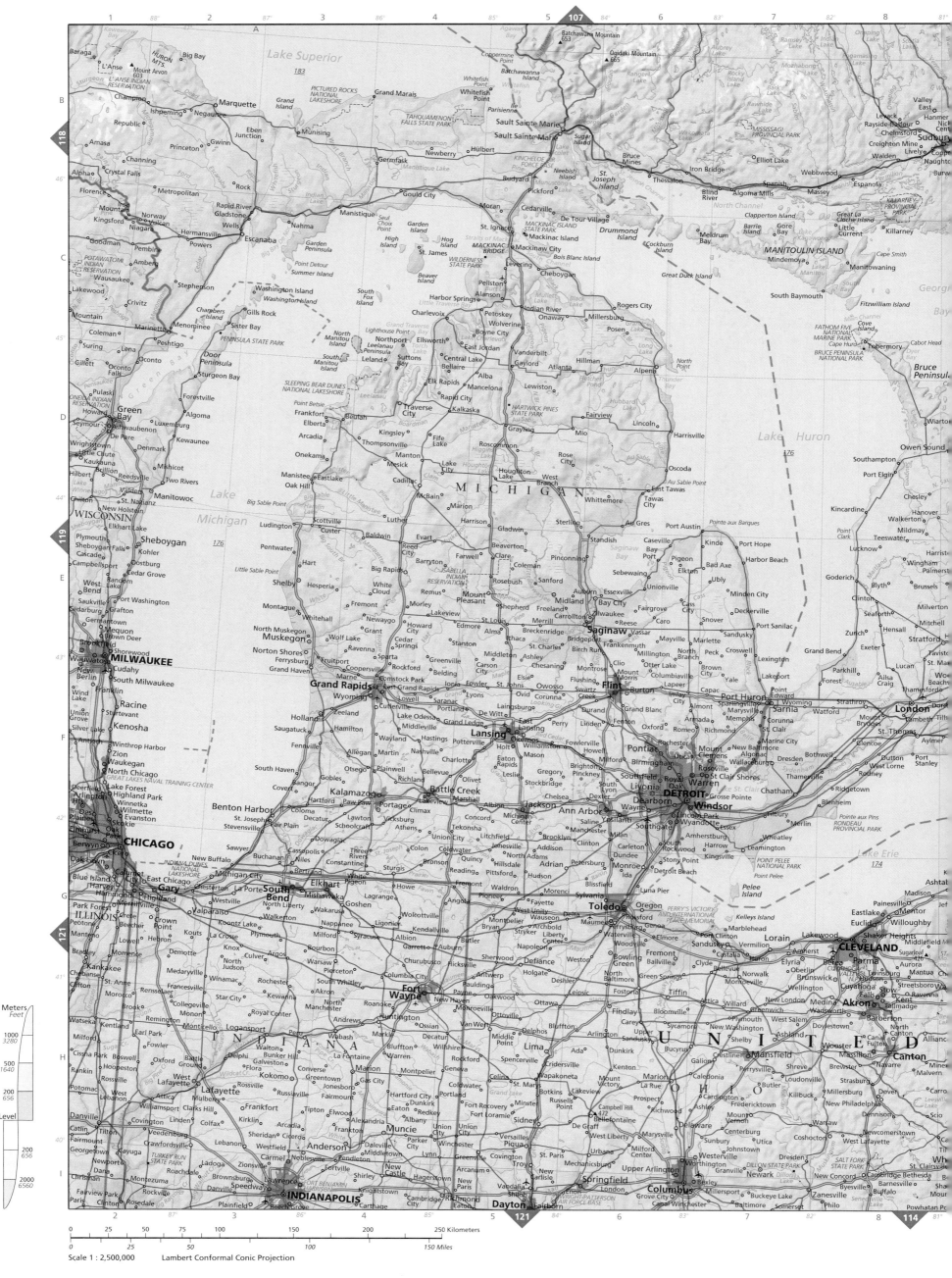

Meters
Feet

1000
3280

500
1640

200
656

Sea Level

200
656

2000
6560

0 25 50 75 100   150   200   250 Kilometers

0   25   50   100   150 Miles

Scale 1 : 2,500,000   Lambert Conformal Conic Projection

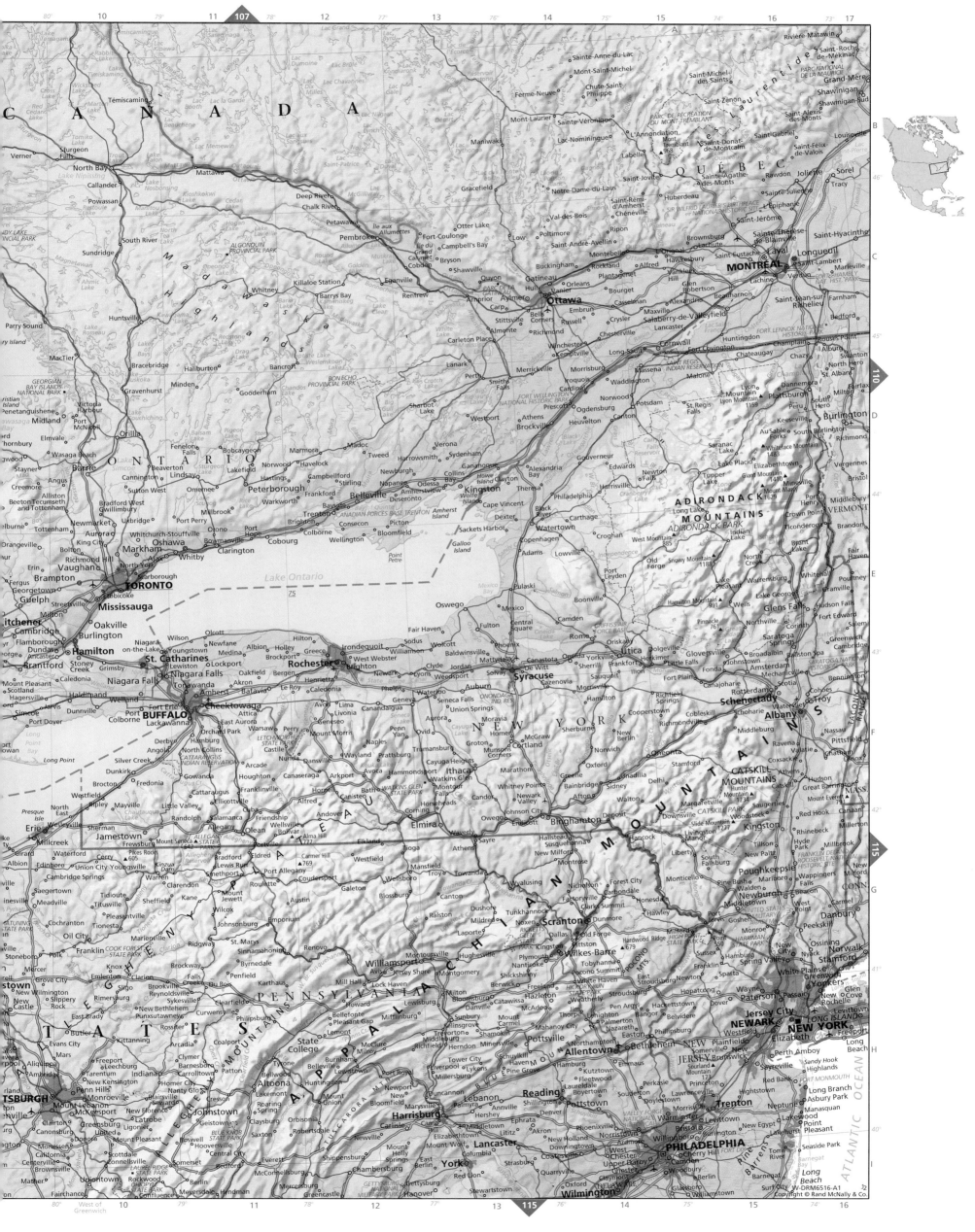

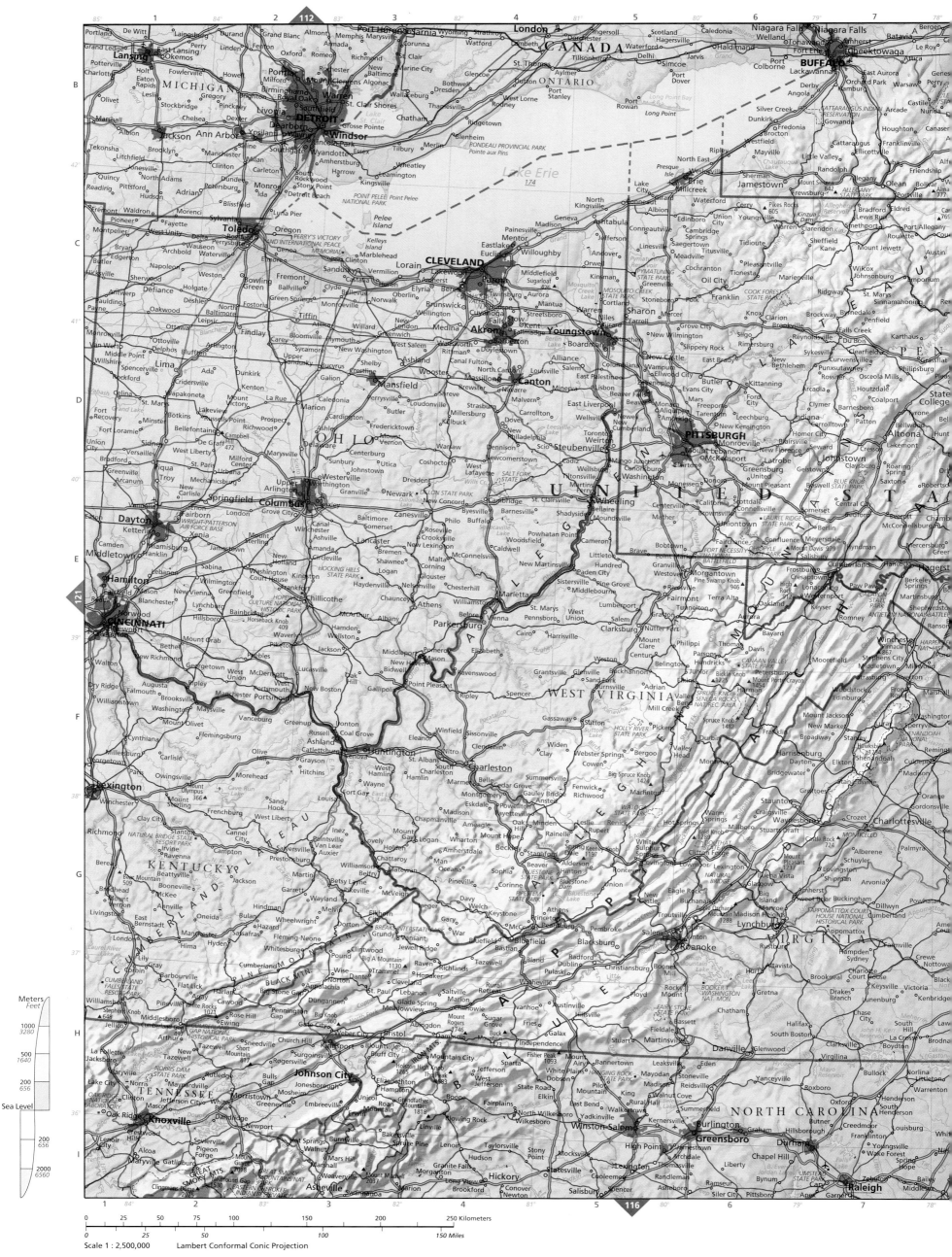

Meters/Feet

1000
3280

500
1640

200
656

Sea Level

200
656

2000
6560

Scale 1 : 2 500 000   Lambert Conformal Conic Projection

0   25   50   75   100   200   250 Kilometers

0   50   100   150 Miles

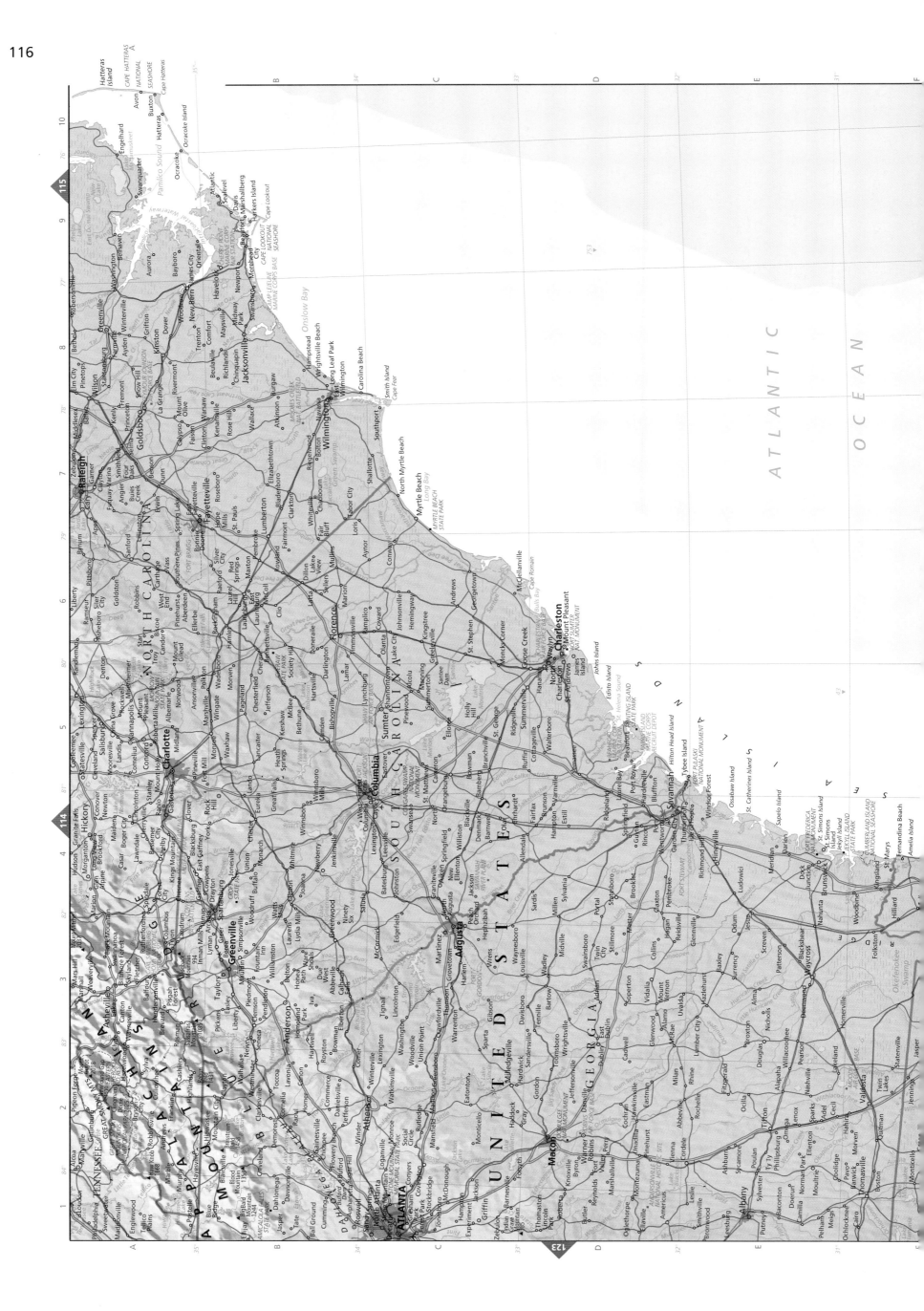

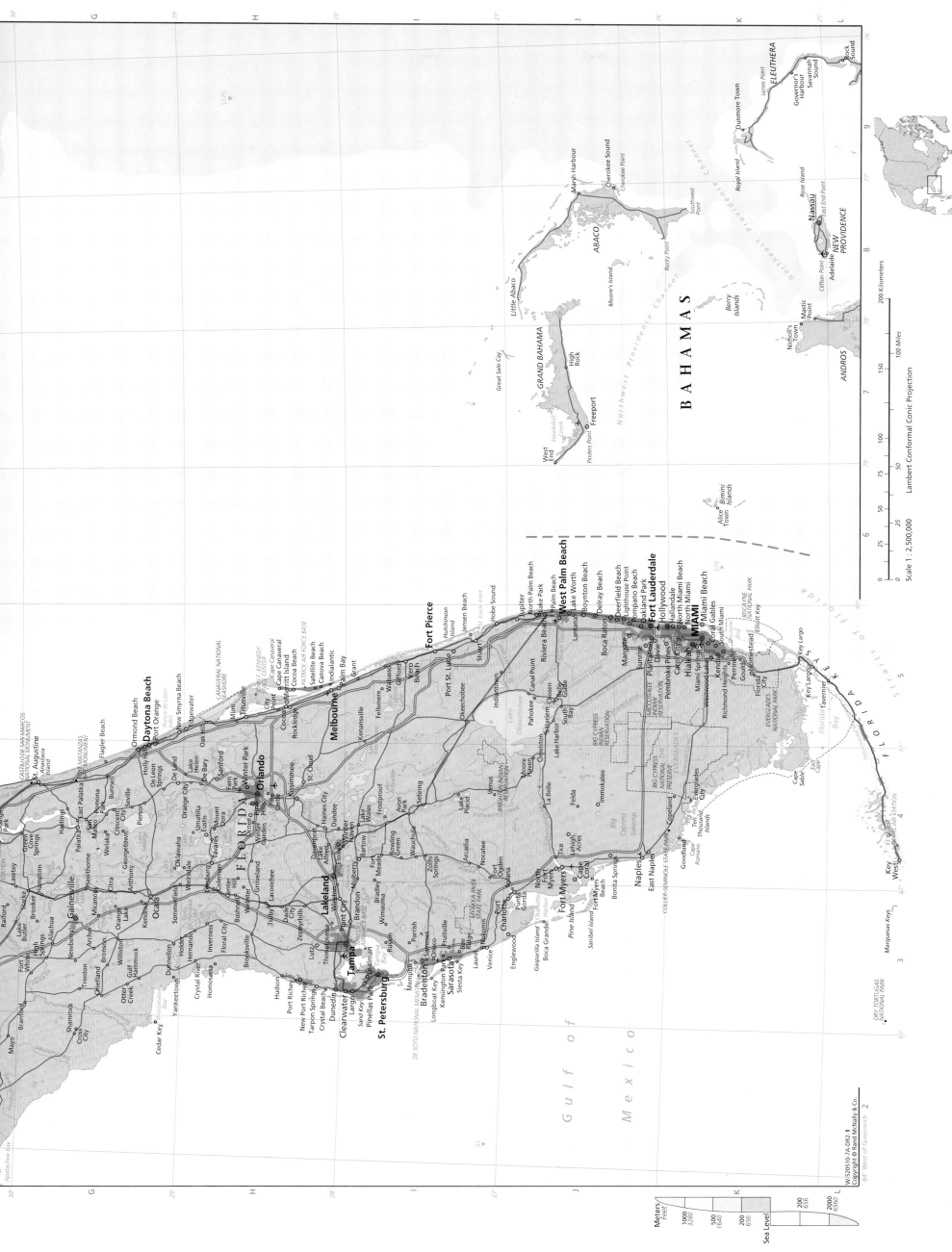

ELEUTHERA
Rock Sound
James Point
Governor's
Harbour
Savannah
Sound

Dunmore Town

ABACO
Marsh Harbour
Cherokee Sound
Cherokee Point

Royal Island
Rose Island
Nassau
NEW
PROVIDENCE
East End Point
Clifton Point
Adelaide

Southwest
Point
Rocky Point

Mastic Point
Berry
Islands

Nicholl's
Town

ANDROS

B A H A M A S

Moore's Island

GRAND BAHAMA

Great Sale Cay

High
Rock

Little Abaco

Hawksbill
Creek
Freeport

West
End
Pinders Point

Northwest Providence Channel

Northern Providence Channel

Alice
Town
Bimini
Islands

200 Kilometers
100 Miles

Scale 1 : 2,500,000

Lambert Conformal Conic Projection

Jupiter
North Palm Beach
Palm Beach
West Palm Beach
Lake Worth
Lantana
Boynton Beach
Delray Beach
Boca Raton
Deerfield Beach
Lighthouse Point
Pompano Beach
Margate
Oakland Park
Sunrise
Fort Lauderdale
Plantation
Davie
Hollywood
Pembroke Pines
Hallandale
North Miami Beach
Carol City
Miami Springs
North Miami
Hialeah
MIAMI
Miami Beach
Coral Gables
Kendall
Westwood Lakes
South Miami
Richmond Heights
Perrine
Gould's
Homestead
Florida
City

BISCAYNE
NATIONAL PARK
Elliott Key

Key Largo
Key Largo
Tavernier

FLORIDA KEYS

Stuart
Hobe Sound
Jupiter Inlet
Jensen Beach
Port St. Lucie
St. Lucie Inlet
Hutchinson
Island

Fort Pierce
Vero
Beach
Gifford
Wabasso
Fellsmere

Sebastian
Micco
Grant
Palm Bay
Malabar
Indialantic
Melbourne
Eau Gallie
Canova Beach
Satellite Beach
Cocoa Beach
Rockledge
Cocoa
Merritt Island
Cape Canaveral
Cape
Canaveral

CANAVERAL NATIONAL
SEASHORE

JOHN F. KENNEDY
SPACE CENTER

PATRICK AIR FORCE BASE

Titusville
Mims

City
Point

New Smyrna Beach
Edgewater

Daytona Beach
Ormond Beach
Port Orange
Holly Hill

Ponce de Leon
Inlet

Flagler Beach

Bunnell

De Land
De Leon
Springs
Lake Helen
De Bary
Sanford
Orange City
Lake
Mary

FLORIDA

Orlando
Winter Park
Fern
Park
Maitland
Apopka
Ocoee
Winter
Garden
Pine
Hills
Conway

Kissimmee
St. Cloud

CASTILLO DE SAN MARCOS
NATIONAL MONUMENT

St. Augustine
Anastasia
Island

FT. MATANZAS
NAT. MON.

Orange
Park

Green
Cove
Springs

East Palatka
Palatka
San
Mateo
Crescent
City
Pomona
Park
Seville
Pierson

Welaka
Georgetown

Hastings

Bostwick

Hawthorne
Melrose
Interlachen

Gainesville

Micanopy
Orange
Lake
Citra
Anthony

Ocala

Silver Springs
Belleview
Summerfield

Oklawaha
Weirsdale
Lady
Lake

Eustis
Tavares
Mount
Dora
Umatilla

Leesburg
Fruitland
Park

Coleman
Wildwood
Bushnell
Webster

Center
Hill

Groveland
Clermont

Mascotte

Minneola

Winter Haven
Auburndale
Lakeland
Mulberry
Bartow
Eagle
Lake
Lake
Alfred
Haines City
Davenport

Lake
Wales

Dundee

Frostproof

Avon
Park
Sebring
Lake
Placid

Venus

Lake
Okeechobee

Okeechobee

Port St. Lucie

Indiantown

Canal Point
Pahokee
Belle
Glade
South
Bay

Clewiston

Moore
Haven

La Belle

Felda

Immokalee

BIG CYPRESS
SEMINOLE INDIAN
RESERVATION

BRIGHTON INDIAN
RESERVATION

Fisheating Creek

MICCOSUKEE
INDIAN
RESERVATION

BIG CYPRESS
NATIONAL
PRESERVE

EVERGLADES
NATIONAL
PARK

THE
EVERGLADES

Florida
Bay

Cape
Sable
East
Cape

Flamingo

Cape
Romano

Goodland
Copeland

Ochopee
Everglades
City

COLLIER-SEMINOLE STATE PARK

Ten
Thousand
Islands

Marco

Naples
East Naples

Bonita Springs

Cape
Coral
North
Fort
Myers
Fort Myers
Fort Myers
Beach

Lehigh
Acres

Tice

Sanibel Island

Pine Island

Englewood

Boca Grande
Gasparilla Island
Charlotte
Harbour

Port
Charlotte
Punta
Gorda

Arcadia

Nocatee

Fort
Ogden

Solana

Zolfo
Springs
Wauchula

Bowling
Green

Fort
Meade

Brewster

Venice

Laurel
Osprey

Siesta Key
Longboat Key
Kensington Park

Sarasota

Bradenton
Palmetto
Ellenton
Parrish
Ruskin

Memphis
Samoset

Oneco
Fruitville

Bee
Ridge

Sun
City

St. Petersburg
Clearwater
Largo
Pinellas Park
Gulfport

Sand Key

Dunedin
Safety
Harbor

Tampa
Brandon
Plant City
Seffner

Thonotosassa
Lutz

Zephyrhills
Dade
City

San
Antonio

Trilby

Inverness
Floral City
Hernando

Crystal River
Homosassa

Chassahowitzka
Bay

Holder
Dunnellon

Morriston
Williston
Bronson

Archer
Newberry

Gulf
Hammock

Otter
Creek

Cedar Key

Yankeetown

Waccasassa
Bay

Hudson
Port Richey
New Port Richey
Tarpon Springs
Crystal Beach

Elfers

Gulf   of   Mexico

DE SOTO NATIONAL MEMORIAL

MYAKKA RIVER
STATE PARK

Key
West
Key West

Marquesas Keys

DRY TORTUGAS
NATIONAL PARK

SUGARLOAF
KEY AIR FORCE
STATION

Straits   of   Florida

Alachua
High
Springs

Fort
White

Branford

Mayo

Cross
City

Shamrock

Old
Town

Trenton

Bell

Chiefland

Lawtey
Starke
Lake
Butler
Brooker

Raiford

Lake City

Lake
City

Lulu

Santa Fe River

84° West of Greenwich   2

W-520510-7A-DR2-1
Copyright © Rand McNally & Co.

Meters
Feet

1000
3280

500
1640

200
656

200
656

2000
6560

Sea Level

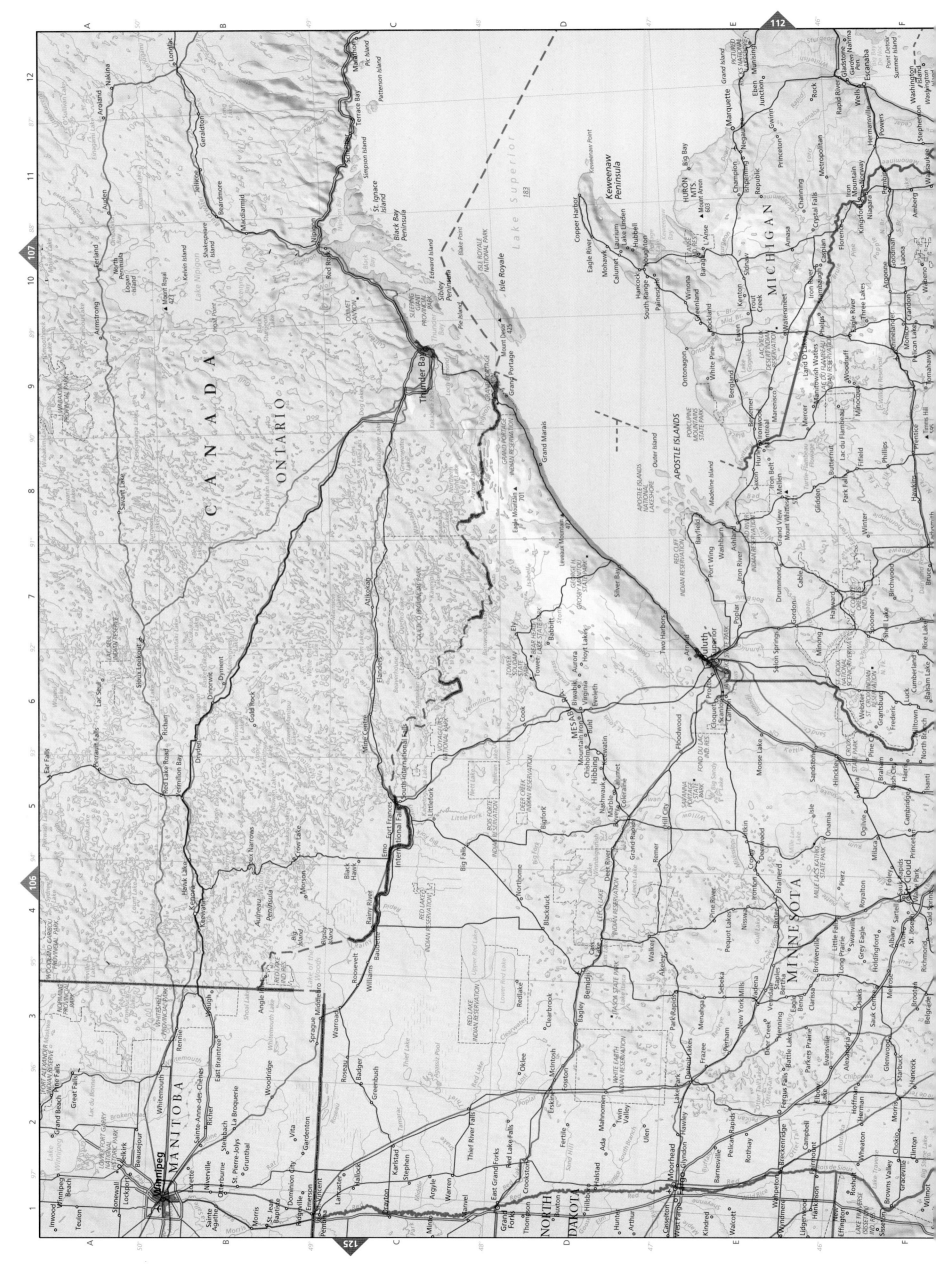

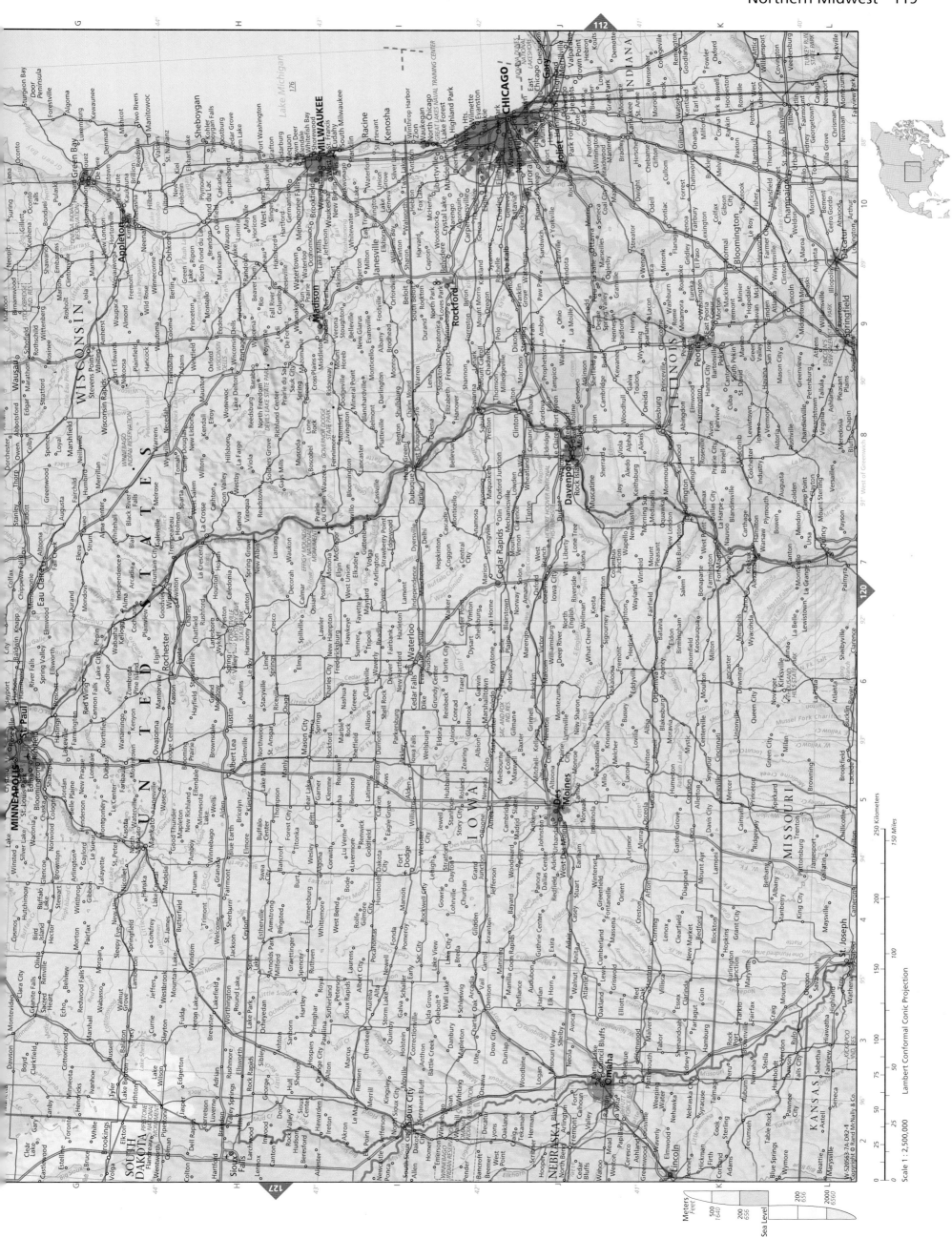

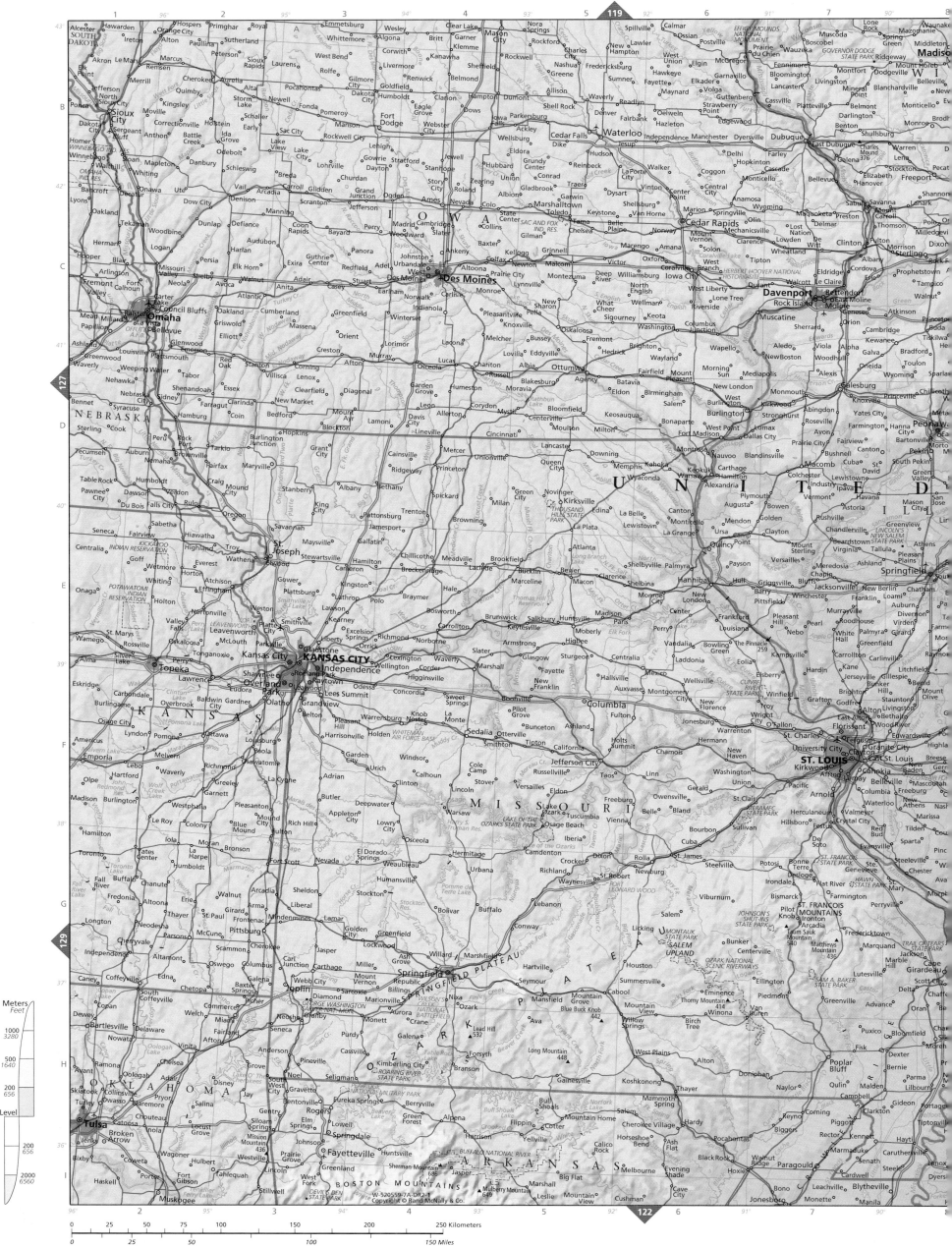

Scale 1 : 2,500,000   Lambert Conformal Conic Projection

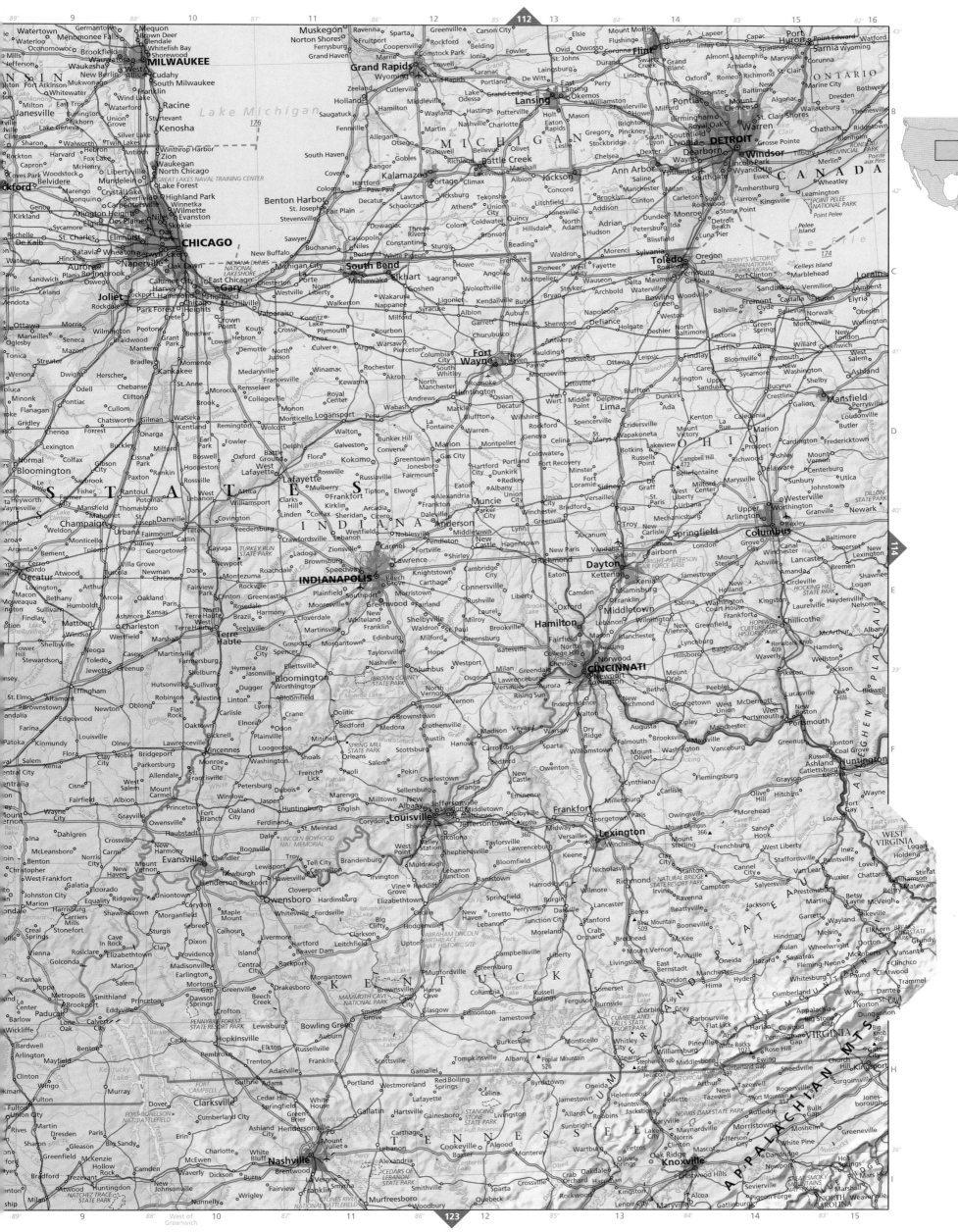

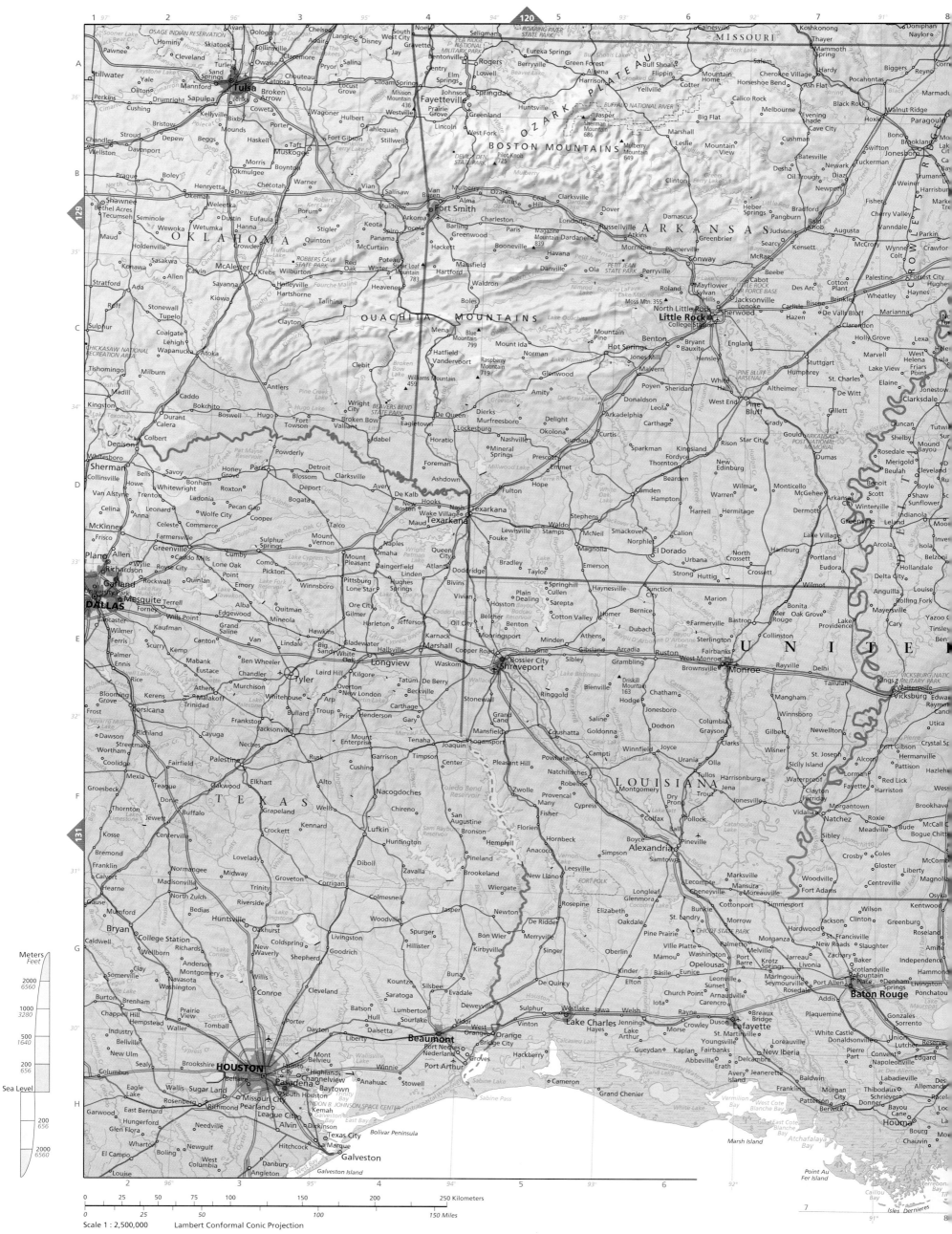

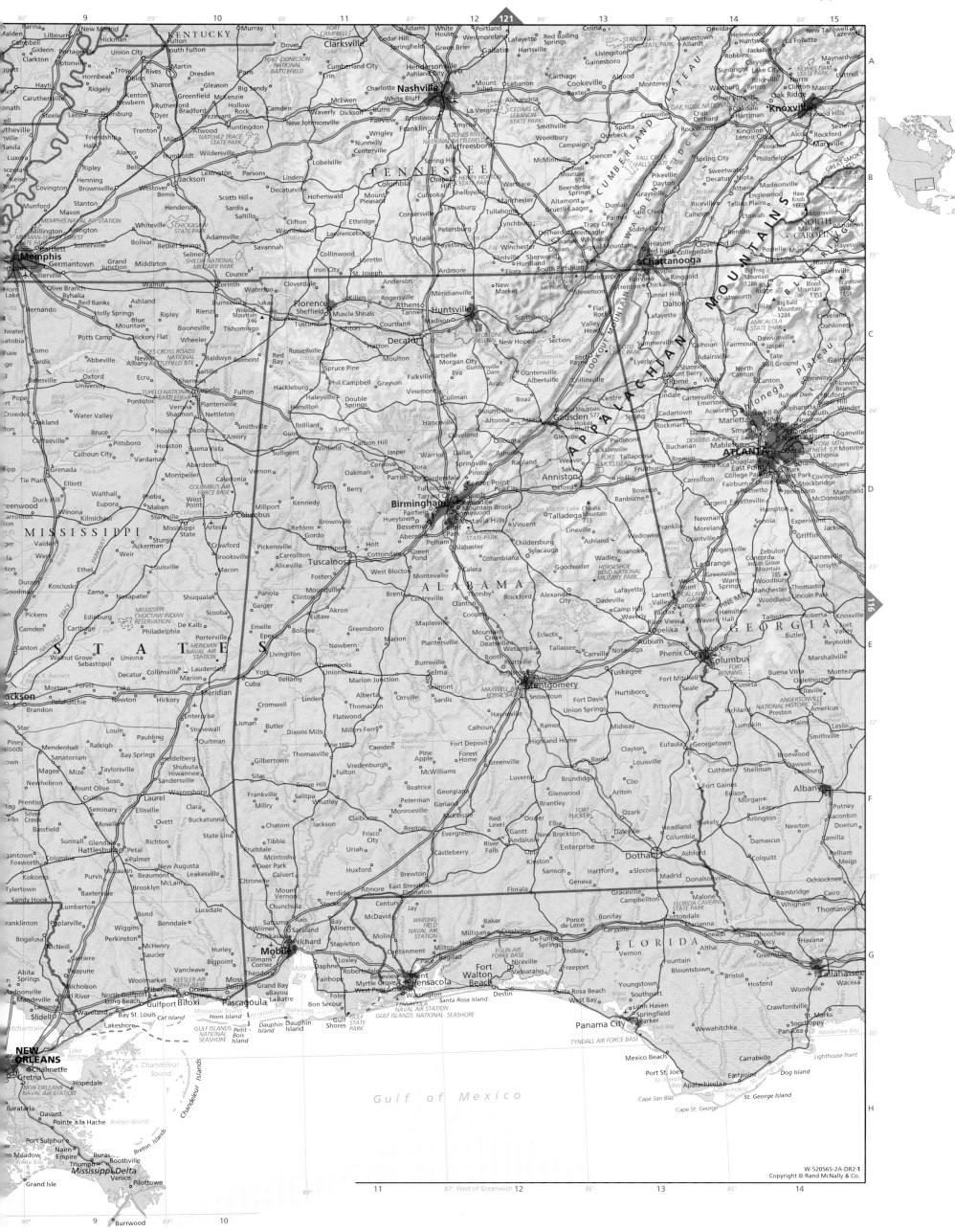

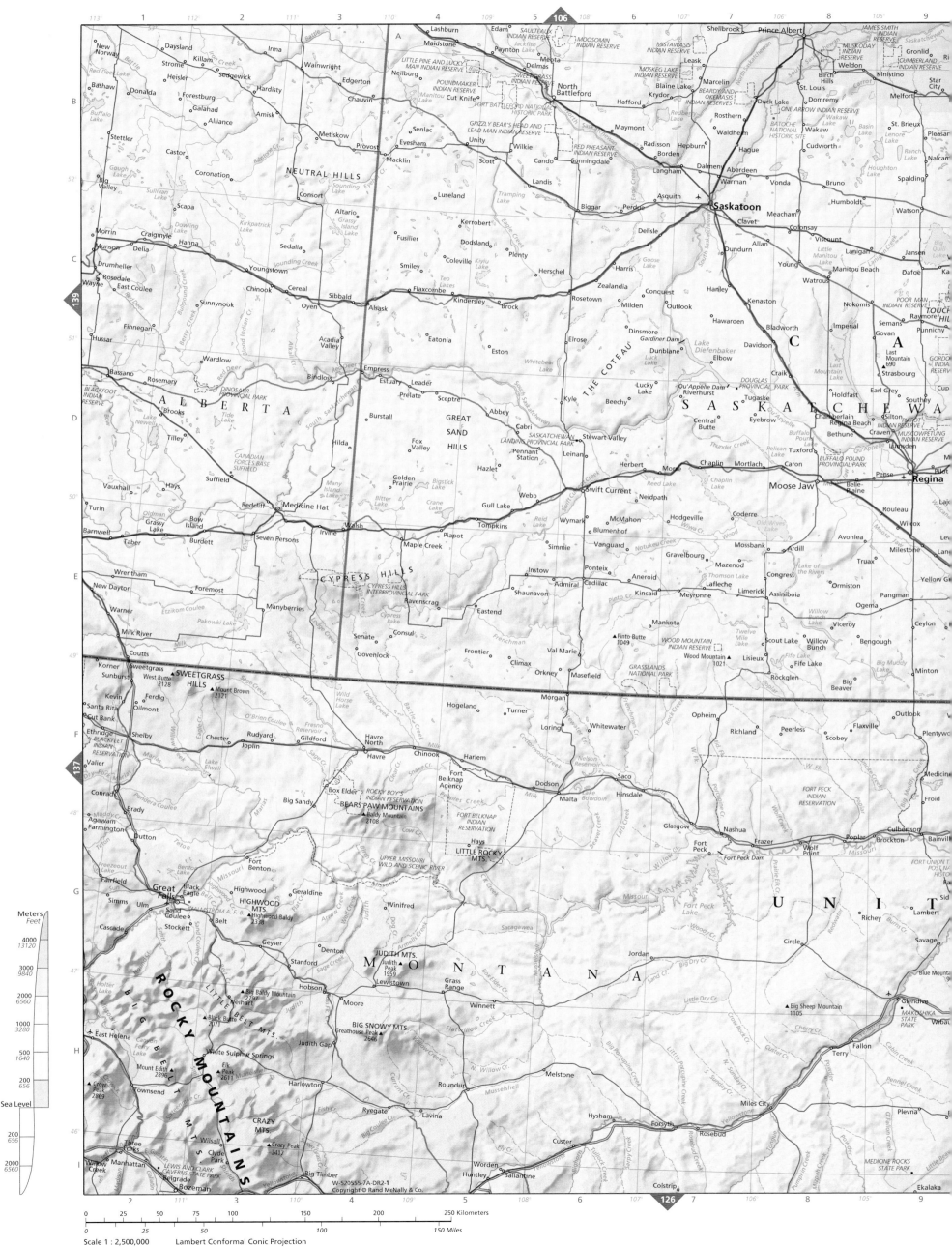

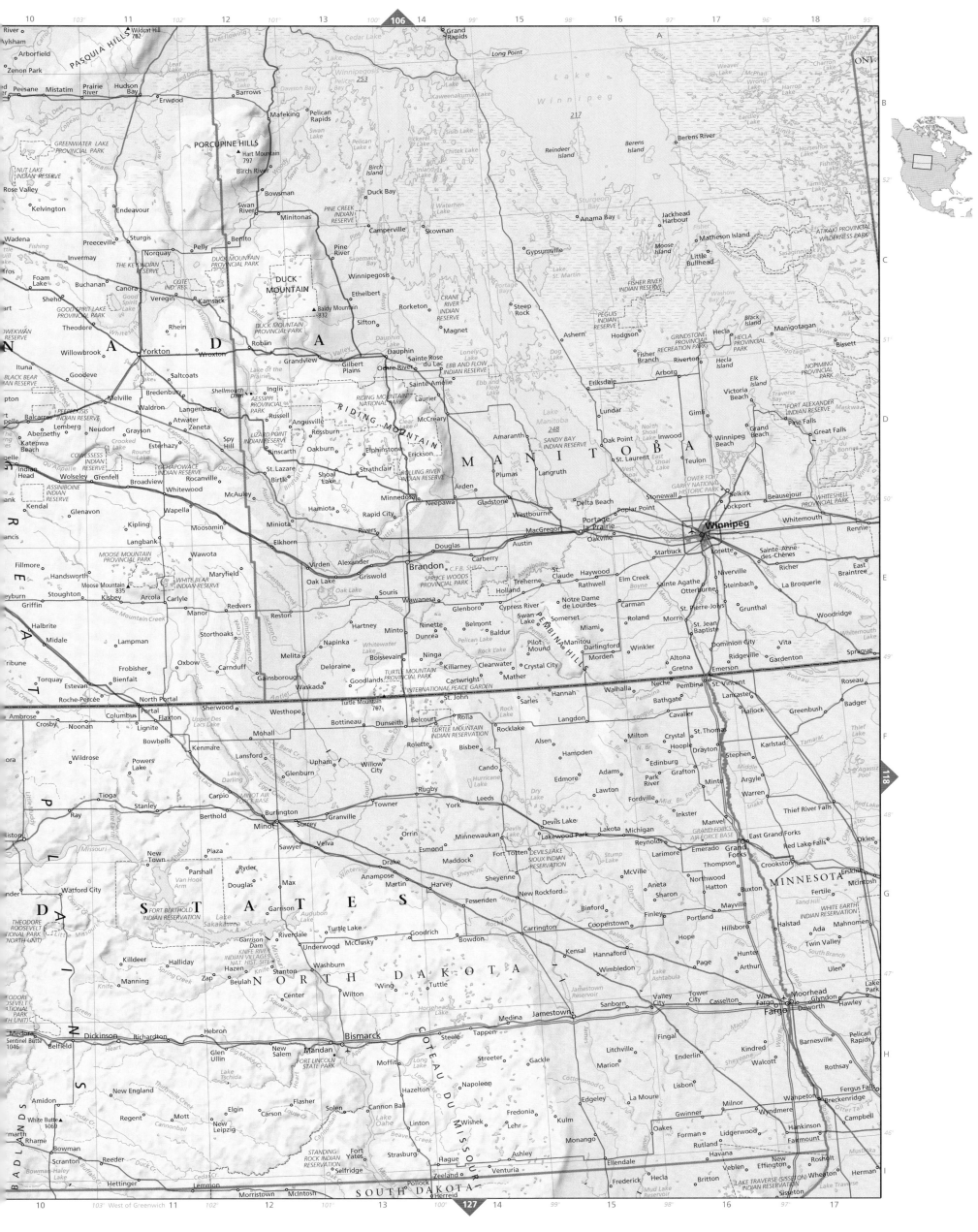

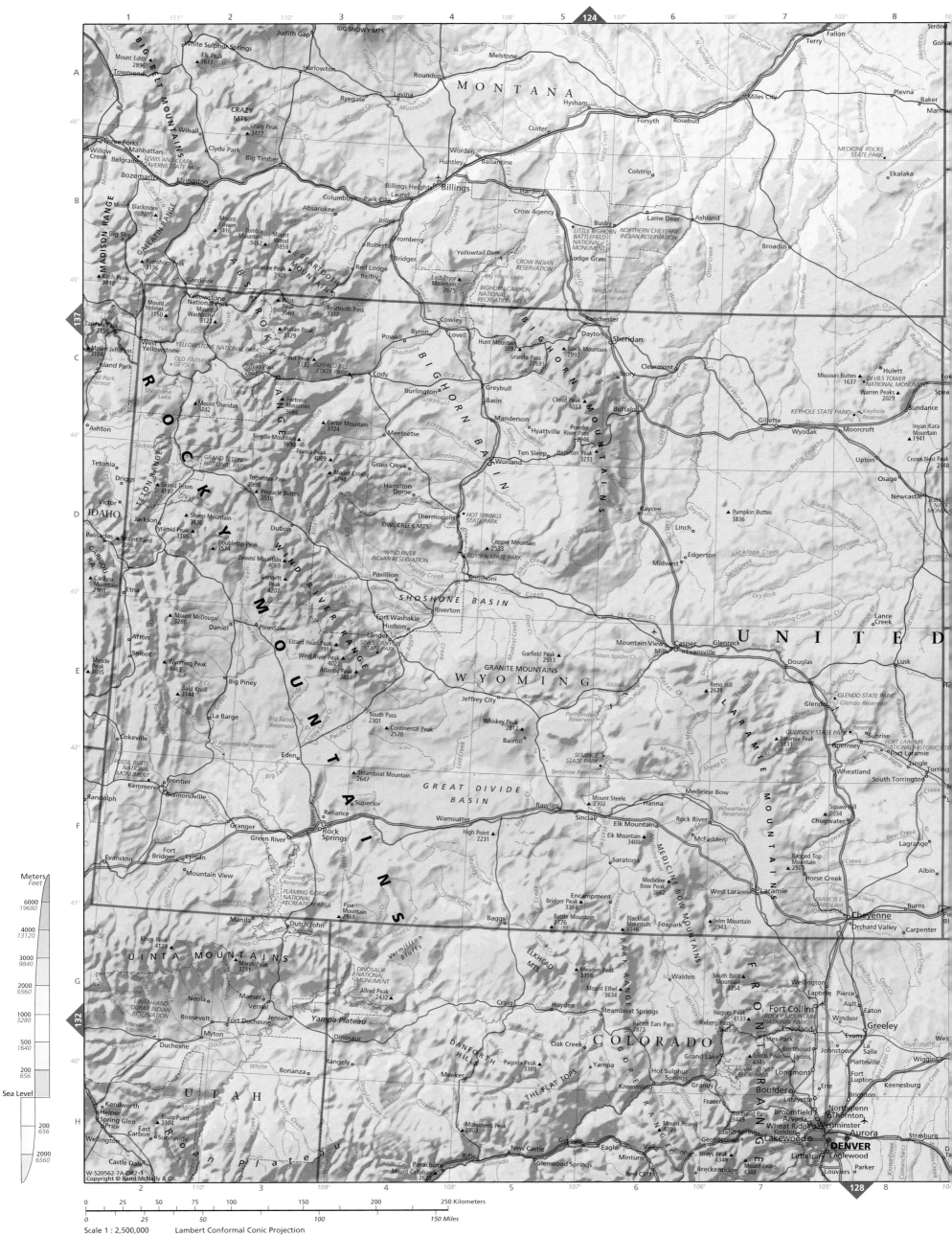

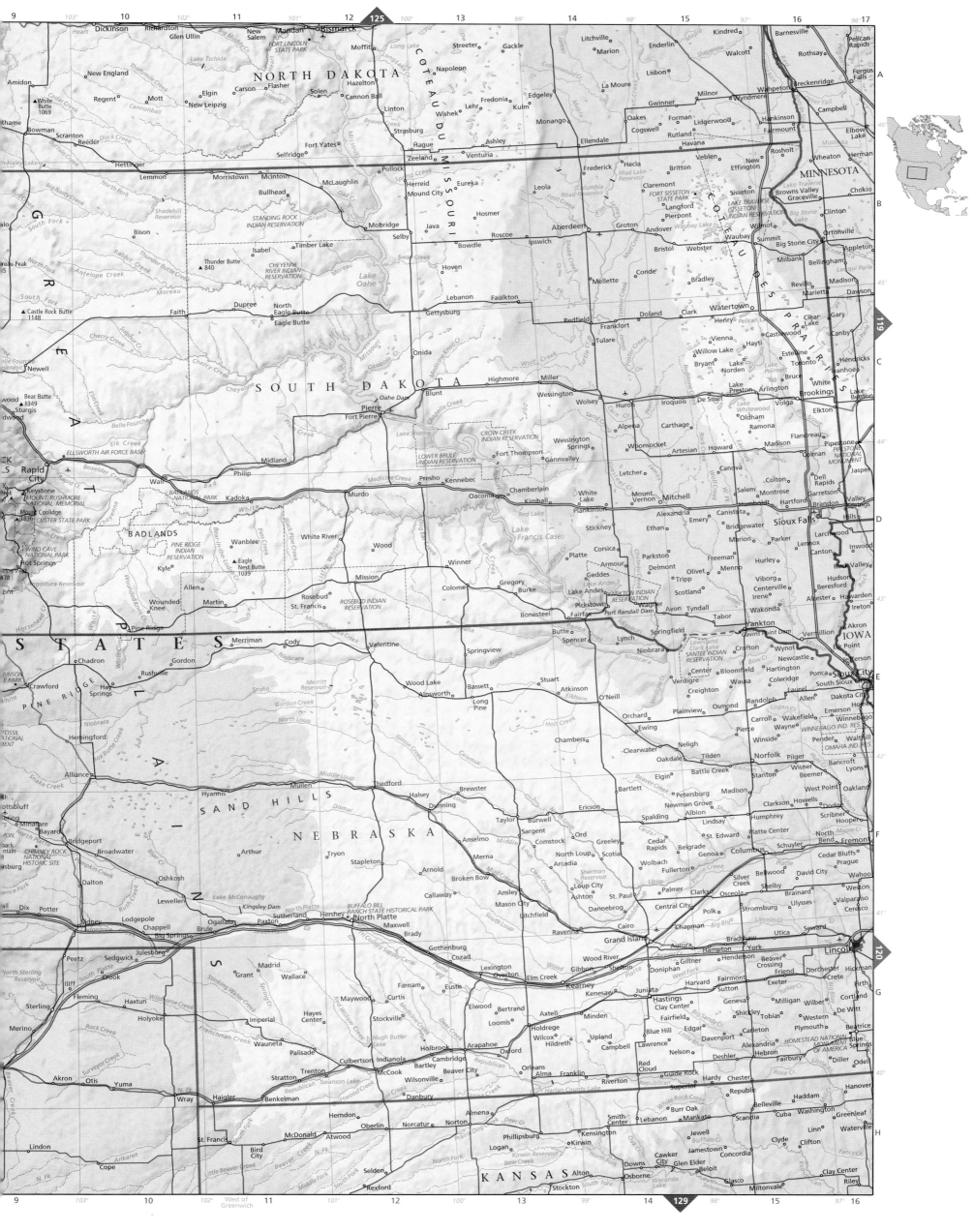

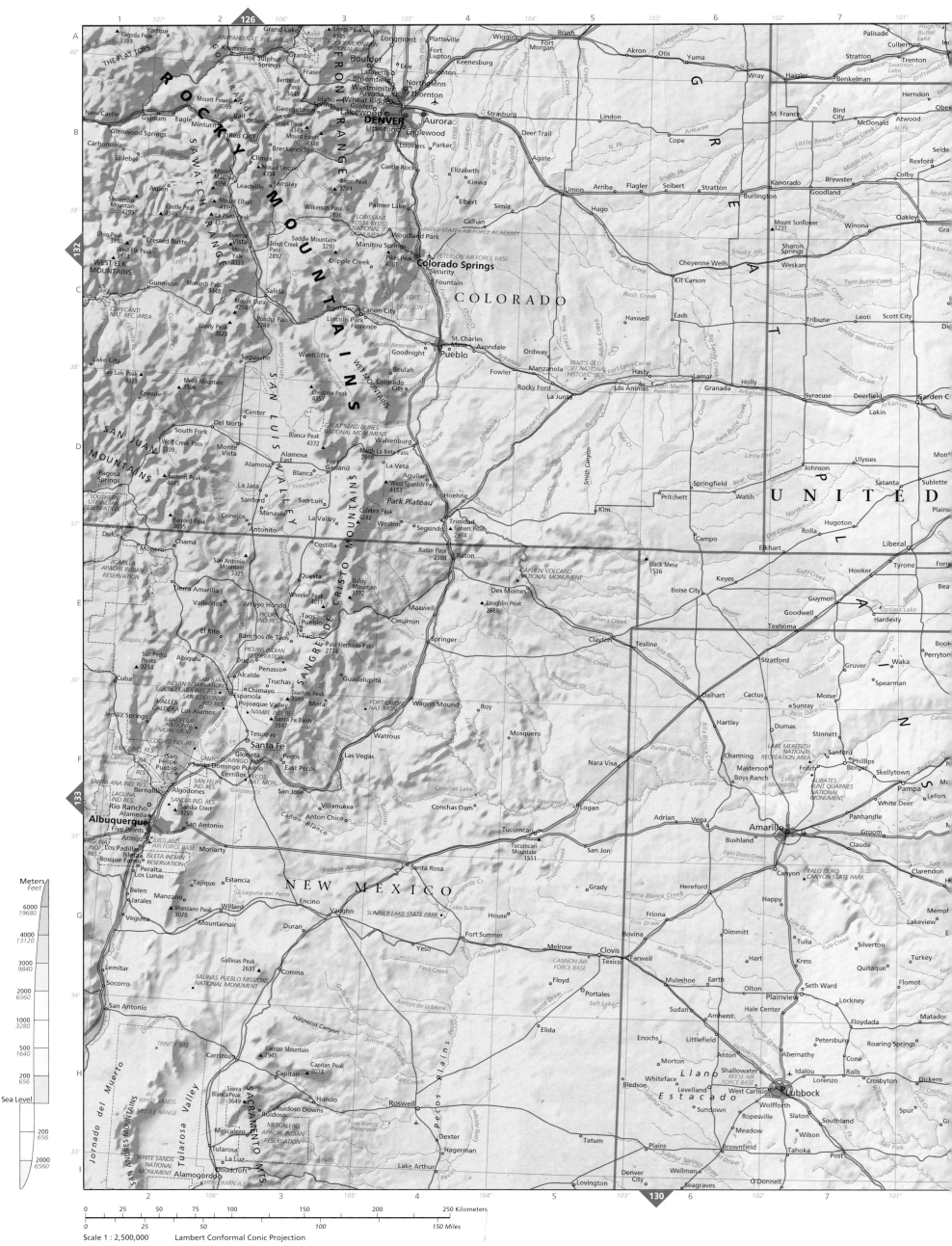

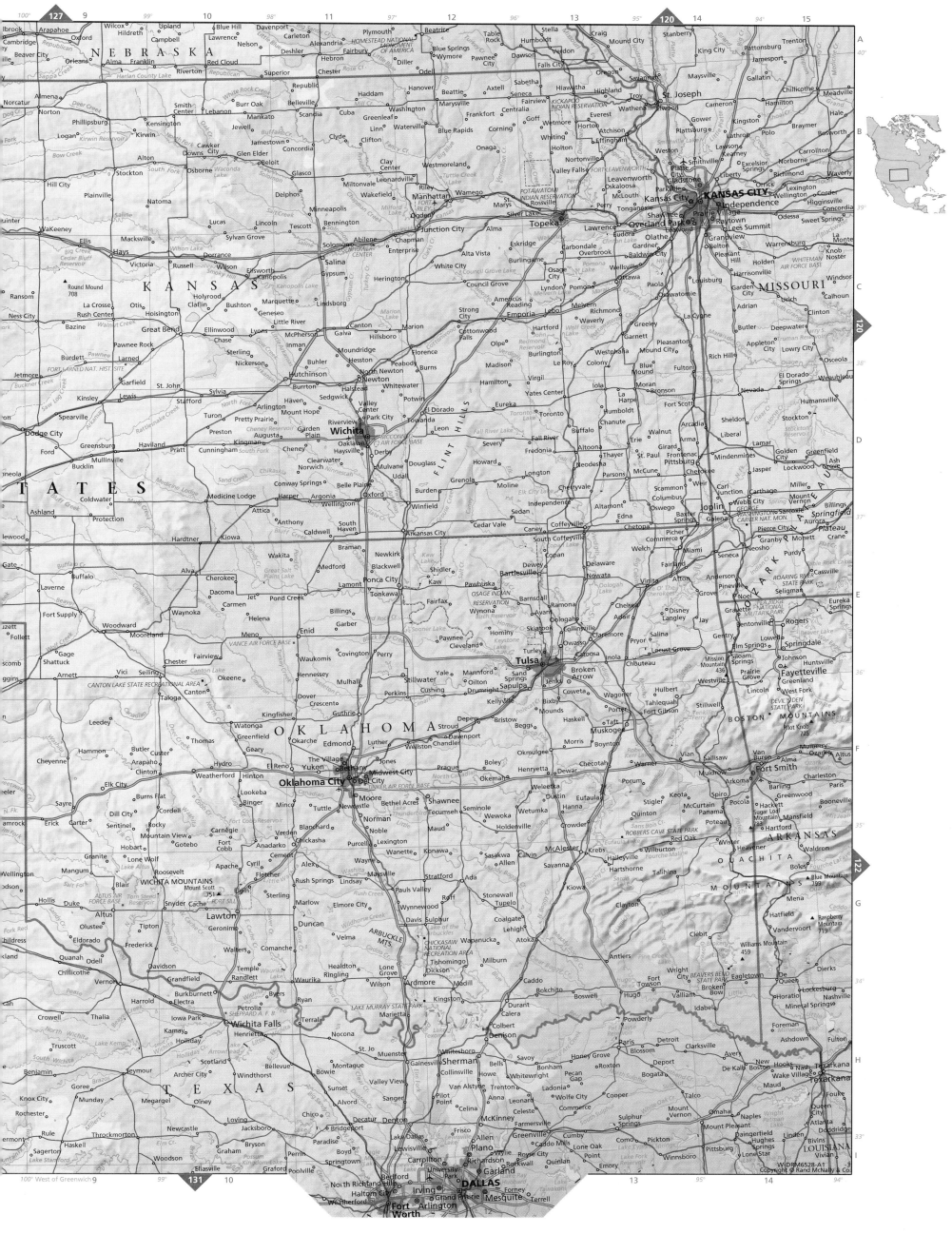

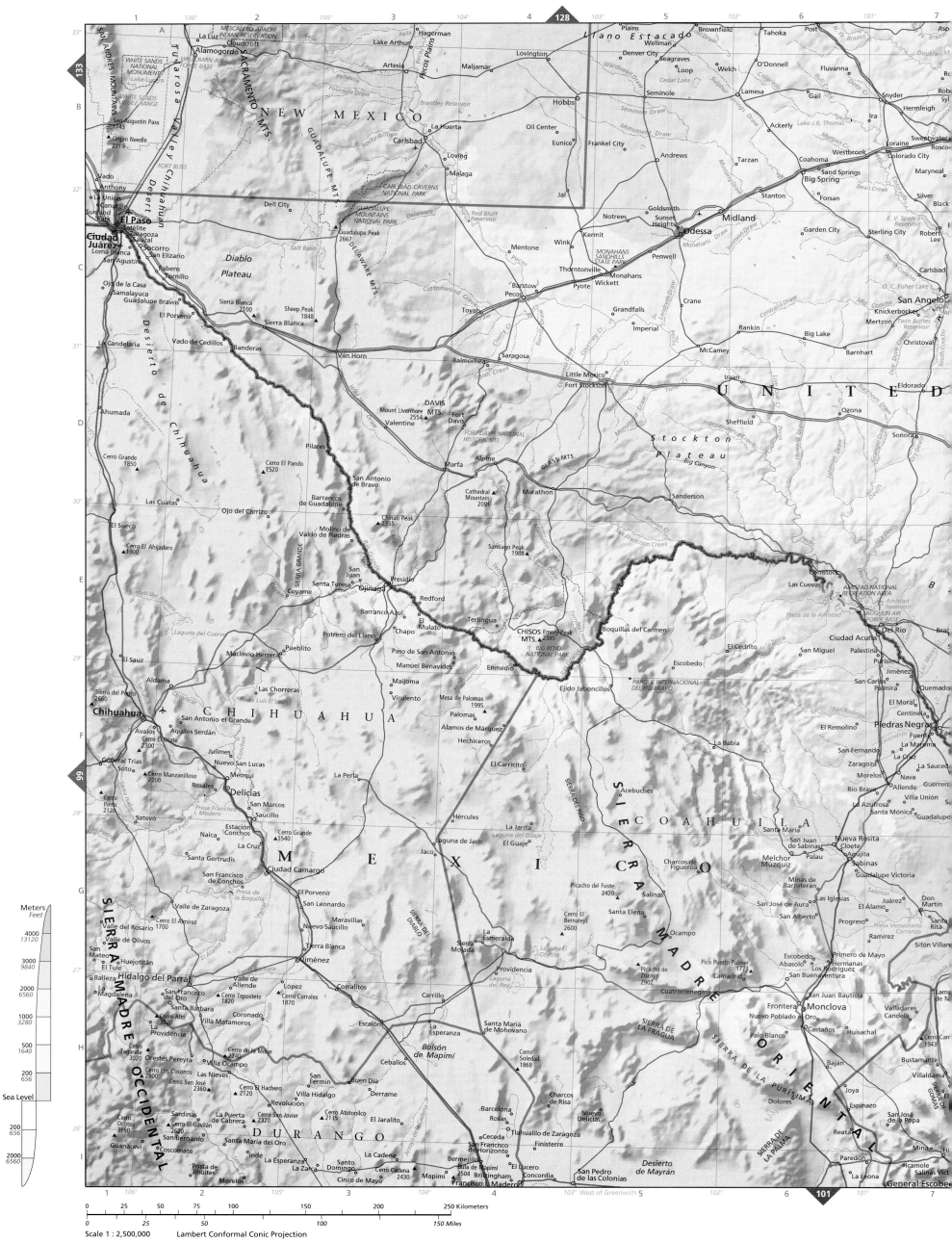

Meters
Feet

4000
13120

3000
9840

2000
6560

1000
3280

500
1640

200
656

Sea Level

200
656

2000
6560

0   25   50   75   100   150   200   250 Kilometers

0   25   50   100   150 Miles

Scale 1 : 2,500,000   Lambert Conformal Conic Projection

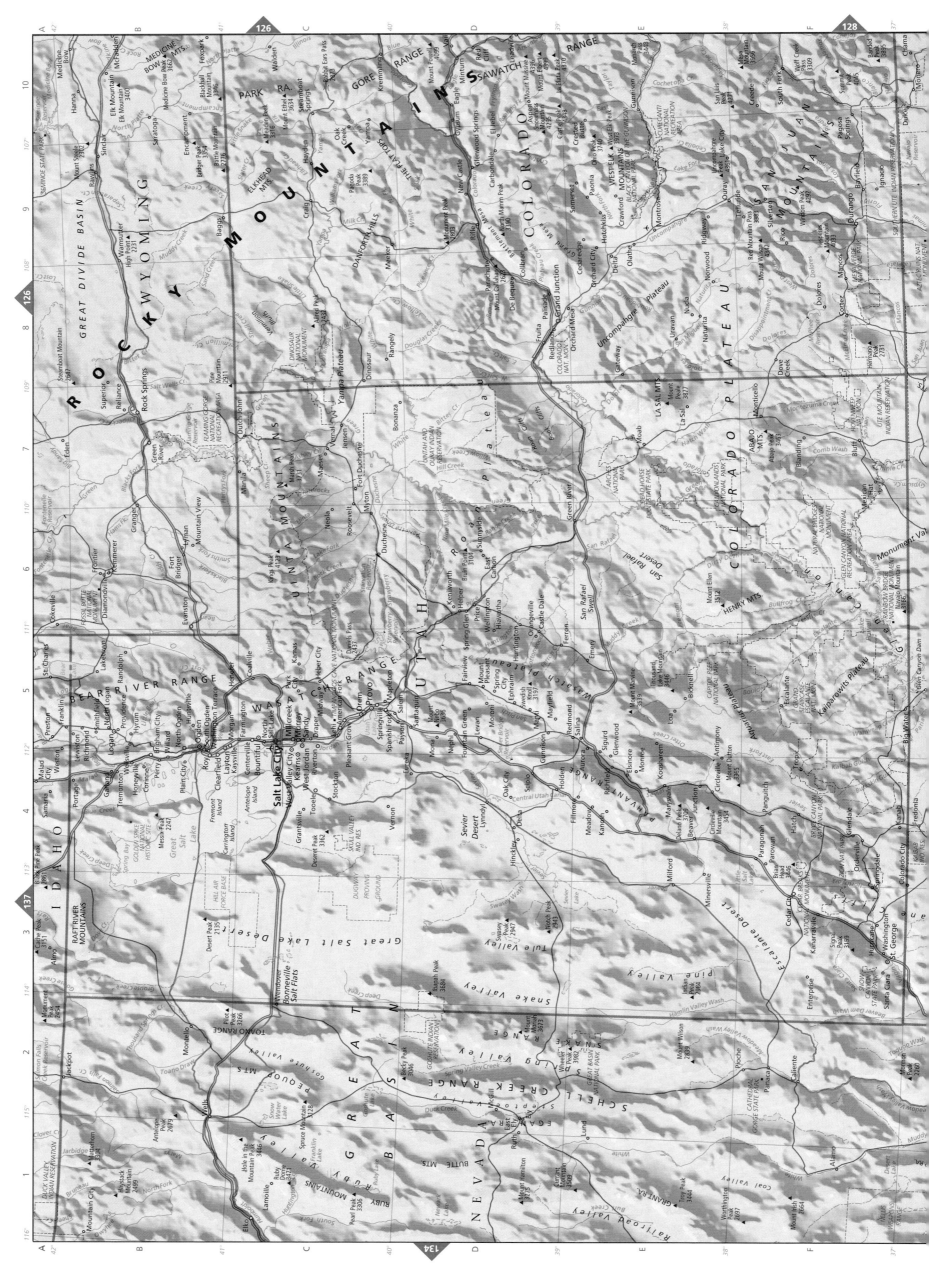

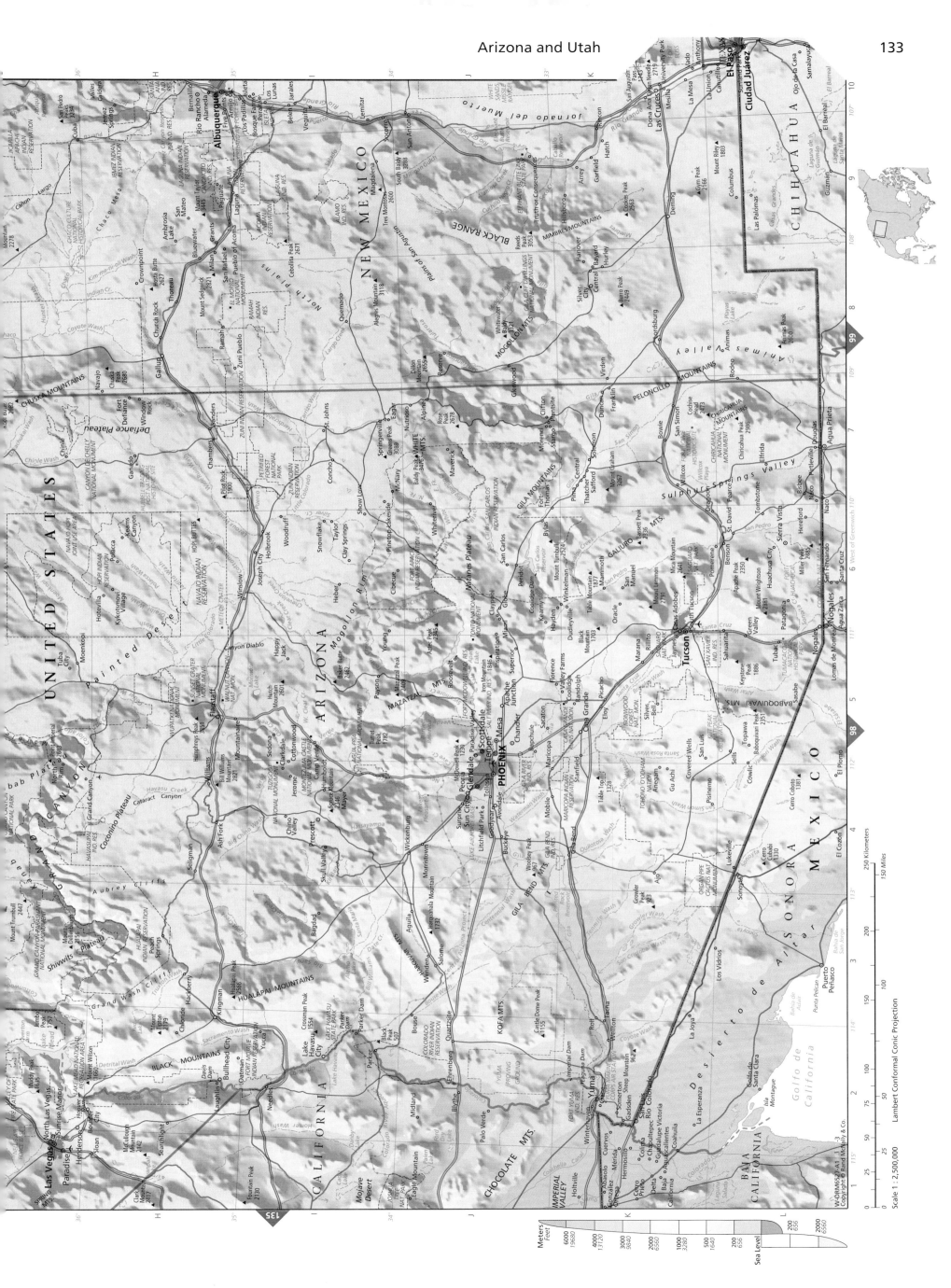

Scale 1 : 2,500,000

Lambert Conformal Conic Projection

Meters	Feet
6000	19680
4000	13120
3000	9840
2000	6560
1000	3280
500	1640
200	656
Sea Level	
200	656
2000	6560

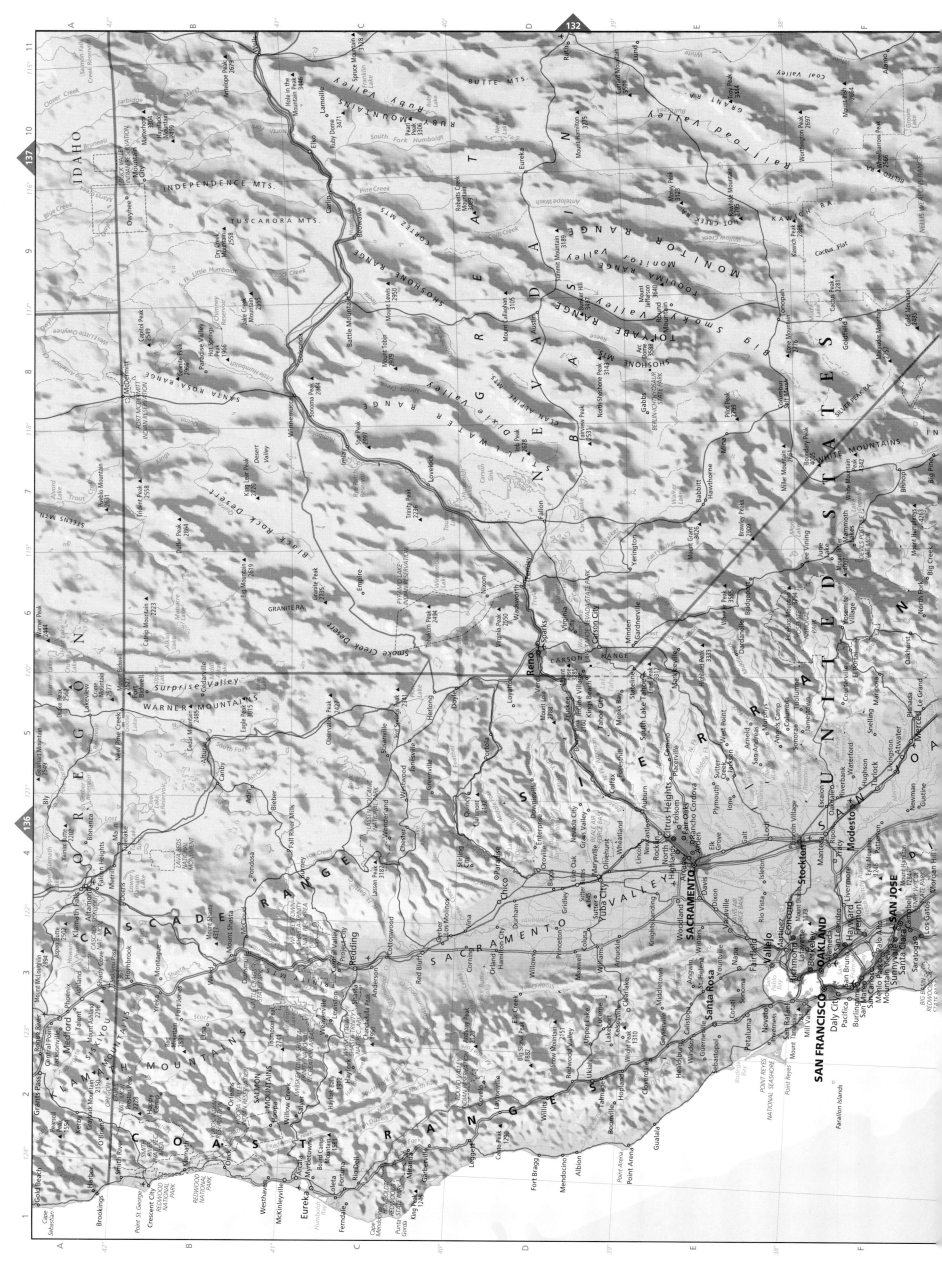

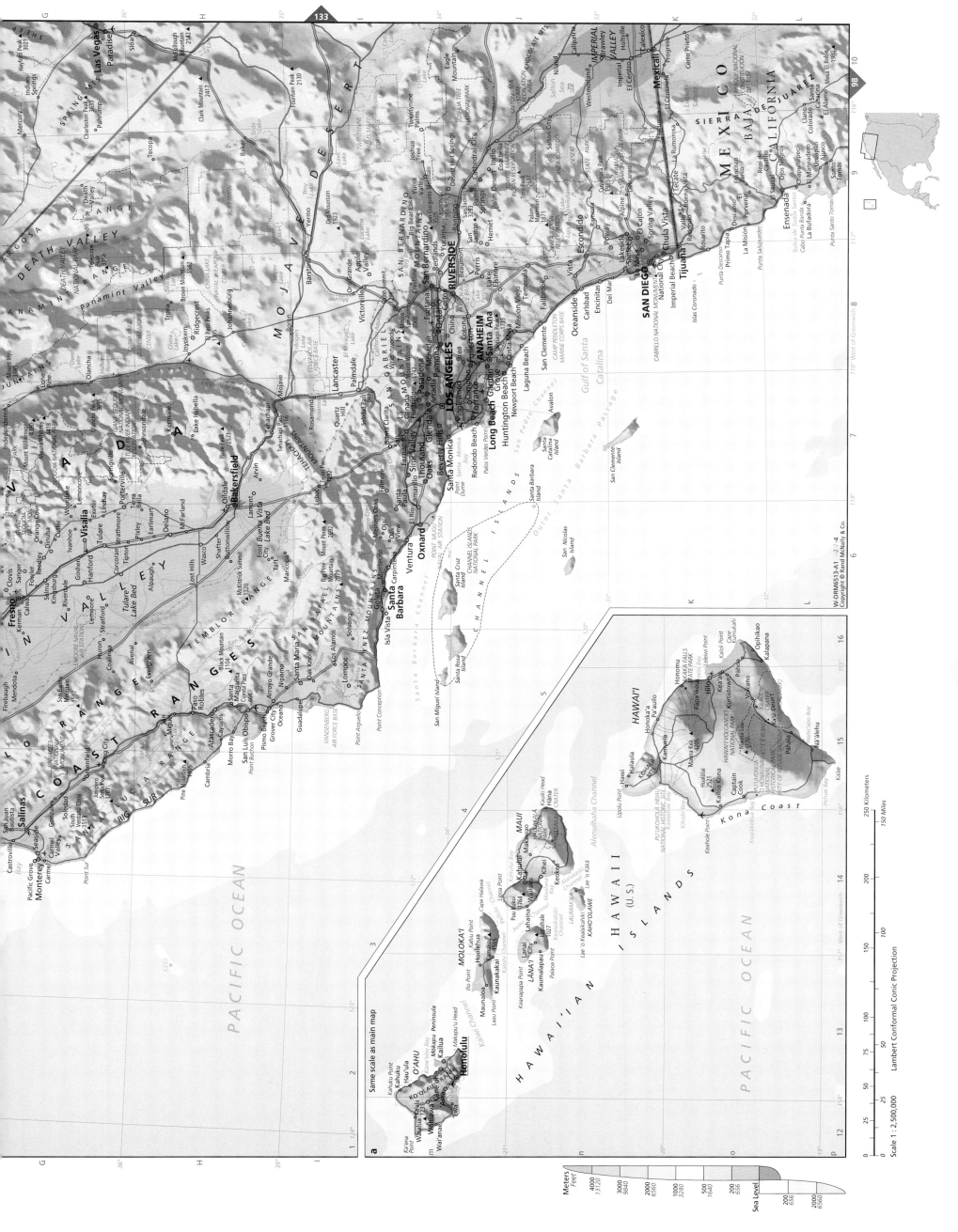

Scale 1 : 2,500,000

Lambert Conformal Conic Projection

W-DRM6513-A1 -2 -4
Copyright © Rand McNally & Co.

Same scale as main map

Meters / Feet
4000 / 13120
3000 / 9840
2000 / 6560
1000 / 3280
500 / 1640
200 / 656
Sea Level
200 / 656
2000 / 6560

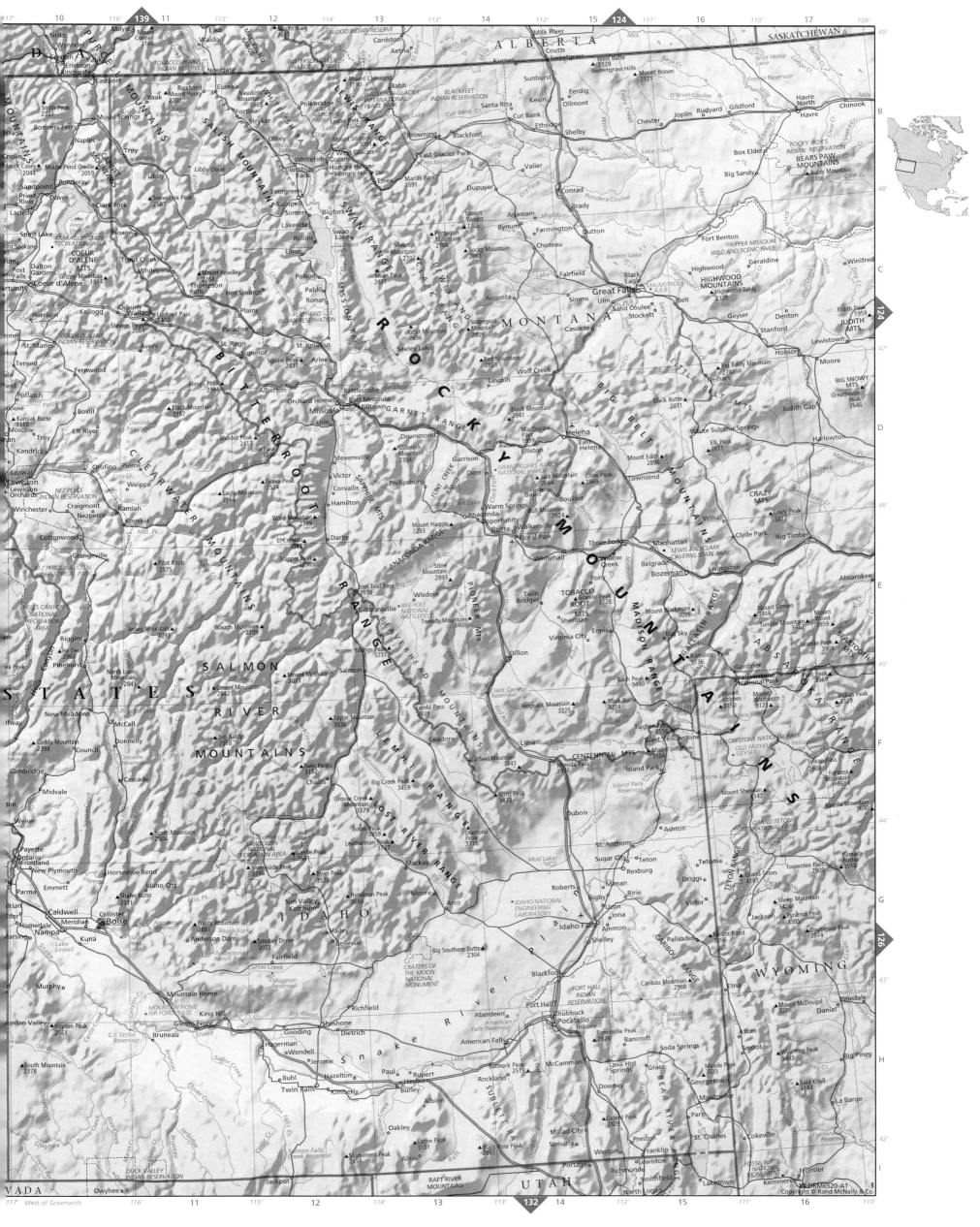

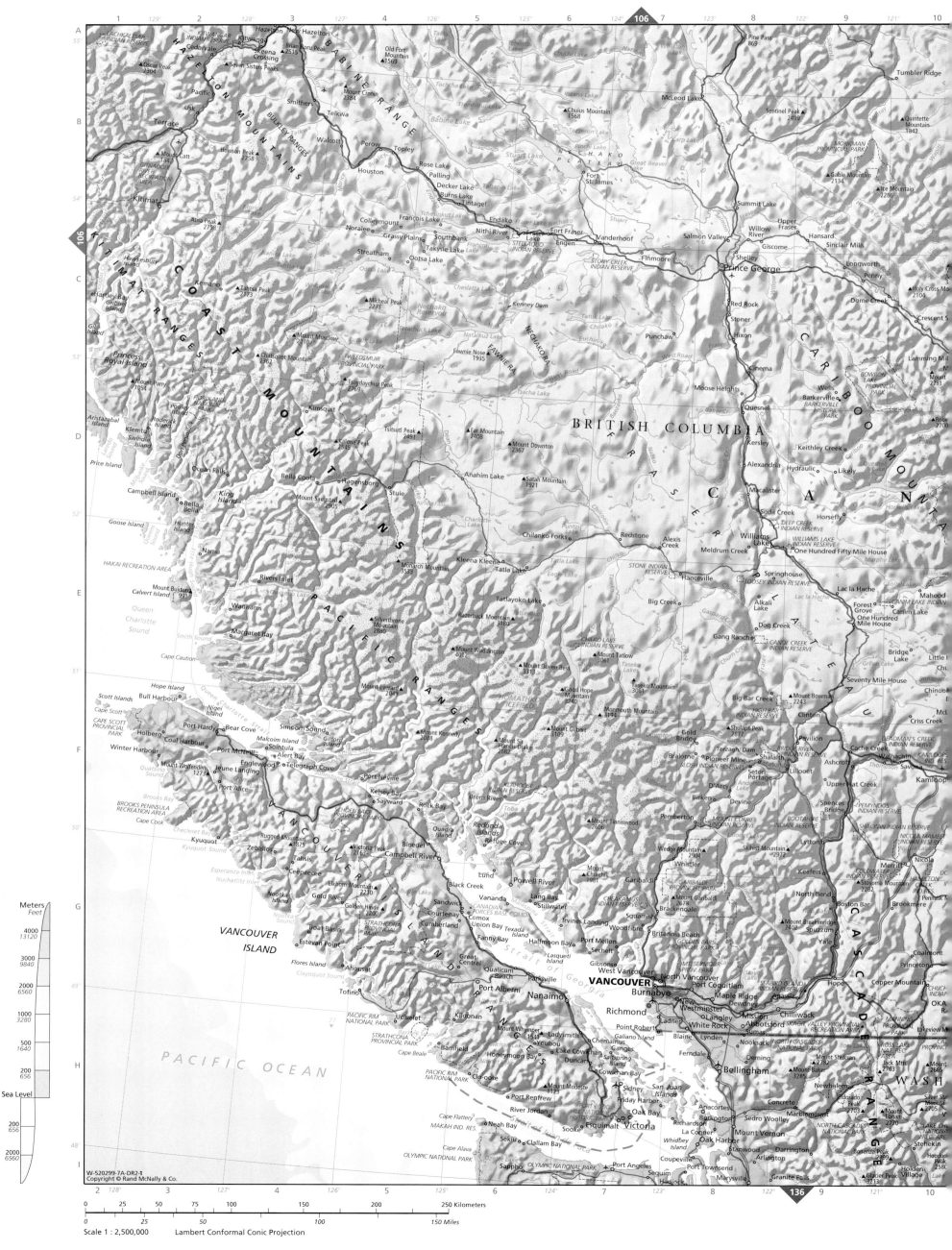

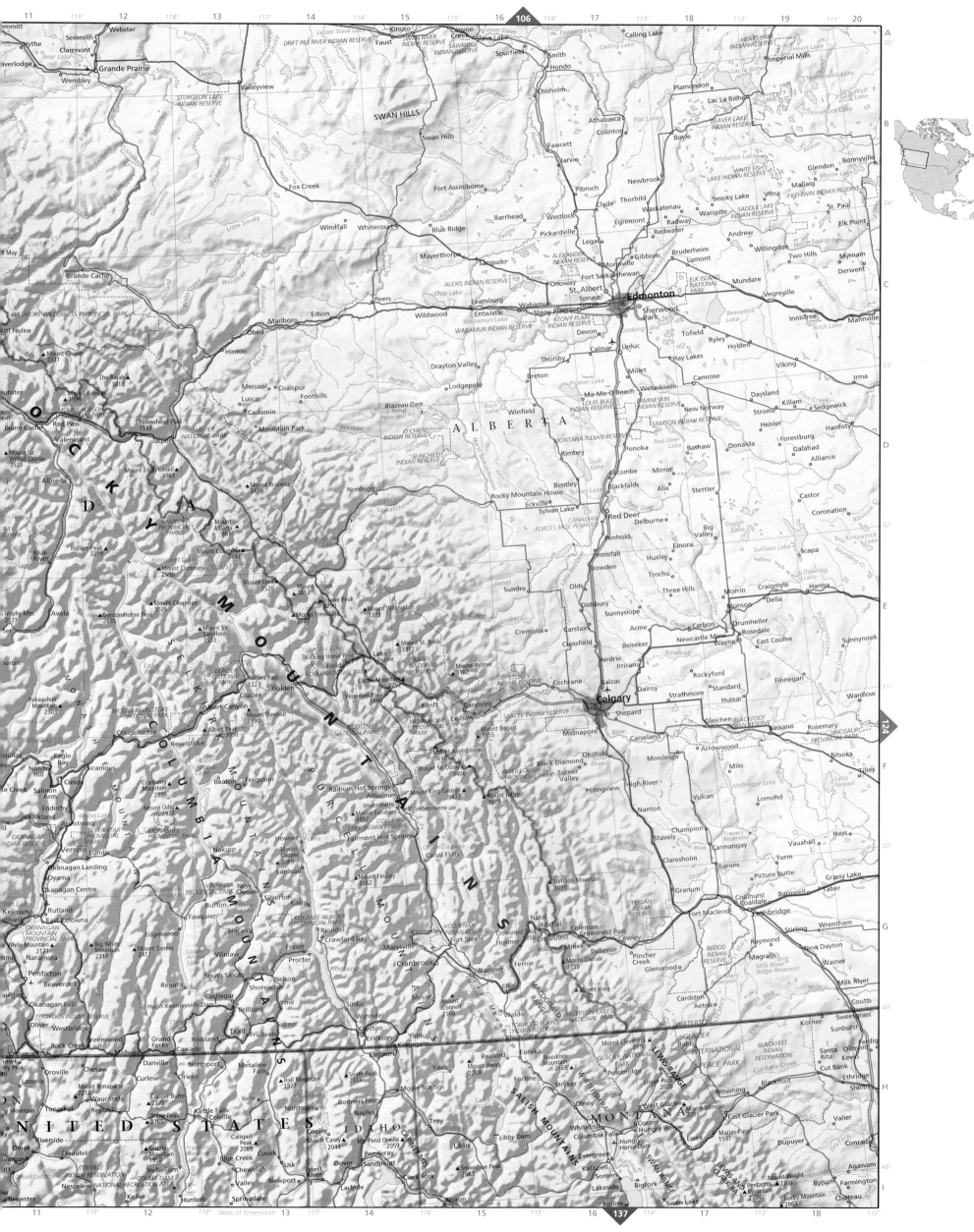

Meters
Feet
4000
13120
3000
9840
2000
6560
1000
3280
500
1640
200
656

Sea Level

200
656
2000
6560

ARCTIC OCEAN

BEAUFORT SEA

CHUKCHI SEA

OSTROV VRANGELJA (WRANGEL ISLAND)

RUSSIA

Cukotskij poluostrov (Chukotsk Peninsula)

BROOKS RANGE

DE LONG MTS.

LOOKOUT RIDGE

SCHWATKA MTS.

BAIRD MTS.

ENDICOTT MOUNTAINS

PHILIP SMITH MTS.

ROMANZOF MTS.

BRITISH MTS.

DAVIDSON MTS.

RICHARDSON MOUNTAINS

NORTHWEST TERRITORIES

CANADA

YUKON

UNITED STATES

Seward Peninsula

KAIYUH MTS.

ALASKA

KUSKOKWIM MTS.

ALASKA RANGE

TALKEETNA MOUNTAINS

WRANGELL MOUNTAINS

CHUGACH MOUNTAINS

ST. ELIAS MOUNTAINS

COAST MOUNTAINS

BRITISH COLUMBIA

OGILVIE MOUNTAINS

SELWYN MOUNTAINS

MACKENZIE MOUNTAINS

PELLY MOUNTAINS

DAWSON RANGE

CASSIAR MOUNTAINS

STIKINE MOUNTAINS

KILBUCK MTS.

BERING SEA

Pribilof Islands

St. Paul Island

St. George Island

St. Matthew Island

Nunivak Island

ST. LAWRENCE ISLAND

Gulf of Alaska

KODIAK ISLAND

Anchorage

Fairbanks

Mount McKinley 6194

Mount Foraker 5304

ALASKA PENINSULA

ALEUTIAN RANGE

ALEXANDER ARCHIPELAGO

CHICHAGOF ISLAND

BARANOF ISLAND

PRINCE OF WALES ISLAND

FOX ISLANDS

Umnak Island

Unalaska Island

Makushin Volcano 2036

Mount Vsevidof 2109

Shishaldin Volcano 2857

Unimak Island

QUEEN CHARLOTTE ISLANDS

M-DRM4700-A1- -2-2-2
Copyright © Rand McNally & Co.

BANKS ISLAND

VICTORIA ISLAND

MELVILLE ISLAND

PRINCE PATRICK ISLAND

NUNAVUT

a

BERING SEA

ALEUTIAN ISLANDS

NEAR ISLANDS

Attu

Agattu Island

RAT ISLANDS

Kiska Volcano 1220

Kiska Island

Amchitka Island

ANDREANOF ISLANDS

Adak Island

Kanaga Island

Great Sitkin Island

Atka Island

Amlia Island

Korovin Volcano 1478

ISLANDS OF FOUR MOUNTAINS

Yunaska Island

Chuginadak Island

FOX ISLANDS

Umnak Island

Unalaska Island

Makushin Volcano 2036

Mount Vsevidof 2109

Nikolski

Akutan Island

Akun Island

Tigalda Island

PACIFIC OCEAN

International Date Line

Same scale as main map

0   100   200   400   600   800   1000 Kilometers

0   100   200   400   600 Miles

Scale 1 : 10,000,000   Lambert Conformal Conic Projection

Scale 1 : 10,000,000   Lambert Conformal Conic Projection

M-DRM4702-A1- -2-2-3
Copyright © Rand McNally & Co.

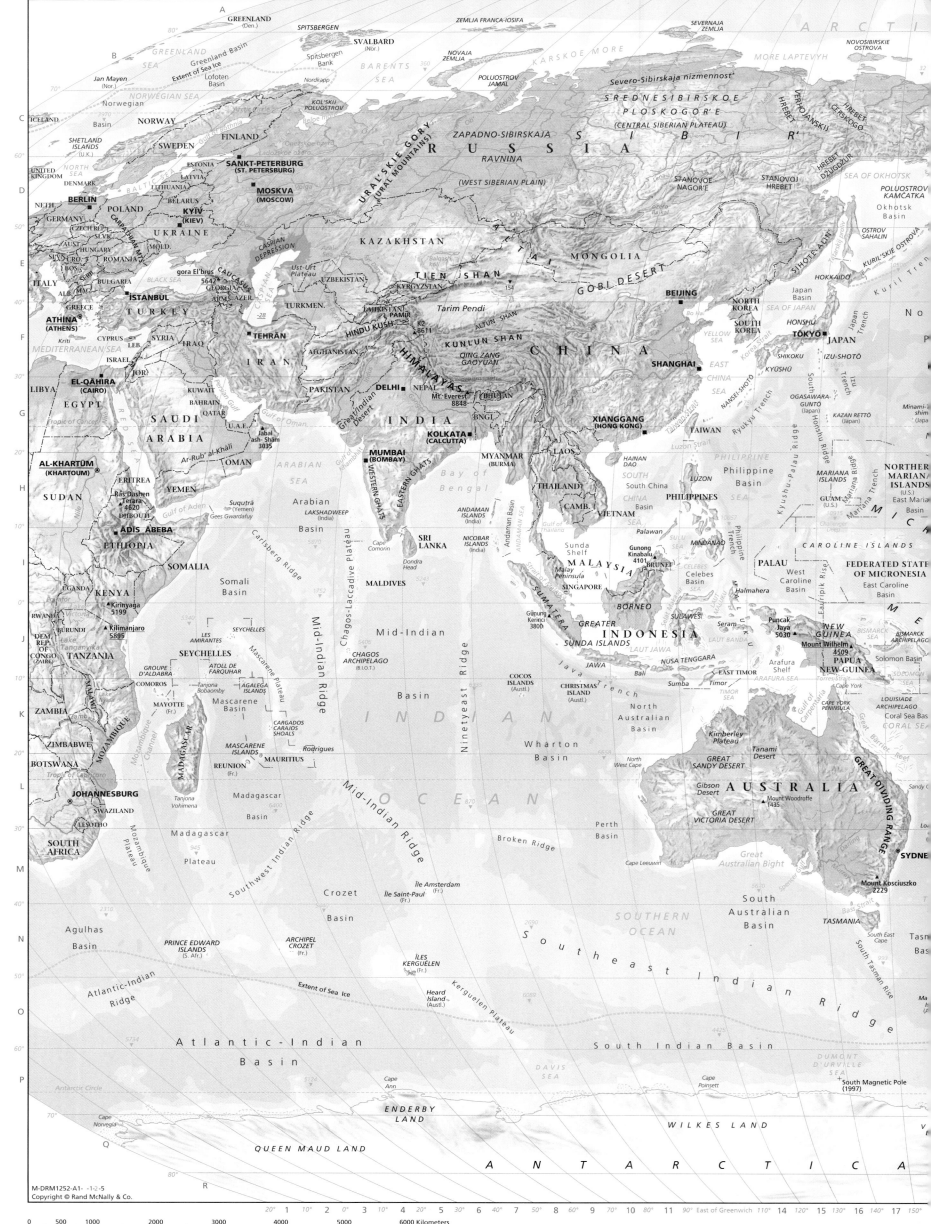

Meters
Feet

6000
19680

4000
13120

3000
9840

2000
6560

1000
3280

500
1640

200
656

Sea Level

200
656

2000
6560

4000
13120

6000
19680

M-DRM1252-A1- -1-2-5
Copyright © Rand McNally & Co.

0   500 1000   2000   3000   4000   5000   6000 Kilometers

0   500 1000   2000   3000   4000 Miles

Scale 1 : 60,000,000   Robinson Projection

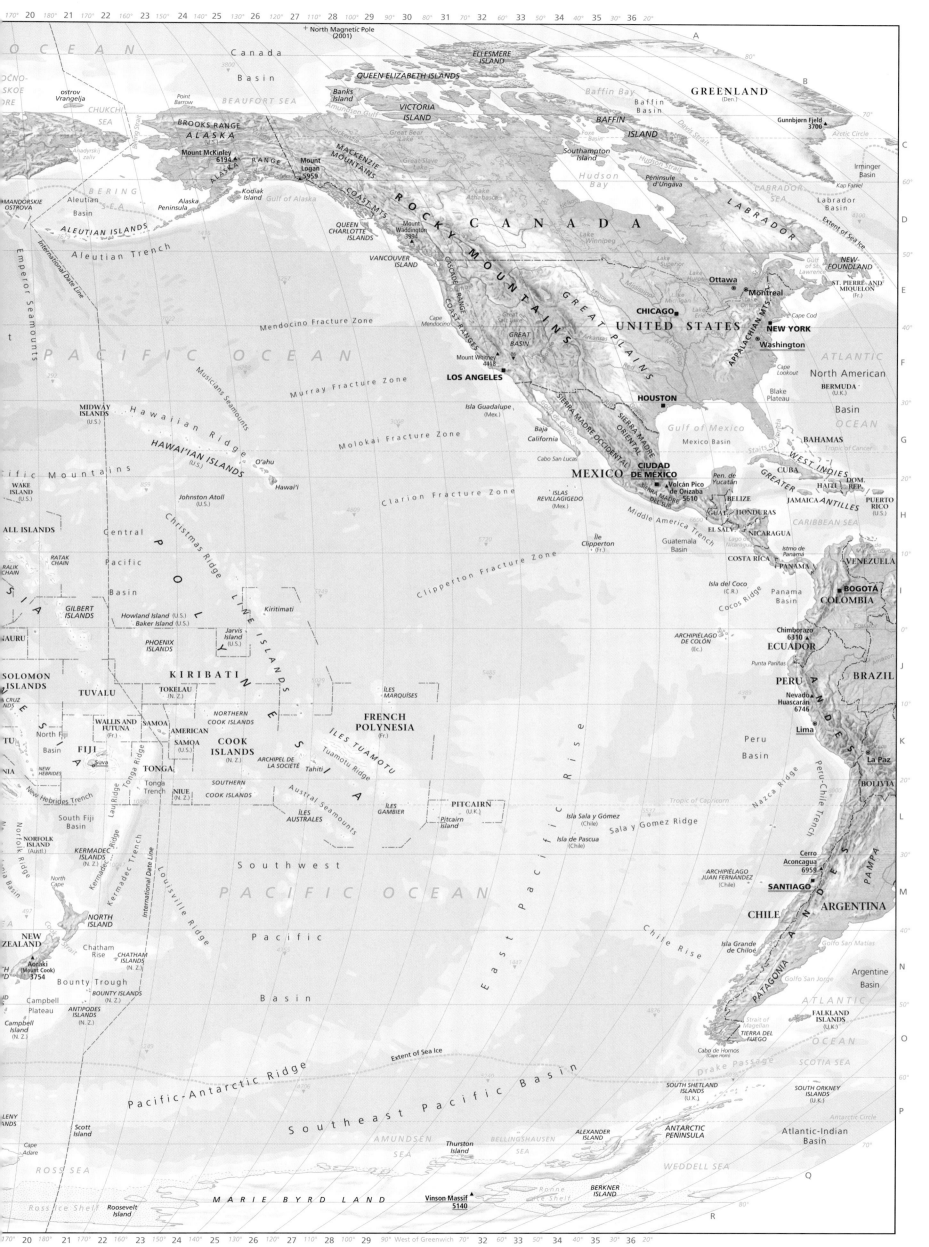

O C E A N
Canada
+ North Magnetic Pole
(2001)
A
OČNO-
SKOE
ORE
ostrov
Vrangelja
Basin
BEAUFORT SEA
Point
Barrow
Bering Strait
CHUKCHI
SEA
Anadyrskij
zaliv
ostrov
Vrangelja
ELLESMERE
ISLAND
QUEEN ELIZABETH ISLANDS
Banks
Island
VICTORIA
ISLAND
Amundsen Gulf
Great Bear
Lake
GREENLAND
(Den.)
Baffin Bay
BAFFIN
Baffin
Basin
ISLAND
Southampton
Island
Foxe
Basin
Gunnbjørn Fjeld
3700
Arctic Circle
B

BROOKS RANGE
ALASKA
(U.S.)
Mount McKinley
6194
RANGE
Mount
Logan
5959
MACKENZIE
MOUNTAINS
Great-Slave
Lake
Hudson
Bay
Hudson Strait
Péninsule
d'Ungava
Kap Farvel
Irminger
Basin
C

MANDORSKIE
OSTROVA
BERING
SEA
Aleutian
Basin
Alaska
Peninsula
Kodiak
Island
Gulf of Alaska
COAST MTS.
QUEEN
CHARLOTTE
ISLANDS
ROCKY
CANADA
Lake
Winnipeg
Lake
Athabasca
LABRADOR
Labrador
Basin
Extent of Sea Ice
D

ALEUTIAN ISLANDS
Aleutian Trench
Emperor Seamounts
International Date Line
VANCOUVER
ISLAND
CASCADE
RANGE
MOUNTAINS
GREAT
Lake
Superior
Lake
Winnipeg
Ottawa
Montreal
NEW-
FOUNDLAND
ST. PIERRE-AND-
MIQUELON
(Fr.)
Gulf of
St. Lawrence
E

Mendocino Fracture Zone
Cape
Mendocino
Mount Waddington
3994
COAST RANGES
GREAT
BASIN
PLAINS
CHICAGO
UNITED   STATES
Lake
Huron
Lake
Michigan
Lake
Erie
Lake
Ontario
Missouri
Arkansas
APPALACHIAN MTS.
NEW YORK
Washington
Cape Cod
ATLANTIC
F

PACIFIC   OCEAN
Murray Fracture Zone
Mount Whitney
4418
LOS ANGELES
SIERRA MADRE OCCIDENTAL
HOUSTON
Red
Gulf of Mexico
Mexico Basin
Cape
Lookout
North American
BERMUDA
(U.K.)
Blake
Plateau
Basin
G

MIDWAY
ISLANDS
(U.S.)
Hawaiian Ridge
Musicians Seamounts
Molokai Fracture Zone
Isla Guadalupe
(Mex.)
Baja
California
SIERRA MADRE ORIENTAL
CIUDAD
DE MÉXICO
Pen. de
Yucatán
Straits of Florida
BAHAMAS
WEST INDIES
Tropic of Cancer
CUBA
GREATER
OCEAN

HAWAI'IAN ISLANDS
O'ahu
(U.S.)
cific Mountains
Christmas Ridge
Hawai'i
Clarion Fracture Zone
Cabo San Lucas
MEXICO
Volcán Pico
de Orizaba 5610
SIERRA MADRE
DEL SUR
ISLAS
REVILLAGIGEDO
(Mex.)
BELIZE
GUAT.
HONDURAS
EL SALV.
NICARAGUA
HAITI
DOM.
REP.
JAMAICA
ANTILLES
PUERTO
RICO
(U.S.)
CARIBBEAN SEA
H

WAKE
ISLAND
(U.S.)
Johnston Atoll
(U.S.)
Central
Pacific
Basin
Île
Clipperton
(Fr.)
Guatemala
Basin
Middle America Trench
COSTA RICA
Lago de
Nicaragua
Istmo de
Panamá
PANAMA
VENEZUELA

ALL ISLANDS
Clipperton Fracture Zone
Isla del Coco
(C.R.)
Cocos Ridge
Panama
Basin
BOGOTÁ
COLOMBIA
I

RATAK
CHAIN
RALIK
CHAIN
GILBERT
ISLANDS
Howland Island (U.S.)
Baker Island (U.S.)
Kiritimati
Jarvis
Island
(U.S.)
LINE ISLANDS
ARCHIPIÉLAGO
DE COLÓN
(Ec.)
Chimborazo
6310
ECUADOR
Punta Pariñas
Equator
0°

NAURU
PHOENIX
ISLANDS
KIRIBATI
PERU
BRAZIL
J

SOLOMON
ISLANDS
CRUZ
NDS
TUVALU
TOKELAU
(N.Z.)
NORTHERN
COOK
ISLANDS
ÎLES
MARQUÎSES
Nevado
Huascarán
6746
10°

TU
North Fiji
Basin
WALLIS AND
FUTUNA
(Fr.)
SAMOA
AMERICAN
SAMOA
(U.S.)
COOK
ISLANDS
(N.Z.)
FRENCH
POLYNESIA
(Fr.)
ÎLES TUAMOTU
East Pacific Rise
Peru
Basin
Lima
K

NIA
NEW
HEBRIDES
FIJI
Suva
TONGA
Tahiti
Tuamotu Ridge
ARCHIPEL DE
LA SOCIÉTÉ
La Paz
NA

NIA
New Hebrides Trench
Lau Ridge
Tonga Ridge
Tonga
Trench
NIUE
(N.Z.)
SOUTHERN
COOK
ISLANDS
(N.Z.)
Austral Seamounts
ÎLES
GAMBIER
PITCAIRN
(U.K.)
Pitcairn
Island
Isla Sala y Gómez
(Chile)
Sala y Gomez Ridge
Nazca Ridge
Peru-Chile Trench
Cerro
Aconcagua
6959
BOLIVIA
L

NORFOLK
ISLAND
(Aust.)
South Fiji
Basin
KERMADEC
ISLANDS
(N.Z.)
ÎLES
AUSTRALES
Isla de Pascua
(Chile)
Tropic of Capricorn
ARCHIPIÉLAGO
JUAN FERNÁNDEZ
(Chile)
SANTIAGO
ARGENTINA
M

oa
Ridge
Norfolk
Ridge
North Cape
Kermadec Trench
International Date Line
Louisville Ridge
Southwest
PACIFIC   OCEAN
East Pacific Rise
Chile Rise
Isla Grande
de Chiloé
PAMPA
CHILE
ANDES
Golfo San Matías
PATAGONIA

NEW
ZEALAND
NORTH
ISLAND
Cook Strait
Chatham Rise
CHATHAM
ISLANDS
(N.Z.)
Pacific
Basin
Argentine
Basin
Golfo San Jorge
ATLANTIC
N

 H
D
Aoraki
(Mount Cook)
3754
Bounty Trough
BOUNTY ISLANDS
(N.Z.)
Strait of
Magellan
FALKLAND
ISLANDS
(U.K.)
OCEAN

UD
Campbell
Plateau
Campbell
Island
(N.Z.)
ANTIPODES
ISLANDS
(N.Z.)
Extent of Sea Ice
TIERRA DEL
FUEGO
Cabo de Hornos
(Cape Horn)
SCOTIA SEA
O

LENY
NDS
Cape
Adare
Scott
Island
Pacific-Antarctic Ridge
Southeast   Pacific   Basin
SOUTH SHETLAND
ISLANDS
(U.K.)
Drake Passage
ANTARCTIC
PENINSULA
ALEXANDER
ISLAND
SOUTH ORKNEY
ISLANDS
(U.K.)
Antarctic Circle
Atlantic-Indian
Basin
P

ROSS SEA
Ross Ice Shelf
Roosevelt
Island
MARIE   BYRD   LAND
AMUNDSEN
SEA
Thurston
Island
BELLINGSHAUSEN
SEA
Vinson Massif
5140
WEDDELL SEA
Ronne
Ice Shelf
BERKNER
ISLAND
Q

R

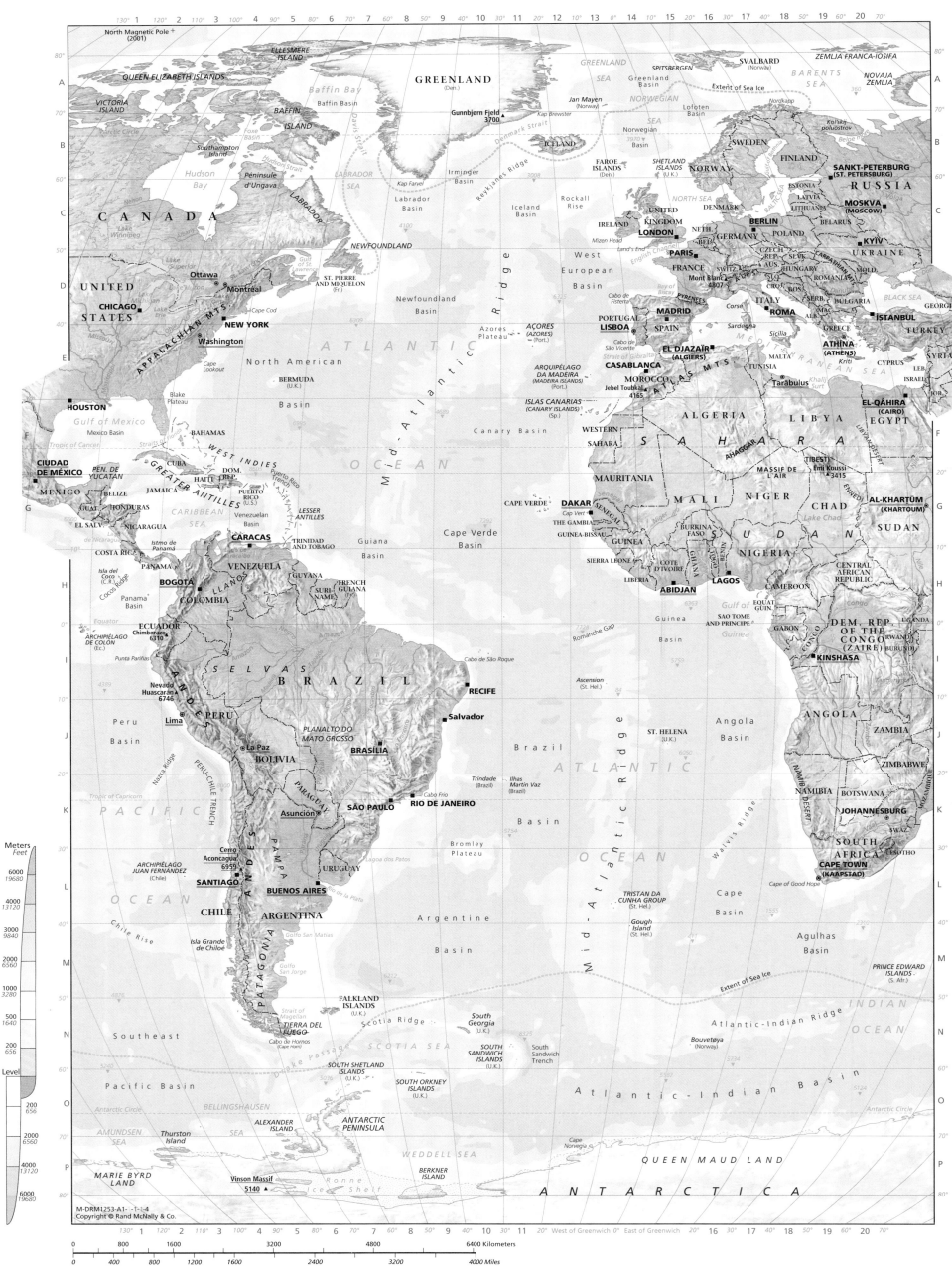

M-DRM1253-A1- -T-1-4
Copyright © Rand McNally & Co.

Scale 1 : 60,000,000   Robinson Projection

Index to World Reference Maps

Introduction to the Index

This index includes in a single alphabetical list approximately 54,000 names of places and geographical features that appear on the reference maps. Each name is followed by the name of the country or continent in which it is located, an alpha-numeric map reference key, and a page reference.

Names The names of cities and towns appear in the index in regular type. The names of all other features appear in *italics*, followed by descriptive terms (hill, mtn., state) to indicate their nature.

Abbreviations of names on the maps have been standardized as much as possible. Names that are abbreviated on the maps are generally spelled out in full in the index.

Country names and names of features that extend beyond the boundaries of one country are followed by the name of the continent in which each is located. Country designations follow the names of all other places in the index. The locations of places in the United States, Canada, and the United Kingdom are further defined by abbreviations that indicate the state, province, or other political division in which each is located.

All abbreviations used in the index are defined in the List of Abbreviations to the right.

Alphabetization Names are alphabetized in the order of the letters of the English alphabet. Spanish *ll* and *ch*, for example, are not treated as distinct letters. Furthermore, diacritical marks are disregarded in alphabetization—German or Scandinavian *ä* or *ö* are treated as *a* or *o*.

The names of physical features may appear inverted, since they are always alphabetized under the proper, not the generic, part of the name, thus: "Gibraltar, Strait of". Otherwise every entry, whether consisting of one word or more, is alphabetized as a single continuous entity. "Lakeland", for example, appears after "La Crosse" and before "La Salle". Names beginning with articles (Le Havre, Den Helder, Al-Manāmah) are not inverted. Names beginning "St.", "Ste." and "Sainte" are alphabetized as though spelled "Saint".

In the case of identical names, towns are listed first, then political divisions, then physical features. Entries that are completely identical are listed alphabetically by country name.

Map Reference Keys and Page References The map reference keys and page references are found in the last two columns of each entry.

Each map reference key consists of a letter and number. The letters correspond to letters along the sides of the maps. Lowercase letters refer to inset maps. The numbers correspond to numbers that appear across the tops and bottoms of the maps.

Map reference keys for point features, such as cities and mountain peaks, indicate the locations of the symbols for these features. For other features, such as countries, mountain ranges, or rivers, the map reference keys indicate the locations of the names.

The page number generally refers to the main map for the country in which the feature is located. Page references for two-page maps always refer to the left-hand page.

List of Abbreviations

Ab., Can.	Alberta, Can.
Afg.	Afghanistan
Afr.	Africa
Ak., U.S.	Alaska, U.S.
Al., U.S.	Alabama, U.S.
Alb.	Albania
Alg.	Algeria
Am. Sam.	American Samoa
anch.	anchorage
And.	Andorra
Ang.	Angola
Ant.	Antarctica
Antig.	Antigua and Barbuda
aq.	aqueduct
Ar., U.S.	Arkansas, U.S.
Arg.	Argentina
Arm.	Armenia
at.	atoll
Aus.	Austria
Austl.	Australia
Az., U.S.	Arizona, U.S.
Azer.	Azerbaijan
b.	bay, gulf, inlet, lagoon
B.C., Can.	British Columbia, Can.
Bah.	Bahamas
Bahr.	Bahrain
Barb.	Barbados
bas.	basin
Bdi.	Burundi
Bel.	Belgium
Bela.	Belarus
Ber.	Bermuda
Bhu.	Bhutan
B.I.O.T.	British Indian Ocean Territory
Blg.	Bulgaria
Bngl.	Bangladesh
Bol.	Bolivia
Bos.	Bosnia and Hercegovina
Bots.	Botswana
Braz.	Brazil
Bru.	Brunei
Br. Vir. Is.	British Virgin Islands
Burkina	Burkina Faso
c.	cape, point
Ca., U.S.	California, U.S.
Cam.	Cameroon
Camb.	Cambodia
Can.	Canada
can.	canal
C.A.R.	Central African Republic
Cay. Is.	Cayman Islands
Christ. I.	Christmas Island
C. Iv.	Cote d'Ivoire
clf.	cliff, escarpment
Co., U.S.	Colorado, U.S.
co.	county, district, etc.
Cocos Is.	Cocos (Keeling) Islands
Col.	Colombia
Com.	Comoros
cont.	continent
Cook Is.	Cook Islands
C.R.	Costa Rica
crat.	crater
Cro.	Croatia
cst.	coast, beach
Ct., U.S.	Connecticut, U.S.
ctry.	independent country
C.V.	Cape Verde
cv.	cave
Cyp.	Cyprus
Czech Rep.	Czech Republic
D.C., U.S.	District of Columbia, U.S.
De., U.S.	Delaware, U.S.
Den.	Denmark
dep.	dependency, colony
depr.	depression
des.	desert
Dji.	Djibouti
Dom.	Dominica
Dom. Rep.	Dominican Republic
D.R.C.	Democratic Republic of the Congo
Ec.	Ecuador
El Sal.	El Salvador
Eng., U.K.	England, U.K.
Eq. Gui.	Equatorial Guinea
Erit.	Eritrea
Est.	Estonia
est.	estuary
Eth.	Ethiopia
E. Timor	East Timor
Eur.	Europe
Falk. Is.	Falkland Islands
Fin.	Finland
Fl., U.S.	Florida, U.S.
for.	forest, moor
Fr.	France
Fr. Gu.	French Guiana
Fr. Poly.	French Polynesia
Ga., U.S.	Georgia, U.S.
Gam.	The Gambia
Gaza	Gaza Strip
Geor.	Georgia
Ger.	Germany
Gib.	Gibraltar
Golan	Golan Heights
Grc.	Greece
Gren.	Grenada
Grnld.	Greenland

Guad.	Guadeloupe
Guat.	Guatemala
Guern.	Guernsey
Gui.	Guinea
Gui.-B.	Guinea-Bissau
Guy.	Guyana
gysr.	geyser
Hi., U.S.	Hawaii, U.S.
hist.	historic site, ruins
hist. reg.	historic region
Hond.	Honduras
Hung.	Hungary
i.	island
Ia., U.S.	Iowa, U.S.
Ice.	Iceland
ice	ice feature, glacier
Id., U.S.	Idaho, U.S.
Il., U.S.	Illinois, U.S.
In., U.S.	Indiana, U.S.
Indon.	Indonesia
I. of Man	Isle of Man
Ire.	Ireland
is.	islands
Isr.	Israel
isth.	isthmus
Jam.	Jamaica
Jer.	Jericho Area
Jord.	Jordan
Kaz.	Kazakhstan
Kir.	Kiribati
Kor., N.	Korea, North
Kor., S.	Korea, South
Ks., U.S.	Kansas, U.S.
Kuw.	Kuwait
Ky., U.S.	Kentucky, U.S.
Kyrg.	Kyrgyzstan
l.	lake, pond
La., U.S.	Louisiana, U.S.
Lat.	Latvia
lav.	lava flow
Leb.	Lebanon
Leso.	Lesotho
Lib.	Liberia
Liech.	Liechtenstein
Lith.	Lithuania
Lux.	Luxembourg
Ma., U.S.	Massachusetts, U.S.
Mac.	Macedonia
Madag.	Madagascar
Malay.	Malaysia
Mald.	Maldives
Marsh. Is.	Marshall Islands
Mart.	Martinique
Maur.	Mauritania
May.	Mayotte
Mb., Can.	Manitoba, Can.
Md., U.S.	Maryland, U.S.
Me., U.S.	Maine, U.S.
Mex.	Mexico
Mi., U.S.	Michigan, U.S.
Micron.	Micronesia, Federated States of
Mid. Is.	Midway Islands
misc. cult.	miscellaneous cultural
Mn., U.S.	Minnesota, U.S.
Mo., U.S.	Missouri, U.S.
Mol.	Moldova
Mon.	Monaco
Mong.	Mongolia
Monts.	Montserrat
Mor.	Morocco
Moz.	Mozambique
Mrts.	Mauritius
Ms., U.S.	Mississippi, U.S.
Mt., U.S.	Montana, U.S.
mth.	river mouth or channel
mtn.	mountain
mts.	mountains
Mwi.	Malawi
Mya.	Myanmar
N.A.	North America
N.B., Can.	New Brunswick, Can.
N.C., U.S.	North Carolina, U.S.
N. Cal.	New Caledonia
N. Cyp.	North Cyprus
N.D., U.S.	North Dakota, U.S.
Ne., U.S.	Nebraska, U.S.
Neth.	Netherlands
Neth. Ant.	Netherlands Antilles
Nf., Can.	Newfoundland, Can.
ngh.	neighborhood
N.H., U.S.	New Hampshire, U.S.
Nic.	Nicaragua
Nig.	Nigeria
N. Ire., U.K.	Northern Ireland, U.K.
N.J., U.S.	New Jersey, U.S.
N.M., U.S.	New Mexico, U.S.
N. Mar. Is.	Northern Mariana Islands
Nmb.	Namibia
Nor.	Norway
Norf. I.	Norfolk Island
N.S., Can.	Nova Scotia, Can.
N.T., Can.	Northwest Territories, Can.
Nu., Can.	Nunavut, Can.
Nv., U.S.	Nevada, U.S.
N.Y., U.S.	New York, U.S.
N.Z.	New Zealand
Oc.	Oceania
Oh., U.S.	Ohio, U.S.

Ok., U.S.	Oklahoma, U.S.
On., Can.	Ontario, Can.
Or., U.S.	Oregon, U.S.
p.	pass
Pa., U.S.	Pennsylvania, U.S.
Pak.	Pakistan
Pan.	Panama
Pap. N. Gui.	Papua New Guinea
Para.	Paraguay
P.E., Can.	Prince Edward Island, Can.
pen.	peninsula
Phil.	Philippines
Pit.	Pitcairn
pl.	plain, flat
plat.	plateau, highland
p.o.i.	point of interest
Pol.	Poland
Port.	Portugal
P.R.	Puerto Rico
Qc., Can.	Quebec, Can.
r.	rock, rocks
reg.	physical region
res.	reservoir
Reu.	Reunion
rf.	reef, shoal
R.I., U.S.	Rhode Island, U.S.
Rom.	Romania
Rw.	Rwanda
S.A.	South America
S. Afr.	South Africa
Samoa	Samoa
sand	sand area
Sau. Ar.	Saudi Arabia
S.C., U.S.	South Carolina, U.S.
sci.	scientific station
Scot., U.K.	Scotland, U.K.
S.D., U.S.	South Dakota, U.S.
Sen.	Senegal
Sey.	Seychelles
S. Geor.	South Georgia
Sing.	Singapore
Sk., Can.	Saskatchewan, Can.
S.L.	Sierra Leone
Slov.	Slovakia
Slvn.	Slovenia
S. Mar.	San Marino
Sol. Is.	Solomon Islands
Som.	Somalia
Sp. N. Afr.	Spanish North Africa
Sri L.	Sri Lanka
state	state, province, etc.
St. Hel.	St. Helena
St. K./N.	St. Kitts and Nevis
St. Luc.	St. Lucia
stm.	stream (river, creek)
S. Tom./P.	Sao Tome and Principe
St. P./M.	St. Pierre and Miquelon
strt.	strait, channel, etc.
St. Vin.	St. Vincent and the Grenadines
Sur.	Suriname
sw.	swamp, marsh
Swaz.	Swaziland
Swe.	Sweden
Switz.	Switzerland
Tai.	Taiwan
Taj.	Tajikistan
Tan.	Tanzania
T./C. Is.	Turks and Caicos Islands
Thai.	Thailand
Tn., U.S.	Tennessee, U.S.
Tok.	Tokelau
Trin.	Trinidad and Tobago
Tun.	Tunisia
Tur.	Turkey
Turkmen.	Turkmenistan
Tx., U.S.	Texas, U.S.
U.A.E.	United Arab Emirates
Ug.	Uganda
U.K.	United Kingdom
Ukr.	Ukraine
unds.	undersea feature
Ur.	Uruguay
U.S.	United States
Ut., U.S.	Utah, U.S.
Uzb.	Uzbekistan
Va., U.S.	Virginia, U.S.
val.	valley, watercourse
Vat.	Vatican City
Ven.	Venezuela
Viet.	Vietnam
V.I.U.S.	Virgin Islands (U.S.)
vol.	volcano
Vt., U.S.	Vermont, U.S.
Wa., U.S.	Washington, U.S.
Wake I.	Wake Island
Wal./F.	Wallis and Futuna
W.B.	West Bank
well	well, spring, oasis
Wi., U.S.	Wisconsin, U.S.
W. Sah.	Western Sahara
wtfl.	waterfall, rapids
W.V., U.S.	West Virginia, U.S.
Wy., U.S.	Wyoming, U.S.
Yk., Can.	Yukon Territory, Can.
Yugo.	Yugoslavia
Zam.	Zambia
Zimb.	Zimbabwe

Index

A

Name	Map Ref.	Page
Alcolea del Pinar, Spain	C8	20
Alcolu, S.C., U.S.	C5	116
Alcorn, Ms., U.S.	F7	122
Alcorta, Arg.	F7	92
Alcoutim, Port.	G3	20
Alcoy see Alcoi, Spain	F10	20
Alcúdia, Spain	E14	20
Alcúdia, Badia d', b., Spain	E14	20
Aldabra, Groupe d', is., Sey.	k11	69b
Aldama, Mex.	D9	100
Aldama, Mex.	A5	100
Aldan, Russia	E14	34
Aldan, stm., Russia	D15	34
Aldan Plateau see Aldanskoe nagor'e, plat., Russia	E14	34
Aldanskoe nagor'e (Aldan Plateau), plat., Russia	E14	34
Aldarchaan, Mong.	B4	36
Aldeia Nova de São Bento, Port.	G3	20
Alden, Mn., U.S.	H5	118
Alderney, i., Guern.	E6	14
Aldershot, Eng., U.K.	J12	12
Alderson, W.V., U.S.	G5	114
Aledo, Il., U.S.	C7	120
Aleg, Maur.	F2	64
Alegre, Braz.	K5	88
Alegrete, Braz.	D10	92
Alej, stm., Russia	D14	32
Alejandro Roca, Arg.	F5	92
Alejandro Selkirk, Isla, i., Chile	I6	82
Alejsk, Russia	D14	32
Aleksandrov, Russia	D21	10
Aleksandrovskij Zavod, Russia	F12	34
Aleksandrovskoe, Russia	B13	32
Aleksandrovsk-Sahalinskij, Russia	F17	34
Aleksandrów Kujawski, Pol.	D14	16
Alekseevka, Kaz.	D12	32
Alekseevka, Kaz.	E14	32
Alekseevka, Russia	D5	32
Alekseevsk, Russia	C19	32
Aleksejevka see Alekseevka, Kaz.	D12	32
Alekseyevka see Alekseevka, Kaz.	D12	32
Aleksin, Russia	F19	10
Aleksinac, Yugo.	F8	26
Alemania, Arg.	B5	92
Além Paraíba, Braz.	K4	88
Alençon, Fr.	F9	14
Alenquer, Braz.	D7	84
Alentejo, hist. reg., Port.	F3	20
Alenuihaha Channel, strt., Hi., U.S.	C5	78a
Aleppo see Halab, Syria	B8	58
Aléria, Fr.	G15	18
Alert, Nu., Can.	A13	141
Alert Bay, B.C., Can.	F4	138
Alert Point, c., Nu., Can.	A8	141
Alès, Fr.	E10	18
Alëšnja, Russia	G16	10
Alessándria, Italy	F5	22
Ålesund, Nor.	E1	8
Aleutian Basin, unds.	D20	142
Aleutian Islands, is., Ak., U.S.	g22	140a
Aleutian Range, mts., Ak., U.S.	E8	140
Aleutian Trench, unds.	E21	142
Aleutka, Russia	G19	34
Alevina, mys, c., Russia	E19	34
Alex, Ok., U.S.	G11	128
Alexander, Mb., Can.	E13	124
Alexander, N.D., U.S.	G10	124
Alexander, Kap, c., Grnld.	B11	141
Alexander Archipelago, is., Ak., U.S.	E12	140
Alexander Bay, S. Afr.	F3	70
Alexander City, Al., U.S.	E12	122
Alexander Island, i., Ant.	B33	81
Alexandra, N.Z.	G3	80
Alexandra, stm., Austl.	B3	76
Alexandra Falls, wtfl, N.T., Can.	C7	106
Alexandretta see İskenderun, Tur.	B6	58
Alexandretta, Gulf of see İskenderun Körfezi, b., Tur.	B6	58
Alexandria, Braz.	D6	88
Alexandria, B.C., Can.	D8	138
Alexandria, On., Can.	E2	110
Alexandria see El-Iskandarîya, Egypt	A6	62
Alexandria, Rom.	F12	26
Alexandria, La., U.S.	F6	122
Alexandria, Mn., U.S.	F3	118
Alexandria, Mo., U.S.	D6	120
Alexandria, S.D., U.S.	D15	126
Alexandria, Tn., U.S.	H11	120
Alexandria, Va., U.S.	F8	114
Alexandria Bay, N.Y., U.S.	D14	112
Alexandrina, Lake, l., Austl.	J2	76
Alexandroúpoli, Grc.	C8	28
Alexis, Il., U.S.	C7	120
Alfambra, Spain	D9	20
Alfaro, Spain	B9	20
Alfarràs, Spain	C11	20
Alfarrás see Alfarràs, Spain	C11	20
Al-Fāshir, Sudan	E5	62
Alfeiós, stm., Grc.	F4	28
Alfeld, Ger.	D5	16
Alfenas, Braz.	K3	88
Alföld, pl., Hung.	C7	26
Alfonsine, Italy	F9	22
Alfred, On., Can.	E2	110
Alfred, Me., U.S.	G6	110
Alfred, N.Y., U.S.	B8	114
Al-Fujayrah, U.A.E.	D8	56
Al-Fuqahā', Libya	B3	62
Al-Furāt see Euphrates, stm., Asia	C6	56
Alga, Kaz.	E9	32
Ålgård, Nor.	G1	8
Algarrobal, Chile	D2	92
Algarrobo, Chile	F2	92
Algarrobo del Águila, Arg.	H4	92
Algarve, hist. reg., Port.	G2	20
Algeciras, Col.	F4	86
Algeciras, Spain	H5	20
Algemesí, Spain	E10	20
Algeria, ctry., Afr.	D5	64
Algérie see Algeria, ctry., Afr.	D5	64
Al-Ghāb, sw., Syria	C7	58
Al-Ghaydah, Yemen	F7	56
Al-Ghāzīyah, Leb.	E6	58
Alghero, Italy	D2	24
Algiers see El Djazaïr, Alg.	B5	64
Alginet, Spain	E10	20
Algoabaai, b., S. Afr.	H7	70
Algoa Bay see Algoabaai, b., S. Afr.	H7	70
Algodón, stm., Peru	I5	86
Algodones, N.M., U.S.	F2	128
Algoma Mills, On., Can.	B7	112
Algona, Ia., U.S.	A3	120
Algonac, Mi., U.S.	B3	114
Algonquin, Il., U.S.	B9	120
Algorta, Spain	A7	20
Algorta, Ur.	F9	92
Al-Haffah, Syria	C7	58
Al-Hajarah, reg., Asia	C5	56
Al-Hamād, pl., Sau. Ar.	C4	56
Alhama de Murcia, Spain	G9	20
Alhandra, Braz.	D8	88
Al-Harrah, lav., Sau. Ar.	C4	56
Al-Harūj al-Aswad, hills, Libya	B3	62
Al-Hasakah, Syria	B5	56
Alhaurín el Grande, Spain	H6	20
Al-Hawātah, Sudan	E7	62
Al-Hawrah, Yemen	G6	56
Al-Hijāz (Hejaz), reg., Sau. Ar.	D4	56
Al-Hillah, Iraq	C5	56
Al-Hirmil, Leb.	D7	58
Al-Hoceima, Mor.	B4	64
Al-Hudaydah (Hodeida), Yemen	G5	56
Al-Hufrah, reg., Sau. Ar.	J9	58
Al-Hufūf, Sau. Ar.	D6	56
Al Hūj, hills, Sau. Ar.	J9	58
Al-Hulwah, Sau. Ar.	E6	56
Alía, Spain	E5	20
Aliağa, Tur.	E9	28
Aliákmonas, stm., Grc.	C4	28
Aliança, Braz.	D8	88
Alībāg, India	B1	53
Alibates Flint Quarries National Monument, p.o.i., Tx., U.S.	F7	128
Äli Bayramlı, Azer.	B6	56
Alibei, ozero, l., Ukr.	D17	26
Alibey Adası, i., Tur.	D9	28
Alibunar, Yugo.	D7	26
Alicante see Alacant, Spain	F10	20
Alicante see Alacant, co., Spain	F10	20
Alice, S. Afr.	H8	70
Alice, Tx., U.S.	G9	130
Alice, stm., Austl.	D5	76
Alice, Punta, c., Italy	E11	24
Alice Springs, Austl.	D6	74
Alice Town, Bah.	K6	116
Aliceville, Al., U.S.	D10	122
Alick Creek, stm., Austl.	C4	76
Alīgarh, India	E6	54
Alignements de Carnac, hist., Fr.	G5	14
Alīgūdarz, Iran	C6	56
'Alī Kheyl, Afg.	B2	54
Al-Ikhsās al-Qiblīyah, Egypt	I2	58
Alima, stm., Congo	E3	66
Alim Island, i., Pap. N. Gui.	a4	79a
Alindao, C.A.R.	C4	66
Alingsås, Swe.	G5	8
Alīpur, Pak.	D3	54
Alīpur Duār, India	E12	54
Aliquippa, Pa., U.S.	D5	114
Alīrājpur, India	G5	54
Aliseda, Spain	E4	20
Alitak, Cape, c., Ak., U.S.	E9	140
Alivéri, Grc.	E7	28
Aliwal North, S. Afr.	G8	70
Alix, Ab., Can.	D17	138
Al-Jabalayn, Sudan	E6	62
Al-Jafr, Jord.	H7	58
Al-Jaghbūb, Libya	B4	62
Al-Jahrah, Kuw.	D6	56
Al-Jawārah, Oman	F8	56
Al-Jawf, Libya	C4	62
Al-Jawf, Sau. Ar.	D4	56
Al-Jazaïr see El Djazaïr, Alg.	B5	64
Al-Jazīrah, reg., Sudan	E6	62
Al-Jifārah (Jeffara), pl., Afr.	C7	64
Al-Jubayl, Sau. Ar.	D6	56
Al-Junaynah, Sudan	E4	62
Aljustrel, Port.	G2	20
Al-Kafr, Syria	F7	58
Al-Karak, Jord.	G6	58
Al-Karak, state, Jord.	G6	58
Al-Khalīl (Hebron), W.B.	G5	58
Al-Khālis, Iraq	C5	56
Al-Khandaq, Sudan	D6	62
Al-Khartām Bahrī, Sudan	D6	62
Al-Khartūm (Khartoum), Sudan	D6	62
Al-Khasab, Oman	D8	56
Al-Khums, Libya	A2	62
Alkmaar, Neth.	B13	14
Al-Kufrah, Libya	C4	62
Al-Kūt, Iraq	C6	56
Al-Kuwayt (Kuwait), Kuw.	D6	56
Al-Labwah, Leb.	D7	58
Al-Lādhiqīyah (Latakia), Syria	C6	58
Al-Lādhiqīyah, state, Syria	C6	58
Allagash, stm., Me., U.S.	D7	110
Allahābād, India	F8	54
Allah-Jun', Russia	D16	34
Allakaket, Ak., U.S.	C9	140
Allan, Sk., Can.	C7	124
Allanmyo, Mya.	C2	48
Allanridge, S. Afr.	E8	70
Allatoona Lake, res., Ga., U.S.	C14	122
Alldays, S. Afr.	C9	70
Allegan, Mi., U.S.	F4	112
Allegany, N.Y., U.S.	B7	114
Allegheny, stm., U.S.	D6	114
Allegheny Mountains, mts., U.S.	E6	114
Allegheny Plateau, plat., U.S.	D5	114
Allegheny Reservoir, res., U.S.	C7	114
Allemands, Lac des, l., La., U.S.	H8	122
Allen, Ne., U.S.	I2	118
Allen, Ok., U.S.	C2	122
Allen, Tx., U.S.	D2	122
Allen, Lough, l., Ire.	G4	12
Allendale, Il., U.S.	F10	120
Allendale, S.C., U.S.	C4	116
Allende, Mex.	A8	100
Allenstein see Olsztyn, Pol.	C16	16
Allentown, Pa., U.S.	D10	114
Alleppey, India	G3	53
Aller, stm., Ger.	D5	16
Allevard, Fr.	D12	18
Allgäu see Kempten, Ger.	I6	16
Allgäu, reg., Ger.	I6	16
Alliance, Ab., Can.	D19	138
Alliance, Ne., U.S.	E10	126
Alliance, Oh., U.S.	D4	114
Al-Lidām, Sau. Ar.	E5	56
Allier, state, Fr.	C9	18
Allier, stm., Fr.	C9	18
Alligator Pond, Jam.	j13	104d
Allinagaram, India	F3	53
Allison, Ia., U.S.	B5	120
Al-Līth, Sau. Ar.	E5	56
Alloa, Scot., U.K.	E9	12
Allos, Fr.	E12	18
Allouez, Wi., U.S.	G11	118
Allred Peak, mtn., Co., U.S.	C8	132
All Saints, Antig.	f4	105b
Al-Luhayyah, Yemen	F5	56
Allumette Lake, l., Can.	C12	112
Allumettes, Île aux, i., Qc., Can.	C12	112
Alma, N.B., Can.	E12	110
Alma, Qc., Can.	B5	110
Alma, Ar., U.S.	B4	122
Alma, Ga., U.S.	E3	116
Alma, Ks., U.S.	E1	120
Alma, Mi., U.S.	E5	112
Alma, Wi., U.S.	G7	118
Almada, Port.	F1	20
Almaden, Austl.	A5	76
Almadén, Spain	F6	20
Al-Madīnah (Medina), Sau. Ar.	E4	56
Al-Mafraq, Jord.	F7	58
Al-Mafraq, state, Jord.	F8	58
Almafuerte, Arg.	F5	92
Almagro, Spain	F7	20
Alma Hill, hill, N.Y., U.S.	B8	114
Al Mālihah, Sudan	D5	62
Almalyk, Uzb.	F11	32
Al-Manāmah (Manama), Bahr.	D7	56
Almanor, Lake, res., Ca., U.S.	C4	134
Almansa, Spain	F9	20
Almanza, Spain	B5	20
Almanzor, mtn., Spain	D5	20
Al-Marj, Libya	A4	62
Almas, Braz.	F2	88
Almas, Pico das, mtn., Braz.	G4	88
Al-Mashrafah, Syria	D7	58
Almaty, Kaz.	F13	32
Al-Mawsil, Iraq	B5	56
Almeida, Port.	D3	20
Almejas, Bahía, b., Mex.	C3	100
Almelo, Neth.	B15	14
Almena, Ks., U.S.	B9	128
Almenara, Braz.	I5	88
Almendra, Embalse de, res., Spain	C4	20
Almendralejo, Spain	F4	20
Almería, Spain	H8	20
Almería, co., Spain	G8	20
Almería, Golfo de, b., Spain	H8	20
Al'metevsk, Russia	D8	32
Al-Mijlad, Sudan	E5	62
Al-Mīnā', Leb.	D6	58
Almira, Wa., U.S.	C7	136
Almirante, Pan.	H6	102
Almirante Latorre, Chile	D2	92
Almo, Id., U.S.	A3	132
Almodóvar del Campo, Spain	F6	20
Almont, Mi., U.S.	B2	114
Almonte, On., Can.	C13	112
Almonte, Spain	G4	20
Almonte, stm., Spain	E4	20
Almora, India	D7	54
Al-Mubarraz, Sau. Ar.	E6	56
Al-Mubarraz, Sau. Ar.	D6	56
Al-Mudawwarah, Jord.	I6	58
Almudévar, Spain	B10	20
Al-Muharraq, Bahr.	D7	56
Al-Mukallā, Yemen	G6	56
Al-Mukhā, Yemen	G5	56
Almuñécar, Spain	H7	20
Al-Muwaylih, Sau. Ar.	K6	58
Almyrós, Grc.	D5	28
Almyroú, Órmos, b., Grc.	H7	28
Alnwick, Eng., U.K.	F11	12
Alofi, Île, i., Wal./F.	E9	72
Alónnisos, Grc.	D6	28
Alónnisos, i., Grc.	D6	28
Alor, Pulau, i., Indon.	G7	44
Alor, Selat, strt., Indon.	G7	44
Alor Setar, Malay.	I5	48
Alosno, Spain	G3	20
Alost see Aalst, Bel.	D13	14
Alotau, Pap. N. Gui.	c5	79a
Aloysius, Mount, mtn., Austl.	E5	74
Alpachiri, Arg.	H5	92
Alpaugh, Ca., U.S.	H6	134
Alpena, Mi., U.S.	C6	112
Alpena, S.D., U.S.	C14	126
Alpercatas, stm., Braz.	D3	88
Alpes-de-Haute-Provence, state, Fr.	E12	18
Alpes-Maritimes, state, Fr.	F13	18
Alpha, Austl.	D6	76
Alpha, Il., U.S.	C7	120
Alpha, Mi., U.S.	B1	112
Alpharetta, Ga., U.S.	B1	116
Alphonse, i., Sey.	k12	69b
Alpine, Ca., U.S.	K9	134
Alpine, Tx., U.S.	D4	130
Alpine National Park, p.o.i., Austl.	K6	76
Alpinópolis, Braz.	K2	88
Alps, mts., Eur.	D6	22
Al-Qadārif, Sudan	E7	62
Al-Qadīmah, Sau. Ar.	E4	56
Al-Qāmishlī, Syria	B5	56
Al-Qaryah ash-Sharqīyah, Libya	A2	62
Al-Qaryatayn, Syria	D8	58
Al-Qatīf, Sau. Ar.	D6	56
Al-Qatrānah, Jord.	G7	58
Al-Qatrūn, Libya	C2	62
Al-Qaysūmah, Sau. Ar.	D6	56
Al-Qunaytirah, Syria	E6	58
Al-Qunaytirah, state, Syria	E6	58
Al-Qunfudhah, Sau. Ar.	F5	56
Al-Qutayfah, Syria	E7	58
Al-Qutaynah, Sudan	E6	62
Als, i., Den.	I3	8
Alsace, hist. reg., Fr.	F16	14
Al'šany, Bela.	H10	10
Alsask, Sk., Can.	C4	124
Alsasua, Spain	B8	20
Alsea, Or., U.S.	F3	136
Alsek, stm., N.A.	D3	106
Alsen, N.D., U.S.	F15	124
Alsfeld, Ger.	F5	16
Alta, Nor.	B10	8
Altaelva, stm., Nor.	B10	8
Alta Gracia, Arg.	E5	92
Altagracia, Ven.	B6	86
Altagracia de Orituco, Ven.	C8	86
Altai, mts., Asia	E15	32
Altaj, state, Russia	D15	32
Altajskij, Russia	D14	32
Altamaha, stm., Ga., U.S.	E4	116
Altamira, Braz.	D7	84
Altamira, Chile	B3	92
Altamirano, Mex.	I10	130
Altamont, Ks., U.S.	G2	120
Altamont, Or., U.S.	A4	134
Altamont, Tn., U.S.	B13	122
Altamura, Italy	D10	24
Altamura, Isla, i., Mex.	C4	100
Altanbulag, Mong.	A6	36
Altar, Mex.	F7	98
Altar, stm., Mex.	F7	98
Altar, Desierto de, des., Mex.	F6	98
Altar de Los Sacrificios, hist., Guat.	D2	102
Altario, Ab., Can.	C3	124
Altata, Mex.	C4	100
Alta Vista, Ks., U.S.	C12	128
Altay, China	E15	32
Altay, Mong.	B4	36
Altay see Altaj, state, Russia	D15	32
Altay Mountains see Altai, mts., Asia	E15	32
Altdorf, Switz.	D5	22
Altenburg, Ger.	E8	16
Altentreptow, Ger.	C9	16
Alter do Chão, Port.	E3	20
Altevatnet, l., Nor.	B8	8
Altha, Fl., U.S.	G13	122
Altheimer, Ar., U.S.	C7	122
Altınekin, Tur.	E15	28
Altinho, Braz.	E7	88
Altınova, Tur.	D9	28
Altıntaş, Tur.	D13	28
Altiplano, plat., S.A.	G4	84
Altmark, reg., Ger.	D7	16
Altmühl, stm., Ger.	G6	16
Alto, Tx., U.S.	F3	122
Alto Araguaia, Braz.	G7	84
Alto Chicapa, Ang.	C2	68
Alto Garças, Braz.	G7	84
Alto Longá, Braz.	C4	88
Altomünster, Ger.	H7	16
Alton, Eng., U.K.	J11	12
Alton, Il., U.S.	F7	120
Alton, Ia., U.S.	B1	120
Alton, Ks., U.S.	B9	128
Alton, N.H., U.S.	G5	110
Altona, Mb., Can.	E16	124
Altoona, Al., U.S.	C12	122
Altoona, Ia., U.S.	C4	120
Altoona, Pa., U.S.	D7	114
Altoona, Wi., U.S.	G7	118
Alto Paraguai, Braz.	F6	84
Alto Paraíso de Goiás, Braz.	G2	88
Alto Paraná, state, Para.	B10	92
Alto Parnaíba, Braz.	E2	88
Alto Río Mayo, Arg.	I2	90
Alto Río Senguer, Arg.	I2	90
Altos, Braz.	C4	88
Alto Santo, Braz.	C6	88
Altötting, Ger.	H8	16
Altun Shan, mts., China	D2	36
Alturas, Ca., U.S.	B5	134
Altus, Ar., U.S.	B5	122
Altus, Ok., U.S.	G9	128
Alu see Shortland Island, i., Sol. Is.	d6	79b
Al-'Ubaylah, Sau. Ar.	E7	56
Al-Ubayyid, Sudan	E6	62
Alubijid, Phil.	F5	52
Al-Udayyah, Sudan	E5	62
Alūksne, Lat.	C9	10
Al-'Ulā, Sau. Ar.	D4	56
Al-'Uqaylah, Libya	A3	62
Al-'Uwaynāt, Libya	B2	62
Alva, Ok., U.S.	E10	128
Alvaiázere, Port.	E2	20
Alvarado, Mex.	F11	100
Alvarado, Tx., U.S.	B10	130
Álvaro Obregón, Presa, res., Mex.	B4	100
Alvear, Arg.	D9	92
Alverca, Port.	F1	20
Alvernia, Mount, hill, Bah.	C10	96
Alvesta, Swe.	H6	8
Alvin, Tx., U.S.	H3	122
Alvinópolis, Braz.	K4	88
Älvkarleby, Swe.	F7	8
Alvord, Tx., U.S.	H11	128
Alvord Desert, des., Or., U.S.	H8	136
Al-Wajh, Sau. Ar.	D4	56
Alwar, India	E6	54
Alwaye, India	F3	53
Alxa Zuoqi, China	B1	42
Alytus, Lith.	F6	10
Alzey, Ger.	G4	16
Alzira, Spain	E10	20
Amacuro (Amakura), stm., S.A.	C11	86
Amadeus, Lake, l., Austl.	D6	74
Amadjuak Lake, l., Nu., Can.	B16	106
Amagasaki, Japan	E8	40
Amagi, Japan	F3	40
Amahai, Indon.	F8	44
Amaichá del Valle, Arg.	C4	92
Amaimon, Pap. N. Gui.	b4	79a
Amajac, stm., Mex.	E9	100
Amakura (Amacuro), stm., S.A.	D11	86
Amakusa-nada, Japan	G2	40
Amakusa-shotō, is., Japan	G2	40
Åmål, Swe.	G5	8
Amalāpuram, India	C6	53
Amalfi, Col.	B2	84
Amaliáda, Grc.	F4	28
Amalner, India	H5	54
Amambaí, Braz.	D5	90
Amami Islands see Amami-Ō-shima, i., Japan	k19	39a
Amami-Ō-shima, i., Japan	k19	39a
Amami-shotō, is., Japan	I19	39a
Amana, Ia., U.S.	C6	120
Amana, stm., Ven.	C10	86
Amaná, Lago, l., Braz.	I9	86
Amanda, Oh., U.S.	E3	114
Amantea, Italy	E9	24
Amapá, Braz.	C7	84
Amapá, state, Braz.	C7	84
Amarante, Braz.	D4	88
Amaranth, Mb., Can.	D15	124
Amarapura, Mya.	B3	48
Amărăștii de Jos, Rom.	F11	26
Amarāvati, stm., India	F3	53
Amares, Port.	C2	20
Amargosa, Braz.	G6	88
Amargosa, stm., U.S.	H9	134
Amarillo, Tx., U.S.	F7	128
Amarkantak, India	G8	54
Amaro, Monte, mtn., Italy	H11	22
Amasra, Tur.	B15	28
Amasya, Tur.	A4	56
aMatikulu, S. Afr.	F10	70
Amatsu-kominato, Japan	D13	40
Amawbia Awka, Nig.	H6	64
Amazar, Russia	F13	34
Amazon (Amazonas) (Solimões), stm., S.A.	D7	84
Amazonas, state, Braz.	D4	84
Amazonas, state, Col.	H6	86
Amazonas, state, Ven.	F8	86
Ambājogāi, India	B3	53
Ambāla, India	C6	54
Ambalangoda, Sri L.	H4	53
Ambalavao, Madag.	E8	68
Ambam, Cam.	D2	66
Ambanja, Madag.	C8	68
Ambarčik, Russia	C21	34
Ambargasta, Salinas de, pl., Arg.	D5	92
Ambato, Ec.	H2	86
Ambatolampy, Madag.	D8	68
Ambatondrazaka, Madag.	D8	68
Ambelau, Pulau, i., Indon.	F8	44
Amberg, Ger.	G7	16
Amberg, Wi., U.S.	C2	112
Ambergris Cay, i., Belize	C4	102
Ambérieu-en-Bugey, Fr.	D11	18
Ambert, Fr.	D9	18
Ambidédi, Mali	G2	64
Ambikāpur, India	G9	54
Ambilobe, Madag.	C8	68
Ambla, Est.	A8	10
Amble, Eng., U.K.	F11	12
Ambo, Peru	F2	84
Ambodifototra, Madag.	D8	68
Ambohimahasoa, Madag.	E8	68
Amboise, Fr.	G10	14
Ambon, Indon.	F8	44
Ambon, Pulau, i., Indon.	F8	44
Amboseli, Lake, l., Afr.	E7	66
Amboseli National Park, p.o.i., Kenya	E7	66
Ambositra, Madag.	E8	68
Ambovombe, Madag.	F8	68
Amboy, Il., U.S.	C8	120
Amboy, Mn., U.S.	H4	118
Ambridge, Pa., U.S.	D5	114
Ambriz, Ang.	B1	68
Ambrosia Lake, N.M., U.S.	H9	132
Ambrym, state, Vanuatu	k17	79d
Ambrym, i., Vanuatu	k17	79d
Ambuntentimur, Indon.	G8	50
Ambunti, Pap. N. Gui.	a3	79a
Āmbūr, India	E4	53
Amchitka Island, i., Ak., U.S.	g22	140a
Amchitka Pass, strt., Ak., U.S.	g22	140a
Am Dam, Chad	E4	62
Amdo, China	B13	54
Ameagle, W.V., U.S.	G4	114
Ameca, Mex.	E6	100
Ameca, stm., Mex.	E6	100
Ameghino, Arg.	G6	92
Ameland, i., Neth.	A14	14
Amelia Court House, Va., U.S.	G8	114
Amelia Island, i., Fl., U.S.	F4	116
Āmer, India	E5	54
American, North Fork, stm., Ca., U.S.	D5	134
American, South Fork, stm., Ca., U.S.	E5	134
Americana, Braz.	L2	88
American Falls Reservoir, res., Id., U.S.	H13	136
American Fork, Ut., U.S.	C5	132
American Highland, plat., Ant.	C12	81
Americanos, Barra de los, i., Mex.	C10	100
American Samoa, dep., Oc.	h12	79c
Americus, Ga., U.S.	D1	116
Americus, Ks., U.S.	F1	120
Amersfoort, Neth.	B14	14
Amery, Wi., U.S.	F6	118
Amery Ice Shelf, ice, Ant.	B12	81
Ames, Ia., U.S.	B4	120
Amesbury, Ma., U.S.	B14	114
Amfilochía, Grc.	E4	28
Ámfissa, Grc.	E5	28
Amga, Russia	D15	34
Amga, stm., Russia	D15	34
Amguema, stm., Russia	C24	34
Amguid, Alg.	D6	64
Amgun', stm., Russia	F16	34
Amherst, N.S., Can.	E12	110
Amherst, Ma., U.S.	B13	114
Amherst, N.Y., U.S.	A7	114
Amherst, Oh., U.S.	C3	114
Amherst, Tx., U.S.	G6	128
Amherst, Wi., U.S.	G9	118
Amherstburg, On., Can.	F6	112
Amherstdale, W.V., U.S.	G4	114
Amherst Island, i., On., Can.	D13	112
Amherstview, On., Can.	D13	112
Amiens, Austl.	G8	76
Amiens, Fr.	E11	14
Amīndīvi Islands, is., India	F3	46
Amino, Japan	D8	40
Aminuis, Nmb.	C4	70
Amirantes, Les, is., Sey.	k12	69b
Amisk, Ab., Can.	B2	124
Amisk Lake, l., Sk., Can.	E10	106
Amistad, Parque Internacional de la, p.o.i., C.R.	H6	102
Amistad, Presa de la (Amistad Reservoir), res., N.A.	E6	130
Amistad National Recreation Area, p.o.i., Tx., U.S.	E6	130
Amistad Reservoir (Amistad, Presa de la), res., N.A.	E6	130
Amite, La., U.S.	G8	122
Amite, stm., La., U.S.	G8	122
Amity, Ar., U.S.	C5	122
Āmla, India	H7	54
Åmli, Nor.	G3	8
'Ammān, Jord.	G6	58
'Ammān, state, Jord.	G7	58
Ämmänsaari, Fin.	D13	8
'Ammār, Tall, hill, Syria	F7	58
Ammasalik see Angmagssalik, Grnld.	D18	141
Ammon, Id., U.S.	G15	136
Amnat Charoen, Thai.	E7	48
Amnok-kang (Yalu), stm., Asia	D7	38
Amo (Torsa), stm., Asia	E12	54
Amo, stm., China	A5	48
Āmol, Iran	B7	56
Amorgós, i., Grc.	G8	28
Amory, Ms., U.S.	D10	122
Amos, Qc., Can.	F15	106
Åmot, Nor.	G2	8
Amoy see Xiamen, China	I7	42
Ampanihy, Madag.	E7	68
Amparo, Braz.	L2	88
Ampasimanolotra, Madag.	D8	68
Amposta, Spain	D11	20
Amqui, Qc., Can.	B9	110
Amrāvati, India	H6	54
Amreli, India	H3	54
Amritsar, India	C5	54
Amroha, India	D7	54
Amrum, i., Ger.	B4	16
Amsterdam, Neth.	B13	14
Amsterdam, S. Afr.	E10	70
Amsterdam, N.Y., U.S.	B11	114
Amsterdam, Île, i., Afr.	M10	142
Amstetten, Aus.	B11	22
Am Timan, Chad	E4	62
Amu Darya, stm., Asia	F10	32
Amugulang see Xin Barag Zuoqi, China	B8	36
Amund Ringnes Island, i., Nu., Can.	B6	141
Amundsen Gulf, b., Can.	B14	140
Amundsen-Scott, sci., Ant.	D19	81
Amundsen Sea, Ant.	P27	142
Amuntai, Indon.	E9	50
Amur (Heilong), stm., Asia	F16	34
Amursk, Russia	F16	34
Amuzhong, China	C10	54
Amvrakikós Kólpos, b., Grc.	E3	28
An, Mya.	C2	48
Ana, Parque Nacional dedo see Doñana, Parque Nacional de, p.o.i., Spain	H4	20
Anaa, at., Fr. Poly.	E12	72
Anabar, stm., Russia	B11	34
Anaco, Ven.	C9	86
Anaconda, Mt., U.S.	D14	136
Anaconda Range, mts., Mt., U.S.	E13	136
Anacortes, Wa., U.S.	B4	136
Anadarko, Ok., U.S.	F10	128
Anadolu (Anatolia), hist. reg., Tur.	H15	6
Anadyr', Russia	D24	34
Anadyr, stm., Russia	C23	34
Anadyr, Gulf of see Anadyrskij zaliv, b., Russia	C21	142
Anadyr Mountains see Anadyrskoe ploskogor'e, plat., Russia	C23	34
Anadyrskij liman, b., Russia	D24	34
Anadyrskij zaliv, b., Russia	C21	142
Anadyrskoe ploskogor'e, plat., Russia	C23	34
Anáfi, i., Grc.	G8	28
Anagni, Italy	C7	24
Anaheim, Ca., U.S.	J8	134
Anahim Lake, B.C., Can.	D5	138
Anáhuac, Mex.	I10	130
Ānai Mudi, mtn., India	F3	53
Anajás, Braz.	D8	84
Anakāpalle, India	C6	53
Anaktuvuk Pass, Ak., U.S.	C9	140
Analalava, Madag.	C8	68
Anamã, Braz.	D5	84
Anama Bay, Mb., Can.	C15	124
Ana María, Golfo de, b., Cuba	B8	102
Anambas, Kepulauan (Anambas Islands), is., Indon.	B5	50
Anambas Islands see Anambas, Kepulauan, is., Indon.	B5	50
Anamizu, Japan	B9	40
Anamoose, N.D., U.S.	G13	124
Anamur, Tur.	B3	58
Anamur Burnu, c., Tur.	B3	58
Anan, Japan	F7	40
Ānand, India	G4	54
Ānandapur, India	H11	54
Ananindeua, Braz.	A1	88
Anan'ïv, Ukr.	B16	26
Anantapur, India	D3	53
Anantnāg, India	B5	54
Anápolis, Braz.	I1	88
Anapurus, Braz.	B4	88
Añasco, P.R.	B1	104a
Anastasia Island, i., Fl., U.S.	G4	116
Anatahan, i., N. Mar. Is.	B5	72
Anatolia see Anadolu, hist. reg., Tur.	H15	6
Anatolikí Makedonía kai Thráki, state, Grc.	B8	28
Anatom, i., Vanuatu	m17	79d
Añatuya, Arg.	D6	92
Anauá, stm., Braz.	G11	86
Anavilhanas, Arquipélago das, is., Braz.	I11	86
Anbei, China	F17	32
Anbianbu, China	C2	42
Anbyŏn-ŭp, Kor., N.	E7	38
Ancaster, On., Can.	E9	112
Ancasti, Sierra de, mts., Arg.	D5	92
Anchiang see Qianyang, China	H3	42
Anch'ing see Anqing, China	F7	42
Anchorage, Ak., U.S.	D10	140
Anchuras, Spain	E6	20
Ancona, Italy	G10	22
Ancón de Sardinas, Bahía de, b., S.A.	G2	86
Ancuabe, Moz.	C6	68
Ancud, Chile	H2	90
Ancy-le-Franc, Fr.	G13	14
Anda, China	B10	36
Andacollo, Arg.	H2	92
Andahuaylas, Peru	F3	84
Andalgalá, Arg.	C4	92
Andalucía, state, Spain	G6	20
Andalusia see Jan Kempdorp, S. Afr.	E7	70
Andalusia, Al., U.S.	F12	122
Andalusia see Andalucía, state, Spain	G6	20
Andaman and Nicobar Islands, state, India	F7	46
Andaman Basin, unds.	H12	142
Andaman Islands, is., India	F7	46
Andaman Sea, Asia	G8	46
Andamook, Austl.	F7	74
Andapa, Madag.	C8	68
Andenes, Nor.	B6	8
Andéramboukane, Mali	F5	64
Andernach, Ger.	F3	16
Anderson, Ca., U.S.	C3	134
Anderson, In., U.S.	H4	112
Anderson, Mo., U.S.	H3	120
Anderson, S.C., U.S.	B3	116
Anderson, Tx., U.S.	G3	122
Anderson, stm., N.T., Can.	B5	106
Anderson, Mount, mtn., Wa., U.S.	C3	136
Anderson Dam, Id., U.S.	G11	136
Andes, Col.	E4	86
Andes, mts., S.A.	F7	82
Andfjorden, strt., Nor.	B7	8
Andhra Lake, res., India	B1	53
Andhra Pradesh, state, India	C4	53
Andilamena, Madag.	D8	68
Andingpu, China	B2	42
Andirlang, China	A5	46
Andižan, Uzb.	F12	32
Andkhvoy, Afg.	B10	56
Andoany, Madag.	C8	68
Andoga, stm., Russia	A19	10
Andong, Kor., S.	C1	40
Andong-chŏsuji, res., Kor., S.	C1	40
Andorra, ctry., Eur.	B12	20
Andorra, ctry., Eur.	B12	20
Andorra-la-Vella, And.	B12	20
Andover, Eng., U.K.	J11	12
Andover, Me., U.S.	F6	110
Andover, Ma., U.S.	H5	110
Andover, Oh., U.S.	C5	114
Andover, S.D., U.S.	B15	126
Andøya, i., Nor.	B6	8
Andradina, Braz.	D6	90
Andranopasy, Madag.	E7	68
Andreanof Islands, is., Ak., U.S.	g23	140a
Andreapol', Russia	D15	10
Andrews, In., U.S.	H4	112
Andrews, N.C., U.S.	A2	116
Andrews, S.C., U.S.	C6	116
Andrews, Tx., U.S.	B5	130
Andria, Italy	C10	24
Andriamena, Madag.	D8	68
Andriievo-Ivanivka, Ukr.	B17	26
Androka, Madag.	F7	68
Andronovskoe, Russia	F16	8
Andros, i., Bah.	C9	96
Ándros, i., Grc.	F7	28
Androscoggin, stm., Me., U.S.	F6	110
Āndrott Island, i., India	F1	53
Andrupene, Lat.	D10	10
Andudu, D.R.C.	D5	66
Andújar, Spain	F6	20
Andulo, Ang.	C2	68
Anduze, Fr.	E9	18
Anegada, Bahía, b., Arg.	H4	90
Anegada Passage, strt., N.A.	h15	96a
Aného, Togo	H5	64
Añelo, Arg.	I3	92
Anemata, Passe d', strt., N. Cal.	m16	79d
Anenii Noi, Mol.	C16	26
Aneroid, Sk., Can.	E6	124
Aneta, N.D., U.S.	G16	124
Anétis, Mali	F5	64
Aneto, mtn., Spain	B11	20
Anfu, China	H6	42
Angamos, Punta, c., Chile	D2	90
Ang'angxi, China	B9	36
Angara, stm., Russia	E8	34
Angarsk, Russia	D18	32
Angas Downs, Austl.	D6	74
Angastaco, Arg.	B4	92
Angaul, Russia	D18	32
Ånge, Swe.	E6	8
Ángel, Salto (Angel Falls), wtfl, Ven.	E10	86
Ángel de la Guarda, Isla, i., Mex.	G6	98
Angeles, Phil.	C3	52
Angel Falls see Ángel, Salto, wtfl, Ven.	E10	86
Ängelholm, Swe.	H5	8
Angelina, stm., Tx., U.S.	F4	122
Angellala Creek, stm., Austl.	F6	76
Angels Camp, Ca., U.S.	E5	134
Angemuk, mtn., Indon.	F10	44
Ångermanälven, stm., Swe.	E7	8
Angermünde, Ger.	C9	16
Angers, Fr.	G8	14
Angical, Braz.	F3	88
Angical do Piauí, Braz.	D4	88
Angicos, Braz.	C7	88
Angijak Island, i., Nu., Can.	D13	141
Angikuni Lake, l., Nu., Can.	C11	106
Angkor Wat, hist., Camb.	F6	48
Ângk Tasaôm, Camb.	G7	48
Angle Inlet, Mn., U.S.	B3	118
Anglem, Mount, mtn., N.Z.	H2	80
Anglesey, i., Wales, U.K.	H8	12
Anglet, Fr.	F4	18
Angleton, Tx., U.S.	H3	122
Anglona, reg., Italy	D2	24
Angmagssalik (Ammasalik), Grnld.	D18	141
Angoche, Moz.	D6	68
Angol, Chile	H1	92
Angola, In., U.S.	G5	112
Angola, N.Y., U.S.	B6	114
Angola, ctry., Afr.	C2	68
Angola Basin, unds.	J14	144
Angora see Ankara, Tur.	D15	28
Angoram, Pap. N. Gui.	a3	79a

Name	Map Ref.	Page
Angostura, Presa de la, res., Mex.	H12	100
Angoulême, Fr.	D6	18
Angoumois, hist. reg., Fr.	D5	18
Angra dos Reis, Braz.	L3	88
Angren, Uzb.	F12	32
Angu, D.R.C.	D4	66
Angualasto, Arg.	D3	92
Anguilla, Ms., U.S.	E8	122
Anguilla, dep., N.A.	h15	96a
Anguille, Cape, c., Nf., Can.	C17	110
Anguli Nur, l., China	A6	42
Anguo, China	B6	42
Angus, On., Can.	D10	112
Angusville, Mb., Can.	D13	124
Anhalt, hist. reg., Ger.	D7	16
Anholt, i., Den.	H4	8
Anhua, China	G4	42
Anhui, state, China	F7	42
Anhwei see Anhui, state, China	F7	42
Aniak, Ak., U.S.	D8	140
Anibare Bay, b., Nauru	q17	78f
Anie, Pic d', mtn., Fr.	F5	18
Anil, Braz.	B3	88
Animas, N.M., U.S.	L8	132
Animas, stm., U.S.	G9	132
Animas Valley, val., N.A.	L8	132
Anina, Rom.	D8	26
Anita, Ia., U.S.	C3	120
Anıtkaya, Tur.	E13	28
Aniva, mys, c., Russia	B13	36
Aniva, zaliv, b., Russia	G17	34
Aniwa, i., Vanuatu	l17	79d
Anjangaon, India	H6	54
Anjār, India	G2	54
'Anjar, Leb.	E6	58
Anjou, hist. reg., Fr.	G8	14
Anjouan see Nzwani, i., Com.	C7	68
Anjudin, Russia	B9	32
Anjujsk, Russia	C21	34
Anjujskij hrebet, mts., Russia	C21	34
Anju-ŭp, Kor., N.	E6	38
Anka, Nig.	G6	64
Ankaboa, Tanjona, c., Madag.	E7	68
Ankang, China	E3	42
Ankara, Tur.	D15	28
Ankara, state, Tur.	D15	28
Ankavandra, Madag.	D8	68
Ankazoabo, Madag.	E7	68
Ankazobe, Madag.	D8	68
Ankeny, Ia., U.S.	C4	120
Anking see Anqing, China	F7	42
Ankleshwar, India	H4	54
Ankoro, D.R.C.	F5	66
Anlong, China	F6	36
Ânlóng Vêng, Camb.	E6	48
Anlu, China	F5	42
An Muileann gCearr see Mullingar, Ire.	H5	12
Ånn, l., Swe.	E5	8
Ann, Cape, c., Ant.	B10	81
Ann, Cape, pen., Ma., U.S.	H6	110
Anna, Il., U.S.	G8	120
Anna, Lake, res., Va., U.S.	F8	114
Annaba, Alg.	B6	64
An-Nabaṭīyah, state, Leb.	E6	58
An-Nabaṭīyah at-Taḥtā, Leb.	E6	58
Annaberg-Buchholz, Ger.	F9	16
An-Nabk, Syria	D7	58
An-Nafūd, des., Sau. Ar.	D5	56
An-Najaf, Iraq	C5	56
Annam see Trung Phan, hist. reg., Viet.	D8	48
Annamitique, Chaîne, mts., Asia	D8	48
Annan, Scot., U.K.	G9	12
Annandale, Austl.	C7	76
Annandale, Mn., U.S.	F4	118
Annandale, val., Scot., U.K.	F9	12
Anna Plains, Austl.	C4	74
Annapolis, Md., U.S.	F9	114
Annapolis Royal, N.S., Can.	F11	110
Annapūrṇa, mtn., Nepal	D9	54
Ann Arbor, Mi., U.S.	B2	114
An Nás see Naas, Ire.	H6	12
An-Nāṣirīyah, Iraq	C6	56
An-Nāṣirīyah, Syria	E7	58
An-Nawfalīyah, Libya	A3	62
Annecy, Fr.	D12	18
Annecy, Lac d', l., Fr.	D12	18
Annemasse, Fr.	C12	18
Annenkov Island, i., S. Geor.	J9	90
An Nhon, Viet.	F9	48
Anning, China	G5	36
Anniston, Al., U.S.	D13	122
Annobón, i., Eq. Gui.	J6	64
Annonay, Fr.	D10	18
An-Nuhūd, Sudan	E5	62
Annville, Ky., U.S.	G2	114
Annville, Pa., U.S.	D9	114
Anoka, Mn., U.S.	F5	118
Anori, Braz.	D5	84
Anpu, China	K3	42
Anqing, China	F7	42
Anqiu, China	C8	42
Anren, China	H5	42
Ansai, China	C3	42
Ansbach, Ger.	G6	16
Anse-d'Hainault, Haiti	C10	102
Anse La Raye, St. Luc.	m6	105c
Anselmo, Ne., U.S.	F13	126
Anserma, Col.	E4	86
Anshan, China	D5	38
Anshun, China	H1	42
Ansina, Ur.	E10	92
Ansley, Ne., U.S.	F13	126
Anson Bay, b., Austl.	B5	74
Anson Bay, b., Norf. I.	y24	78i
Ansongo, Mali	F5	64
Ansonville, N.C., U.S.	A5	116
Ansted, W.V., U.S.	F4	114
Antakya see Hatay, Tur.	B7	58
Antalaha, Madag.	C9	68
Antalieptė, Lith.	E8	10
Antalya, Tur.	G13	28
Antalya, state, Tur.	F14	28
Antalya, Gulf of see Antalya Körfezi, b., Tur.	G14	28
Antalya Körfezi (Antalya, Gulf of), b., Tur.	G14	28
Antananarivo, Madag.	D8	68
An tAonach see Nenagh, Ire.	I4	12
Antarctica, cont.	D11	81
Antarctic Peninsula, pen., Ant.	C35	81
Antas, Braz.	F6	88
Antas, stm., Braz.	D12	92
Antelope Island, i., Ut., U.S.	C4	132
Antelope Mine, Zimb.	B9	70
Antelope Peak, mtn., Nv., U.S.	B1	132
Antenor Navarro, Braz.	D6	88
Antequera, Para.	A9	92
Antequera, Spain	H6	20
Anthon, Ia., U.S.	B2	120
Anthony, Ks., U.S.	D10	128
Anthony, N.M., U.S.	K10	132
Anthony, Tx., U.S.	E9	98
Anti-Atlas, mts., Mor.	D3	64
Antibes, Fr.	F13	18
Anticosti, Île d', i., Qc., Can.	F18	106
Antifer, Cap d', c., Fr.	E8	14
Antigonish, N.S., Can.	E14	110
Antigua, i., Antig.	f4	105b
Antigua and Barbuda, ctry., N.A.	h15	96a
Antigua International Airport, Antig.	f4	105b
Antiguo Morelos, Mex.	D9	100
Antikýthira, i., Grc.	H6	28
Anti-Lebanon (Sharqī, Al-Jabal ash-), mts., Asia	E7	58
Antilla, Cuba	B10	102
Antillen, Nederlandse see Netherlands Antilles, dep., N.A.	i14	96a
Antimony, Ut., U.S.	E5	132
Antioch see Hatay, Tur.	B7	58
Antioch, Il., U.S.	F1	112
Antioquia, Col.	D4	86
Antioquia, state, Col.	D4	86
Antipajuta, Russia	C4	34
Antipodes Islands, is., N.Z.	H9	72
Antisana, vol., Ec.	H2	86
Antler, stm., N.A.	E12	124
Antofagasta, Chile	A2	92
Antofagasta, state, Chile	B3	92
Antofagasta de la Sierra, Arg.	C4	92
Antofalla, Salar de, pl., Arg.	C3	92
Antofalla, Volcán, vol., Arg.	B4	92
Antón, Pan.	H7	102
Anton, Tx., U.S.	H6	128
Anton Chico, N.M., U.S.	F3	128
Antongila, Helodrano, b., Madag.	D8	68
Antonina, Braz.	B13	92
Antonina do Norte, Braz.	D5	88
Antônio Prado, Braz.	D12	92
Antonito, Co., U.S.	D2	128
Antón Lizardo, Punta, c., Mex.	F10	100
Antopal', Bela.	H7	10
Antrim, N. Ire., U.K.	G6	12
Antropovo, Russia	G20	8
Antsalova, Madag.	D7	68
Antsirabe, Madag.	D8	68
Antsirañana, Madag.	C8	68
Antsohihy, Madag.	C8	68
Antulai, Gunong, mtn., Malay.	A10	50
Antun', Russia	G16	34
Antung see Dandong, China	D5	38
Antwerp see Antwerpen, Bel.	C13	14
Antwerp, Oh., U.S.	C1	114
Antwerpen (Antwerp), Bel.	C13	14
An Uaimh see Navan, Ire.	H6	12
Anugul, India	H10	54
Anūpgarh, India	D4	54
Anuradhapura, Sri L.	G5	53
Anvers see Antwerpen, Bel.	C13	14
Anvers Island, i., Ant.	B34	81
Anvik, Ak., U.S.	D7	140
Anxi, China	C4	36
Anxi, China	I8	42
Anxiang, China	G5	42
Anxious Bay, b., Austl.	F6	74
Anyang, China	C6	42
Anyang, Kor., S.	F7	38
A'nyêmaqên Shan, mts., China	D4	36
Anyer Kidul, Indon.	G4	50
Anykščiai, Lith.	E7	10
Anyuan, China	I6	42
Anyuanyi see Tianzhu, China	D5	36
Anyue, China	F1	42
Anze, China	C5	42
Anžero-Sudžensk, Russia	C15	32
Anzio, Italy	C6	24
Anzoátegui, state, Ven.	C9	86
Anžu, ostrova, is., Russia	A17	34
Aoba, i., Vanuatu	j16	79d
Aoba / Maéwo, state, Vanuatu	j17	79d
Aoga-shima, i., Japan	G12	40
Aohan Qi, China	C3	38
Aojiang, China	H9	42
Aoji-ri, Kor., N.	C9	38
Ao Luk, Thai.	H4	48
Aomar, Alg.	H14	20
Aomen (Macau), China	J5	42
Aomori, Japan	D14	38
Aonla, India	D7	54
Aóös (Vjosës), stm., Eur.	D13	24
A'opo, Samoa	g11	79c
Aoraki (Cook, Mount), mtn., N.Z.	F4	80
Aôral, Phnum, mtn., Camb.	F7	48
Aore, i., Vanuatu	j16	79d
Aosta (Aoste), Italy	E4	22
Aoste see Aosta, Italy	E4	22
Aouderas, Niger	F6	64
Aouk, Bahr, stm., Afr.	F3	62
Aoukâr, reg., Maur.	F3	64
Aoya, Japan	D7	40
Aozou, Chad	C3	62
Apache Junction, Az., U.S.	J5	132
Apache Peak, mtn., Az., U.S.	L6	132
Apalachee, stm., Ga., U.S.	C2	116
Apalachicola, Fl., U.S.	H13	122
Apalachicola, stm., Fl., U.S.	H14	122
Apalachicola Bay, b., Fl., U.S.	H13	122
Apaporis, stm., S.A.	H7	86
Aparados da Serra, Parque Nacional de, p.o.i., Braz.	D12	92
Aparri, Phil.	A3	52
Apartadó, Col.	D3	86
Apatin, Yugo.	D5	26
Apatity, Russia	C15	8
Apatzingán de la Constitución, Mex.	F7	100
Apaxtla de Castrejón, Mex.	F8	100
Apeldoorn, Neth.	B15	14
Apennines see Appennino, mts., Italy	G11	6
Apex, N.C., U.S.	I7	114
Api, mtn., Nepal	D8	54
Apía, Col.	E4	86
Apia, Samoa	g12	79c
Apiacás, Serra dos, plat., Braz.	E6	84
Apiaí, Braz.	B13	92
Apiaú, stm., Braz.	F11	86
Apishapa, stm., Co., U.S.	D4	128
Apizaco, Mex.	F9	100
Apo, Mount, mtn., Phil.	G5	52
Apodi, Braz.	C7	88
Apodi, stm., Braz.	C7	88
Apolakkiá, Grc.	G10	28
Apolda, Ger.	E7	16
Apolinario Saravia, Arg.	B6	92
Apolo, Bol.	B3	90
Apón, stm., Ven.	B5	86
Aponguao, stm., Ven.	E11	86
Apopka, Lake, l., Fl., U.S.	H4	116
Aporá, Braz.	F6	88
Aporé, Braz.	C6	90
Apostle Islands, is., Wi., U.S.	E8	118
Apostle Islands National Lakeshore, p.o.i., Wi., U.S.	D8	118
Apóstoles, Arg.	C10	92
Apostolove, Ukr.	E4	32
Appalaches, Les see Appalachian Mountains, mts., N.A.	D12	108
Appalachia, Va., U.S.	H3	114
Appalachian Mountains, mts., N.A.	D12	108
Appennino see Apennines, mts., Italy	G11	6
Appennino, Calabro, mts., Italy	E10	24
Appennino Abruzzese, mts., Italy	B7	24
Appennino Ligure, mts., Italy	F6	22
Appennino Lucano, mts., Italy	D9	24
Appennino Tosco-Emiliano, mts., Italy	F8	22
Appennino Umbro-Marchigiano, mts., Italy	G9	22
Appenzell, Switz.	C6	22
Apple Orchard Mountain, mtn., Va., U.S.	G6	114
Appleton, Mn., U.S.	F3	118
Appleton, Wi., U.S.	G10	118
Appleton City, Mo., U.S.	F3	120
Apple Valley, Ca., U.S.	I8	134
Appomattox, Va., U.S.	G7	114
Appomattox, stm., Va., U.S.	G7	114
Aprelevka, Russia	E20	10
Aprilia, Italy	C6	24
Apšeronsk, Russia	F5	32
Apt, Fr.	F11	18
Apucarana, Braz.	A12	92
Apulia see Puglia, state, Italy	C10	24
Apure, state, Ven.	D7	86
Apure, stm., Ven.	D8	86
Apurímac, stm., Peru	F3	84
Apurito, Ven.	D7	86
Aqaba, Gulf of, b.	J5	58
Āqchah, Afg.	B10	56
'Aqīq, Sudan	D7	62
Aqtaū see Aktau, Kaz.	F8	32
Aqtöbe see Aktjubinsk, Kaz.	D9	32
Aquidabã, Braz.	F7	88
Aquidauana, Braz.	D5	90
Aquila, Mex.	F7	100
Aquiles Serdán, Mex.	A6	100
Aquiles Serdán, Mex.	C9	100
Aquin, Haiti	C11	102
Aquio, stm., Col.	F8	86
Ara, India	F10	54
Ara, stm., Japan	D12	40
Arab, Al., U.S.	C12	122
'Arab, Bahr al-, stm., Sudan	E5	62
'Araba, Wadi ('Arabah, Wādī), stm., Egypt	I3	58
'Arabah, Wādī al- (Ha'Arava), val., Asia	H6	58
Arabako, co., Spain	B8	20
Araban, Tur.	A8	58
Arabian Basin, unds.	H9	142
Arabian Desert (Eastern Desert), des., Egypt	B6	62
Arabian Gulf see Persian Gulf, b., Asia	D7	56
Arabian Peninsula, pen., Asia	E6	56
Arabian Sea	F9	56
Araçá, stm., Braz.	G10	86
Aracaju, Braz.	F7	88
Aracataca, Col.	B4	86
Aracati, Braz.	C7	88
Araçatuba, Braz.	D6	90
Aracena, Spain	G4	20
Araci, Braz.	F6	88
Aracides, Cape, c., Sol. Is.	e9	79b
Aracoiaba, Braz.	C6	88
Aracruz, Braz.	J5	88
Araçuaí, Braz.	I4	88
Araçuaí, stm., Braz.	I4	88
'Arad, Isr.	G6	58
Arad, Rom.	C8	26
Arad, state, Rom.	C8	26
Aradhíppou, Cyp.	D4	58
Arafura Sea	J16	142
Arafura Shelf, unds.	K16	142
Aragarças, Braz.	G7	84
Aragats Lerr, mtn., Arm.	A5	56
Aragón, state, Spain	C10	20
Aragón, stm., Spain	B9	20
Aragona, Italy	G7	24
Aragua, state, Ven.	B8	86
Araguacema, Braz.	E8	84
Araguaçu, Braz.	F8	84
Aragua de Barcelona, Ven.	C9	86
Araguaia, stm., Braz.	E8	84
Araguaína, Braz.	D1	88
Araguao, Caño, stm., Ven.	C11	86
Araguari, Braz.	J1	88
Araguari, stm., Braz.	C7	84
Araguari, stm., Braz.	J1	88
Araguatins, Braz.	C1	88
Arahal, Spain	G5	20
Arai, Japan	B11	40
Araioses, Braz.	B4	88
Ârak, Alg.	D5	64
Arāk, Iran	C6	56
Arakan see Rakhine, state, Mya.	C1	48
Arakan Yoma, mts., Mya.	C2	48
Arakkonam, India	E4	53
Araks see Aras, stm., Asia	B6	56
Araks see Araz, stm., Asia	B6	56
Aral Sea, l., Asia	E9	32
Aral'sk, Kaz.	E10	32
Aralsk see Aral'sk, Kaz.	E10	32
Aramac, Austl.	D5	76
Aramac, stm., Austl.	D5	76
Ārāmbāg, India	G11	54
Aramberri, Mex.	C8	100
Ārān, Iran	C7	56
Aranda de Duero, Spain	C7	20
Arandas, Mex.	E7	100
Arandis, Nmb.	C2	70
Arang, India	H8	54
Ārani, India	E4	53
Aran Island, i., Ire.	G4	12
Aran Islands, is., Ire.	H3	12
Aranjuez, Spain	D7	20
Aranos, Nmb.	D4	70
Aransas, stm., Tx., U.S.	F10	130
Arantāngi, India	F4	53
Aranyaprathet, Thai.	F6	48
Arao, Japan	G3	40
Araouane, Mali	F4	64
Arapaho, Ok., U.S.	F9	128
Arapahoe, Ne., U.S.	A9	128
Arapey Grande, stm., Ur.	E9	92
Arapiraca, Braz.	E7	88
Arapongas, Braz.	D6	90
Arapoti, Braz.	B12	92
Araranguá, Braz.	D13	92
Araraquara, Braz.	K1	88
Araras, Braz.	L2	88
Araras, Açude, res., Braz.	C5	88
Ararat, Austl.	K4	76
Ararat, Mount see Ağrı Dağı, mtn., Tur.	B5	56
Arari, Braz.	B3	88
Arāria, India	E11	54
Araripe, Braz.	D5	88
Araripe, Chapada do, plat., Braz.	D6	88
Araripina, Braz.	D5	88
Ararirá, stm., Braz.	H10	86
Araruama, Lagoa de, b., Braz.	L4	88
Araruna, Braz.	D8	88
Aras (Araz), stm., Asia	B6	56
Aratuípe, Braz.	G6	88
Arauca, Col.	D6	86
Arauca, state, Col.	D6	86
Arauca, stm., S.A.	D8	86
Araucária, Braz.	B13	92
Arauquita, Col.	D6	86
Araure, Ven.	C7	86
Arāvalli Range, mts., India	F4	54
Arawa, Pap. N. Gui.	d6	79b
Araxá, Braz.	J2	88
Araya, Ven.	B9	86
Araya, Punta de, c., Ven.	B9	86
Araz (Aras), stm., Asia	B6	56
Ārba Minch', Eth.	F7	62
Arbatax, Italy	E3	24
Arboga, Swe.	G6	8
Arboledas, Arg.	H7	92
Arbon, Switz.	C6	22
Arboréa, Italy	E2	24
Arborea, reg., Italy	E2	24
Arborfield, Sk., Can.	A10	124
Arbroath, Scot., U.K.	E10	12
Arbuckle, Ca., U.S.	D3	134
Arc, stm., Fr.	D12	18
Arcachon, Fr.	E4	18
Arcachon, Bassin d', b., Fr.	E4	18
Arcade, Ca., U.S.	E4	134
Arcade, N.Y., U.S.	B7	114
Arcadia, Ca., U.S.	I7	134
Arcadia, Fl., U.S.	I4	116
Arcadia, Ia., U.S.	B2	120
Arcadia, Ks., U.S.	G3	120
Arcadia, La., U.S.	E6	122
Arcadia, Mi., U.S.	D3	112
Arcadia, Mo., U.S.	G7	120
Arcadia, S.C., U.S.	B3	116
Arcadia, Wi., U.S.	G7	118
Arcanum, Oh., U.S.	D1	114
Arcas, Cayos, is., Mex.	E12	100
Arcata, Ca., U.S.	C1	134
Arc Dome, mtn., Nv., U.S.	E8	134
Arcelia, Mex.	F8	100
Arcevia, Italy	G9	22
Archangel see Arhangel'sk, Russia	D19	8
Archbold, Oh., U.S.	C1	114
Archer, Fl., U.S.	G3	116
Archer, stm., Austl.	B8	74
Archer, Mount, mtn., Austl.	D8	76
Archer City, Tx., U.S.	H10	128
Archer's Post, Kenya	D7	66
Arches National Park, p.o.i., Ut., U.S.	E7	132
Archiac, Fr.	D5	18
Archidona, Spain	G6	20
Arcis-sur-Aube, Fr.	F13	14
Arco, Id., U.S.	G13	136
Arcola, Il., U.S.	E9	120
Arcola, Ms., U.S.	D8	122
Arcos, Braz.	K3	88
Arcos de la Frontera, Spain	H5	20
Arcot, India	E4	53
Arcoverde, Braz.	E7	88
Arctic Bay see Tununirusiq, Nu., Can.	A14	106
Arctic Ocean	A21	4
Arctic Red, stm., N.T., Can.	B4	106
Arctic Village, Ak., U.S.	C10	140
Arda, stm., Eur.	H12	26
Ardabīl, Iran	B6	56
Ardahan, Tur.	A5	56
Ardakān, Iran	C7	56
Ardatov, Russia	I20	8
Ardèche, state, Fr.	E10	18
Arden, Ca., U.S.	E4	134
Ardennes, state, Fr.	E13	14
Ardennes, reg., Eur.	D14	14
Ardennes, Canal des, can., Fr.	E13	14
Ardestān, Iran	C7	56
Ardila, stm., Eur.	F3	20
Ardill, Sk., Can.	E8	124
Ardlethan, Austl.	J6	76
Ardmore, Al., U.S.	B12	122
Ardmore, Ok., U.S.	G11	128
Ardmore, Pa., U.S.	D10	114
Åre, Swe.	E5	8
Areado, Braz.	K2	88
Arecibo, P.R.	B2	104a
Arecibo, Observatorio de, sci., P.R.	B2	104a
Arecibo Observatory see Arecibo, Observatorio de, sci., P.R.	B2	104a
Arèḫausk, Bela.	F13	10
Areia, Braz.	D8	88
Areia, stm., Braz.	H3	88
Areia Branca, Braz.	C7	88
Arena, Point, c., Ca., U.S.	E2	134
Arena, Punta, c., Mex.	D4	100
Arena de la Ventana, Punta, c., Mex.	C4	100
Arenal, P.R.	C3	104a
Arenas, Cayo, i., Mex.	D13	100
Arenas, Punta de, c., Arg.	J3	90
Arenas de San Pedro, Spain	D5	20
Arendal, Nor.	G3	8
Arenys de Mar, Spain	C13	20
Arequipa, Peru	G3	84
Arequito, Arg.	F7	92
Arévalo, Spain	C6	20
Arezzo, Italy	G8	22
Arga, stm., Spain	B9	20
Argadargada, Austl.	D7	74
Argamasilla de Alba, Spain	E7	20
Arganda del Rey, Spain	D7	20
Arga-Sala, stm., Russia	C10	34
Argelès-Gazost, Fr.	F5	18
Argens, stm., Fr.	F12	18
Argent, Côte d', cst., Fr.	F4	18
Argenta, Italy	F8	22
Argentan, Fr.	F8	14
Argentat, Fr.	D7	18
Argenteuil, Fr.	F11	14
Argentina, ctry., S.A.	G3	90
Argentine Basin, unds.	L10	144
Argentino, Lago, l., Arg.	J2	90
Argenton-sur-Creuse, Fr.	H10	14
Argeș, state, Rom.	E11	26
Argeș, stm., Rom.	E13	26
Arghandāb, stm., Afg.	C10	56
Argolikós Kólpos (Argolis, Gulf of), b., Grc.	F6	28
Argolis, Gulf of see Argolikós Kólpos, b., Grc.	F6	28
Argonia, Ks., U.S.	D11	128
Argonne, Wi., U.S.	F10	118
Argonne, reg., Fr.	E14	14
Árgos, Grc.	F5	28
Argos, In., U.S.	G3	112
Argostóli, Grc.	E3	28
Arguello, Point, c., Ca., U.S.	I5	134
Argun' (Ergun), stm., Asia	F12	34
Argungu, Nig.	G5	64
Argyle, Lake, l., Austl.	C5	74
Arhangel'sk, Russia	D19	8
Arhangel'skaja oblast', co., Russia	E20	8
Arhangel'skoe, Russia	G20	10
Arhara, Russia	G15	34
Arhipovo, Russia	C21	8
Århus, Den.	H4	8
Århus, state, Den.	H4	8
Ariake-kai, b., Japan	F3	40
Ariana, Tun.	H4	24
Ariano Irpino, Italy	C9	24
Ariari, stm., Col.	F5	86
Arias, Arg.	F6	92
Ari Atoll, at., Mald.	i12	46a
Arica, Chile	C2	90
Arica, Col.	I6	86
Arichat, N.S., Can.	E16	110
Arichuna, Ven.	D8	86
Arid, Cape, c., Austl.	F4	74
Arida, Japan	E8	40
Aridaía, Grc.	C5	28
Ariège, state, Fr.	G7	18
Ārifwāla, Pak.	C4	54
Ariguaní, stm., Col.	C5	86
Arīḥā (Jericho), Gaza	G6	58
Arīḥā, Syria	C7	58
Arikaree, stm., U.S.	B6	128
Arima, Trin.	s12	105f
Arinos, stm., Braz.	F6	84
Ariogala, Lith.	E6	10
Ariporo, stm., Col.	D6	86
Aripuanã, Braz.	E5	84
Aripuanã, stm., Braz.	E5	84
Ariquemes, Braz.	E5	84
Arisa, stm., Ven.	D9	86
Arish, Wadi el- ('Arīsh, Wādī al-), stm., Egypt	H4	58
Aristazabal Island, i., B.C., Can.	E5	106
Ariton, Al., U.S.	F13	122
Arivonimamo, Madag.	D8	68
Ariyalūr, India	F4	53
Arizaro, Salar de, pl., Arg.	B4	92
Arizgoiti, Spain	A8	20
Arizona, Arg.	G5	92
Arizona, state, U.S.	I5	132
Arizpe, Mex.	F7	98
Arja, Russia	H22	8
Arjasa, Indon.	G9	50
Arjona, Col.	B4	86
Arjona, Spain	G6	20
Arka, Russia	D17	34
Arkadelphia, Ar., U.S.	C5	122
Arkalyk, Kaz.	D11	32
Arkansas, state, U.S.	B6	122
Arkansas, stm., U.S.	E9	108
Arkansas, Salt Fork, stm., U.S.	D7	122
Arkansas City, Ar., U.S.	D7	122
Arkansas City, Ks., U.S.	D11	128
Arkanū, Jabal, mtn., Libya	C4	62
Arkhara see Arhara, Russia	G15	34
Arklow, Ire.	I6	12
Arkoma, Ok., U.S.	B4	122
Arkona, Kap, c., Ger.	B9	16
Arkport, N.Y., U.S.	B8	114
Arktičeskogo Instituta, ostrova, is., Russia	A5	34
Arlanza, stm., Spain	B7	20
Arlanzón, stm., Spain	B7	20
Arles, Fr.	F10	18
Arlington, S. Afr.	E8	70
Arlington, Ga., U.S.	F14	122
Arlington, Ks., U.S.	D10	128
Arlington, Ky., U.S.	H9	120
Arlington, Ne., U.S.	C1	120
Arlington, Oh., U.S.	D2	114
Arlington, Or., U.S.	E6	136
Arlington, Tn., U.S.	B9	122
Arlington, Tx., U.S.	B10	130
Arlington, Vt., U.S.	G3	110
Arlington, Va., U.S.	F8	114
Arlington, Wa., U.S.	B4	136
Arlington Heights, Il., U.S.	F2	112
Arlit, Niger	F6	64
Arlon, Bel.	E14	14
Arm, stm., Sk., Can.	D8	124
Arma, Ks., U.S.	G3	120
Armada, Mi., U.S.	B3	114
Armadale, Austl.	F3	74
Armageddon see Tel Megiddo, hist., Isr.	F6	58
Armagh, N. Ire., U.K.	G6	12
Armançon, stm., Fr.	G13	14
Armavir, Russia	E6	32
Armenia, Col.	E4	86
Armenia, ctry., Asia	A5	56
Armenija see Armenia, ctry., Asia	A5	56
Armenistis, Grc.	F9	28
Armentières, Fr.	D11	14
Armería, Mex.	F6	100
Armero, Col.	E4	86
Armidale, Austl.	H8	76
Armijo, N.M., U.S.	H10	132
Armour, S.D., U.S.	D14	126
Armstrong, Arg.	F7	92
Armstrong, B.C., Can.	F11	138
Armstrong, On., Can.	A9	118
Armstrong, Mo., U.S.	E5	120
Armstrong, Mount, mtn., Yk., Can.	C4	106
Ārmūr, India	B4	53
Armutlu, Tur.	C11	28
Arnarfjörður, b., Ice.	k27	8a
Arnaud, stm., Qc., Can.	D16	106
Arnaudville, La., U.S.	G6	122
Arnay-le-Duc, Fr.	G13	14
Arnedo, Spain	B8	20
Arneiros, Braz.	D5	88
Arnhem, Neth.	B14	14
Arnhem, Cape, c., Austl.	B7	74
Arnhem Bay, b., Austl.	B7	74
Arnhem Land, reg., Austl.	B6	74
Arno, at., Marsh. Is.	C8	72
Arno, stm., Italy	G7	22
Arnold, Ca., U.S.	E5	134
Arnold, Mn., U.S.	E6	118
Arnold, Mo., U.S.	F7	120
Arnold, Ne., U.S.	F12	126
Arnolds Park, Ia., U.S.	H3	118
Arnon, stm., Fr.	C8	18
Arnprior, On., Can.	C13	112
Arnsberg, Ger.	E4	16
Arnstadt, Ger.	F6	16
Aro, stm., Ven.	D9	86
Aroa, Ven.	B7	86
Aroa, Pointe, c., Fr. Poly.	u20	78h
Aroab, Nmb.	E4	70
Aroland, On., Can.	A12	118
Arolsen, Ger.	E5	16
Arona, Italy	E5	22
Arona, Pap. N. Gui.	b4	79a
Aroostook, stm., N.A.	D8	110
Arop Island (Long Island), i., Pap. N. Gui.	b4	79a
Arorae, i., Kir.	D8	72
Aroroy, Phil.	D4	52
Arosa, Ría de see Arousa, Ría de, est., Spain	B1	20
Arousa, Ría de, est., Spain	B1	20
Arp, Tx., U.S.	E3	122
Arqalyq see Arkalyk, Kaz.	D11	32
Arquata Scrivia, Italy	F5	22
Arraga, Arg.	D5	92
Ar-Rahad, Sudan	E6	62
Arraial do Cabo, Braz.	L5	88
Arraias, Braz.	G2	88
Ar-Ramādī, Iraq	C5	56
Ar-Ramthā, Jord.	F7	58
Arran, Island of, i., Scot., U.K.	F7	12
Ar-Rank, Sudan	E6	62
Ar-Raqqah, Syria	B9	58
Ar-Raqqah, state, Syria	B9	58
Arras, Fr.	D11	14
Ar-Rastan, Syria	D7	58
Arrecifes, Arg.	G7	92
Arrey, N.M., U.S.	K9	132
Arriaga, Mex.	G11	100
Ar-Riyāḍ (Riyadh), Sau. Ar.	E6	56
Arroio Grande, Braz.	F11	92
Arrojado, stm., Braz.	G3	88
Arronches, Port.	E3	20
Arros, stm., Fr.	F6	18
Arroux, stm., Fr.	B10	18
Arrowhead, Lake, res., Tx., U.S.	H10	128
Arrowwood, Ab., Can.	F17	138
Arroyito, Arg.	E6	92
Arroyo, P.R.	C3	104a
Arroyo de la Luz, Spain	E4	20
Arroyo Grande, Ca., U.S.	H5	134
Arroyo Hondo, N.M., U.S.	E3	128
Arroyo Seco, Arg.	F7	92
Arroyos y Esteros, Para.	B9	92
Ar-Rub' al-Khālī, des., Asia	E6	56
Ar-Ruqayyah, hist., Syria	F8	58
Ar-Ruṣāfah, hist., Syria	C9	58
Ar-Ruṣayfah, Jord.	F7	58
Ar-Ruṣayriṣ, Sudan	E6	62
Ar-Ruṭbah, Iraq	C5	56
Arsenev, Russia	B10	38
Arsenevka, stm., Russia	B10	38
Arsikere, India	E3	53
Ársos, Cyp.	D3	58
Art, Île, i., N. Cal.	I14	79d
Árta, Grc.	D3	28
Artà, Spain	E14	20
Artá see Artà, Spain	E14	20
Arteaga, Mex.	F7	100
Art'em, Russia	C9	38
Artemisa, Cuba	A6	102
Artëmovsk, Russia	D16	32
Artëmovskij, Russia	E12	34
Artëmovskij, Russia	C10	38
Artesia, Ms., U.S.	D10	122
Artesia, N.M., U.S.	B3	130
Arthabaska, ngh., Qc., Can.	D5	110
Arthal, India	B6	54
Arthur, On., Can.	E9	112
Arthur, Il., U.S.	E9	120
Arthur, N.D., U.S.	D1	118
Arthur, Tn., U.S.	H2	114
Arthur, stm., Austl.	n12	77a
Arthur's Pass National Park, p.o.i., N.Z.	F5	80
Arthur's Town, Bah.	C9	96
Artibonite, stm., Haiti	C11	102
Artigas, Ur.	E9	92
Artillery Lake, l., N.T., Can.	C9	106
Artois, hist. reg., Fr.	D11	14
Artsyz, Ukr.	D16	26
Artyk, Russia	D18	34
Aru, Kepulauan (Aru Islands), is., Indon.	G10	44
Aru, Tanjung, c., Indon.	E10	50
Arua, Ug.	D6	66
Aruanã, Braz.	F7	84
Aruba, dep., N.A.	F12	102
Aru Islands see Aru, Kepulauan, is., Indon.	G10	44
Arunāchal Pradesh, state, India	C7	46
Arun Qi, China	B9	36
Aruppukkottai, India	G4	53
Arurandeua, stm., Braz.	C1	88
Arusha, Tan.	E7	66
Arut, stm., Indon.	E7	50
Aruvi, stm., Sri L.	G5	53
Aruwimi, stm., D.R.C.	D4	66
Arvada, Co., U.S.	B3	128
Arvayheer, Mong.	B5	36
Arvi, India	H7	54
Arviat, Nu., Can.	C12	106
Arvidsjaur, Swe.	D8	8
Arvika, Swe.	G5	8
Arvin, Ca., U.S.	H7	134
Arvon, Mount, mtn., Mi., U.S.	B1	112
Arvorezinha, Braz.	D11	92
Arxan, China	B8	36
Arys', Kaz.	F11	32
Arys, ozero, l., Kaz.	E11	32
Arzachena, Italy	C3	24
Arzamas, Russia	I20	8
Arzignano, Italy	E8	22
Arz Lubnān, for., Leb.	D7	58
Aš, Czech Rep.	F8	16
Aša, Russia	D9	32
Asa, stm., Ven.	D10	86
Asaba, Nig.	H6	64
Asad, Buḥayrat al- (Assad, Lake), res., Syria	B9	58
Asadābād, Afg.	C11	56
Asadābād, Iran	B8	56
Aşağibostancı, N. Cyp.	C3	58
Asahan, stm., Indon.	B1	50
Asahi, Japan	D13	40
Asahi, stm., Japan	E6	40
Asahi-dake, vol., Japan	C15	38
Asahigawa see Asahikawa, Japan	C15	38
Asahikawa, Japan	C15	38
Asama-yama, vol., Japan	C11	40
Asan-man, b., Kor., S.	F7	38
Āsānsol, India	G11	54
Åsarna, Swe.	E6	8
Asaro, Ven.	q20	104g
Asbest, Russia	C10	32
Asbestos, Qc., Can.	E4	110
Asbestos Range National Park, p.o.i., Austl.	n13	77a
Asbury Park, N.J., U.S.	D12	114
Ascensión, Mex.	F9	98
Ascension, i., St. Hel.	G4	60
Aschaffenburg, Ger.	G5	16
Aschersleben, Ger.	E7	16
Ascoli Piceno, Italy	H10	22
Ascoli Satriano, Italy	C9	24
Ascör (Ostër), stm., Eur.	G14	10
Āseb, Erit.	E8	62
Åseda, Swe.	H6	8
Āsela, Eth.	F7	62
Åsele, Swe.	D7	8
Āsendabo, Eth.	F7	62
Asenovgrad, Blg.	G11	26
Aseri, Est.	A9	10
Ašgabat, Turkmen.	B8	56
Ashāqif, Jabal al-, hills, Jord.	F8	58
Ashburton, N.Z.	F4	80
Ashburton, stm., Austl.	D3	74
Ashcroft, B.C., Can.	F9	138
Ashdod, Isr.	G5	58
Ashdod, Tel, hist., Isr.	G5	58
Ashdown, Ar., U.S.	D4	122
Asheboro, N.C., U.S.	I6	114
Ashern, Mb., Can.	C15	124
Asheville, N.C., U.S.	I3	114
Ash Flat, Ar., U.S.	H6	120
Ashford, Eng., U.K.	J13	12
Ashford, Al., U.S.	F13	122
Ash Fork, Az., U.S.	H4	132
Ashgabat see Ašgabat, Turkmen.	B8	56
Ash Grove, Mo., U.S.	G4	120
Ashibe, Japan	F2	40
Ashikaga, Japan	C12	40
Ashington, Eng., U.K.	F11	12
Ashio, Japan	C12	40
Ashizuri-misaki, c., Japan	G6	40
Ashland, Al., U.S.	D13	122
Ashland, Il., U.S.	E7	120
Ashland, Ks., U.S.	D9	128
Ashland, Ky., U.S.	F3	114
Ashland, Mo., U.S.	F5	120
Ashland, Mt., U.S.	B6	126
Ashland, Ne., U.S.	C1	120
Ashland, N.H., U.S.	G5	110
Ashland, Oh., U.S.	D3	114
Ashland, Or., U.S.	A3	134
Ashland, Va., U.S.	G8	114
Ashland, Wi., U.S.	E7	118
Ashland, Mount, mtn., Or., U.S.	A3	134
Ashley, Austl.	G7	76
Ashley, Il., U.S.	F8	120
Ashley, Mi., U.S.	E5	112
Ashley, Oh., U.S.	D3	114
Ashmore, Il., U.S.	E9	120
Ashmore Islands, is., Austl.	B4	74
Ashoknagar, India	F6	54
Ashqelon, Isr.	G5	58
Ash-Shamāl, state, Leb.	D7	58
Ash-Shaqrā' see Shaqrā', Sau. Ar.	D6	56
Ash-Shāriqah, U.A.E.	D8	56
Ash-Shawbak, Jord.	H6	58
Ash-Shiḥr, Yemen	G6	56
Ash-Shurayf, Sau. Ar.	D4	56
Ashta, India	C2	53
Ashta, India	G6	54
Ashtabula, Oh., U.S.	C5	114
Ashtabula, Lake, res., N.D., U.S.	G16	124
Ashton, St. Vin.	p11	105e
Ashton, S. Afr.	H5	70
Ashton, Id., U.S.	F15	136
Ashton, Il., U.S.	C8	120
Ashton, Ne., U.S.	F14	126
Ashuanipi Lake, l., Nf., Can.	E17	106

Ashu-Bala I•5

Name	Map Ref.	Page
Ashuapmushuan, stm., Qc., Can.	B3	110
Ashûm, Egypt	H1	58
Ashville, Al., U.S.	D12	122
Ashwaubenon, Wi., U.S.	D1	112
Asi see Orontes, stm., Asia	B7	58
Asia, cont.	C19	4
Asia, Kepulauan, is., Indon.	E9	44
Asia Minor, hist. reg., Tur.	E13	28
Āsika, India	I10	54
Asinara, Golfo dell', b., Italy	D2	24
Asinara, Isola, i., Italy	C2	24
Asíni, hist., Grc.	F5	28
Asino, Russia	C15	32
Asintorf, Bela.	F13	10
Asipovičy, Bela.	G11	10
'Asīr, reg., Sau. Ar.	F5	56
Askham, S. Afr.	E5	70
Askiz, Russia	D16	32
Askja, vol., Ice.	k31	8a
Aslanapa, Tur.	D12	28
Aslantaş Barajı, res., Tur.	A7	58
Asmara see Asmera, Erit.	D7	62
Asmera, Erit.	D7	62
Ašmjany, Bela.	F8	10
Asola, Italy	E7	22
Asomante, P.R.	B2	104a
Āsosa, Eth.	E6	62
Asoteriba, Jabal, mtn., Sudan	C7	62
Asotin, Wa., U.S.	D9	136
Asouf, Oued, stm., Alg.	D5	64
Asp, Spain	F10	20
Aspe see Asp, Spain	F10	20
Aspen, Co., U.S.	D10	132
Aspendos, hist., Tur.	G14	28
Aspermont, Tx., U.S.	A7	130
Aspiring, Mount, mtn., N.Z.	G3	80
Assad, Lake see Asad, Buḩayrat al-, res., Syria	B9	58
As-Safīrah, Syria	B8	58
Aş-Şāfiyah, Sudan	D6	62
As-Salṭ, Jord.	F6	58
Assam, state, India	C7	46
As-Samāwah, Iraq	C6	56
Aş-Şanamayn, Syria	E7	58
Aş-Şarafand, Leb.	E6	58
Assaré, Braz.	D6	88
Assateague Island, i., U.S.	F10	114
Assateague Island National Seashore, p.o.i., U.S.	G10	114
Assemini, Italy	E2	24
Assen, Neth.	A15	14
Asseria, hist., Cro.	F12	22
Assiniboia, Sk., Can.	E8	124
Assiniboine, stm., Can.	E16	124
Assiniboine, Mount, mtn., Can.	F15	138
Assis, Braz.	D6	90
Assis Chateaubriand, Braz.	B11	92
Assisi, Italy	G9	22
Assomption, i., Sey.	k11	69b
Assu, Braz.	C7	88
As-Sudd, reg., Sudan	F6	62
As-Sufāl, Yemen	G6	56
As-Sulaymānīyah, Iraq	B6	56
As-Sulaymānīyah, Sau. Ar.	E6	56
As-Sulayyil, Sau. Ar.	E6	56
Assumption, Il., U.S.	E8	120
As-Suwaydā', Syria	F7	58
As-Suwaydā', state, Syria	F7	58
Astakós, Grc.	E3	28
Astana (Akmola), Kaz.	D12	32
Astara, Azer.	B6	56
Asti, Italy	F5	22
Astica, Arg.	E4	92
Astola Island, i., Pak.	D9	56
Astorga, Spain	B4	20
Astoria, Il., U.S.	D7	120
Astoria, Or., U.S.	D3	136
Astove, i., Sey.	I11	69b
Astrahan', Russia	E7	32
Astrakhan see Astrahan', Russia	E7	32
Astrašycki Haradok, Bela.	F10	10
Astrolabe, Cape, c., Sol. Is.	e9	79b
Astrolabe, Récifs de l', rf., N. Cal.	I15	79d
Astrolabe Reefs see Astrolabe, Récifs de l', rf., N. Cal.	I15	79d
Astrouna, Bela.	E12	10
Astudillo, Spain	B6	20
Asturias, state, Spain	A5	20
Astypálaia, i., Grc.	G9	28
Asunción, Para.	B9	92
Asunción, Bahía la, b., Mex.	B1	100
Asunción Nochixtlán, Mex.	G10	100
Åsunden, l., Swe.	H5	8
Asveja, Bela.	E11	10
Asvejskae, vozero, l., Bela.	D10	10
Aswân, Egypt	C6	62
Aswan High Dam see Aali, Sadd el-, dam, Egypt	C6	62
Asyût, Egypt	K2	58
Asyûti, Wadi el- (Asyūṭī, Wādī al-), stm., Egypt	K2	58
'Ata, i., Tonga	F9	72
Atabapo, stm., S.A.	F8	86
Atacama, state, Chile	C3	92
Atacama, Desierto de, des., Chile	E2	90
Atacama, Puna de, plat., S.A.	B4	92
Atacama, Salar de, pl., Chile	D3	90
Atacama Desert see Atacama, Desierto de, des., Chile	B3	92
Ataco, Col.	F4	86
Atagaj, Russia	C17	32
Atakpamé, Togo	H5	64
Atalaia, Braz.	E7	88
Atambua, Indon.	G7	44
Atami, Japan	D12	40
Atangmik, Grnld.	E15	141
Aṭar, Maur.	E2	64
Atascadero, Ca., U.S.	H5	134
Atascosa, stm., Tx., U.S.	F9	130
Atasu, Kaz.	E12	32
Atata, i., Tonga	n14	78e
Atatürk Barajı, res., Tur.	A9	58
Atauro, Pulau, i., E. Timor	G8	44
'Aṭbarah, Sudan	D6	62
'Aṭbarah, stm., Afr.	D7	62
Atbasar, Kaz.	D11	32
Atchafalaya, stm., La., U.S.	G7	122
Atchafalaya Bay, b., La., U.S.	H7	122
Atchison, Ks., U.S.	E2	120
Ateca, Spain	C9	20
Aterno, stm., Italy	H10	22
Atfîh, Egypt	I2	58
Ath, Bel.	D12	14
Athabasca, Ab., Can.	B17	138
Athabasca, stm., Ab., Can.	D8	106
Athabasca, Lake, l., Can.	D9	106
Athalmer, B.C., Can.	F14	138
Athboy, Ire.	H6	12
Athena, Or., U.S.	E8	136
Athens, On., Can.	D14	112
Athens see Athína, Grc.	E6	28
Athens, Al., U.S.	C11	122
Athens, Ga., U.S.	C2	116
Athens, Il., U.S.	E8	120
Athens, La., U.S.	E5	122
Athens, Mi., U.S.	F4	112
Athens, Oh., U.S.	E3	114
Athens, Pa., U.S.	C9	114
Athens, Tn., U.S.	B14	122
Athens, Tx., U.S.	E3	122
Athens, W.V., U.S.	G5	114
Atherton, Austl.	A5	76
Athi, stm., Kenya	E7	66
Athiaínou, Cyp.	C4	58
Athína (Athens), Grc.	E6	28
Athlone, Ire.	H4	12
Athni, India	C2	53
Athok, Mya.	D2	48
Athol, Ma., U.S.	B13	114
Áthos, mtn., Grc.	C7	28
Athos, Mount see Áthos, mtn., Grc.	C7	28
Ati, Chad	E3	62
Atiak, Ug.	D6	66
Atico, Peru	G3	84
Atienza, Spain	C8	20
Atikokan, On., Can.	C7	118
Atirāmpattinam, India	F4	53
Atiu, i., Cook Is.	F11	72
Atka, Russia	D19	34
Atka Island, i., Ak., U.S.	g24	140a
Atkarsk, Russia	D6	32
Atkins, Ar., U.S.	B6	122
Atkinson, Il., U.S.	C8	120
Atkinson, N.C., U.S.	B7	116
Atlanta, Ga., U.S.	C1	116
Atlanta, Il., U.S.	D8	120
Atlanta, Mi., U.S.	C5	112
Atlanta, Mo., U.S.	E5	120
Atlantic, Ia., U.S.	C2	120
Atlantic, N.C., U.S.	B9	116
Atlantic Beach, Fl., U.S.	F4	116
Atlantic City, N.J., U.S.	E11	114
Atlantic-Indian Basin, unds.	O5	142
Atlantic-Indian Ridge, unds.	N15	144
Atlántico, state, Col.	B4	86
Atlantic Ocean	E9	144
Atlantic Peak, mtn., Wy., U.S.	E3	126
Atlas Mountains, mts., Afr.	C4	64
Atlasova, ostrov, i., Russia	F20	34
Atlas Saharien, mts., Alg.	C4	64
Atlin, B.C., Can.	D4	106
Atlin Lake, l., Can.	D4	106
'Atlit, Isr.	F5	58
Ātmakūr, India	D4	53
Atmore, Al., U.S.	F11	122
Atnarko, stm., B.C., Can.	D5	138
Atocha, Bol.	D3	90
Atoka, Ok., U.S.	C2	122
Atotonilco, Cerro, mtn., Mex.	H3	130
Atoyac, stm., Mex.	F9	100
Atoyac de Álvarez, Mex.	G8	100
Atrak (Atrek), stm., Asia	B7	56
Ätran, stm., Swe.	H5	8
Atrato, stm., Col.	D3	86
Atrauli, India	D7	54
Atrek (Atrak), stm., Asia	B7	56
Atri, Italy	H10	22
Atsumi, Japan	E10	40
Atsumi-hantō, pen., Japan	E10	40
Aṭ-Ṭafīlah, Jord.	H6	58
Aṭ-Ṭafīlah, state, Jord.	H6	58
At-Tā'if, Sau. Ar.	E5	56
At-Tall, Syria	E7	58
Attalla, Al., U.S.	C12	122
Attapu, Laos	E8	48
Attawapiskat, On., Can.	E14	106
Attawapiskat, stm., On., Can.	E13	106
Attawapiskat Lake, l., On., Can.	E13	106
Aṭ-Ṭawīl, mts., Sau. Ar.	D4	56
Aṭ-Ṭayyibah, Syria	C9	58
Attendorn, Ger.	E3	16
Attersee, l., Aus.	C10	22
Attica, In., U.S.	H2	112
Attica, Ks., U.S.	D10	128
Attica, N.Y., U.S.	B7	114
Attica see Attikí, hist. reg., Grc.	E6	28
Attikí, state, Grc.	F6	28
Attikí, hist. reg., Grc.	E6	28
Attleboro, Ma., U.S.	C14	114
Attock, Pak.	B4	54
Attu, Ak., U.S.	g21	140a
Attu Island, i., Ak., U.S.	g21	140a
Āttūr, India	F4	53
Aṭ-Ṭuwayshah, Sudan	E5	62
Atuel, stm., Arg.	G3	92
Atuel, Bañados del, sw., Arg.	H4	92
Atuntaqui, Ec.	G2	86
Atuona, Fr. Poly.	s18	78g
Atwater, Ca., U.S.	F5	134
Atwater, Mn., U.S.	F4	118
Atwood, Il., U.S.	E9	120
Atwood, Ks., U.S.	B7	128
Atwood, Tn., U.S.	I9	120
Atyrau, Kaz.	E8	32
Aua Island, i., Pap. N. Gui.	a3	79a
Auari, stm., Braz.	F9	86
Auau Channel, strt., Hi., U.S.	C5	78a
Aubagne, Fr.	F11	18
Aube, state, Fr.	F13	14
Aube, stm., Fr.	F13	14
Aubigny-sur-Nère, Fr.	G11	14
Aubinadong, stm., On., Can.	A6	112
Aubrey Cliffs, clf, Az., U.S.	H3	132
Aubrey Lake, res., On., Can.	A6	112
Aubry Lake, l., N.T., Can.	B5	106
Auburn, Al., U.S.	E13	122
Auburn, Ca., U.S.	E4	134
Auburn, Il., U.S.	E8	120
Auburn, In., U.S.	G4	112
Auburn, Ky., U.S.	H11	120
Auburn, Me., U.S.	F6	110
Auburn, Ma., U.S.	B14	114
Auburn, Mi., U.S.	E5	112
Auburn, N.Y., U.S.	B9	114
Auburn, Wa., U.S.	C4	136
Auburn, stm., Austl.	E8	76
Aubusson, Fr.	D8	18
Auca Mahuida, Cerro, mtn., Arg.	H3	92
Auce, Lat.	D5	10
Auch, Fr.	F6	18
Auchi, Nig.	H6	64
Aucilla, stm., U.S.	F2	116
Auckland, N.Z.	C6	80
Auckland Islands, is., N.Z.	I7	72
Aude, state, Fr.	F8	18
Aude, stm., Fr.	F9	18
Auden, On., Can.	A11	118
Audenarde see Oudenaarde, Bel.	D12	14
Audierne, Fr.	F4	14
Audincourt, Fr.	G15	14
Audubon Lake, res., N.D., U.S.	G12	124
Aue, Ger.	F8	16
Augathella, Austl.	E6	76
Augrabies Falls National Park, p.o.i., S. Afr.	F4	70
Augrabiesvalle, wtfl, S. Afr.	F5	70
Augsburg, Ger.	H6	16
Augusta, Austl.	F2	74
Augusta, Italy	G9	24
Augusta, Ar., U.S.	B7	122
Augusta, Ga., U.S.	C3	116
Augusta, Il., U.S.	D6	120
Augusta, Ky., U.S.	F1	114
Augusta, Me., U.S.	F7	110
Augusta, Mt., U.S.	C14	136
Augusta, Wi., U.S.	G7	118
Augusto Severo, Braz.	C7	88
Augustów, Pol.	C18	16
Augustowski, Kanał, can., Eur.	C19	16
Augustus, Mount, mtn., Austl.	D3	74
Auki, Sol. Is.	e9	79b
Aukstaitijos nacionalnis parkas, p.o.i., Lith.	E8	10
Aulander, N.C., U.S.	H8	114
Auld, Lake, l., Austl.	D4	74
Aulla, Italy	F6	22
Aulne, stm., Fr.	F5	14
Aulneau Peninsula, pen., On., Can.	B4	118
Aumale, Fr.	E10	14
Auna, Nig.	G5	64
Auob, stm., Afr.	E5	70
Auraiya, India	E7	54
Aurangābād, India	B2	53
Aurangābād, India	F10	54
Aure, Nor.	E3	8
Aurelia, Ia., U.S.	B2	120
Aurich, Ger.	C3	16
Aurilândia, Braz.	G7	84
Aurillac, Fr.	E8	18
Aurine, Alpi (Zillertaler Alpen), mts., Eur.	C8	22
Aurora, On., Can.	D10	112
Aurora, Co., U.S.	B4	128
Aurora, Il., U.S.	C9	120
Aurora, In., U.S.	E13	120
Aurora, Me., U.S.	F8	110
Aurora, Mn., U.S.	D6	118
Aurora, N.Y., U.S.	B9	114
Aurora, N.C., U.S.	A9	116
Aurora, Oh., U.S.	C4	114
Aurora, Ut., U.S.	E4	132
Aurora, W.V., U.S.	E6	114
Aurora do Norte, Braz.	G2	88
Aursunden, l., Nor.	E4	8
Aurukun, Austl.	B8	74
Aus, Nmb.	E3	70
Ausable, stm., On., Can.	E8	112
Au Sable, stm., Mi., U.S.	D6	112
Au Sable Forks, N.Y., U.S.	F3	110
Au Sable Point, c., Mi., U.S.	D6	112
Auschwitz see Oświęcim, Pol.	F15	16
Aust-Agder, state, Nor.	G3	8
Austin, In., U.S.	F12	120
Austin, Mn., U.S.	H6	118
Austin, Nv., U.S.	D8	134
Austin, Pa., U.S.	C7	114
Austin, Tx., U.S.	D10	130
Austin, Lake, l., Austl.	E3	74
Australes, Îles, is., Fr. Poly.	F11	72
Australia, ctry., Oc.	D5	74
Australian Capital Territory, state, Austl.	J7	76
Austral Islands see Australes, Îles, is., Fr. Poly.	F11	72
Austral Seamounts, unds.	L24	142
Austria, ctry., Eur.	C11	22
Austvågøya, i., Nor.	B6	8
Ausuittuq (Grise Fiord), Nu., Can.	B9	141
Autlán de Navarro, Mex.	F6	100
Autun, Fr.	H13	14
Auvergne, hist. reg., Fr.	D8	18
Auxerre, Fr.	G12	14
Auxier, Ky., U.S.	G3	114
Auxi-le-Château, Fr.	D11	14
Auxvasse, Mo., U.S.	E6	120
Auyán Tepuy, mtn., Ven.	E10	86
Auzances, Fr.	C8	18
Auzangate, Nevado, mtn., Peru	F3	84
Ava, Mo., U.S.	H5	120
Avaí, Braz.	L1	88
Avala, hist., Yugo.	E7	26
Avallon, Fr.	G12	14
Avalon, Ca., U.S.	J7	134
Ávalos, Mex.	A5	100
Avanersuaq see Nordgrønland, state, Grnld.	B14	141
Avant, Ok., U.S.	H1	120
Avaré, Braz.	L1	88
Avarua, Cook Is.	a26	78j
Avarua Harbour, b., Cook Is.	a26	78j
Avatiu Harbour, b., Cook Is.	a26	78j
'Avedat, Horvot, hist., Isr.	H5	58
Aveiro, Port.	D2	20
Aveiro, state, Port.	D2	20
Aveiro, Ria de, mth., Port.	D1	20
Avellaneda, Arg.	D8	92
Avellaneda, Arg.	G8	92
Avellino, Italy	D8	24
Averøya, i., Nor.	E2	8
Aversa, Italy	D8	24
Avery, Id., U.S.	C11	136
Avery, Tx., U.S.	D4	122
Avery Island, La., U.S.	H6	122
Aves, Islas de, is., Ven.	B8	86
Avesnes-sur-Helpe, Fr.	D12	14
Avesta, Swe.	F6	8
Aveyron, state, Fr.	E8	18
Aveyron, stm., Fr.	E7	18
Avezzano, Italy	H10	22
Avigliano, Italy	D9	24
Avignon, Fr.	F10	18
Ávila, Spain	D6	20
Ávila, co., Spain	D6	20
Ávila, Sierra de, mts., Spain	D5	20
Avilés, Spain	A4	20
Aviño, Spain	A2	20
Avinurme, Est.	B9	10
Avispa, Cerro, mtn., Ven.	G9	86
Avoca, Austl.	K4	76
Avoca, Ia., U.S.	C2	120
Avoca, N.Y., U.S.	B8	114
Avoca, stm., Austl.	K4	76
Avola, B.C., Can.	E11	138
Avola, Italy	H9	24
Avon, Il., U.S.	D7	120
Avon, Mn., U.S.	F4	118
Avon, N.Y., U.S.	B8	114
Avon, N.C., U.S.	A10	116
Avon, stm., Eng., U.K.	K11	12
Avon, stm., Eng., U.K.	I11	12
Avon, stm., Eng., U.K.	J10	12
Avondale, Az., U.S.	J4	132
Avondale, Co., U.S.	C4	128
Avon Downs, Austl.	D7	74
Avon Park, Fl., U.S.	I4	116
Avontuur, S. Afr.	H6	70
Avranches, Fr.	F7	14
Awaaso, Ghana	H4	64
Awaji, Japan	E8	40
Awaji-shima, i., Japan	E7	40
Awara, Japan	C9	40
Āwarē, Eth.	F8	62
Āwasa, Eth.	F7	62
Āwash, Eth.	F8	62
Āwash, stm., Eth.	E8	62
Awa-shima, i., Japan	A12	40
Awbārī, Libya	B2	62
Awbārī, Şaḩrā', reg., Libya	B2	62
Awe, Loch, l., Scot., U.K.	E7	12
Awegyun, Mya.	F4	48
Awjilah, Libya	B4	62
Awled Djellal, Alg.	C6	64
Awlef, Alg.	D5	64
Awul, Pap. N. Gui.	b5	79a
Axel Heiberg Island, i., Nu., Can.	A7	141
Axim, Ghana	I4	64
Axiós (Vardar), stm., Eur.	C5	28
Axis, Al., U.S.	G10	122
Axixá, Braz.	B3	88
Axtell, Ks., U.S.	L2	118
Axtell, Ne., U.S.	G13	126
Ayabe, Japan	D8	40
Ayacucho, Arg.	H8	92
Ayacucho, Peru	F3	84
Ayakkum Hu, l., China	D2	36
Ayakoz see Ajaguz, Kaz.	E13	32
Ayam, C. Iv.	H4	64
Ayamonte, Spain	G3	20
Ayapel, Col.	C4	86
Ayaş, Tur.	C15	28
Ayaviri, Peru	F3	84
Aydın, Tur.	F10	28
Aydın, state, Tur.	F11	28
Aydınkent, Tur.	F14	28
Ayer, Ma., U.S.	B14	114
Ayers Rock see Uluru, mtn., Austl.	E6	74
Ayeyarwady, state, Mya.	D2	48
Ayeyarwady (Irrawaddy), stm., Mya.	E8	46
Ayeyarwady, Mouths of the, mth., Mya.	E7	46
Aylesbury, Eng., U.K.	J12	12
Aylmer, On., Can.	F8	112
Aylmer, Qc., Can.	C14	112
Aylmer Lake, l., N.T., Can.	C9	106
Aylsham, Sk., Can.	A10	124
'Ayn Dār, Sau. Ar.	D6	56
Aynor, S.C., U.S.	B6	116
'Aynūnah, Sau. Ar.	J6	58
Ayon Island see Aën, ostrov, i., Russia	B22	34
Ayora see Aiora, Spain	E9	20
Ayorou, Niger	G5	64
'Ayoûn el 'Atroûs, Maur.	F3	64
Ayr, Austl.	B6	76
Ayr, Scot., U.K.	F8	12
Ayrancı, Tur.	A4	58
Ayre, Point of, c., I. of Man	G8	12
Āysha, Eth.	E8	62
Aytos see Ajtos, Blg.	G14	26
Ayutla, Mex.	E6	100
Ayutla de los Libres, Mex.	G9	100
Ayvacık, Tur.	D9	28
Ayvalık, Tur.	D9	28
Azaila, Spain	C10	20
Āzamgarh, India	E9	54
Azángaro, Peru	F3	84
Azaouâd, reg., Mali	F4	64
Azare, Nig.	G6	64
Azaryčy, Bela.	H12	10
A'zāz, Syria	B8	58
Azdavay, Tur.	B16	28
Azeffâl, sand, Afr.	E2	64
Azerbaijan, ctry., Asia	A6	56
Azëry, Bela.	G7	10
Āzezo, Eth.	E7	62
Azhikode, India	F2	53
Azilal, Mor.	C3	64
Azogues, Ec.	I2	86
Azores see Açores, is., Port.	C3	60
Azores Plateau, unds.	E10	144
Azov, Russia	E5	32
Azov, Sea of, Eur.	E5	32
Azovskoje more see Azov, Sea of, Eur.	E5	32
Azraq, Al-Baḩr al- see Blue Nile, stm., Afr.	E6	62
Aztec, N.M., U.S.	G9	132
Aztec Peak, mtn., Az., U.S.	J5	132
Aztec Ruins National Monument, p.o.i., N.M., U.S.	G8	132
Azua, Dom. Rep.	C12	102
Azuaga, Spain	F5	20
Azuay, state, Ec.	I2	86
Azuer, stm., Spain	F7	20
Azuero, Península de, pen., Pan.	D1	86
Azufre, Volcán, vol., S.A.	B3	92
Azuga, Rom.	D12	26
Azul, Arg.	H8	92
Azur, Côte d', cst., Fr.	F13	18
Azurduy, Bol.	C4	90
Azure Lake, l., B.C., Can.	D10	138
Az-Zahrān, Sau. Ar.	D6	56
Az-Zarqā', Jord.	F7	58
Az-Zarqā', state, Jord.	G8	58
Az-Zāwiyah, Libya	A2	62
Azzel Matti, Sebkha, pl., Alg.	D5	64

B

Name	Map Ref.	Page
Ba, Fiji	p18	79e
Ba, stm., China	F6	42
Ba, stm., China	F2	42
Ba, stm., Viet.	F9	48
Baa, Indon.	H7	44
Baaba, Île, i., N. Cal.	I14	79d
Baao, Phil.	D4	52
Baardheere, Som.	D8	66
Baba Burnu, c., Tur.	D9	28
Babadağ, Tur.	F11	28
Babaeski, Tur.	B10	28
Babaevo, Russia	A18	10
Babahoyo, Ec.	H2	86
Babak, Phil.	G5	52
Babanango, S. Afr.	F10	70
Babanūsah, Sudan	E5	62
Babar, Kepulauan, is., Indon.	G8	44
Babbitt, Mn., U.S.	D7	118
Babbitt, Nv., U.S.	E7	134
B'abdā, Leb.	E6	58
Babeldaob, i., Palau	g7	78b
Bab el Mandeb see Mandeb, Bab el, strt.	E8	62
Babia, Arroyo de la, stm., Mex.	F5	130
Babian, stm., China	A5	48
Babičy, Bela.	H12	10
Babīna, India	F7	54
Babinda, Austl.	A5	76
Babine, stm., B.C., Can.	D5	106
Babine Lake, l., B.C., Can.	B5	138
Babine Range, mts., B.C., Can.	B4	138
Babino, Russia	A14	10
Babiogórski Park Narodowy, p.o.i., Pol.	G15	16
Babo, Indon.	F9	44
Bābol, Iran	B7	56
Baboquivari Peak, mtn., Az., U.S.	L5	132
Baborów, Pol.	F13	16
Babrujsk, Bela.	G12	10
Babuškin, Russia	F10	34
Babuyan Channel, strt., Phil.	A3	52
Babuyan Island, i., Phil.	A4	52
Babuyan Islands, is., Phil.	A3	52
Bacabal, Braz.	C3	88
Bacadéhuachi, Mex.	G8	98
Bacatuba, Braz.	C4	88
Bacău, Rom.	C13	26
Bacău, state, Rom.	C13	26
Bac Binh, Viet.	G9	48
Baccarat, Fr.	F15	14
Bačėjkava, Bela.	F12	10
Bac Giang, Viet.	B8	48
Bachaquero, Ven.	B6	86
Bachiniva, Mex.	A5	100
Bach Ma, Viet.	D8	48
Bach Thong, Viet.	A7	48
Bachu, China	B12	56
Back, stm., Nu., Can.	B11	106
Bačka, reg., Eur.	E16	22
Bačka Palanka, Yugo.	D6	26
Bačka Topola, Yugo.	D6	26
Back Creek, stm., Va., U.S.	F6	114
Backnang, Ger.	H5	16
Backstairs Passage, strt., Austl.	J1	76
Bac Lieu, Viet.	H7	48
Bac Ninh, Viet.	B8	48
Baco, Mount, mtn., Phil.	D3	52
Bacoachi, Mex.	F8	98
Bacolod, Phil.	E4	52
Baconton, Ga., U.S.	E1	116
Bacoor, Phil.	C3	52
Bac Phan, hist. reg., Viet.	A7	48
Bács-Kiskun, state, Hung.	C6	26
Bâcu, stm., Mol.	C15	26
Bacuri, Lago do, l., Braz.	B4	88
Bād, Iran	C7	56
Bad, stm., Mi., U.S.	E5	112
Bad, stm., S.D., U.S.	C12	126
Badagara, India	F2	53
Badajós, Lago, l., Braz.	D5	84
Badajoz, Spain	F4	20
Badajoz, co., Spain	F4	20
Badalona, Spain	C13	20
Bādāmi, India	D2	53
Badanah, Sau. Ar.	C5	56
Badarīnāth, India	C7	54
Badas, Bru.	A9	50
Badas, Kepulauan, is., Indon.	C5	50
Bad Axe, Mi., U.S.	E7	112
Bad Bergzabern, Ger.	G3	16
Bad Bevensen, Ger.	C6	16
Bad Bramstedt, Ger.	C5	16
Baddeck, N.S., Can.	D16	110
Bad Doberan, Ger.	B7	16
Bad Dürrenberg, Ger.	E8	16
Bad Ems, Ger.	F3	16
Baden, Switz.	C5	22
Baden-Baden, Ger.	H4	16
Badenoch, hist. reg., Scot., U.K.	E8	12
Badenweiler, Ger.	I3	16
Baden-Württemberg, state, Ger.	H4	16
Bad Freienwalde, Ger.	D9	16
Badgastein, Aus.	C10	22
Badger, Mn., U.S.	C3	118
Bad Hall, Aus.	B11	22
Bad Harzburg, Ger.	E6	16
Bad Hersfeld, Ger.	F5	16
Bad Homburg vor der Höhe, Ger.	F4	16
Bad Honnef, Ger.	F3	16
Badin Lake, res., N.C., U.S.	A5	116
Bad Ischl, Aus.	C10	22
Bad Kissingen, Ger.	F6	16
Bad Kreuznach, Ger.	G3	16
Badlands, hills, U.S.	A9	126
Badlands, hills, S.D., U.S.	D10	126
Badlands National Park, p.o.i., S.D., U.S.	D10	126
Bad Langensalza, Ger.	E6	16
Bad Lauterberg im Harz, Ger.	E6	16
Bad Mergentheim, Ger.	G5	16
Bad Muskau, Ger.	E10	16
Bad Nauheim, Ger.	F4	16
Badnera, India	H6	54
Bad Neustadt an der Saale, Ger.	F6	16
Bad Oeynhausen, Ger.	D4	16
Bad Oldesloe, Ger.	C6	16
Badong, China	F4	42
Bad Orb, Ger.	F5	16
Bad Pyrmont, Ger.	E5	16
Bad Reichenhall, Ger.	I8	16
Bad Salzuflen, Ger.	D4	16
Bad Salzungen, Ger.	F6	16
Bad Schwalbach, Ger.	F3	16
Bad Schwartau, Ger.	C6	16
Bad Segeberg, Ger.	C6	16
Bādshāhpur, India	F9	54
Bad Tölz, Ger.	I7	16
Badulla, Sri L.	H5	53
Badvel, India	D4	53
Bad Vöslau, Aus.	C13	22
Bad Waldsee, Ger.	I5	16
Bad Wildungen, Ger.	E4	16
Bad Wörishofen, Ger.	I6	16
Badžalskij hrebet, mts., Russia	F15	34
Baena, Spain	G6	20
Baependi, Braz.	K3	88
Baer, Russia	C17	32
Baeza, Spain	G7	20
Baezaeko, stm., B.C., Can.	D7	138
Bafang, Cam.	C1	66
Bafatá, Gui.-B.	G2	64
Baffin Basin, unds.	A7	144
Baffin Bay, b., N.A.	C12	141
Baffin Bay, b., Tx., U.S.	G10	130
Baffin Island, i., Nu., Can.	B16	106
Bafia, Cam.	D2	66
Bafing, stm., Afr.	G2	64
Bafoulabé, Mali	G2	64
Bafoussam, Cam.	C2	66
Bafra, Tur.	A4	56
Bāft, Iran	D8	56
Bafwaboli, D.R.C.	D5	66
Bafwasende, D.R.C.	D5	66
Bagaces, C.R.	G5	102
Bagagem, stm., Braz.	H1	88
Bagaha, India	E9	54
Bāgalkot, India	C2	53
Bagamoyo, Tan.	F7	66
Bagan Datuk, Malay.	K5	48
Baganga, Phil.	G6	52
Bagansiapiapi, Indon.	B2	50
Bagasra, India	H3	54
Bagdad, Az., U.S.	I3	132
Bagdad, Fl., U.S.	G11	122
Bagdarin, Russia	F11	34
Bagé, Braz.	E10	92
Bagenkop, Den.	B6	16
Bāgerhāt, Bngl.	G12	54
Bāgevādi, India	C2	53
Baghdād, Iraq	C5	56
Bagheria, Italy	F7	24
Baghlān, Afg.	B10	56
Bagley, Mn., U.S.	D3	118
Bagnères-de-Luchon, Fr.	G6	18
Bagni di Lucca, Italy	F7	22
Bagnols-sur-Cèze, Fr.	E10	18
Bago (Pegu), Mya.	D3	48
Bago, state, Mya.	C2	48
Bagodar, India	F10	54
Bagoé, stm., Afr.	G3	64
Bağpınar, Tur.	A9	58
Baguio, Phil.	B3	52
Bāh, India	E7	54
Bahādurgarh, India	D6	54
Bahama, Canal Viejo de, strt., N.A.	A8	102
Bahamas, ctry., N.A.	C9	96
Baharampur, India	F11	54
Bahau, Malay.	K6	48
Bahau, stm., Indon.	B9	50
Bahāwalnagar, Pak.	C4	54
Bahāwalpur, Pak.	D3	54
Bahçe, Tur.	A7	58
Baheri, India	D7	54
Bahi, Phil.	D4	52
Bahia see Salvador, Braz.	G6	88
Bahia, state, Braz.	G4	88
Bahía, Islas de la, is., Hond.	D4	102
Bahía Blanca, Arg.	I6	92
Bahía Bustamante, Arg.	I3	90
Bahía de Caráquez, Ec.	H1	86
Bahía Kino, Mex.	A3	100
Bahir Dar, Eth.	E7	62
Bahraich, India	E8	54
Bahrain, ctry., Asia	D7	56
Bahta, Russia	B15	32
Bahtîm, Egypt	H2	58
Bahty, Kaz.	E14	32
Bahušèųsk, Bela.	F13	10
Bai, stm., China	A7	42
Bai, stm., China	E5	42
Baia de Aramă, Rom.	E9	26
Baia di Terra Nova, sci., Ant.	C21	81
Baía Farta, Ang.	C1	68
Baia Mare, Rom.	B10	26
Baião, Braz.	B1	88
Baicheng, China	F14	32
Baicheng, China	B9	36
Baidoa see Baydhabo, Som.	D8	66
Baie-Comeau, Qc., Can.	A8	110
Baiersbronn, Ger.	H4	16
Baie-Saint-Paul, Qc., Can.	C6	110
Baie-Trinité, Qc., Can.	A9	110
Baie Verte, Nf., Can.	j22	107a
Baihe, China	B11	46
Baijnāth, India	D7	54
Baikal, Lake see Bajkal, ozero, l., Russia	F10	34
Baikal Mountains see Bajkal'skij hrebet, mts., Russia	F10	34
Baikonur see Bajkonur, Kaz.	E11	32
Bailadores, Ven.	C6	86
Baile Átha Cliath see Dublin, Ire.	H6	12
Baile Átha Luain see Athlone, Ire.	H4	12
Băile Govora, Rom.	D11	26
Bailén, Spain	F7	20
Băileşti, Rom.	F10	26
Bailey, N.C., U.S.	I7	114
Bail Hongal, India	D2	53
Bailicun, China	I4	42
Bailique, Ilha, i., Braz.	C8	84
Baillie Islands, is., N.T., Can.	B14	140
Baillif, Guad.	h5	105c
Bailong, stm., China	E1	42
Bailu Hu, l., China	G5	42
Bailundo, Ang.	C2	68
Baimamiao, China	C2	42
Baima Shan, mtn., China	H4	42
Baimuru, Pap. N. Gui.	b3	79a
Bainbridge, Ga., U.S.	G14	122
Bainbridge, N.Y., U.S.	B10	114
Bain-de-Bretagne, Fr.	G7	14
Baing, Indon.	I12	50
Bainville, Mt., U.S.	F9	124
Baio Grande, Spain	A2	20
Baiona, Spain	B2	20
Baipeng, China	I3	42
Baipu, China	E9	42
Baiquan, China	B10	36
Baird, Tx., U.S.	B8	130
Baird Mountains, mts., Ak., U.S.	C7	140
Baird Peninsula, pen., Nu., Can.	B15	106
Bairiki, Kir.	C8	72
Bairin Zuoqi, China	C8	36
Bairnsdale, Austl.	K6	76
Baïse, stm., Fr.	F6	18
Baisha, China	G2	42
Baisha, China	L3	42
Baisha, China	I8	42
Baishe, China	H7	42
Baishuijiang, China	E2	42
Baisogala, Lith.	E6	10
Baiwang, China	I3	42
Baixingt, China	C4	38
Baixio, Braz.	D6	88
Baiyan Shan, mtn., China	H8	42
Baiyin, China	D5	36
Baiyü, China	E4	36
Baja, Hung.	C5	26
Baja, Punta, c., Chile	e29	78l
Baja California, state, Mex.	F5	98
Baja California, pen., Mex.	B2	96
Baja California Sur, state, Mex.	C2	100
Bajada del Agrio, Arg.	I2	92
Baján, Mex.	H6	130
Bajan, Mong.	B7	36
Bajanaul, Kaz.	D13	32
Bajangol, Russia	F9	34
Bajánsenye, Hung.	C3	26
Bajawa, Indon.	H12	50
Bajdarackaja guba, b., Russia	C2	34
Bajestān, Iran	C8	56
Bajkal, Russia	F9	34
Bajkal, ozero (Baikal, Lake), l., Russia	F10	34
Bajkal'skij hrebet, mts., Russia	F10	34
Bajkit, Russia	B17	32
Bajkonur, Kaz.	E11	32
Bajmak, Russia	D9	32
Bajmok, Yugo.	D6	26
Bajo, Indon.	H11	50
Bajo Boquete, Pan.	H6	102
Bajool, Austl.	D8	76
Bajramaly, Turkmen.	B9	56
Bajsun, Uzb.	G11	32
Bakacak, Tur.	C10	28
Bakala, C.A.R.	C4	66
Bakanas, Kaz.	F13	32
Bake, Indon.	E2	50
Bakel, Sen.	G2	64
Baker, Ca., U.S.	H9	134
Baker, Fl., U.S.	G12	122
Baker, La., U.S.	G7	122
Baker, Mt., U.S.	A8	126
Baker, Or., U.S.	F9	136
Baker, Mount, vol., Wa., U.S.	B5	136
Baker Butte, mtn., Az., U.S.	I5	132
Baker Island, i., Oc.	C9	72
Baker Lake see Qamani'tuaq, Nu., Can.	C11	106
Baker Lake, l., Austl.	E5	74
Baker Lake, l., Nu., Can.	C11	106
Bakersfield, Ca., U.S.	H7	134
Bâ Kêv, Camb.	F8	48
Bakharden, Turkmen.	B8	56
Bakhardok, Turkmen.	B8	56
Bakhtegān, Daryācheh-ye, l., Iran	D7	56
Bakı (Baku), Azer.	A6	56
Bakkafjörður, Ice.	j32	8a
Bakkaflói, b., Ice.	j32	8a
Baklan, Tur.	F12	28
Bako, C. Iv.	H3	64
Bako, Eth.	F7	62
Bakony, mts., Hung.	C4	26
Bakouma, C.A.R.	C4	66
Baku see Bakı, Azer.	A6	56
Bakumpai, Indon.	D8	50
Bakung, Pulau, i., Indon.	C4	50
Bakungan, Indon.	K3	48
Bakwanga see Mbuji-Mayi, D.R.C.	F4	66
Balâ, Tur.	D16	28
Balabac, Phil.	F1	52
Balabac Island, i., Phil.	G1	52
Balabac Strait, strt., Asia	G1	52
Ba'labakk, Leb.	D7	58
Balabalagan, Kepulauan, is., Indon.	E10	50
Balabanovo, Russia	E19	10
Balabio, Île, i., N. Cal.	m15	79d
Balad, Iraq	C5	56
Baladëk, Russia	F15	34
Bālāghāt, India	H8	54
Bālāghāt Range, mts., India	B3	53
Balagne, reg., Fr.	G14	18
Balaguer, Spain	C11	20
Balahna, Russia	H20	8
Balaikarangan, Indon.	C7	50
Balaisepuah, Indon.	C7	50
Balakirevo, Russia	D21	10
Balaklava, Austl.	J2	76
Balakovo, Russia	D7	32
Balama, Moz.	C6	68
Balambangan, Pulau, i., Malay.	G1	52
Bālā Morghāb, Afg.	B9	56
Balanga, Phil.	C3	52
Balāngīr, India	H9	54
Balapulang, Indon.	G6	50
Balarāmpur, India	G11	54

I • 6 Bala-Bayo

Name — Map Ref. — Page

Balašiha, Russia E20 10
Balašov, Russia D6 32
Balassagyarmat, Hung. A6 26
Balatina, Mol. B14 26
Balaton, Mn., U.S. G3 118
Balaton, l., Hung. C4 26
Balayan, Phil. D3 52
Balbieriškis, Lith. F6 10
Balbina, Represa, res., Braz. H12 86
Balcanoona, Austl. H2 76
Balcarce, Arg. H8 92
Balcarres, Sk., Can. D10 124
Bălcești, Rom. E10 26
Balcones Escarpment, clf, Tx., U.S. D9 130
Balde, Arg. F4 92
Bald Knob, Ar., U.S. B7 122
Bald Knob, mtn., Va., U.S. G6 114
Bald Mountain, mtn., Or., U.S. G5 136
Bald Mountain, mtn., Or., U.S. F3 136
Baldock Lake, l., Mb., Can. D11 106
Baldone, Lat. D7 10
Baldwin, La., U.S. H7 122
Baldwin, Mi., U.S. E4 112
Baldwin, Wi., U.S. G6 118
Baldwinsville, N.Y., U.S. E13 112
Baldwyn, Ms., U.S. C10 122
Baldy Mountain, mtn., Mb., Can. C13 124
Baldy Mountain, mtn., N.M., U.S. E3 128
Baldy Peak, mtn., Az., U.S. J7 132
Bâle see Basel, Switz. C4 22
Baleares see Balears, state, Spain E13 20
Baleares, Islas see Balears, Illes, is., Spain E12 20
Balearic Islands see Balears, state, Spain E13 20
Balearic Islands see Balears, Illes, is., Spain E12 20
Balears, state, Spain E13 20
Balears, Illes (Balearic Islands), is., Spain E12 20
Balease, Gunung, mtn., Indon. E12 50
Baleh, stm., Malay. C8 50
Baleia, Ponta da, c., Braz. I6 88
Baleine, stm., Qc., Can. D17 106
Baleine, Grande rivière de la, stm., Qc., Can. D15 106
Baleine, Petite rivière de la, stm., Qc., Can. D15 106
Balej, Russia F12 34
Baler, Phil. C3 52
Baler Bay, b., Phil. C3 52
Bāleshwar, India H11 54
Balezino, Russia C8 32
Balfate, Hond. E4 102
Balfour, N.C., U.S. A3 116
Balgazyn, Russia D17 32
Balhaš, ozero (Balkhash Lake), l., Kaz. E13 32
Bāli, India F4 54
Bali, state, Indon. G9 50
Bali, i., Indon. G9 50
Bali, Laut (Bali Sea), Indon. G9 50
Bali, Selat, strt., Indon. H9 50
Bali Barat National Park, p.o.i., Indon. H9 50
Baliceaux, i., St. Vin. p11 105e
Balige, Indon. B1 50
Balıkesir, Tur. D10 28
Balıkesir, state, Tur. D10 28
Balīkh, stm., Syria B10 58
Balikpapan, Indon. D10 50
Balimbing, Indon. F4 50
Balimbing, Phil. H2 52
Balimo, Pap. N. Gui. b3 79a
Balingen, Ger. H4 16
Balingian, Malay. B8 50
Balintang Channel, strt., Phil. K9 42
Bali Sea see Bali, Laut, Indon. G9 50
Bali Strait see Bali, Selat, strt., Indon. H9 50
Baliza, Braz. G7 84
Balkan Mountains, mts., Eur. G11 26
Balkan Peninsula, pen., Eur. B6 28
Balkaria see Kabardino-Balkarija, state, Russia F6 32
Balkh, Afg. B10 56
Balkhash, Lake see Balhaš, ozero, l., Kaz. E13 32
Ballachulish, Scot., U.K. E7 12
Balladonia, Austl. F4 74
Ballālpur, India B4 53
Ballangen, Nor. B7 8
Ballantine, Mt., U.S. B4 126
Ballarat, Austl. K4 76
Ballard, Lake, l., Austl. E4 74
Ballater, Scot., U.K. D9 12
Ball Bay, b., Norf. I. y25 78i
Ballenas, Bahía de, b., Mex. B2 100
Ballenita, Punta, c., Chile B2 92
Balleny Islands, is., Ant. B21 81
Balleza, Mex. B5 100
Balleza, stm., Mex. B5 100
Ball Ground, Ga., U.S. B1 116
Ballia, India F10 54
Ballina, Austl. G9 76
Ballina, Ire. G3 12
Ballina, Ire. I4 12
Ballinrobe, Ire. H3 12
Ballston Spa, N.Y., U.S. G2 110
Ballville, Oh., U.S. C2 114
Ballybunnion, Ire. I3 12
Ballyhaunis, Ire. H4 12
Ballymena, N. Ire., U.K. G6 12
Ballymoney, N. Ire., U.K. F6 12
Ballyrogan, Lake, l., Austl. I6 76
Balmaceda, Chile I2 90
Balmoral, Austl. K3 76
Balmorhea, Tx., U.S. C4 130
Balnearia, Arg. E6 92
Baloda Bāzār, India H9 54
Balombo, Ang. C1 68
Balong, Indon. G7 50
Balonne, stm., Austl. G7 76
Bālotra, India F4 54
Balphakram National Park, p.o.i., India F13 54
Balqash Köli see Balhaš, ozero, l., Kaz. E13 32
Balrāmpur, India E8 54
Balranald, Austl. J4 76
Balș, Rom. E11 26
Balsam Lake, Wi., U.S. F6 118
Balsam Lake, l., On., Can. D11 112
Balsas, Braz. D2 88
Balsas, stm., Braz. F2 88
Balsas, stm., Braz. D3 88
Balsas, stm., Mex. F8 100
Balsas, stm., Pan. C3 86
Balsthal, Switz. C4 22
Balta, Ukr. B16 26
Baltasar Brum, Ur. E9 92
Bălți, Mol. B14 26
Baltic Sea, Eur. D12 6
Baltijsk, Russia F2 10
Baltijskaja kosa, spit, Eur. F2 10
Baltijskoje more see Baltic Sea, Eur. D12 6
Baltim, Egypt G2 58
Baltimore, Ire. J3 12
Baltimore, Md., U.S. E9 114
Baltimore, Oh., U.S. E3 114
Ba Lu, stm., Viet. E9 48
Baluchistān, state, Pak. C2 54
Baluchistan, hist. reg., Asia D9 56
Balui, stm., Malay. B8 50
Bālurghāt, India F12 54
Balvi, Lat. C10 10
Balygyčan, Russia D19 34
Balykši, Kaz. E8 32
Balzac, Ab., Can. E16 138
Balzar, Ec. H2 86
Bam, Iran D8 56
Bama, China I2 42
Bama, Nig. G7 64
Bamaga, Austl. B8 74
Bamako, Mali G3 64
Bamba, Mali F4 64
Bambamarca, Peru E2 84
Bambana, stm., Nic. F6 102
Bambari, C.A.R. C4 66
Bambaroo, Austl. B6 76
Bamberg, Ger. G6 16
Bamberg, S.C., U.S. C4 116
Bambio, C.A.R. D3 66
Bambuí, Braz. K2 88
Bam Co, l., China C13 54
Bamenda, Cam. C1 66
Bami, Turkmen. B8 56
Bāmīān, Afg. C10 56
Bamingui, C.A.R. C4 66
Bampūr, Iran D9 56
Bāmra Hills, hills, India H10 54
Bamumo, China B14 54
Banaba, i., Kir. D7 72
Banabuiú, stm., Braz. C6 88
Banabuiú, Açude, l., Braz. C6 88
Banalia, D.R.C. D5 66
Banamba, Mali G3 64
Banana Islands, is., S.L. H2 64
Bananal, stm., Braz. E1 88
Bananal, Ilha do, i., Braz. F7 84
Banarlı, Tur. B10 28
Banās, stm., India E6 54
Banâs, Râs, c., Egypt C7 62
Banat, hist. reg., Eur. D7 26
Banaz, Tur. E12 28
Ban Ban, Laos C6 48
Ban Bouang-nom, Laos E8 48
Banbridge, N. Ire., U.K. G6 12
Ban Bung Na Rang, Thai. D5 48
Banbury, Eng., U.K. I11 12
Ban Cha La, Laos D7 48
Bancroft, On., Can. C12 112
Bancroft, Id., U.S. H15 136
Bancroft, Ia., U.S. H4 118
Bancroft, Ne., U.S. C1 120
Bānda, India F8 54
Banda, Kepulauan, is., Indon. F9 44
Banda, Laut (Banda Sea), Indon. G8 44
Banda Aceh, Indon. J2 48
Bānda Dāūd Shāh, Pak. B3 54
Banda del Río Salí, Arg. C5 92
Bandai-Asahi-kokuritsu-kōen, p.o.i., Japan B12 40
Bandai-san, vol., Japan B13 40
Bandama, stm., C. Iv. H3 64
Bandama Blanc, stm., C. Iv. H3 64
Ban Dan, Thai. E7 48
Ban Dangtai, Laos D7 48
Bandar Beheshtī, Iran D9 56
Bandarbeyla, Som. C10 66
Bandar-e ʿAbbās, Iran D8 56
Bandar-e Anzalī, Iran B6 56
Bandar-e Būshehr, Iran D7 56
Bandar-e Deylam, Iran D7 56
Bandar-e Lengeh, Iran D7 56
Bandar-e Māh Shahr, Iran C6 56
Bandar-e Moghūyeh, Iran D7 56
Bandar-e Torkeman, Iran B7 56
Bandar Seri Begawan, Bru. A9 50
Banda Sea see Banda, Laut, Indon. G8 44
Bandeira, Pico da, mtn., Braz. K5 88
Bandeirantes, Braz. F7 84
Bandelier National Monument, p.o.i., N.M., U.S. F2 128
Bandera, Arg. D6 92
Bandera, Alto, mtn., Dom. Rep. C12 102
Banderas, Mex. C2 130
Banderas, Bahía de, b., Mex. E6 100
Bandhavgarh National Park, p.o.i., India G8 54
Bāndhi, Pak. E2 54
Bandiagara, Mali G4 64
Bandiantaolehai, China C5 36
Bāndīkūi, India E6 54
Bandipura, India A5 54
Bandipur Tiger Reserve, India F3 53
Bandırma, Tur. C11 28
Bandon, Or., U.S. G2 136
Ban Don, Ao, b., Thai. H4 48
Ban Donhiang, Laos C5 48
Bandundu, D.R.C. E3 66
Bandung, Indon. G5 50
Banes, Cuba B10 102
Banff, Ab., Can. E15 138
Banff, Scot., U.K. D10 12
Banff National Park, p.o.i., Ab., Can. E15 138
Banfora, Burkina G4 64
Banga, D.R.C. F4 66
Banga, India C6 54
Banga, stm., Phil. G5 52
Bangalore, India E3 53
Bangaon, India G12 54
Bangassou, C.A.R. D4 66
Bangdag Co, l., China A8 54
Banggai, Indon. F7 44
Banggai, Kepulauan, is., Indon. F7 44
Banggi, Pulau, i., Malay. G1 52
Banggong Co, l., China B7 54
Banghāzī (Bengasi), Libya A3 62
Banghiang, stm., Laos D7 48
Bangil, Indon. G8 50
Bangka, Pulau, i., Indon. E5 50
Bangka, Selat, strt., Indon. E4 50
Bangkalan, Indon. G8 50
Bangkaru, Pulau, i., Indon. L3 48
Bangkinang, Indon. C2 50
Bangkir, Indon. C12 50
Bangko, Indon. E3 50
Bangkog Co, l., China C12 54
Bangkok see Krung Thep, Thai. F5 48
Bangladesh, ctry., Asia G13 54
Bang Lamung, Thai. F5 48
Bang Mun Nak, Thai. D5 48
Bangor, N. Ire., U.K. G7 12
Bangor, Wales, U.K. H8 12
Bangor, Me., U.S. F8 110
Bangor, Pa., U.S. D10 114
Bangriposi, India G11 54
Bangs, Tx., U.S. C8 130
Bangs, Mount, mtn., Az., U.S. G3 132
Bang Saphan, Thai. G4 48
Bangued, Phil. B3 52
Bangui, C.A.R. D3 66
Bangweulu, Lake, l., Zam. C4 68
Bangweulu Swamps, sw., Zam. C5 68
Bangxu, China J2 42
Ban Hatgnao, Laos E8 48
Ban Hèt, Laos E8 48
Ban Hom, Thai. E4 48
Ban Hong Muang, Laos D7 48
Ban Houayxay, Laos B5 48
Bani, C.A.R. C4 66
Baní, Dom. Rep. C12 102
Bani, Jbel, mts., Mor. D3 64
Baniara, Pap. N. Gui. b4 79a
Bani Bangou, Niger F5 64
Banihāl Pass, p., India B4 46
Banī Walīd, Libya A2 62
Bāniyās, Golan E6 58
Bāniyās, Syria C6 58
Banja Luka, Bos. E4 26
Banjarmasin, Indon. E9 50
Banjul (Bathurst), Gam. G1 64
Bānka, India F11 54
Banka Banka, Austl. C6 74
Ban Katèp, Laos D7 48
Ban Kèngkabao, Laos D7 48
Ban Kèngtangan, Laos D7 48
Ban Kheun, Laos B5 48
Ban Khuan Mao, Thai. I4 48
Ban Kruat, Thai. E6 48
Banks, Al., U.S. F13 122
Banks, Îles (Banks Islands), is., Vanuatu i16 79d
Banks Island, i., B.C., Can. E4 106
Banks Island, i., N.T., Can. B15 140
Banks Islands see Banks, Îles, is., Vanuatu i16 79d
Banks Lake, res., Wa., U.S. C7 136
Banks Peninsula, pen., N.Z. F5 80
Banks Strait, strt., Austl. n13 77a
Banks / Torres, state, Vanuatu i16 79d
Bānkura, India G11 54
Ban Mae La Luang, Thai. C3 48
Ban Mit, Laos C5 48
Ban Muangngat, Laos C6 48
Bann, stm., N. Ire., U.K. F6 12
Ban Nadou, Laos E7 48
Ban Nahin, Laos C7 48
Ban Nalan, Laos E7 48
Ban Nam Chan, Thai. C6 48
Ban Namnga, Laos B6 48
Ban Nam Thaeng, Thai. E7 48
Ban Naxouang, Laos C7 48
Bannertown, N.C., U.S. H5 114
Banning, Ca., U.S. J9 134
Ban Nong Lumphuk, Thai. E6 48
Bannu, Pak. B3 54
Bañolas see Banyoles, Spain B13 20
Baños, Ec. H2 86
Banow, Afg. B10 56
Ban Pak Bong, Thai. C4 48
Ban Pakkhop, Laos C5 48
Ban Pak Nam, Thai. G4 48
Ban Phai, Thai. D6 48
Ban Phai, Thai. D6 48
Ban Pho, Thai. F5 48
Ban Phông Pho, Laos E7 48
Ban Pong, Thai. F4 48
Ban Sa-ang, Laos D7 48
Ban Salik, Thai. C5 48
Ban Sam Pong, Laos C6 48
Ban Samrong, Thai. E6 48
Bānsda, India H4 54
Banshadhāra, stm., India B6 53
Banská Bystrica, Slov. H15 16
Banská Štiavnica, Slov. H14 16
Bansko, Blg. H10 26
Ban Songkhon, Laos C7 48
Bānswāra, India G5 54
Bantaeng, Indon. F11 50
Ban Takhlo, Thai. E5 48
Bantarkawung, Indon. G6 50
Bantayan, Phil. E4 52
Ban Thabôk, Laos C6 48
Ban Thapayi, Laos D7 48
Ban Tian Sa, Laos C6 48
Bantry, Ire. J3 12
Bantry Bay, b., Ire. J3 12
Ban Van Hom, Laos C7 48
Ban Xènkhalôk, Laos C5 48
Banya, Testa de la, c., Spain D11 20
Banyak, Kepulauan, is., Indon. K3 48
Ban Ya Plong, Thai. H4 48
Banyo, Cam. C2 66
Banyoles, Spain B13 20
Banyuwangi, Indon. H9 50
Banzare Coast, cst., Ant. B17 81
Baode, China B4 42
Baoding, China B6 42
Baofeng, China E5 42
Bao Ha, Viet. A7 48
Baoji, China D2 42
Baojing, China G3 42
Bao Lac, Viet. G8 48
Bao Lac, Viet. A7 48
Baolunyuan, China E1 42
Baoqing, China B11 36
Baoshan, China F4 36
Baoting, China L3 42
Baotou, China A4 42
Baoulé, stm., Mali G3 64
Baowei, China A8 48
Baoyi, China E7 42
Baoying, China E8 42
Bāpatla, India D5 53
Bapaume, Fr. D11 14
Baptiste Lake, res., On., Can. C12 112
Bāqa el Gharbiyya, Isr. F6 58
Baqing, China B14 54
Baʿqūbah, Iraq C5 56
Baquedano, Chile A3 92
Bar, Yugo. G6 26
Bara, Nig. G7 64
Baraawe, Som. D8 66
Barabinsk, Russia C13 32
Barabinskaja step', pl., Russia C13 32
Baraboo, Wi., U.S. H9 118
Baraboo, stm., Wi., U.S. H8 118
Baracaldo see Barakaldo, Spain A8 20
Baracoa, Cuba B10 102
Baradero, Arg. F8 92
Baradine, Austl. H7 76
Baraga, Mi., U.S. B1 112
Bārah, Sudan E6 62
Barahona, Dom. Rep. C12 102
Barak, Tur. B8 58
Barāk, stm., India F14 54
Barakaldo, Spain A8 20
Baraki, Afg. B2 54
Barakula, Austl. F8 76
Baralaba, Austl. E7 76
Baram, stm., Malay. A9 50
Barama, stm., Guy. D12 86
Bārāmati, India B2 53
Bāramūla, India A5 54
Baran', Bela. F13 10
Bārān, India F6 54
Baranagar, India G12 54
Baranavičy, Bela. G9 10
Barangbarang, Indon. G12 50
Baranoa, Col. B4 86
Baranof Island, i., Ak., U.S. E12 140
Barany, Russia C12 10
Baranya, state, Hung. D5 26
Barão de Grajaú, Braz. D4 88
Barão de Melgaço, Braz. G6 84
Barão de Tromai, Braz. A3 88
Baraški, Russia D24 8
Barataria, La., U.S. H8 122
Barataria Bay, b., La., U.S. H8 122
Barat Daya, Kepulauan (Barat Daya Islands), is., Indon. G8 44
Barat Daya Islands see Barat Daya, Kepulauan, is., Indon. G8 44
Barauana, stm., Braz. G11 86
Barauni, India F10 54
Baraut, India D6 54
Baraya, Col. F4 86
Barbacena, Braz. K4 88
Barbacoas, Col. G2 86
Barbadillo del Mercado, Spain B7 20
Barbados, ctry., N.A. h16 96a
Barbalha, Braz. D6 88
Barbar, Sudan D6 62
Barbaria, Cap de, c., Spain F12 20
Barbas, Cap, c., W. Sah. E1 64
Barbaši, Russia C11 10
Barbastro, Spain B10 20
Barbate, Spain H4 20
Barbeau Peak, mtn., Nu., Can. A10 141
Barberena, Guat. E2 102
Barberton, S. Afr. D10 70
Barberton, Oh., U.S. C4 114
Barbil, India G10 54
Barbosa, Col. E5 86
Barbuda, i., Antig. e4 105b
Barby, Ger. E7 16
Bârca, Rom. F10 26
Barcaldine, Austl. D5 76
Barcău (Berettyó), stm., Eur. B8 26
Barcellona Pozzo di Gotto, Italy F9 24
Barcelona, Mex. B7 100
Barcelona, Spain C13 20
Barcelona, Ven. B9 86
Barcelona, co., Spain C13 20
Barceloneta, P.R. B2 104a
Barcelos, Braz. H10 86
Barcelos, Port. C2 20
Barcin, Pol. D13 16
Barcoo, stm., Austl. E4 76
Barczewo, Pol. C16 16
Barda del Medio, Arg. I3 92
Bardaï, Chad C3 62
Bardawīl, Sabkhet el-, b., Egypt G4 58
Barddhamān, India G11 54
Bardejov, Slov. G17 16
Bardeskan, Iran B8 56
Bardīyah, Libya A5 62
Bardo, Tun. H4 24
Bārdoli, India H4 54
Bardstown, Ky., U.S. G12 120
Bardwell Lake, res., Tx., U.S. E2 122
Bareilly, India D7 54
Barentsburg, Nor. B29 141
Barentsøya, i., Nor. B30 141
Barents Sea, Eur. B7 30
Bareta, India D5 54
Barfleur, Fr. E7 14
Bargaal, Som. B10 66
Bargara, Austl. E9 76
Bargarh, India D5 46
Barguzin, stm., Russia F11 34
Barguzinskij hrebet, mts., Russia F11 34
Bar Harbor, Me., U.S. F8 110
Barharwa, India F11 54
Barhi, India F10 54
Bāri, India E6 54
Bari, Italy C10 24
Baria, stm., Ven. G8 86
Barī Gāv, Afg. B1 54
Barigua, Salina de, pl., Ven. p20 104g
Barillas, Guat. E2 102
Barīm, i., Yemen G5 56
Barima, stm., S.A. C12 86
Barima-Waini, state, Guy. D12 86
Barinas, P.R. B2 104a
Barinas, Ven. C6 86
Barinas, state, Ven. C7 86
Baring, Cape, c., N.T., Can. A7 106
Baringo, Lake, l., Kenya D7 66
Bāripada, India H11 54
Bariri, Braz. L1 88
Bârîs, Egypt C6 62
Bari Sādri, India F5 54
Barisāl, Bngl. G13 54
Barisāl, state, Bngl. G13 54
Barisan, Pegunungan, mts., Indon. E2 50
Barito, stm., Indon. E9 50
Barjols, Fr. F11 18
Barkam, China E5 36
Barkava, Lat. D9 10
Barkerville, B.C., Can. C9 138
Bark Lake, l., On., Can. C12 112
Barkley, Lake, res., U.S. H10 120
Barkley Sound, strt., B.C., Can. H5 138
Barkly East, S. Afr. G8 70
Barkly Tableland, plat., Austl. C7 74
Barkly West, S. Afr. F7 70
Barkol, China C3 36
Bârlad, Rom. C14 26
Bârlad, stm., Rom. D14 26
Bar-le-Duc, Fr. F14 14
Barlee, Lake, l., Austl. E3 74
Barletta, Italy C10 24
Barlinek, Pol. D11 16
Barling, Ar., U.S. B4 122
Barlow, Ky., U.S. G8 120
Barmedman, Austl. J6 76
Bārmer, India F3 54
Barmera, Austl. J3 76
Barnagar, India G5 54
Barnard Castle, Eng., U.K. G11 12
Barnaul, Russia D14 32
Barn Bluff, mtn., Austl. n12 77a
Barnegat, N.J., U.S. E11 114
Barnegat Bay, b., N.J., U.S. E11 114
Barnes Ice Cap, ice, Nu., Can. A16 106
Barnesville, Ga., U.S. C1 116
Barnesville, Mn., U.S. E2 118
Barnesville, Oh., U.S. E4 114
Barneville-Carteret, Fr. E7 14
Barnsdall, Ok., U.S. E12 128
Barnsley, Eng., U.K. H11 12
Barnstable, Ma., U.S. C15 114
Barnstaple, Eng., U.K. J8 12
Barnstaple Bay, b., Eng., U.K. J8 12
Barnwell, Ab., Can. G18 138
Barnwell, S.C., U.S. C4 116
Baro, stm., Afr. F7 62
Baron Bluff, clf, V.I.U.S. g10 104c
Baron'ki, Bela. G15 10
Barora Fa Island, i., Sol. Is. d8 79b
Barora Ite Island, i., Sol. Is. d8 79b
Baroua, Niger G7 64
Barpeta, India E13 54
Barqah (Cyrenaica), hist. reg., Libya A4 62
Barques, Pointe aux, c., Mi., U.S. D7 112
Barquisimeto, Ven. B7 86
Barra, Braz. F4 88
Barra, i., Scot., U.K. D5 12
Barra, Ponta da, c., Moz. C12 70
Barraba, Austl. H8 76
Barra da Estiva, Braz. G5 88
Barra del Colorado, C.R. G6 102
Barra de Rio Grande, Nic. F6 102
Barra do Corda, Braz. C3 88
Barra do Cuanza, Ang. B1 68
Barra do Garças, Braz. G7 84
Barra do Mendes, Braz. F4 88
Barra do Piraí, Braz. L3 88
Barra do Ribeiro, Braz. E12 92
Barra Falsa, Ponta da, c., Moz. C12 70
Barra Mansa, Braz. L3 88
Barranca, Peru F2 84
Barrancabermeja, Col. D4 86
Barrancas, Ven. C10 86
Barrancas, Ven. C7 86
Barrancas, stm., Arg. H2 92
Barranco Azul, Mex. E3 130
Barranco do Velho, Port. G3 20
Barranqueras, Arg. C8 92
Barranquilla, Col. B4 86
Barranquitas, P.R. B3 104a
Barras, Braz. C4 88
Barre, Vt., U.S. F4 110
Barreal, Arg. E3 92
Barreiras, Braz. G3 88
Barreirinha, Braz. D6 84
Barreiro, Port. F1 20
Barreiros, Braz. E8 88
Barren, stm., Ky., U.S. H11 120
Barren, Nosy, is., Madag. D7 68
Barren Islands, is., Ak., U.S. E9 140
Barren River Lake, res., Ky., U.S. H11 120
Barretos, Braz. K1 88
Barrhead, Ab., Can. B16 138
Barrie, On., Can. D10 112
Barrie Island, i., On., Can. C7 112
Barrière, B.C., Can. E10 138
Barrier Range, mts., Austl. H3 76
Barrigada, Guam j10 78c
Barrington, N.S., Can. G11 110
Barrington Tops National Park, p.o.i., Austl. I8 76
Barringun, Austl. G5 76
Barrouallie, St. Vin. o11 105e
Barrow, Arg. I7 92
Barrow, Ak., U.S. B8 140
Barrow, stm., Ire. I5 12
Barrow, Point, c., Ak., U.S. B8 140
Barrow Creek, Austl. D6 74
Barrow-in-Furness, Eng., U.K. G9 12
Barrow Island, i., Austl. D2 74
Barrows, Mb., Can. B12 124
Barrow Strait, strt., Nu., Can. C6 141
Barry, Wales, U.K. J9 12
Barry, Il., U.S. E6 120
Barryton, Mi., U.S. E4 112
Barsalpur, India D4 54
Bārsi, India B2 53
Barsinghausen, Ger. D5 16
Barstow, Ca., U.S. I8 134
Barstow, Tx., U.S. C4 130
Bar-sur-Seine, Fr. F13 14
Bartang, Taj. B11 56
Barth, Ger. B8 16
Barthélemy, Deo, p., Viet. C6 48
Bartholomew, Bayou, stm., U.S. E7 122
Bartibougou, Burkina G5 64
Bartica, Guy. B6 84
Bartın, Tur. B15 28
Bartın, state, Tur. B15 28
Bartle Frere, mtn., Austl. A5 76
Bartlesville, Ok., U.S. H2 120
Bartlett, N.H., U.S. F5 110
Bartlett, Tn., U.S. B9 122
Bartlett, Tx., U.S. D10 130
Bartley, Ne., U.S. A8 128
Barton, Vt., U.S. F4 110
Bartoszyce, Pol. B16 16
Bartow, Fl., U.S. I4 116
Bartow, Ga., U.S. D3 116
Barú, Volcán, vol., Pan. H6 102
Bārūk, Jabal al-, mtn., Leb. E6 58
Barumini, Italy E2 24
Barumun, stm., Indon. C2 50
Barung, Nusa, i., Indon. H8 50
Barus, Indon. L4 48
Baruun-Urt, Mong. B7 36
Barvas, Scot., U.K. C6 12
Barview, Or., U.S. G2 136
Barwāh, India G5 54
Barwāni, India H5 54
Barwick, Ga., U.S. F2 116
Barwon, stm., Austl. H6 76
Barybino, Russia E20 10
Barycz, stm., Pol. E13 16
Barysau, Bela. F11 10
Basail, Arg. C8 92
Basalt, stm., Austl. B5 76
Basankusu, D.R.C. D3 66
Basarabeasca, Mol. C15 26
Basatongwula Shan, mtn., China B13 54
Basavakalyān, India C3 53
Basavilbaso, Arg. F8 92
Bascuñán, Cabo, c., Chile D2 92
Basel (Bâle), Switz. C4 22
Basella see Bassella, Spain B12 20
Basey, Phil. E5 52
Bashi Channel, strt., Asia K9 42
Bashkortostan see Baškirija, state, Russia D9 32
Basilan Island, i., Phil. G4 52
Basilan Strait, strt., Phil. G4 52
Basildon, Eng., U.K. J13 12
Basile, La., U.S. G6 122
Basilicata, state, Italy D10 24
Basin, Mt., U.S. D14 136
Basin, Wy., U.S. C4 126
Basingstoke, Eng., U.K. J11 12
Basin Lake, l., Sk., Can. B8 124
Basīrhat, India G12 54
Baskahegan Lake, l., Me., U.S. E8 110
Baskakovka, Russia F17 10
Başkale, Tur. B5 56
Baskatong, Réservoir, res., Qc., Can. B13 112
Basket Lake, l., On., Can. B6 118
Baškirija, state, Russia D9 32
Baskomutan Milli Parkı, p.o.i., Tur. E13 28
Basmat, India B3 53
Bāsoda, India G6 54
Basoko, D.R.C. D4 66
Basora, Punt, c., Aruba p20 104g
Basque Provinces see Euskal Herriko, state, Spain A8 20
Basra see Al-Başrah, Iraq C6 56
Bas-Rhin, state, Fr. F16 14
Bassano, Ab., Can. F18 138
Bassano del Grappa, Italy E8 22
Bassari, Togo H5 64
Bassas da India, rf., Reu. E6 68
Bassein, stm., Mya. D2 48
Bassella, Spain B12 20
Basse Santa Su, Gam. G2 64
Basse-Terre, Guad. i5 105c
Basseterre, St. K./N. C2 105a
Basse Terre, Trin. s12 105f
Basse-Terre, i., Guad. h5 105c
Bassett, Ne., U.S. E13 126
Bassett, Va., U.S. H6 114
Bassfield, Ms., U.S. F9 122
Bassikounou, Maur. F3 64
Bassila, Benin H5 64
Bass River, N.S., Can. E13 110
Bass Strait, strt., Austl. L6 76
Basswood Lake, l., N.A. C6 118
Båstad, Swe. H5 8
Bastenaken see Bastogne, Bel. D14 14
Bastersberge, hill, S. Afr. G5 70
Basti, India E9 54
Bastia, Fr. G15 18
Bastogne, Bel. D14 14
Bastrop, La., U.S. E6 122
Bastrop, Tx., U.S. D10 130
Basu, Pulau, i., Indon. D3 50
Basutoland see Lesotho, ctry., Afr. F9 70
Bata, Eq. Gui. I6 64
Bataan Peninsula, pen., Phil. C3 52
Batabanó, Golfo de, b., Cuba A6 102
Batac, Phil. A3 52
Batagaj, Russia C15 34
Batagaj-Alyta, Russia C15 34
Batak, Blg. H11 26
Batala, India C5 54
Batalha, Braz. E7 88
Batalha, Port. E2 20
Batam, Pulau, i., Indon. C3 50
Batamaj, Russia D14 34
Batang, China E4 36
Batangafo, C.A.R. C3 66
Batangas, Phil. D3 52
Batangtoru, Indon. C1 50
Batan Islands, is., Phil. K9 42
Batanta, Pulau, i., Indon. F9 44
Batatais, Braz. K2 88
Batavia, Arg. G5 92
Batavia see Jakarta, Indon. G5 50
Batavia, Il., U.S. C9 120
Batavia, Ia., U.S. D5 120
Batavia, N.Y., U.S. A7 114
Batchelor, Austl. B6 74
Bătdâmbâng, Camb. F6 48
Bateckij, Russia B13 10
Batemans Bay, Austl. J8 76
Bates, Mount, mtn., Norf. I. y24 78i
Batesburg, S.C., U.S. C4 116
Batesville, Ar., U.S. B7 122
Batesville, Ms., U.S. C9 122
Batesville, Tx., U.S. F8 130
Bath, N.B., Can. D9 110
Bath, Eng., U.K. J10 12
Bath, Me., U.S. G7 110
Bath, N.Y., U.S. B8 114
Batha, stm., Chad E3 62
Bathgate, N.D., U.S. F16 124
Bathinda, India C5 54
Bathsheba, Barb. n8 105d
Bathurst, Austl. I7 76
Bathurst, N.B., Can. C11 110
Bathurst see Banjul, Gam. G1 64
Bathurst, Cape, c., N.T., Can. A5 106
Bathurst Inlet see Kingaok, Nu., Can. B9 106
Bathurst Island, i., Austl. B5 74
Bathurst Island, i., Nu., Can. B5 141
Batlow, Austl. J6 76
Batman, Tur. B5 56
Batna, Alg. B6 64
Ba To, Viet. E9 48
Baton Rouge, La., U.S. G7 122
Batouri, Cam. D2 66
Batsawul, Afg. A3 54
Batson, Tx., U.S. G4 122
Batterie, Pointe de la, c., Mart. k7 105c
Batticaloa, Sri L. H5 53
Battipaglia, Italy D8 24
Battle, stm., Can. D19 138
Battle Creek, Mi., U.S. F4 112
Battle Creek, Ne., U.S. F15 126
Battle Creek, stm., N.A. F4 124
Battle Ground, In., U.S. H3 112
Battle Ground, Wa., U.S. E4 136
Battle Harbour, Nf., Can. i22 107a
Battle Mountain, Nv., U.S. C8 134
Battle Mountain, mtn., Wy., U.S. B9 132
Batu, mtn., Eth. F7 62
Batu, Kepulauan, is., Indon. F2 44
Batu-Batu, Indon. F11 50
Batu Berincang, Gunong, mtn., Malay. J5 48
Batubrok, Bukit, mtn., Indon. C9 50
Batu Gajah, Malay. J5 48
Batukelau, Indon. C9 50
Batumi, Geor. F6 32
Batu Pahat, Malay. L6 48
Batupanjang, Indon. C2 50
Baturaja, Indon. F3 50
Baturino, Russia C15 32
Baturité, Braz. C6 88
Baturusa, Indon. D5 50
Batusangkar, Indon. D2 50
Batz, Île de, i., Fr. F4 14
Bau, Malay. C7 50
Baubau, Indon. G7 44
Bauchi, Nig. G6 64
Bauda, India H10 54
Baudette, Mn., U.S. C4 118
Baudó, stm., Col. E3 86
Bauld, Cape, c., Nf., Can. i22 107a
Bauman Fiord, b., Nu., Can. B8 141
Baume-les-Dames, Fr. G15 14
Baures, Bol. B4 90
Bauru, Braz. L1 88
Bauska, Lat. D7 10
Bautzen, Ger. E10 16
Bauxite, Ar., U.S. C6 122
Bavaria see Bayern, state, Ger. H7 16
Bavarian Alps, mts., Eur. I7 16
Båven, l., Swe. G7 8
Bavispe, Mex. F8 98
Bavispe, stm., Mex. F8 98
Bawang, Indon. G6 50
Bawdwin, Mya. A3 48
Bawean, Pulau, i., Indon. F8 50
Bawiti, Egypt B5 62
Bawmi, Mya. D2 48
Baxaya, mtn., Som. B9 66
Baxian, China G2 42
Baxian, China B7 42
Baxter, Ia., U.S. C4 120
Baxter, Mn., U.S. E4 118
Baxter, Tn., U.S. H12 120
Baxterville, Ms., U.S. F9 122
Bay, Ar., U.S. B8 122
Bay, Laguna de, l., Phil. C3 52
Bayamo, Cuba B9 102
Bayamón, P.R. B3 104a
Bayan, China A7 38
Bayan, Indon. H10 50
Bayāna, India E6 54
Bayan Har Shan, mts., China E4 36
Bayanhongor, Mong. B5 36
Bayannaobao, China B2 42
Bayano, Lago, res., Pan. H8 102
Bayan Obo, China C7 36
Bayard, Ia., U.S. C3 120
Bayard, N.M., U.S. K8 132
Bayard, W.V., U.S. E6 114
Bayawan, Phil. F4 52
Baybay, Phil. E5 52
Bayboro, N.C., U.S. A9 116
Bayburt, Tur. A5 56
Bay City, Mi., U.S. E6 112
Bay City, Or., U.S. E3 136
Bay City, Tx., U.S. F12 130
Baydhabo (Baidoa), Som. D8 66
Baydrag, stm., Mong. B4 36
Bayern (Bavaria), state, Ger. H7 16
Bayeux, Braz. D8 88
Bayeux, Fr. E8 14
Bayfield, Co., U.S. F9 132
Bayfield, Wi., U.S. E8 118
Bayındır, Tur. E10 28
Baykonur see Bajkonur, Kaz. E11 32
Bay Minette, Al., U.S. G11 122
Bayombong, Phil. B3 52
Bayona see Baiona, Spain B2 20
Bayonne, Fr. F4 18
Bayou Bodcau Reservoir, res., La., U.S. E5 122
Bayou Cane, La., U.S. H8 122

Name	Map Ref.	Page

Name	Map Ref.	Page
Bor, Russia	E20	8
Bor, Sudan	F6	62
Bor, Tur.	B3	56
Bor, Yugo.	E9	26
Bor, Lak, stm., Kenya	D7	66
Bora-Bora, i., Fr. Poly.	E11	72
Borabu, Thai.	E6	48
Borah Peak, mtn., Id., U.S.	F13	136
Borås, Swe.	H5	8
Borba, Braz.	D6	84
Bordeaux, Fr.	E5	18
Bordeaux Mountain, hill, V.I.U.S.	e8	104b
Borden, Sk., Can.	B6	124
Borden Peninsula, pen., Nu., Can.	A14	106
Bordertown, Austl.	K3	76
Bordesholm, Ger.	B6	16
Bordighera, Italy	G4	22
Bordj Menaïel, Alg.	H14	20
Bordj Omar Idriss, Alg.	D6	64
Borđoy, i., Far. Is.	m34	8b
Borgå see Porvoo, Fin.	F11	8
Borgarnes, Ice.	k28	8a
Børgefjell Nasjonalpark, p.o.i., Nor.	D5	8
Borger, Tx., U.S.	F7	128
Borgholm, Swe.	H7	8
Borgne, Lake, b., La., U.S.	G9	122
Borgnesse, Pointe, c., Mart.	I7	105c
Borgomanero, Italy	E5	22
Borgo San Dalmazzo, Italy	F4	22
Borgosesia, Italy	E5	22
Borgo Val di Taro, Italy	F6	22
Borgworm see Waremme, Bel.	D14	14
Borikhan, Laos	C6	48
Borisoglebsk, Russia	D6	32
Borisoglebskij, Russia	C21	10
Borjas Blancas see Les Borges Blanques, Spain	C11	20
Borkavičy, Bela.	E11	10
Borken, Ger.	E2	16
Borkou, reg., Chad	D3	62
Borkum, i., Ger.	C2	16
Borlänge, Swe.	F6	8
Bormes, Fr.	F12	18
Borna, Ger.	E9	16
Borneo (Kalimantan), i., Asia	E5	44
Bornholm, state, Den.	I6	8
Bornholm, i., Den.	I6	8
Borocay Island, i., Phil.	E3	52
Borodino, Russia	C17	32
Borogoncy, Russia	D15	34
Borohoro Shan, mts., China	F14	32
Boromo, Burkina	G4	64
Boron, Ca., U.S.	H8	134
Boronga Islands, is., Mya.	I14	54
Borongan, Phil.	E5	52
Borovan, Blg.	F10	26
Boroviči, Russia	B16	10
Borovljanka, Russia	D14	32
Borovsk, Russia	E19	10
Borovskij, Russia	C11	32
Borovskoj, Kaz.	D10	32
Borrachudo, stm., Braz.	J3	88
Borrazópolis, Braz.	A12	92
Borriana, Spain	E10	20
Borroloola, Austl.	C7	74
Borş, Rom.	B8	26
Borşa, Rom.	B11	26
Borsad, India	G4	54
Borščovočnyj hrebet, mts., Russia	F12	34
Borsod-Abaúj-Zemplén, state, Hung.	A8	26
Bort-les-Orgues, Fr.	D8	18
Borūjerd, Iran	C6	56
Borzja, Russia	F12	34
Bosa, Italy	D2	24
Bosanska Dubica, Bos.	D3	26
Bosanska Gradiška, Bos.	D4	26
Bosanska Krupa, Bos.	E3	26
Bosanski Novi, Bos.	D3	26
Bosanski Šamac, Bos.	D5	26
Bosavi, Mount, mtn., Pap. N. Gui.	b3	79a
Boscobel, Wi., U.S.	A7	120
Bose, China	J2	42
Boshan, China	C7	42
Boshof, S. Afr.	F7	70
Bosilegrad, Yugo.	G9	26
Bosna, stm., Bos.	E5	26
Bosnia and Herzegovina, ctry., Eur.	E3	26
Bosnik, Indon.	F10	44
Bošnjakovo, Russia	G17	34
Bosobolo, D.R.C.	D3	66
Bōsō-hantō, pen., Japan	D13	40
Bosporus see İstanbul Boğazı, strt., Tur.	B12	28
Bossangoa, C.A.R.	C3	66
Bossembélé, C.A.R.	C3	66
Bossey Bangou, Niger	G5	64
Bossier City, La., U.S.	E5	122
Bosten Hu, l., China	C2	36
Boston, Eng., U.K.	H12	12
Boston, Ga., U.S.	F2	116
Boston, Ma., U.S.	B14	114
Boston Bar, B.C., Can.	G9	138
Boston Mountains, mts., Ar., U.S.	B5	122
Boswell, In., U.S.	H2	112
Boswell, Ok., U.S.	C3	122
Bosworth, Mo., U.S.	E4	120
Botād, India	G3	54
Botany Bay, b., Austl.	J8	76
Boteti, stm., Bots.	E3	68
Bothaville, S. Afr.	E8	70
Bothnia, Gulf of, b., Eur.	E9	8
Bothwell, On., Can.	F8	112
Boticas, Port.	C3	20
Botna, stm., Mol.	C15	26
Botoşani, Rom.	B13	26
Botoşani, state, Rom.	B13	26
Bo Trach, Viet.	D8	48
Botrange, mtn., Bel.	D15	14
Botswana, ctry., Afr.	E3	68
Botte Donato, Monte, mtn., Italy	E10	24
Bottineau, N.D., U.S.	F13	124
Botucatu, Braz.	L1	88
Botwood, Nf., Can.	j22	107a
Bouaflé, C. Iv.	H3	64
Bouaké, C. Iv.	H3	64
Bouar, C.A.R.	C3	66
Bouârfa, Mor.	C4	64
Bouca, C.A.R.	C3	66
Boucher, stm., Qc., Can.	A7	110
Bouches-du-Rhône, state, Fr.	F11	18
Bouctouche, N.B., Can.	D12	110
Boufarik, Alg.	H13	20
Bou Ficha, Tun.	H4	24
Bougainville, i., Pap. N. Gui.	d7	79b
Bougainville, Détroit de, strt., Vanuatu	j16	79d
Bougainville Strait, strt., Oc.	d7	79b
Bougouni, Mali	G3	64
Bouillante, Guad.	h5	105c
Bouillon, Bel.	E14	14
Bouïra, Alg.	B5	64
Boujdour, Cap, c., W. Sah.	D2	64
Boularderie Island, i., N.S., Can.	D16	110
Boulder, Co., U.S.	A3	128
Boulder, Mt., U.S.	D14	136
Boulder, stm., Mt., U.S.	D15	136
Boulder City, Nv., U.S.	H2	132
Boulia, Austl.	D2	76
Boulogne-sur-Mer, Fr.	D10	14
Bouloupari, N. Cal.	m15	79d
Boulsa, Burkina	G4	64
Bou Medfaa, Alg.	H13	20
Bouna, C. Iv.	H4	64
Boundary Peak, mtn., Nv., U.S.	F7	134
Boundiali, C. Iv.	H3	64
Boun Nua, Laos	B5	48
Bountiful, Ut., U.S.	C4	132
Bounty Bay, b., Pit.	c28	78k
Bounty Islands, is., N.Z.	H8	80
Bounty Trough, unds.	N20	142
Bourail, N. Cal.	m15	79d
Bourbeuse, stm., Mo., U.S.	F6	120
Bourbon, In., U.S.	G3	112
Bourbonnais, hist. reg., Fr.	C9	18
Bourbonne-les-Bains, Fr.	G14	14
Bourem, Mali	F4	64
Bourg, La., U.S.	H8	122
Bourg-en-Bresse, Fr.	C11	18
Bourges, Fr.	G11	14
Bourget, On., Can.	E1	110
Bourget, Lac du, l., Fr.	D11	18
Bourgogne (Burgundy), hist. reg., Fr.	B10	18
Bourgogne, Canal de, can., Fr.	G13	14
Bourgoin-Jallieu, Fr.	D11	18
Bourke, Austl.	H5	76
Bournemouth, Eng., U.K.	K11	12
Bou Saâda, Alg.	B5	64
Bou Salem, Tun.	H2	24
Bouse Wash, stm., Az., U.S.	J3	132
Bou Smail, Alg.	H13	20
Boussac, Fr.	C8	18
Bousso, Chad	E3	62
Boutilimit, Maur.	F2	64
Bouvetøya, i., Ant.	A5	81
Bouza, Niger	G6	64
Bøvågen, Nor.	F1	8
Bovec, Slvn.	D10	22
Bovey, Mn., U.S.	D5	118
Bovill, Id., U.S.	D10	136
Bovina, Tx., U.S.	G6	128
Bow, stm., Ab., Can.	G19	138
Bo-Wadrif, S. Afr.	H4	70
Bowbells, N.D., U.S.	F11	124
Bow Creek, stm., Ks., U.S.	B9	128
Bowden, Ab., Can.	E16	138
Bowdle, S.D., U.S.	B13	126
Bowdon, N.D., U.S.	G14	124
Bowen, Arg.	G4	92
Bowen, Austl.	C7	76
Bowen, Il., U.S.	D7	120
Bowen, stm., Austl.	C6	76
Bowie, Az., U.S.	K7	132
Bowie, Md., U.S.	F9	114
Bowling Green, Fl., U.S.	I4	116
Bowling Green, Ky., U.S.	H11	120
Bowling Green, Mo., U.S.	E6	120
Bowling Green, Oh., U.S.	C2	114
Bowling Green, Va., U.S.	F8	114
Bowling Green, Cape, c., Austl.	B6	76
Bowling Green Bay National Park, p.o.i., Austl.	B6	76
Bowman, N.D., U.S.	A9	126
Bowman, S.C., U.S.	C5	116
Bowman, Mount, mtn., B.C., Can.	E9	138
Bowmanville, On., Can.	E11	112
Bowral, Austl.	J8	76
Bowraville, Austl.	H9	76
Bowron, stm., B.C., Can.	C9	138
Bowsman, Mb., Can.	B12	124
Boxelder Creek, stm., U.S.	B8	126
Box Elder Creek, stm., Mt., U.S.	G5	124
Boxelder Creek, stm., S.D., U.S.	C10	126
Boxing, China	C8	42
Boyacá, state, Col.	E5	86
Boyang, China	G7	42
Boyce, La., U.S.	F6	122
Boyceville, Wi., U.S.	F6	118
Boyd, Tx., U.S.	A10	130
Boyd, stm., Austl.	G9	76
Boydton, Va., U.S.	H7	114
Boyer, stm., Ia., U.S.	C2	120
Boyertown, Pa., U.S.	D10	114
Boykins, Va., U.S.	H8	114
Boyle, Ms., U.S.	D8	122
Boylston, Al., U.S.	E12	122
Boyne, stm., Austl.	E8	76
Boyne, stm., Mb., Can.	E16	124
Boyne, stm., Ire.	H5	12
Boyne City, Mi., U.S.	C5	112
Boynton Beach, Fl., U.S.	J5	116
Boysen Reservoir, res., Wy., U.S.	D4	126
Boys Ranch, Tx., U.S.	F6	128
Bozburun, Tur.	G11	28
Bozburun Yarımadası, pen., Tur.	G11	28
Boz Dağ, mtn., Tur.	E11	28
Boz Dağlar, mts., Tur.	E10	28
Bozdoğan, Tur.	F11	28
Bozeman, Mt., U.S.	E15	136
Bozen see Bolzano, Italy	D8	22
Bozhen, China	B7	42
Bozhou, China	E6	42
Bozkurt, Tur.	F12	28
Bozoum, C.A.R.	C3	66
Bozova, Tur.	A9	58
Bozovici, Rom.	E9	26
Bozšakol', Kaz.	D12	32
Bozüyük, Tur.	D13	28
Bra, Italy	F4	22
Brač, Otok, i., Cro.	G13	22
Bracciano, Italy	H9	22
Bracciano, Lago di, l., Italy	H9	22
Bracebridge, On., Can.	C10	112
Brackendale, B.C., Can.	G7	138
Brackettville, Tx., U.S.	E7	130
Bracknell, Eng., U.K.	J12	12
Braço do Norte, Braz.	D13	92
Brad, Rom.	C9	26
Bradano, stm., Italy	D10	24
Bradenton, Fl., U.S.	I3	116
Bradford, Eng., U.K.	H11	12
Bradford, Ar., U.S.	B7	122
Bradford, Pa., U.S.	C7	114
Bradford, Tn., U.S.	H9	120
Bradford, Vt., U.S.	G4	110
Bradford West Gwillimbury, On., Can.	D10	112
Bradley, Ar., U.S.	D5	122
Bradley, Fl., U.S.	I3	116
Bradley, Il., U.S.	G2	112
Bradley, S.D., U.S.	B15	126
Brady, Mt., U.S.	B15	136
Brady, Ne., U.S.	F12	126
Brady, Tx., U.S.	C8	130
Brady Creek, stm., Tx., U.S.	C8	130
Braga, Port.	C2	20
Braga, state, Port.	C2	20
Bragado, Arg.	G7	92
Bragança, Braz.	D8	84
Bragança, Port.	C4	20
Bragança, state, Port.	C4	20
Bragança Paulista, Braz.	L2	88
Brāhmanbāria, Bngl.	F13	54
Brāhmani, stm., India	H10	54
Brahmapur, India	B7	53
Brahmaputra (Yarlung), stm., Asia	C7	46
Braich y Pwll, c., Wales, U.K.	I8	12
Braidwood, Austl.	J7	76
Braidwood, Il., U.S.	C9	120
Brăila, Rom.	D14	26
Brăila, state, Rom.	D14	26
Brainard, Ne., U.S.	F15	126
Brainerd, Mn., U.S.	E4	118
Braintree, Eng., U.K.	J13	12
Brak, stm., S. Afr.	G6	70
Brake, Ger.	C4	16
Bralorne, B.C., Can.	F8	138
Brampton, On., Can.	E10	112
Bramsche, Ger.	D3	16
Branchville, S.C., U.S.	C5	116
Branco, stm., Braz.	H11	86
Branco, stm., Braz.	F3	88
Brandaris, hill, Neth. Ant.	p23	104g
Brandberg, mtn., Nmb.	B2	70
Brandbu, Nor.	F4	8
Brandenburg, Ger.	D8	16
Brandenburg, Ky., U.S.	G11	120
Brandenburg, state, Ger.	D9	16
Brandfort, S. Afr.	F8	70
Brandon, Mb., Can.	E14	124
Brandon, Fl., U.S.	I3	116
Brandon, Ms., U.S.	E9	122
Brandon, S.D., U.S.	H2	118
Brandon, Vt., U.S.	G3	110
Brandsen, Arg.	G8	92
Brandvlei, S. Afr.	G5	70
Brandy Peak, mtn., Or., U.S.	H3	136
Brandýs nad Labem-Stará Boleslav, Czech Rep.	F10	16
Branford, Fl., U.S.	G2	116
Braniewo, Pol.	B15	16
Bransby, Austl.	G4	76
Bransby Point, c., Monts.	D3	105a
Bransfield Strait, strt., Ant.	B35	81
Branson, Mo., U.S.	H4	120
Brantford, On., Can.	E9	112
Brantley, Al., U.S.	F12	122
Brantley Tank, res., N.M., U.S.	B3	130
Brantôme, Fr.	D6	18
Brantville, N.B., Can.	C12	110
Bras d'Or Lake, l., N.S., Can.	E16	110
Brasiléia, Braz.	F4	84
Brasília, Braz.	H1	88
Brasília, Parque Nacional de, p.o.i., Braz.	H1	88
Brasília de Minas, Braz.	I3	88
Braslau, Bela.	E9	10
Braşov, Rom.	D12	26
Braşov, state, Rom.	D12	26
Brassey, Banjaran, mts., Malay.	A10	50
Brass Islands, is., V.I.U.S.	e7	104b
Brasstown Bald, mtn., Ga., U.S.	B2	116
Bratca, Rom.	C9	26
Bratislava, Slov.	H13	16
Bratislava, state, Slov.	H13	16
Bratsk, Russia	C18	32
Bratskoe vodohranilišče, res., Russia	C18	32
Bratsk Reservoir see Bratskoe vodohranilišče, res., Russia	C18	32
Brattleboro, Vt., U.S.	B13	114
Braulio Carrillo, Parque Nacional, p.o.i., C.R.	G5	102
Braúnas, Braz.	J4	88
Braunau am Inn, Aus.	B10	22
Braunschweig (Brunswick), Ger.	D6	16
Brava, i., C.V.	I10	65a
Brava, Costa, cst., Spain	C14	20
Brava, Laguna, l., Arg.	D3	92
Brava, Punta, c., Ur.	G9	92
Brave, Pa., U.S.	E5	114
Bravo (Rio Grande), stm., N.A.	H13	98
Bravo, Cerro, mtn., Peru	E2	84
Bravo del Norte see Bravo, stm., N.A.	H13	98
Brawley, Ca., U.S.	K10	134
Bray, Ire.	H6	12
Bray Island, i., Nu., Can.	B15	106
Brazeau, stm., Ab., Can.	D15	138
Brazeau, Mount, mtn., Ab., Can.	D13	138
Brazeau Dam, dam, Ab., Can.	C15	138
Brazil, In., U.S.	E10	120
Brazil, ctry., S.A.	F9	82
Brazil Basin, unds.	J11	144
Brazoria, Tx., U.S.	E12	130
Brazos, stm., Tx., U.S.	E8	108
Brazos, Clear Fork, stm., Tx., U.S.	B8	130
Brazos, Double Mountain Fork, stm., Tx., U.S.	H8	128
Brazos, North Fork, stm., Tx., U.S.	H3	122
Brazzaville, Congo	E2	66
Brčko, Bos.	E5	26
Brda, stm., Pol.	C13	16
Bré see Bray, Ire.	H6	12
Brea, Ca., U.S.	J8	134
Bream Bay, b., N.Z.	B6	80
Brea Pozo, Arg.	D6	92
Breaux Bridge, La., U.S.	G7	122
Brebes, Indon.	G6	50
Brechin, Scot., U.K.	E10	12
Breckenridge, Mi., U.S.	E5	112
Breckenridge, Mn., U.S.	E2	118
Breckenridge, Mo., U.S.	E4	120
Brecknock, Península, pen., Chile	J2	90
Břeclav, Czech Rep.	H12	16
Brecon, Wales, U.K.	J9	12
Brecon Beacons, hills, Wales, U.K.	J9	12
Brecon Beacons National Park, p.o.i., Wales, U.K.	J9	12
Breda, Neth.	C13	14
Breda, Ia., U.S.	B3	120
Bredasdorp, S. Afr.	I5	70
Bredenbury, Sk., Can.	D11	124
Bredy, Russia	D9	32
Breë, stm., S. Afr.	I5	70
Breese, Il., U.S.	F8	120
Bregalnica, stm., Mac.	A5	28
Bregenz, Aus.	C6	22
Bregovo, Blg.	E9	26
Bréhat, Île de, i., Fr.	F6	14
Breiðafjörður, b., Ice.	k28	8a
Brejinho de Nazaré, Braz.	F1	88
Brejo, Braz.	B4	88
Brejo Grande, Braz.	F7	88
Brejo Santo, Braz.	D6	88
Brekstad, Nor.	E3	8
Bremen, Ger.	C4	16
Bremen, Ga., U.S.	D13	122
Bremen, Oh., U.S.	E3	114
Bremen, state, Ger.	C4	16
Bremer Bay, Austl.	F3	74
Bremer Bay, b., Austl.	F3	74
Bremerhaven, Ger.	C4	16
Bremerton, Wa., U.S.	C4	136
Bremervörde, Ger.	C4	16
Bremond, Tx., U.S.	F2	122
Brenham, Tx., U.S.	G2	122
Brenner Pass, p., Eur.	C8	22
Brent, Fl., U.S.	G11	122
Brenta, stm., Italy	D8	22
Brentwood, Eng., U.K.	J13	12
Brentwood, N.Y., U.S.	D12	114
Brentwood, Tn., U.S.	H11	120
Breo, Italy	F4	22
Brescia, Italy	E7	22
Breslau see Wrocław, Pol.	E13	16
Bressanone, Italy	D8	22
Bressay, i., Scot., U.K.	n18	12a
Bresse, reg., Fr.	C11	18
Bressuire, Fr.	H8	14
Brèst, Bela.	H6	10
Brest, Fr.	F4	14
Brèst, state, Bela.	H8	10
Bretagne (Brittany), hist. reg., Fr.	F5	14
Bretenoux, Fr.	E7	18
Breton, Ab., Can.	C16	138
Breton Islands, is., La., U.S.	H9	122
Breton Sound, strt., La., U.S.	H9	122
Brett, Cape, c., N.Z.	B6	80
Bretten, Ger.	G4	16
Breueh, Pulau, i., Indon.	J2	48
Breuil-Cervinia, Italy	E4	22
Brevard, N.C., U.S.	A3	116
Breves, Braz.	D7	84
Brevoort Island, i., Nu., Can.	E13	141
Brewarrina, Austl.	G6	76
Brewer, Me., U.S.	F8	110
Brewster, Mn., U.S.	H3	118
Brewster, Ne., U.S.	F13	126
Brewster, Wa., U.S.	B7	136
Brewster, Kap, c., Grnld.	C21	141
Brewton, Al., U.S.	F11	122
Breyten, S. Afr.	E10	70
Březnice, Czech Rep.	G9	16
Brezno, Slov.	H15	16
Bria, C.A.R.	C4	66
Brian Boru Peak, mtn., B.C., Can.	A3	138
Briançon, Fr.	E12	18
Brian Head, mtn., Ut., U.S.	F4	132
Briare, Canal de, can., Fr.	G11	14
Bribie Island, i., Austl.	F9	76
Bricelyn, Mn., U.S.	H5	118
Briceni, Mol.	A14	26
Briceville, Tn., U.S.	A14	122
Bri Chuallan see Bray, Ire.	H6	12
Bridge, stm., B.C., Can.	F7	138
Bridge City, Tx., U.S.	G5	122
Bridge Lake, B.C., Can.	E10	138
Bridgend, Wales, U.K.	J9	12
Bridgeport, Ca., U.S.	E6	134
Bridgeport, Ct., U.S.	C12	114
Bridgeport, Mi., U.S.	E6	112
Bridgeport, Ne., U.S.	F9	126
Bridgeport, Tx., U.S.	H11	128
Bridgeport, Wa., U.S.	C7	136
Bridgeport, Lake, res., Tx., U.S.	H10	128
Bridger, Mt., U.S.	B4	126
Bridger Peak, mtn., Wy., U.S.	B9	132
Bridgeton, N.J., U.S.	E10	114
Bridgetown, Austl.	F3	74
Bridgetown, Barb.	n8	105d
Bridgetown, N.S., Can.	F11	110
Bridgeville, De., U.S.	F10	114
Bridgewater, N.S., Can.	F12	110
Bridgewater, Ma., U.S.	B15	114
Bridgewater, S.D., U.S.	D15	126
Bridgewater, Va., U.S.	F6	114
Bridgwater, Eng., U.K.	J9	12
Bridgwater Bay, b., Eng., U.K.	J9	12
Bridlington, Eng., U.K.	G12	12
Bridport, Eng., U.K.	K10	12
Brie, reg., Fr.	F12	14
Brier Creek, stm., Ga., U.S.	C4	116
Brig, Switz.	D5	22
Briggs, Tx., U.S.	D10	130
Brigham City, Ut., U.S.	B4	132
Bright, Austl.	K6	76
Brighton, On., Can.	D12	112
Brighton, Eng., U.K.	K12	12
Brighton, Co., U.S.	A4	128
Brighton, Ia., U.S.	C6	120
Brighton, Mi., U.S.	B2	114
Brighton, N.Y., U.S.	E12	112
Brighton Downs, Austl.	D3	76
Brignoles, Fr.	F11	18
Brijuni, i., Cro.	F10	22
Brilliant, B.C., Can.	G13	138
Brilliant, Al., U.S.	C11	122
Brillion, Wi., U.S.	D1	112
Brilon, Ger.	E4	16
Brindisi, Italy	D11	24
Brinkworth, Austl.	I2	76
Brion, Île, i., Qc., Can.	C15	110
Brioude, Fr.	D9	18
Brisbane, Austl.	F9	76
Brisighella, Italy	F8	22
Bristol, Eng., U.K.	J10	12
Bristol, Ct., U.S.	C12	114
Bristol, Fl., U.S.	G14	122
Bristol, N.H., U.S.	G5	110
Bristol, Pa., U.S.	D11	114
Bristol, R.I., U.S.	C14	114
Bristol, Tn., U.S.	H3	114
Bristol, Vt., U.S.	F3	110
Bristol Bay, b., Ak., U.S.	E7	140
Bristol Channel, strt., U.K.	J8	12
Bristol Island, i., S. Geor.	A2	81
Bristol Lake, l., Ca., U.S.	I10	134
Bristow, Ok., U.S.	B2	122
Britannia Beach, B.C., Can.	G7	138
British Columbia, state, Can.	E5	106
British Guiana see Guyana, ctry., S.A.	C6	84
British Honduras see Belize, ctry., N.A.	D3	102
British Indian Ocean Territory, dep., Afr.	G17	2
British Isles, is., Eur.	C12	4
British Mountains, mts., N.A.	C11	140
British Solomon Islands see Solomon Islands, ctry., Oc.	D7	72
British Virgin Islands, dep., N.A.	h15	96a
Brits, S. Afr.	D8	70
Britstown, S. Afr.	G6	70
Britt, Ia., U.S.	A4	120
Brittany see Bretagne, hist. reg., Fr.	F5	14
Britton, S.D., U.S.	B15	126
Brive-la-Gaillarde, Fr.	D7	18
Brixen see Bressanone, Italy	D8	22
Brixham, Eng., U.K.	K9	12
Brixton, Austl.	D5	76
Brjanka, Russia	C16	32
Brjansk, Russia	G17	10
Brjanskaja oblast', co., Russia	H16	10
Brno, Czech Rep.	G12	16
Broa, Ensenada de la, b., Cuba	A6	102
Broad, stm., U.S.	B4	116
Broad, stm., Ga., U.S.	B2	116
Broadalbin, N.Y., U.S.	G2	110
Broad Sound, b., Austl.	D7	76
Broad Sound Channel, strt., Austl.	C8	76
Broadus, Mt., U.S.	B7	126
Broadwater, Ne., U.S.	F10	126
Broadway, Va., U.S.	F7	114
Brocēni, Lat.	D5	10
Brochet, Mb., Can.	D10	106
Brock, Sk., Can.	C5	124
Brockman, Mount, mtn., Austl.	D3	74
Brockton, Ma., U.S.	B14	114
Brockton, Mt., U.S.	F9	124
Brockville, On., Can.	D14	112
Brockway, Pa., U.S.	C7	114
Brocton, N.Y., U.S.	B6	114
Brodeur Peninsula, pen., Nu., Can.	A13	106
Brodhead, Wi., U.S.	B8	120
Brodick, Scot., U.K.	F7	12
Brodnax, Va., U.S.	H7	114
Brodnica, Pol.	C15	16
Brogan, Or., U.S.	F9	136
Brok, Pol.	D17	16
Broken Arrow, Ok., U.S.	H2	120
Broken Bay, b., Austl.	I8	76
Broken Bow, Ok., U.S.	C4	122
Broken Bow Lake, res., Ok., U.S.	C4	122
Broken Hill, Austl.	H3	76
Broken Hill see Kabwe, Zam.	C4	68
Broken Ridge, unds.	M12	142
Brokopondo, Sur.	B6	84
Brokopondo Stuwmeer, res., Sur.	C6	84
Bromley Plateau, unds.	K10	144
Bromptonville, Qc., Can.	E4	110
Bromsgrove, Eng., U.K.	I10	12
Bronkhorstspruit, S. Afr.	D9	70
Bronlund Peak, mtn., B.C., Can.	D5	106
Bronnae, Bela.	H13	10
Bronnicy, Russia	E21	10
Bronson, Fl., U.S.	G3	116
Bronson, Ks., U.S.	G2	120
Bronson, Mi., U.S.	G4	112
Bronte, Italy	G8	24
Bronte, Tx., U.S.	C7	130
Brook, In., U.S.	H2	112
Brookeland, Tx., U.S.	F5	122
Brooker, Fl., U.S.	G3	116
Brookfield, N.S., Can.	E13	110
Brookfield, Wi., U.S.	E1	112
Brookford, N.C., U.S.	I4	114
Brookhaven, Ms., U.S.	F8	122
Brookings, Or., U.S.	A1	134
Brookings, S.D., U.S.	G2	118
Brookland, Ar., U.S.	B8	122
Brooklyn, N.S., Can.	F12	110
Brooklyn, Ia., U.S.	J6	118
Brooklyn, Mi., U.S.	B1	114
Brooklyn Center, Mn., U.S.	F5	118
Brookmere, B.C., Can.	G10	138
Brookneal, Va., U.S.	G7	114
Brookport, Il., U.S.	G9	120
Brooks, Ab., Can.	F19	138
Brooks Bay, b., B.C., Can.	F2	138
Brookshire, Tx., U.S.	H3	122
Brooks Range, mts., Ak., U.S.	C8	140
Brooksville, Fl., U.S.	H3	116
Brooksville, Ms., U.S.	D10	122
Brookville, In., U.S.	E12	120
Brookville, Pa., U.S.	C6	114
Brookville Lake, res., In., U.S.	E13	120
Broome, Austl.	C4	74
Broomfield, Co., U.S.	B3	128
Brooten, Mn., U.S.	F3	118
Brora, Scot., U.K.	C9	12
Brosna, stm., Ire.	H5	12
Brotas de Macaúbas, Braz.	G4	88
Brou, Fr.	F10	14
Broughton, Mount, mtn., Austl.	K5	76
Broughty Ferry, Scot., U.K.	E10	12
Browerville, Mn., U.S.	E4	118
Brown, Mount, mtn., Mt., U.S.	B15	136
Brown, Point, c., Wa., U.S.	D2	136
Brown Deer, Wi., U.S.	E2	112
Browne Bay, b., Nu., Can.	A11	106
Brownfield, Tx., U.S.	A5	130
Browning, Mo., U.S.	D4	120
Browning, Mt., U.S.	B13	136
Brownlee Reservoir, res., U.S.	F9	136
Brownsburg, Qc., Can.	E2	110
Brownsburg, In., U.S.	I3	112
Brownsdale, Mn., U.S.	H5	118
Browns Town, Jam.	i13	104d
Brownstown, In., U.S.	F11	120
Brownsville, Ky., U.S.	G11	120
Brownsville, La., U.S.	E6	122
Brownsville, Or., U.S.	F4	136
Brownsville, Tn., U.S.	B9	122
Brownsville, Tx., U.S.	I10	130
Brownton, Mn., U.S.	G4	118
Brownville, Me., U.S.	E7	110
Brownville, Ne., U.S.	D2	120
Brownville Junction, Me., U.S.	E7	110
Brownwood, Tx., U.S.	C8	130
Brownwood, Lake, res., Tx., U.S.	C9	130
Browse Island, i., Austl.	B4	74
Broxton, Ga., U.S.	E3	116
Broža, Bela.	H12	10
Bruay-en-Artois, Fr.	D11	14
Bruce, S.D., U.S.	G2	118
Bruce, Wi., U.S.	F7	118
Bruce, Mount, mtn., Austl.	D3	74
Bruce Mines, On., Can.	B6	112
Bruce Peninsula, pen., On., Can.	C8	112
Bruce Peninsula National Park, p.o.i., On., Can.	C8	112
Bruce Rock, Austl.	F3	74
Bruchsal, Ger.	G4	16
Bruck an der Leitha, Aus.	B13	22
Bruck an der Mur, Aus.	C12	22
Bruges see Brugge, Bel.	C12	14
Brugg, Switz.	C5	22
Brugge (Bruges), Bel.	C12	14
Brühl, Ger.	F2	16
Bruit, Pulau, i., Malay.	B7	50
Brule, Ne., U.S.	F11	126
Brumado, Braz.	H5	88
Brundidge, Al., U.S.	F13	122
Bruneau, Id., U.S.	H11	136
Bruneau, stm., U.S.	H11	136
Bruneck see Brunico, Italy	D8	22
Brunei, ctry., Asia	A9	50
Brunico, Italy	D8	22
Brunsbüttel, Ger.	C4	16
Brunson, S.C., U.S.	D4	116
Brunswick see Braunschweig, Ger.	D6	16
Brunswick, Ga., U.S.	E4	116
Brunswick, Me., U.S.	G6	110
Brunswick, Md., U.S.	E8	114
Brunswick, Mo., U.S.	E4	120
Brunswick, Oh., U.S.	C4	114
Brunswick, Península, pen., Chile	J2	90
Bruntál, Czech Rep.	F13	16
Brus, Laguna de, b., Hond.	E5	102
Brush, Co., U.S.	A5	128
Brusovo, Russia	C18	10
Brusque, Braz.	C13	92
Brussel see Bruxelles, Bel.	D13	14
Brussels see Bruxelles, Bel.	D13	14
Brussels, On., Can.	E8	112
Bruthen, Austl.	K6	76
Bruxelles (Brussels), Bel.	D13	14
Bruzual, Ven.	D7	86
Bryan, Oh., U.S.	C1	114
Bryan, Tx., U.S.	G2	122
Bryan, Mount, mtn., Austl.	I2	76
Bryant, Ar., U.S.	C6	122
Bryce Canyon National Park, p.o.i., Ut., U.S.	F4	132
Bryli, Bela.	G13	10
Bryson, Qc., Can.	C13	112
Bryson, Tx., U.S.	A9	130
Brzeg, Pol.	F13	16
Brześć Kujawski, Pol.	D14	16
Brzesko, Pol.	F16	16
Brzeziny, Pol.	E15	16
Bsharrī, Leb.	D6	58
Bua, Fiji	p19	79e
Bua Bay, b., Fiji	p19	79e
Buada Lagoon, b., Nauru	q17	78f
Buala, Sol. Is.	e8	79b
Bua Yai, Thai.	E6	48
Bubanza, Bdi.	E5	66
Bubaque, Gui.-B.	G1	64
Bubi, stm., Zimb.	B10	70
Būbiyān, i., Kuw.	D6	56
Bubuduo, China	C10	54
Bucak, Tur.	F13	28
Bucaramanga, Col.	D5	86
Buccaneer Archipelago, is., Austl.	C4	74
Buchanan, Sk., Can.	C11	124
Buchanan, Lib.	H2	64
Buchanan, Ga., U.S.	D13	122
Buchanan, Mi., U.S.	G3	112
Buchanan, Lake, l., Austl.	C5	76
Buchanan, Lake, l., Tx., U.S.	D9	130
Buchan Ness, c., Scot., U.K.	D11	12
Buchans, Nf., Can.	j22	107a
Bucharest see Bucureşti, Rom.	E13	26
Buchen, Ger.	G5	16
Buchholz in der Nordheide, Ger.	C5	16
Buchloe, Ger.	H6	16
Buchon, Point, c., Ca., U.S.	H4	134
Buchs, Switz.	C6	22
Buckatunna, Ms., U.S.	F10	122
Buckatunna Creek, stm., Ms., U.S.	F10	122
Bückeburg, Ger.	D5	16
Buckeye, Az., U.S.	J4	132
Buckeye Lake, Oh., U.S.	I7	112
Buckhaven, Scot., U.K.	E9	12
Buckholts, Tx., U.S.	D10	130
Buckhorn Draw, stm., Tx., U.S.	D7	130
Buckie, Scot., U.K.	D10	12
Buckingham, Qc., Can.	C14	112
Buckingham, Va., U.S.	G7	114
Buckingham Bay, b., Austl.	B7	74
Buck Island, i., V.I.U.S.	g11	104c
Buck Island Reef National Monument, p.o.i., V.I.U.S.	g11	104c
Buck Lake, l., Ab., Can.	D16	138
Buckland, Ak., U.S.	C7	140
Buckley, Wa., U.S.	C4	136
Bucklin, Ks., U.S.	D9	128
Bucklin, Mo., U.S.	E5	120
Buck Mountain, mtn., Wa., U.S.	B7	136
Bucovăţ, Mol.	B15	26
Buco Zau, Ang.	A1	68
Bucureşti (Bucharest), Rom.	E13	26
Bucureşti, state, Rom.	E13	26
Bucyrus, Oh., U.S.	D3	114
Buda, Il., U.S.	C8	120
Buda, Tx., U.S.	D10	130
Budalin, Mya.	A2	48
Budapest, Hung.	B6	26
Budapest, state, Hung.	B6	26
Budaun, India	D7	54
Budd Coast, cst., Ant.	B16	81
Buddh Gaya see Bodh Gaya, India	F10	54
Buddusò, Italy	D3	24
Bude, Ms., U.S.	F8	122
Bude Bay, b., Eng., U.K.	K8	12
Budënnovsk, Russia	F6	32
Budeşti, Rom.	E13	26
Büdingen, Ger.	F5	16
Budišov nad Budišovkou, Czech Rep.	G13	16
Budjala, D.R.C.	D3	66
Budogovišči, Russia	G19	10
Budrio, Italy	F8	22
Budweis see České Budějovice, Czech Rep.	H10	16
Buea, Cam.	D1	66
Buena Esperanza, Arg.	G5	92
Buenaventura, Col.	F3	86
Buenaventura, Mex.	G9	98
Buena Vista, Bol.	C4	90
Buena Vista, Mex.	K9	134
Buenavista, Phil.	G4	52
Buena Vista, Co., U.S.	C2	128
Buena Vista, Ga., U.S.	E14	122
Buena Vista, Va., U.S.	G6	114
Buena Vista Lake Bed, reg., Ca., U.S.	H6	134
Buendía, Embalse de, res., Spain	D8	20
Buenópolis, Braz.	I3	88
Buenos Aires, Arg.	G8	92
Buenos Aires, Col.	F3	86
Buenos Aires, C.R.	H6	102
Buenos Aires, state, Arg.	G5	90
Buenos Aires, Lago see General Carrera, Lago, l., S.A.	I2	90
Buen Pasto, Arg.	I3	90
Buerarema, Braz.	H6	88
Buffalo, Ks., U.S.	G2	120
Buffalo, Mn., U.S.	F5	118
Buffalo, Mo., U.S.	G4	120
Buffalo, N.Y., U.S.	B7	114
Buffalo, Oh., U.S.	E4	114
Buffalo, S.C., U.S.	B4	116
Buffalo, S.D., U.S.	B9	126
Buffalo, Tx., U.S.	F2	122
Buffalo, stm., Can.	C8	106
Buffalo, stm., Ar., U.S.	H4	120
Buffalo, stm., Tn., U.S.	B11	122
Buffalo Creek, stm., Mn., U.S.	G4	118
Buffalo Lake, Mn., U.S.	G4	118
Buffalo Lake, l., Ab., Can.	D18	138
Buffalo Lake, l., N.T., Can.	C7	106
Buffalo Narrows, Sk., Can.	D8	106
Buffalo Pound Lake, l., Sk., Can.	D8	124
Buffels, stm., S. Afr.	F10	70
Buffels, stm., S. Afr.	F3	70
Buford, Ga., U.S.	B2	116
Buford Dam, dam, Ga., U.S.	B1	116
Buftea, Rom.	E12	26
Bug (Buh) (Zakhidnyy Buh), stm., Eur.	D17	16
Buga, Col.	F3	86
Bugala Island, i., Ug.	E6	66
Bugeat, Fr.	D7	18
Bugojno, Bos.	E4	26
Bugrino, Russia	B23	8
Bugsuk Island, i., Phil.	F1	52
Bugt, China	C4	38
Bugul'ma, Russia	D8	32
Buguruslan, Russia	D8	32
Buh, stm., China	D4	36
Buh (Bug) (Zakhidnyy Buh), stm., Eur.	D19	16
Buhara, Uzb.	G10	32
Buhl, Mn., U.S.	D6	118
Buhler, Ks., U.S.	C11	128
Buhuşi, Rom.	C13	26
Buies Creek, N.C., U.S.	A7	116
Builth Wells, Wales, U.K.	I9	12
Buin, Chile	F2	92
Buin, Pap. N. Gui.	d6	79b
Buíque, Braz.	E7	88
Buitsivango (Rietfontein), stm., Afr.	B4	70
Buj, Russia	G19	8
Bujalance, Spain	G6	20
Buje, Cro.	E10	22
Bujnaksk, Russia	F7	32
Bujumbura, Bdi.	E5	66
Bukačača, Russia	F12	34
Bukama, D.R.C.	F5	66
Bukan', Russia	G17	10
Bukavu, D.R.C.	E5	66
Bukeya, D.R.C.	G5	66
Bukhara see Buhara, Uzb.	G10	32
Bukittinggi, Indon.	D2	50
Bükki Nemzeti Park, p.o.i., Hung.	A7	26
Bukoba, Tan.	E6	66
Bukovica, reg., Cro.	F12	22
Bukovina, hist. reg., Eur.	B12	26

Name	Map Ref.	Page
Bukuru, Nig.	H6	64
Bula, Indon.	F9	44
Bulaevo, Kaz.	C12	32
Bulajevo see Bulaevo, Kaz.	C12	32
Bulan, Phil.	D4	52
Bulandshahr, India	D6	54
Bulawayo, Zimb.	B9	70
Bulbul, Syria	B7	58
Buldan, Tur.	E11	28
Buldāna, India	H6	54
Buldir Island, i., Ak., U.S.	g22	140a
Bulgan, Mong.	B3	36
Bulgan, Mong.	B5	36
Bulgaria, ctry., Eur.	G12	26
Bulkley, stm., B.C., Can.	B3	138
Bullard, Tx., U.S.	E3	122
Bulla Regia, hist., Tun.	H2	24
Bullas, Spain	F9	20
Bullaxaar, Som.	B8	66
Bulle, Switz.	D4	22
Buller, stm., N.Z.	E5	80
Buller, Mount, mtn., Austl.	K6	76
Bullfinch, Austl.	F3	74
Bull Harbour, B.C., Can.	F2	138
Bullhead, S.D., U.S.	B11	126
Bullhead City, Az., U.S.	H2	132
Bullock, N.C., U.S.	H7	114
Bullock Creek, Austl.	A5	76
Bullock Creek, stm., Austl.	C5	76
Bulloo, stm., Austl.	G4	76
Bullpound Creek, stm., Ab., Can.	E19	138
Bulls Gap, Tn., U.S.	H2	114
Bull Shoals, Ar., U.S.	H5	120
Bull Shoals Lake, res., U.S.	H5	120
Bulnes, Chile	H1	92
Bulolo, Pap. N. Gui.	b4	79a
Bulsār, India	H4	54
Buluan, Phil.	G5	52
Bulukumba, Indon.	F12	50
Bululawang, Indon.	H8	50
Bumba, D.R.C.	D4	66
Bumpus, Mount, hill, Nu., Can.	B8	106
Bumu Hu, l., China	C13	54
Buna, Kenya	D7	66
Bunawan, Phil.	F5	52
Bunbury, Austl.	F3	74
Bunceton, Mo., U.S.	F5	120
Bundaberg, Austl.	E9	76
Bundarra, Austl.	H8	76
Bünde, Ger.	D4	16
Būndi, India	F5	54
Bundoran, Ire.	G4	12
Būndu, India	G10	54
Bungamas, Indon.	E3	50
Bungo-suidō, strt., Japan	G5	40
Bungo-takada, Japan	F4	40
Bungtlang, India	G14	54
Bunia, D.R.C.	D6	66
Bunker, Mo., U.S.	G6	120
Bunker Group, is., Austl.	D9	76
Bunker Hill, In., U.S.	H3	112
Bunker Hill, Or., U.S.	G2	136
Bunker Hill, mtn., Nv., U.S.	D8	134
Bunkie, La., U.S.	G6	122
Bunnell, Fl., U.S.	G4	116
Buñol see Bunyolo, Spain	E10	20
Buntok, Indon.	D9	50
Bunyolo, Spain	E10	20
Bunyu, Pulau, i., Indon.	B10	50
Buolkalah, Russia	B12	34
Buolkalakh see Buolkalah, Russia	B12	34
Buon Ma Thuot, Viet.	F9	48
Buor-Haja, guba, b., Russia	B15	34
Buor-Haja, mys, c., Russia	B15	34
Bupul, Indon.	G11	44
Buqayq, Sau. Ar.	D6	56
Bura, Kenya	E7	66
Burām, Sudan	E5	62
Burang, China	C8	54
Buranhém, stm., Braz.	I6	88
Burāq, Syria	E7	58
Burauen, Phil.	E5	52
Burbank, Wa., U.S.	D8	136
Burç, Tur.	A8	58
Burcher, Austl.	I6	76
Burco, Som.	C9	66
Burdekin, stm., Austl.	C6	76
Burdekin Falls, wtfl, Austl.	C6	76
Burden, Ks., U.S.	D12	128
Burdett, Ks., U.S.	C9	128
Burdur, Tur.	F13	28
Burdur, state, Tur.	F13	28
Burdur Gölü, l., Tur.	F12	28
Bureinskij hrebet, mts., Russia	G15	34
Bureja, Russia	G15	34
Bureja, stm., Russia	F15	34
Büren, Ger.	E4	16
Bürenhayrhan, Mong.	B3	36
Burford, On., Can.	E9	112
Burg, Ger.	D7	16
Burg, Den see Den Burg, Neth.	A13	14
Burgas, Blg.	G14	26
Burgas, state, Blg.	G13	26
Burgas, Gulf of see Burgaski Zaliv, b., Blg.	G14	26
Burgaski Zaliv, b., Blg.	G14	26
Burg auf Fehmarn, Ger.	B7	16
Burgaw, N.C., U.S.	B8	116
Burgdorf, Switz.	C4	22
Burgenland, state, Aus.	C13	22
Burgeo, Nf., Can.	j22	107a
Burgersdorp, S. Afr.	G8	70
Burghausen, Ger.	H8	16
Burghead, Scot., U.K.	D9	12
Burgin, Ky., U.S.	G13	120
Burgo de Osma, Spain	C7	20
Burgos, Mex.	C9	100
Burgos, Phil.	C3	52
Burgos, Spain	B7	20
Burgos, co., Spain	B7	20
Burgstädt, Ger.	F8	16
Burgundy see Bourgogne, hist. reg., Fr.	B10	18
Burhan Budai Shan, mts., China	D4	36
Burhaniye, Tur.	D9	28
Burhānpur, India	H5	54
Burias Island, i., Phil.	D4	52
Burica, Punta, c., N.A.	I6	102
Burien, Wa., U.S.	C4	136
Burila Mare, Rom.	E9	26
Buri Ram, Thai.	E6	48
Buriti, Braz.	B4	88
Buriti Bravo, Braz.	C4	88
Buriticupu, stm., Braz.	C2	88
Buriti dos Lopes, Braz.	B5	88
Buritizeiro, Braz.	I3	88
Burjasot see Burjassot, Spain	E10	20
Burjassot, Spain	E10	20
Burjatija, state, Russia	F11	34
Burkburnett, Tx., U.S.	G10	128
Burke, S.D., U.S.	D13	126
Burke, stm., Austl.	D2	76
Burketown, Austl.	A2	76
Burkina Faso, ctry., Afr.	G4	64
Burleson, Tx., U.S.	B10	130
Burley, Id., U.S.	H13	136
Burlingame, Ca., U.S.	F3	134
Burlingame, Ks., U.S.	F2	120
Burlington, On., Can.	E10	112
Burlington, Co., U.S.	B6	128
Burlington, Ia., U.S.	D6	120
Burlington, Ks., U.S.	F2	120
Burlington, N.C., U.S.	H6	114
Burlington, Vt., U.S.	F3	110
Burlington, Wa., U.S.	B4	136
Burlington, Wi., U.S.	B9	120
Burlington, Wy., U.S.	C4	126
Burlington Junction, Mo., U.S.	D2	120
Burma see Myanmar, ctry., Asia	D8	46
Burnaby, B.C., Can.	G7	138
Burnet, Tx., U.S.	D9	130
Burnett, stm., Austl.	E8	76
Burnett Bay, b., N.T., Can.	B14	140
Burney, Ca., U.S.	C4	134
Burnie, Austl.	n12	77a
Burnley, Eng., U.K.	H10	12
Burns, Ks., U.S.	C12	128
Burns, Or., U.S.	G7	136
Burns, Tn., U.S.	H10	120
Burns, Wy., U.S.	F8	126
Burnside, Ky., U.S.	G13	120
Burnside, stm., Nu., Can.	B8	106
Burnside, Lake, l., Austl.	E4	74
Burns Lake, B.C., Can.	B5	138
Burnsville, Ms., U.S.	C10	122
Burnsville, N.C., U.S.	I3	114
Burnsville, W.V., U.S.	F5	114
Burnt, stm., Or., U.S.	F9	136
Burnt Pine, Norf. I.	y25	78i
Burntwood, stm., Mb., Can.	D11	106
Burqin, China	B2	36
Burra, Austl.	I2	76
Burragorang, Lake, res., Austl.	J7	76
Burrel, Alb.	C13	24
Burreli see Burrel, Alb.	C13	24
Burrendong, Lake, res., Austl.	I7	76
Burren Junction, Austl.	H7	76
Burriana see Borriana, Spain	E10	20
Burrinjuck Reservoir, res., Austl.	J7	76
Burr Oak, Ks., U.S.	B10	128
Burrton, Ks., U.S.	C11	128
Burruyacú, Arg.	E4	90
Bursa, Tur.	C11	28
Bursa, state, Tur.	C11	28
Bûr Sa'îd (Port Said), Egypt	G3	58
Burstall, Sk., Can.	D4	124
Būr Sūdān (Port Sudan), Sudan	D7	62
Burt, Ia., U.S.	H4	118
Burt Lake, l., Mi., U.S.	C5	112
Burtnieks ezers, l., Lat.	C8	10
Burton, Mi., U.S.	E6	112
Burton, Tx., U.S.	G2	122
Burton upon Trent, Eng., U.K.	I11	12
Buru, i., Indon.	F8	44
Burullus, Buheirat el-, l., Egypt	G1	58
Burundi, ctry., Afr.	E6	66
Burun-Šibertuj, gora, mtn., Russia	G10	34
Bururi, Bdi.	E5	66
Burwash, On., Can.	B9	112
Burwell, Ne., U.S.	F13	126
Bury, Eng., U.K.	H10	12
Buryatia see Burjatija, state, Russia	F11	34
Bury Saint Edmunds, Eng., U.K.	I13	12
Burzil, Pak.	A5	54
Busa, Mount, mtn., Phil.	G5	52
Busan see Pusan-jikhalsi, state, Kor., S.	D2	40
Busanga, D.R.C.	E4	66
Busby, Mt., U.S.	B5	126
Bûsh, Egypt	I2	58
Bushire see Bandar-e Būshehr, Iran	D7	56
Bushland, Tx., U.S.	F6	128
Bushman Land, reg., S. Afr.	F4	70
Bushnell, Fl., U.S.	H3	116
Bushnell, Il., U.S.	D7	120
Bushtyna, Ukr.	A10	26
Busia, Ug.	D6	66
Businga, D.R.C.	D4	66
Busira, stm., D.R.C.	E3	66
Buskerud, state, Nor.	F3	8
Busko-Zdrój, Pol.	F16	16
Buṣrá ash-Shām, Syria	F7	58
Busselton, Austl.	F3	74
Bussey, Ia., U.S.	C5	120
Bussum, Neth.	B14	14
Bustamante, Mex.	B8	100
Busto Arsizio, Italy	E5	22
Busuanga Island, i., Phil.	D2	52
Busu-Djanoa, D.R.C.	D4	66
Büsum, Ger.	B4	16
Buta, D.R.C.	D4	66
Buta Ranquil, Arg.	H2	92
Butare, Rw.	E5	66
Butaritari, at., Kir.	C8	72
Bute, Island of, i., Scot., U.K.	F7	12
Bute Inlet, b., B.C., Can.	F5	138
Butembo, D.R.C.	D5	66
Butera, Italy	G8	24
Butere, Kenya	D6	66
Butha-Buthe, Leso.	F9	70
Buthidaung, Mya.	D7	46
Butiá, Braz.	E11	92
Butler, Ga., U.S.	D1	116
Butler, In., U.S.	C1	114
Butler, Mo., U.S.	F3	120
Butler, Oh., U.S.	D3	114
Butler, Pa., U.S.	D6	114
Butner, N.C., U.S.	H7	114
Buto, hist., Egypt	G1	58
Buton, Pulau, i., Indon.	F7	44
Butrint, hist., Alb.	E14	24
Butru, Austl.	C2	76
Butte, Mt., U.S.	D14	136
Butte, Ne., U.S.	E14	126
Butte Creek, stm., Ca., U.S.	D4	134
Butte Falls, Or., U.S.	H4	136
Butternut, Wi., U.S.	E8	118
Butterworth, Malay.	J5	48
Butterworth, S. Afr.	H9	70
Buttle Lake, l., B.C., Can.	G5	138
Button Islands, is., Nu., Can.	C17	106
Buttonwillow, Ca., U.S.	H6	134
Butuan, Phil.	F5	52
Buturlino, Russia	I21	8
Buṭwal, Nepal	E9	54
Butzbach, Ger.	F4	16
Bützow, Ger.	C7	16
Buulobarde, Som.	D9	66
Buur Gaabo, Som.	E8	66
Buurgplaatz, mtn., Lux.	D15	14
Buxtehude, Ger.	C5	16
Buxton, S. Afr.	E7	70
Buxton, Eng., U.K.	H11	12
Buxton, N.C., U.S.	A10	116
Buxton, Mount, mtn., B.C., Can.	E2	138
Buyr nuur, l., Asia	B8	36
Büyükada, Tur.	C12	28
Büyükçekmece, Tur.	B11	28
Büyükkarıştıran, Tur.	B10	28
Büyükkemikli Burnu, c., Tur.	C9	28
Büyükmenderes, stm., Tur.	F10	28
Buzău, Rom.	D13	26
Buzău, state, Rom.	D13	26
Buzău, stm., Rom.	D13	26
Buzen, Japan	F4	40
Búzi, stm., Moz.	A12	70
Buziaș, Rom.	D8	26
Buzuluk, Russia	D8	32
Byādgi, India	D2	53
Byam Channel, strt., Nu., Can.	A19	140
Byam Martin Island, i., Nu., Can.	B19	140
Bycen', Bela.	H8	10
Byčki, Russia	F17	10
Byczyna, Pol.	E14	16
Bydgoszcz, Pol.	C13	16
Bydgoszcz, state, Pol.	C13	16
Byelorussia see Belarus, ctry., Eur.	E14	6
Byers, Tx., U.S.	G10	128
Byesville, Oh., U.S.	E4	114
Bygdin, l., Nor.	F3	8
Byhalia, Ms., U.S.	C9	122
Byhau, Bela.	G13	10
Bykle, Nor.	G2	8
Bylnice, Czech Rep.	G14	16
Bylot Island, i., Nu., Can.	A15	106
Byng Inlet, On., Can.	C9	112
Bynum, Mt., U.S.	C14	136
Bynum, N.C., U.S.	I6	114
Byrd, Lac, l., Qc., Can.	A13	112
Byrnedale, Pa., U.S.	C7	114
Byro, Austl.	E3	74
Byron, Ga., U.S.	D2	116
Byron, Il., U.S.	B8	120
Byron, Cape, c., Austl.	G9	76
Byron Bay, Austl.	G9	76
Byrranga, gory, mts., Russia	B8	34
Bystřice pod Hostýnem, Czech Rep.	G13	16
Bytantaj, stm., Russia	C15	34
Bytča, Slov.	G14	16
Bytom, Pol.	F14	16
Bytoš', Russia	G17	10
Bytów, Pol.	B13	16

C

Name	Map Ref.	Page
Ca, stm., Asia	C7	48
Caacupé, Para.	B9	92
Caaguazú, Para.	B9	92
Caaguazú, state, Para.	B10	92
Caála, Ang.	C2	68
Caapiranga, Braz.	I11	86
Caatinga, Braz.	I3	88
Caazapá, Para.	C9	92
Caazapá, state, Para.	C9	92
Cabaiguán, Cuba	A8	102
Cabaliana, Lago, l., Braz.	I11	86
Caballococha, Peru	D3	84
Caballo Reservoir, res., N.M., U.S.	K9	132
Cabanatuan, Phil.	C3	52
Cabano, Qc., Can.	C8	110
Cabarroguis, Phil.	B3	52
Cabedelo, Braz.	D8	88
Cabeza del Buey, Spain	F5	20
Cabezas, Bol.	C4	90
Cabildo, Arg.	I7	92
Cabimas, Ven.	B6	86
Cabinda, Ang.	B1	68
Cabinda, state, Ang.	B1	68
Cabinet Mountains, mts., U.S.	B10	136
Cable, Wi., U.S.	E7	118
Cabo, Braz.	E8	88
Cabo Blanco, Arg.	I3	90
Cabo Frio, Braz.	L4	88
Cabonga, Réservoir, res., Qc., Can.	F15	106
Cabool, Mo., U.S.	G5	120
Caboolture, Austl.	F9	76
Caborca, Mex.	F6	98
Cabo Rojo, P.R.	B1	104a
Cabot, Ar., U.S.	C7	122
Cabot Head, c., On., Can.	C8	112
Cabot Strait, strt., Can.	j21	107a
Cabourg, Fr.	E8	14
Cabra Corral, Embalse, res., Arg.	B5	92
Cabramurra, Austl.	J7	76
Cabrera, stm., Col.	F4	86
Cabrera, Illa de, i., Spain	E13	20
Cabri, Sk., Can.	D5	124
Cabriel, stm., Spain	E9	20
Cabrillo National Monument, p.o.i., Ca., U.S.	K8	134
Cabrobó, Braz.	E6	88
Cabruta, Ven.	D8	86
Čabullónes, Punta, c., P.R.	C2	104a
Čabusy, Bela.	H11	10
Cabuyaro, Col.	E5	86
Caçador, Braz.	C12	92
Čačak, Yugo.	F7	26
Caçapava, Braz.	L3	88
Caçapava do Sul, Braz.	E11	92
Cacapon, stm., W.V., U.S.	E7	114
Cacequi, Braz.	D10	92
Cáceres, Braz.	G6	84
Cáceres, Col.	D4	86
Cáceres, Spain	E4	20
Cáceres, co., Spain	E4	20
Čačèrsk, Bela.	H13	10
Cache, stm., Ar., U.S.	B7	122
Cache, stm., Il., U.S.	G8	120
Cache Creek, B.C., Can.	F9	138
Cache Creek, stm., Ca., U.S.	E3	134
Cache la Poudre, stm., Co., U.S.	G7	126
Cache Peak, mtn., Id., U.S.	A3	132
Cachi, Arg.	B4	92
Cachimbo, Braz.	E7	84
Cachimbo, Serra do, mts., Braz.	E6	84
Cachoeira Alta, Braz.	C6	90
Cachoeira de Manteiga, Braz.	I3	88
Cachoeira do Sul, Braz.	E11	92
Cachoeiro de Itapemirim, Braz.	K5	88
Cachos, Punta, c., Chile	C2	92
Cachuela Esperanza, Bol.	B3	90
Căciulați, Rom.	E13	26
Cacolo, Ang.	C2	68
Caconda, Ang.	C2	68
Cactus, Tx., U.S.	E6	128
Cactus Flat, pl., Nv., U.S.	F9	134
Cacuaco, Ang.	B1	68
Caculé, Braz.	H4	88
Çacuri, Ven.	E9	86
Čadan, Russia	D16	32
Čadca, Slov.	G14	16
Caddo, Ok., U.S.	C2	122
Caddo, stm., Ar., U.S.	C5	122
Caddo Lake, res., U.S.	E4	122
Caddo Mills, Tx., U.S.	D2	122
Cadell, stm., Austl.	D3	76
Cadena, Cerro, mtn., Mex.	I3	130
Cadena, Punta, c., P.R.	B1	104a
Cadillac, Sk., Can.	E6	124
Cadillac, Fr.	E5	18
Cadillac, Mi., U.S.	D4	112
Cádiz, Spain	H4	20
Cadiz, Ky., U.S.	H10	120
Cádiz, co., Spain	H5	20
Cádiz, Bahía de, b., Spain	H4	20
Cadiz Lake, l., Ca., U.S.	I1	132
Čadobec, stm., Russia	C17	32
Cadomin, Ab., Can.	C13	138
Cadore, reg., Italy	D9	22
Cadott, Wi., U.S.	G7	118
Çadwell, Ga., U.S.	D2	116
Čaek, Kyrg.	F12	32
Caen, Fr.	E8	14
Caengo (Kwenge), stm., Afr.	B2	68
Caernarfon, Wales, U.K.	H8	12
Caernarfon Bay, b., Wales, U.K.	H8	12
Caerphilly, Wales, U.K.	J9	12
Caesarea see Qesari, Horbat, hist., Isr.	F5	58
Caeté, Braz.	J4	88
Caetité, Braz.	H4	88
Cafayate, Arg.	C4	92
Cagayan, stm., Phil.	A3	52
Cagayan de Oro, Phil.	F5	52
Cagayan Islands, is., Phil.	F3	52
Çagayan Sulu Island, i., Phil.	G2	52
Čagda, Russia	E15	34
Çağış, Tur.	D10	28
Cagliari, Italy	E3	24
Cagliari, Golfo di, b., Italy	E3	24
Cagliari, Stagno di, l., Italy	E2	24
Cagnes-sur-Mer, Fr.	F13	18
Čagoda, stm., Russia	A17	10
Čagodošča, stm., Russia	A18	10
Caguán, stm., Col.	G4	86
Caguas, P.R.	B3	104a
Cahaba, stm., Al., U.S.	E11	122
Cahama, Ang.	D1	68
Caher, Ire.	I4	12
Cahokia, Il., U.S.	F7	120
Cahora Bassa, Albufeira, res., Moz.	D5	68
Cahors, Fr.	E7	18
Cahto Peak, mtn., Ca., U.S.	D2	134
Cahuinari, stm., Col.	H6	86
Cahul, Mol.	D15	26
Caí, stm., Braz.	D12	92
Caianda, Ang.	C3	68
Caiapó, Serra do, mts., Braz.	G7	84
Caibarién, Cuba	A8	102
Cai Bau, Dao, i., Viet.	B8	48
Caiçara, Braz.	D8	88
Caicara, Caño, stm., Ven.	D7	86
Caicara de Maturín, Ven.	C10	86
Caicara de Orinoco, Ven.	D8	86
Caicedonia, Col.	E4	86
Caicó, Braz.	D7	88
Caicos Islands, is., T./C. Is.	B11	102
Caicos Passage, strt., N.A.	B11	102
Caijiapo, China	D2	42
Caima Bay, b., Phil.	D4	52
Caimanera, Cuba	C10	102
Caimanero, Laguna del, l., Mex.	D5	100
Cain Creek, stm., S.D., U.S.	C14	126
Cai Nuoc, Viet.	H7	48
Cairari, Braz.	B1	88
Caird Coast, cst., Ant.	C3	81
Cairns, Austl.	A5	76
Cairo see El-Qâhira, Egypt	H2	58
Cairo, Ga., U.S.	F1	116
Cairo, Il., U.S.	G8	120
Cairo, Ne., U.S.	F14	126
Cairo, W.V., U.S.	E4	114
Cairo Montenotte, Italy	F5	22
Cairu, Braz.	G6	88
Caisleán an Bharraigh see Castlebar, Ire.	H3	12
Caiundo, Ang.	D2	68
Caiwan, China	I4	42
Caizi Hu, l., China	F7	42
Caja de Muertos, Isla, i., P.R.	C2	104a
Cajamarca, Peru	E2	84
Cajapió, Braz.	B3	88
Cajazeiras, Braz.	D6	88
Cajon Summit, p., Ca., U.S.	I8	134
Cajuru, Braz.	K2	88
Caka, China	D4	36
Çakmak, Tur.	A5	58
Čakovec, Cro.	D13	22
Calabar, Nig.	H6	64
Calabozo, Ven.	C8	86
Calabozo, Ensenada de, b., Ven.	B6	86
Calabria, state, Italy	F10	24
Calafat, Rom.	F9	26
Calagua Islands, is., Phil.	C4	52
Calahorra, Spain	B8	20
Calais, Fr.	C10	14
Calalaste, Sierra de, mts., Arg.	B4	92
Calama, Chile	D3	90
Calamar, Col.	B4	86
Calamar, Col.	F5	86
Calamian Group, is., Phil.	E3	52
Calamus, stm., Ne., U.S.	E13	126
Calañas, Spain	G4	20
Calang, Indon.	J2	48
Calapan, Phil.	D3	52
Călărași, Mol.	B15	26
Călărași, Rom.	E14	26
Călărași, state, Rom.	E14	26
Calarcá, Col.	E4	86
Calatafimi, Italy	G6	24
Calatayud, Spain	C9	20
Calau, Ger.	E9	16
Calavite Passage, strt., Phil.	D3	52
Calayan Island, i., Phil.	A3	52
Calbayog, Phil.	D5	52
Calbe, Ger.	E7	16
Calbuco, Chile	H2	90
Calcasieu, stm., La., U.S.	G5	122
Calcasieu Lake, l., La., U.S.	G5	122
Calceta, Ec.	H1	86
Calchaquí, Arg.	D7	92
Calchaquí, stm., Arg.	B4	92
Calçoene, Braz.	C7	84
Calcutta see Kolkata, India	G12	54
Caldaro, Italy	D8	22
Caldas, Col.	D4	86
Caldas, state, Col.	E4	86
Caldas da Rainha, Port.	E1	20
Caldas de Reis, Spain	B2	20
Caldas de Reyes see Caldas de Reis, Spain	B2	20
Caldas Novas, Braz.	I1	88
Caldera, Chile	C2	92
Caldwell, Id., U.S.	G10	136
Caldwell, Ks., U.S.	D11	128
Caldwell, Oh., U.S.	E4	114
Caldwell, Tx., U.S.	G2	122
Caledon, S. Afr.	I4	70
Caledon (Mohokare), stm., Afr.	F8	70
Caledonia, Belize	C3	102
Caledonia, N.S., Can.	F11	110
Caledonia, Ms., U.S.	D10	122
Caledonia, N.Y., U.S.	A8	114
Caledonia, Oh., U.S.	D3	114
Calella, Spain	C13	20
Calen, Austl.	C7	76
Calera, Al., U.S.	D12	122
Caleta Olivia, Arg.	I3	90
Caleufú, Arg.	G5	92
Calexico, Ca., U.S.	K10	134
Calgary, Ab., Can.	E16	138
Calhan, Co., U.S.	B4	128
Calhoun, Al., U.S.	E12	122
Calhoun, Ga., U.S.	C14	122
Calhoun, Mo., U.S.	F4	120
Calhoun, Tn., U.S.	B14	122
Calhoun City, Ms., U.S.	D9	122
Cali, Col.	F3	86
Calico Rock, Ar., U.S.	H5	120
Calicut see Kozhikode, India	F2	53
Caliente, Nv., U.S.	F2	132
California, Mo., U.S.	F5	120
California, state, U.S.	D3	108
California, Golfo de (California, Gulf of), b., Mex.	B2	96
California, Gulf of see California, Golfo de, b., Mex.	B2	96
California Aqueduct, aq., Ca., U.S.	I8	134
Calilegua, Parque Nacional, p.o.i., Arg.	A5	92
Calimere, Point, c., India	F4	53
Calingasta, Arg.	E3	92
Calion, Ar., U.S.	D6	122
Calipatria, Ca., U.S.	J10	134
Calispell Peak, mtn., Wa., U.S.	B9	136
Calistoga, Ca., U.S.	E3	134
Calitri, Italy	D9	24
Calitzdorp, S. Afr.	H5	70
Callabonna, Lake, l., Austl.	G2	76
Callabonna Creek, stm., Austl.	G3	76
Callahan, Mount, mtn., Co., U.S.	D8	132
Callan, Ire.	I5	12
Callander, On., Can.	B10	112
Callao, Peru	F2	84
Callaquén, Volcán, vol., Chile	H2	92
Callaway, Ne., U.S.	F12	126
Calliaqua, St. Vin.	o11	105e
Calling Lake, Ab., Can.	A17	138
Calling Lake, l., Ab., Can.	A17	138
Callosa de Segura, Spain	F9	20
Calmar, Ab., Can.	C17	138
Calmar, Ia., U.S.	A6	120
Çalm Lake, l., On., Can.	C6	118
Çal'mny-Varre, Russia	C17	8
Čalna, Russia	F15	8
Caloundra, Austl.	F9	76
Calp, Spain	F11	20
Calpe see Calp, Spain	F11	20
Caltagirone, Italy	G8	24
Caltanissetta, Italy	G8	24
Călugăreni, Rom.	E12	26
Calulo, Ang.	B2	68
Calumet, Mn., U.S.	D5	118
Calumet City, Il., U.S.	G2	112
Calunda, Ang.	C3	68
Caluula, Som.	B10	66
Calvados, state, Fr.	E8	14
Calvert, Al., U.S.	F10	122
Calvert, Tx., U.S.	G2	122
Calvert Island, i., B.C., Can.	E2	138
Calvillo, Mex.	E7	100
Calvin, Ok., U.S.	C2	122
Calvinia, S. Afr.	G4	70
Calw, Ger.	H4	16
Calwa, Ca., U.S.	G6	134
Calypso, N.C., U.S.	A7	116
Camabatela, Ang.	B2	68
Camaçari, Braz.	G6	88
Camacupa, Ang.	C2	68
Camaguán, Ven.	C8	86
Camagüey, Cuba	B9	102
Camaiore, Italy	G7	22
Camajuaní, Cuba	A8	102
Camaná, Peru	G3	84
Camaná, stm., Peru	G3	84
Camanaú, stm., Braz.	H11	86
Camanche Reservoir, res., Ca., U.S.	E4	134
Camapuã, Braz.	C6	90
Camaquã, Braz.	E12	92
Camaquã, stm., Braz.	E11	92
Camará, Braz.	D5	84
Camarajibe, Braz.	D8	88
Camararé, stm., Braz.	F6	84
Camarat, Cap, c., Fr.	F12	18
Camarès, Fr.	F8	18
Camargo, Bol.	D3	90
Camargue, reg., Fr.	F10	18
Camarillo, Ca., U.S.	I6	134
Camarón, Arroyo, stm., Mex.	G7	130
Camarón, Cabo, c., Hond.	D5	102
Camarones, Arg.	H3	90
Camarones, Bahía, b., Arg.	H3	90
Camas Creek, stm., Id., U.S.	F14	136
Camatagua, Embalse de, l., Ven.	C8	86
Ca Mau, Viet.	H7	48
Ca Mau, Mui, c., Viet.	H7	48
Camba, Indon.	F11	50
Cambodia, ctry., Asia	C3	48
Camboon, Austl.	E8	76
Camboriú, Braz.	C13	92
Camborne, Eng., U.K.	K7	12
Cambrai, Fr.	D12	14
Cambria, Ca., U.S.	H4	134
Cambrian Mountains, mts., Wales, U.K.	I9	12
Cambridge, On., Can.	E9	112
Cambridge, N.Z.	C6	80
Cambridge, Eng., U.K.	I12	12
Cambridge, Il., U.S.	C7	120
Cambridge, Ia., U.S.	C4	120
Cambridge, Md., U.S.	F9	114
Cambridge, Ma., U.S.	B14	114
Cambridge, Mn., U.S.	F5	118
Cambridge, Ne., U.S.	A8	128
Cambridge, N.Y., U.S.	G3	110
Cambridge, Oh., U.S.	D4	114
Cambridge Bay see Ikaluktutiak, Nu., Can.	B10	106
Cambridge Fiord, b., Nu., Can.	A15	106
Cambridge Springs, Pa., U.S.	C5	114
Cambrils, Spain	C11	20
Cambuí, Braz.	L2	88
Cambulo, Ang.	B3	68
Cambundi-Catembo, Ang.	C2	68
Camden, Austl.	J8	76
Camden, Al., U.S.	F11	122
Camden, Ar., U.S.	D6	122
Camden, Me., U.S.	F7	110
Camden, N.J., U.S.	E10	114
Camden, N.Y., U.S.	E14	112
Camden, N.C., U.S.	H9	114
Camden, Oh., U.S.	E1	114
Camden, S.C., U.S.	B5	116
Camden, Tn., U.S.	H9	120
Camden Bay, b., Ak., U.S.	B11	140
Camdenton, Mo., U.S.	G5	120
Camels Hump, mtn., Vt., U.S.	F3	110
Camenca, Mol.	A15	26
Camerino, Italy	G10	22
Cameron, Mo., U.S.	E3	120
Cameron, Tx., U.S.	D10	130
Cameron, W.V., U.S.	E5	114
Cameron, Wi., U.S.	F7	118
Cameron Hills, hills, Can.	D7	106
Cameroon, ctry., Afr.	C2	66
Cameroon Mountain, vol., Cam.	D1	66
Camerota, Italy	D9	24
Cametá, Braz.	B1	88
Çamiçi Gölü, l., Tur.	F10	28
Camiguin Island, i., Phil.	F5	52
Camiguin Island, i., Phil.	A3	52
Camiling, Phil.	C3	52
Camilla, Ga., U.S.	E1	116
Camino, Ca., U.S.	E5	134
Camiranga, Braz.	A2	88
Camiri, Bol.	D4	90
Camissombo, Ang.	B3	68
Çamlıdere, Tur.	C15	28
Çamlıdere, Tur.	A10	58
Cam Lo, Viet.	D8	48
Camocim, Braz.	B5	88
Camooweal, Austl.	C7	74
Camorta Island, i., India	G7	46
Camotes Islands, is., Phil.	E5	52
Camotes Sea, Phil.	E5	52
Campagna di Roma, reg., Italy	C6	24
Campaign, Tn., U.S.	B13	122
Campana, Arg.	G8	92
Campana, Isla, i., Chile	I1	90
Campanario, Spain	F5	20
Campania, state, Italy	D8	24
Campano, Appennino, mts., Italy	C8	24
Campaspe, stm., Austl.	C6	76
Campbell, S. Afr.	F6	70
Campbell, Ca., U.S.	F4	134
Campbell, Mo., U.S.	H7	120
Campbell, Ne., U.S.	A10	128
Campbell, Cape, c., N.Z.	E6	80
Campbellford, On., Can.	D12	112
Campbell Hill, hill, Oh., U.S.	D2	114
Campbell Hills, hill, St. Vin.	p11	105e
Campbell Island, B.C., Can.	D2	138
Campbell Island, i., N.Z.	I7	72
Campbell Lake, l., B.C., Can.	G5	138
Campbell Plateau, unds.	O20	142
Campbellpore, Pak.	B4	54
Campbell River, B.C., Can.	F5	138
Campbell's Bay, Qc., Can.	C13	112
Campbellsport, Wi., U.S.	E1	112
Campbellton, N.B., Can.	C10	110
Campbellton, P.E., Can.	D12	110
Campbellton, Fl., U.S.	G13	122
Campbelltown, Austl.	J8	76
Campbell Town, Austl.	n13	77a
Campbeltown, Scot., U.K.	F7	12
Campeche, Mex.	C2	102
Campeche, state, Mex.	C2	102
Campeche, Bahía de, b., Mex.	D6	96
Campeche, Gulf of see Campeche, Bahía de, b., Mex.	E13	100
Campechuela, Cuba	B9	102
Câmpeni, Rom.	C10	26
Camperdown, Austl.	L4	76
Camperville, Mb., Can.	C13	124
Cam Pha, Viet.	B8	48
Camp Hill, Al., U.S.	E13	122
Camp Hill, Pa., U.S.	H12	112
Câmpia Turzii, Rom.	C10	26
Campidano, val., Italy	E2	24
Campiglia Marittima, Italy	G7	22
Campillos, Spain	G6	20
Câmpina, Rom.	D12	26
Campina, reg., Spain	G5	20
Campina Grande, Braz.	D7	88
Campinas, Braz.	L2	88
Campina Verde, Braz.	J1	88
Campoalegre, Col.	F4	86
Campo Alegre de Goiás, Braz.	I2	88
Campobasso, Italy	C8	24
Campo Belo, Braz.	K3	88
Campo de Criptana, Spain	E7	20
Campo Erê, Braz.	C11	92
Campo Florido, Braz.	J1	88
Campo Formoso, Braz.	F5	88
Campo Gallo, Arg.	C6	92
Campo Grande, Braz.	D6	90
Campo Largo, Arg.	C7	92
Campo Largo, Braz.	B13	92
Campo Maior, Braz.	C4	88
Campo Maior, Port.	F3	20
Campo Mourão, Braz.	A11	92
Campo Novo, Braz.	C11	92
Campos, Braz.	K5	88
Campos Altos, Braz.	J2	88
Campo Santo, Arg.	B5	92
Campos Belos, Braz.	G2	88
Campos do Jordão, Braz.	L3	88
Campos Gerais, Braz.	K2	88
Campos Novos, Braz.	C12	92
Campos Sales, Braz.	D5	88
Camp Point, Il., U.S.	D6	120
Campti, La., U.S.	F5	122
Campton, Ky., U.S.	G2	114
Câmpulung, Rom.	D11	26
Câmpulung Moldovenesc, Rom.	B12	26
Campuya, stm., Peru	H4	86
Camp Verde, Az., U.S.	I4	132
Cam Ranh, Viet.	G9	48
Cam Ranh, Vinh, b., Viet.	G9	48
Cam Ranh Bay see Cam Ranh, Vinh, b., Viet.	G9	48
Camrose, Ab., Can.	C18	138
Camsell, stm., N.T., Can.	B7	106
Camuy, P.R.	B2	104a
Çan, Tur.	C10	28
Canaan, Vt., U.S.	E5	110
Cana-brava, stm., Braz.	G1	88
Cana-brava, stm., Braz.	G1	88
Canada, ctry., N.A.	D9	106
Canada Basin, unds.	A25	142
Cañada de Gómez, Arg.	F7	92
Cañada Honda, Arg.	F3	92
Canadian, Tx., U.S.	F8	128
Canadian, stm., U.S.	F13	128
Canadian, Deep Fork, stm., Ok., U.S.	F13	128
Canaguá, stm., Ven.	D7	86
Canaima, Parque Nacional, p.o.i., Ven.	E10	86
Canajoharie, N.Y., U.S.	B11	114
Çanakkale, Tur.	C9	28
Çanakkale, state, Tur.	D9	28
Çanakkale Boğazı (Dardanelles), strt., Tur.	C9	28
Canala, N. Cal.	m15	79d
Canal Fulton, Oh., U.S.	D4	114
Canal Point, Fl., U.S.	J5	116
Canals, Arg.	F6	92
Canal Winchester, Oh., U.S.	E3	114
Canandaigua, N.Y., U.S.	B8	114
Cananea, Mex.	F7	98
Canápolis, Braz.	J1	88
Cañar, Ec.	I2	86
Cañar, state, Ec.	I2	86
Canarias, Islas (Canary Islands), is., Spain	D1	64
Canarreos, Archipiélago de los, is., Cuba	B6	102
Canary Basin, unds.	F11	144
Canary Islands see Canarias, Islas, is., Spain	D1	64
Cañas, C.R.	G5	102
Canaseraga, N.Y., U.S.	B8	114
Canastota, N.Y., U.S.	E14	112
Canatlán, Mex.	C6	100
Canaveral, Cape, c., Fl., U.S.	H5	116
Canaveral National Seashore, p.o.i., Fl., U.S.	H5	116
Cañaveras, Spain	D8	20
Canavese, hist. reg., Italy	E4	22
Canavieiras, Braz.	H6	88
Canbelego, Austl.	H6	76
Canberra, Austl.	J7	76
Canby, Ca., U.S.	B5	134
Canby, Mn., U.S.	G2	118
Canby, Or., U.S.	E4	136
Cancon, Fr.	E6	18
Cancún, Mex.	B4	102
Cancún, Punta, c., Mex.	B4	102
Çandarlı Körfezi, b., Tur.	E9	28
Candé, Fr.	G7	14
Candeias, Braz.	G6	88
Candeias, Braz.	K3	88
Candela, stm., Mex.	B8	100
Candelaria, Arg.	C10	92
Candelária, Braz.	D11	92
Candelaria, stm., Mex.	C2	102
Candelo, Austl.	K7	76
Cándido Aguilar, Mex.	C9	100
Cândido Mendes, Braz.	A3	88
Candlemas Islands, is., S. Geor.	K12	82
Candlestick, Ms., U.S.	E8	122
Cando, N.D., U.S.	F14	124
Candon, Phil.	B3	52
Candor, N.Y., U.S.	B9	114
Candor, N.C., U.S.	A6	116
Canea see Chaniá, Grc.	H7	28
Canela, Braz.	D12	92
Canelas, Mex.	C5	100
Canelli, Italy	F5	22

Name	Map Ref.	Page

Name | Map Ref. | Page

Crevillente see Crevillent, Spain F10 20
Crewe, Eng., U.K. H10 12
Crewe, Va., U.S. G7 114
Cricaré, stm., Braz. J5 88
Criciúma, Braz. D13 92
Crikvenica, Cro. E11 22
Crimea see Kryms'kyi pivostriv, pen., Ukr. E4 32
Crimean Peninsula see Kryms'kyi pivostriv, pen., Ukr. E4 32
Crimmitschau, Ger. F8 16
Cripple Creek, Co., U.S. C3 128
Crisfield, Md., U.S. F10 114
Criss Creek, B.C., Can. E10 138
Crissiumal, Braz. C10 92
Cristal, Monts de, mts., Afr. I7 64
Cristalândia, Braz. F1 88
Cristália, Braz. I4 88
Cristalina, Braz. I2 88
Cristinápolis, Braz. F7 88
Cristino Castro, Braz. E3 88
Cristóbal Colón, Pico, mtn., Col. B5 86
Crişul Alb, stm., Eur. C8 26
Crişul Negru, stm., Eur. C8 26
Crişul Repede (Sebes Körös), stm., Eur. B8 26
Crivitz, Wi., U.S. C1 112
Crna, stm., Mac. B4 28
Crna Gora (Montenegro), state, Yugo. G6 26
Crni Drim (Drinit të Zi), stm., Eur. C14 24
Črnomelj, Slvn. E12 22
Croajingolong National Park, p.o.i., Austl. K7 76
Croatia, ctry., Eur. E13 22
Croche, stm., Qc., Can. C4 110
Crocker, Mo., U.S. G5 120
Crocker, Banjaran, mts., Malay. H1 52
Crockett, Tx., U.S. F3 122
Crocodilopilos, hist., Egypt I1 58
Crocus Hill, hill, Anguilla A1 105a
Crofton, Ky., U.S. G10 120
Croghan, N.Y., U.S. E14 112
Croix, Lac la, l., N.A. C6 118
Croker, Cape, c., Austl. B6 74
Croker, Cape, c., On., Can. D9 112
Croker Island, i., Austl. B6 74
Cromer, Eng., U.K. I14 12
Cromínia, Braz. I1 88
Crompton Point, c., Dom. i6 105c
Cromwell, N.Z. G3 80
Cromwell, Al., U.S. E10 122
Crooked, stm., Or., U.S. F5 136
Crooked Creek, Ak., U.S. D8 140
Crooked Creek, stm., U.S. D8 128
Crooked Island, i., Bah. A10 102
Crooked Island Passage, strt., Bah. A10 102
Crooked River, Sk., Can. B10 124
Crookston, Mn., U.S. D2 118
Crooksville, Oh., U.S. E3 114
Crosby, Mn., U.S. E5 118
Crosby, N.D., U.S. F10 124
Crosby, Mount, mtn., Wy., U.S. D3 126
Crosbyton, Tx., U.S. H7 128
Cross, stm., Afr. H6 64
Crossett, Ar., U.S. D7 122
Cross Lake, res., Mb., Can. E11 106
Crossman Peak, mtn., Az., U.S. I2 132
Cross Plains, Tx., U.S. B8 130
Cross Plains, Wi., U.S. H9 118
Cross Sound, strt., Ak., U.S. E12 140
Crossville, Il., U.S. F9 120
Crossville, Tn., U.S. I12 120
Croswell, Mi., U.S. E7 112
Crotone, Italy E11 24
Crow, North Fork, stm., Mn., U.S. F5 118
Crow, South Fork, stm., Mn., U.S. G4 118
Crow Agency, Mt., U.S. B5 126
Crow Creek, stm., U.S. G8 126
Crowder, Ms., U.S. C8 122
Crowduck Lake, l., Mb., Can. A3 118
Crowdy Head, c., Austl. H9 76
Crowell, Tx., U.S. H9 128
Crow Lake, On., Can. B5 118
Crowley, La., U.S. G6 122
Crowleys Ridge, mts., U.S. B8 122
Crown Mountain, mtn., V.I.U.S. e7 104b
Crown Point, In., U.S. G2 112
Crownpoint, N.M., U.S. H8 132
Crown Point, N.Y., U.S. G3 110
Crown Prince Frederik Island, i., Nu., Can. A13 106
Crowsnest Pass, Ab., Can. G16 138
Crowsnest Pass, p., Can. G16 138
Crows Nest Peak, mtn., S.D., U.S. C8 126
Crow Wing, stm., Mn., U.S. E4 118
Croydon, Austl. B4 76
Croydon Station, B.C., Can. C11 138
Crozet, Va., U.S. F7 114
Crozet, Îles, is., Afr. J16 4
Crozet Basin, unds. M9 142
Crucea, Rom. E15 26
Cruces, Cuba A7 102
Cruger, Ms., U.S. D8 122
Crump Lake, l., Or., U.S. A6 134
Cruz, Cabo, c., Cuba C9 102
Cruz Alta, Arg. F6 92
Cruz Alta, Braz. D11 92
Cruz Bay, V.I.U.S. e7 104b
Cruz del Eje, Arg. E5 92
Cruzeiro, Braz. L3 88
Cruzeiro do Oeste, Braz. A11 92
Cruzeiro do Sul, Braz. E3 84
Cruzeta, Braz. D7 88
Cruz Grande, Chile D2 92
Crysler, On., Can. C14 112
Crystal, Mn., U.S. F5 118
Crystal, N.D., U.S. F16 124
Crystal Brook, Austl. I2 76
Crystal City, Mb., Can. E15 124
Crystal City, Mo., U.S. F7 120
Crystal City, Tx., U.S. F8 130
Crystal Falls, Mi., U.S. B1 112
Crystal Lake, Il., U.S. B9 120
Crystal Lake, l., Mi., U.S. D3 112
Crystal Springs, Ms., U.S. E8 122
Csongrád, Hung. C7 26
Csongrád, state, Hung. C7 26
Csorna, Hung. B4 26
Cu, stm., Asia F11 32
Cúa, Ven. B8 86
Cuajinicuilapa, Mex. G9 100
Cuamba, Moz. C6 68
Cuando (Kwando), stm., Afr. D3 68
Cuangar, Ang. D2 68
Cuango, Ang. B2 68
Cuango see Kwango, stm., Afr. F3 66
Cuanza, stm., Ang. C2 68
Cuao, stm., Ven. E8 86
Cuareim (Quaraí), stm., S.A. E9 92
Cuaró, Ur. E9 92
Cuarto, stm., Arg. F5 92
Cuatrociénegas, Mex. B7 100
Cuauhtémoc, Mex. A5 100
Cuautitlán, Mex. F6 100
Cuba, Port. F3 20
Cuba, Al., U.S. E10 122
Cuba, Il., U.S. D7 120
Cuba, Mo., U.S. F6 120
Cuba, N.M., U.S. G10 132
Cuba, ctry., N.A. C9 96
Cubagua, Isla, i., Ven. B9 86
Cubal, Ang. C1 68
Cubango (Okavango), stm., Afr. D2 68
Cubati, Braz. D7 88
Čublas, Russia D21 8
Çubuk, Tur. C15 28
Čuchi, stm., Ang. C2 68
Cuchillo Co, Arg. I5 92
Cuchivero, stm., Ven. D9 86
Cucuí, Braz. G8 86
Cucurpe, Mex. F7 98
Cúcuta, Col. D5 86
Cucuy, Piedra de, hill, Ven. G8 86
Cudahy, Wi., U.S. F2 112
Cuddalore, India F4 53
Cuddapah, India D4 53
Čudovo, Russia A14 10
Cudworth, Sk., Can. B8 124
Čudzin, Bela. H9 10
Cue, Austl. E3 74
Cuemba, Ang. C2 68
Cuenca, Ec. I2 86
Cuenca, Spain D8 20
Cuenca, co., Spain E9 20
Cuencamé de Ceniceros, Mex. C7 100
Cuernavaca, Mex. F9 100
Cuero, Tx., U.S. E10 130
Cuers, Fr. F12 18
Cuervo, Laguna del, l., Mex. A6 100
Cuesta Pass, p., Ca., U.S. H5 134
Cueto, Cuba B9 102
Cugir, Rom. D10 26
Čuguevka, Russia B10 38
Čuhlomskoe, ozero, l., Russia G19 8
Cuiabá, Braz. G6 84
Cuiabá, stm., Braz. G6 84
Cuiari, Braz. G7 86
Cuicatlán, Mex. G10 100
Cuilapa, Guat. E2 102
Cuilco see Grijalva, stm., N.A. G12 100
Cuilo (Kwilu), stm., Afr. F3 66
Cuité, Braz. D7 88
Cuíto, stm., Ang. D2 68
Cuito Cuanavale, Ang. D2 68
Cuitzeo, Lago de, l., Mex. F8 100
Cuiuni, stm., Braz. H10 86
Cukai, Malay. J6 48
Cukas, Indon. D4 50
Čukotskij, mys, c., Russia D26 34
Čukotskij poluostrov (Chukotsk Peninsula), pen., Russia C26 34
Čulakkurgan, Kaz. F11 32
Culbertson, Mt., U.S. F9 124
Cul de Sac, Guad. A1 105a
Cul de Sac, Neth. Ant. A1 105a
Culebra, P.R. B5 104a
Culebra, Isla de, i., P.R. B5 104a
Culebra Peak, mtn., Co., U.S. D3 128
Culfa, Azer. B6 56
Culgoa, stm., Austl. G6 76
Culiacán, Mex. C5 100
Culiacán, Mex. C5 100
Culion Island, i., Phil. E2 52
Cúllar, Spain G8 20
Cullen, La., U.S. E5 122
Culleoka, Tn., U.S. B12 122
Cullera, Spain E10 20
Cullman, Al., U.S. C12 122
Cullom, Il., U.S. D9 120
Čul'man, Russia E13 34
Culpeper, Va., U.S. F7 114
Culpina, Bol. D4 90
Culuene, stm., Braz. F7 84
Culver, In., U.S. G3 112
Culver, Or., U.S. F5 136
Culverden, N.Z. F5 80
Čulym, Russia C14 32
Čulym, stm., Russia C14 32
Čum, Russia C1 34
Cumaná, Ven. B9 86
Cumare, Cerro, hill, Col. G5 86
Cumari, Braz. J1 88
Cumbal, Nevado, vol., Col. G2 86
Cumbe, Braz. F7 88
Cumberland, B.C., Can. G5 138
Cumberland, Ky., U.S. G2 114
Cumberland, Md., U.S. E7 114
Cumberland, Va., U.S. G7 114
Cumberland, Wi., U.S. F6 118
Cumberland, stm., U.S. H2 114
Cumberland, Lake, res., Ky., U.S. H13 120
Cumberland, South Fork, stm., U.S. H13 120
Cumberland Gap, p., U.S. H2 114
Cumberland Island National Seashore, p.o.i., Ga., U.S. F4 116
Cumberland Islands, is., Austl. C7 76
Cumberland Lake, l., Sk., Can. E10 106
Cumberland Peninsula, pen., Nu., Can. B17 106
Cumberland Plateau, plat., U.S. G14 120
Cumberland Sound, strt., Nu., Can. B17 106
Cumbernauld, Scot., U.K. F9 12
Cumbrian Mountains, mts., Eng., U.K. G9 12
Cumby, Tx., U.S. D3 122
Čumikan, Russia F16 34
Cumming, Ga., U.S. B1 116
Cummins, Austl. F7 74
Cumnock, Scot., U.K. F8 12
Cumpas, Mex. F8 98
Çumra, Tur. F15 28
Čumyš, stm., Russia D15 32
Čuna, stm., Russia C17 32
Cunani, Braz. C7 84
Cunaviche, Ven. D8 86
Cunco, Chile G2 90
Cundinamarca, state, Col. E4 86
Čundža, Kaz. F13 32
Cunene (Kunene), stm., Afr. D1 68
Cuneo (Coni), Italy F4 22
Cunha Porã, Braz. C11 92
Čunja, stm., Russia B17 32
Cunnamulla, Austl. G5 76
Cunningham, Ks., U.S. D10 128
Čunskij, Russia C17 32
Cunucunuma, stm., Ven. F9 86
Čuny, Russia G17 8
Cuorgnè, Italy E4 22
Cupar, Sk., Can. D9 124
Cupar, Scot., U.K. E9 12
Cupica, Golfo de, b., Col. D3 86
Čuprovo, Russia D22 8
Cuquenán, stm., Ven. E11 86
Curaçá, Braz. E6 88
Curaçao, i., Neth. Ant. p21 104g
Curacautín, Chile I2 92
Curanilahue, Chile H1 92
Curanipe, Chile G1 92
Čurapča, Russia D15 34
Curaray, stm., S.A. H4 86
Curepipe, Mrts. i10 69a
Curepto, Chile G1 92
Curicó, Chile G2 92
Curicuriari, stm., Braz. H8 86
Curimatá, Braz. E3 88
Curitiba, Braz. B13 92
Curitibanos, Braz. C12 92
Curiuaú, stm., Braz. H11 86
Curiúva, Braz. B12 92
Curlew, Wa., U.S. B8 136
Curnamona, Austl. H2 76
Čurovići, Russia H15 10
Currais Novos, Braz. D7 88
Curralinho, Braz. D8 84
Currant Mountain, mtn., Nv., U.S. E1 132
Current, stm., U.S. H7 120
Currie, Austl. m12 77a
Currituck, N.C., U.S. H9 114
Currituck Sound, strt., N.C., U.S. H10 114
Curtea de Argeş, Rom. D11 26
Curtina, Ur. F9 92
Curtis, Ar., U.S. D5 122
Curtis, Ne., U.S. G12 126
Curtis, Port, b., Austl. D8 76
Curtis Channel, strt., Austl. D8 76
Curtis Island, i., Austl. D8 76
Curtis Island, i., N.Z. G9 72
Curu, stm., Braz. B6 88
Curuá, stm., Braz. D7 84
Curuá, stm., Braz. E7 84
Curuá, Ilha do, i., Braz. C7 84
Curuá-Una, stm., Braz. D7 84
Curuçá, Braz. D8 84
Curumu, Braz. D7 84
Curup, Indon. E3 50
Curupá, Braz. E2 88
Cururupu, Braz. A3 88
Curuzú Cuatiá, Arg. D8 92
Curvelo, Braz. J3 88
Cusco, Peru F3 84
Cushing, Ok., U.S. B2 122
Cushing, Tx., U.S. F4 122
Cushman, Ar., U.S. I6 120
Cusiana, stm., Col. E5 86
Cusihuiriachic, Mex. A5 100
Čusovaja, stm., Russia C9 32
Čusovoj, Russia C9 32
Cusset, Fr. C9 18
Cusseta, Ga., U.S. E14 122
Čust, Uzb. F12 32
Custer, Mi., U.S. E3 112
Custer, Mt., U.S. A5 126
Custer, S.D., U.S. D9 126
Custódia, Braz. E7 88
Cut, Nuhu, i., Indon. G9 44
Cut Bank, Mt., U.S. B14 136
Cutbank, stm., Ab., Can. B12 138
Cut Bank Creek, stm., U.S. F12 124
Cut Bank Creek, stm., Mt., U.S. B14 136
Cutervo, Peru E2 84
Cuthbert, Ga., U.S. F14 122
Cutler, Ca., U.S. G6 134
Cutler, Me., U.S. F9 110
Cutlerville, Mi., U.S. F4 112
Cutral-Có, Arg. G3 90
Cutro, Italy E10 24
Cuttack, India H10 54
Cutzamalá, stm., Mex. F8 100
Čuvašija, state, Russia C7 32
Cuvier, Cape, c., Austl. D2 74
Cuvo, stm., Ang. C1 68
Cuxhaven, Ger. C4 16
Cuyahoga Falls, Oh., U.S. C4 114
Cuyama, stm., Ca., U.S. I6 134
Cuyamaca Peak, mtn., Ca., U.S. J9 134
Cuyarí, stm., S.A. G7 86
Cuyo, Phil. E3 52
Cuyo East Pass, strt., Phil. E3 52
Cuyo Islands, is., Phil. E3 52
Cuyo West Pass, strt., Phil. E3 52
Cuyubini, stm., Ven. D11 86
Cuyuni, stm., S.A. B6 84
Cuyuni-Mazaruni, state, Guy. D11 86
Cwmbran, Wales, U.K. J10 12
Cyclades see Kikládes, is., Grc. F7 28
Cypress, La., U.S. F5 122
Cypress Hills, hills, Can. E4 124
Cypress River, Mb., Can. E14 124
Cypress Springs, Lake, res., Tx., U.S. D3 122
Cyprus, ctry., Asia C4 58
Cyprus, i., Asia D15 4
Cyprus, North, ctry., Asia C4 58
Cyrenaica see Barqah, hist. reg., Libya A4 62
Cyril, Ok., U.S. G10 128
Cyril E. King Airport, V.I.U.S. e7 104b
Cyrus Field Bay, b., Nu., Can. E13 141
Čyrvonae, vozero, l., Bela. H10 10
Cythera see Kýthira, i., Grc. G5 28
Czaplinek, Pol. C12 16
Czarna Woda, Pol. C14 16
Czarnków, Pol. D12 16
Czechoslovakia see Czech Republic, ctry., Eur. G11 16
Czechowice-Dziedzice, Pol. G15 16
Czech Republic, ctry., Eur. G11 16
Czerniejewo, Pol. D13 16
Czerwieńsk, Pol. D11 16
Częstochowa, Pol. F15 16
Częstochowa, state, Pol. F15 16
Człuchów, Pol. C13 16

D

Da, stm., China G8 42
Da, Song see Black, stm., Asia D9 46
Da'an, China J4 42
Dabajuro, Ven. B6 86
Daba Ling, mtn., China I5 42
Daba Shan, mts., China E3 42
Dabat, Eth. E7 62
Dabeiba, Col. D3 86
Dabhoi, India G4 54
Dąbie, Pol. D14 16
Dabie Shan, mts., China F6 42
Dabnou, Niger G5 64
Dabola, Gui. G2 64
Dabou, C. Iv. H4 64
Daboya, Ghana H4 64
Dabra, India F7 54
Dąbrowa Białostocka, Pol. C19 16
Dabu, China I7 42
Dacca see Dhaka, Bngl. G13 54
Dac Glei, Viet. E8 48
Dachau, Ger. H7 16
Dačice, Czech Rep. G11 16
Dacoma, Ok., U.S. E10 128
Dadanawa, Guy. F12 86
Dade City, Fl., U.S. H3 116
Dadeldhurā, Nepal D8 54
Dadeville, Al., U.S. E13 122
Dādra and Nagar Haveli, state, India I4 54
Dādu, Pak. D10 56
Daegu see Taegu, Kor., S. D1 40
Daejeon see Taejŏn, Kor., S. F7 38
Daerhanwangfu, China B5 38
Daet, Phil. C4 52
Dafang, China F6 36
Dafeng, China E9 42
Dáfni, Grc. F5 28
Dafoe, Sk., Can. C9 124
Dafu, stm., China F5 42
Dagā, stm., Mya. D2 48
Dagana, Sen. F1 64
Daga Post, Sudan F6 62
Dağardı, Tur. D12 28
Dagda, Lat. D10 10
Dagestan, state, Russia F7 32
Daglung, China D13 54
Dagu, China B7 42
Dagua, Pap. N. Gui. a3 79a
Daguan, China F5 36
Daguan Hu, l., China F7 42
Daguao, P.R. B4 104a
Dagujia, China C6 38
Dagupan, Phil. B3 52
Dagzê Co, l., China B11 54
Dahab, Egypt J5 58
Dahei, India H4 54
Daheiding Shan, mtn., China B10 36
Da Hinggan Ling (Greater Khingan Range), mts., China B9 36
Dahlak Archipelago, is., Erit. D8 62
Dahlonega, Ga., U.S. B1 116
Dahlonega Plateau, plat., U.S. C14 122
Dahmani, Tun. I2 24
Dahme, Ger. E9 16
Dāhod, India G5 54
Dahomey see Benin, ctry., Afr. G5 64
Dahra, Libya B3 62
Dahra, mts., Alg. H11 20
Dahshur, Pyramides de (Dashur, Pyramids of), hist., Egypt I1 58
Dai, i., Sol. Is. d9 79b
Daia, Rom. E12 26
Dai Hai, l., China A5 42
Daik-u, Mya. D3 48
Dā'il, Syria F7 58
Daimiel, Spain E7 20
Daingean, Ire. H5 12
Daingerfield, Tx., U.S. D4 122
Dainkog, China E4 36
Daireaux, Arg. H7 92
Dairen see Dalian, China B9 42
Dairût, Egypt K1 58
Dai-sen, vol., Japan D6 40
Daisetta, Tx., U.S. G4 122
Daixian, China B5 42
Daiyun Shan, mts., China I8 42
Dajarra, Austl. C2 76
Dajian Shan, mtn., China F5 36
Dakar, Sen. G1 64
Dakeng, China H6 42
Dakhin Shāhbāzpur Island, i., Bngl. G13 54
Dakhla, W. Sah. E1 64
Dākoānk, India G7 46
Dakoro, Niger G6 64
Dakota City, Ia., U.S. B3 120
Dakota City, Ne., U.S. B1 120
Đakovica, Yugo. G7 26
Đakovo, Cro. E15 22
Dala, Sol. Is. e9 79b
Dalaba, Gui. G2 64
Dalad Qi, China A4 42
Dalälven, stm., Swe. F7 8
Dalaman, stm., Tur. G11 28
Dalāmī, Sudan E6 62
Dalandzadgad, Mong. C5 36
Dalarna, state, Swe. F6 8
Da Lat, Viet. F9 48
Dālbandin, Pak. D9 56
Dalbosjön, b., Swe. G5 8
Dalby, Austl. F8 76
Dale, Nor. F1 8
Dale, In., U.S. F10 120
Dale Hollow Lake, res., U.S. H12 120
Dalet, Mya. B1 48
Daleville, In., U.S. H4 112
Dalga, Egypt K1 58
Dalhart, Tx., U.S. E6 128
Dalhousie, N.B., Can. B10 110
Dalhousie, India B5 54
Dalhousie, Cape, c., N.T., Can. B14 140
Dali, China F5 36
Dali, China D3 42
Dalian (Dairen), China B9 42
Daliang Shan, mts., China F5 36
Dalin, China C5 38
Daling, stm., China D4 38
Dalj, Cro. E15 22
Dālkola, India F11 54
Dallas, Ga., U.S. D14 122
Dallas, Or., U.S. F3 136
Dallas, Pa., U.S. C9 114
Dallas, Tx., U.S. B11 130
Dallas, Wi., U.S. F7 118
Dallas Center, Ia., U.S. J4 118
Dallas City, Il., U.S. D6 120
Dalli Rājhara, India H8 54
Dall Island, i., Ak., U.S. F13 140
Dall Lake, l., Ak., U.S. D7 140
Dalmacija see Dalmatia, hist. reg., Eur. G12 22
Dalmatia, hist. reg., Eur. G12 22
Dalmau, India E8 54
Dal'negorsk, Russia B11 38
Dal'nerečensk, Russia B11 36
Dal'nyk, Ukr. C17 26
Daloa, C. Iv. H3 64
Dalqū, Sudan C6 62
Dalroy, Ab., Can. E17 138
Dalrymple, Mount, mtn., Austl. C7 76
Dalsing Sarai, India F10 54
Dāltenganj, India F10 54
Dalton, Ga., U.S. C13 122
Dalton, Ma., U.S. B12 114
Dalton, Ne., U.S. F10 126
Daludalu, Indon. C2 50
Dalupiri Island, i., Phil. A3 52
Dalwallinu, Austl. F3 74
Daly, stm., Austl. B6 74
Daly Bay, b., Nu., Can. C13 106
Daly City, Ca., U.S. F3 134
Daly Lake, l., Sk., Can. D9 106
Daly Waters, Austl. C6 74
Dam, stm., China B14 54
Damaia, Port. F1 20
Damān, India H4 54
Damān and Diu, state, India H4 54
Damanhûr, Egypt G1 58
Damar, Pulau, i., Indon. G8 44
Damaraland, hist. reg., Nmb. E2 68
Damascus see Dimashq, Syria E7 58
Damascus, Ar., U.S. B6 122
Damascus, Ga., U.S. F14 122
Damascus, Md., U.S. E8 114
Damaturu, Nig. G7 64
Damāvand, Qolleh-ye, vol., Iran B7 56
Damba, Ang. B2 68
Dambarta, Nig. G6 64
Damboa, Nig. G7 64
Dâmboviţa, state, Rom. E12 26
Dâmboviţa, stm., Rom. D12 26
Dam Doi, Viet. H7 48
Damen Dao, i., China H9 42
Dāmghān, Iran B7 56
Damiao, China C1 42
Damietta, Egypt G2 58
Damietta Mouth see Dumyât, Masabb, mth., Egypt G3 58
Daming, China C6 42
Dāmodar, stm., India G11 54
Damoh, India G7 54
Damongo, Ghana H4 64
Dampier, Austl. D3 74
Dampier, Selat, strt., Indon. F9 44
Dampier Land, pen., Austl. C4 74
Dampier Strait, strt., Pap. N. Gui. b4 79a
Dâmrei, Chuŏr Phnum, mts., Camb. G7 48
Damxung, China C13 54
Dan, stm., China E4 42
Dan, stm., U.S. H6 114
Dana, In., U.S. I2 112
Danai, Indon. C3 50
Danakil, reg., Afr. E8 62
Danané, C. Iv. H3 64
Da Nang, Viet. D9 48
Danao, Phil. E5 52
Dānāpur, India F10 54
Danba, China E5 36
Danbury, Ct., U.S. C12 114
Danbury, Ia., U.S. B2 120
Danbury, Ne., U.S. A8 128
Danby Lake, l., Ca., U.S. I1 132
Dandeli, India D2 53
Dandenong, Austl. K5 76
Dandong, China D5 38
Dandridge, Tn., U.S. H2 114
Danfeng, China E4 42
Danforth, Me., U.S. E9 110
Dang, stm., China F16 32
Dangan Liedao, is., China K6 42
Dangara, Taj. B10 56
Dangchang, China E5 36
Danger Point, c., S. Afr. I4 70
Danggali Conservation Park, p.o.i., Austl. I3 76
Dangila, Eth. E7 62
Dangriga, Belize D3 102
Dangshan, China D7 42
Dangtu, China F8 42
Dan-Gulbi, Nig. G6 64
Dangyang, China F4 42
Daniel, Wy., U.S. H16 136
Daniel-Johnson, Barrage, dam, Qc., Can. E17 106
Daniëlskuil, S. Afr. F6 70
Danielson, Ct., U.S. C13 114
Daniels Pass, p., Ut., U.S. C5 132
Danielsville, Ga., U.S. B2 116
Danilov, Russia G18 8
Danilovka, Kaz. D12 32
Daning, China I4 42
Danjiangkou Shuiku, res., China E4 42
Danjo-guntō, is., Japan G1 40
Danlí, Hond. F4 102
Danmark Fjord, b., Grnld. A22 141
Dannebrog, Ne., U.S. F14 126
Dannenberg, Ger. C6 16
Dannevirke, N.Z. E7 80
Danshui, China J6 42
Dansville, N.Y., U.S. B8 114
Dante, Va., U.S. H3 114
Dantewāra, India B5 53
Danube, stm., Eur. F11 6
Danube, Mouths of the, mth., Eur. E16 26
Danubyu, Mya. D2 48
Danvers, Il., U.S. D8 120
Danville, Qc., Can. E4 110
Danville, Ga., U.S. D2 116
Danville, Il., U.S. H2 112
Danville, Ky., U.S. G13 120
Danville, Pa., U.S. D9 114
Danville, Vt., U.S. F4 110
Danville, Va., U.S. H6 114
Danville, Wa., U.S. B8 136
Danxian, China L3 42
Danyang, China F8 42
Danzig see Gdańsk, Pol. B14 16
Danzig, Gulf of see Gdansk, Gulf of, b., Eur. B15 16
Daocheng, China F5 36
Daodi, China B8 42
Daohu, China G7 42
Daosa, India E6 54
Daotiandi, China B10 36
Daoukro, C. Iv. H4 64
Daoxian, China I4 42
Daozhen, China G2 42
Dapaong, Togo G5 64
Dapchi, Nig. G7 64
Daphnae, hist., Egypt H3 58
Daphne, Al., U.S. G11 122
Dapingshan, China I3 42
Da Qaidam, China D4 36
Daqiu, China I8 42
Dara, Sen. F1 64
Dar'ā, Syria F7 58
Dar'ā, state, Syria F7 58
Dārāb, Iran D7 56
Darāban, Pak. C3 54
Darabani, Rom. A13 26
Darasun, Russia F11 34
Đaravica, mtn., Yugo. G7 26
Darâw, Egypt C6 62
Dārayyā, Syria E7 58
Darb al-Ḩajj, Jabal, mtn., Jord. H6 58
Darbhanga, India E10 54
D'Arbonne, Bayou, stm., La., U.S. E6 122
Darby, Mt., U.S. D12 136
Dardanelle, Ar., U.S. B5 122
Dardanelle Lake, res., Ar., U.S. B5 122
Dardanelles see Çanakkale Boğazı, strt., Tur. C9 28
Dar-el-Beida see Casablanca, Mor. C3 64
Dar es Salaam, Tan. F7 66
Darfo, Italy E7 22
Dargai, Pak. A3 54
Dargan-Ata, Turkmen. A9 56
Dargaville, N.Z. B5 80
Dargol, Niger G5 64
Darhan, Mong. B6 36
Darıca, Tur. C12 28
Darién, Col. F3 86
Darien, Ga., U.S. E4 116
Darien, Parque Nacional, p.o.i., Pan. D2 86
Darién, Serranía del, mts. C3 86
Dārjiling, India E12 54
Dark Head, c., St. Vin. o11 105e
Darlag, China E4 36
Darling, S. Afr. H4 70
Darling, Ms., U.S. C8 122
Darling, stm., Austl. I4 76
Darling Downs, reg., Austl. F8 76
Darlingford, Mb., Can. E15 124
Darling Range, mts., Austl. F3 74
Darlington, Eng., U.K. G11 12
Darlington, Wi., U.S. B7 120
Darlington Dam, res., S. Afr. H7 70
Darlot, Lake, l., Austl. E4 74
Darłowo, Pol. B12 16
Darmstadt, Ger. G4 16
Darnah, Libya A4 62
Darnall, S. Afr. F10 70
Darney, Fr. F15 14
Darnley, Cape, c., Ant. B11 81
Darnley Bay, b., N.T., Can. B6 106
Darr, stm., Austl. D4 76
Darregueira, Arg. H6 92
Darreh Gaz, Iran B8 56
Darrington, Wa., U.S. B5 136
Darrouzett, Tx., U.S. E8 128
Dart, Cape, c., Ant. C27 81
Dartmoor, Austl. K3 76
Dartmoor, for., Eng., U.K. K9 12
Dartmoor National Park, p.o.i., Eng., U.K. K9 12
Dartmouth, N.S., Can. F13 110
Dartmouth, Eng., U.K. K9 12
Dartmouth, Lake, l., Austl. E5 76
Dartmouth Reservoir, res., Austl. K6 76
Daru, Pap. N. Gui. b3 79a
Daruvar, Cro. E14 22
Darvaza, Turkmen. A8 56
Dārwha, India H6 54
Darwin, Austl. B6 74
Darwin, Bahía, b., Chile I2 90
Darya Khān, Pak. C3 54
Dashbalbar, Mong. B7 36
Dashitou, China C8 38
Dašhovuz, Turkmen. A8 56
Dasht, stm., Pak. D9 56
Dashur, Pyramids of see Dahshur, Pyramides de, hist., Egypt I1 58
Dashutang, China A6 48
Dasol Bay, b., Phil. C2 52
Dastgardān, Iran C8 56
Datang, China I3 42
Datça, Tur. G10 28
Date, Japan C14 38
Datia, India F7 54
Datian, China I7 42
Datian Ding, mtn., China J4 42
Datong, China D5 36
Datong, China B9 36
Datong, China A5 42
Datong Shan, mts., China D4 36
Datu, Cape, c., Asia E4 44
Datumakuta, Indon. B10 50
Datu Piang, Phil. G5 52
Daua (Dawa), stm., Afr. G8 62
Daudnagar, India F10 54
Daugai, Lith. F7 10
Daugavpils, Lat. E9 10
Dauhinava, Bela. F10 10
Daule, Ec. H2 86
Daule, stm., Ec. H1 86
Daund, India B2 53
Daung Kyun, i., Mya. F3 48
Dauphin, Mb., Can. C13 124
Dauphin, stm., Mb., Can. C15 124
Dauphiné, hist. reg., Fr. E11 18
Dauphin Island, Al., U.S. G10 122
Dauphin Island, i., Al., U.S. G10 122
Dauphin Lake, l., Mb., Can. C13 124
Daura, Nig. G6 64
Dāvangere, India D2 53
Davant, La., U.S. H9 122
Davao, Phil. G5 52
Davao Gulf, b., Phil. G5 52
Dāvarzan, Iran B8 56
Davenport, Fl., U.S. H4 116
Davenport, Ia., U.S. C7 120
Davenport, Ok., U.S. B2 122
Davenport, Wa., U.S. C8 136
Davenport Downs, Austl. E3 76
Davey, Port, b., Austl. o12 77a
David, Pan. H6 102
David City, Ne., U.S. F15 126
Davidson, Sk., Can. C7 124
Davidson Mountains, mts., Ak., U.S. C11 140
Davie, Fl., U.S. J5 116
Davis, Ca., U.S. E4 134
Davis, N.C., U.S. B9 116
Davis, Ok., U.S. G11 128
Davis, W.V., U.S. E6 114
Davis, stm., Austl. D4 74
Davis, sci., Ant. B12 81
Davis, Mount, mtn., Pa., U.S. E6 114
Davisboro, Ga., U.S. C3 116
Davis Dam, dam, U.S. H2 132
Davis Inlet, Nf., Can. D18 106
Davis Mountains, mts., Tx., U.S. D3 130
Davis Sea, Ant. P11 142
Davis Strait, strt., N.A. D14 141
Davos, Switz. D6 22
Davy, W.V., U.S. G4 114
Davyd-Haradok, Bela. H9 10
Dawa (Daua), stm., Afr. G7 62
Dawei (Tavoy), Mya. E4 48
Dawen, stm., China D7 42
Dawlan, Mya. D4 48
Dawna Range, mts., Mya. D4 48
Dawson, Yk., Can. C3 106
Dawson, Ga., U.S. F14 122
Dawson, Ne., U.S. D2 120
Dawson, Tx., U.S. F2 122
Dawson, stm., Austl. D7 76
Dawson, Isla, i., Chile J2 90
Dawson Bay, b., Mb., Can. B13 124
Dawson Creek, B.C., Can. D7 106
Dawson Inlet, b., Nu., Can. C12 106
Dawson Range, mts., Yk., Can. C3 106
Dawsonville, Ga., U.S. B1 116
Dax, Fr. F4 18
Daxian, China F2 42
Daxing, China B7 42
Daxu, China I4 42
Daxue Shan, mts., China F5 36
Dayang, stm., China D5 38
Dayangshu, China B9 36
Dayao, China F5 36
Daye, China F6 42
Daying, China B5 42
Daylesford, Austl. K5 76
Daymán, stm., Ur. E9 92
Dayong, China G4 42
Dayr az-Zawr, Syria B4 56
Dayr Ḩāfir, Syria B8 58
Daysland, Ab., Can. D18 138
Dayton, Oh., U.S. E1 114
Dayton, Or., U.S. E3 136
Dayton, Tn., U.S. B13 122
Dayton, Tx., U.S. G4 122
Dayton, Wa., U.S. D9 136
Dayton, Wy., U.S. C5 126
Daytona Beach, Fl., U.S. G5 116
Dayu, China I6 42
Dayu Ling, mts., China I6 42
Da Yunhe (Grand Canal), can., China E8 42
Dayville, Or., U.S. F7 136
Dazhu, China F2 42
Dazkırı, Tur. F12 28
De Aar, S. Afr. G7 70
Deadhorse, Ak., U.S. B10 140
Deadman's Cay, Bah. A10 102
Dead Sea, l., Asia G6 58
Deadwood, S.D., U.S. C9 126
Deakin, Austl. F5 74
Deal, Eng., U.K. J14 12
Dealesville, S. Afr. F7 70
Deal Island, Md., U.S. F10 114
De'an, China G6 42
Dean, stm., B.C., Can. D4 138
Deán Funes, Arg. E5 92
Deans Dundas Bay, b., N.T., Can. B16 140
Dearborn, Mi., U.S. B2 114
Dearg, Beinn, mtn., Scot., U.K. D8 12
Dease, stm., B.C., Can. D5 106
Dease Arm, b., N.T., Can. B6 106
Dease Strait, strt., Nu., Can. B9 106
Death Valley, Ca., U.S. G9 134
Death Valley, val., Ca., U.S. G9 134
Death Valley National Park, p.o.i., U.S. G8 134
Deatsville, Al., U.S. E12 122
Deauville, Fr. E8 14
Deba, Nig. G7 64
Debao, China J2 42
Debar, Mac. B3 28
De Bary, Fl., U.S. H4 116
Debe, Trin. s12 105f
De Berry, Tx., U.S. E4 122
Dębica, Pol. F17 16
Dęblin, Pol. E17 16
Débo, Lac, l., Mali F4 64
Deborah West, Lake, l., Austl. F3 74
Deboyne Islands, is., Pap. N. Gui. B10 74
Debre Birhan, Eth. F7 62

Name — Map Ref. — Page

Doraville, Ga., U.S. D14 122
Dorcheat, Bayou, stm., U.S. D5 122
Dorchester, N.B., Can. E12 110
Dorchester, On., Can. F8 112
Dorchester, Eng., U.K. K10 12
Dorchester, Ne., U.S. G15 126
Dorchester, Cape, c., Nu., Can. B15 106
Dordabis, Nmb. C3 70
Dordogne, state, Fr. D6 18
Dordogne, stm., Fr. D8 18
Dordrecht, Neth. C13 14
Dordrecht, S. Afr. G8 70
Dore Lake, l., Sk., Can. E9 106
Dorena, Or., U.S. G4 136
Dores do Indaiá, Braz. J3 88
Dorfen, Ger. H8 16
Dorgali, Italy D3 24
Dörgön nuur, l., Mong. B3 36
Dori, Burkina G4 64
Doring, stm., S. Afr. G4 70
Dornbirn, Aus. C6 22
Dornoch, Scot., U.K. D8 12
Dorog, Hung. B5 26
Dorogobuž, Russia F16 10
Dorohoi, Rom. A13 26
Dorokempo, Indon. H11 50
Dorre Island, i., Austl. E2 74
Dorrigo, Austl. H9 76
Dorris, Ca., U.S. B4 134
Dorsale, mts., Tun. I3 24
Dort see Dordrecht, Neth. C13 14
Dortmund, Ger. E3 16
Dorton, Ky., U.S. G3 114
Dörtyol, Tur. B7 58
Doruma, D.R.C. D5 66
Dos, Canal Numero, can., Arg. H9 92
Dosatuj, Russia A8 36
Dos Bahías, Cabo, c., Arg. H3 90
Dos Bocas, P.R. B2 104a
Döşemealtı, Tur. F13 28
Dos Hermanas, Spain G4 20
Do Son, Viet. B8 48
Dos Pos, Neth. Ant. p23 104g
Dos Quebradas, Col. E4 86
Dosso, Niger G5 64
Dossor, Kaz. E8 32
Dothan, Al., U.S. F13 122
Dotnuva, Lith. E6 10
Dou, stm., China B8 42
Douai, Fr. D11 14
Douala, Cam. D1 66
Douarnenez, Fr. F4 14
Doublé, Pointe, c., Guad. h7 105c
Double Island Point, c., Austl. E9 76
Double Springs, Al., U.S. C11 122
Doubletop Peak, mtn., Wy., U.S. G16 136
Doubs, state, Fr. G15 14
Doubs, stm., Eur. H14 14
Doubtful Sound, strt., N.Z. G2 80
Doubtless Bay, b., N.Z. B5 80
Douentza, Mali F4 64
Dougga, hist., Tun. H3 24
Douglas, Mb., Can. E14 124
Douglas, I. of Man G8 12
Douglas, S. Afr. F6 70
Douglas, Ak., U.S. E13 140
Douglas, Az., U.S. L7 132
Douglas, Ga., U.S. E3 116
Douglas, Wy., U.S. E7 126
Douglas Channel, strt., B.C., Can. C1 138
Douglas Lake, B.C., Can. F10 138
Douglas Lake, res., Tn., U.S. H2 114
Douglasville, Ga., U.S. D14 122
Doullens, Fr. D11 14
Dourada, Serra, plat., Braz. G1 88
Dourados, Braz. D6 90
Dourbali, Chad E3 62
Douro (Duero), stm., Eur. C2 20
Dousk, Bela. G13 10
Douz, Tun. C6 64
Dove Bugt, strt., Grnld. B21 141
Dove Creek, Co., U.S. F7 132
Dover, Austl. o13 77a
Dover, Eng., U.K. J14 12
Dover, De., U.S. E10 114
Dover, Id., U.S. B10 136
Dover, N.H., U.S. G6 110
Dover, N.J., U.S. D11 114
Dover, N.C., U.S. A8 116
Dover, Oh., U.S. D4 114
Dover, Ok., U.S. E11 128
Dover, Tn., U.S. H10 120
Dover, Strait of, strt., Eur. K14 12
Dover-Foxcroft, Me., U.S. E7 110
Dovrefjell Nasjonalpark, p.o.i., Nor. E3 8
Dow City, Ia., U.S. C2 120
Dowlatābād, Iran D8 56
Downey, Id., U.S. H14 136
Downieville, Ca., U.S. D5 134
Downing, Mo., U.S. D5 120
Downingtown, Pa., U.S. D10 114
Downpatrick, N. Ire., U.K. G7 12
Downs, Ks., U.S. B10 128
Downton, Mount, mtn., B.C., Can. D6 138
Dows, Ia., U.S. B4 120
Dowshī, Afg. B10 56
Doyle, Ca., U.S. C5 134
Doyles, Nf., Can. C17 110
Doylestown, Pa., U.S. D10 114
Doyline, La., U.S. E5 122
Dōzen, is., Japan C5 40
Dozier, Al., U.S. F12 122
Dra, Cap, c., Mor. D2 64
Dra'a, Hamada du, des., Alg. D3 64
Drâa, Oued, stm., Afr. D2 64
Drac, stm., Fr. E2 22
Dracena, Braz. D6 90
Drachten, Neth. A15 14
Dracut, Ma., U.S. B14 114
Dragalina, Rom. E14 26
Drăgănești-Vlașca, Rom. E12 26
Drăgășani, Rom. E11 26
Dragonera, Sa, i., Spain E13 20
Dragons Mouths, strt. s12 105f
Dragoon, Az., U.S. K6 132
Draguignan, Fr. F12 18
Drahičyn, Bela. H8 10
Drake, N.D., U.S. G13 124
Drakensberg, mts., Afr. F9 70
Drake Passage, strt. K8 82
Drakesboro, Ky., U.S. G10 120
Drakes Branch, Va., U.S. H7 114
Dráma, Grc. B7 28
Drammen, Nor. G3 8
Drang, stm., Asia F8 48
Drangajökull, ice, Ice. j28 8a
Dranov, Ostrovul, i., Rom. E16 26
Drau (Dráva), stm., Eur. D11 22
Dráva (Drau), stm., Eur. D14 22
Dravograd, Slvn. D12 22
Drawsko Pomorskie, Pol. C11 16
Drayton, N.D., U.S. C1 118
Drayton, S.C., U.S. B4 116
Drayton Valley, Ab., Can. C15 138
Dresden, On., Can. F7 112
Dresden, Ger. E9 16
Dresden, Oh., U.S. D3 114
Drètun', Bela. E12 10
Dreux, Fr. F10 14
Drew, Ms., U.S. D8 122
Drienov, Slov. H17 16
Driftwood, B.C., Can. D5 106
Driftwood, stm., In., U.S. E12 120
Driggs, Id., U.S. G15 136
Drin, stm., Alb. C13 24
Drina, stm., Eur. F16 22
Drinit, Gjiri i, b., Alb. C13 24
Drinit të Zi (Crni Drim), stm., Eur. C14 24
Driskill Mountain, hill, La., U.S. E6 122
Drissa (Drysa), stm., Eur. E11 10
Drniš, Cro. G13 22
Drobeta-Turnu Severin, Rom. E9 26
Drochia, Mol. A14 26
Drogheda, Ire. H6 12
Droichead Átha see Drogheda, Ire. H6 12
Droichead Nua, Ire. H6 12
Drôme, state, Fr. E11 18
Dronero, Italy F4 22
Dronne, stm., Fr. D6 18
Dronning Louise Land, reg., Grnld. B20 141
Druc', stm., Bela. G12 10
Druif, Aruba o19 104g
Druja, Bela. E10 10
Drūkšiai, l., Eur. E9 10
Drumheller, Ab., Can. E18 138
Drummond, Mt., U.S. D13 136
Drummond, Wi., U.S. E7 118
Drummond Island, i., Mi., U.S. C6 112
Drummondville, Qc., Can. E4 110
Druskininkai, Lith. F7 10
Družba, Kaz. E14 32
Druzhba see Družba, Kaz. E14 32
Družina, Russia C18 34
Drvar, Bos. E3 26
Dry Arm, b., Mt., U.S. G7 124
Dry Bay, b., Ak., U.S. E12 140
Dryberry Lake, l., On., Can. B4 118
Dry Cimarron, stm., U.S. B2 122
Dry Creek Mountain, mtn., Nv., U.S. B9 134
Dryden, On., Can. B6 118
Dry Devils, stm., Tx., U.S. D7 130
Dry Prong, La., U.S. F6 122
Dry Ridge, Ky., U.S. F1 114
Drysdale, stm., Austl. C5 74
Dry Tortugas, is., Fl., U.S. G11 108
Dry Tortugas National Park, p.o.i., Fl., U.S. L3 116
Drzewica, Pol. E16 16
Dschang, Cam. C1 66
Du, stm., China E4 42
Du'an, China I3 42
Duaringa, Austl. D7 76
Duarte, Pico, mtn., Dom. Rep. C12 102
Duartina, Braz. L1 88
Dubā, Sau. Ar. K6 58
Dubach, La., U.S. E6 122
Dubai see Dubayy, U.A.E. D8 56
Dubăsari, Mol. B16 26
Dubăsari, Lacul, res., Mol. B15 26
Dubawnt, stm., Can. C10 106
Dubawnt Lake, l., Can. C10 106
Dubayy (Dubai), U.A.E. D8 56
Dubbo, Austl. I7 76
Dubh Artach, r., Scot., U.K. E6 12
Dublin (Baile Átha Cliath), Ire. H6 12
Dublin, Ga., U.S. D3 116
Dublin, Tx., U.S. B9 130
Dublin, Va., U.S. G5 114
Dublin, state, Ire. H6 12
Dubna, Russia F19 10
Dubna, Russia D20 10
Dubna, stm., Russia D21 10
Dubnica nad Váhom, Slov. H14 16
Dubois, In., U.S. F11 120
Du Bois, Ne., U.S. D1 120
Du Bois, Pa., U.S. C7 114
Dubois, Wy., U.S. D3 126
Dubossary Reservoir see Dubăsari, Lacul, res., Mol. B15 26
Dubovka, Russia E6 32
Dubrājpur, India G11 54
Dubréka, Gui. H2 64
Dubrouna, Bela. F13 10
Dubrovka, Russia G16 10
Dubrovnik, Cro. H15 22
Dubrovnoe, Russia C11 32
Dubuque, Ia., U.S. B7 120
Dubysa, stm., Lith. E6 10
Duchang, China G7 42
Duchesne, Ut., U.S. C6 132
Duchesne, stm., Ut., U.S. C7 132
Duchess, Austl. C2 76
Duck, stm., Tn., U.S. B11 122
Duck Creek, stm., Nv., U.S. D2 132
Duck Hill, Ms., U.S. D9 122
Duck Lake, Sk., Can. B7 124
Ducktown, Tn., U.S. B14 122
Duda, stm., Col. F4 86
Dudačkino, Russia A15 10
Duderstadt, Ger. E6 16
Dudinka, Russia C6 34
Dudley, Eng., U.K. I10 12
Dudleyville, Az., U.S. K6 132
Dudna, stm., India B2 53
Dudorovskij, Russia G18 10
Dudwa National Park, p.o.i., India D8 54
Dueré, stm., Braz. F1 88
Duero (Douro), stm., Eur. C2 20
Due West, S.C., U.S. B3 116
Dufourspitze, mtn., Eur. D13 18
Dufur, Or., U.S. E5 136
Duga-Zapadnaja, mys, c., Russia E18 34
Dugdemona, stm., La., U.S. F6 122
Dugi Otok, i., Cro. F11 22
Dugna, Russia F19 10
Du Gué, stm., Qc., Can. D16 106
Duhovščina, Russia E15 10
Duida, Cerro, mtn., Ven. F9 86
Duisburg, Ger. E2 16
Duitama, Col. E5 86
Duiwelskloof, S. Afr. C10 70
Dujuuma, Som. D8 66
Duke, Ok., U.S. G9 128
Duke of York Bay, b., Nu., Can. B13 106
Duk Fadiat, Sudan F6 62
Dukhān, Qatar D7 56
Duki, Pak. C2 54
Dukla Pass, p., Eur. G17 16
Dukou, China F5 36
Dūkštas, Lith. E9 10
Dulan, China D4 36
Dulce, N.M., U.S. G9 132
Dulce, stm., Arg. D6 92
Dulce, Golfo, b., C.R. H6 102
Dul'durga, Russia F11 34
Dulgalah, stm., Russia C15 34
Dullstroom, S. Afr. D10 70
Dulovka, Russia C11 10
Dulq Maghār, Syria B9 58
Duluth, Ga., U.S. C14 122
Duluth, Mn., U.S. E6 118
Dūmā, Syria E7 58
Dumaguete, Phil. F4 52
Dumai, Indon. C2 50
Dumalag, Phil. E4 52
Dumali Point, c., Phil. D3 52
Dumaran Island, i., Phil. E2 52
Dumaresq, stm., Austl. G8 76
Dumaring, Indon. C11 50
Dumas, Tx., U.S. F7 128
Dumbarton, Scot., U.K. F8 12
Dumbrăveni, Rom. C11 26
Dume, Point, c., Ca., U.S. J7 134
Dumfries, Scot., U.K. F9 12
Dumka, India F11 54
Dumlupınar, Tur. E12 28
Dummar, Syria E7 58
Dumoine, Lac, l., Qc., Can. B12 112
Dumont, Ia., U.S. B4 120
Dumont d'Urville, sci., Ant. B18 81
Dumpu, Pap. N. Gui. b4 79a
Dumraon, India F10 54
Dumyât, Masabb (Damietta Mouth), mth., Egypt G3 58
Duna see Danube, stm., Eur. F11 6
Dunaharaszti, Hung. B6 26
Dunaj see Danube, stm., Eur. F11 6
Dunajec, stm., Eur. F16 16
Dunajská Streda, Slov. H13 16
Dunakeszi, Hung. B6 26
Dunărea Veche, Brațul, stm., Rom. E15 26
Dunaújváros, Hung. C5 26
Dunavățu de Sus, Rom. E16 26
Duna-völgyi-főcsatorna, can., Hung. C6 26
Dunav-Tisa-Dunav, Kanal, can., Yugo. D6 26
Dunbar, Scot., U.K. E10 12
Dunblane, Sk., Can. C6 124
Duncan, B.C., Can. H7 138
Duncan, Az., U.S. K7 132
Duncan, Ok., U.S. G11 128
Duncan, stm., B.C., Can. F13 138
Duncan Lake, res., B.C., Can. F14 138
Duncannon, Pa., U.S. D8 114
Duncan Passage, strt., India F7 46
Duncans, Jam. i13 104d
Duncansby Head, c., Scot., U.K. C9 12
Dundaga, Lat. C5 10
Dundalk, On., Can. D9 112
Dundalk (Dún Dealgan), Ire. G6 12
Dundalk, Md., U.S. E9 114
Dundalk Bay, b., Ire. H6 12
Dundas, On., Can. E9 112
Dundas, Lake, l., Austl. F4 74
Dundas Peninsula, pen., Can. B17 140
Dundas Strait, strt., Austl. B6 74
Dún Dealgan see Dundalk, Ire. G6 12
Dundee, S. Afr. F10 70
Dundee, Scot., U.K. E10 12
Dundee, Fl., U.S. H4 116
Dundee, Mi., U.S. C2 114
Dundurn, Sk., Can. C7 124
Dunedin, N.Z. G4 80
Dunedin, Fl., U.S. H3 116
Dunedoo, Austl. I7 76
Dunfermline, Scot., U.K. E9 12
Dungannon, N. Ire., U.K. G6 12
Dūngarpur, India G4 54
Dungarvan, Ire. I5 12
Dungeness, c., Eng., U.K. K13 12
Dungog, Austl. I8 76
Dungu, D.R.C. D5 66
Dungun, Malay. J6 48
Dunhua, China C8 38
Dunhuang, China C3 36
Dunilovo, Russia C21 10
Dunkerque (Dunkirk), Fr. C11 14
Dunkirk see Dunkerque, Fr. C11 14
Dunkirk, In., U.S. H4 112
Dunkirk, N.Y., U.S. B6 114
Dunkirk, Oh., U.S. D2 114
Dunkwa, Ghana H4 64
Dún Laoghaire, Ire. H6 12
Dunlap, Tn., U.S. B13 122
Dunmore, Pa., U.S. C10 114
Dunmore Town, Bah. K9 116
Dunn, N.C., U.S. A7 116
Dunnellon, Fl., U.S. G3 116
Dunnet Head, c., Scot., U.K. C9 12
Dunning, Ne., U.S. F12 126
Dunnville, On., Can. F10 112
Dunoon, Scot., U.K. F8 12
Dunqulah, Sudan D5 62
Dunqunāb, Sudan C7 62
Duns, Scot., U.K. F10 12
Dunseith, N.D., U.S. F13 124
Dunsmuir, Ca., U.S. B3 134
Dunstable, Eng., U.K. J12 12
Dunster, B.C., Can. C11 138
Dunyāpur, Pak. D3 54
Duolun, China C2 38
Duolundabohuer, China B14 54
Duomula, China A9 54
Duozhu, China J6 42
Dupang Ling, mts., China I4 42
Dupnica, Blg. G10 26
Dupnitsa see Dupnica, Blg. G10 26
Dupuyer, Mt., U.S. B14 136
Duque Bacelar, Braz. C4 88
Duque de Caxias, Braz. L4 88
Duque de York, Isla, i., Chile J1 90
Duran, N.M., U.S. G3 128
Durance, stm., Fr. F11 18
Durand, Il., U.S. B8 120
Durand, Wi., U.S. G7 118
Durand, Récif, rf., N. Cal. n17 79d
Durand Reef see Durand, Récif, rf., N. Cal. n17 79d
Durango, Mex. C6 100
Durango, Spain A8 20
Durango, Co., U.S. F9 132
Durango, state, Mex. C6 100
Durant, Ia., U.S. C6 120
Durant, Ms., U.S. D9 122
Durant, Ok., U.S. D2 122
Duras, Fr. E6 18
Durazno, Ur. F9 92
Durban, S. Afr. F10 70
Đurđevac, Cro. D14 22
Düren, Ger. F2 16
Durg, India H8 54
Durgāpur, India G11 54
Durham, On., Can. D9 112
Durham, Eng., U.K. G11 12
Durham, Ca., U.S. D4 134
Durham, N.H., U.S. G5 110
Durham, N.C., U.S. H6 114
Durham Downs, Austl. F3 76
Durham Heights, mtn., N.T., Can. A6 106
Durlas éile see Thurles, Ire. I5 12
Durlești, Mol. B15 26
Durmitor, mtn., Yugo. F5 26
Durmitor Nacionalni Park, p.o.i., Yugo. F6 26
Dürnkrut, Aus. B13 22
Durrës, Alb. C13 24
Durrësi see Durrës, Alb. C13 24
Durrie, Austl. E3 76
Dursunbey, Tur. D11 28
Duru Gölü, l., Tur. B11 28
Durūz, Jabal ad-, mtn., Syria F7 58
D'Urville, Tanjung, c., Indon. F10 44
D'Urville Island, i., N.Z. E5 80
Dušak, Turkmen. B9 56
Dusa Marreb see Dhuusamarreeb, Som. C9 66
Dušanbe, Taj. B10 56
Dušekan, Russia B19 32
Dusetos, Lith. E8 10
Dushan, China I2 42
Du Shan, mtn., China A8 42
Dushanzi, China C1 36
Duson, La., U.S. G6 122
Düsseldorf, Ger. E2 16
Dustin, Ok., U.S. B2 122
Dutch John, Ut., U.S. C7 132
Dutton, Mt., U.S. C15 136
Dutton, stm., Austl. C4 76
Duvno, Bos. F4 26
Duxun, China J7 42
Duyfken Point, c., Austl. B8 74
Duyun, China H2 42
Düzce, Tur. C14 28
Dve Mogili, Blg. F12 26
Dvine, ozero, l., Russia D14 10
Dvinskaja guba, b., Russia D17 8
Dvuh Cirkov, gora, mtn., Russia C22 34
Dvůr Králové nad Labem, Czech Rep. F11 16
Dwārka, India G2 54
Dwight, Il., U.S. C9 120
Dworshak Reservoir, res., Id., U.S. D11 136
Dwyka, stm., S. Afr. H5 70
Dyer, Tn., U.S. H8 120
Dyer, Cape, c., Nu., Can. D13 141
Dyer Bay, b., On., Can. C8 112
Dyersburg, Tn., U.S. H8 120
Dyje (Thaya), stm., Eur. H12 16
Dyment, On., Can. B6 118
Dynów, Pol. G18 16
Dysart, Sk., Can. D9 124
Dysart, Ia., U.S. B5 120
Dysna (Dzisna), stm., Eur. E9 10
Dytikí Elláda, state, Grc. E4 28
Dytikí Makedonía, state, Grc. C4 28
Džagdy, hrebet, mts., Russia F15 34
Džalal-Abad, Kyrg. F12 32
Džalinda, Russia F13 34
Džambejty, Kaz. D8 32
Džanybek, Kaz. E7 32
Dzaoudzi, May. C8 68
Džardžan, Russia C13 34
Dzavhan, stm., Mong. B3 36
Dzeržinsk, Russia H20 8
Dzeržinskoe, Russia C16 32
Džetygara, Kaz. D10 32
Dzhankoi, Ukr. E4 32
Dzhugdzhur Mountains see Džugdžur, hrebet, mts., Russia E16 34
Dzhungarian Alatau Mountains, mts., Asia E14 32
Działoszyce, Pol. F16 16
Dzibilchaltún, hist., Mex. B3 102
Dzierżoniów, Pol. F12 16
Dzilam González, Mex. B3 102
Dzisna, Bela. E11 10
Dzisna (Dysna), stm., Eur. E9 10
Dzitbalché, Mex. B2 102
Dziwnów, Pol. B10 16
Džizak, Uzb. F11 32
Dzjarèčyn, Bela. G7 10
Dzjaršynskaja, hara, hill, Bela. G9 10
Dzjaržynsk, Bela. G9 10
Dzjatlavičy, Bela. H9 10
Dzöölön, Mong. F8 34
Džugdžur, hrebet, mts., Russia E16 34
Dzūkijos nacionalinis parkas, p.o.i., Lith. F7 10
Dzungarian Basin see Junggar Pendi, bas., China B2 36
Dzungarian Gate, p., Asia E14 32
Džusaly, Kaz. E10 32
Dzüünharaa, Mong. B6 36
Dzuunmod, Mong. B6 36
Dzyhivka, Ukr. A15 26

E

Eads, Co., U.S. C6 128
Eagle, Ak., U.S. D11 140
Eagle, Co., U.S. D10 132
Eagle, stm., Co., U.S. B2 128
Eagle Bay, B.C., Can. F11 138
Eagle Butte, S.D., U.S. C11 126
Eagle Creek, stm., Sk., Can. B6 124
Eagle Grove, Ia., U.S. B4 120
Eaglehawk, Austl. K4 76
Eagle Lake, Tx., U.S. H2 122
Eagle Lake, l., On., Can. B5 118
Eagle Lake, l., Ca., U.S. C5 134
Eagle Lake, l., Me., U.S. D7 110
Eagle Mountain, Ca., U.S. J1 132
Eagle Mountain, mtn., Id., U.S. D11 136
Eagle Mountain, mtn., Mn., U.S. D8 118
Eagle Mountain Lake, res., Tx., U.S. A10 130
Eagle Pass, Tx., U.S. F7 130
Eagle Peak, mtn., Ca., U.S. B5 134
Eagle River, Mi., U.S. D10 118
Eagle River, Wi., U.S. F9 118
Eagletown, Ok., U.S. C4 122
Ear Falls, On., Can. A5 118
Earle, Ar., U.S. B8 122
Earl Grey, Sk., Can. D9 124
Earlham, Ia., U.S. C3 120
Earlimart, Ca., U.S. H6 134
Earlville, Il., U.S. C8 120
Early, Ia., U.S. B2 120
Early, Tx., U.S. C9 130
Eas, Vanuatu k17 79d
Easley, S.C., U.S. B3 116
East Alton, Il., U.S. F7 120
East Angus, Qc., Can. E5 110
East Antarctica, reg., Ant. C8 81
East Aurora, N.Y., U.S. B7 114
East Bay, b., Tx., U.S. H4 122
East Bend, N.C., U.S. H5 114
East Bernard, Tx., U.S. H2 122
East Bernstadt, Ky., U.S. G1 114
East Borneo see Kalimantan Timur, state, Indon. C10 50
Eastbourne, Eng., U.K. K13 12
East Brady, Pa., U.S. D6 114
East Brewton, Al., U.S. F11 122
East Cache Creek, stm., Ok., U.S. G10 128
East Caicos, i., T./C. Is. B12 102
East Cape, c., N.Z. C8 80
East Cape, c., Fl., U.S. K4 116
East Carbon, Ut., U.S. D6 132
East Caroline Basin, unds. I17 142
East Chicago, In., U.S. G2 112
East China Sea, Asia F9 36
East Cote Blanche Bay, b., La., U.S. H7 122
East Coulee, Ab., Can. E18 138
East Dereham, Eng., U.K. I13 12
East Dismal Swamp, sw., N.C., U.S. A9 116
East Dubuque, Il., U.S. B7 120
East Ely, Nv., U.S. D2 132
East End, V.I.U.S. e8 104b
Easter Island see Pascua, Isla de, i., Chile f30 78l
Eastern Cape, state, S. Afr. G8 70
Eastern Channel see Tsushima-kaikyō, strt., Japan F2 40
Eastern Creek, stm., Austl. C3 76
Eastern Desert see Arabian Desert, des., Egypt B6 62
Eastern Division, state, Fiji q20 79e
Eastern Ghāts, mts., India E4 53
Eastern Point, c., Guad. A1 105a
Eastern Sayans see Vostočnyj Sajan, mts., Russia D17 32
East Falkland, i., Falk. Is. J5 90
East Fayetteville, N.C., U.S. A7 116
East Frisian Islands see Ostfriesische Inseln, is., Ger. C3 16
East Gaffney, S.C., U.S. A4 116
East Germany see Germany, ctry., Eur. E6 16
East Glacier Park, Mt., U.S. B13 136
East Grand Forks, Mn., U.S. D2 118
East Grand Rapids, Mi., U.S. F4 112
East Grinstead, Eng., U.K. J12 12
Easthampton, Ma., U.S. B13 114
East Java see Jawa Timur, state, Indon. G8 50
East Jordan, Mi., U.S. C4 112
East Kelowna, B.C., Can. G11 138
East Kilbride, Scot., U.K. F8 12
Eastlake, Mi., U.S. D3 112
Eastlake, Oh., U.S. C4 114
Eastland, Tx., U.S. B9 130
East Lansing, Mi., U.S. B1 114
East Laurinburg, N.C., U.S. B6 116
Eastleigh, Eng., U.K. K11 12
East Liverpool, Oh., U.S. D5 114
East London (Oos-Londen), S. Afr. H9 70
Eastmain, Qc., Can. E15 106
Eastmain, stm., Qc., Can. E15 106
Eastmain-Opinaca, Réservoir, res., Qc., Can. E15 106
Eastman, Ga., U.S. D2 116
East Mariana Basin, unds. H18 142
East Matagorda Bay, b., Tx., U.S. F11 130
East Missoula, Mt., U.S. D13 136
East Moline, Il., U.S. C7 120
East Naples, Fl., U.S. J4 116
East Nishnabotna, stm., Ia., U.S. C2 120
East Nusa Tenggara see Nusa Tenggara Timur, state, Indon. H12 50
East Olympia, Wa., U.S. D3 136
Easton, Md., U.S. F9 114
Easton, Pa., U.S. D10 114
East Pacific Rise, unds. N27 142
East Palatka, Fl., U.S. G4 116
East Pecos, N.M., U.S. F3 128
East Peoria, Il., U.S. D8 120
Eastpoint, Fl., U.S. H14 122
East Point, Ga., U.S. D14 122
East Point, c., P.E., Can. D15 110
East Point, c., V.I.U.S. g11 104c
Eastport, Id., U.S. B10 136
Eastport, Me., U.S. F9 110
East Prairie, Mo., U.S. H8 120
East Prairie, stm., Ab., Can. A14 138
East Pryor Mountain, mtn., Mt., U.S. B4 126
East Retford, Eng., U.K. H12 12
East Saint Louis, Il., U.S. F7 120
East Sea (Japan, Sea of), Asia D11 38
East Shoal Lake, l., Mb., Can. D16 124
East Siberian Sea see Vostočno-Sibirskoe more, Russia B20 34
East Sister Island, i., Austl. L6 76
East Slovakia see Východoslovenský Kraj, state, Slov. H17 16
East Stroudsburg, Pa., U.S. D11 114
East Timor, dep., Asia G8 44
East Troy, Wi., U.S. B9 120
Eastville, Va., U.S. G10 114
East Wenatchee, Wa., U.S. C6 136
East Wilmington, N.C., U.S. B8 116
Eaton, In., U.S. H4 112
Eaton, Oh., U.S. E1 114
Eaton Rapids, Mi., U.S. B1 114
Eatonton, Ga., U.S. C2 116
Eatonville, Wa., U.S. D4 136
Eau Claire, Wi., U.S. G7 118
Eau Claire, Lac à l', l., Qc., Can. D16 106
Eauripik, at., Micron. C5 72
Eauripik Rise, unds. I17 142
Eauze, Fr. F6 18
Ebano, Mex. D9 100
Ebb and Flow Lake, l., Mb., Can. D14 124
Ebbw Vale, Wales, U.K. J9 12
Ebebiyín, Eq. Gui. I7 64
Eben Junction, Mi., U.S. B2 112
Ebensee, Aus. C10 22
Eberbach, Ger. G4 16
Eber Gölü, l., Tur. E14 28
Ebern, Ger. F6 16
Ebersbach, Ger. E10 16
Eberswalde-Finow, Ger. D9 16
Ebetsu, Japan C14 38
Ebino, Japan G3 40
Ebinur Hu, l., China F14 32
Eboli, Italy D9 24
Ebolowa, Cam. D2 66
Ebon, at., Marsh. Is. C7 72
Ebre see Ebro, stm., Spain C11 20
Ebre, Delta de l', Spain D11 20
Ebro (Ebre), stm., Spain C11 20
Ebro, Delta del see Ebre, Delta de l', Spain D11 20
Ebro, Embalse del, res., Spain B7 20
Eceabat, Tur. C9 28
Ech Cheliff, Alg. B5 64
Echeng, China E7 36
Echínos, Grc. B7 28
Echt, Neth. E1 16
Echuca, Austl. K5 76
Écija, Spain G5 20
Eckernförde, Ger. B5 16
Eckerö, i., Fin. F8 8
Eckville, Ab., Can. D16 138
Eclectic, Al., U.S. E12 122
Eclipse Sound, strt., Nu., Can. A14 106
Ecoporanga, Braz. J5 88
Écorce, Lac de l', res., Qc., Can. B13 112
Écrins, Barre des, mtn., Fr. E12 18
Écrins, Massif des, plat., Fr. E12 18
Ecru, Ms., U.S. C9 122
Ecuador, ctry., S.A. D2 84
Ed, Swe. G4 8
Edam, Sk., Can. A5 124
Eddrachillis Bay, b., Scot., U.K. C7 12
Eddystone Rocks, r., Eng., U.K. K8 12
Eddyville, Ia., U.S. C5 120
Eddyville, Ky., U.S. G9 120
Ede, Neth. B14 14
Ede, Nig. H5 64
Edéa, Cam. D2 66
Edehon Lake, l., Nu., Can. C11 106
Edelény, Hung. A7 26
Eden, Austl. K7 76
Eden, Ms., U.S. D8 122
Eden, N.C., U.S. H6 114
Eden, Wy., U.S. A7 132
Eden, stm., Eng., U.K. G10 12
Edendale, S. Afr. F10 70
Eden Valley, Mn., U.S. F4 118
Edenville, S. Afr. E8 70
Eder, stm., Ger. E4 16
Édessa, Grc. C4 28
Edfu, Egypt C6 62
Edgar, Ne., U.S. G14 126
Edgar, Wi., U.S. G8 118
Edgard, La., U.S. H8 122
Edgartown, Ma., U.S. C15 114
Edgeley, N.D., U.S. A14 126
Edgell Island, i., Grnld. E13 141
Edgemont, S.D., U.S. D9 126
Edgeøya, i., Nor. B30 141
Edgeroi, Austl. H7 76
Edgerton, Ab., Can. B3 124
Edgerton, Mn., U.S. H2 118
Edgerton, Oh., U.S. C1 114
Edgerton, Wi., U.S. B8 120
Edgewater, Fl., U.S. H5 116
Edgewood, Il., U.S. F9 120
Edgewood, Ia., U.S. B6 120
Edgewood, Md., U.S. E9 114
Edgewood, Tx., U.S. E3 122
Edina, Mn., U.S. G5 118
Edina, Mo., U.S. D5 120
Edinburg, Il., U.S. E8 120
Edinburg, In., U.S. E11 120
Edinburg, Ms., U.S. E9 122
Edinburg, Tx., U.S. H9 130
Edinburg, Va., U.S. F7 114
Edinburgh, Scot., U.K. F9 12
Edincik, Tur. C10 28
Edineț, Mol. A14 26
Edirne, Tur. B9 28
Edirne, state, Tur. B9 28
Edison, Ga., U.S. F14 122
Edisto, stm., S.C., U.S. D5 116
Edisto, North Fork, stm., S.C., U.S. C4 116
Edisto Island, i., S.C., U.S. D5 116
Edith, Mount, mtn., Mt., U.S. D15 136
Edith Cavell, Mount, mtn., Ab., Can. D12 138
Edjeleh, Alg. D6 64
Edmond, Ok., U.S. F11 128
Edmonds, Wa., U.S. C4 136
Edmonton, Austl. A5 76
Edmonton, Ab., Can. C17 138
Edmonton, Ky., U.S. G12 120
Edmore, N.D., U.S. F15 124
Edmundston, N.B., Can. C8 110
Edna, Ks., U.S. G2 120
Edna, Tx., U.S. E11 130
Edremit, Tur. D10 28
Edremit Körfezi, b., Tur. D9 28
Edrovo, Russia C16 10
Edson, Ab., Can. C14 138
Eduardo Castex, Arg. G5 92
Eduni, Mount, mtn., N.T., Can. C5 106
Edward, stm., Austl. J5 76
Edward, Lake, l., Afr. E5 66
Edward Island, i., On., Can. C10 118
Edwards, Ms., U.S. E8 122
Edwards Air Force Base, Ca., U.S. I8 134
Edwards Plateau, plat., Tx., U.S. D7 130
Edwardsville, Il., U.S. F8 120
Edward VII Peninsula, pen., Ant. C25 81
Eek, Ak., U.S. D7 140
Eeklo, Bel. C12 14
Eel, stm., Ca., U.S. D2 134
Eel, stm., In., U.S. G4 112
Eel, stm., In., U.S. E10 120
Eems (Ems), stm., Eur. A16 14
Éfaté, state, Vanuatu k17 79d
Éfaté, i., Vanuatu k17 79d
Eferding, Aus. B10 22
Efes (Ephesus), hist., Tur. F10 28
Effigy Mounds National Monument, p.o.i., Ia., U.S. A6 120
Effingham, Il., U.S. E9 120
Effingham, Ks., U.S. E2 120
Eflâni, Tur. B15 28
Eforie Nord, Rom. E15 26
Eforie Sud, Rom. F15 26
Efremov, Russia G20 10
Eg, stm., Mong. F9 34
Egadi, Isole, is., Italy G5 24
Egaña, Arg. H8 92
Egan Range, mts., Nv., U.S. D2 132
Egedesminde (Aasiaat), Grnld. D15 141
Egegik, Ak., U.S. E8 140
Eger, Hung. B7 26
Egersund, Nor. G1 8
Eggenfelden, Ger. H8 16
Egg Harbor City, N.J., U.S. E11 114
Égletons, Fr. D7 18
Egmont, Cape, c., N.Z. D5 80
Egmont, Mount see Taranaki, Mount, vol., N.Z. D6 80
Egmont Bay, b., P.E., Can. D12 110
Egmont National Park, p.o.i., N.Z. D5 80
Egorevsk, Russia E22 10
Egremont, Ab., Can. B17 138
Eğridir, Tur. F13 28
Eğridir Gölü, l., Tur. E13 28
Éguas, stm., Braz. G3 88
Egvekinot, Russia C25 34
Egypt, ctry., Afr. B5 62
Eha-Amufu, Nig. H6 64
Ehime, state, Japan F5 40
Ehingen, Ger. H5 16
Ehrhardt, S.C., U.S. C4 116
Eibar, Spain A8 20
Eibiswald, Aus. D12 22
Eichstätt, Ger. H7 16
Eidsvold, Austl. E8 76
Eifel, mts., Ger. F2 16
Eigg, i., Scot., U.K. E6 12
Eight Degree Channel, strt., Asia h12 46a
Eights Coast, cst., Ant. C31 81
Eighty Mile Beach, cst., Austl. C4 74
Eildon, Austl. K5 76
Eildon, Lake, res., Austl. K5 76
Eilenburg, Ger. E8 16
Eiler Rasmussen, Kap, c., Grnld. A21 141
Einasleigh, Austl. B5 76
Einasleigh, stm., Austl. A4 76
Einbeck, Ger. E5 16
Eindhoven, Neth. C14 14
Einme, Mya. D2 48
Eirunepé, Braz. E4 84
Eiseb, stm., Afr. B4 70
Eisenach, Ger. E6 16
Eisenberg, Ger. F7 16
Eisenerz, Aus. C11 22
Eisenhüttenstadt, Ger. D10 16
Eisenstadt, Aus. C13 22
Eisfeld, Ger. F6 16
Eišiškės, Lith. F7 10
Eislingen, Ger. H5 16
Eitorf, Ger. F3 16
Eivissa (Iviza), Spain F12 20
Eivissa (Ibiza), i., Spain F12 20
Ejea de los Caballeros, Spain B9 20
Ejeda, Madag. E7 68
Ejido Jaboncillos, Mex. A7 100
Ejin Horo Qi, China B3 42
Ejin Qi, China C5 36
Ejsk, Russia E5 32
Ejura, Ghana H4 64
Ejutla de Crespo, Mex. G10 100
Ekaterinburg, Russia C10 32
Ekaterinino, Russia E16 10
Ekateriny, proliv, strt., Russia B17 38
Ekenäs see Tammisaari, Fin. G10 8
Ekibastuz, Kaz. D13 32
Ekimčan, Russia F15 34
Ekonda, Russia C10 34
Ekwan, stm., On., Can. E14 106
Ela, Mya. C3 48

Name	Map Ref.	Page

I • 20 Fort-Gasp

Name	Map Ref.	Page
Forte dei Marmi, Italy	G7	22
Fort Edward, N.Y., U.S.	G3	110
Fort Erie, On., Can.	F10	112
Fortescue, stm., Austl.	D3	74
Fortezza, Italy	D8	22
Fort Frances, On., Can.	C5	118
Fort Fraser, B.C., Can.	B6	138
Fort Frederica National Monument, p.o.i., Ga., U.S.	E4	116
Fort Gaines, Ga., U.S.	F13	122
Fort Garland, Co., U.S.	D3	128
Fort Gibson, Ok., U.S.	I2	120
Fort Good Hope, N.T., Can.	B5	106
Forth, Firth of, b., Scot., U.K.	E10	12
Fort Hall, Id., U.S.	G14	136
Fortine, Mt., U.S.	B12	136
Fortín Uno, Arg.	I5	92
Fort Jones, Ca., U.S.	B3	134
Fort Klamath, Or., U.S.	H4	136
Fort Knox, Ky., U.S.	G12	120
Fort-Lamy see N'Djamena, Chad	E3	62
Fort Laramie, Wy., U.S.	E8	126
Fort Lauderdale, Fl., U.S.	J5	116
Fort Liard, N.T., Can.	C6	106
Fort Loramie, Oh., U.S.	D1	114
Fort Loudoun Lake, res., Tn., U.S.	B15	122
Fort Lyon Canal, can., Co., U.S.	C5	128
Fort MacKay, Ab., Can.	D8	106
Fort Macleod, Ab., Can.	G17	138
Fort Madison, Ia., U.S.	D6	120
Fort Matanzas National Monument, p.o.i., Fl., U.S.	G4	116
Fort McMurray, Ab., Can.	D8	106
Fort McPherson, N.T., Can.	B4	106
Fort Meade, Fl., U.S.	I4	116
Fort Mill, S.C., U.S.	A5	116
Fort Morgan, Co., U.S.	A5	128
Fort Myers, Fl., U.S.	J3	116
Fort Myers Beach, Fl., U.S.	J3	116
Fort Nelson, B.C., Can.	D6	106
Fort Nelson, stm., B.C., Can.	D6	106
Fort Ogden, Fl., U.S.	I4	116
Fort Payne, Al., U.S.	C13	122
Fort Peck, Mt., U.S.	F7	124
Fort Peck Dam, dam, Mt., U.S.	G7	124
Fort Peck Lake, res., Mt., U.S.	G7	124
Fort Pierce, Fl., U.S.	I5	116
Fort Plain, N.Y., U.S.	B11	114
Fort Portal, Ug.	D6	66
Fort Providence, N.T., Can.	C7	106
Fort Pulaski National Monument, p.o.i., Ga., U.S.	E5	116
Fort Qu'Appelle, Sk., Can.	D10	124
Fort Randall Dam, dam, S.D., U.S.	D14	126
Fort Recovery, Oh., U.S.	D1	114
Fort Resolution, N.T., Can.	C8	106
Fort Rixon, Zimb.	B9	70
Fort Saint James, B.C., Can.	B6	138
Fort Saint John, B.C., Can.	D6	106
Fort Saskatchewan, Ab., Can.	C17	138
Fort Scott, Ks., U.S.	G3	120
Fort-Ševčenko, Kaz.	F7	32
Fort Severn, On., Can.	D13	106
Fort Simpson, N.T., Can.	C6	106
Fort Smith, N.T., Can.	C8	106
Fort Smith, Ar., U.S.	B4	122
Fort Stockton, Tx., U.S.	D4	130
Fort Sumner, N.M., U.S.	G4	128
Fort Sumter National Monument, p.o.i., S.C., U.S.	D6	116
Fort Supply, Ok., U.S.	E9	128
Fort Thomas, Az., U.S.	J7	132
Fort Totten, N.D., U.S.	G14	124
Fort Towson, Ok., U.S.	D3	122
Fortuna, Arg.	G5	92
Fortuna, C.R.	G5	102
Fortuna, Ca., U.S.	C1	134
Fortuna, V.I.U.S.	e6	104b
Fortune Bay, b., Nf., Can.	j22	107a
Fortuneswell, Eng., U.K.	K10	12
Fort Union National Monument, p.o.i., N.M., U.S.	F3	128
Fort Valley, Ga., U.S.	D2	116
Fort Vermilion, Ab., Can.	D7	106
Fort Victoria, hist., Ber.	k16	104e
Fort Walton Beach, Fl., U.S.	G12	122
Fort Wayne, In., U.S.	G4	112
Fort White, Fl., U.S.	G3	116
Fort William, Scot., U.K.	E7	12
Fort Worth, Tx., U.S.	B10	130
Fort Yates, N.D., U.S.	A12	126
Fort Yukon, Ak., U.S.	C10	140
Foshan, China	J5	42
Fosheim Peninsula, pen., Nu., Can.	B9	141
Foso, Ghana	H4	64
Fossano, Italy	F4	22
Fossil, Or., U.S.	F6	136
Fossil Butte National Monument, p.o.i., Wy., U.S.	B6	132
Fossil Lake, l., Or., U.S.	G6	136
Fossombrone, Italy	G9	22
Fosston, Mn., U.S.	D3	118
Foster, Austl.	L6	76
Foster Bugt, strt., Grnld.	C21	141
Fosters, Al., U.S.	D11	122
Fostoria, Oh., U.S.	C2	114
Fougamou, Gabon	E2	66
Fougères, Fr.	F7	14
Fouhsin see Fuxin, China	C4	38
Fou-kien see Fujian, state, China	I7	42
Foula, i., Scot., U.K.	n17	12a
Fouling see Fuling, China	G2	42
Foulwind, Cape, c., N.Z.	E4	80
Foumban, Cam.	C2	66
Foum-el-Hassan, Mor.	D3	64
Foum-Zguid, Mor.	C3	64
Foundiougne, Sen.	G1	64
Fountain, Co., U.S.	C4	128
Fountain, Fl., U.S.	G13	122
Fountain City, Wi., U.S.	G7	118
Fountain Green, Ut., U.S.	D5	132
Fountain Peak, mtn., Ca., U.S.	I1	132
Fountain Place, La., U.S.	G7	122
Fourche LaFave, stm., Ar., U.S.	C6	122
Fourchu, N.S., Can.	E16	110
Four Corners, Or., U.S.	F4	136
Fourmies, Fr.	D13	14
Four Mountains, Islands of, is., Ak., U.S.	g24	140a
Four Oaks, N.C., U.S.	A7	116
Fourth Cataract see Rābiʿ, Ash-Shallāl ar-, wtfl, Sudan	D6	62
Fous, Pointe des, c., Dom.	j6	105c
Fouta Djalon, reg., Gui.	G2	64
Foux, Cap à, c., Haiti	C11	102
Fouyang see Fuyang, China	E6	42
Foveaux Strait, strt., N.Z.	H3	80
Fowler, Co., U.S.	C4	128
Fowler, In., U.S.	H2	112
Fowler, Mi., U.S.	E5	112
Fowlers Bay, Austl.	F6	74
Fowlerville, Mi., U.S.	B1	114
Fox, stm., U.S.	C9	120
Fox, stm., U.S.	D5	120
Fox, stm., Wi., U.S.	H10	118
Fox Creek, Ab., Can.	B14	138
Foxe Basin, b., Nu., Can.	B15	106
Foxe Channel, strt., Nu., Can.	C15	106
Foxe Peninsula, pen., Nu., Can.	C15	106
Foxford, Ire.	H3	12
Fox Islands, is., Ak., U.S.	g25	140a
Fox Lake, Il., U.S.	B9	120
Foxpark, Wy., U.S.	B10	132
Fox Valley, Sk., Can.	D4	124
Foxworth, Ms., U.S.	F9	122
Foyle, Lough, b., Eur.	F5	12
Foz do Areia, Represa de, res., Braz.	B12	92
Foz do Cunene, Ang.	D1	68
Foz do Iguaçu, Braz.	B10	92
Foz do Jordão, Braz.	E3	84
Foz Giraldo, Port.	E3	20
Fraga, Spain	C11	20
Fraile Muerto, Ur.	F10	92
Framingham, Ma., U.S.	B14	114
França, Braz.	F5	88
Franca, Braz.	K2	88
Franca-Iosifa, Zemlja, is., Russia	B9	30
Francavilla al Mare, Italy	H11	22
Francavilla Fontana, Italy	D11	24
France, ctry., Eur.	C8	18
Frances, stm., Yk., Can.	C5	106
Frances Lake, l., Yk., Can.	C4	106
Francés Viejo, Cabo, c., Dom. Rep.	C13	102
Franceville, Gabon	E2	66
Franche-Comté, hist. reg., Fr.	B12	18
Francis, Sk., Can.	D10	124
Francis Case, Lake, res., S.D., U.S.	D13	126
Francisco Beltrão, Braz.	B11	92
Francisco I. Madero, Mex.	C6	100
Francisco I. Madero, Mex.	I4	130
Francisco Murguía, Mex.	C7	100
Francisco Sá, Braz.	I4	88
Francistown, Bots.	B8	70
Francofonte, Italy	G8	24
François Lake, B.C., Can.	B5	138
François Lake, l., B.C., Can.	C5	138
Francs Peak, mtn., Wy., U.S.	C3	126
Frankel City, Tx., U.S.	B5	130
Franken, hist. reg., Ger.	G6	16
Frankenberg, Ger.	F9	16
Frankenberg, Ger.	E4	16
Frankenmuth, Mi., U.S.	E6	112
Frankford, On., Can.	D12	112
Frankford, Mo., U.S.	E6	120
Frankfort, S. Afr.	E9	70
Frankfort, In., U.S.	H3	112
Frankfort, Ks., U.S.	B12	128
Frankfort, Ky., U.S.	F13	120
Frankfort, N.Y., U.S.	A10	114
Frankfort, Oh., U.S.	E2	114
Frankfort, S.D., U.S.	C14	126
Frankfurt, Ger.	D10	16
Frankfurt am Main, Ger.	F4	16
Franklin, Az., U.S.	K7	132
Franklin, Ga., U.S.	D13	122
Franklin, Id., U.S.	A5	132
Franklin, Il., U.S.	E7	120
Franklin, In., U.S.	E11	120
Franklin, Ma., U.S.	B14	114
Franklin, Ne., U.S.	A9	128
Franklin, N.H., U.S.	G5	110
Franklin, N.J., U.S.	C11	114
Franklin, N.C., U.S.	A2	116
Franklin, Oh., U.S.	E1	114
Franklin, Pa., U.S.	C6	114
Franklin, Tn., U.S.	I11	120
Franklin, Tx., U.S.	F2	122
Franklin, Va., U.S.	H9	114
Franklin, Wi., U.S.	F2	112
Franklin Bay, b., N.T., Can.	B5	106
Franklin D. Roosevelt Lake, res., Wa., U.S.	B4	108
Franklin Gordon Wild Rivers National Park, p.o.i., Austl.	o12	77a
Franklin Grove, Il., U.S.	C8	120
Franklin Lake, l., Nu., Can.	B12	106
Franklin Mountains, mts., N.T., Can.	B5	106
Franklin Strait, strt., Nu., Can.	A11	106
Franklinton, La., U.S.	G8	122
Franklinville, N.Y., U.S.	B7	114
Frankston, Tx., U.S.	E3	122
Frankton, In., U.S.	H4	112
Fransfontein, Nmb.	B2	70
Franzensfeste see Fortezza, Italy	D8	22
Franz Josef Land see Franca-Iosifa, Zemlja, is., Russia	B9	30
Frascati, Italy	I9	22
Fraser, B.C., Can.	G13	138
Fraser, Co., U.S.	B3	128
Fraser, stm., B.C., Can.	G9	138
Fraser, Mount, mtn., Austl.	E3	74
Fraserburgh, Scot., U.K.	D11	12
Fraser Island, i., Austl.	E9	76
Fraser Lake, B.C., Can.	B6	138
Fraser Lake, l., B.C., Can.	B6	138
Fraser Plateau, plat., B.C., Can.	E8	138
Fraser Range, Austl.	F4	74
Frauenfeld, Switz.	C5	22
Fray Bentos, Ur.	F8	92
Fray Jorge, Parque Nacional, p.o.i., Chile	E2	92
Fray Marcos, Ur.	G10	92
Frazer, Mt., U.S.	F7	124
Frederic, Wi., U.S.	F6	118
Frederica, De., U.S.	E10	114
Fredericia, Den.	I3	8
Frederick, Md., U.S.	E8	114
Frederick, S.D., U.S.	B14	126
Frederick Hills, hills, Austl.	B7	74
Frederick Reef, rf., Austl.	C10	76
Fredericksburg, Ia., U.S.	B5	120
Fredericksburg, Tx., U.S.	D9	130
Fredericksburg, Va., U.S.	F8	114
Fredericktown, Oh., U.S.	D3	114
Frederico Westphalen, Braz.	C11	92
Fredericton, N.B., Can.	E10	110
Fredericton Junction, N.B., Can.	E10	110
Frederiksborg, state, Den.	H5	8
Frederiksdal, Grnld.	E17	141
Frederikshåb (Paamiut), Grnld.	E15	141
Frederikshavn, Den.	H4	8
Frederiksted, V.I.U.S.	h10	104c
Fredonia, Ks., U.S.	G2	120
Fredonia, N.Y., U.S.	B6	114
Fredonia, N.D., U.S.	A13	126
Fredrika, Swe.	D8	8
Fredrikstad, Nor.	G4	8
Freeburg, Il., U.S.	F8	120
Freeland, Mi., U.S.	E5	112
Freeland, Pa., U.S.	C9	114
Freel Peak, mtn., Ca., U.S.	E5	134
Freels, Cape, c., Nf., Can.	j23	107a
Freeman, S.D., U.S.	D15	126
Freeport, Bah.	B9	96
Freeport, N.S., Can.	F10	110
Freeport, Fl., U.S.	G12	122
Freeport, Il., U.S.	B8	120
Freeport, N.Y., U.S.	H16	112
Freeport, Pa., U.S.	D6	114
Freeport, Tx., U.S.	F12	130
Free State, state, S. Afr.	F8	70
Freetown, Antig.	f4	105b
Freetown, S.L.	H2	64
Fregenal de la Sierra, Spain	F4	20
Freiberg, Ger.	F9	16
Freiburg see Fribourg, Switz.	D4	22
Freiburg im Breisgau, Ger.	I3	16
Freirina, Chile	D2	92
Freising, Ger.	H7	16
Freistadt, Aus.	B11	22
Freital, Ger.	F9	16
Fréjus, Fr.	F12	18
Fremantle, Austl.	F3	74
Fremont, Ca., U.S.	F4	134
Fremont, In., U.S.	C1	114
Fremont, Ia., U.S.	C5	120
Fremont, Mi., U.S.	E4	112
Fremont, Ne., U.S.	C1	120
Fremont, Oh., U.S.	C2	114
Fremont, Wi., U.S.	G10	118
Fremont, stm., Ut., U.S.	E6	132
French, stm., On., Can.	B9	112
French Broad, stm., U.S.	I3	114
Frenchcap Cay, i., V.I.U.S.	f7	104b
French Guiana, dep., S.A.	C7	84
French Island, i., Austl.	L5	76
French Lick, In., U.S.	F11	120
Frenchman (Frenchman Creek), stm., N.A.	E5	124
Frenchman Creek (Frenchman), stm., N.A.	E5	124
Frenchman Creek, stm., U.S.	G11	126
Frenchmans Cap, mtn., Austl.	o12	77a
French Polynesia, dep., Oc.	K24	142
French Somaliland see Djibouti, ctry., Afr.	E8	62
Fresco, C. Iv.	H3	64
Fresco, stm., Braz.	E7	84
Fresnillo, Mex.	D7	100
Fresno, Ca., U.S.	G6	134
Fresno, stm., Ca., U.S.	F6	134
Fresno Reservoir, res., Mt., U.S.	B16	136
Freu, Cap des, c., Spain	E14	20
Freudenstadt, Ger.	H4	16
Frewena, Austl.	C7	74
Frewsburg, N.Y., U.S.	B6	114
Freycinet National Park, p.o.i., Austl.	o14	77a
Freycinet Peninsula, pen., Austl.	o14	77a
Freyre, Arg.	E6	92
Fria, Gui.	G2	64
Fria, Cape, c., Nmb.	D1	68
Friant, Ca., U.S.	G6	134
Friars Point, Ms., U.S.	C8	122
Frías, Arg.	D5	92
Fribourg (Freiburg), Switz.	D4	22
Fridley, Mn., U.S.	F5	118
Fridtjof Nansen, Mount, mtn., Ant.	D25	81
Friedberg, Aus.	C12	22
Friedberg, Ger.	F4	16
Friedberg, Ger.	H7	16
Friedland, Ger.	C9	16
Friedrichshafen, Ger.	I5	16
Friend, Ne., U.S.	G15	126
Friendship, N.Y., U.S.	B7	114
Friendship, Tn., U.S.	I8	120
Fries, Va., U.S.	H4	114
Friesach, Aus.	D11	22
Frio, stm., Tx., U.S.	F9	130
Frio, Cabo, c., Braz.	L5	88
Frio Draw, stm., U.S.	G6	128
Friona, Tx., U.S.	G6	128
Frisco, Tx., U.S.	D2	122
Frisian Islands, is., Eur.	A14	14
Fritch, Tx., U.S.	F7	128
Fritzlar, Ger.	E5	16
Friuli, hist. reg., Italy	E9	22
Friuli-Venezia Giulia, state, Italy	D9	22
Frjazino, Russia	E21	10
Frobisher, Sk., Can.	E11	124
Frobisher Bay, b., Nu., Can.	C17	106
Frobisher Lake, l., Sk., Can.	D9	106
Froid, Mt., U.S.	F9	124
Frolovo, Russia	E6	32
Frome, Eng., U.K.	J10	12
Frome, stm., Austl.	G2	76
Frome, Lake, l., Austl.	H2	76
Fronteiras, Braz.	D5	88
Frontenac, Ks., U.S.	G3	120
Frontera, Mex.	F12	100
Frontera, Mex.	B8	100
Frontier, Sk., Can.	E5	124
Frontier, Wy., U.S.	B6	132
Frontino, Col.	B2	84
Frontino, Páramo, mtn., Col.	D3	86
Front Range, mts., Co., U.S.	H7	126
Front Royal, Va., U.S.	F7	114
Frosinone, Italy	C7	24
Frostburg, Md., U.S.	E6	114
Frostproof, Fl., U.S.	I4	116
Frøya, i., Nor.	E3	8
Fruges, Fr.	D11	14
Fruita, Co., U.S.	D8	132
Fruitdale, Or., U.S.	H3	136
Fruithurst, Al., U.S.	D13	122
Fruitland, Id., U.S.	F10	136
Fruitport, Mi., U.S.	E3	112
Fruitvale, B.C., Can.	G13	138
Fruitvale, Wa., U.S.	D6	136
Frunzivka, Ukr.	B16	26
Frutal, Braz.	J1	88
Frutigen, Switz.	D4	22
Frýdek-Místek, Czech Rep.	G14	16
Fryeburg, Me., U.S.	G6	110
Fu, stm., China	G7	42
Fu, stm., China	F2	42
Fu, stm., China	G6	42
Fua'amotu International Airport, Tonga	n14	78e
Fu'an, China	H8	42
Fuchou see Fuzhou, China	H8	42
Fuchow see Fuzhou, China	G7	42
Fuchū, Japan	E6	40
Fuchun, stm., China	G8	42
Fuding, China	H9	42
Fuego, Volcán de, vol., Guat.	E2	102
Fuencaliente, Spain	F6	20
Fuengirola, Spain	H6	20
Fuensalida, Spain	D6	20
Fuente, Mex.	F7	130
Fuente de Cantos, Spain	F4	20
Fuente de Oro, Col.	F5	86
Fuentes de Ebro, Spain	C10	20
Fuerte, stm., Mex.	B4	100
Fuerte Olimpo, Para.	D5	90
Fuga Island, i., Phil.	A3	52
Fugou, China	D6	42
Fuhai, China	B2	36
Fuhsien see Wafangdian, China	B9	42
Fuji, Japan	D11	40
Fuji, Mount see Fuji-san, vol., Japan	D11	40
Fujian, state, China	I7	42
Fujieda, Japan	E11	40
Fujin, China	B11	36
Fujinomiya, Japan	D11	40
Fuji-san (Fuji, Mount), vol., Japan	D11	40
Fujisawa, Japan	D12	40
Fujiyama see Fuji-san, vol., Japan	D11	40
Fuji-yoshida, Japan	D11	40
Fukagawa, Japan	C14	38
Fukang, China	C2	36
Fukave, i., Tonga	n14	78e
Fukaya, Japan	C12	40
Fukien see Fujian, state, China	I7	42
Fukuchiyama, Japan	D8	40
Fukue, Japan	G1	40
Fukue-jima, i., Japan	G1	40
Fukui, Japan	C9	40
Fukui, state, Japan	D9	40
Fukuoka, Japan	F3	40
Fukuoka, state, Japan	F3	40
Fukuroi, Japan	E10	40
Fukushima, Japan	B13	40
Fukushima, state, Japan	B12	40
Fukuyama, Japan	E6	40
Fūlādī, Kūh-e, mtn., Afg.	C10	56
Fulaga Passage, strt., Fiji	q20	79e
Fulda, Ger.	F5	16
Fulda, Mn., U.S.	H3	118
Fulda, stm., Ger.	E5	16
Fuling, China	G2	42
Fullarton, stm., Austl.	C3	76
Fullerton, Ca., U.S.	J8	134
Fullerton Point, c., Antig.	f4	105b
Fulong, China	J2	42
Fulton, Al., U.S.	F11	122
Fulton, Ar., U.S.	D5	122
Fulton, Il., U.S.	C7	120
Fulton, Ks., U.S.	F3	120
Fulton, Ky., U.S.	H9	120
Fulton, Mo., U.S.	F5	120
Fulton, N.Y., U.S.	E13	112
Fulton, Tx., U.S.	F10	130
Fumay, Fr.	D13	14
Funabashi, Japan	D12	40
Funafuti, i., Tuvalu	D8	72
Funan, China	E6	42
Funchal, Port.	C1	64
Fundación, Col.	B4	86
Fundão, Port.	D3	20
Fundy, Bay of, b., Can.	F10	110
Fundy National Park, p.o.i., N.B., Can.	E11	110
Funhalouro, Moz.	C12	70
Funing, China	E8	42
Funiu Shan, mts., China	E5	42
Funsi, Ghana	G4	64
Funtua, Nig.	G6	64
Fuping, China	D3	42
Fuqing, China	I8	42
Fuquay-Varina, N.C., U.S.	A7	116
Furculeşti, Rom.	F12	26
Furmanov, Russia	H19	8
Furnas, Represa de, res., Braz.	K2	88
Furneaux Group, is., Austl.	m13	77a
Furnes see Veurne, Bel.	C11	14
Fürstenberg / Havel, Ger.	C9	16
Fürstenfeld, Aus.	C12	22
Fürstenfeldbruck, Ger.	H7	16
Fürstenwalde, Ger.	D9	16
Fürth, Ger.	G6	16
Furth im Wald, Ger.	G8	16
Furukawa, Japan	C10	40
Furukawa, Japan	A13	40
Fury and Hecla Strait, strt., Nu., Can.	B14	106
Fusagasugá, Col.	E4	86
Fusan see Pusan, Kor., S.	D2	40
Fushan, China	C9	42
Fushan, China	D4	42
Fushih see Yan'an, China	C3	42
Fushun, China	D5	38
Fushun, China	G1	42
Fusilier, Sk., Can.	C4	124
Fusong, China	C7	38
Füssen, Ger.	I6	16
Fuste, Picacho del, mtn., Mex.	G5	130
Fusui, China	J2	42
Futun, stm., China	H7	42
Futuna, Île, i., Wal./F.	E9	72
Futuyu, China	B6	42
Fuwa, Egypt	G1	58
Fuxian Hu, l., China	G5	36
Fuxin, China	C4	38
Fuyang, China	E6	42
Fuyang, stm., China	C6	42
Fuyu, China	B9	36
Fuyu, China	B6	38
Fuyuan see Tongjiang, China	B11	36
Fuyuan, China	F5	36
Fuyuan, China	B11	36
Fuzhou, China	G7	42
Fuzhou, China	H8	42
Fylí, hist., Grc.	E6	28
Fyn, state, Den.	I4	8
Fyn, i., Den.	I4	8
Fyne, Loch, b., Scot., U.K.	E7	12
Fyresvatnet, l., Nor.	G2	8

G

Name	Map Ref.	Page
Gaalkacyo, Som.	C9	66
Gabare, Blg.	F10	26
Gabarus, N.S., Can.	E16	110
Gabela, Ang.	C1	68
Gaberones see Gaborone, Bots.	D7	70
Gabès, Tun.	C7	64
Gabiarra, Braz.	I6	88
Gabon, ctry., Afr.	E2	66
Gaborone, Bots.	D7	70
Gabras, Sudan	E5	62
Gabriel Strait, strt., Nu., Can.	C17	106
Gabriel y Galán, Embalse de, res., Spain	D4	20
Gabrovo, Blg.	G12	26
Gacé, Fr.	F9	14
Gackle, N.D., U.S.	A13	126
Gadag, India	D2	53
Gādarwāra, India	G7	54
Gäddede, Swe.	D6	8
Gado Bravo, Ilha do, i., Braz.	F4	88
Gádor, Spain	H8	20
Gadsden, Al., U.S.	C12	122
Gadsden, Az., U.S.	K2	132
Gadwāl, India	C3	53
Gael Hamke Bugt, b., Grnld.	C22	141
Găeşti, Rom.	E12	26
Gaeta, Italy	C7	24
Gaeta, Golfo di, b., Italy	C7	24
Gaferut, i., Micron.	C5	72
Gaffney, S.C., U.S.	A4	116
Gafour, Tun.	H3	24
Gafsa, Tun.	C6	64
Gag, Pulau, i., Indon.	F8	44
Gagarin, Russia	E17	10
Gage, Ok., U.S.	E9	128
Gaggenau, Ger.	H4	16
Gagliano del Capo, Italy	E12	24
Gagnoa, C. Iv.	H3	64
Gagra, Geor.	F5	32
Gaibandha, Bngl.	F12	54
Gail, Tx., U.S.	B6	130
Gaillac, Fr.	F7	18
Gaillimh see Galway, Ire.	H3	12
Gaimán, Arg.	H3	90
Gainesboro, Tn., U.S.	H12	120
Gainesville, Fl., U.S.	G3	116
Gainesville, Ga., U.S.	B2	116
Gainesville, Mo., U.S.	H5	120
Gainesville, Tx., U.S.	H11	128
Gainsborough, Eng., U.K.	H12	12
Gainsborough Creek, stm., Can.	E12	124
Gairdner, Lake, l., Austl.	F7	74
Gaithersburg, Md., U.S.	E8	114
Gaixian, China	A10	42
Gaizina Kalns, hill, Lat.	D8	10
Gajendragarh, India	D2	53
Gajny, Russia	B8	32
Gajuapara, stm., Braz.	C2	88
Gajutino, Russia	B21	10
Gakarosa, mtn., S. Afr.	E6	70
Gakona, Ak., U.S.	D10	140
Galahad, Ab., Can.	D19	138
Galâla el Baharîya, Gebel el-, mts., Egypt	I3	58
Galâla el-Qiblîya, Gebel el-, mts., Egypt	J3	58
Galán, Cerro, mtn., Arg.	C4	92
Galana, stm., Kenya	E7	66
Galanta, Slov.	H13	16
Galapagos Islands see Colón, Archipiélago de, is., Ec.	h12	84a
Galashiels, Scot., U.K.	F9	12
Galaţi, Rom.	D14	26
Galaţi, state, Rom.	D14	26
Galatia, Il., U.S.	G9	120
Galatina, Italy	D12	24
Galaxídi, Grc.	E5	28
Galdhøpiggen, mtn., Nor.	F2	8
Galeana, Mex.	F9	98
Galeana, Mex.	C8	100
Galela, Indon.	E8	44
Galena, Ak., U.S.	D8	140
Galena, Il., U.S.	B7	120
Galena, Mo., U.S.	H4	120
Galena Park, Tx., U.S.	E12	130
Galeota Point, c., Trin.	s13	105f
Galera, Punta, c., Chile	G2	90
Galera, Punta, c., Ec.	G1	86
Galera Point, c., Trin.	s13	105f
Galeras, Volcán, vol., Col.	G3	86
Galesburg, Il., U.S.	D7	120
Galesville, Wi., U.S.	G7	118
Galeton, Pa., U.S.	C8	114
Galiano Island, i., B.C., Can.	H7	138
Galič, Russia	G20	8
Galicia, state, Spain	B3	20
Galicia, hist. reg., Eur.	G18	16
Galičica Nacionalni Park, p.o.i., Mac.	C3	28
Galičskaja vozvyšennost', hills, Russia	G20	8
Galičskoe, ozero, l., Russia	G20	8
Galilee, Lake, l., Austl.	D5	76
Galilee, Sea of see Kinneret, Yam, l., Isr.	F6	58
Galiléia, Braz.	J5	88
Galina Point, c., Jam.	i14	104d
Galion, Oh., U.S.	D3	114
Galite, Canal de la, strt., Tun.	G3	24
Gallarate, Italy	E5	22
Gallatin, Tn., U.S.	H11	120
Gallatin, stm., U.S.	E15	136
Galle, Sri L.	H5	53
Gállego, stm., Spain	B10	20
Gallegos, stm., Arg.	J3	90
Galliano, La., U.S.	H8	122
Gallinas, stm., N.M., U.S.	F4	128
Gallinas, Punta, c., Col.	A6	86
Gallipoli, Italy	D11	24
Gallipoli see Gelibolu, Tur.	C9	28
Gallipoli Peninsula see Gelibolu Yarımadası, pen., Tur.	C9	28
Gallipolis, Oh., U.S.	F3	114
Gällivare, Swe.	C9	8
Gallo, Capo, c., Italy	F7	24
Gallo Arroyo, stm., N.M., U.S.	G3	128
Galloo Island, i., N.Y., U.S.	E13	112
Galloway, hist. reg., Scot., U.K.	G8	12
Galloway, Mull of, c., Scot., U.K.	G8	12
Gallup, N.M., U.S.	H8	132
Gallura, reg., Italy	C3	24
Galoa Harbour, b., Fiji	q19	79e
Galt, Ca., U.S.	E4	134
Galtat Zemmour, W. Sah.	D2	64
Galty Mountains, mts., Ire.	I4	12
Galva, Il., U.S.	C7	120
Galva, Ks., U.S.	C11	128
Galveston, In., U.S.	H3	112
Galveston, Tx., U.S.	H4	122
Galveston Bay, b., Tx., U.S.	H4	122
Galveston Island, i., Tx., U.S.	E13	130
Gálvez, Arg.	F7	92
Galway (Gaillimh), Ire.	H3	12
Galway, state, Ire.	H4	12
Galway Bay, b., Ire.	H3	12
Gam (Jin), stm., Asia	A7	48
Gama, Isla, i., Arg.	H4	90
Gamagōri, Japan	E10	40
Gamarra, Col.	C5	86
Gamay, Phil.	D5	52
Gamba, China	D12	54
Gambaga, Ghana	G4	64
Gambēla, Eth.	F6	62
Gambell, Ak., U.S.	D5	140
Gambia (Gambie), stm., Afr.	G1	64
Gambia, The, ctry., Afr.	G1	64
Gambie (Gambia), stm., Afr.	G2	64
Gambier, Îles, is., Fr. Poly.	F13	72
Gamboa, Pan.	C2	86
Gamboma, Congo	E3	66
Gamboula, C.A.R.	D2	66
Gamka, stm., S. Afr.	H5	70
Gamlakarleby see Kokkola, Fin.	E10	8
Gamleby, Swe.	H7	8
Gammon Ranges National Park, p.o.i., Austl.	H2	76
Ga-Mogara, stm., S. Afr.	E6	70
Gan, stm., China	B10	36
Gan, stm., China	G6	42
Ganado, Az., U.S.	H7	132
Ganado, Tx., U.S.	E11	130
Gananoque, On., Can.	D13	112
Gäncä, Azer.	A6	56
Gand see Gent, Bel.	C12	14
Ganda, Ang.	C1	68
Gandadiwata, Bulu, mtn., Indon.	E11	50
Gandajika, D.R.C.	F4	66
Gandak (Nārāyani), stm., Asia	E10	54
Gándara, Spain	A2	20
Gander, Nf., Can.	j23	107a
Ganderkesee, Ger.	C4	16
Gandesa, Spain	C11	20
Gandevi, India	H4	54
Gāndhinagar, India	G4	54
Gandhi Reservoir see Gāndhi Sāgar, res., India	F5	54
Gāndhi Sāgar, res., India	F5	54
Gandia, Spain	F10	20
Gandu, Braz.	G6	88
Ganga see Ganges, stm., Asia	F11	54
Gan Gan, Arg.	H3	90
Gangānagar, India	D4	54
Gangāpur, India	B2	53
Gangāpur, India	F5	54
Gangāpur, India	E6	54
Gangārāmpur, India	F12	54
Gangaw, Mya.	A2	48
Gangāwati, India	D3	53
Gangdhār, India	G5	54
Gangdisê Shan, mts., China	C9	54
Ganges, B.C., Can.	H7	138
Ganges (Ganga) (Padma), stm., Asia	G13	54
Ganges, Mouths of the, mth., Asia	H12	54
Ganghu, China	B11	54
Gangmar Co, l., China	B10	54
Gangneung see Kangnŭng, Kor., S.	B1	40
Gangoa, China	D5	36
Gangotri, India	C7	54
Gangotri, India	C7	54
Gangoumen, China	D2	38
Gangtok, India	E12	54
Gangu, China	D1	42
Gangweon see Kangwŏn-do, state, Kor., S.	B1	40
Gannan, China	B9	36
Gannett Peak, mtn., Wy., U.S.	D3	126
Gannvalley, S.D., U.S.	C14	126
Ganquan, China	C3	42
Gansbaai, S. Afr.	I4	70
Gansu, state, China	D5	36
Gantang, China	H8	42
Gantt, Al., U.S.	F12	122
Gantung, Indon.	E6	50
Ganyanchi, China	C1	42
Ganyesa, S. Afr.	E7	70
Ganzê, China	E4	36
Ganzhou, China	I6	42
Gao, Mali	F4	64
Gao'an, China	G6	42
Gaochun, China	F8	42
Gaohebu, China	F7	42
Gaojian, China	F9	36
Gaolan, China	D5	36
Gaolong, China	H5	42
Gaona, Arg.	B5	92
Gaoping, China	D5	42
Gaotan, China	E3	42
Gaotang, China	C7	42
Gaoua, Burkina	G4	64
Gaoual, Gui.	G2	64
Gaoxian, China	F5	36
Gaoyi, China	C6	42
Gaoyou, China	E8	42
Gaoyou Hu, l., China	E8	42
Gaozhou, China	K4	42
Gap, Fr.	E12	18
Gar, China	B8	54
Gar, stm., China	C8	54
Gara, Lough, l., Ire.	H4	12
Garagumskij kanal (Kara-Kum Canal), can., Turkmen.	B9	56
Garagumy (Kara-Kum), des., Turkmen.	A8	56
Garaina, Pap. N. Gui.	b4	79a
Garanhuns, Braz.	E7	88
Garapan, N. Mar. Is.	B5	72
Garara, Pap. N. Gui.	b4	79a
Garber, Ok., U.S.	E11	128
Garberville, Ca., U.S.	C2	134
Gârbovu, Rom.	E10	26
Garça, Braz.	L1	88
García, Mex.	G8	98
García de Sola, Embalse de, res., Spain	E5	20
Gard, state, Fr.	F10	18
Garda, Italy	E7	22
Garda, Lago di, l., Italy	E7	22
Gardelegen, Ger.	D7	16
Garden City, Ks., U.S.	C8	128
Garden City, Mo., U.S.	F3	120
Garden City, Tx., U.S.	C6	130
Gardendale, Al., U.S.	D12	122
Garden Grove, Ca., U.S.	J7	134
Garden Grove, Ia., U.S.	D4	120
Garden Island, i., Mi., U.S.	C4	112
Garden Peninsula, pen., Mi., U.S.	C3	112
Garden Reach, India	G11	54
Gardenton, Mb., Can.	E17	124
Gardey, Arg.	H8	92
Gardeyz, Afg.	C10	56
Gardiner, Mt., U.S.	E16	136
Gardiner, Or., U.S.	G2	136
Gardiner Dam, dam, Sk., Can.	C6	124
Gardner, Ks., U.S.	F2	120
Gardner, Ma., U.S.	B13	114
Gardner Canal, b., B.C., Can.	C2	138
Gardnerville, Nv., U.S.	E6	134
Garessio, Italy	F5	22
Garet, Mont, vol., Vanuatu	j16	79d
Garfield, Ks., U.S.	C9	128
Garfield, N.M., U.S.	K9	132
Garfield Mountain, mtn., Mt., U.S.	F14	136
Gargano, Promontorio del, mts., Italy	I12	22
Gargano, Testa del, c., Italy	I13	22
Gargždai, Lith.	E4	10
Garhākota, India	G7	54
Garibaldi, Braz.	D12	92
Garibaldi, B.C., Can.	G7	138
Garibaldi, Or., U.S.	E2	136
Garibaldi, Mount, vol., B.C., Can.	G8	138
Gariep Dam, res., S. Afr.	G7	70
Garies, S. Afr.	G4	70
Garigliano, stm., Italy	C7	24
Gariglione, Monte, mtn., Italy	E10	24
Garissa, Kenya	E7	66
Garland, Tx., U.S.	E2	122
Garland, Ut., U.S.	B4	132
Garlasco, Italy	E5	22
Garlin, Fr.	F5	18
Garm, Taj.	B11	56
Garmisch-Partenkirchen, Ger.	I7	16
Garnavillo, Ia., U.S.	B6	120
Garner, Ia., U.S.	A4	120
Garner, N.C., U.S.	I7	114
Garnpung Lake, l., Austl.	I4	76
Garona (Garonne), stm., Eur.	E5	18
Garonne (Garona), stm., Eur.	E5	18
Garoowe, Som.	C9	66
Garoua, Cam.	C2	66
Garoua Boulaï, Cam.	C2	66
Garqu Yan, China	B14	54
Garqu Yan, China	A14	54
Garrel, Ger.	D3	16
Garretson, S.D., U.S.	H2	118
Garrett, In., U.S.	G4	112
Garrett, Ky., U.S.	G3	114
Garrison, N.D., U.S.	G12	124
Garrison, Tx., U.S.	F4	122
Garrison Dam, dam, N.D., U.S.	G12	124
Garry Bay, b., Nu., Can.	B13	106
Garry Lake, l., Nu., Can.	B10	106
Garsen, Kenya	E7	66
Garson, On., Can.	B9	112
Garut, Indon.	G5	50
Garwolin, Pol.	E17	16
Garwood, Tx., U.S.	H2	122
Gary, In., U.S.	G2	112
Gary, Tx., U.S.	E4	122
Gary, W.V., U.S.	G4	114
Garyarsa, China	C8	54
Garza, Arg.	D6	92
Garza Ayala, Mex.	H7	130
Garzón, Col.	F4	86
Garzón, Ur.	G10	92
Gasan-Kuli, Turkmen.	B7	56
Gas City, In., U.S.	H4	112
Gascogne (Gascony), hist. reg., Fr.	F6	18
Gasconade, stm., Mo., U.S.	F6	120
Gasconade, Osage Fork, stm., Mo., U.S.	G5	120
Gascony see Gascogne, hist. reg., Fr.	F6	18
Gascoyne, stm., Austl.	D2	74
Gashaka, Nig.	H7	64
Gashua, Nig.	G7	64
Gaspar, Braz.	C13	92

Guay-Haut I•23

Name	Map Ref.	Page
Guaymallén, Arg.	F3	92
Guaymas, Mex.	B3	100
Guaynabo, P.R.	B3	104a
Guayquiraró, stm., Arg.	E8	92
Guazapares, Mex.	B4	100
Guazárachi, Mex.	B5	100
Guba, D.R.C.	G5	66
Gubaha, Russia	C9	32
Gûbâl, Madîq (Jubal, Strait of), strt., Egypt	K4	58
Gubavica, wtfl, Cro.	G13	22
Gubbi, India	E3	53
Gubbio, Italy	G9	22
Guben, Ger.	E10	16
Gubin, Pol.	E10	16
Gucheng, China	E4	42
Gūdalūr, India	G3	53
Gúdar, Sierra de, mts., Spain	D10	20
Gudauta, Geor.	F6	32
Gudermes, Russia	F7	32
Gudivāda, India	C5	53
Gudiyāttam, India	E4	53
Güdül, Tur.	C15	28
Gūdūr, India	D4	53
Guebwiller, Fr.	G16	14
Güejar, stm., Col.	F5	86
Guékédou, Gui.	H2	64
Guélengdeng, Chad	E3	62
Guelma, Alg.	B6	64
Guelmime, Mor.	D2	64
Guelph, On., Can.	E9	112
Guérande, Fr.	G6	14
Guercif, Mor.	C4	64
Guerdjoumane, Djebel, mtn., Alg.	H13	20
Güere, stm., Ven.	C9	86
Guéréda, Chad	E4	62
Guéret, Fr.	C7	18
Guerla Mandata Shan, mtn., China	C8	54
Guernesey see Guernsey, dep., Eur.	L10	12
Guerneville, Ca., U.S.	E3	134
Guernica see Gernika, Spain	A8	20
Guernica y Luno see Gernika, Spain	A8	20
Guernsey, dep., Eur.	E6	14
Guernsey, i., Guern.	E6	14
Guerrero, Mex.	A5	100
Guerrero, Mex.	F7	130
Guerrero, state, Mex.	G8	100
Guerrero Negro, Mex.	B1	100
Gueydan, La., U.S.	G6	122
Guga, Russia	F16	34
Gugē, mtn., Eth.	F7	62
Guguan, i., N. Mar. Is.	B5	72
Gui, stm., China	I4	42
Guiana Basin, unds.	G9	144
Guiana Highlands (Guayana, Macizo de), mts., S.A.	E10	86
Güicán, Col.	D5	86
Guichi, China	F7	42
Guide, China	D5	36
Guidimouni, Niger	G6	64
Guiding, China	H2	42
Guier, Lac de, l., Sen.	F1	64
Guijuelo, Spain	D5	20
Guilarte, Monte, mtn., P.R.	B2	104a
Guildford, Eng., U.K.	J12	12
Guildhall, Vt., U.S.	F5	110
Guilford, Me., U.S.	E7	110
Guilin, China	I4	42
Guillaume-Delisle, Lac, l., Qc., Can.	D15	106
Guillestre, Fr.	E12	18
Guimarães, Braz.	B3	88
Guimaras Island, i., Phil.	E4	52
Guimba, Phil.	C3	52
Guin, Al., U.S.	D11	122
Guinan, China	D5	36
Guindulman, Phil.	F5	52
Guinea, ctry., Afr.	G2	64
Guinea, Gulf of, b., Afr.	I6	64
Guinea Basin, unds.	H13	144
Guinea-Bissau, ctry., Afr.	G1	64
Güines, Cuba	A7	102
Guingamp, Fr.	F5	14
Güinope, Hond.	F4	102
Guiping, China	J4	42
Guipúzcoa see Gipuzkoako, co., Spain	A8	20
Guiratinga, Braz.	G7	84
Güiria, Ven.	B10	86
Guitry, C. Iv.	H3	64
Guiuan, Phil.	E5	52
Guixian, China	J3	42
Guiyang, China	I5	42
Guiyang, China	H2	42
Güiza, stm., Col.	G2	86
Guizhou, state, China	F6	36
Gujarāt, state, India	G3	54
Gūjar Khān, Pak.	B4	54
Gujrānwāla, Pak.	B4	54
Gujrāt, Pak.	B4	54
Gukou, China	H8	42
Gulargambone, Austl.	H7	76
Gulbarga, India	C3	53
Gulbene, Lat.	C9	10
Güldüzü, Tur.	B8	58
Guledagudda, India	C2	53
Gülek Boğazı, p., Tur.	A5	58
Gulf Islands National Seashore, p.o.i., U.S.	G10	122
Gulfport, Ms., U.S.	G9	122
Gulf Shores, Al., U.S.	G11	122
Gulgong, Austl.	I7	76
Gulian, China	F13	34
Gulistan, Uzb.	F11	32
Gulkana, Ak., U.S.	D10	140
Gull, stm., On., Can.	B9	118
Gullfoss, wtfl, Ice.	k29	8a
Gull Lake, Sk., Can.	D5	124
Gull Lake, l., Ab., Can.	D17	138
Gull Lake, l., Mn., U.S.	E4	118
Güllük, Tur.	F10	28
Güllük Körfezi, b., Tur.	F10	28
Gülpınar, Tur.	D9	28
Gulu, Ug.	D6	66
Guluogongba, China	A10	54
Gumaca, Phil.	D4	52
Gumal (Gowmal), stm., Asia	B2	54
Gumbalie, Austl.	G5	76
Gumdag, Turkmen.	B7	56
Gumel, Nig.	G6	64
Gumla, India	G10	54
Gumma, state, Japan	C11	40
Gummersbach, Ger.	E3	16
Gümüşhane, Tur.	A4	56
Gümüşsu, Tur.	E12	28
Guna, India	F6	54
Gundagai, Austl.	J7	76
Gundji, D.R.C.	D4	66
Gundlupet, India	F3	53
Gündoğdu, Tur.	C9	28
Güney, Tur.	E12	28
Gungu, D.R.C.	F3	66
Gunmi, Nig.	G6	64
Gunnar, Sk., Can.	D9	106
Gunnarn, Swe.	D7	8
Gunnbjørn Fjeld, mtn., Grnld.	D19	141
Gunnedah, Austl.	H7	76
Gunnison, Ut., U.S.	D5	132
Gunnison, stm., Co., U.S.	E8	132
Gunong Mulu National Park, p.o.i., Malay.	A9	50
Gun Point, c., Gren.	p11	105e
Gunpowder Creek, stm., Austl.	B2	76
Gunsan see Kunsan, Kor., S.	F7	38
Guntakal, India	D3	53
Guntersville, Al., U.S.	C12	122
Guntersville Dam, dam, Al., U.S.	C12	122
Guntersville Lake, res., Al., U.S.	C12	122
Guntūr, India	C5	53
Gunungkencana, Indon.	G4	50
Gunungsahilan, Indon.	C2	50
Gunungsitoli, Indon.	L3	48
Gunupur, India	B6	53
Günzburg, Ger.	H6	16
Gunzenhausen, Ger.	G6	16
Guo, stm., China	E7	42
Guoyang, China	E7	42
Guoyangzhen, China	B5	42
Gupis, Pak.	B11	56
Gurabo, P.R.	B4	104a
Gura Humorului, Rom.	B12	26
Gurais, India	A5	54
Gurdāspur, India	B5	54
Gurdon, Ar., U.S.	D5	122
Güre, Tur.	E12	28
Gurevsk, Russia	D15	32
Gurgueia, stm., Braz.	D4	88
Gurha, India	F3	54
Guri, Embalse de, res., Ven.	D10	86
Gurskoe, Russia	F16	34
Gurskøya, i., Nor.	E1	8
Gürsu, Tur.	C12	28
Gurupá, Braz.	D7	84
Gurupi, Braz.	F1	88
Gurupi, stm., Braz.	D8	84
Guru Sikhar, mtn., India	F4	54
Gurvan Sayhan uul, mts., Mong.	C5	36
Gusau, Nig.	G6	64
Gusev, Russia	F5	10
Gušgy, Turkmen.	B9	56
Gushan, China	B10	42
Gushi, China	E6	42
Gus'-Hrustal'nyj, Russia	I19	8
Gusino, Russia	F14	10
Gusinoozersk, Russia	F10	34
Gus'-Khrustal'nyy see Gus'-Hrustal'nyj, Russia	I19	8
Guspini, Italy	E2	24
Güssing, Aus.	C13	22
Gustav Holm, Kap, c., Grnld.	D19	141
Gustavus, Ak., U.S.	E12	140
Gustine, Ca., U.S.	F5	134
Gustine, Tx., U.S.	C9	130
Güstrow, Ger.	C8	16
Gütersloh, Ger.	E4	16
Guthrie, Ok., U.S.	F11	128
Guthrie, Tx., U.S.	H8	128
Guthrie Center, Ia., U.S.	C3	120
Gutian, China	H8	42
Gutiérrez Zamora, Mex.	E10	100
Guttenberg, Ia., U.S.	B6	120
Guwāhāti, India	E13	54
Guxian, China	E5	42
Guyana, ctry., S.A.	C6	84
Guyang, China	A4	42
Guye, China	B8	42
Guy Fawkes River National Park, p.o.i., Austl.	H9	76
Guymon, Ok., U.S.	E7	128
Guyot, Mount, mtn., U.S.	I2	114
Guyra, Austl.	H8	76
Guyton, Ga., U.S.	D4	116
Guyuan, China	D2	42
Guzar, Uzb.	G11	32
Güzelyurt, N. Cyp.	C3	58
Güzelyurt Körfezi, b., N. Cyp.	C3	58
Guzhen, China	E7	42
Guzmán, Mex.	F9	98
Guzmán, Mex.	F7	100
Gvardejsk, Russia	F4	10
Gwa, Mya.	D2	48
Gwaai, Zimb.	D4	68
Gwādar, Pak.	D9	56
Gwalia, Austl.	E4	74
Gwalior (Lashkar), India	E7	54
Gwanda, Zimb.	B9	70
Gwane, D.R.C.	D5	66
Gwangju see Kwangju, Kor., S.	G7	38
Gwardafuy, Gees, c., Som.	B10	66
Gwātar Bay, b., Asia	E9	56
Gwayi, stm., Zimb.	D4	68
Gwda, stm., Pol.	C12	16
Gweedore, Ire.	F4	12
Gweru, Zimb.	D4	68
Gwinn, Mi., U.S.	B2	112
Gwydir, stm., Austl.	G7	76
Gyangtse see Gyangzê, China	D12	54
Gyangzê, China	D12	54
Gyaring Co, l., China	C12	54
Gyaring Hu, l., China	E4	36
Gyda, Russia	B4	34
Gydanskaja guba, b., Russia	B4	34
Gydanskij poluostrov, pen., Russia	B4	34
Gyeongju see Kyŏngju, Kor., S.	D2	40
Gyirong, China	D10	54
Gyldenløves Fjord, b., Grnld.	E17	141
Gym Peak, mtn., N.M., U.S.	K9	132
Gympie, Austl.	F9	76
Gyobingauk, Mya.	C2	48
Gyoma, Hung.	C7	26
Gyöngyös, Hung.	B6	26
Győr (Raab), Hung.	B4	26
Győr-Moson-Sopron, state, Hung.	B4	26
Gypsum, Co., U.S.	D10	132
Gypsum, Ks., U.S.	C11	128
Gypsumville, Mb., Can.	C15	124
Gyula, Hung.	C8	26
Gyulafehérvár see Alba Iulia, Rom.	C10	26
Gyzylarbat, Turkmen.	B8	56

H

Name	Map Ref.	Page
Haag in Oberbayern, Ger.	H8	16
Haaksbergen, Neth.	D2	16
Haapiti, Fr. Poly.	v20	78h
Haapsalu, Est.	G10	8
Haar, Ger.	H7	16
Ha'Arava ('Arabah, Wādī al-), val., Asia	H6	58
Ha'Arava (Jayb, Wādī al-), stm., Asia	H6	58
Haarlem, Neth.	B13	14
Habaqila, China	C6	36
Habarovsk, Russia	G16	34
Habary, Russia	D13	32
Ḥabashīyah, Jabal, mts., Yemen	F7	56
Ḥabbān, Yemen	G6	56
Habermehl Peak, mtn., Ant.	C6	81
Habiganj, Bngl.	F13	54
Habomai Islands see Malaja Kuril'skaja Grjada, is., Russia	C17	38
Hachijō-jima, i., Japan	F12	40
Hachiman, Japan	D9	40
Hachinohe, Japan	D14	38
Hachiōji, Japan	D12	40
Hackberry, La., U.S.	H5	122
Hackberry Creek, stm., Ks., U.S.	C8	128
Hackett, Ar., U.S.	B4	122
Hackettstown, N.J., U.S.	D11	114
Hadāli, Pak.	B4	54
HaDarom, state, Isr.	H5	58
Ḥadd, Ra's al-, c., Oman	E8	56
Haddam, Ks., U.S.	B11	128
Haddington, Scot., U.K.	F10	12
Haddock, Ga., U.S.	C2	116
Haddon Downs, Austl.	F3	76
Hadejia, Nig.	G7	64
Hadejia, stm., Nig.	G6	64
Haden, Austl.	F8	76
Ḥadera, Isr.	F5	58
Haderslev, Den.	I3	8
Hadībū, Yemen	G7	56
Ḥadīthah, Iraq	C5	56
Hadley Bay, b., Nu., Can.	A9	106
Hadlock, Wa., U.S.	B4	136
Ha Dong, Viet.	B7	48
Ḥaḍramawt, reg., Yemen	F6	56
Hadrian's Wall, misc. cult., Eng., U.K.	G10	12
Hadzilavičy, Bela.	G13	10
Haeju, Kor., N.	E6	38
Haenam, Kor., S.	G7	38
Haerhpin see Harbin, China	B7	38
Haffner Bjerg, mtn., Grnld.	B13	141
Hafford, Sk., Can.	B6	124
Haffouz, Tun.	I3	24
Hāfizābād, Pak.	B4	54
Hāflong, India	F14	54
Hafnarfjörður, Ice.	k28	8a
Haft Gel, Iran	C6	56
Hagan, Ga., U.S.	D3	116
Hagari, stm., India	D3	53
Hagåtña (Agana), Guam	j10	78c
Hagemeister Island, i., Ak., U.S.	E7	140
Hagen, Ger.	E3	16
Hagenow, Ger.	C7	16
Hagensborg, B.C., Can.	D4	138
Hagerman, N.M., U.S.	A3	130
Hagerstown, In., U.S.	I4	112
Hagerstown, Md., U.S.	E8	114
Hagersville, On., Can.	F9	112
Hagfors, Swe.	F5	8
Haggin, Mount, mtn., Mt., U.S.	D13	136
Hagi, Japan	E4	40
Ha Giang, Viet.	A7	48
Hagondange, Fr.	E15	14
Hags Head, c., Ire.	I3	12
Hague, Sk., Can.	B7	124
Hague, Cap de la, c., Fr.	E7	14
Haguenau, Fr.	F16	14
Hagues Peak, mtn., Co., U.S.	G7	126
Hahira, Ga., U.S.	F2	116
Hai'an, China	E9	42
Haibei, China	B10	36
Haicheng, China	A10	42
Haichow Bay see Haizhou Wan, b., China	D8	42
Haidargarh, India	E8	54
Hai Duong, Viet.	B8	48
Haifa see Ḥefa, Isr.	F5	58
Haifa see Ḥefa, state, Isr.	F5	58
Haifeng, China	J6	42
Haig, Austl.	F5	74
Haigler, Ne., U.S.	A7	128
Haikang, China	K3	42
Haikou, China	K4	42
Haikou, China	G9	42
Ḥā'il, Sau. Ar.	D5	56
Hailākāndi, India	F14	54
Hailar, China	B8	36
Hailar, stm., China	B8	36
Haileyville, Ok., U.S.	C3	122
Hailin, China	B8	38
Hailun, China	B10	36
Hailuoto, i., Fin.	D11	8
Haimen, China	J7	42
Haimen, China	G9	42
Hainan, state, China	L3	42
Hainan Dao (Hainan Island), i., China	L4	42
Hainan Island see Hainan Dao, i., China	L4	42
Hainan Strait see Qiongzhou Haixia, strt., China	K4	42
Haines, Ak., U.S.	E12	140
Haines, Or., U.S.	F8	136
Haines City, Fl., U.S.	H4	116
Haines Junction, Yk., Can.	C3	106
Haining, China	F9	42
Hai Ninh, Viet.	B8	48
Hai Phong, Viet.	B8	48
Haiphong see Hai Phong, Viet.	B8	48
Haiti, ctry., N.A.	C11	102
Haitun, China	D4	36
Haivoron, Ukr.	A16	26
Haiyuan, China	C1	42
Haizhou, China	D8	42
Haizhou Wan, b., China	D8	42
Hajdú-Bihar, state, Hung.	B8	26
Hajdúböszörmény, Hung.	B8	26
Hajdúnánás, Hung.	B8	26
Hajdúszoboszló, Hung.	B8	26
Hājīpur, India	F10	54
Hajnówka, Pol.	D19	16
Hakasija, state, Russia	D16	32
Hakha, Mya.	A1	48
Hakken-san, mtn., Japan	E8	40
Hakodate, Japan	D14	38
Hakone-yama, vol., Japan	D12	40
Hakui, Japan	C9	40
Haku-san, vol., Japan	C9	40
Haku-san-kokuritsu-kōen, p.o.i., Japan	C9	40
Hal see Halle, Bel.	D13	14
Ḥalab (Aleppo), Syria	B8	58
Ḥalab, state, Syria	B8	58
Halachó, Mex.	B2	102
Halahai, China	B6	38
Ḥalā'ib, Sudan	C7	62
Halawa, Cape, c., Hi., U.S.	B5	78a
Halberstadt, Ger.	E7	16
Halbrite, Sk., Can.	E10	124
Halcon, Mount, mtn., Phil.	D3	52
Halden, Nor.	G4	8
Haldensleben, Ger.	D7	16
Haldimand, On., Can.	F10	112
Haldwāni, India	D7	54
Hale, Mo., U.S.	E4	120
Haleakala Crater, crat., Hi., U.S.	C5	78a
Haleakala National Park, p.o.i., Hi., U.S.	C5	78a
Hale Center, Tx., U.S.	G7	128
Halenkov, Czech Rep.	G14	16
Halfmoon Bay, B.C., Can.	G6	138
Halfway, Md., U.S.	E8	114
Halfway, Or., U.S.	F9	136
Halicarnassus, hist., Tur.	F10	28
Halifax, Austl.	B6	76
Halifax, N.S., Can.	F13	110
Halifax, Eng., U.K.	H11	12
Halifax, N.C., U.S.	H8	114
Halifax, Va., U.S.	H6	114
Halifax Bay, b., Austl.	B6	76
Haliyāl, India	D2	53
Haljala, Est.	A9	10
Halkapınar, Tur.	A5	58
Halland, state, Swe.	H5	8
Hallandale, Fl., U.S.	K5	116
Ḥallānīyah, Juzur al- (Kuria Muria Islands), is., Oman	F8	56
Halla-san, mtn., Kor., S.	H7	38
Hall Basin, b., N.A.	A13	141
Halle, Bel.	D13	14
Halle, Ger.	E7	16
Hällefors, Swe.	G6	8
Hallein, Aus.	C10	22
Hallettsville, Tx., U.S.	E11	130
Halley, sci., Ant.	C2	81
Halligen, is., Ger.	B4	16
Hall in Tirol, Aus.	C8	22
Hall Islands, is., Micron.	C6	72
Hall Lake, l., Nu., Can.	B14	106
Hall Land, reg., Grnld.	A14	141
Hall Mountain, mtn., Wa., U.S.	B9	136
Hallock, Mn., U.S.	C2	118
Hallowell, Me., U.S.	F7	110
Hall Peninsula, pen., Nu., Can.	C17	106
Halls, Tn., U.S.	I8	120
Hallsberg, Swe.	G6	8
Halls Creek, Austl.	C5	74
Hallstahammar, Swe.	G7	8
Hallstavik, Swe.	F8	8
Hallstead, Pa., U.S.	C10	114
Hallsville, Mo., U.S.	E5	120
Halmahera, i., Indon.	E8	44
Halmahera, Laut (Halmahera Sea), Indon.	F8	44
Halmahera Sea see Halmahera, Laut, Indon.	F8	44
Hal'mer-Ju, Russia	A10	32
Halmstad, Swe.	H5	8
Haloŭčyn, Bela.	F12	10
Hal'šany, Bela.	F8	10
Halsey, Ne., U.S.	F12	126
Halsey, Or., U.S.	F3	136
Halstead, Ks., U.S.	D11	128
Haltern, Ger.	E3	16
Haltiatunturi, mtn., Eur.	B9	8
Haltom City, Tx., U.S.	B10	130
Halton Hills see Georgetown, On., Can.	E9	112
Halvorson, Mount, mtn., B.C., Can.	C10	138
Ham, stm., Nmb.	F4	70
Hamada, Japan	E4	40
Hamadān, Iran	C6	56
Ḥamāh, Syria	C7	58
Ḥamāh, state, Syria	C8	58
Hamamatsu, Japan	E10	40
Haman, Kor., S.	D1	40
Hamana-ko, l., Japan	E10	40
Hamar, Nor.	F4	8
Ha Marakabei, Leso.	F9	70
Hamar-Daban, hrebet, mts., Russia	F9	34
Hamburg, Ger.	C6	16
Hamburg, Ar., U.S.	D7	122
Hamburg, Ia., U.S.	D2	120
Hamburg, N.J., U.S.	C11	114
Hamburg, N.Y., U.S.	B7	114
Hamburg, state, Ger.	C6	16
Hamden, Ct., U.S.	C13	114
Hamden, Oh., U.S.	E3	114
Häme, state, Fin.	F11	8
Hämeenlinna (Tavastehus), Fin.	F10	8
Hamelin, Austl.	E2	74
Hameln, Ger.	D5	16
HaMerkaz, state, Isr.	F5	58
Hamersley Range, mts., Austl.	D3	74
Hamgyŏng-sanjulgi, mts., Kor., N.	D8	38
Hamhŭng, Kor., N.	E7	38
Hami, China	C3	36
Hamilton, Austl.	K4	76
Hamilton, Ber.	k15	104e
Hamilton, On., Can.	E10	112
Hamilton, N.Z.	C6	80
Hamilton, Scot., U.K.	F8	12
Hamilton, Al., U.S.	C11	122
Hamilton, Ga., U.S.	E14	122
Hamilton, Il., U.S.	D6	120
Hamilton, Mi., U.S.	F4	112
Hamilton, Mo., U.S.	E3	120
Hamilton, Mt., U.S.	D12	136
Hamilton, N.Y., U.S.	B10	114
Hamilton, Oh., U.S.	E1	114
Hamilton, stm., Austl.	D3	76
Hamilton, Lake, res., Ar., U.S.	C5	122
Hamilton, Mount, mtn., Ca., U.S.	F4	134
Hamilton City, Ca., U.S.	D3	134
Hamilton Dome, Wy., U.S.	D4	126
Hamilton Hotel, Austl.	D3	76
Hamilton Mountain, mtn., N.Y., U.S.	G2	110
Hamina, Fin.	F12	8
Hamiota, Mb., Can.	D13	124
Hamīrpur, India	F7	54
Hamlin, Tx., U.S.	B7	130
Hamlin, W.V., U.S.	F3	114
Hamlin Valley Wash, stm., U.S.	E3	132
Hamm, Ger.	E3	16
Hammamet, Tun.	H4	24
Hammamet, Golfe de, b., Tun.	H4	24
Hammam Lif, Tun.	H4	24
Hammelburg, Ger.	F5	16
Hammerdal, Swe.	E6	8
Hammerfest, Nor.	A10	8
Hammon, Ok., U.S.	F9	128
Hammond, In., U.S.	G2	112
Hammond, La., U.S.	G8	122
Hammondsport, N.Y., U.S.	F12	112
Hampden, Me., U.S.	F8	110
Hampden, N.D., U.S.	F15	124
Hampi, India	D3	53
Hampshire, Il., U.S.	I10	118
Hampstead, N.C., U.S.	B8	116
Hampton, N.B., Can.	E11	110
Hampton, Ar., U.S.	D6	122
Hampton, Fl., U.S.	G3	116
Hampton, Ga., U.S.	C1	116
Hampton, Ne., U.S.	G15	126
Hampton, N.H., U.S.	H6	110
Hampton, Tn., U.S.	H3	114
Hampton, Va., U.S.	G9	114
Hampton Butte, mtn., Or., U.S.	G6	136
Hampton Tableland, plat., Austl.	F5	74
Hamra, Swe.	F6	8
Hamrā',Al-Ḥamādah al-, des., Libya	B2	62
Hamra, As Saquia al, stm., W. Sah.	D2	64
Hamsara, stm., Russia	D16	32
Hams Fork, stm., Wy., U.S.	F2	126
Hamṭa, Gebel (Ḥamāṭah, Jabal), mtn., Egypt	C6	62
Ham Tan, Viet.	G8	48
Hāmūn, Daryācheh-ye, l., Iran	C9	56
Han, stm., China	I7	42
Han, stm., China	F6	42
Han, Nong, l., Thai.	D7	48
Hana, Hi., U.S.	C6	78a
Hanahan, S.C., U.S.	D5	116
Hanamaki, Japan	E14	38
Hananui see Anglem, Mount, mtn., N.Z.	H2	80
Hanapepe, Hi., U.S.	B2	78a
Hanateio, Fr. Poly.	s18	78g
Hanatetena, Fr. Poly.	s18	78g
Hanau am Main, Ger.	F4	16
Hanbury, stm., N.T., Can.	C9	106
Hancavičy, Bela.	H9	10
Hâncești, Mol.	C15	26
Hanceville, Al., U.S.	C12	122
Hancheng, China	D7	36
Hancheng, China	D4	42
Hanchung see Hanzhong, China	E2	42
Hancock, Md., U.S.	E7	114
Hancock, Mi., U.S.	D10	118
Hancock, Mn., U.S.	F3	118
Hancock, N.Y., U.S.	C10	114
Handa, Japan	E9	40
Handan, China	C6	42
Handlová, Slov.	H14	16
Handsworth, Sk., Can.	E10	124
Handyga, Russia	D16	34
HaNegev (Negev Desert), reg., Isr.	H5	58
Hanford, Ca., U.S.	G6	134
Hanga Roa, Chile	e29	78l
Hangayn nuruu, mts., Mong.	B4	36
Hangchou see Hangzhou, China	F9	42
Hangchow see Hangzhou, China	F9	42
Hangchow Bay see Hangzhou Wan, b., China	F9	42
Hanggin Houqi, China	A2	42
Hanggin Qi, China	B3	42
Hangman Creek, stm., U.S.	C9	136
Hangö see Hanko, Fin.	G10	8
Hangokurt, Russia	B10	32
Hangu, China	B7	42
Hangu, Pak.	B3	54
Hanguang, China	I5	42
Hangzhou, China	F9	42
Hangzhou Wan, b., China	F9	42
Hanino, Russia	F19	10
Ḥanīsh, is., Yemen	G5	56
Hanish Islands see Ḥanīsh, is., Yemen	G5	56
Hanjiang, China	I8	42
Hankinson, N.D., U.S.	E2	118
Hanko, Fin.	G10	8
Hankow see Wuhan, China	F6	42
Hanku see Hangu, China	B7	42
Hānle, India	B7	54
Hanley, Sk., Can.	C7	124
Hanna, Ab., Can.	E19	138
Hanna, Ok., U.S.	B3	122
Hanna, Wy., U.S.	B10	132
Hanna City, Il., U.S.	D8	120
Hannah, N.D., U.S.	F15	124
Hannah Bay, b., On., Can.	E14	106
Hannibal, Mo., U.S.	E6	120
Hannover, Ger.	D5	16
Ha Noi (Hanoi), Viet.	B7	48
Hanoi see Ha Noi, Viet.	B7	48
Hanover, On., Can.	D8	112
Hanover see Hannover, Ger.	D5	16
Hanover, S. Afr.	G7	70
Hanover, Il., U.S.	B7	120
Hanover, In., U.S.	F12	120
Hanover, N.H., U.S.	G4	110
Hanover, N.M., U.S.	K8	132
Hanover, Pa., U.S.	E9	114
Hanover, Va., U.S.	G8	114
Hanover, Isla, i., Chile	J2	90
Hansdiha, India	F11	54
Hānsi, India	D5	54
Hanska, Mn., U.S.	G4	118
Hantajskoe, ozero, l., Russia	C6	34
Hantan see Handan, China	C6	42
Hantau, Kaz.	F12	32
Hantsport, N.S., Can.	E12	110
Hanty-Mansijsk, Russia	B11	32
Hantzsch, stm., Nu., Can.	B16	106
Hanumāngarh, India	C3	46
Hanumangarh, India	D4	54
Hanuy, stm., Mong.	B5	36
Hanyin, China	E3	42
Hanzhong, China	E2	42
Hanzhuang, China	D7	42
Haojiadian, China	F5	42
Haoli see Hegang, China	B11	36
Hāora, India	G12	54
Haparanda, Swe.	D10	8
Hapčeranga, Russia	G11	34
Happy, Tx., U.S.	G7	128
Happy Jack, Az., U.S.	I5	132
Happy Valley-Goose Bay, Nf., Can.	E18	106
Hāpur, India	D6	54
Ḥaql, Sau. Ar.	I5	58
Ḥaraḍ, Sau. Ar.	E6	56
Haradok, Bela.	E13	10
Haradzec, Bela.	H7	10
Haradzec, Bela.	G13	10
Haradzišča, Bela.	G9	10
Haramachi, Japan	B13	40
Haranor, Russia	A8	36
Harar see Hārer, Eth.	F8	62
Harare, Zimb.	D5	68
Harazé Mangueigne, Chad	E4	62
Harbala, Russia	D13	34
Harbavičy, Bela.	G13	10
Harbin, China	B7	38
Harbiye, Tur.	B7	58
Harbor, Or., U.S.	A1	134
Harbor Beach, Mi., U.S.	E7	112
Harbour Breton, Nf., Can.	j22	107a
Harbourville, N.S., Can.	E12	110
Harda, India	G6	54
Hardangerfjorden, b., Nor.	F2	8
Hardangerjøkulen, ice, Nor.	F2	8
Hardangervidda Nasjonalpark, p.o.i., Nor.	F2	8
Hardap, state, Nmb.	D3	70
Hardeeville, S.C., U.S.	D4	116
Harderwijk, Neth.	B14	14
Hardin, Il., U.S.	E7	120
Hardin, Mt., U.S.	B5	126
Harding, S. Afr.	G9	70
Harding, Lake, res., U.S.	E13	122
Hardinsburg, Ky., U.S.	G11	120
Hardisty Lake, l., N.T., Can.	C7	106
Hardoi, India	E7	54
Hardtner, Ks., U.S.	D10	128
Hardwick, Ga., U.S.	C2	116
Hardwick, Vt., U.S.	F4	110
Hardy, Ar., U.S.	H6	120
Hardy, Ne., U.S.	G15	126
Hardy Bay, b., N.T., Can.	B16	140
Hare Bay, b., Nf., Can.	i22	107a
Hare Indian, stm., N.T., Can.	B5	106
Hareøen, i., Grnld.	C14	141
Hārer, Eth.	F8	62
Hargeysa, Som.	C8	66
Harghita, state, Rom.	C12	26
Har Hu, l., China	D4	36
Hari, stm., Indon.	D3	50
Ḥarīb, Yemen	G6	56
Haridwār, India	D7	54
Harihar, India	D2	53
Ḥārim, Syria	B7	58
Harīpur, Pak.	B4	54
Harīrūd (Tedžen), stm., Asia	C9	56
Harischandra Range, mts., India	B1	53
Haritonovo, Russia	F22	8
Harkers Island, N.C., U.S.	B9	116
Harlan, Ky., U.S.	H2	114
Harlan County Lake, res., Ne., U.S.	A9	128
Harlem, Fl., U.S.	J5	116
Harlem, Ga., U.S.	C3	116
Harleton, Tx., U.S.	E4	122
Harlingen, Neth.	A14	14
Harlingen, Tx., U.S.	H10	130
Harlovka, Russia	B17	8
Harlow, Eng., U.K.	J13	12
Harlowton, Mt., U.S.	D17	136
Harman, W.V., U.S.	F6	114
Harmancık, Tur.	D12	28
Harmanli, Blg.	H12	26
Harmony, In., U.S.	E10	120
Harnai, India	C1	53
Harney Basin, bas., Or., U.S.	G8	136
Harney Lake, l., Or., U.S.	G7	136
Harney Peak, mtn., S.D., U.S.	D9	126
Härnösand, Swe.	E8	8
Har nuur, l., Mong.	B3	36
Haro, Spain	B8	20
Haro, Cabo, c., Mex.	B3	100
Harovsk, Russia	F18	8
Harpanahalli, India	D3	53
Harper, Lib.	I3	64
Harper, Ks., U.S.	D10	128
Harper, Tx., U.S.	D8	130
Harper, Mount, mtn., Ak., U.S.	D11	140
Harqin Qi, China	D3	38
Harrai, India	G7	54
Harricana, stm., Can.	E15	106
Harriman, Tn., U.S.	I13	120
Harrington, De., U.S.	F10	114
Harrington, Me., U.S.	F9	110
Harris, Sk., Can.	C6	124
Harris, Monts.	D3	105a
Harris, Mn., U.S.	F5	118
Harris, reg., Scot., U.K.	D6	12
Harris, Lake, l., Fl., U.S.	H4	116
Harrisburg, Ar., U.S.	B8	122
Harrisburg, Ne., U.S.	F9	126
Harrisburg, Or., U.S.	F3	136
Harrisburg, Pa., U.S.	D8	114
Harrismith, S. Afr.	F9	70
Harrison, Ar., U.S.	H4	120
Harrison, Mi., U.S.	D5	112
Harrison, Ne., U.S.	E9	126
Harrison Bay, b., Ak., U.S.	B9	140
Harrisonburg, La., U.S.	F7	122
Harrisonburg, Va., U.S.	F6	114
Harrison Islands, is., Nu., Can.	B13	106
Harrison Lake, l., B.C., Can.	G9	138
Harriston, On., Can.	E9	112
Harriston, Ms., U.S.	F7	122
Harrisville, N.Y., U.S.	D14	112
Harrisville, W.V., U.S.	E4	114
Harrodsburg, Ky., U.S.	G13	120
Harrogate, Eng., U.K.	H11	12
Harrold, Tx., U.S.	G9	128
Harrowsmith, On., Can.	D13	112
Harry S. Truman Reservoir, res., Mo., U.S.	F4	120
Har Sai Shan, mtn., China	D4	36
Harsīn, Iran	C6	56
Hârșova, Rom.	E14	26
Harstad, Nor.	B7	8
Harsūd, India	G6	54
Hart, Mi., U.S.	E3	112
Hart, Tx., U.S.	G6	128
Hart, stm., Yk., Can.	B3	106
Hartbees, stm., S. Afr.	F5	70
Hartberg, Aus.	C12	22
Hartford, Ar., U.S.	C4	122
Hartford, Ct., U.S.	C13	114
Hartford, Ks., U.S.	F2	120
Hartford, Mi., U.S.	F3	112
Hartford, S.D., U.S.	H2	118
Hartford, Wi., U.S.	H10	118
Hartford City, In., U.S.	H4	112
Hartland, N.B., Can.	D9	110
Hartland, Me., U.S.	F7	110
Hartlepool, Eng., U.K.	G11	12
Hartley, Ia., U.S.	H3	118
Hartley Bay, B.C., Can.	C1	138
Hart Mountain, mtn., Mb., Can.	B12	124
Hartney, Mb., Can.	E13	124
Harts, stm., S. Afr.	E7	70
Hartselle, Al., U.S.	C12	122
Hartshorne, Ok., U.S.	C3	122
Hartsville, S.C., U.S.	B5	116
Hartville, Mo., U.S.	G5	120
Hartwell, Ga., U.S.	B3	116
Hartwell Lake, res., U.S.	B2	116
Hartz Mountains National Park, p.o.i., Austl.	o13	77a
Hārūnābād, Pak.	D4	54
Haruniye, Tur.	A7	58
Harūr, India	E4	53
Har-Us nuur, l., Mong.	B3	36
Hārūt, stm., Afg.	C9	56
Harvard, Ne., U.S.	G14	126
Harvey, N.B., Can.	E12	110
Harvey, Il., U.S.	G2	112
Harvey, N.D., U.S.	G14	124
Harwich, Eng., U.K.	J14	12
Haryāna, state, India	D6	54
Haryn', stm., Eur.	H10	10
Harz, mts., Ger.	E6	16
Hasavjurt, Russia	F7	32
Hasdo, stm., India	G9	54
Hase, stm., Ger.	D3	16
Hasenkamp, Arg.	E8	92
Hashima, Japan	D9	40
Hashimoto, Japan	E8	40
Hāsilpur, Pak.	D4	54
Haskell, Ok., U.S.	I2	120
Haskell, Tx., U.S.	A8	130
Haskovo, Blg.	H12	26
Haskovo, state, Blg.	G12	26
Haslemere, Eng., U.K.	J12	12
Hasperos Canyon, val., N.M., U.S.	H3	128
Ḥaṣṣ, Jabal al-, hill, Syria	C8	58
Hassa, Tur.	B7	58
Hassan, India	E3	53
Hassayampa, stm., Az., U.S.	J4	132
Hassel Sound, strt., Nu., Can.	B6	141
Hasselt, Bel.	D14	14
Hassfurt, Ger.	F6	16
Hassi Messaoud, Alg.	C6	64
Hässleholm, Swe.	H5	8
Hastings, Barb.	n8	105d
Hastings, On., Can.	D11	112
Hastings, N.Z.	D7	80
Hastings, Eng., U.K.	K13	12
Hastings, Mi., U.S.	F4	112
Hastings, Mn., U.S.	G6	118
Hastings, Ne., U.S.	G14	126
Haswell, Co., U.S.	C5	128
Hatanga, Russia	B9	34
Hatanga, stm., Russia	B9	34
Hatangskij zaliv, b., Russia	B10	34
Hatay (Antioch), Tur.	B7	58
Hatay, state, Tur.	B7	58
Hatch, N.M., U.S.	K9	132
Hatch, Ut., U.S.	F4	132
Hat Chao Mai National Park, p.o.i., Thai.	I4	48
Hatchie, stm., U.S.	B9	122
Hatfield, Austl.	I4	76
Hatfield, Ar., U.S.	C4	122
Hatfield, Ma., U.S.	B13	114
Hatgal, Mong.	F9	34
Hāthras, India	E7	54
Ha Tien, Viet.	G7	48
Hatillo, P.R.	A2	104a
Ha Tinh, Viet.	C7	48
Hatip, Tur.	F15	28
Hato, Bocht van, b., Neth. Ant.	p21	104g
Hato Mayor del Rey, Dom. Rep.	C13	102
Hāt Pīplia, India	G6	54
Hatta, India	F7	54
Hatteras, N.C., U.S.	A10	116
Hatteras, Cape, c., N.C., U.S.	A10	116
Hatteras Island, i., N.C., U.S.	A10	116
Hattiesburg, Ms., U.S.	F9	122
Hatton, Al., U.S.	C11	122
Hatton, N.D., U.S.	G16	124
Hatunsaray, Tur.	A3	58
Hatvan, Hung.	B6	26
Hat Yai, Thai.	I5	48
Hatyrka, Russia	D24	34
Haugesund, Nor.	G1	8
Haukeligrend, Nor.	G2	8
Haukivesi, l., Fin.	E12	8
Hauraki Gulf, b., N.Z.	C6	80
Hausach, Ger.	H4	16
Haut, Isle au, i., Me., U.S.	F8	110

Name	Map Ref.	Page

I • 26 Indi-Jare

Name	Map Ref.	Page
Indian Head, Sk., Can.	D10	124
Indian Lake, N.Y., U.S.	G2	110
Indian Lake, l., On., Can.	A7	112
Indian Lake, l., Mi., U.S.	B3	112
Indian Ocean	K11	142
Indianola, Ia., U.S.	C4	120
Indianola, Ms., U.S.	D8	122
Indianola, Ne., U.S.	A8	128
Indian Peak, mtn., Ut., U.S.	E3	132
Indian River, Mi., U.S.	C5	112
Indian Rock, mtn., Wa., U.S.	E6	136
Indiantown, Fl., U.S.	I5	116
Indiera Alta, P.R.	B2	104a
Indiga, Russia	C23	8
Indigirka, stm., Russia	C18	34
Indin, Mya.	H14	54
Indio, Ca., U.S.	J9	134
Indira Gandhi Canal, can., India	E4	54
Indispensable Strait, strt., Sol. Is.	e9	79b
Indochina, reg., Asia	D7	48
Indonesia, ctry., Asia	J16	30
Indore, India	G5	54
Indragiri, stm., Indon.	D2	50
Indramayu, Indon.	G6	50
Indrāvati, stm., India	B5	53
Indravati Tiger Reserve, p.o.i., India	B5	53
Indre, state, Fr.	C7	18
Indre, stm., Fr.	G10	14
Indre-et-Loire, state, Fr.	G9	14
Indus, stm., Asia	D2	46
Industry, Tx., U.S.	H2	122
İnece, Tur.	B10	28
In Ecker, Alg.	E6	64
İnegöl, Tur.	C12	28
Ineu, Rom.	C8	26
Inez, Ky., U.S.	G3	114
Inez, Tx., U.S.	F11	130
Inferior, Laguna, b., Mex.	G11	100
Infiernillo, Canal del, strt., Mex.	G6	98
Infiernillo, Presa del, res., Mex.	F7	100
Ing, stm., Thai.	C5	48
Ingá, Braz.	D8	88
Ingabu, Mya.	D2	48
Ingal, Niger	F6	64
Ingall Point, c., On., Can.	B10	118
Ingelheim, Ger.	G4	16
Ingende, D.R.C.	E3	66
Ingeniero Jacobacci, Arg.	H3	90
Ingeniero Luiggi, Arg.	G5	92
Ingham, Austl.	B6	76
Inglefield Land, reg., Grnld.	B12	141
Ingleside, Tx., U.S.	G10	130
Inglewood, Austl.	G8	76
Inglewood, Austl.	K4	76
Inglewood, Ca., U.S.	J7	134
Inglis, Mb., Can.	D12	124
Ingolf Fjord, b., Grnld.	A22	141
Ingolstadt, Ger.	H7	16
Ingonish, N.S., Can.	D16	110
Ingrāj Bāzār, India	F12	54
Ingrid Christensen Coast, cst., Ant.	B12	81
In Guezzam, Alg.	F6	64
Ingušetija, state, Russia	F6	32
Ingushetia see Ingušetija, state, Russia	F6	32
Inhaca, Ilha da, i., Moz.	E11	70
Inhambane, Moz.	C12	70
Inhambane, state, Moz.	C12	70
Inhambane, Baía de, b., Moz.	C12	70
Inhambupe, Braz.	F6	88
Inhaminga, Moz.	D5	68
Inhapim, Braz.	J4	88
Inharrime, Moz.	D12	70
Inhassoro, Moz.	B12	70
Inhuma, Braz.	D5	88
Inhumas, Braz.	I1	88
Inimutaba, Braz.	J3	88
Ining see Yining, China	F14	32
Inírida, stm., Col.	F7	86
Inis see Ennis, Ire.	I3	12
Inis Córthaidh see Enniscorthy, Ire.	I6	12
Inishbofin, i., Ire.	H2	12
Inishmore, i., Ire.	H3	12
Inishowen, pen., Ire.	F5	12
Inishturk, i., Ire.	H2	12
Inja, Russia	E17	34
Inja, stm., Russia	D18	34
Injune, Austl.	E7	76
Inkom, Id., U.S.	H14	136
Inkster, N.D., U.S.	F16	124
Inland Lake, l., Mb., Can.	B14	124
Inland Sea see Seto-naikai, Japan	E5	40
Inle Lake, l., Mya.	B3	48
Inman, Ks., U.S.	C11	128
Inman Mills, S.C., U.S.	A3	116
Inn, stm., Eur.	B10	22
Innamincka, Austl.	F3	76
Inner Channel, strt., Belize	D3	102
Inner Hebrides, is., Scot., U.K.	E6	12
Inner Mongolia see Nei Monggol, state, China	C7	36
Inner Sister Island, i., Austl.	m13	77a
Innisfail, Austl.	A6	76
Innisfail, Ab., Can.	D17	138
Innisfree, Ab., Can.	C19	138
Innokentevka, Russia	G16	34
Innoko, stm., Ak., U.S.	D8	140
Innoshima, Japan	E6	40
Innsbruck, Aus.	C8	22
Innviertel, reg., Aus.	B10	22
Inola, Ok., U.S.	H2	120
Inongo, D.R.C.	E3	66
İnönü, Tur.	D13	28
Inowrocław, Pol.	D14	16
In Salah, Alg.	D5	64
Instow, Sk., Can.	E5	124
Inta, Russia	A10	32
Intendente Alvear, Arg.	G6	92
İntepe, Tur.	D9	28
Interlaken, Switz.	D4	22
Interlândia, Braz.	I1	88
International Falls, Mn., U.S.	C5	118
Inthanon, Doi, mtn., Thai.	C4	48
Intiyaco, Arg.	D7	92
Intracoastal Waterway, strt., U.S.	L5	116
Intracoastal Waterway, strt., U.S.	H10	130
Intu, Indon.	D9	50
Inubō-saki, c., Japan	D13	40
Inukjuak, Qc., Can.	D15	106
Inuvik, N.T., Can.	B4	106
Inverbervie, Scot., U.K.	E10	12
Invercargill, N.Z.	H3	80
Inverell, Austl.	G8	76
Inverloch, Austl.	L5	76
Invermay, Sk., Can.	C10	124
Invermere, B.C., Can.	F14	138
Inverness, N.S., Can.	D15	110
Inverness, Scot., U.K.	D8	12
Inverness, Ca., U.S.	E3	134
Inverness, Fl., U.S.	H3	116
Inverurie, Scot., U.K.	D10	12
Inverway, Austl.	C5	74
Investigator Strait, strt., Austl.	G7	74
Inwood, Mb., Can.	D16	124
Inyangani, mtn., Zimb.	D5	68
Inyathi, Zimb.	D4	68
Inyo, Mount, mtn., Ca., U.S.	G8	134
Inyokern, Ca., U.S.	H8	134
Inyo Mountains, mts., Ca., U.S.	G7	134
Inzana Lake, l., B.C., Can.	B6	138
Ioánnina, Grc.	D3	28
Iokanga, stm., Russia	C18	8
Iola, Ks., U.S.	G2	120
Ioma, Pap. N. Gui.	b4	79a
Iona, Ang.	D1	68
Iona, N.S., Can.	D16	110
Iona, Id., U.S.	G15	136
Iona, i., Scot., U.K.	E6	12
Ione, Ca., U.S.	E5	134
Ione, Wa., U.S.	B9	136
Ionia, Mi., U.S.	E4	112
Ionian Islands see Iónioi Nísoi, is., Grc.	E3	28
Ionian Sea, Eur.	F11	24
Iónioi Nísoi, state, Grc.	E3	28
Iónioi Nísoi (Ionian Islands), is., Grc.	E3	28
Iony, ostrov, i., Russia	E17	34
Íos, i., Grc.	G8	28
Iosegun Lake see Fox Creek, Ab., Can.	B14	138
Iowa, La., U.S.	G5	122
Iowa, state, U.S.	I5	118
Iowa, stm., Ia., U.S.	C6	120
Iowa City, Ia., U.S.	C6	120
Iowa Falls, Ia., U.S.	B4	120
Iowa Park, Tx., U.S.	H10	128
Ipameri, Braz.	I1	88
Ipanema, stm., Braz.	E7	88
Ipanguaçu, Braz.	C7	88
Ipatinga, Braz.	J4	88
Ipatovo, Russia	E6	32
Ipaumirim, Braz.	D6	88
Ipeiros, state, Grc.	D3	28
Ipeiros, hist. reg., Grc.	D3	28
Ipel' (Ipoly), stm., Eur.	I14	16
Ipiales, Col.	G3	86
Ipiaú, Braz.	H6	88
Ipin see Yibin, China	F5	36
Ipirá, Braz.	G6	88
Ipixuna, Braz.	C3	88
Ipoh, Malay.	J5	48
Ipojuca, stm., Braz.	E7	88
Ipoly (Ipel'), stm., Eur.	I14	16
Iporã, Braz.	G7	84
Iporã, Braz.	A11	92
Ipota, Vanuatu	I17	79d
Ipsala, Tur.	C9	28
Ipswich, Austl.	F9	76
Ipswich, Eng., U.K.	I14	12
Ipswich, Ma., U.S.	B15	114
Ipswich, S.D., U.S.	B13	126
Ipu, Braz.	C5	88
Ipubi, Braz.	D5	88
Ipuc' (Iput'), stm., Eur.	H14	10
Ipueiras, Braz.	C5	88
Iput' (Ipuc'), stm., Eur.	H14	10
Iqaluit, Nu., Can.	C17	106
Iqfahs, Egypt	J1	58
Iquique, Chile	D2	90
Iquitos, Peru	D3	84
Ira, Tx., U.S.	B7	130
Iracema, Braz.	C6	88
Irákleia, i., Grc.	G8	28
Irákleio, Grc.	H8	28
Iran, ctry., Asia	C7	56
Iran Mountains, mts., Asia	C9	50
Īrānshahr, Iran	D9	56
Irapa, Ven.	B10	86
Irapuato, Mex.	E8	100
Iraq, ctry., Asia	C5	56
Irará, Braz.	F6	88
Irati, Braz.	B12	92
Irazú, Volcán, vol., C.R.	G6	102
Irbejskoe, Russia	C17	32
Irbid, Jord.	F6	58
Irbid, state, Jord.	F6	58
Irbīl, Iraq	B5	56
Irbit, Russia	C10	32
Irdning, Aus.	C11	22
Irebu, D.R.C.	E3	66
Irecê, Braz.	F5	88
Ireland, ctry., Eur.	H4	12
Ireland Island North, i., Ber.	k15	104e
Irene, S.D., U.S.	D15	126
Ireng (Maú), stm., S.A.	F12	86
Ireton, Ia., U.S.	B1	120
Irgiz, Kaz.	E10	32
Iri, Kor., S.	G7	38
Iriba, Chad	E4	62
Iriga, Phil.	D4	52
Irîgui, reg., Afr.	F3	64
Iringa, Tan.	F7	66
Irinjālakuda, India	F3	53
Iriomote-jima, i., Japan	G9	36
Iriri, stm., Braz.	D7	84
Irish, Mount, mtn., Nv., U.S.	F1	132
Irish Sea, Eur.	H7	12
Irituia, Braz.	A2	88
Irkutsk, Russia	D18	32
Irma, Ab., Can.	D19	138
Irminger Basin, unds.	B10	144
Irnijärvi, l., Fin.	D13	8
Iroise, b., Fr.	F4	14
Iron Bottom Sound, strt., Sol. Is.	e8	79b
Iron Bridge, On., Can.	B6	112
Iron City, Tn., U.S.	B11	122
Irondale, Al., U.S.	D12	122
Irondale, Mo., U.S.	G7	120
Irondequoit, N.Y., U.S.	E12	112
Iron Gate, val., Eur.	E9	26
Iron Knob, Austl.	F7	74
Iron Mountain, Mi., U.S.	C1	112
Iron Range, Austl.	B8	74
Iron River, Mi., U.S.	E10	118
Ironton, Mn., U.S.	E4	118
Ironton, Mo., U.S.	G7	120
Ironton, Oh., U.S.	F3	114
Ironwood, Mi., U.S.	E8	118
Iroquois, On., Can.	D14	112
Iroquois, stm., U.S.	H2	112
Iroquois Falls, On., Can.	F14	106
Irō-zaki, c., Japan	E11	40
Irrawaddy see Ayeyarwady, stm., Mya.	E8	46
Irricana, Ab., Can.	E17	138
Irrigon, Or., U.S.	E7	136
Irshava, Ukr.	A10	26
Irsina, Italy	D10	24
Irtyš see Irtysh, stm., Asia	C11	32
Irtysh (Irtyš) (Ertix), stm., Asia	C11	32
Irtyšsk, Kaz.	D12	32
Irún, Spain	A9	20
Iruña see Pamplona, Spain	B9	20
Irurzun, Spain	B9	20
Irú Tepuy, mtn., Ven.	E11	86
Irvine, Ab., Can.	E3	124
Irvine, Scot., U.K.	F8	12
Irvines Landing, B.C., Can.	G6	138
Irving, Tx., U.S.	B10	130
Irvington, Ky., U.S.	G11	120
Isa, Nig.	G6	64
Isaac, stm., Austl.	D7	76
Isaac Lake, l., B.C., Can.	C10	138
Isabel, state, Sol. Is.	d8	79b
Isabela, Phil.	G3	52
Isabela, P.R.	A1	104a
Isabela, Cabo, c., Dom. Rep.	C12	102
Isabela, Isla, i., Ec.	i11	84a
Isabelia, Cordillera, mts., Nic.	F5	102
Isaccea, Rom.	D15	26
Isachsen, Cape, c., Nu., Can.	B4	141
Ísafjarðardjúp, b., Ice.	j28	8a
Ísafjörður, Ice.	j28	8a
Isahaya, Japan	G3	40
Isak, Indon.	J3	48
Isaka, Tan.	E6	66
Īsa Khel, Pak.	B3	54
Işalnița, Rom.	E10	26
Isana (Içana), stm., S.A.	G7	86
Isangel, Vanuatu	I17	79d
Isanti, Mn., U.S.	F5	118
Isar, stm., Eur.	H8	16
Isarog, Mount, vol., Phil.	D4	52
İscehisar, Tur.	E13	28
Ischia, Italy	D7	24
Ischia, Isola d', i., Italy	D7	24
Ise, Japan	E9	40
Iseo, Lago d', l., Italy	E6	22
Isère, state, Fr.	D11	18
Isère, stm., Fr.	D11	18
Iserlohn, Ger.	E3	16
Isernia, Italy	C8	24
Isesaki, Japan	C12	40
Ise-shima-kokuritsu-kōen, p.o.i., Japan	E9	40
Ise-wan, b., Japan	E9	40
Iseyin, Nig.	H5	64
Isezaki see Isesaki, Japan	C12	40
Isfahan see Eşfahān, Iran	C7	56
Isfara, Taj.	A11	56
Isherton, Guy.	F12	86
Ishigaki, Japan	G9	36
Ishikari, stm., Japan	C14	38
Ishikari-wan, b., Japan	C14	38
Ishikawa, state, Japan	C9	40
Ishim (Išim), stm., Asia	C12	32
Ishinomaki, Japan	A14	40
Ishioka, Japan	C13	40
Ishizuchi-san, mtn., Japan	F5	40
Ishpeming, Mi., U.S.	B2	112
Ishurdi, Bngl.	F12	54
Isigny-sur-Mer, Fr.	E7	14
Işıklı, Tur.	E12	28
Isil'kul', Russia	C12	32
Išim, Russia	C11	32
Išimskaja ravnina, pl., Asia	C11	32
Isiolo, Kenya	D7	66
Isipingo, ngh., S. Afr.	G10	70
Isiro, D.R.C.	D5	66
Isis, Austl.	E9	76
Iskăr, stm., Blg.	F11	26
Iskăr, Jazovir, res., Blg.	G10	26
İskenderun (Alexandretta), Tur.	B6	58
İskenderun Körfezi, b., Tur.	B6	58
Iskitim, Russia	D14	32
Iskut, stm., B.C., Can.	D4	106
Isla, Mex.	G11	100
Isla, Salar de la, pl., Chile	B3	92
İslâhiye, Tur.	A7	58
Islāmābād, Pak.	B4	54
Islāmkot, Pak.	F3	54
Islāmpur, India	C2	53
Islāmpur, India	F10	54
Islāmpur, India	E12	54
Island, Ky., U.S.	G10	120
Island Falls, Me., U.S.	E8	110
Island Harbour, Anguilla	A1	105a
Island Lake, l., Mb., Can.	E12	106
Island Park, Id., U.S.	F15	136
Island Pond, Vt., U.S.	F5	110
Islands, Bay of, b., Nf., Can.	j22	107a
Isla Patrulla, Ur.	F10	92
Isla Vista, Ca., U.S.	I5	134
Islay, i., Scot., U.K.	F6	12
Isle, Mn., U.S.	E5	118
Isle, stm., Fr.	E5	18
Isle of Man, dep., Eur.	G8	12
Isle of Wight, Va., U.S.	H9	114
Isle Royale National Park, p.o.i., Mi., U.S.	C10	118
Islesboro Island, i., Me., U.S.	F8	110
Isleta, N.M., U.S.	I10	132
Isleton, Ca., U.S.	E4	134
Islón, Chile	D2	92
Ismailia (Al-Ismā'īlīyah), Egypt	H3	58
Isna, Egypt	B6	62
Isny, Ger.	I5	16
Isoka, Zam.	C5	68
Isola del Liri, Italy	I10	22
Isola di Capo Rizzuto, Italy	F11	24
Isonzo, stm., Eur.	E10	22
Isparta, Tur.	F13	28
Isparta, state, Tur.	F13	28
Ispica, Italy	H8	24
Israel, ctry., Asia	G5	58
Isrā'īl see Israel, ctry., Asia	G5	58
Issa, stm., Russia	D11	10
Isser, Oued, stm., Alg.	H14	20
Issia, C. Iv.	H3	64
Issoire, Fr.	D9	18
Issoudun, Fr.	H10	14
Issuna, Tan.	F6	66
Issyk-Kul', Kyrg.	F13	32
Issyk-Kul, Lake see Issyk-Kul', ozero, l., Kyrg.	F13	32
Issyk-Kul', ozero, l., Kyrg.	F13	32
Īstādeh-ye Moqor, Āb-e, l., Afg.	B2	54
İstanbul, Tur.	B12	28
İstanbul, state, Tur.	B11	28
İstanbul Boğazı (Bosporus), strt., Tur.	B12	28
Istiaía, Grc.	E6	28
Istmina, Col.	E3	86
Isto, Mount, mtn., Ak., U.S.	C11	140
Istra, Russia	E19	10
Istria, pen., Eur.	E10	22
Itá, Para.	B9	92
Itabaiana, Braz.	D8	88
Itabaiana, Braz.	F7	88
Itabaianinha, Braz.	F7	88
Itabapoana, Braz.	K5	88
Itaberaba, Braz.	G5	88
Itaberaí, Braz.	G8	84
Itabi, Braz.	F7	88
Itabira, Braz.	J4	88
Itabuna, Braz.	H6	88
Itacajá, Braz.	E2	88
Itacambiruçu, stm., Braz.	I4	88
Itacoatiara, Braz.	D6	84
Itacurubí del Rosario, Para.	B9	92
Itaeté, Braz.	G5	88
Itaguajé, Braz.	D6	90
Itaguara, Braz.	K3	88
Itaguari, stm., Braz.	H3	88
Itagüí, Col.	D4	86
Itaí, Braz.	A13	92
Itaiçaba, Braz.	C7	88
Itaim, stm., Braz.	D5	88
Itainópolis, Braz.	D5	88
Itaipu Reservoir, res., S.A.	B10	92
Itäisen Suomenlahden kansallispuisto, p.o.i., Fin.	F12	8
Itaituba, Braz.	D6	84
Itajaí, Braz.	C13	92
Itajubá, Braz.	L3	88
Itaju do Colônia, Braz.	H6	88
Itajuípe, Braz.	H6	88
Itala Game Reserve, S. Afr.	E10	70
Itálica, hist., Spain	G4	20
Italy, Tx., U.S.	B11	130
Italy, ctry., Eur.	G11	6
Itamaraju, Braz.	I6	88
Itamarandiba, Braz.	I4	88
Itamarandiba, stm., Braz.	I4	88
Itamari, Braz.	G6	88
Itambacuri, Braz.	I5	88
Itambé, Braz.	H5	88
Itami, Japan	E8	40
Itampolo, Madag.	E7	68
Itānagar, India	E14	54
Itanhaém, Braz.	B14	92
Itanhém, Braz.	I5	88
Itaobim, Braz.	I5	88
Itapagipe, Braz.	J1	88
Itapajé, Braz.	B6	88
Itaparica, Ilha de, i., Braz.	G6	88
Itaparica, Represa de, res., Braz.	E6	88
Itapebi, Braz.	H6	88
Itapecerica, Braz.	K3	88
Itapecuru-Mirim, Braz.	B3	88
Itapemirim, Braz.	K5	88
Itaperuna, Braz.	K5	88
Itapetim, Braz.	D7	88
Itapetinga, Braz.	H5	88
Itapetininga, Braz.	L1	88
Itapetininga, stm., Braz.	A14	92
Itapeva, Braz.	L1	88
Itapicuru, Braz.	F6	88
Itapicuru, stm., Braz.	B3	88
Itapicuru, stm., Braz.	F6	88
Itapipoca, Braz.	B6	88
Itapiranga, Braz.	D6	84
Itapirapuã, Braz.	G7	84
Itapiúna, Braz.	C6	88
Itápolis, Braz.	K1	88
Itaporã de Goiás, Braz.	D1	88
Itaporanga, Braz.	D6	88
Itaporanga d'Ajuda, Braz.	F7	88
Itapúa, state, Para.	C10	92
Itaquara, Braz.	G6	88
Itaquari, Braz.	K5	88
Itaqui, Braz.	D9	92
Itarantim, Braz.	H5	88
Itararé, Braz.	B13	92
Itararé, stm., Braz.	A13	92
Itārsi, India	G6	54
Itarumã, Braz.	C6	90
Itasca, Tx., U.S.	B10	130
Itasca, Lake, l., Mn., U.S.	D3	118
Itata, stm., Chile	H1	92
Itatinga, Braz.	L1	88
Itatira, Braz.	C6	88
Itatupã, Braz.	D7	84
Itaueira, Braz.	D4	88
Itaueira, stm., Braz.	D4	88
Itaúna, Braz.	K3	88
Itbayat Island, i., Phil.	K9	42
Itéa, Grc.	E5	28
Iténez (Guaporé), stm., S.A.	F5	84
Ithaca, Mi., U.S.	E5	112
Ithaca, N.Y., U.S.	B9	114
Ithaca see Itháki, i., Grc.	E3	28
Itháki, i., Grc.	E3	28
Itimbiri, stm., D.R.C.	D4	66
Itinga, Braz.	I5	88
Itiquira, stm., Braz.	G6	84
Itiruçu, Braz.	G5	88
Itiúba, Braz.	F5	88
Itla el-Bâsha, hill, Egypt	K3	58
Itō, Japan	E12	40
Itoigawa, Japan	B10	40
Iton, stm., Fr.	F9	14
Itororó, Braz.	H5	88
Itsuki, Japan	G3	40
Ittiri, Italy	D2	24
Ittoqqortoormiit see Scoresbysund, Grnld.	C21	141
Itu, Braz.	L2	88
Itu, stm., Braz.	D10	92
Ituaçu, Braz.	G5	88
Ituango, Col.	D4	86
Ituberá, Braz.	G6	88
Itueta, Braz.	J5	88
Ituí, stm., Braz.	E3	84
Ituiutaba, Braz.	J1	88
Itumbiara, Braz.	J1	88
Ituna, Sk., Can.	C10	124
Itupiranga, Braz.	E8	84
Ituporanga, Braz.	C13	92
Iturama, Braz.	C6	90
Iturbide, Mex.	C3	102
Iturup, ostrov (Etorofu-tō), i., Russia	B17	38
Ituverava, Braz.	K2	88
Ituxi, stm., Braz.	E4	84
Ituzaingó, Arg.	C9	92
Itzehoe, Ger.	C5	16
Iuka, Ms., U.S.	C10	122
Iul'tin, Russia	C25	34
Iúna, Braz.	K5	88
Ivacevičy, Bela.	H8	10
Ivačovo, Russia	F17	8
Ivaí, stm., Braz.	D6	90
Ivaiporã, Braz.	B12	92
Ivalo, Fin.	B12	8
Ivalojoki, stm., Fin.	B12	8
Ivanava, Bela.	H8	10
Ivančice, Czech Rep.	G12	16
Ivangorod, Russia	A11	10
Ivangrad, Yugo.	G6	26
Ivanhoe, Austl.	I5	76
Ivanhoe, Ca., U.S.	G6	134
Ivanhoe, Mn., U.S.	G2	118
Ivanhoe, Va., U.S.	H4	114
Ivanišči, Russia	D18	10
Ivanjica, Yugo.	F7	26
Ivan'kovo, Russia	F20	10
Ivan'kovskoe vodohranilišče, res., Russia	D19	10
Ivano-Frankivs'k, Ukr.	F13	6
Ivano-Frankivs'k, co., Ukr.	A11	26
Ivanovka, Russia	F14	34
Ivanovo, Russia	H19	8
Ivanovskaja oblast', co., Russia	H19	8
Ivanovskoe, Russia	A11	10
Ivanpah Lake, l., Ca., U.S.	H1	132
Ivdel', Russia	B9	32
Ivigtut, Grnld.	E16	141
Ivindo, stm., Gabon	D2	66
Ivinheíma, stm., Braz.	D6	90
Iviza see Eivissa, Spain	F12	20
Ivjanec, Bela.	G9	10
Ivohibe, Madag.	E8	68
Ivory Coast see Cote d'Ivoire, ctry., Afr.	H3	64
Ivory Coast, cst., C. Iv.	I3	64
Ivrea, Italy	E4	22
İvrindi, Tur.	D10	28
Ivujivik, Qc., Can.	C15	106
Iwaki, Japan	B13	40
Iwaki-san, vol., Japan	D14	38
Iwakuni, Japan	E5	40
Iwami, Japan	D7	40
Iwanuma, Japan	A13	40
Iwata, Japan	E10	40
Iwate, state, Japan	A14	40
Iwate-san, vol., Japan	E14	38
'Iweibid, Gebel, mtn., Egypt	H3	58
Iwo, Nig.	H5	64
Ixmiquilpan, Mex.	E9	100
Ixopo, S. Afr.	G10	70
Ixtapa, Mex.	G8	100
Ixtepec, Mex.	G11	100
Ixtlán del Río, Mex.	E6	100
Iyang see Yiyang, China	G5	42
Iyo, Japan	F5	40
Iyo-mishima, Japan	F6	40
Iyo-nada, Japan	F5	40
Izabal, Lago de, l., Guat.	E3	102
Izamal, Mex.	B3	102
Izapa, hist., Mex.	H12	100
Izberbaš, Russia	F7	32
Izbica, Pol.	F19	16
Izegem, Bel.	D12	14
Iževsk, Russia	C8	32
Izium, Ukr.	E5	32
Ižma, stm., Russia	B8	32
Izmail, Ukr.	D15	26
Izmalkovo, Russia	H21	10
Izmayil see Izmail, Ukr.	D15	26
İzmir (Smyrna), Tur.	E10	28
İzmir, state, Tur.	E10	28
İzmir Körfezi, b., Tur.	E9	28
İzmit (Kocaeli), Tur.	C12	28
İzmit Körfezi, b., Tur.	C12	28
İznik, Tur.	C12	28
İznik Gölü, l., Tur.	C12	28
Iznoski, Russia	E18	10
Izozog, Bañados del, sw., Bol.	C4	90
Izra', Syria	F7	58
Izsák, Hung.	C6	26
Iztaccíhuatl, Volcán, vol., Mex.	F9	100
Iztaccíhuatl y Popocatéptl, Parques Nacionales, p.o.i., Mex.	F9	100
Izucar de Matamoros, Mex.	F9	100
Izu-hantō, pen., Japan	E11	40
Izuhara, Japan	E2	40
Izu Islands see Izu-shotō, is., Japan	E12	40
Izumi, Japan	G3	40
Izumi, Japan	A13	40
Izumi, Japan	E8	40
Izumo, Japan	D5	40
Izu-shotō (Izu Islands), is., Japan	E12	40
Izu Trench, unds.	G17	142
Izvestij CIK, ostrova, is., Russia	A5	34
Izvorul Muntelui, Lacul, l., Rom.	C12	26

J

Name	Map Ref.	Page
Jabal, Bahr al- see Mountain Nile, stm., Afr.	F6	62
Jabal al-Awliyā', Sudan	D6	62
Jabal Lubnān, state, Leb.	D6	58
Jabalón, stm., Spain	F7	20
Jabalpur, India	G7	54
Jabālyah, Gaza	G5	58
Jabbūl, Sabkhat al-, l., Syria	C8	58
Jabiru, Austl.	B6	74
Jablah, Syria	C6	58
Jablanica, Bos.	F4	26
Jablaničko jezero, res., Bos.	F4	26
Jablonec nad Nisou, Czech Rep.	F11	16
Jabłonka, Pol.	G15	16
Jablonovyj hrebet, mts., Russia	F11	34
Jablunkov, Czech Rep.	G14	16
Jaboticabal, Braz.	K1	88
Jaca, Spain	B10	20
Jacala, Mex.	E9	100
Jacaré, stm., Braz.	F5	88
Jacareí, Braz.	L2	88
Jacarezinho, Braz.	D7	90
Jáchal, stm., Arg.	E4	92
Jaciara, Braz.	G6	84
Jacinto, Braz.	I5	88
Jacinto Aráuz, Arg.	I6	92
Jacinto City, Tx., U.S.	H3	122
Jackfish Lake, l., Sk., Can.	A5	124
Jackhead Harbour, Mb., Can.	C16	124
Jack Mountain, mtn., Mt., U.S.	D14	136
Jackpot, Nv., U.S.	B2	132
Jacksboro, Tn., U.S.	H1	114
Jacksboro, Tx., U.S.	H10	128
Jackson, Ca., U.S.	E5	134
Jackson, Ky., U.S.	G2	114
Jackson, La., U.S.	G7	122
Jackson, Mi., U.S.	B1	114
Jackson, Mn., U.S.	H4	118
Jackson, Ms., U.S.	E8	122
Jackson, N.C., U.S.	H8	114
Jackson, Oh., U.S.	E3	114
Jackson, S.C., U.S.	C4	116
Jackson, Tn., U.S.	B10	122
Jackson, Wy., U.S.	G16	136
Jackson, stm., Va., U.S.	G6	114
Jackson, Mount, mtn., Ant.	C34	81
Jackson, Mount, mtn., Austl.	F3	74
Jackson Creek, stm., Can.	E12	124
Jackson Lake, l., Wy., U.S.	G16	136
Jacksonville, Al., U.S.	D13	122
Jacksonville, Ar., U.S.	C6	122
Jacksonville, Fl., U.S.	F4	116
Jacksonville, Il., U.S.	E7	120
Jacksonville, N.C., U.S.	B8	116
Jacksonville, Or., U.S.	A2	134
Jacksonville, Tx., U.S.	F3	122
Jacksonville Beach, Fl., U.S.	F4	116
Jacmel, Haiti	C11	102
Jaco, Mex.	B6	100
Jacobābād, Pak.	D2	54
Jacobina, Braz.	F5	88
Jacobsdal, S. Afr.	F7	70
Jacques-Cartier, Mont, mtn., Qc., Can.	A11	110
Jacu, stm., Braz.	D8	88
Jacuí, stm., Braz.	D11	92
Jacuípe, stm., Braz.	F5	88
Jacumba, Ca., U.S.	K9	134
Jacundá, Braz.	D8	84
Jacupiranga, Braz.	B13	92
Jacuriaí, stm., Braz.	F6	88
Jadebusen, b., Ger.	C4	16
J.A.D. Jensens Nunatakker, mtn., Grnld.	E16	141
Jadraque, Spain	D8	20
Jādū, Libya	A2	62
Jaén, Peru	E2	84
Jaén, Spain	G7	20
Jaén, co., Spain	G7	20
Jāfarābād, India	H3	54
Jaffa, Cape, c., Austl.	K2	76
Jaffna, Sri L.	G4	53
Jaffna Lagoon, b., Sri L.	G4	53
Jaffrey, N.H., U.S.	B13	114
Jafr, Qā' al-, depr., Jord.	H7	58
Jagalūr, India	D3	53
Jagannāthganj Ghāt, Bngl.	F12	54
Jagatsingpur, India	H11	54
Jagdalpur, India	B6	53
Jageljurta, gora, hill, Russia	C17	8
Jagersfontein, S. Afr.	F7	70
Jaggayyapeta, India	C5	53
Jagodnoe, Russia	D18	34
Jagraon, India	C5	54
Jagtiāl, India	B4	53
Jaguaquara, Braz.	G6	88
Jaguarão, Braz.	F11	92
Jaguarão (Yaguarón), stm., S.A.	F11	92
Jaguarari, Braz.	F5	88
Jaguari, Braz.	D10	92
Jaguariaíva, Braz.	B13	92
Jaguaribara, Braz.	C6	88
Jaguaribe, Braz.	C6	88
Jaguaribe, stm., Braz.	C7	88
Jaguaruna, Braz.	D13	92
Jagüey Grande, Cuba	A7	102
Jahānābād, India	F10	54
Jahrom, Iran	D7	56
Jahroma, Russia	D20	10
Jaicós, Braz.	D5	88
Jailolo, Indon.	E8	44
Jaintiāpur, Bngl.	F14	54
Jaipur, India	E5	54
Jaipur Hāt, Bngl.	F12	54
Jais, India	E8	54
Jaisalmer, India	E3	54
Jaito, India	C5	54
Jaja, Russia	C15	32
Jājapur, India	H11	54
Jajce, Bos.	E4	26
Jakarta, Indon.	G5	50
Jakarta, Teluk, b., Indon.	F5	50
Jakaulevičy, Bela.	F13	10
Jakhāu, India	G2	54
Jakobshavn (Ilulissat), Grnld.	D15	141
Jakobstad see Pietarsaari, Fin.	E10	8
Jakovlevka, Russia	B10	38
Jakša, Russia	B9	32
Jakutija, state, Russia	C14	34
Jakutsk, Russia	D14	34
Jal, N.M., U.S.	B4	130
Jalaid Qi, China	B9	36
Jalālābād, Afg.	C11	56
Jalālpur, India	E9	54
Jalandhar, India	C5	54
Jalapa, Guat.	E3	102
Jalapa see Xalapa, Mex.	F10	100
Jālaun, India	E7	54
Jales, Braz.	D6	90
Jalesar, India	E7	54
Jaleshwar, India	H11	54
Jālgaon, India	H5	54
Jālgaon, India	H6	54
Jalingo, Nig.	H7	64
Jalisco, state, Mex.	E6	100
Jālna, India	B2	53
Jalón, stm., Spain	C9	20
Jālor, India	F4	54
Jalostotitlán, Mex.	E7	100
Jalpa, Mex.	E7	100
Jalpāiguri, India	E12	54
Jaluit, at., Marsh. Is.	C7	72
Jalutorovsk, Russia	C11	32
Jamaame, Som.	E8	66
Jamaica, ctry., N.A.	D8	102
Jamaica Channel, strt., N.A.	D9	102
Jamal, poluostrov, pen., Russia	B2	34
Jam-Alin', hrebet, mts., Russia	F15	34
Jamālpur, Bngl.	F12	54
Jamālpur, India	F11	54
Jamanota, hill, Aruba	o20	104g
Jamantau, gora, mtn., Russia	D9	32
Jamanxim, stm., Braz.	E6	84
Jamari, stm., Braz.	E5	84
Jamarovka, Russia	F11	34
Jambelí, Canal de, strt., Ec.	I2	86
Jambi, Indon.	D3	50
Jambi, state, Indon.	D3	50
Jamboaye, stm., Indon.	J3	48
Jambol, Blg.	G13	26
Jambongan, Pulau, i., Malay.	G1	52
Jambuair, Tanjung, c., Indon.	J3	48
Jambusar, India	G4	54
James, stm., U.S.	C8	108
James, stm., Mo., U.S.	H4	120
James, stm., Va., U.S.	G8	114
James, Isla, i., Chile	H2	90
James Bay, b., Can.	E14	106
James City, N.C., U.S.	A8	116
James Craik, Arg.	F6	92
James Island, S.C., U.S.	D5	116
James Point, c., Bah.	K9	116
Jamesport, Mo., U.S.	E4	120
James Ross, Cape, c., N.T., Can.	B17	140
James Ross Island, i., Ant.	B35	81
James Ross Strait, strt., Nu., Can.	A11	106
Jamestown, Austl.	I2	76
Jamestown, S. Afr.	G8	70
Jamestown, Ca., U.S.	F5	134
Jamestown, Ky., U.S.	H12	120
Jamestown, N.Y., U.S.	B6	114
Jamestown, N.C., U.S.	I6	114
Jamestown, N.D., U.S.	H15	124
Jamestown, Tn., U.S.	H13	120
Jamestown, misc. cult., Va., U.S.	G9	114
Jām Jodhpur, India	H3	54
Jamkhandi, India	C2	53
Jamm, Russia	B10	10
Jammerbugten, b., Den.	H3	8
Jammu, India	B5	54
Jammu and Kashmir see Kashmir, hist. reg., Asia	B4	46
Jamnagar (Navanagar), India	G3	54
Jampang-kulon, Indon.	G5	50
Jāmpur, Pak.	D3	54
Jämsä, Fin.	F11	8
Jamshedpur, India	G10	54
Jamsk, Russia	E19	34
Jämtland, state, Swe.	E6	8
Jamūi, India	F11	54
Jamuna, stm., Bngl.	F12	54
Jana, stm., Russia	C16	34
Janaúba, Braz.	H4	88
Janaucu, Ilha, i., Braz.	C7	84
Jand, Pak.	B4	54
Jandaia, Braz.	G7	84
Jandiāla, India	C5	54
Jandowae, Austl.	F8	76
Jándula, stm., Spain	F7	20
Janeiro, stm., Braz.	F3	88
Janesville, Ca., U.S.	C5	134
Janesville, Mn., U.S.	G5	118
Janesville, Wi., U.S.	B9	120
Jangamo, Moz.	D12	70
Jangeru, Indon.	E10	50
Jangijul', Uzb.	F11	32
Jangīpur, India	F11	54
Jangoon, India	C4	53
Janīn, W.B.	F6	58
Janisjarvi, ozero, l., Russia	E14	8
Janiuay, Phil.	E4	52
Jankan, hrebet, mts., Russia	E12	34
Jan Kempdorp, S. Afr.	E7	70
Janlohong, Indon.	B10	50
Jan Mayen, i., Nor.	B22	94
Janos, Mex.	F8	98
Jánosháza, Hung.	B4	26
Janowiec Wielkopolski, Pol.	D13	16
Janskij, Russia	C15	34
Janskij zaliv, b., Russia	B16	34
Jantra, stm., Blg.	F12	26
Januária, Braz.	H3	88
Januário Cicco, Braz.	D8	88
Jaora, India	G5	54
Japan, ctry., Asia	E12	38
Japan, Sea of (East Sea), Asia	D11	38
Japan Basin, unds.	E16	142
Japan Trench, unds.	F17	142
Japaratinga, Braz.	E8	88
Japi, Braz.	D7	88
Japonskoje more see East Sea, Asia	D11	38
Japonskoje more see Japan, Sea of, Asia	D11	38
Japtiksalja, Russia	C3	34
Japurá, Braz.	H8	86
Japurá (Caquetá), stm., S.A.	D5	84
Jaqué, Pan.	D2	86
Jarābulus, Syria	B9	58
Jaraguá, Braz.	H1	88
Jaraguá do Sul, Braz.	C13	92
Jaraíz de la Vera, Spain	D5	20
Jarales, N.M., U.S.	I10	132
Jarama, stm., Spain	D7	20
Jaramānah, Syria	E7	58
Jaransk, Russia	C7	32
Jarānwāla, Pak.	C4	54
Jarash, Jord.	F6	58
Jarash, hist., Jord.	F6	58
Jarcevo, Russia	E15	10
Jardim, Braz.	D6	88
Jardim, Braz.	D5	90
Jardim de Piranhas, Braz.	D7	88
Jardín América, Arg.	C10	92
Jardines de la Reina, Archipiélago de los, is., Cuba	B8	102
Jardinópolis, Braz.	K1	88
Jarej-Uliga-Delap, Marsh. Is.	C8	72
Jarenga, Russia	E23	8
Jarensk, Russia	E23	8

I • 28 Kala-Kemu

Name	Map Ref.	Page
Kalaotoa, Pulau, i., Indon.	G7	44
Kalar, stm., Russia	E12	34
Kalasin, Thai.	D6	48
Kalašnikovo, Russia	C18	10
Kalāt, Pak.	D10	56
Kalávryta, Grc.	E5	28
Kalaw, Mya.	B3	48
Kalbarri, Austl.	E2	74
Kale, Tur.	F11	28
Kale, Tur.	G12	28
Kaleden, B.C., Can.	G11	138
Kalegauk Island, i., Mya.	E3	48
Kalehe, D.R.C.	E5	66
Kalemie, D.R.C.	F5	66
Kalemyo, Mya.	D7	46
Kaletwa, Mya.	H14	54
Kalevala, Russia	D14	8
Kalewa, Mya.	D7	46
Kálfafell, Ice.	k31	8a
Kalgan see Zhangjiakou, China	A6	42
Kalgoorlie-Boulder, Austl.	F4	74
Kaliakra, nos, c., Blg.	F15	26
Kalianda, Indon.	F4	50
Kalibo, Phil.	E4	52
Kalima, D.R.C.	E5	66
Kalimantan (Borneo), i., Asia	F5	44
Kalimantan Barat, state, Indon.	D7	50
Kalimantan Selatan, state, Indon.	E9	50
Kalimantan Tengah, state, Indon.	D8	50
Kalimantan Timur, state, Indon.	C10	50
Kālimpang, India	E12	54
Kālīnadi, stm., India	D2	53
Kalinin see Tver', Russia	D18	10
Kaliningrad (Königsberg), Russia	F3	10
Kaliningradskaja oblast', co., Russia	F4	10
Kalinkavičy, Bela.	H12	10
Kaliro, Ug.	D6	66
Kalisat, Indon.	H8	50
Kāli Sindh, stm., India	F6	54
Kalispell, Mt., U.S.	B12	136
Kalisz, Pol.	E14	16
Kalisz, state, Pol.	E13	16
Kalisz Pomorski, Pol.	C11	16
Kaliua, Tan.	E6	66
Kaliveli Tank, l., India	E4	53
Kalixälven, stm., Swe.	C9	8
Kaljazin, Russia	C20	10
Kālka, India	C6	54
Kalkaska, Mi., U.S.	D4	112
Kalkfonteindam, res., S. Afr.	F7	70
Kalkım, Tur.	D10	28
Kalkrand, Nmb.	D3	70
Kallar Kahār, Pak.	B4	54
Kallavesi, l., Fin.	E12	8
Kallsjön, l., Swe.	E5	8
Kalmar, Swe.	H6	8
Kalmar, state, Swe.	H7	8
Kalmarsund, strt., Swe.	H7	8
Kalmykia see Kalmykija, state, Russia	E7	32
Kalmykija, state, Russia	E7	32
Kalmykovo, Kaz.	E8	32
Kālna, India	G12	54
Kalocsa, Hung.	C5	26
Kalofer, Blg.	G12	26
Kalohi Channel, strt., Hi., U.S.	B4	78a
Kalol, India	G4	54
Kālol, India	G4	54
Kalomo, Zam.	D4	68
Kalona, Ia., U.S.	J7	118
Kalone Peak, mtn., B.C., Can.	D4	138
Kalpeni Island, i., India	F1	53
Kālpi, India	E7	54
Kalpin, China	A12	56
Kalsūbai, mtn., India	B1	53
Kaltag, Ak., U.S.	D8	140
Kaluga, Russia	F19	10
Kalukalukuang, Pulau, i., Indon.	F10	50
Kalumburu, Austl.	B5	74
Kałuszyn, Pol.	D17	16
Kalutara, Sri L.	H4	53
Kalužskaja oblast', co., Russia	F18	10
Kalyān, India	B1	53
Kalyāndurg, India	D3	53
Kálymnos, Grc.	G9	28
Kálymnos, i., Grc.	F9	28
Kama, stm., Russia	C8	32
Kamae, Japan	G4	40
Kamaishi, Japan	E14	38
Kamakou, mtn., Hi., U.S.	B5	78a
Kamakura, Japan	D12	40
Kamālia, Pak.	C4	54
Kamamaung, Mya.	D3	48
Kaman, stm., Laos	E8	48
Kamanjab, Nmb.	D1	68
Kamarān, i., Yemen	F5	56
Kāmāreddi, India	B4	53
Kama Reservoir see Kamskoe vodohranilišče, res., Russia	C9	32
Kamas, Ut., U.S.	C5	132
Kamay, Tx., U.S.	H10	128
Kambalda, Austl.	F4	74
Kambam, India	G3	53
Kambarka, Russia	C8	32
Kambja, Est.	B9	10
Kambove, D.R.C.	G5	66
Kamčatka, stm., Russia	E21	34
Kamčatka, poluostrov, pen., Russia	E19	34
Kamčatskij poluostrov, pen., Russia	E21	34
Kamčatskij zaliv, b., Russia	E21	34
Kamchatka Peninsula see Kamčatka, poluostrov, pen., Russia	E20	34
Kameda, Japan	B12	40
Kámeiros, hist., Grc.	G10	28
Kamen', gora, mtn., Russia	C8	34
Kameng, stm., India	E14	54
Kamenjak, Rt, c., Cro.	F10	22
Kamenka, Kaz.	D11	32
Kamenka, Russia	D21	8
Kamenka, Russia	D6	32
Kamen'-na-Obi, Russia	D14	32
Kameno, Blg.	G14	26
Kamen-Rybolov, Russia	B9	38
Kamenskoe, Russia	D22	34
Kamensk-Ural'skij, Russia	C10	32
Kamenz, Ger.	E10	16
Kāmet, mtn., Asia	C7	54
Kam'ians'ke, Ukr.	D16	26
Kamień Krajeński, Pol.	C13	16
Kamienna Góra, Pol.	F12	16
Kamieńsk, Pol.	E15	16
Kamieskroon, S. Afr.	G3	70
Kamiiso, Japan	D14	38
Kamilukuak Lake, l., Can.	C10	106
Kamina, D.R.C.	F4	66
Kaminak Lake, l., Nu., Can.	C12	106
Kaminoyama, Japan	A13	40
Kaminuriak Lake, l., Nu., Can.	C12	106
Kamioka, Japan	C10	40
Kamjanec, Bela.	H6	10
Kamkhat Muḥaywir, hill, Jord.	G7	58
Kamloops, B.C., Can.	F10	138
Kamnik, Slvn.	D11	22
Kamo, Japan	B12	40
Kamoa Mountains, mts., Guy.	C6	84
Kamojima, Japan	E7	40
Kāmoke, Pak.	B5	54
Kampala, Ug.	D6	66
Kampar, Malay.	J5	48
Kampar, stm., Indon.	C3	50
Kamparkalns, hill, Lat.	C5	10
Kampar Kanan, stm., Indon.	C2	50
Kampen, Neth.	B14	14
Kamphaeng Phet, Thai.	D4	48
Kampinoski Park Narodowy, p.o.i., Pol.	D16	16
Kâmpóng Cham, Camb.	F7	48
Kâmpóng Chhnăng, Camb.	F7	48
Kâmpóng Kântuŏt, Camb.	G7	48
Kâmpóng Saôm, Camb.	G6	48
Kâmpóng Saôm, Chhâk, b., Camb.	G6	48
Kâmpóng Thum, Camb.	F7	48
Kampong Ulu, Mya.	G4	48
Kâmpôt, Camb.	G7	48
Kampsville, Il., U.S.	E7	120
Kampti, Burkina	G4	64
Kampuchea see Cambodia, ctry., Asia	C3	48
Kampungbaru, Indon.	D3	50
Kampung Litang, Malay.	A11	50
Kamrau, Teluk, b., Indon.	F9	44
Kamsack, Sk., Can.	C12	124
Kamskoe vodohranilišče, res., Russia	C9	32
Kāmthi, India	H7	54
Kamuela, Hi., U.S.	D6	78a
Kámuk, Cerro, mtn., C.R.	H6	102
Kamundan, stm., Indon.	F9	44
Kamyšin, Russia	D7	32
Kamyšlov, Russia	C10	32
Kan, stm., Russia	C17	32
Kanaaupscow, stm., Qc., Can.	E15	106
Kanab, Ut., U.S.	F4	132
Kanab Creek, stm., U.S.	G4	132
Kanaga Island, i., Ak., U.S.	g23	140a
Kanagawa, state, Japan	D12	40
Kanakapura, India	E3	53
Kananga (Luluabourg), D.R.C.	F4	66
Kananggar, Indon.	I12	50
Kanangra-Boyd National Park, p.o.i., Austl.	I7	76
Kanaš, Russia	C7	32
Kanawha, Ia., U.S.	B4	120
Kanawha, stm., W.V., U.S.	F4	114
Kanazawa, Japan	C9	40
Kanbauk, Mya.	E3	48
Kanchanaburi, Thai.	F4	48
Kanchanjanggā (Kānchenjunga), mtn., Asia	E11	54
Kānchenjunga (Kanchanjanggā), mtn., Asia	E11	54
Kānchipuram, India	E4	53
Kanchow see Ganzhou, China	I6	42
Kańczuga, Pol.	F18	16
Kanda, Japan	F3	40
Kandahar, Sk., Can.	C9	124
Kandalakša, Russia	C15	8
Kandalakšskaja guba, b., Russia	C15	8
Kandale, D.R.C.	F3	66
Kandang, Indon.	K3	48
Kandangan, Indon.	E9	50
Kandanghaur, Indon.	G6	50
Kandé, Togo	H5	64
Kandhkot, Pak.	D2	54
Kandi, India	G12	54
Kandi, Tanjung, c., Indon.	E7	44
Kandıra, Tur.	B13	28
Kandla, India	G3	54
Kandos, Austl.	I7	76
Kandreho, Madag.	D8	68
Kandy, Sri L.	H5	53
Kane, Pa., U.S.	C7	114
Kane Basin, b., N.A.	B12	141
Kanem, state, Chad	E3	62
Kaneohe, Hi., U.S.	B4	78a
Kanëvka, Russia	C18	8
Kang, Bots.	C6	70
Kangaba, Mali	G3	64
Kangalassy, Russia	D15	34
Kangâmiut, Grnld.	D15	141
Kangān, Iran	D7	56
Kangar, Malay.	I5	48
Kangaroo Island, i., Austl.	G7	74
Kangāvar, Iran	C6	56
Kangbao, China	C7	36
Kangding, China	C9	46
Kangean, Kepulauan (Kangean Islands), is., Indon.	G9	50
Kangean, Pulau, i., Indon.	G9	50
Kangean Islands see Kangean, Kepulauan, is., Indon.	G9	50
Kangeeak Point, c., Nu., Can.	B18	106
Kangerlussuaq, b., Grnld.	D19	141
Kangersuatsiaq see Prøven, Grnld.	C14	141
Kanger Valley National Park, p.o.i., India	B6	53
Kanggye, Kor., N.	D7	38
Kanghwa-do, i., Kor., S.	F7	38
Kangiqsliniq (Rankin Inlet), Nu., Can.	C12	106
Kangiqsualujjuaq, Qc., Can.	D17	106
Kangiqsujuaq, Qc., Can.	C16	106
Kangiqtugaapik (Clyde River), Nu., Can.	A16	106
Kangirsuk, Qc., Can.	C17	106
Kangmar, China	D12	54
Kangnŭng, Kor., S.	B1	40
Kango, Gabon	D2	66
Kangping, China	C5	38
Kangpu, China	F4	36
Kangrinboqê Feng, mtn., China	C8	54
Kangshan, Tai.	J9	42
Kangsŏ, Kor., N.	E6	38
Kangto, mtn., Asia	D14	54
Kangwŏn-do, state, Kor., S.	B1	40
Kanha National Park, p.o.i., India	G8	54
Kanhar, stm., India	F9	54
Kanhsien see Ganzhou, China	I6	42
Kani, Mya.	A2	48
Kaniama, D.R.C.	F4	66
Kanibadam, Taj.	A11	56
Kaniet Islands, is., Pap. N. Gui.	a4	79a
Kanigiri, India	D4	53
Kanin, poluostrov, pen., Russia	C21	8
Kanin-Kamen', mts., Russia	B21	8
Kanin Nos, Russia	B20	8
Kanin Nos, mys, c., Russia	B20	8
Kaniva, Austl.	K3	76
Kanjiža, Yugo.	C7	26
Kankaanpää, Fin.	F10	8
Kankakee, Il., U.S.	G2	112
Kankan, Gui.	G3	64
Kānker, India	H8	54
Kankunskij, Russia	E14	34
Kanmaw Kyun, i., Mya.	G4	48
Kannack, Viet.	E9	48
Kannad, India	H5	54
Kannapolis, N.C., U.S.	A5	116
Kannauj, India	E7	54
Kanniyākumari, India	G3	53
Kannod, India	G6	54
Kannur see Cannanore, India	F2	53
Kannus, Fin.	E10	8
Kano, Nig.	G6	64
Kanonji, Japan	E6	40
Kanopolis, Ks., U.S.	C10	128
Kanorado, Ks., U.S.	B6	128
Kanosh, Ut., U.S.	E4	132
Kanoya, Japan	H3	40
Kanpetlet, Mya.	B1	48
Kānpur (Cawnpore), India	E7	54
Kansas, state, U.S.	C10	128
Kansas, stm., Ks., U.S.	B13	128
Kansas City, Ks., U.S.	E3	120
Kansas City, Mo., U.S.	E3	120
Kansk, Russia	C17	32
Kansŏng, Kor., S.	A1	40
Kan-sou see Gansu, state, China	D5	36
Kansu see Gansu, state, China	D5	36
Kantang, Thai.	I4	48
Kantchari, Burkina	G5	64
Kānth, India	D7	54
Kantishna, stm., Ak., U.S.	D9	140
Kantō-heiya, pl., Japan	D12	40
Kanton, i., Kir.	D9	72
Kantō-sanchi, mts., Japan	D11	40
Kantu-long, Mya.	C3	48
Kantunilkín, Mex.	B4	102
Kanuku Mountains, mts., Guy.	F12	86
Kanuma, Japan	C12	40
Kanye, Bots.	D7	70
Kanyutkwin, Mya.	C3	48
Kaohiung see Kaohsiung, Tai.	J8	42
Kaohsiung, Tai.	J8	42
Kaohsiunghsien, Tai.	J9	42
Kaoka Bay, b., Sol. Is.	e9	79b
Kaoko Veld, plat., Nmb.	D1	68
Kaolack, Sen.	G1	64
Kaolinovo, Blg.	F14	26
Kaoma, Zam.	C3	68
Kaouar, reg., Niger	F7	64
Kapaa, Hi., U.S.	A2	78a
Kapadvanj, India	G4	54
Kapanga, D.R.C.	F4	66
Kapaonik, mts., Yugo.	G8	26
Kapatkevičy, Bela.	H11	10
Kapčagaj, Kaz.	F13	32
Kapčagajskoe vodohranilišče, res., Kaz.	F13	32
Kapchagay Reservoir see Kapčagajskoe vodohranilišče, res., Kaz.	F13	32
Kapfenberg, Aus.	C12	22
Kapıdağ Yarımadası, pen., Tur.	C10	28
Kapikotongwa, stm., On., Can.	A11	118
Kapingamarangi, at., Micron.	C6	72
Kapiri Mposhi, Zam.	C4	68
Kapisigdlit, Grnld.	E16	141
Kapiskau, stm., On., Can.	E14	106
Kapit, Malay.	C8	50
Kaplan, La., U.S.	G6	122
Kaplice, Czech Rep.	H10	16
Kapoeta, Sudan	G6	62
Kapona, D.R.C.	F5	66
Kapos, stm., Hung.	C5	26
Kaposvár, Hung.	C4	26
Kaposvar Creek, stm., Sk., Can.	D11	124
Kappeln, Ger.	B5	16
Kaptai, Bngl.	G14	54
Kaptai Lake see Karnaphuli Reservoir, res., Bngl.	G14	54
Kapuas, stm., Indon.	D6	50
Kapuas, stm., Indon.	E9	50
Kapunda, Austl.	J2	76
Kapūrthala, India	C5	54
Kapuskasing, On., Can.	F14	106
Kapuvár, Hung.	B4	26
Kapyl', Bela.	G9	10
Kara, Russia	C1	34
Kara-Balta, Kyrg.	F12	32
Karabanovo, Russia	D21	10
Karabaš, Russia	C9	32
Kara-Bogaz-Gol, zaliv, b., Turkmen.	A7	56
Kara-Bogaz-Gol Gulf see Kara-Bogaz-Gol, zaliv, b., Turkmen.	A7	56
Karabük, Tur.	B15	28
Karabula, Russia	C17	32
Karaburun, Tur.	E9	28
Karabutak, Kaz.	D10	32
Karacabey, Tur.	C11	28
Karačaevo-Čerkesija, state, Russia	F6	32
Karacasu, Tur.	F11	28
Karačev, Russia	G17	10
Karachay see Karačaevo-Čerkesija, state, Russia	F6	32
Karachay-Cherkessia see Karačaevo-Čerkesija, state, Russia	F6	32
Karāchi, Pak.	E10	56
Karād, India	C2	53
Karaftit, Russia	F11	34
Karaganda, Kaz.	E12	32
Karagayly see Karkaralinsk, Kaz.	E13	32
Karaginskij, ostrov, i., Russia	E21	34
Karaginskij zaliv, b., Russia	E21	34
Karagoš, gora, mtn., Russia	D15	32
Karahallı, Tur.	E12	28
Kāraikkudi, India	F4	53
Karaisalı, Tur.	A6	58
Karaj, Iran	B7	56
Kara-Kala, Turkmen.	B8	56
Karakaralong, Pulau, is., Indon.	E8	44
Karakax, stm., China	A7	54
Karakojyn, ozero, l., Kaz.	E11	32
Karakol, Kyrg.	F13	32
Karakoram Pass, p., Asia	A6	54
Karakoram Range, mts., Asia	A4	46
Karakul', Uzb.	G10	32
Kara-Kum Canal see Garagumskij kanal, can., Turkmen.	B9	56
Karama, stm., Indon.	E11	50
Karamai see Karamay, China	B1	36
Karaman, Tur.	A4	58
Karaman, state, Tur.	A4	58
Karamanlı, Tur.	F12	28
Karamay, China	B1	36
Karamea Bight, b., N.Z.	E4	80
Karamürsel, Tur.	C12	28
Karamyševo, Russia	C18	32
Karamzino, Russia	D17	10
Karangasem, Indon.	H9	50
Karangnunggal, Indon.	G6	50
Kāranja, India	H6	54
Karanjia, India	H10	54
Karapınar, Tur.	A4	58
Karas, state, Nmb.	E3	70
Karaşar, Tur.	C14	28
Karasburg, Nmb.	F4	70
Kara Sea see Karskoe more, Russia	B10	30
Karasjok, Nor.	B11	8
Karasu, Tur.	B13	28
Karasu, stm., Tur.	B4	56
Karasuk, Russia	D13	32
Karatal, Kaz.	E15	32
Karatal, stm., Kaz.	E13	32
Karataş Burun, c., Tur.	B6	58
Karatau, Kaz.	F11	32
Karatau, hrebet, mts., Kaz.	F11	32
Karatau Range see Karatau, hrebet, mts., Kaz.	F11	32
Karatobe, Kaz.	E8	32
Karaton, Kaz.	E8	32
Karatsu, Japan	F2	40
Karaul, Kaz.	E13	32
Karaul, Russia	B5	34
Karauli, India	E6	54
Karawa, D.R.C.	D4	66
Karawang, Indon.	G5	50
Karawang, Tanjung, c., Indon.	F5	50
Karawanken, mts., Eur.	D11	22
Karažal, Kaz.	E12	32
Karbalā', Iraq	C5	56
Kårböle, Swe.	E6	8
Karcag, Hung.	B7	26
Kardámaina, Grc.	G9	28
Kardeljevo, Cro.	G14	22
Kardítsa, Grc.	D4	28
Kärdla, Est.	G10	8
Kărdžali, Blg.	H12	26
Karelia see Karelija, state, Russia	D15	8
Karelia, hist. reg., Eur.	E14	8
Karelija, state, Russia	D15	8
Karelija see Karelia, hist. reg., Eur.	E14	8
Karel'skij Gorodok, Russia	B19	10
Karema, Tan.	F6	66
Karen, India	F7	46
Karesuando, Swe.	B9	8
Kärevere, Est.	B9	10
Kargasok, Russia	C14	32
Kargat, Russia	C14	32
Kargil, India	A5	54
Kargopol', Russia	F18	8
Kariba, Zimb.	D4	68
Kariba, Lake, res., Afr.	D4	68
Karibib, Nmb.	B2	70
Kariega, stm., S. Afr.	H6	70
Karimata, Kepulauan, is., Indon.	D6	50
Karimata, Selat, strt., Indon.	E6	50
Karīmganj, India	F14	54
Karīmnagar, India	B4	53
Karimunjawa, Kepulauan, is., Indon.	F7	50
Karimunjawa, Pulau, i., Indon.	F7	50
Karisimbi, vol., Afr.	E5	66
Káristos, Grc.	E7	28
Kariya, Japan	D10	40
Kārkal, India	E2	53
Karkaralinsk, Kaz.	E13	32
Karkar Island, i., Pap. N. Gui.	a4	79a
Karkonoski Park Narodowy, p.o.i., Pol.	F11	16
Karkūk, Iraq	B5	56
Karleby see Kokkola, Fin.	E10	8
Karlino, Pol.	B11	16
Karl-Marx-Stadt see Chemnitz, Ger.	F8	16
Karlovac, Cro.	E12	22
Karlovo, Blg.	G11	26
Karlovy Vary, Czech Rep.	F8	16
Karlsborg, Swe.	D10	8
Karlsburg see Alba Iulia, Rom.	C10	26
Karlshamn, Swe.	H6	8
Karlskoga, Swe.	G6	8
Karlskrona, Swe.	H6	8
Karlsruhe, Ger.	G4	16
Karlstad, Swe.	G5	8
Karlstadt, Ger.	G5	16
Karluk, Ak., U.S.	E9	140
Karma, Bela.	H14	10
Karma, Niger	G5	64
Karmah an Nuzul, Sudan	D6	62
Karmāla, India	B2	53
Karmøy, i., Nor.	G1	8
Karnack, Tx., U.S.	E4	122
Karnak, Il., U.S.	G9	120
Karnāl, India	D6	54
Karṇālī, stm., Asia	D8	54
Karnāli, stm., Nepal	D8	54
Karnaphuli Reservoir, res., Bngl.	G14	54
Karnātaka, state, India	D2	53
Karnobat, Blg.	G13	26
Kärnten, state, Aus.	D10	22
Karoli, India	G7	54
Karonga, Mwi.	B5	68
Karoo National Park, p.o.i., S. Afr.	H6	70
Karoonda, Austl.	J2	76
Karor, Pak.	C3	54
Kárpathos, Grc.	H10	28
Kárpathos, i., Grc.	H10	28
Karpats'kyi Pryrodnyi Natsional'nyi Park, p.o.i., Ukr.	A11	26
Karpenísi, Grc.	E4	28
Karpogory, Russia	D21	8
Karpuzlu, Tur.	F10	28
Karratha, Austl.	D3	74
Karrats Fjord, b., Grnld.	C14	141
Kars, Tur.	A5	56
Karsakpaj, Kaz.	E11	32
Karsantı, Tur.	A6	58
Karši, Uzb.	G11	32
Karsin, Pol.	C13	16
Karskoe more (Kara Sea), Russia	B10	30
Kartala, vol., Com.	C7	68
Kartaly, Russia	D10	32
Kartārpur, India	C5	54
Karthaus, Pa., U.S.	C7	114
Kartuzy, Pol.	B14	16
Karufa, Indon.	F9	44
Karumba, Austl.	A3	76
Karungi, Swe.	C10	8
Karunjie, Austl.	C5	74
Karūr, India	F4	53
Karviná, Czech Rep.	G14	16
Kārwār, India	D1	53
Karyés, Grc.	C7	28
Karymskoe, Russia	F11	34
Kasai (Cassai), stm., Afr.	E3	66
Kasaji, D.R.C.	G4	66
Kasama, Japan	C13	40
Kasama, Zam.	C5	68
Kasane, Bots.	D3	68
Kasanga, Tan.	F6	66
Kasangulu, D.R.C.	E3	66
Kasaoka, Japan	E6	40
Kāsaragod, India	E2	53
Kasba, India	F11	54
Kasba Lake, l., Can.	C10	106
Kascjukouka, Bela.	H13	10
Kascjukovičy, Bela.	G14	10
Kaseda, Japan	H3	40
Kasempa, Zam.	C4	68
Kasenga, D.R.C.	G5	66
Kasenye, D.R.C.	D6	66
Kasese, D.R.C.	E5	66
Kasese, Ug.	D6	66
Kaset Sombun, Thai.	D5	48
Kāsganj, India	E7	54
Kāshān, Iran	C7	56
Kashgar see Kashi, China	B12	56
Kashi, China	B12	56
Kashihara, Japan	E8	40
Kashima, Japan	F3	40
Kashima-nada, Japan	C13	40
Kashing see Jiaxing, China	F9	42
Kāshīpur, India	D7	54
Kashiwazaki, Japan	B11	40
Kāshmar, Iran	B8	56
Kashmir, hist. reg., Asia	A3	46
Kasia, India	E9	54
Kasimbar, Indon.	D12	50
Kasimov, Russia	I19	8
Kašin, Russia	C20	10
Kašira, Russia	F21	10
Kasiruta, Pulau, i., Indon.	F8	44
Kaskaskia, stm., Il., U.S.	E9	120
Kaskinen, Fin.	E9	8
Kaslo, B.C., Can.	G13	138
Kasnja, Russia	E17	10
Kasongo, D.R.C.	E5	66
Kasongo-Lunda, D.R.C.	F3	66
Kásos, i., Grc.	H9	28
Kasota, Mn., U.S.	G5	118
Kaspijsk, Russia	F7	32
Kaspijskij, Russia	E7	32
Kaspijskoje more see Caspian Sea	F7	32
Kasplja, stm., Eur.	E13	10
Kasr, Ra's, c., Afr.	D7	62
Kassab, Syria	C6	58
Kassalā, Sudan	D7	62
Kassándra, pen., Grc.	C6	28
Kassandra, Gulf of see Kassándras, Kólpos, b., Grc.	C6	28
Kassándras, Kólpos, b., Grc.	C6	28
Kassel, Ger.	E5	16
Kasserine, Tun.	B6	64
Kastamonu, Tur.	A3	56
Kastamonu, state, Tur.	B16	28
Kastélli, Grc.	H6	28
Kastoria, Grc.	C4	28
Kastorías, Límni, l., Grc.	C4	28
Kastrakíou, Technití Límni, res., Grc.	E4	28
Kasugai, Japan	D9	40
Kasulu, Tan.	E6	66
Kasumi, Japan	D7	40
Kasumiga-ura, l., Japan	C13	40
Kasungan, Indon.	E8	50
Kasūr, Pak.	C5	54
Kaszuby, hist. reg., Pol.	B13	16
Kataba, Zam.	D4	68
Katahdin, Mount, mtn., Me., U.S.	E7	110
Katako-Kombe, D.R.C.	E4	66
Katanga, hist. reg., D.R.C.	F4	66
Katanga, stm., Russia	C18	32
Katangi, India	G7	54
Katangli, Russia	F17	34
Katanning, Austl.	F3	74
Katchall Island, i., India	G7	46
Katepwa Beach, Sk., Can.	D10	124
Kateríni, Grc.	C5	28
Kates Needle, mtn., N.A.	D4	106
Katete, Zam.	C5	68
Katha, Mya.	D8	46
Katherîna, Gebel, mtn., Egypt	J4	58
Katherine, Austl.	B6	74
Katherine, stm., Austl.	B6	74
Katherine Creek, stm., Austl.	D4	76
Kāthiāwār Peninsula, pen., India	H3	54
Kathla, India	C6	54
Kāṭhmāṇḍau (Kathmandu), Nepal	E10	54
Kathmandu see Kāṭhmāṇḍau, Nepal	E10	54
Kathor, India	H4	54
Kathua, India	B5	54
Kati, Mali	G3	64
Katibas, stm., Malay.	C8	50
Katihār, India	F11	54
Katimik Lake, l., Mb., Can.	B14	124
Katiola, C. Iv.	H4	64
Katipunan, Phil.	F4	52
Ka Tiriti o te Moana see Southern Alps, mts., N.Z.	F4	80
Katmai, Mount, vol., Ak., U.S.	E8	140
Káto Achaía, Grc.	E4	28
Kātol, India	H7	54
Katoomba, Austl.	I8	76
Katowice, Pol.	F14	16
Katowice, state, Pol.	F15	16
Katrineholm, Swe.	G7	8
Katsina, Nig.	G6	64
Katsina Ala, stm., Afr.	H6	64
Katsuta, Japan	C13	40
Katsuura, Japan	D13	40
Katsuyama, Japan	C9	40
Katsuyama, Japan	D6	40
Kattakurgan, Uzb.	G11	32
Kattegat, strt., Eur.	H4	8
Katul, Jabal, mtn., Sudan	E5	62
Katun', stm., Russia	D15	32
Katunino, Russia	G21	8
Kātwa, India	G11	54
Katwijk aan Zee, Neth.	B13	14
Katyn, Russia	F14	10
Katzenbuckel, mtn., Ger.	G5	16
Kauai, i., Hi., U.S.	B2	78a
Kauai Channel, strt., Hi., U.S.	B3	78a
Kaufbeuren, Ger.	I6	16
Kaufman, Tx., U.S.	E2	122
Kaukauna, Wi., U.S.	D1	112
Kaukau Veld, plat., Afr.	D3	68
Kaulakahi Channel, strt., Hi., U.S.	B2	78a
Kaumalapau, Hi., U.S.	C4	78a
Kaunas, Lith.	F6	10
Kaura-Namoda, Nig.	G6	64
Kauriālā (Ghāghara), stm., Asia	D8	54
Kautokeino, Nor.	B10	8
Kau-ye Kyun, i., Mya.	G4	48
Kavača, Russia	D23	34
Kavadarci, Mac.	B5	28
Kavaja see Kavajë, Alb.	C13	24
Kavajë, Alb.	C13	24
Kavaklıdere, Tur.	F11	28
Kavála, Grc.	C7	28
Kavalerovo, Russia	B11	38
Kāvali, India	D4	53
Kavaratti, India	F3	46
Kavaratti Island, i., India	F3	46
Kāveri (Cauvery), stm., India	F4	53
Kāveri Falls, wtfl, India	E3	53
Kavieng, Pap. N. Gui.	a5	79a
Kavīr, Dasht-e, des., Iran	C8	56
Kaw, Ok., U.S.	E12	128
Kawa, Mya.	D3	48
Kawagama Lake, l., On., Can.	C10	112
Kawagoe, Japan	D12	40
Kawaguchi, Japan	D12	40
Kawaihoa, c., Hi., U.S.	B1	78a
Kawaikini, mtn., Hi., U.S.	A2	78a
Kawambwa, Zam.	B4	68
Kawanoe, Japan	E6	40
Kawardha, India	H8	54
Kawasaki, Japan	D12	40
Kawatana, Japan	F2	40
Kawdut, Mya.	E3	48
Kaweenakumik Lake, l., Mb., Can.	B14	124
Kawhia Harbour, b., N.Z.	D6	80
Kawich Peak, mtn., Nv., U.S.	F9	134
Kawkareik, Mya.	D4	48
Kaw Lake, res., Ok., U.S.	E12	128
Kawludo, Mya.	C3	48
Kawnipi Lake, l., On., Can.	C7	118
Kawthaung, Mya.	H4	48
Kaxgar, stm., China	B12	56
Kaya, Burkina	G4	64
Kayah, state, Mya.	C3	48
Kayak Island, i., Ak., U.S.	E11	140
Kāyalpattinam, India	G4	53
Kayan, Mya.	D3	48
Kayan, stm., Indon.	B10	50
Kāyankulam, India	G3	53
Kaycee, Wy., U.S.	D6	126
Kayenta, Az., U.S.	G6	132
Kayes, Mali	G2	64
Kayin, state, Mya.	D3	48
Kaymaz, Tur.	D14	28
Kayseri, Tur.	B4	56
Kaysville, Ut., U.S.	B4	132
Kayuadi, Pulau, i., Indon.	G12	50
Kayuagung, Indon.	E4	50
Kayumas, Indon.	G9	50
Kazače, Russia	B16	34
Kazačinskoe, Russia	C19	32
Kazačinskoe, Russia	E7	34
Kazahskij melkosopočnik (Kazakh Hills), hills, Kaz.	D12	32
Kazakh Hills see Kazahskij melkosopočnik, hills, Kaz.	D12	32
Kazakhstan, ctry., Asia	E10	32
Kazaki, Russia	H21	10
Kazalinsk, Kaz.	E10	32
Kazan', Russia	C7	32
Kazan, stm., Can.	C11	106
Kazanlăk, Blg.	G12	26
Kazanlı, Tur.	B5	58
Kazan-rettō, is., Japan	G18	30
Kazanskoe, Russia	C11	32
Kāzerūn, Iran	D7	56
Kazimierza Wielka, Pol.	F16	16
Kazincbarcika, Hung.	A7	26
Kaziranga National Park, p.o.i., India	E14	54
Kazlų Rūda, Lith.	F6	10
Kaztalovka, Kaz.	E7	32
Kazula, Moz.	D5	68
Kazym, Russia	B11	32
Kazym, stm., Russia	B11	32
Kazyr, stm., Russia	D16	32
Kbal Dâmrei, Camb.	E7	48
Kdyně, Czech Rep.	G9	16
Kéa, Grc.	F7	28
Kéa, i., Grc.	F7	28
Keahole Point, c., Hi., U.S.	D5	78a
Kealaikahiki Channel, strt., Hi., U.S.	C5	78a
Keams Canyon, Az., U.S.	H6	132
Keanapapa Point, c., Hi., U.S.	C4	78a
Kearney, Mo., U.S.	E3	120
Kearney, Ne., U.S.	G13	126
Kearns, Ut., U.S.	C4	132
Kearny, Az., U.S.	J6	132
Keban Barajı, res., Tur.	B4	56
Keban Reservoir see Keban Barajı, res., Tur.	B4	56
Kébèmer, Sen.	F1	64
Kebnekaise, mtn., Swe.	B8	8
K'ebrī Dehar, Eth.	F8	62
Kech, stm., Pak.	D9	56
Kechika, stm., B.C., Can.	D5	106
Keçiborlu, Tur.	F13	28
Kecskemét, Hung.	C6	26
Kedah, state, Malay.	J5	48
Kėdainiai, Lith.	E6	10
Kediri, Indon.	G8	50
Kedon, Russia	D20	34
Kédougou, Sen.	G2	64
Kędzierzyn-Koźle, Pol.	F14	16
Keefers, B.C., Can.	F9	138
Keele, stm., N.T., Can.	C5	106
Keele Peak, mtn., Yk., Can.	C4	106
Keeling Islands see Cocos Islands, dep., Oc.	K12	142
Keelung see Chilung, Tai.	I9	42
Keene, Ky., U.S.	G13	120
Keene, N.H., U.S.	B13	114
Keene, Tx., U.S.	B10	130
Keeney Knob, mtn., W.V., U.S.	G5	114
Keer-Weer, Cape, c., Austl.	B8	74
Keeseville, N.Y., U.S.	F3	110
Keetmanshoop, Nmb.	E3	70
Keewatin, On., Can.	B4	118
Keewatin, Mn., U.S.	D5	118
Kefalloniá, i., Grc.	E3	28
Kefamenanu, Indon.	G7	44
Kefar Naḥum (Capernaum), hist., Isr.	F6	58
Kefar Sava, Isr.	F5	58
Keffi, Nig.	H6	64
Keflavík, Ice.	k28	8a
Ke Ga, Mui, c., Viet.	F9	48
Kegalla, Sri L.	H5	53
Keg River, Ab., Can.	D7	106
Kegums, Lat.	D7	10
Ke-hsi Mānsām, Mya.	B3	48
Keighley, Eng., U.K.	H10	12
Keila, Est.	G11	8
Keimoes, S. Afr.	F5	70
Keith, Scot., U.K.	D9	12
Keith Arm, b., N.T., Can.	B6	106
Keithley Creek, B.C., Can.	D9	138
Keithsburg, Il., U.S.	J8	118
Keiyasi, Fiji	p18	79e
Keizer, Or., U.S.	F3	136
Kejimkujik National Park, p.o.i., N.S., Can.	F11	110
Kejvy, mts., Russia	C17	8
Kekaha, Hi., U.S.	B2	78a
Kékes, mtn., Hung.	B7	26
Kekri, India	E5	54
K'elafo, Eth.	F8	62
Kelai, stm., Indon.	C10	50
Kelani, stm., Sri L.	H5	53
Kelantan, state, Malay.	J6	48
Kelantan, stm., Malay.	J6	48
Kelapa, Indon.	D4	50
Kelbia, Sebkhet, l., Tun.	I4	24
Kelheim, Ger.	H7	16
Kelibia, Tun.	H5	24
Kéllé, Congo	E2	66
Kellerberrin, Austl.	F3	74
Keller Lake, l., N.T., Can.	C6	106
Kellett, Cape, c., N.T., Can.	B14	140
Kelleys Island, i., Oh., U.S.	C3	114
Kellogg, Id., U.S.	C10	136
Kellogg, Ia., U.S.	C5	120
Kellogg, Mn., U.S.	G6	118
Kelloselkä, Fin.	C13	8
Kells, Ire.	H6	12
Kelmė, Lith.	E5	10
Kélo, Chad	F3	62
Kelolokan, Indon.	C10	50
Kelowna, B.C., Can.	G11	138
Kelsey Bay, B.C., Can.	F5	138
Kelseyville, Ca., U.S.	D3	134
Kelso, Scot., U.K.	F10	12
Kelso, Wa., U.S.	D4	136
Keluang, Malay.	K6	48
Kelvington, Sk., Can.	B10	124
Kelvin Island, i., On., Can.	B10	118
Kem', Russia	D16	8
Kem', stm., Russia	D15	8
Kemano, B.C., Can.	C2	138
Kemena, stm., Malay.	B8	50
Kemer, Tur.	F13	28
Kemer Barajı, res., Tur.	F11	28
Kemerhisar, Tur.	A5	58
Kemerovo, Russia	C15	32
Kemi, Fin.	D11	8
Kemijärvi, Fin.	C12	8
Kemijärvi, l., Fin.	C12	8
Kemijoki, stm., Fin.	C12	8
Kemmerer, Wy., U.S.	B6	132
Kemmuna (Comino), i., Malta	H8	24
Kemnath, Ger.	G7	16
Kemp, Tx., U.S.	E2	122
Kemp, Lake, res., Tx., U.S.	H9	128
Kempner, Tx., U.S.	C9	130
Kempsey, Austl.	H9	76
Kempt, Lac, l., Qc., Can.	F16	106
Kempten, Ger.	I6	16
Kemptville, On., Can.	C14	112
Kemujan, Pulau, i., Indon.	F7	50

Name	Map Ref.	Page

Name	Map Ref.	Page
Lincoln Park, Co., U.S.	C3	128
Lincoln Park, Mi., U.S.	B2	114
Lincoln Sea, N.A.	A13	141
Lincolnton, Ga., U.S.	C3	116
Lincolnton, N.C., U.S.	A4	116
Lincoln Village, Ca., U.S.	F4	134
Lindale, Ga., U.S.	C13	122
Lindale, Tx., U.S.	E3	122
Lindau, Ger.	I5	16
Linde, stm., Russia	C13	34
Linden, Guy.	B6	84
Linden, Al., U.S.	E11	122
Linden, In., U.S.	H3	112
Linden, Mi., U.S.	B2	114
Linden, Tn., U.S.	B11	122
Lindesnes, c., Nor.	H2	8
Lindi, Tan.	F7	66
Lindi, stm., D.R.C.	D5	66
Líndos, hist., Grc.	G10	28
Lind Point, c., V.I.U.S.	e7	104b
Lindsay, On., Can.	D11	112
Lindsay, Ca., U.S.	G6	134
Lindsay, Ne., U.S.	F15	126
Lindsay, Ok., U.S.	G11	128
Line Islands, is., Oc.	D11	72
Linesville, Pa., U.S.	C5	114
Lineville, Al., U.S.	D13	122
Lineville, Ia., U.S.	D4	120
Linfen, China	C4	42
Linganamakki Reservoir, res., India	D2	53
Lingao, China	L3	42
Lingayen, Phil.	B3	52
Lingayen Gulf, b., Phil.	B3	52
Lingbi, China	E7	42
Lingbo, Swe.	F7	8
Lingchuan, China	D5	42
Lingen, Ger.	D3	16
Lingfengwei, China	I6	42
Lingga, Kepulauan, is., Indon.	C4	50
Lingga, Pulau, i., Indon.	D4	50
Lingomo II, D.R.C.	D4	66
Lingqiu, China	B6	42
Lingshan, China	J3	42
Lingshi, China	C4	42
Lingshui, China	L4	42
Linguère, Sen.	F2	64
Lingwu, China	B2	42
Lingxian, China	H5	42
Lingyuan, China	A8	42
Linh, Ngoc, mtn., Viet.	E9	48
Linhai, China	G9	42
Linhares, Braz.	J5	88
Linhe, China	A2	42
Linhsia see Linxia, China	D5	36
Lini see Linyi, China	D8	42
Linjiang, China	D7	38
Linköping, Swe.	G6	8
Linkou, China	B9	38
Linksmakalnis, Lith.	F6	10
Linkuva, Lith.	D6	10
Linn, Ks., U.S.	B11	128
Linn, Mo., U.S.	F6	120
Linnansaaren kansallispuisto, p.o.i., Fin.	E13	8
Linnhe, Loch, b., Scot., U.K.	E7	12
Linqi, China	D5	42
Linqing, China	C6	42
Linqu, China	C8	42
Linquan, China	E6	42
Linru, China	D5	42
Lins, Braz.	K1	88
Linstead, Jam.	i13	104d
Lintan, China	E5	36
Linton, In., U.S.	E10	120
Linton, N.D., U.S.	A12	126
Lintong, China	D3	42
Linwu, China	I5	42
Linxi, China	C8	36
Linxi, China	C3	38
Linxia, China	D5	36
Linxian, China	C4	42
Linxian, China	C5	42
Linyi, China	D8	42
Linyi, China	C7	42
Linyü see Shanhaiguan, China	A8	42
Linz, Aus.	B11	22
Lio Matoh, Malay.	B9	50
Lion, Golfe du, b., Fr.	G10	18
Lion, Gulf of see Lion, Golfe du, b., Fr.	G10	18
Lionel Town, Jam.	j13	104d
Liouesso, Congo	D3	66
Lipa, Phil.	D3	52
Lipan, Tx., U.S.	B9	130
Lipari, Italy	F8	24
Lipari, Isola, i., Italy	F9	24
Lipari, Isole see Eolie, Isole, is., Italy	F8	24
Lipcani, Mol.	A13	26
Lipeck, Russia	D6	32
Lipez, Cerro, mtn., Bol.	D3	90
Lipicy, Russia	G20	10
Liping, China	H3	42
Lipki, Russia	G20	10
Lipník nad Bečvou, Czech Rep.	G13	16
Lipno, Pol.	D15	16
Lipno, údolní nádrž, res., Czech Rep.	H10	16
Lipova, Rom.	C8	26
Lipovcy, Russia	B9	38
Lippe, stm., Ger.	E2	16
Lippstadt, Ger.	E4	16
Lipscomb, Tx., U.S.	E8	128
Liptovská Teplička, Slov.	G15	16
Liptovský Mikuláš, Slov.	G15	16
Liptrap, Cape, c., Austl.	L5	76
Lipu, China	I4	42
Lira, Ug.	D6	66
Liri, stm., Italy	C7	24
Liria see Llíria, Spain	E10	20
Liro, Vanuatu	k17	79d
Lisala, D.R.C.	D4	66
Lisboa (Lisbon), Port.	F1	20
Lisboa, state, Port.	E1	20
Lisbon see Lisboa, Port.	F1	20
Lisbon, N.H., U.S.	F5	110
Lisbon, N.D., U.S.	A15	126
Lisbon, Oh., U.S.	D5	114
Lisburn, N. Ire., U.K.	G6	12
Lisburne, Cape, c., Ak., U.S.	C6	140
Lishi, China	C4	42
Lishu, China	C6	38
Lishui, China	G8	42
Lishuzhen, China	B9	38
Lisicy, Russia	D19	10
Lisieux, Sk., Can.	E7	124
Lisieux, Fr.	E9	14
Liski, Russia	D5	32
L'Isle-Jourdain, Fr.	C6	18
Lisman, Al., U.S.	E10	122
Lismore, Austl.	G9	76
Lismore, N.S., Can.	E14	110
Lišov, Czech Rep.	G10	16
Listowel, On., Can.	E9	112
Listowel, Ire.	I3	12
Litang, China	E5	36
Litang, China	J3	42
Litchfield, Il., U.S.	E8	120
Litchfield, Mn., U.S.	F4	118
Litchfield, Ne., U.S.	F13	126
Litchville, N.D., U.S.	A14	126
Lithgow, Austl.	I8	76
Líthino, Ákra, c., Grc.	I7	28
Lithonia, Ga., U.S.	D14	122
Lithuania, ctry., Eur.	E7	10
Litija, Slvn.	D11	22
Lititz, Pa., U.S.	D9	114
Litoměřice, Czech Rep.	F10	16
Litomyšl, Czech Rep.	G12	16
Litovko, Russia	G16	34
Little, stm., U.S.	D5	122
Little, stm., U.S.	B8	122
Little, stm., Ga., U.S.	C3	116
Little, stm., N.C., U.S.	A7	116
Little, stm., Ok., U.S.	F11	128
Little, stm., Tx., U.S.	D11	130
Little, Mountain Fork, stm., U.S.	C4	122
Little Abaco, i., Bah.	B9	96
Little Andaman, i., India	F7	46
Little Arkansas, stm., Ks., U.S.	C11	128
Little Beaver Creek, stm., U.S.	A8	126
Little Beaver Creek, stm., U.S.	B7	128
Little Belt see Lillebælt, strt., Den.	I3	8
Little Belt Mountains, mts., Mt., U.S.	D16	136
Little Bighorn, stm., U.S.	B5	126
Little Bighorn Battlefield National Monument, p.o.i., Mt., U.S.	B5	126
Little Blue, stm., U.S.	G15	126
Little Buffalo, stm., Can.	C8	106
Little Carpathians see Malé Karpaty, mts., Slov.	H13	16
Little Cayman, i., Cay. Is.	C7	102
Little Chute, Wi., U.S.	D1	112
Little Colorado, stm., Az., U.S.	H5	132
Little Current, On., Can.	C8	112
Little Current, stm., On., Can.	A12	118
Little Deep Creek, stm., N.D., U.S.	F12	124
Little Deschutes, stm., Or., U.S.	G5	136
Little Desert, des., Austl.	K3	76
Little Desert National Park, p.o.i., Austl.	K3	76
Little Dry Creek, stm., Mt., U.S.	G7	124
Little Falls, Mn., U.S.	E4	118
Little Falls, N.Y., U.S.	E15	112
Littlefork, Mn., U.S.	C5	118
Little Fork, stm., Mn., U.S.	C5	118
Little Hurricane Creek, stm., Ga., U.S.	E3	116
Little Inagua, i., Bah.	B11	102
Little Kanawha, stm., W.V., U.S.	E4	114
Little Karroo (Klein Karroo), plat., S. Afr.	H5	70
Little Lake, l., La., U.S.	H8	122
Little London, Jam.	i12	104d
Little Lost, stm., Id., U.S.	F13	136
Little Mexico, Tx., U.S.	D4	130
Little Missouri, stm., U.S.	B7	108
Little Missouri, stm., Ar., U.S.	D5	122
Little Namaqualand (Klein Namaland), hist. reg., S. Afr.	F3	70
Little Nicobar, i., India	G7	46
Little Osage, stm., U.S.	G3	120
Little Pee Dee, stm., S.C., U.S.	B6	116
Little Pic, stm., On., Can.	C12	118
Little Powder, stm., U.S.	B7	126
Little Quill Lake, l., Sk., Can.	C10	124
Little Rann of Kachchh, reg., India	G3	54
Little Red, stm., Ar., U.S.	B7	122
Little Red, Middle Fork, stm., Ar., U.S.	B6	122
Little Red Deer, stm., Ab., Can.	E16	138
Little River, Ks., U.S.	C10	128
Little Rock, Ar., U.S.	C6	122
Little Rock, stm., U.S.	H2	118
Little Sable Point, c., Mi., U.S.	E3	112
Little Saint Bernard Pass, p., Eur.	D12	18
Little Sandy Creek, stm., Wy., U.S.	E3	126
Little Sioux, stm., U.S.	J3	118
Little Sioux, West Fork, stm., Ia., U.S.	B2	120
Little Smoky, stm., Ab., Can.	A14	138
Little Snake, stm., U.S.	C8	132
Littlestown, Pa., U.S.	E8	114
Little Tallapoosa, stm., U.S.	D13	122
Little Tennessee, stm., U.S.	A1	116
Little Tobago, i., Trin.	r13	105f
Littleton, Co., U.S.	B3	128
Littleton, N.H., U.S.	F5	110
Littleton, W.V., U.S.	E5	114
Little Valley, N.Y., U.S.	B7	114
Little Wabash, stm., Il., U.S.	F9	120
Little White, stm., S.D., U.S.	D12	126
Little Wood, stm., Id., U.S.	G12	136
Litvínov, Czech Rep.	F9	16
Liu, stm., China	C6	38
Liu, stm., China	C5	38
Liu, stm., China	I3	42
Liuaniua see Ontong Java, at., Sol. Is.	D7	72
Liuba, China	E2	42
Liuboml', Ukr.	E20	16
Liuchen, China	J4	42
Liucheng, China	I3	42
Liuchow see Liuzhou, China	I3	42
Liucura, Chile	I2	92
Liufang, China	H7	42
Liuhe, China	C6	38
Liuheng Dao, i., China	G10	42
Liujiazi, China	A9	42
Liupan Shan, mts., China	D2	42
Liushuquan, China	F16	32
Liuxi, stm., China	J5	42
Liuyang, China	G5	42
Liuyang, stm., China	G5	42
Liuzhou, China	I3	42
Livada, Rom.	B10	26
Livadija, Russia	C10	38
Līvāni, Lat.	D9	10
Livanjsko Polje, val., Bos.	F3	26
Lively, On., Can.	B8	112
Lively Island, i., Falk. Is.	J5	90
Live Oak, Ca., U.S.	D4	134
Live Oak, Fl., U.S.	F2	116
Liveringa, Austl.	C4	74
Livermore, Ca., U.S.	F4	134
Livermore, Ia., U.S.	B3	120
Livermore, Ky., U.S.	G10	120
Livermore, Mount, mtn., Tx., U.S.	D3	130
Livermore Falls, Me., U.S.	F6	110
Liverpool, N.S., Can.	F12	110
Liverpool, Eng., U.K.	H10	12
Liverpool, Cape, c., Nu., Can.	C10	141
Liverpool Bay, b., N.T., Can.	A5	106
Liverpool Bay, b., Eng., U.K.	H9	12
Lívingston, Guat.	E3	102
Livingston, Al., U.S.	E10	122
Livingston, Il., U.S.	F8	120
Livingston, La., U.S.	G8	122
Livingston, Mt., U.S.	E16	136
Livingston, Tn., U.S.	H12	120
Livingston, Tx., U.S.	G4	122
Livingston, Wi., U.S.	B7	120
Livingston, Lake, res., Tx., U.S.	G3	122
Livingstone, Zam.	D4	68
Livingstone Falls, wtfl, Afr.	A1	68
Livingstonia, Mwi.	C5	68
Livingston Manor, N.Y., U.S.	C11	114
Livno, Bos.	F4	26
Livny, Russia	H20	10
Livonia, La., U.S.	G7	122
Livonia, Mi., U.S.	B2	114
Livonia, N.Y., U.S.	B8	114
Livorno (Leghorn), Italy	G7	22
Livramento do Brumado, Braz.	G5	88
Liwale, Tan.	F7	66
Lixi, China	G6	42
Lixian, China	G4	42
Lixian, China	D1	42
Lixian see Black, stm., Asia	D9	56
Lixin, China	E7	42
Lixoúri, Grc.	E3	28
Liyang, China	F8	42
Lizarda, Braz.	E2	88
Lizard Point, c., Eng., U.K.	L7	12
Lizarra see Estella, Spain	B8	20
Ljady, Bela.	F14	10
Ljahavičy, Bela.	G9	10
Ljahovskie ostrova, is., Russia	B17	34
Ljamca, Russia	D17	8
Ljaskavičy, Bela.	H11	10
Ljasnaja, Bela.	G8	10
Ljuban', Bela.	H10	10
Ljuban', Russia	A14	10
Ljubercy, Russia	E20	10
Ljubimec, Blg.	H12	26
Ljubljana, Slvn.	D11	22
Ljubnica, Russia	C15	10
Ljubohna, Russia	G17	10
Ljubuški, Bos.	F4	26
Ljudinovo, Russia	G17	10
Ljudkovo, Russia	F17	10
Ljungan, stm., Swe.	E5	8
Ljungby, Swe.	H5	8
Ljusdal, Swe.	F7	8
Ljusina, Bela.	H9	10
Ljusnan, stm., Swe.	F6	8
Llancanelo, Laguna, l., Arg.	G3	92
Llandeilo, Wales, U.K.	J8	12
Llandrindod Wells, Wales, U.K.	I9	12
Llandudno, Wales, U.K.	H9	12
Llanelli, Wales, U.K.	J8	12
Llangefni, Wales, U.K.	H8	12
Llanidloes, Wales, U.K.	I9	12
Llano, stm., Tx., U.S.	D8	130
Llano Colorado, Mex.	L9	134
Llanos, pl., S.A.	E7	86
Llanquihue, Lago, l., Chile	H2	90
Lleida, Spain	C11	20
Lleida, co., Spain	B12	20
Llera de Canales, Mex.	D9	100
Llerena, Spain	F4	20
Lleulleu, Lago, l., Chile	I1	92
Llico, Chile	G1	92
Llíria, Spain	E10	20
Llivia, Spain	B12	20
Llobregat, stm., Spain	C12	20
Lloydminster, Sk., Can.	E9	106
Llucena, Spain	D10	20
Lluchmayor see Llucmajor, Spain	E13	20
Llucmajor, Spain	E13	20
Llullaillaco, Volcán, vol., S.A.	B3	92
Lo (Panlong), stm., Asia	A7	48
Loa, Ut., U.S.	E5	132
Loa, stm., Chile	D3	90
Loanda, Braz.	D6	90
Loange (Luangue), stm., Afr.	F3	66
Lobamba, Swaz.	E10	70
Lobanovo, Russia	G21	10
Lobatse, Bots.	D7	70
Löbau, Ger.	E10	16
Lobaye, stm., C.A.R.	D3	66
Lobelville, Tn., U.S.	B11	122
Lobería, Arg.	I8	92
Lobnja, Russia	D20	10
Lobos, Arg.	G8	92
Lobos, Cay, i., Bah.	A9	102
Lobos, Isla, i., Mex.	B3	100
Lobskoe, Russia	E16	8
Łobżenica, Pol.	C13	16
Locarno, Switz.	D5	22
Loches, Fr.	G10	14
Loch Garman see Wexford, Ire.	I6	12
Lochinver, Scot., U.K.	C7	12
Lochsa, stm., Id., U.S.	D12	136
Lock, Austl.	F7	74
Lockeport, N.S., Can.	G11	110
Lockerbie, Scot., U.K.	F9	12
Lockesburg, Ar., U.S.	D4	122
Lockhart, Austl.	J6	76
Lock Haven, Pa., U.S.	C8	114
Lockney, Tx., U.S.	G7	128
Lockport, Il., U.S.	C9	120
Lockport, La., U.S.	H8	122
Lockport, N.Y., U.S.	E11	112
Lockwood, Mo., U.S.	G4	120
Locminé, Fr.	G6	14
Loc Ninh, Viet.	G8	48
Locust Creek, stm., U.S.	D4	120
Locust Fork, stm., Al., U.S.	D11	122
Locust Grove, Ok., U.S.	H2	120
Lod (Lydda), Isr.	G5	58
Lodalskåpa, mtn., Nor.	F2	8
Loddon, stm., Austl.	K4	76
Lodejnoe Pole, Russia	F15	8
Lodève, Fr.	F9	18
Lodge Creek, stm., N.A.	F4	124
Lodge Grass, Mt., U.S.	B5	126
Lodgepole, Ab., Can.	C15	138
Lodgepole, Ne., U.S.	F10	126
Lodgepole Creek, stm., U.S.	F10	126
Lodhrān, Pak.	D3	54
Lodi, Italy	E6	22
Lodi, Ca., U.S.	E4	134
Lodi, Wi., U.S.	H9	118
Lodja, D.R.C.	E4	66
Lodwar, Kenya	D7	66
Łódź, Pol.	E15	16
Łódź, state, Pol.	E15	16
Loei, Thai.	D5	48
Loei, stm., Thai.	D5	48
Loeriesfontein, S. Afr.	G4	70
Lofer, Aus.	C9	22
Lofoten, is., Nor.	B5	8
Lofoten Basin, unds.	A14	144
Loga, Niger	G5	64
Logan, Ia., U.S.	C2	120
Logan, Ks., U.S.	B9	128
Logan, Oh., U.S.	E3	114
Logan, Ut., U.S.	B5	132
Logan, W.V., U.S.	G4	114
Logan, Mount, mtn., Yk., Can.	C2	106
Logan Creek, stm., Ne., U.S.	E15	126
Logan Island, i., On., Can.	A10	118
Logan Martin Lake, res., Al., U.S.	D12	122
Logan Mountains, mts., Yk., Can.	C5	106
Logan Pass, p., Mt., U.S.	B13	136
Logansport, In., U.S.	H3	112
Logansport, La., U.S.	F5	122
Loganville, Ga., U.S.	C2	116
Logone, stm., Afr.	F3	62
Logroño, Spain	B8	20
Løgstør, Den.	H3	8
Logudoro, reg., Italy	D2	24
Lohārdaga, India	G10	54
Lohiniva, Fin.	C11	8
Lohne, Ger.	D4	16
Loho see Luohe, China	E6	42
Lohrville, Ia., U.S.	B3	120
Loi (Nanlei), stm., Asia	B4	48
Loi, Phou, mtn., Laos	B6	48
Loi-kaw, Mya.	C3	48
Loi Mwe, Mya.	B4	48
Loing, stm., Fr.	F11	14
Loing, Canal du, can., Fr.	F11	14
Loir, stm., Fr.	G8	14
Loire, state, Fr.	D10	18
Loire, stm., Fr.	B4	18
Loire, Canal latéral à la, can., Fr.	C9	18
Loire-Atlantique, state, Fr.	G7	14
Loiret, state, Fr.	F11	14
Loir-et-Cher, state, Fr.	G10	14
Loja, Ec.	D2	84
Loja, Spain	G6	20
Lokandu, D.R.C.	E5	66
Lokan Reservoir see Lokan tekojärvi, res., Fin.	C12	8
Lokan tekojärvi, res., Fin.	C12	8
Lokeren, Bel.	C13	14
Loket, Czech Rep.	F8	16
Lokichar, Kenya	D7	66
Lokichokio, Kenya	D6	66
Loknja, Russia	D13	10
Lokoja, Nig.	H6	64
Lokolama, D.R.C.	E3	66
Lokot', Russia	H17	10
Loksa, Est.	A8	10
Loks Land, i., Nu., Can.	E13	141
Lola, Gui.	H3	64
Loleta, Ca., U.S.	C1	134
Loliondo, Tan.	E7	66
Lolita, Tx., U.S.	F11	130
Lolland, i., Den.	I4	8
Lolo, Mt., U.S.	D12	136
Lolodorf, Cam.	D2	66
Lolo Pass, p., U.S.	D12	136
Lolowai, Vanuatu	j16	79d
Loltong, Vanuatu	j16	79d
Lolvavana, Passage, strt., Vanuatu	j16	79d
Lom, Blg.	F10	26
Lom, Nor.	F3	8
Lom, stm., Afr.	F2	62
Lomami, stm., D.R.C.	D4	66
Lomas de Zamora, Arg.	G8	92
Lomax, Il., U.S.	D6	120
Łomazy, Pol.	E19	16
Lombardia, state, Italy	E6	22
Lombardy see Lombardia, state, Italy	E6	22
Lomblen, Pulau, i., Indon.	G7	44
Lombok, Indon.	H10	50
Lombok, i., Indon.	H10	50
Lombok, Selat, strt., Indon.	H9	50
Lomé, Togo	H5	64
Lomela, D.R.C.	E4	66
Lomela, stm., D.R.C.	E4	66
Lometa, Tx., U.S.	C9	130
Lomié, Cam.	D2	66
Lomira, Wi., U.S.	H10	118
Lommel, Bel.	C14	14
Lomond, Loch, l., Scot., U.K.	E8	12
Lomonosov, Russia	A12	10
Lomonosovka, Kaz.	D11	32
Lomovoe, Russia	D19	8
Lompobatang, Gunung, mtn., Indon.	F11	50
Lompoc, Ca., U.S.	I5	134
Lom Sak, Thai.	D5	48
Łomża, Pol.	C18	16
Łomża, state, Pol.	C18	16
Lonaconing, Md., U.S.	E7	114
Lonāvale, India	B1	53
Loncoche, Chile	G2	90
Loncopué, Arg.	I2	92
London, On., Can.	F8	112
London, Eng., U.K.	J12	12
London, Ar., U.S.	B5	122
London, Ky., U.S.	G1	114
London, Tx., U.S.	D8	130
Londonderry, N.S., Can.	E13	110
Londonderry (Derry), N. Ire., U.K.	F6	12
Londonderry, Cape, c., Austl.	B5	74
Londonderry, Isla, i., Chile	K2	90
Londrina, Braz.	D6	90
Lone Grove, Ok., U.S.	G11	128
Lone Oak, Ky., U.S.	G9	120
Lone Pine, Ca., U.S.	G7	134
Lone Rock, Wi., U.S.	A7	120
Lone Tree, Ia., U.S.	C6	120
Lone Wolf, Ok., U.S.	G9	128
Long, stm., China	I3	42
Longa, Ang.	C2	68
Longá, stm., Braz.	B5	88
Longa, proliv, strt., Russia	B24	34
Long Akah, Malay.	B9	50
Longana, Vanuatu	j17	79d
Longarone, Italy	D9	22
Longaví, Chile	G2	92
Longbangun, Indon.	C9	50
Long Bay, b., U.S.	C7	116
Long Beach, Ca., U.S.	J7	134
Long Beach, Ms., U.S.	G9	122
Long Beach, N.Y., U.S.	D12	114
Long Beach, Wa., U.S.	D2	136
Long Beach, cst., N.J., U.S.	E11	114
Longboat Key, Fl., U.S.	I3	116
Long Branch, N.J., U.S.	D12	114
Long Cay, i., Bah.	m18	104f
Longchang, China	G1	42
Longchuan, China	I6	42
Long Creek, stm., N.A.	E10	124
Longde, China	D2	42
Long Eaton, Eng., U.K.	I11	12
Longford, Austl.	L6	76
Longford, Ire.	H5	12
Longford, state, Ire.	H5	12
Long Hu, l., China	F6	42
Longhua, China	A7	42
Longhui, China	H4	42
Longiram, Indon.	C9	50
Long Island, i., Antig.	f4	105b
Long Island, i., Austl.	D7	76
Long Island, i., Bah.	A10	102
Long Island, i., Nu., Can.	E14	106
Long Island, i., N.S., Can.	F10	110
Long Island, i., N.Y., U.S.	D12	114
Long Island Sound, strt., U.S.	D12	114
Longitudinal, Valle, val., Chile	H1	92
Longjiang, China	B9	36
Longkou, China	C9	42
Long Lake, N.Y., U.S.	G2	110
Long Lake, l., On., Can.	B11	118
Longleaf, La., U.S.	F6	122
Long Leaf Park, N.C., U.S.	B8	116
Longli, China	H2	42
Longlin, China	G6	36
Longling, China	G4	36
Longmeadow, Ma., U.S.	B13	114
Long Moc, Viet.	C7	48
Longmont, Co., U.S.	A3	128
Long Mountain, mtn., Mo., U.S.	H5	120
Longnan, China	I6	42
Longnawan, Indon.	C9	50
Long Pine, Ne., U.S.	E13	126
Long Point, c., Bah.	n18	104f
Long Point, c., N.S., Can.	D16	110
Long Point, pen., Mb., Can.	A15	124
Long Point, pen., On., Can.	F9	112
Long Point Bay, b., On., Can.	F9	112
Longquan, China	G8	42
Long Range Mountains, mts., Nf., Can.	j22	107a
Longreach, Austl.	D5	76
Long-Sault, On., Can.	E2	110
Longsegah, Indon.	B10	50
Longshan, China	G3	42
Longsheng, China	I3	42
Longs Peak, mtn., Co., U.S.	A3	128
Long Swamp, Br. Vir. Is.	e8	104b
Long Thanh, Viet.	G8	48
Longton, Ks., U.S.	G1	120
Longtown, Eng., U.K.	F10	12
Longueuil, Qc., Can.	E3	110
Longuyon, Fr.	E14	14
Longview, Ab., Can.	F16	138
Long View, N.C., U.S.	I4	114
Longview, Tx., U.S.	E4	122
Longview, Wa., U.S.	D4	136
Longwai, Indon.	C10	50
Longwy, Fr.	E14	14
Longxi, China	E5	36
Longxian, China	D2	42
Long Xuyen, Viet.	G7	48
Longyan, China	I7	42
Longyou, China	G8	42
Longzhen, China	B10	36
Longzhou, China	J2	42
Lonigo, Italy	E8	22
Löningen, Ger.	D3	16
Lonja, stm., Cro.	E13	22
Lonoke, Ar., U.S.	C7	122
Lonquimay, Volcán, vol., Chile	I2	92
Lonsdale, Mn., U.S.	G5	118
Lons-le-Saunier, Fr.	H14	14
Lontra, stm., Braz.	D1	88
Loogootee, In., U.S.	F11	120
Lookout, Cape, c., N.C., U.S.	B9	116
Lookout Mountain, mts., U.S.	C13	122
Lookout Pass, p., U.S.	C11	136
Lookout Ridge, mts., Ak., U.S.	C8	140
Loolmalassin, vol., Tan.	E7	66
Loomis, Ne., U.S.	G13	126
Loomis, Wa., U.S.	B7	136
Loop, Tx., U.S.	B5	130
Loop Head, c., Ire.	I2	12
Lop, China	A5	46
Lop, stm., Viet.	F8	48
Lopatina, gora, mtn., Russia	F17	34
Lopatka, mys, c., Russia	F20	34
Lopatovo, Russia	D12	10
Lop Buri, Thai.	E5	48
Lopévi, i., Vanuatu	k17	79d
Lopez, Cap, c., Gabon	E1	66
Lop Nur, l., China	C3	36
Loptjuga, Russia	E22	8
Lora, Hāmūn-i-, l., Asia	D9	56
Lora del Río, Spain	G5	20
Lorain, Oh., U.S.	C3	114
Loraine, Tx., U.S.	B7	130
Loralai, Pak.	C2	54
Lorca, Spain	G9	20
Lord Howe Island, i., Austl.	G6	72
Lord Howe Rise, unds.	L19	142
Lord Mayor Bay, b., Nu., Can.	B12	106
Lordsburg, N.M., U.S.	K8	132
Loreauville, La., U.S.	G7	122
Loreley, misc. cult., Ger.	F3	16
Lorena, Braz.	L3	88
Lorengau, Pap. N. Gui.	a4	79a
Lorenzo, Tx., U.S.	H7	128
Lorenzo Geyres, Ur.	F9	92
Loreto, Arg.	C9	92
Loreto, Mex.	D8	100
Loreto, Mex.	B3	100
Loreto, state, Peru	H4	86
Loretto, Ky., U.S.	G12	120
Loretto, Tn., U.S.	B11	122
Lorica, Col.	C4	86
Lorient, Fr.	G5	14
Lorimor, Ia., U.S.	C3	120
Loriol-sur-Drôme, Fr.	E10	18
Loris, S.C., U.S.	B7	116
Lorman, Ms., U.S.	F7	122
Lorn, Firth of, b., Scot., U.K.	E7	12
Lorne, Austl.	L5	76
Lorne, N.B., Can.	C10	110
Lörrach, Ger.	I3	16
Lorraine, hist. reg., Fr.	F14	14
Los, Îles de, is., Gui.	H2	64
Losada, stm., Col.	F4	86
Los Alamos, N.M., U.S.	F2	128
Los Aldamas, Mex.	B9	100
Los Andes, Chile	F2	92
Los Angeles, Chile	H1	92
Los Angeles, Ca., U.S.	I7	134
Los Angeles Aqueduct, aq., Ca., U.S.	H7	134
Los Antiguos, Arg.	I2	90
Los Banos, Ca., U.S.	F5	134
Los Blancos, Arg.	D4	90
Los Bolones, Cerro, mtn., Mex.	G12	100
Los Cerrillos, Arg.	E5	92
Los Conquistadores, Arg.	E8	92
Los Fresnos, Tx., U.S.	H10	130
Los Garza, Mex.	H8	130
Los Gatos, Ca., U.S.	F4	134
Loshan see Leshan, China	F5	36
Los Hermanos, Islas, is., Ven.	B9	86
Łosice, Pol.	D18	16
Los Idolos, Parque Arquelógico de, hist., Col.	G3	86
Lošinj, Otok, i., Cro.	F11	22
Losinoborskaja, Russia	C15	32
Los Juríes, Arg.	D6	92
Los Lagos, Chile	G2	90
Los Llanos, P.R.	B3	104a
Los López, Mex.	H8	130
Los Lunas, N.M., U.S.	I10	132
Los Mochis, Mex.	C4	100
Los Nogales, Mex.	H8	130
Losolava, Vanuatu	j16	79d
Los Padillas, N.M., U.S.	I10	132
Los Palacios, Arg.	D3	92
Los Palacios, Cuba	A6	102
Los Palacios y Villafranca, Spain	G4	20
Los Picachos, Parque Nacional, p.o.i., Col.	F4	86
Los Rábanos, P.R.	B2	104a
Los Ríos, state, Ec.	H2	86
Los Roques, Islas, is., Ven.	B8	86
Los Sauces, Chile	H1	92
Lossiemouth, Scot., U.K.	D9	12
Lost, stm., U.S.	A4	134
Los Taques, Ven.	B6	86
Los Teques, Ven.	B8	86
Los Testigos, Islas, is., Ven.	B10	86
Lost Hills, Ca., U.S.	H6	134
Lost Nation, Ia., U.S.	C7	120
Lost River Range, mts., Id., U.S.	F13	136
Lost Trail Pass, p., U.S.	E13	136
Losuia, Pap. N. Gui.	b5	79a
Los Vidrios, Mex.	F6	98
Los Vilos, Chile	E2	92
Los Yébenes, Spain	E6	20
Lot, state, Fr.	E7	18
Lot, stm., Fr.	E7	18
Lota, Chile	H1	92
Lot-et-Garonne, state, Fr.	E6	18
Lothair, S. Afr.	E10	70
Lotošino, Russia	D18	10
Lotsane, stm., Bots.	C8	70
Lotta, stm., Eur.	B13	8
Lotuke, Jabal, mtn., Sudan	G6	62
Lotung, Tai.	I9	42
Louang Namtha, Laos	B5	48
Louangphrabang, Laos	C6	48
Loubomo, Congo	E2	66
Loudon, Tn., U.S.	A1	116
Loudonville, Oh., U.S.	D3	114
Loudun, Fr.	G9	14
Loue, stm., Fr.	H14	14
Louga, Sen.	F1	64
Louge, Arg.	H7	92
Loughborough, Eng., U.K.	I11	12
Loughrea, Ire.	H4	12
Louhi, Russia	C15	8
Louin, Ms., U.S.	E9	122
Louisa, Ky., U.S.	F3	114
Louisbourg, N.S., Can.	E16	110
Louisburg, Ks., U.S.	F3	120
Louisburg, N.C., U.S.	H7	114
Louise, Ms., U.S.	D8	122
Louise, Tx., U.S.	H2	122
Louiseville, Qc., Can.	D3	110
Louisiade Archipelago, is., Pap. N. Gui.	B10	74
Louisiana, Mo., U.S.	E6	120
Louisiana, state, U.S.	F6	122
Louis Trichardt, S. Afr.	C9	70
Louisville, Al., U.S.	F13	122
Louisville, Ga., U.S.	C3	116
Louisville, Ky., U.S.	F12	120
Louisville, Ne., U.S.	D1	120
Louisville, Oh., U.S.	D4	114
Louisville Ridge, unds.	M22	142
Louis-XIV, Pointe, c., Qc., Can.	E14	106
Loulé, Port.	G2	20
Loum, Cam.	D1	66
Lount Lake, l., On., Can.	A4	118
Louny, Czech Rep.	F9	16
Loup, stm., Ne., U.S.	F14	126
Loup City, Ne., U.S.	F14	126
Loups Marins, Lacs des, l., Qc., Can.	D16	106
Lourdes, Fr.	F5	18
Lourenço Marques see Maputo, Moz.	D11	70
Lourinhã, Port.	E1	20
Lousã, Port.	D2	20
Louth, Austl.	H5	76
Louth, Ire.	H6	12
Louth, Eng., U.K.	H13	12
Louth, state, Ire.	H6	12
Loutrá Aidipsoú, Grc.	E6	28
Louvain see Leuven, Bel.	D13	14
Louviers, Fr.	E10	14
Louviers, Co., U.S.	B4	128
Lovat', stm., Russia	B14	10
Loveč, Blg.	F11	26
Loveč, state, Blg.	F11	26
Loveland, Co., U.S.	G7	126
Lovell, Wy., U.S.	C4	126
Lovell Village, St. Vin.	p11	105e
Lovelock, Nv., U.S.	C7	134
Lovely, Ky., U.S.	G3	114
Lovere, Italy	E6	22
Loves Park, Il., U.S.	B8	120
Loving, N.M., U.S.	B3	130
Loving, Tx., U.S.	H10	128
Lovingston, Va., U.S.	G7	114
Lovington, N.M., U.S.	B4	130
Lovosice, Czech Rep.	F9	16
Lovozero, Russia	D13	8
Lovozero, ozero, l., Russia	C16	8
Lóvua, Ang.	B3	68
Low, Qc., Can.	C14	112
Low, Cape, c., Nu., Can.	C13	106
Lowa, D.R.C.	E5	66
Lowa, stm., D.R.C.	E5	66
Lowden, Ia., U.S.	C7	120
Lowell, Ar., U.S.	H3	120
Lowell, In., U.S.	G2	112
Lowell, Ma., U.S.	B14	114
Lowell, Or., U.S.	G4	136
Lowell, Lake, res., Id., U.S.	G10	136
Löwen, stm., Nmb.	E3	70
Löwenberg, Ger.	D8	16
Lower Arrow Lake, res., B.C., Can.	G12	138
Lower Austria see Niederösterreich, state, Aus.	B12	22
Lower California see Baja California, pen., Mex.	B2	96
Lower Egypt see Misr el-Bahrî, hist. reg., Egypt	G2	58
Lower Glenelg National Park, p.o.i., Austl.	L3	76
Lower Hutt, N.Z.	E6	80
Lower Lake, l., U.S.	B5	134
Lower Manitou Lake, l., On., Can.	B6	118
Lower Post, B.C., Can.	D5	106
Lower Red Lake, l., Mn., U.S.	D3	118
Lower Saxony see Niedersachsen, state, Ger.	D4	16
Lower Trajan's Wall, misc. cult., Eur.	D15	26
Lower West End Point, c., Anguilla	A1	105a
Lower Woods Harbour, N.S., Can.	G10	110
Lowestoft, Eng., U.K.	I14	12
Lowgar, state, Afg.	A2	54
Łowicz, Pol.	D15	16
Lowmoor, Va., U.S.	G6	114
Low Rocky Point, c., Austl.	o12	77a
Lowry City, Mo., U.S.	F4	120
Lowville, N.Y., U.S.	E14	112
Loxton, Austl.	J3	76
Loyal, Wi., U.S.	G8	118
Loyalton, Ca., U.S.	D5	134
Loyalty Islands see Loyauté, Îles, is., N. Cal.	m16	79d
Loyang see Luoyang, China	D5	42
Loyauté, Îles (Loyalty Islands), is., N. Cal.	m16	79d
Loyoro, Ug.	D6	66
Lozère, state, Fr.	E9	18
Loznica, Yugo.	E6	26
Lualaba, stm., Afr.	E5	66
Luama, stm., D.R.C.	E5	66
Lu'an, China	F7	42
Luan, stm., China	E3	38
Luancheng, China	J3	42
Luanda, Ang.	B1	68
Luando, stm., Ang.	C2	68
Luang, Khao (Maw Taung), mtn., Asia	G4	48
Luang, Thale, l., Thai.	I5	48
Luang Chiang Dao, Doi, mtn., Thai.	C4	48
Luanginga, stm., Afr.	G4	66
Luang Prabang see Louangphrabang, Laos	C6	48
Luangue (Loange), stm., Afr.	F3	66
Luangwa, stm., Afr.	C5	68
Luanping, China	A7	42
Luanshya, Zam.	C4	68
Luan Toro, Arg.	H5	92
Luanxian, China	B8	42
Luapula, stm., Afr.	C4	68
Luar, Danau, l., Indon.	C8	50
Luarca, Spain	A4	20
Luba, Eq. Gui.	I6	64
Lubaantun, hist., Belize	D3	102
Lubań, Pol.	E11	16
Lubāna, Lat.	D9	10
Lubang Islands, is., Phil.	D2	52
Lubango, Ang.	C1	68
Lubāns, l., Lat.	D9	10
Lubartów, Pol.	E18	16
Lübben, Ger.	E9	16
Lübbenau, Ger.	E9	16
Lubbock, Tx., U.S.	H7	128
Lübeck, Ger.	C6	16
Lubefu, D.R.C.	E4	66
Lubefu, stm., D.R.C.	E4	66
Lubień Kujawski, Pol.	D15	16
Lubilash, stm., D.R.C.	F4	66
Lubin, Pol.	E12	16

Name | Map Ref. | Page

Mali-Mass I•35

Name	Map Ref.	Page
Malita, Phil.	G5	52
Malizhen, China	A7	48
Maljamar, N.M., U.S.	B4	130
Malka, Russia	F20	34
Malkāpur, India	H5	54
Malkara, Tur.	C9	28
Mallāḥ, Syria	F7	58
Mallan luonnonpuisto, p.o.i., Fin.	B9	8
Mallawi, Egypt	K1	58
Mallersdorf-Pfaffenberg, Ger.	H8	16
Mallery Lake, l., Nu, Can.	C11	106
Mallet, Braz.	B12	92
Malligasta, Arg.	D4	92
Mallorca (Majorca), i., Spain	E13	20
Mallow, Ire.	I4	12
Malm, Nor.	D4	8
Malmberget, Swe.	C8	8
Malmesbury, S. Afr.	H4	70
Malmö, Swe.	I5	8
Malmok, c., Neth. Ant.	p23	104g
Malo, i., Vanuatu	j16	79d
Maloelap, at., Marsh. Is.	C8	72
Maloe Skuratovo, Russia	G19	10
Malojaroslavec, Russia	E19	10
Malolos, Phil.	C3	52
Malone, Fl., U.S.	G13	122
Malone, N.Y., U.S.	F2	110
Malonga, D.R.C.	G4	66
Małopolska, reg., Pol.	F17	16
Malošujka, Russia	E17	8
Malott, Wa., U.S.	B7	136
Małowice, Pol.	E11	16
Måløy, Nor.	E1	8
Malozemel'skaja Tundra, reg., Russia	C24	8
Malpas, Austl.	J3	76
Malpe, India	E2	53
Malpeque Bay, b., P.E., Can.	D13	110
Malprabha, stm., India	D2	53
Mālpura, India	E5	54
Malta, Braz.	D7	88
Malta, Lat.	D10	10
Malta, Mt., U.S.	F6	124
Malta, ctry., Eur.	I8	24
Malta, i., Malta	I8	24
Malta Channel, strt., Eur.	H8	24
Maltahöhe, Nmb.	D3	70
Maluku (Moluccas), is., Indon.	F8	44
Maluku, Laut (Molucca Sea), Indon.	F8	44
Ma'lūlā, Syria	E7	58
Malu Mare, Rom.	E10	26
Malunda, Indon.	E11	50
Mālvan, India	C1	53
Malvern, Ar., U.S.	C6	122
Malvern, Ia., U.S.	K3	118
Malvern, Oh., U.S.	D4	114
Malvérnia, Moz.	C10	70
Malvinas Sur, Arg.	D8	92
Malý Dunaj, stm., Slov.	H13	16
Malyja Haradzjaciчy, Bela.	H11	10
Malyj Anjuj, stm., Russia	C21	34
Malyj Enisej, stm., Russia	F8	34
Malyj Tajmyr, ostrov, i., Russia	A10	34
Mama, Russia	E11	34
Mamaia, Rom.	E15	26
Mamanguape, Braz.	D8	88
Mamasa, Indon.	E11	50
Mamasa, stm., Indon.	E11	50
Mambajao, Phil.	F5	52
Mambasa, D.R.C.	D5	66
Mamberamo, stm., Indon.	F10	44
Mamburao, Phil.	D3	52
Mamehaktebo, Indon.	C9	50
Mameigwess Lake, l., On., Can.	B6	118
Ma-Me-O Beach, Ab., Can.	C17	138
Mamfe, Cam.	C1	66
Mamljutka, Kaz.	D11	32
Mammoth, Az., U.S.	K6	132
Mammoth Cave National Park, p.o.i., Ky., U.S.	G11	120
Mammoth Lakes, Ca., U.S.	F7	134
Mammoth Spring, Ar., U.S.	H6	120
Mamonovo, Russia	F2	10
Mamoré, stm., S.A.	F4	84
Mamou, Gui.	G2	64
Mampikony, Madag.	D8	68
Mamry, Jezioro, l., Pol.	B17	16
Mamuju, Indon.	E11	50
Mamuno, Bots.	C5	70
Man, C. Iv.	H3	64
Man, W.V., U.S.	G4	114
Man, Isle of see Isle of Man, dep., Eur.	G8	12
Mana, Hi., U.S.	A2	78a
Manabí, state, Ec.	H2	86
Manacacías, stm., Col.	F5	86
Manacapuru, Braz.	I11	86
Manacapuru, stm., Braz.	I11	86
Manacor, Spain	E14	20
Manado (Menado), Indon.	E7	44
Manaenki, Russia	G19	10
Managua, Nic.	F4	102
Managua, Lago de, l., Nic.	F4	102
Manakara, Madag.	E8	68
Manakau, mtn., N.Z.	F5	80
Manāli, India	B6	54
Manama see Al-Manāmah, Bahr.	D7	56
Manam Island, i., Pap. N. Gui.	a4	79a
Mánamo, Caño, stm., Ven.	C10	86
Mananara Avaratra, Madag.	D8	68
Mananjary, Madag.	E8	68
Manantenina, Madag.	E8	68
Manapire, stm., Ven.	D8	86
Manappārai, India	F4	53
Manār, stm., India	B3	53
Manas, China	C2	36
Manās, stm., Asia	E13	54
Manasarowar Lake see Mapam Yumco, l., China	C8	54
Manas Hu, l., China	B2	36
Manāslu, mtn., Nepal	D10	54
Manasquan, N.J., U.S.	D11	114
Manassas, Va., U.S.	F8	114
Mânăstirea, Rom.	E13	26
Manatí, Col.	B4	86
Manatí, P.R.	B3	104a
Manatuto, E. Timor	G8	44
Manaung, Mya.	C1	48
Manaus, Braz.	D5	84
Manavgat, Tur.	G14	28
Manawa, Wi., U.S.	G10	118
Manāwar, India	G5	54
Manawoka, Pulau, i., Indon.	F9	44
Manban, China	A6	48
Manbij, Syria	B8	58
Mancelona, Mi., U.S.	D4	112
Mancha Real, Spain	G7	20
Manche, state, Fr.	E7	14
Mancheng, China	B6	42
Mancherāl, India	B4	53
Manchester, Eng., U.K.	H10	12
Manchester, Ct., U.S.	C13	114
Manchester, Ga., U.S.	E14	122
Manchester, Ia., U.S.	B6	120
Manchester, Ky., U.S.	G2	114
Manchester, N.H., U.S.	H5	110
Manchester, Oh., U.S.	F2	114
Manchester, Vt., U.S.	G3	110
Manchioneal, Jam.	i14	104d
Manchouli see Manzhouli, China	B8	36
Manchuria see Dong San Shen, hist. reg., China	B5	38
Manciano, Italy	H8	22
Mancos, Co., U.S.	F8	132
Mancos, stm., U.S.	F8	132
Mānd, stm., India	G9	54
Mand, stm., Iran	D7	56
Manda, Tan.	G6	66
Manda, Jabal, mtn., Sudan	F4	62
Mandabe, Madag.	E7	68
Mandaguari, Braz.	A12	92
Manda Island, i., Kenya	E8	66
Mandal, Mong.	B6	36
Mandala, Puncak, mtn., Indon.	F10	44
Mandalay, Mya.	A2	48
Mandalay, state, Mya.	B2	48
Mandan, N.D., U.S.	A11	126
Mandar, Teluk, b., Indon.	E11	50
Mandara, Monts (Mandara Mountains), mts., Afr.	G7	64
Mandara Mountains (Mandara, Monts), mts., Afr.	G7	64
Mandas, Italy	E3	24
Mandaue, Phil.	E4	52
Mandeb, Bab el, strt.	E8	62
Mandera, Kenya	D8	66
Manderson, Wy., U.S.	C5	126
Mandeville, Jam.	i13	104d
Mandi, India	C6	54
Mandi Bahāuddīn, Pak.	B4	54
Mandi Būrewāla, Pak.	C4	54
Mandi Dabwāli, India	D5	54
Mandimba, Moz.	C6	68
Mandioli, Pulau, i., Indon.	F8	44
Mandioré, Lagoa (Mandioré, Laguna), l., S.A.	G6	84
Mandioré, Laguna (Mandioré, Lagoa), l., S.A.	G6	84
Mandla, India	G8	54
Mandlakazi, Moz.	D11	70
Mandora, Austl.	C4	74
Mandra, Pak.	B4	54
Mandritsara, Madag.	D8	68
Mandsaur, India	F5	54
Mandun, China	A4	48
Manduria, Italy	D11	24
Māndvi, India	H4	54
Māndvi, India	G2	54
Mandya, India	E3	53
Manendragarh, India	G9	54
Manfalût, Egypt	K1	58
Manfredonia, Italy	I12	22
Manfredonia, Golfo di, b., Italy	C10	24
Manga, Braz.	H3	88
Manga, reg., Niger	F7	64
Mangabeiras, Chapada das, hills, Braz.	E2	88
Mangagoy, Phil.	F6	52
Mangai, D.R.C.	E3	66
Mangalagiri, India	C5	53
Mangaldai, India	E14	54
Mangalia, Rom.	F15	26
Mangalore, India	E2	53
Mangalvedha, India	C2	53
Mangchang, China	I2	42
Mange, China	B9	54
Mangela, Mount see Nanggala Hill, mtn., Sol. Is.	e7	79b
Manggar, Indon.	E6	50
Mangham, La., U.S.	E7	122
Mangin Range, mts., Mya.	C8	46
Mangkalihat, Tanjung, c., Indon.	C11	50
Manglares, Cabo, c., Col.	G2	86
Mangla Reservoir, res., Pak.	B4	54
Mangnai, China	G16	32
Mangochi, Mwi.	C6	68
Mangoky, stm., Madag.	E7	68
Mangole, Pulau, i., Indon.	F8	44
Mangrol, India	H2	54
Mangrūl Pīr, India	H6	54
Mangsang, Indon.	E4	50
Mangshi see Luxi, China	G4	36
Mangueira, Lagoa, b., Braz.	F11	92
Mangueirinha, Braz.	B11	92
Mangum, Ok., U.S.	G9	128
Mangya, China	D3	36
Manhattan, Ks., U.S.	B12	128
Manhattan, Mt., U.S.	E15	136
Manhiça, Moz.	D11	70
Mān Hpāng, Mya.	A4	48
Manhuaçu, Braz.	K4	88
Manhuaçu, stm., Braz.	J5	88
Manhumirim, Braz.	K4	88
Maniago, Italy	D9	22
Manica, Moz.	D5	68
Manica, state, Moz.	B11	70
Manicaland, state, Zimb.	B11	70
Manic Deux, Réservoir, res., Qc., Can.	A8	110
Manicoré, Braz.	E5	84
Manicouagan, stm., Qc., Can.	E17	106
Manicouagan, Réservoir, res., Qc., Can.	E17	106
Maniganggo, China	E4	36
Manigotagan, Mb., Can.	C17	124
Manigotagan, stm., Can.	C17	124
Manihiki, at., Cook Is.	E10	72
Maniitsoq see Sukkertoppen, Grnld.	D15	141
Mānikganj, Bngl.	G13	54
Mānikpur, India	F8	54
Manila, Phil.	C3	52
Manila, Ar., U.S.	I7	120
Manila, Ut., U.S.	C7	132
Manila Bay, b., Phil.	C3	52
Manilla, Austl.	H8	76
Manily, Russia	D22	34
Maningrida, Austl.	B6	74
Maninjau, Danau, l., Indon.	D1	50
Manipa, Selat, strt., Indon.	F8	44
Manipur, state, India	C7	46
Manipur, stm., Asia	A1	48
Manisa, Tur.	E10	28
Manisa, state, Tur.	E11	28
Manistee, Mi., U.S.	D3	112
Manistee, stm., Mi., U.S.	D3	112
Manistique, Mi., U.S.	C3	112
Manistique Lake, l., Mi., U.S.	B4	112
Manito, Il., U.S.	K9	118
Manitoba, state, Can.	D11	106
Manitoba, Lake, l., Mb., Can.	D15	124
Manitou, stm., On., Can.	B5	118
Manitou, Lake, l., On., Can.	C7	112
Manitou Beach, Sk., Can.	C8	124
Manitou Lake, l., Sk., Can.	B4	124
Manitoulin Island, i., On., Can.	C7	112
Manitou Springs, Co., U.S.	C3	128
Manitowaning, On., Can.	C8	112
Manitowoc, Wi., U.S.	D2	112
Maniwaki, Qc., Can.	B13	112
Manizales, Col.	E4	86
Manja, Madag.	E7	68
Manjakandriana, Madag.	D8	68
Manjeri, India	F3	53
Mānjra, stm., India	B3	53
Mankanza, D.R.C.	D3	66
Mankato, Ks., U.S.	B10	128
Mankato, Mn., U.S.	G4	118
Mankera, Pak.	C3	54
Mankota, Sk., Can.	E6	124
Manley Hot Springs, Ak., U.S.	D9	140
Manlleu, Spain	B13	20
Manmād, India	H5	54
Manna, Indon.	F3	50
Mannahill, Austl.	I3	76
Mannar, Sri L.	G4	53
Mannar, Gulf of, b., Asia	G4	53
Mannārgudi, India	F4	53
Mannford, Ok., U.S.	A2	122
Mannheim, Ger.	G4	16
Manning, N.D., U.S.	G11	124
Manning, S.C., U.S.	C5	116
Manning Strait, strt., Sol. Is.	d7	79b
Mannum, Austl.	J2	76
Mannville, Ab., Can.	C19	138
Manoharpur, India	G10	54
Manokwari, Indon.	F9	44
Manombo Atsimo, Madag.	E7	68
Manono, D.R.C.	F5	66
Manor, Sk., Can.	E11	124
Manor, Tx., U.S.	D10	130
Manosque, Fr.	F11	18
Manouane, Lac, l., Qc., Can.	C2	110
Manouane, Lac, res., Qc., Can.	E16	106
Manp'o, Kor., N.	D7	38
Mānpur, India	H8	54
Manra, at., Kir.	D9	72
Manresa, Spain	C12	20
Mānsa, India	C5	54
Mansa, Zam.	C4	68
Mansafīs, Egypt	J1	58
Mānsehra, Pak.	A4	54
Mansel Island, i., Nu., Can.	C14	106
Mansfield, Eng., U.K.	H11	12
Mansfield, Ga., U.S.	C2	116
Mansfield, Il., U.S.	D9	120
Mansfield, La., U.S.	E5	122
Mansfield, Mo., U.S.	G5	120
Mansfield, Oh., U.S.	D3	114
Mansfield, Pa., U.S.	C8	114
Mansfield, Tx., U.S.	B10	130
Mansfield, Mount, mtn., Vt., U.S.	F4	110
Mansion, St. K./N.	C2	105a
Mansôa, Gui.-B.	G1	64
Manson, Ia., U.S.	B3	120
Mansucum, Pan.	H9	102
Mansura, La., U.S.	F6	122
Manta, Ec.	H1	86
Manta, Bahía de, b., Ec.	H1	86
Mantagao, stm., Mb., Can.	C16	124
Mantalingajan, Mount, mtn., Phil.	F1	52
Mantanani Besar, Pulau, i., Malay.	G1	52
Manteca, Ca., U.S.	F4	134
Mantecal, Ven.	D7	86
Mantena, Braz.	J5	88
Manteo, N.C., U.S.	I10	114
Mantes-la-Jolie, Fr.	F10	14
Manti, Ut., U.S.	D5	132
Mantiqueira, Serra da, mts., Braz.	L3	88
Manton, Mi., U.S.	D4	112
Mántova, Italy	E7	22
Mantua, Cuba	A5	102
Mantua see Mántova, Italy	E7	22
Mantua, Oh., U.S.	C4	114
Manturovo, Russia	G21	8
Mäntyharju, Fin.	F12	8
Manu, Peru	F3	84
Manuae, at., Cook Is.	E11	72
Manuae, at., Fr. Poly.	E11	72
Manua Islands, is., Am. Sam.	h13	79c
Manuel, Mex.	D9	100
Manuel Alves, stm., Braz.	F2	88
Manuel Alves Grande, stm., Braz.	D2	88
Manuel Benavides, Mex.	A6	100
Manuel F. Mantilla see Pedro R. Fernández, Arg.	D8	92
Manuguru, India	B5	53
Manui, Pulau, i., Indon.	F7	44
Manukau, N.Z.	C6	80
Manukau Harbour, b., N.Z.	C6	80
Manus Island, i., Pap. N. Gui.	a4	79a
Mānwat, India	B3	53
Many, La., U.S.	F5	122
Manyara, Lake, l., Tan.	E7	66
Manyberries, Ab., Can.	E3	124
Many Island Lake, l., Can.	D3	124
Manyoni, Tan.	F6	66
Many Peaks, Austl.	E8	76
Manza, D.R.C.	F5	66
Manzala, Bahra el-, l., Egypt	G3	58
Manzanares, Spain	E7	20
Manzanilla Point, c., Trin.	s13	105f
Manzanillo, Cuba	B9	102
Manzanillo, Mex.	F6	100
Manzanillo Bay, b., N.A.	C11	102
Manzano, N.M., U.S.	G2	128
Manzano Peak, mtn., N.M., U.S.	G2	128
Manzhouli, China	B8	36
Manzini, Swaz.	E10	70
Mao, Chad	E3	62
Mao, Dom. Rep.	C12	102
Maó, Spain	E15	20
Maoba, China	F3	42
Maoke, Pegunungan, mts., Indon.	a2	79a
Maolin, China	C5	38
Maoming, China	K4	42
Mapaga, Indon.	D11	50
Mapam Yumco, l., China	C8	54
Mapane, Indon.	D12	50
Mapari, stm., Braz.	I8	86
Mapastepec, Mex.	H12	100
Mapi, Indon.	G10	44
Mapimí, Mex.	C6	100
Mapimí, Bolsón de, des., Mex.	B6	100
Mapire, Ven.	D9	86
Mapiri, Bol.	C3	90
Mapixari, Ilha, i., Braz.	I9	86
Maple, stm., Ia., U.S.	B2	120
Maple, stm., Mi., U.S.	E5	112
Maple, stm., N.D., U.S.	H16	124
Maple Creek, Sk., Can.	E4	124
Maple Lake, Mn., U.S.	F4	118
Maple Mount, Ky., U.S.	G10	120
Maple Ridge, B.C., Can.	G8	138
Mapleton, Ia., U.S.	B2	120
Mapleton, Or., U.S.	F3	136
Mapleton, Ut., U.S.	C5	132
Mapuera, stm., Braz.	C6	84
Maputo, Moz.	D11	70
Maputo, state, Moz.	D11	70
Maputo, stm., Afr.	E11	70
Maqên Gangri, mtn., China	E4	36
Maqna, Sau. Ar.	J5	58
Maquan, stm., China	D10	54
Maquela do Zombo, Ang.	B2	68
Maquereau, Pointe au, c., Qc., Can.	B12	110
Maquinchao, Arg.	H3	90
Maquoketa, Ia., U.S.	B7	120
Maquoketa, stm., Ia., U.S.	B7	120
Maquoketa, North Fork, stm., Ia., U.S.	B7	120
Mar, Serra do, mts., Braz.	B13	92
Mara, stm., Afr.	E7	66
Maraã, Braz.	H9	86
Maraa, Fr. Poly.	v21	78h
Marabá, Braz.	C1	88
Marabahan, Indon.	E9	50
Maraboon, Lake, res., Austl.	D6	76
Maracá, Ilha de, i., Braz.	C7	84
Maracá, Ilha de, i., Braz.	F11	86
Maracaçumé, stm., Braz.	A3	88
Maracaibo, Ven.	B5	86
Maracaibo, Lago de, l., Ven.	C6	86
Maracaju, Braz.	D5	90
Maracanaú, Braz.	B6	88
Maracás, Braz.	G5	88
Maracay, Ven.	B8	86
Marādah, Libya	B3	62
Maradi, Niger	G6	64
Marāghah, Sabkhat al-, l., Syria	C8	58
Marāgheh, Iran	B6	56
Maragogipe, Braz.	G6	88
Maragoji, Braz.	E8	88
Marahuaca, Cerro, mtn., Ven.	F9	86
Maraial, Braz.	E8	88
Marais des Cygnes, stm., U.S.	F3	120
Marajó, Baía de, b., Braz.	D8	84
Marajó, Ilha de, i., Braz.	D8	84
Maralal, Kenya	D7	66
Marali, C.A.R.	C3	66
Maralinga, Austl.	F6	74
Marambio, sci., Ant.	B35	81
Marampa, S.L.	H2	64
Maramsilli Reservoir, res., India	H8	54
Maramureș, state, Rom.	B10	26
Maran, Malay.	K6	48
Marana, Az., U.S.	K5	132
Marand, Iran	B6	56
Marang, Malay.	J6	48
Marangas, Phil.	F1	52
Maranguape, Braz.	B6	88
Maranhão, state, Braz.	C3	88
Maranhão, stm., Braz.	D9	84
Marano, Laguna di, b., Italy	E10	22
Maranoa, stm., Austl.	F7	76
Marañón, stm., Peru	D2	84
Marasende, Pulau, i., Indon.	F10	50
Mărășești, Rom.	D14	26
Maratasã, stm., Braz.	C4	88
Marathon, Austl.	C4	76
Marathon, On., Can.	C12	118
Marathon, Tx., U.S.	D4	130
Marathon, Wi., U.S.	G9	118
Marathónas, Grc.	E6	28
Maratua, Pulau, i., Indon.	B11	50
Maraú, Braz.	H6	88
Marau, Braz.	D11	92
Marauiá, stm., Braz.	H9	86
Maravilha, Braz.	C11	92
Maravillas, Mex.	B6	100
Maravillas Creek, stm., Tx., U.S.	E4	130
Marav Lake, l., Pak.	D2	54
Maravovo, Sol. Is.	e8	79b
Marawi, Phil.	F5	52
Marawwah, i., U.A.E.	E7	56
Marayes, Arg.	E4	92
Marbella, Spain	H6	20
Marble, N.C., U.S.	A2	116
Marble Bar, Austl.	D3	74
Marble Canyon, val., Az., U.S.	G5	132
Marble Falls, Tx., U.S.	D9	130
Marble Hall, S. Afr.	D9	70
Marble Hill, Mo., U.S.	G8	120
Marblemount, Wa., U.S.	B5	136
Marble Rock, Ia., U.S.	I6	118
Marburg, Ger.	F4	16
Marburg, S. Afr.	G10	70
Marca, Ponta da, c., Ang.	D1	68
Marcal, stm., Hung.	B4	26
Marcelin, Sk., Can.	B7	124
Marceline, Mo., U.S.	E5	120
March, Eng., U.K.	I12	12
March (Morava), stm., Eur.	H12	16
Marche, state, Italy	G10	22
Marche, hist. reg., Fr.	C8	18
Marche-en-Famenne, Bel.	D14	14
Marchena, Spain	G5	20
Marches see Marche, state, Italy	G10	22
Mar Chiquita, Laguna, b., Arg.	H9	92
Mar Chiquita, Laguna, l., Arg.	E6	92
Marcigny, Fr.	C10	18
Marco, Braz.	B5	88
Marcos Juárez, Arg.	F6	92
Marcus, Ia., U.S.	B2	120
Marcus Baker, Mount, mtn., Ak., U.S.	D10	140
Marcus Island see Minami-Tori-shima, i., Japan	G19	30
Marcy, Mount, mtn., N.Y., U.S.	F2	110
Mardān, Pak.	A4	54
Mardarivka, Ukr.	B16	26
Mar del Plata, Arg.	H9	92
Mardin, Tur.	B5	56
Maré, i., N. Cal.	m17	79d
Mare a Brăilei, Insula, i., Rom.	D14	26
Marea de Portillo, Cuba	C9	102
Marechal Cândido Rondon, Braz.	B10	92
Marechal Deodoro, Braz.	E8	88
Maree, Loch, l., Scot., U.K.	D7	12
Mareeba, Austl.	A5	76
Maremma, reg., Italy	H8	22
Marengo, Il., U.S.	B9	120
Marengo, Ia., U.S.	C5	120
Marenisco, Mi., U.S.	E9	118
Marennes, Fr.	D4	18
Marettimo, Isola, i., Italy	G5	24
Marfa, Tx., U.S.	D3	130
Margai Caka, l., China	A6	46
Margaree Harbour, N.S., Can.	D15	110
Margaret, stm., Austl.	C5	74
Margaret Bay, B.C., Can.	E3	138
Margaret River, Austl.	F2	74
Margaretville, N.Y., U.S.	B11	114
Margarita, Isla de, i., Ven.	B9	86
Margate, S. Afr.	G10	70
Margate, Eng., U.K.	J14	12
Margate, Fl., U.S.	J5	116
Margecany, Slov.	H16	16
Margelan see Margilan, Uzb.	F12	32
Margherita di Savoia, Italy	C10	24
Margherita Peak, mtn., Afr.	D5	66
Margilan, Uzb.	F12	32
Margonin, Pol.	D13	16
Margosatubig, Phil.	G4	52
Māgow, Dasht-e, des., Afg.	C9	56
Marha, Russia	D13	34
Marha, stm., Russia	C12	34
Maria, Îles, is., Fr. Poly.	F11	72
María Cleofas, Isla, i., Mex.	E5	100
María Elena, Chile	D3	90
María Grande, Arg.	E8	92
María Ignacia, Arg.	H8	92
Maria Island, i., Austl.	B7	74
Maria Island National Park, p.o.i., Austl.	o14	77a
Mariakani, Kenya	E7	66
María Madre, Isla, i., Mex.	E5	100
María Magdalena, Isla, i., Mex.	E5	100
Mariana, Braz.	K4	88
Mariana Islands, is., Oc.	B5	72
Mariana Ridge, unds.	H17	142
Mariana Trench, unds.	H17	142
Marian Lake, l., N.T., Can.	C7	106
Marianna, Ar., U.S.	C8	122
Marianna, Fl., U.S.	G13	122
Mariano I. Loza, Arg.	D8	92
Mariánské Lázně, Czech Rep.	G8	16
Marias, stm., Mt., U.S.	B16	136
Marias Pass, p., Mt., U.S.	B13	136
María Teresa, Arg.	G6	92
Mariato, Punta, c., Pan.	I7	102
Maribo, Den.	B7	16
Maribor, Slvn.	D12	22
Maricao, P.R.	B2	104a
Marico, stm., Afr.	D8	70
Maricopa, Az., U.S.	J4	132
Maricunga, Salar de, pl., Chile	C3	92
Marié, stm., Braz.	H8	86
Marie Byrd Land, reg., Ant.	C29	81
Marie-Galante, i., Guad.	i6	105c
Mariehamn see Maarianhamina, Fin.	F9	8
Mariental, Nmb.	D4	70
Marienville, Pa., U.S.	C6	114
Mariestad, Swe.	G5	8
Marieta, stm., Ven.	E8	86
Marietta, Ga., U.S.	D14	122
Marietta, Mn., U.S.	G2	118
Marietta, Oh., U.S.	E4	114
Marieville, Qc., Can.	E3	110
Marignane, Fr.	F11	18
Marigot, Dom.	i6	105c
Marigot, Guad.	A1	105a
Mariinsk, Russia	C15	32
Mariinskoe, Russia	F17	34
Marijampolė, Lith.	F6	10
Marij El, state, Russia	C7	32
Marília, Braz.	D7	90
Marimba, Ang.	B2	68
Marín, Mex.	I7	130
Marín, Spain	B2	20
Marina di Ravenna, Italy	F9	22
Marina Fall, wtfl, Guy.	E12	86
Mar''ina Horka, Bela.	G11	10
Marinduque, i., Phil.	D3	52
Marine City, Mi., U.S.	B3	114
Marinette, Wi., U.S.	C2	112
Maringá, Braz.	D6	90
Marino, Vanuatu	j16	79d
Marintu, Indon.	C6	50
Marion, Al., U.S.	E11	122
Marion, Ar., U.S.	B8	122
Marion, Il., U.S.	G9	120
Marion, In., U.S.	H4	112
Marion, Ia., U.S.	B6	120
Marion, Ks., U.S.	C12	128
Marion, Ky., U.S.	G9	120
Marion, La., U.S.	E6	122
Marion, Ms., U.S.	E10	122
Marion, N.C., U.S.	I4	114
Marion, N.D., U.S.	A14	126
Marion, Oh., U.S.	D2	114
Marion, S.C., U.S.	B6	116
Marion, Va., U.S.	H4	114
Marion, Lake, res., S.C., U.S.	C5	116
Marion Bay, b., Austl.	o13	77a
Marion County Lake, res., Ks., U.S.	C11	128
Marion Downs, Austl.	D2	76
Marion Junction, Al., U.S.	E11	122
Marion Reef, rf., Austl.	B9	76
Marionville, Mo., U.S.	G4	120
Maripa, Ven.	D9	86
Mariposa, Ca., U.S.	F5	134
Mariquita, Col.	E4	86
Mariscal Estigarribia, Para.	D4	90
Maritime Alps, mts., Eur.	E12	18
Maritsa (Évros) (Marica) (Meriç), stm., Eur.	C9	28
Mariupol', Ukr.	E5	32
Mariusa, Caño, stm., Ven.	C11	86
Mariveles, Phil.	C3	52
Mariyampole see Marijampolė, Lith.	F6	10
Marjanovka, Russia	D12	32
Marka, Som.	D8	66
Markakol', ozero, l., Kaz.	E15	32
Mārkāpur, India	D4	53
Markaryd, Swe.	H5	8
Markdale, On., Can.	D9	112
Marked Tree, Ar., U.S.	B8	122
Markesan, Wi., U.S.	H10	118
Market Harborough, Eng., U.K.	I12	12
Markham, On., Can.	E10	112
Markham, Tx., U.S.	F11	130
Markham Bay, b., Nu., Can.	C16	106
Markit, China	B12	56
Markle, In., U.S.	H4	112
Markleeville, Ca., U.S.	E6	134
Markovo, Russia	D23	34
Marks, Russia	D7	32
Marks, Ms., U.S.	C8	122
Marktheidenfeld, Ger.	G5	16
Marktoberdorf, Ger.	I6	16
Marktredwitz, Ger.	G8	16
Mark Twain Lake, res., Mo., U.S.	E6	120
Marlboro, Ab., Can.	C14	138
Marlboro, N.Y., U.S.	C11	114
Marlborough, Austl.	D7	76
Marlborough, Guy.	B6	84
Marlborough, Ma., U.S.	B14	114
Marlette, Mi., U.S.	E6	112
Marlinton, W.V., U.S.	F5	114
Marlow, Ok., U.S.	G11	128
Marmaduke, Ar., U.S.	H7	120
Marmande, Fr.	E6	18
Marmara, Sea of see Marmara Denizi, Tur.	C11	28
Marmara Adası, i., Tur.	C10	28
Marmara Denizi (Marmara, Sea of), Tur.	C11	28
Marmara Ereğlisi, Tur.	C10	28
Marmara Gölü, l., Tur.	E10	28
Marmaris, Tur.	G11	28
Marmaton, stm., U.S.	G3	120
Marmelos, stm., Braz.	E5	84
Marmet, W.V., U.S.	F4	114
Marmion Lake, l., On., Can.	C7	118
Marmolada, mtn., Italy	D8	22
Marmora, On., Can.	D12	112
Marnay, Fr.	G14	14
Marne, Ger.	C4	16
Marne, Mi., U.S.	E4	112
Marne, state, Fr.	E13	14
Marne, stm., Fr.	E11	14
Marne à la Saône, Canal de la, can., Fr.	F14	14
Maroa, Ven.	F8	86
Maroantsetra, Madag.	D8	68
Maromandia, Madag.	C8	68
Maromme, Fr.	E10	14
Maromokotro, mtn., Madag.	C8	68
Marondera, Zimb.	D5	68
Maroni (Marowijne), stm., S.A.	C7	84
Maros, Indon.	F11	50
Maros (Mureș), stm., Eur.	C7	26
Maroua, Cam.	B2	66
Marovoay, Madag.	D8	68
Marowijne (Maroni), stm., S.A.	C7	84
Marquand, Mo., U.S.	G7	120
Marquard, S. Afr.	F8	70
Marquesas Islands see Marquises, Îles, is., Fr. Poly.	D12	72
Marquesas Keys, is., Fl., U.S.	L3	116
Marquette, Ks., U.S.	C11	128
Marquette, Mi., U.S.	B2	112
Marquis, Gren.	q10	105e
Marquises, Îles, is., Fr. Poly.	D12	72
Marradi, Italy	F8	22
Marrah, Jabal, hill, Sudan	E4	62
Marrakech, Mor.	C3	64
Marrakesh see Marrakech, Mor.	C3	64
Marrawah, Austl.	n12	77a
Marree, Austl.	E7	74
Marrero, La., U.S.	H8	122
Marromeu, Moz.	D6	68
Marrupa, Moz.	C6	68
Marsá al-Burayqah, Libya	A3	62
Marsabit, Kenya	D7	66
Marsala, Italy	G6	24
Marsciano, Italy	H9	22
Marseille, Fr.	F11	18
Marseilles, Il., U.S.	C9	120
Marsfjället, mtn., Swe.	D6	8
Marshall, Lib.	H2	64
Marshall, Ak., U.S.	D7	140
Marshall, Ar., U.S.	I5	120
Marshall, Mi., U.S.	B1	114
Marshall, Mn., U.S.	G3	118
Marshall, Mo., U.S.	E4	120
Marshall, N.C., U.S.	I3	114
Marshall, Tx., U.S.	E4	122
Marshall, Va., U.S.	F8	114
Marshall, stm., Austl.	D7	74
Marshallberg, N.C., U.S.	B9	116
Marshall Islands, ctry., Oc.	H19	142
Marshall Islands, is., Marsh. Is.	B7	72
Marshalltown, Ia., U.S.	B5	120
Marshfield, Mo., U.S.	G4	120
Marshfield, Wi., U.S.	G8	118
Mars Hill, Me., U.S.	D9	110
Mars Hill, N.C., U.S.	I3	114
Marsh Island, i., La., U.S.	H7	122
Marshville, N.C., U.S.	A5	116
Marsing, Id., U.S.	G10	136
Märsta, Swe.	G7	8
Marstal, Den.	B6	16
Martaban, Gulf of, b., Mya.	D3	48
Martapura, Indon.	E9	50
Martapura, Indon.	F4	50
Marte R. Gómez, Presa, res., Mex.	H9	130
Marthaguy Creek, stm., Austl.	H6	76
Martha's Vineyard, i., Ma., U.S.	C15	114
Martí, Cuba	B9	102
Martigny, Switz.	D4	22
Martigues, Fr.	F11	18
Martin, Slov.	G14	16
Martin, Ky., U.S.	G3	114
Martin, Mi., U.S.	F4	112
Martin, N.D., U.S.	G13	124
Martin, Tn., U.S.	H9	120
Martín, stm., Spain	C10	20
Martina Franca, Italy	D11	24
Martindale, Tx., U.S.	E10	130
Mărtinești, Rom.	D14	26
Martinez, Ca., U.S.	E3	134
Martinez, Ga., U.S.	C3	116
Martínez de la Torre, Mex.	E10	100
Martinho Campos, Braz.	J3	88
Martinique, dep., N.A.	i15	96a
Martinique Passage, strt., N.A.	k6	105c
Martin Lake, res., Al., U.S.	E12	122
Martinópole, Braz.	B5	88
Martinsberg, Aus.	B12	22
Martinsburg, W.V., U.S.	E7	114
Martins Ferry, Oh., U.S.	D5	114
Martinsville, Il., U.S.	E10	120
Martinsville, In., U.S.	E11	120
Martinsville, Va., U.S.	H5	114
Martin Vaz, Ilhas, is., Braz.	H12	82
Martos, Spain	G7	20
Martre, Lac la, l., N.T., Can.	C7	106
Martti, Fin.	C13	8
Marudi, Malay.	A9	50
Marudu, Telukan, b., Malay.	G1	52
Marugame, Japan	E6	40
Maruim, Braz.	F7	88
Maruoka, Japan	C9	40
Marutea, at., Fr. Poly.	E12	72
Marv Dasht, Iran	D7	56
Marvine, Mount, mtn., Ut., U.S.	E5	132
Mārwār, India	F4	54
Mary, Turkmen.	B9	56
Mary, stm., Austl.	E9	76
Maryborough, Austl.	E9	76
Maryborough, Austl.	K4	76
Marydale, S. Afr.	F5	70
Maryfield, Sk., Can.	E12	124
Mary Kathleen, Austl.	C2	76
Maryland, state, U.S.	E8	114
Maryneal, Tx., U.S.	B7	130
Maryport, Eng., U.K.	G9	12
Marysvale, Ut., U.S.	E4	132
Marysville, N.B., Can.	D10	110
Marysville, Ca., U.S.	D4	134
Marysville, Ks., U.S.	L2	118
Marysville, Mi., U.S.	B3	114
Marysville, Oh., U.S.	D2	114
Marysville, Wa., U.S.	B4	136
Maryville, Mo., U.S.	D3	120
Maryville, Tn., U.S.	I2	114
Marzagão, Braz.	I1	88
Marzo, Punta, c., Col.	D3	86
Masada see Meẓada, Ḥorvot, hist., Isr.	G6	58
Masai Mara Game Reserve, Kenya	E7	66
Masai Steppe, plat., Tan.	E7	66
Masaka, Ug.	E6	66
Masalembu Besar, Pulau, i., Indon.	F9	50
Masamba, Indon.	E12	50
Masan, Kor., S.	D1	40
Masasi, Tan.	G7	66
Masatepe, Nic.	G4	102
Masaya, Nic.	G4	102
Masbate, Phil.	D4	52
Masbate, i., Phil.	E4	52
Mascarene Basin, unds.	K8	142
Mascarene Islands, is., Afr.	i10	69a
Mascarene Plateau, unds.	J8	142
Mascot, Tn., U.S.	H2	114
Mascota, Mex.	E6	100
Mascoutah, Il., U.S.	F8	120
Maseru, Leso.	F8	70
Mashan, China	J3	42
Mashava, Zimb.	D5	68
Mashhad, Iran	B8	56
Mashi, China	G6	42
Mashiko, Japan	C13	40
Mashra'ar Raqq, Sudan	F5	62
Masi-Manimba, D.R.C.	E3	66
Masindi, Ug.	D6	66
Masira, Gulf of see Maṣīrah, Khalīj, b., Oman	F8	56
Maṣīrah, i., Oman	E8	56
Maṣīrah, Khalīj, b., Oman	F8	56
Masisea, Peru	E3	84
Masjed-e Soleymān, Iran	C6	56
Mask, Lough, l., Ire.	H3	12
Maskanah, Syria	B8	58
Masljanino, Russia	D14	32
Mason, Mi., U.S.	F5	112
Mason, Oh., U.S.	E1	114
Mason, Tx., U.S.	D8	130
Mason, W.V., U.S.	E3	114
Mason City, Il., U.S.	D8	120
Mason City, Ia., U.S.	A4	120
Mason City, Ne., U.S.	F13	126
Masqaṭ (Muscat), Oman	E8	56
Massa, Italy	F7	22
Massachusetts, state, U.S.	B14	114
Massachusetts Bay, b., Ma., U.S.	B15	114
Massafra, Italy	D11	24
Massaguet, Chad	E3	62
Massa Marittima, Italy	G7	22
Massangena, Moz.	B11	70
Massawa (Mitsiwa), Erit.	D7	62
Massena, Ia., U.S.	C3	120
Massena, N.Y., U.S.	F2	110
Massenya, Chad	E3	62
Massey, On., Can.	B7	112
Massey Sound, strt., Nu., Can.	B7	141
Massiac, Fr.	D9	18
Massillon, Oh., U.S.	D4	114

Name — Map Ref. — Page

Massina, reg., Mali G4 64
Massinga, Moz. C12 70
Massingir, Moz. C11 70
Massive, Mount, mtn., Co., U.S. D10 132
Masson Island, i., Ant. B14 81
Mastābah, Sau. Ar. E4 56
Masterson, Tx., U.S. F6 128
Masterton, N.Z. E6 80
Mastic Point, Bah. K8 116
Mastung, Pak. D10 56
Masty, Bela. G7 10
Masuda, Japan E4 40
Masurai, Gunung, mtn., Indon. E2 50
Masuria see Mazury, reg., Pol. C16 16
Masvingo, Zimb. E5 68
Masvingo, state, Zimb. B10 70
Maṣyāf, Syria C7 58
Mata Amarilla, Arg. I2 90
Matabeleland North, state, Zimb. A9 70
Matabeleland South, state, Zimb. B9 70
Matabuena, Spain C7 20
Matacuni, stm., Ven. F9 86
Mata de São João, Braz. G6 88
Matadi, D.R.C. F2 66
Matagalpa, Nic. F5 102
Matagami, Qc., Can. F15 106
Matagorda, Tx., U.S. F12 130
Matagorda Island, i., Tx., U.S. F11 130
Matagorda Peninsula, pen., Tx., U.S. F11 130
Matahiae, Pointe, c., Fr. Poly. w22 78h
Matâi, Egypt J1 58
Mataiea, Fr. Poly. w22 78h
Mataiva, at., Fr. Poly. E12 72
Matak, Pulau, i., Indon. B5 50
Matakana, Austl. I5 76
Matale, Sri L. H5 53
Matam, Sen. F2 64
Matamoros, Mex. C10 100
Matamoros, Mex. C7 100
Matan, Indon. D7 50
Matandu, stm., Tan. F7 66
Matane, Qc., Can. B9 110
Matanni, Pak. B3 54
Matanzas, Cuba A7 102
Matanzas, Mex. E8 100
Maṭapan, Cape see Taínaro, Ákra, c., Grc. G5 28
Matape, stm., Mex. A3 100
Matapédia, Qc., Can. C9 110
Matapédia, Lac, l., Qc., Can. B9 110
Mataquito, stm., Chile G2 92
Matara, Sri L. I5 53
Mataram, Indon. H9 50
Mataranka, Austl. B6 74
Mataró, Spain C13 20
Matasiri, Pulau, i., Indon. F9 50
Matatiele, S. Afr. G9 70
Matatula, Cape, c., Am. Sam. h12 79c
Matā'utu, Wal./F. E9 72
Matavera, Cook Is. a27 78j
Mataveri, Chile e29 78l
Mataveri, Aeropuerto, Chile f29 78l
Mataveri Airstrip see Mataveri, Aeropuerto, Chile f29 78l
Matehuala, Mex. D8 100
Mateke Hills, hills, Zimb. B10 70
Matera, Italy D10 24
Mateur, Tun. G3 24
Matha, Fr. D5 18
Mather, Mb., Can. E14 124
Mather, Pa., U.S. E5 114
Matheson, On., Can. F14 106
Mathews, Va., U.S. G9 114
Mathis, Tx., U.S. F10 130
Mathura (Muttra), India E6 54
Matias Barbosa, Braz. K4 88
Matías Romero, Mex. G11 100
Matícora, stm., Ven. B6 86
Matinha, Braz. B3 88
Matipó, Braz. K4 88
Matiyure, stm., Ven. D7 86
Mātli, Pak. F2 54
Mato, Cerro, mtn., Ven. D9 86
Mato Grosso, state, Braz. F6 84
Mato Grosso, Planalto do, plat., Braz. B5 90
Mato Grosso, Plateau of see Mato Grosso, Planalto do, plat., Braz. B5 90
Mato Grosso do Sul, state, Braz. C6 90
Matola Rio, Moz. D11 70
Matopos, Zimb. B9 70
Matosinhos, Port. C2 20
Matouying, China B8 42
Matozinhos, Braz. J3 88
Maṭraḥ, Oman E8 56
Matsudo, Japan D12 40
Matsue, Japan D6 40
Matsumoto, Japan C10 40
Matsusaka, Japan E9 40
Matsu Tao, i., Tai. H8 42
Matsutō, Japan C9 40
Matsuura, Japan F2 40
Matsuyama, Japan F5 40
Mattagami, stm., On., Can. F14 106
Mattamuskeet, Lake, l., N.C., U.S. A9 116
Mattaponi, stm., Va., U.S. G8 114
Mattawa, On., Can. B11 112
Mattawa, Wa., U.S. D7 136
Mattawamkeag, stm., Me., U.S. E8 110
Matterhorn, mtn., Eur. D13 18
Matterhorn, mtn., Nv., U.S. B1 132
Matthews Mountain, hill, Mo., U.S. G7 120
Matthew Town, Bah. C10 96
Mattighofen, Aus. B10 22
Mattoon, Il., U.S. E9 120
Mattoon, Wi., U.S. F9 118
Mattydale, N.Y., U.S. E13 112
Matua, Indon. E7 50
Matudo see Matsudo, Japan D12 40
Matue see Matsue, Japan D6 40
Matuku, i., Fiji q19 79e
Matumoto see Matsumoto, Japan C10 40
Maturín, Ven. C10 86
Matutina, Braz. J2 88
Matuzaka see Matsusaka, Japan E9 40
Maú (Ireng), stm., S.A. F12 86
Maúa, Moz. C6 68
Mau Aimma, India F8 54
Maubeuge, Fr. D12 14
Maud, Tx., U.S. D4 122
Maudaha, India F7 54
Maude, Austl. J5 76
Maués, Braz. D6 84
Maués, stm., Braz. D6 84
Mauganj, India F8 54
Maui, i., Hi., U.S. C5 78a
Mauk, Indon. F5 50
Mauldin, S.C., U.S. B3 116
Maule, state, Chile G2 92
Maule, stm., Chile G1 92
Maule, Laguna del, l., Chile G2 92
Mauléon-Licharre, Fr. F5 18
Maumee, Oh., U.S. G6 112
Maumee, stm., U.S. G6 112
Maumelle, Lake, res., Ar., U.S. C6 122
Maumere, Indon. G7 44
Maun, Bots. D3 68
Maunabo, P.R. B4 104a
Mauna Kea, vol., Hi., U.S. D6 78a
Maunaloa, Hi., U.S. B4 78a
Mauna Loa, vol., Hi., U.S. D6 78a
Maunath Bhanjan, India F9 54
Maungdaw, Mya. H14 54
Maungmagan, Mya. E3 48
Maunoir, Lac, l., N.T., Can. B6 106
Maupihaa, at., Fr. Poly. E11 72
Mau Rānīpur, India F7 54
Maurepas, Lake, l., La., U.S. G8 122
Maurice, Lake, l., Austl. E6 74
Mauricie, Parc national de la, p.o.i., Qc., Can. D3 110
Mauritania, ctry., Afr. F2 64
Mauritanie see Mauritania, ctry., Afr. F2 64
Mauritius, ctry., Afr. h10 69a
Mauron, Fr. F6 14
Mauston, Wi., U.S. H8 118
Mautau, c., Fr. Poly. r19 78g
Mauterndorf, Aus. C10 22
Mauthen, Aus. D9 22
Mauvais Coulee, stm., N.D., U.S. F14 124
Mava, Pap. N. Gui. b3 79a
Maverick, Az., U.S. J7 132
Mavinga, Ang. D3 68
Mavrovo Nacionalni Park, p.o.i., Mac. B3 28
Mavuradonha Mountains, mts., Zimb. D5 68
Mawchi, Mya. C3 48
Mawlaik, Mya. D7 46
Mawlamyine (Moulmein), Mya. D3 48
Mawson, sci., Ant. B11 81
Maw Taung (Luang, Khao), mtn., Asia G4 48
Max, N.D., U.S. G12 124
Maxaranguape, Braz. C8 88
Maxcanú, Mex. B3 102
Maxixe, Moz. C12 70
Maxville, On., Can. E2 110
Maxwell, Ca., U.S. D3 134
Maxwell, Ne., U.S. F12 126
Maxwell, N.M., U.S. E4 128
May, Tx., U.S. B9 130
May, Cape, pen., N.J., U.S. F11 114
May, Mount, mtn., Ab., Can. B11 138
Maya, Pulau, i., Indon. D6 50
Mayaguana, i., Bah. A11 102
Mayaguana Passage, strt., Bah. A11 102
Mayagüez, P.R. B1 104a
Mayang, China H3 42
Mayarí, Cuba B10 102
Maybole, Scot., U.K. F8 12
Maydena, Austl. o13 77a
Maydh, Som. B9 66
Mayen, Ger. F3 16
Mayenne, Fr. F8 14
Mayenne, state, Fr. F8 14
Mayenne, stm., Fr. F8 14
Mayer, Az., U.S. I4 132
Mayerthorpe, Ab., Can. C15 138
Mayfield, Ky., U.S. H9 120
Mayfield, Ut., U.S. D5 132
Mayflower, Ar., U.S. C6 122
Māyir, Syria B8 58
Maykain see Majkain, Kaz. D13 32
Maymyo, Mya. A3 48
Maynard, Ia., U.S. B6 120
Maynardville, Tn., U.S. H2 114
Mayne, stm., Austl. D3 76
Mayo, Yk., Can. C3 106
Mayo, Fl., U.S. F2 116
Mayo, state, Ire. H3 12
Mayo, stm., Arg. I3 90
Mayo, stm., Mex. B4 100
Mayon Volcano, vol., Phil. D4 52
Mayor Buratovich, Arg. G4 90
Mayotte, dep., Afr. C8 68
Mayoyoque, Col. G4 86
May Pen, Jam. j13 104d
Mayreau, i., St. Vin. p11 105e
Mays Landing, N.J., U.S. E11 114
Maysville, Ky., U.S. F2 114
Maysville, Mo., U.S. E3 120
Maysville, N.C., U.S. B8 116
Maysville, Ok., U.S. G11 128
Mayumba, Gabon E2 66
Māyūram, India F4 53
Mayville, Mi., U.S. E6 112
Mayville, N.Y., U.S. B6 114
Mayville, N.D., U.S. G16 124
Maywood, Ne., U.S. G12 126
Maza, Arg. H6 92
Mazabuka, Zam. D4 68
Mazagão, Braz. D7 84
Mazamet, Fr. F8 18
Mazán, stm., Peru I4 86
Mazara, Val di, reg., Italy G7 24
Mazara del Vallo, Italy G6 24
Mazār-e Sharīf, Afg. B10 56
Mazarrón, Golfo de, b., Spain G9 20
Mazaruni, stm., Guy. D11 86
Mazatenango, Guat. E2 102
Mazatlán, Mex. D5 100
Mažeikiai, Lith. D5 10
Mazenod, Sk., Can. E7 124
Mazinga, mtn., Neth. Ant. C2 105a
Mazirbe, Lat. C5 10
Mazon, Il., U.S. C9 120
Mazowe, stm., Afr. D5 68
Mazury (Masuria), reg., Pol. C16 16
Mazyr, Bela. D3 32
Mbabane, Swaz. E10 70
M'bahiakro, C. Iv. H4 64
Mbaïki, C.A.R. D3 66
Mbaké, Sen. G1 64
Mbala, Zam. B5 68
Mbalabala, Zimb. B9 70
Mbale, Ug. D6 66
Mbalmayo, Cam. D2 66
Mbamba Bay, Tan. G7 66
Mbandaka (Coquilhatville), D.R.C. D3 66
Mbanga, Cam. D1 66
Mbanika Island, i., Sol. Is. e8 79b
M'banza Congo, Ang. B1 68
Mbanza-Ngungu, D.R.C. F3 66
Mbarara, Ug. E6 66
Mbashe, stm., S. Afr. H9 70
Mbava Island, i., Sol. Is. d7 79b
Mbé, Cam. C2 66
Mberengwa, Zimb. B9 70
Mbeya, Tan. F6 66
Mbigou, Gabon E2 66
Mbinda, Congo E2 66
Mbini, Eq. Gui. I6 64
Mbini, stm., Afr. I6 64
Mboi, D.R.C. F4 66
Mboki, C.A.R. C5 66
Mbola, Sol. Is. e9 79b
Mborokua, i., Sol. Is. e8 79b
Mborong, Indon. H12 50
Mbouda, Cam. C2 66
Mbour, Sen. G1 64
Mbout, Maur. F2 64
Mbuji-Mayi (Bakwanga), D.R.C. F4 66
Mbuluzi, stm., Swaz. E10 70
Mbwemkuru, stm., Tan. F7 66
McAdam, N.B., Can. E9 110
McAdoo, Pa., U.S. D9 114
McAlester, Ok., U.S. C3 122
McAllen, Tx., U.S. H9 130
McArthur, Oh., U.S. E3 114
McArthur, stm., Austl. C7 74
McArthur River, Austl. C7 74
McBain, Mi., U.S. D4 112
McBee, S.C., U.S. B5 116
McBeth Fjord, b., Nu., Can. B17 106
McBride, B.C., Can. C10 138
McCall Creek, Ms., U.S. F8 122
McCamey, Tx., U.S. C5 130
McCammon, Id., U.S. H14 136
McCauley Island, i., B.C., Can. E4 106
McCleary, Wa., U.S. C3 136
McClellan Creek, stm., Tx., U.S. F8 128
McClellanville, S.C., U.S. C6 116
McClintock, Mount, mtn., Ant. D21 81
McCloud, Ca., U.S. B3 134
McCloud, stm., Ca., U.S. B3 134
McClure, Il., U.S. G8 120
Mcclusky, N.D., U.S. G13 124
McColl, S.C., U.S. B6 116
McComb, Ms., U.S. F8 122
McConaughy, Lake, res., Ne., U.S. F11 126
McConnellsburg, Pa., U.S. E7 114
McConnelsville, Oh., U.S. E4 114
McCook, Ne., U.S. A8 128
McCormick, S.C., U.S. C3 116
McCreary, Mb., Can. D14 124
McCullough Mountain, mtn., Nv., U.S. H1 132
McCune, Ks., U.S. G2 120
McCurtain, Ok., U.S. B4 122
McDade, Tx., U.S. D10 130
McDermitt, Nv., U.S. B8 134
McDermott, Oh., U.S. F2 114
McDonald, Ks., U.S. B7 128
McDonald, Lake, l., Mt., U.S. B12 136
McDowell Peak, mtn., Az., U.S. J4 132
Mcensk, Russia G19 10
McEwen, Tn., U.S. H10 120
McFadden, Wy., U.S. B10 132
McFarland, Ca., U.S. H6 134
McGehee, Ar., U.S. D7 122
McGill, Nv., U.S. D2 132
McGrath, Ak., U.S. D8 140
McGraw, N.Y., U.S. B9 114
McGregor, Tx., U.S. C10 130
McGregor, stm., B.C., Can. B9 138
McGregor Lake, l., Ab., Can. F18 138
McHenry, Il., U.S. B9 120
McHenry, Ms., U.S. G9 122
Mchinji, Mwi. C5 68
McIntosh, Al., U.S. F10 122
McIntosh, Mn., U.S. D3 118
McIntyre Bay, b., On., Can. B10 118
McKeand, stm., Nu., Can. C17 106
McKee, Ky., U.S. G2 114
McKeesport, Pa., U.S. D6 114
McKenzie, Tn., U.S. H9 120
McKenzie, stm., Or., U.S. F4 136
McKenzie Bridge, Or., U.S. F4 136
McKenzie Island, On., Can. E12 106
McKinlay, Austl. C3 76
McKinlay, stm., Austl. C3 76
McKinley, Mount, mtn., Ak., U.S. D9 140
McKinleyville, Ca., U.S. C1 134
McKinney, Tx., U.S. D2 122
McKittrick Summit, mtn., Ca., U.S. H6 134
McLain, Ms., U.S. F10 122
McLaurin, Ms., U.S. F9 122
McLean, Il., U.S. D8 120
McLean, Tx., U.S. F8 128
McLeansboro, Il., U.S. F9 120
McLennan, Ab., Can. D7 106
McLeod, stm., Ab., Can. C15 138
McLeod Bay, b., N.T., Can. C8 106
McLeod Lake, B.C., Can. B7 138
M'Clintock Channel, strt., Nu., Can. A10 106
McLoughlin, Mount, mtn., Or., U.S. A3 134
McLouth, Ks., U.S. E2 120
M'Clure Strait, strt., N.T., Can. B16 140
McMahon, Sk., Can. D6 124
McMinnville, Or., U.S. E3 136
McMinnville, Tn., U.S. B13 122
McMurdo, sci., Ant. C22 81
McMurdo Sound, strt., Ant. C22 81
McNary, Az., U.S. I7 132
McNeil, Ar., U.S. D5 122
McPherson, Ks., U.S. C11 128
McQueeney, Tx., U.S. E9 130
McRae, Ar., U.S. B7 122
McRae, Ga., U.S. D3 116
McVeigh, Ky., U.S. G3 114
McVille, N.D., U.S. G15 124
McWilliams, Al., U.S. F11 122
Mdantsane, S. Afr. H8 70
M'drak, Viet. F9 48
Mead, Ne., U.S. C1 120
Mead, Lake, res., U.S. G2 132
Meade, Ks., U.S. D8 128
Meaden Peak, mtn., Co., U.S. C9 132
Meadow, Ut., U.S. E4 132
Meadow Lake, Sk., Can. E9 106
Meadow Valley Wash, stm., Nv., U.S. F2 132
Meadowview, Va., U.S. H3 114
Meadville, Ms., U.S. F7 122
Meadville, Mo., U.S. E4 120
Meadville, Pa., U.S. C5 114
Meaford, On., Can. D9 112
Mealhada, Port. D2 20
Meandarra, Austl. F7 76
Meander River, Ab., Can. D7 106
Mearim, stm., Braz. B3 88
Meath, state, Ire. H6 12
Meath, hist. reg., Ire. H6 12
Meaux, Fr. F11 14
Mecaya, stm., Col. G4 86
Mecca see Makkah, Sau. Ar. E4 56
Mechanicsburg, Oh., U.S. D2 114
Mechanicsville, Ia., U.S. C6 120
Mechanicsville, Va., U.S. G8 114
Mechanicville, N.Y., U.S. B12 114
Mechelen (Malines), Bel. C13 14
Mecklenburg, hist. reg., Ger. C7 16
Mecklenburger Bucht, b., Ger. B7 16
Mecklenburg-Vorpommern, state, Ger. C8 16
Mecubúri, Moz. C6 68
Mecula, Moz. C6 68
Meda, Port. D3 20
Medak, India B4 53
Medan, Indon. B1 50
Medanosa, Punta, c., Arg. I3 90
Mede, Italy E5 22
Medeiros Neto, Braz. I5 88
Medellín, Col. D4 86
Médenine, Tun. C6 64
Mederdra, Maur. F1 64
Medford, Ok., U.S. E11 128
Medford, Or., U.S. A2 134
Medford, Wi., U.S. F8 118
Medgidia, Rom. E15 26
Mediapolis, Ia., U.S. C6 120
Mediaș, Rom. C11 26
Medicine Bow, Wy., U.S. B10 132
Medicine Bow, stm., Wy., U.S. A10 132
Medicine Bow Mountains, mts., U.S. F6 126
Medicine Creek, stm., Mo., U.S. E4 120
Medicine Hat, Ab., Can. D3 124
Medicine Lake, Mt., U.S. F9 124
Medicine Lodge, Ks., U.S. D10 128
Medicine Lodge, stm., U.S. D10 128
Medina, Braz. I5 88
Medina see Al-Madīnah, Sau. Ar. E4 56
Medina, N.Y., U.S. E11 112
Medina, Oh., U.S. C4 114
Medina, Tx., U.S. E8 130
Medina, stm., Tx., U.S. E9 130
Medinaceli, Spain C8 20
Medina del Campo, Spain C6 20
Medina-Sidonia, Spain H5 20
Medinīpur, India G11 54
Medio, Punta, c., Chile C2 92
Medio Creek, stm., Tx., U.S. F10 130
Mediterranean Sea A4 62
Medje, D.R.C. D5 66
Medjez el Bab, Tun. H3 24
Medkovec, Blg. F10 26
Mednogorsk, Russia D9 32
Médoc, reg., Fr. D4 18
Medora, N.D., U.S. H10 124
Médouneu, Gabon D2 66
Meductic, N.B., Can. E9 110
Medveđa, Yugo. G8 26
Medvedica, stm., Russia C19 10
Medvedica, stm., Russia D6 32
Medvėgalis, hill, Lith. E5 10
Medvežegorsk, Russia E15 8
Medvežji ostrova, is., Russia B21 34
Medyn', Russia F18 10
Meekatharra, Austl. E3 74
Meeker, Co., U.S. C8 132
Meeks Bay, Ca., U.S. D5 134
Meeladeen, Som. B9 66
Meerane, Ger. F8 16
Meersburg, Ger. I5 16
Meerut, India D6 54
Mēga, Eth. G7 62
Mega, Pulau, i., Indon. E2 50
Megalópoli, Grc. F4 28
Mégantic, Lac, l., Qc., Can. E5 110
Mégara, Grc. E6 28
Megargel, Tx., U.S. H9 128
Meghālaya, state, India F13 54
Meghna, stm., Bngl. G13 54
Megísti, i., Grc. G12 28
Megra, Russia C19 8
Mehakit, Indon. E9 50
Meharry, Mount, mtn., Austl. D3 74
Mehedinți, state, Rom. E10 26
Mehekar, India H6 54
Meherrin, stm., U.S. H7 114
Mehidpur, India G5 54
Mehikoorma, Est. B10 10
Mehndāwal, India E9 54
Mehren'ga, Russia F19 8
Mehrenga, stm., Russia E19 8
Mehtarlām, Afg. C11 56
Mehun-sur-Yèvre, Fr. G11 14
Mei, stm., China I7 42
Mei, stm., China H7 42
Meia Meia, Tan. F7 66
Meia Ponte, stm., Braz. I1 88
Meichuan, China F6 42
Meiganga, Cam. C2 66
Meighen Island, i., Nu., Can. A5 141
Meigs, Ga., U.S. E1 116
Meihekou, China C6 38
Meihsien see Meizhou, China I7 42
Meikeng, China J6 42
Meiktila, Mya. B2 48
Meiners Oaks, Ca., U.S. I6 134
Meiningen, Ger. F6 16
Meishan, China E5 36
Meissen, Ger. E9 16
Meitan, China H2 42
Meizhou, China I7 42
Mejillones, Chile D2 90
Mejillones, Península, pen., Chile A2 92
Mejnypil'gyno, Russia D24 34
Mékambo, Gabon D2 66
Mek'elē, Eth. E7 62
Mékhé, Sen. F1 64
Mekhtar, Pak. C2 54
Mekka see Makkah, Sau. Ar. E4 56
Meknès, Mor. C3 64
Mekong (Mékôngk) (Khong) (Lancang), stm., Asia F9 46
Mekongga, Gunung, mtn., Indon. F7 44
Mékôngk see Mekong, stm., Asia F10 46
Melado, stm., Chile H2 92
Melaka, Malay. K6 48
Melaka, state, Malay. K6 48
Melanesia, is., Oc. D7 72
Melawi, stm., Indon. D8 50
Melbourne, Austl. K5 76
Melbourne, Ar., U.S. H6 120
Melbourne, Fl., U.S. H5 116
Melbourne, Ia., U.S. J5 118
Melbourne Island, i., Nu., Can. B10 106
Melcher, Ia., U.S. C4 120
Melchor, Isla, i., Chile I2 90
Melchor Múzquiz, Mex. B8 100
Meldorf, Ger. B4 16
Meldrum Bay, On., Can. C6 112
Meldrum Creek, B.C., Can. D8 138
Mélé, Baie, b., Vanuatu k17 79d
Melekeok, Palau g8 78b
Melenki, Russia I19 8
Meleuz, Russia D9 32
Mélèzes, stm., Qc., Can. D16 106
Melfi, Chad E3 62
Melfi, Italy C9 24
Melfort, Sk., Can. B9 124
Meliane, Oued, stm., Tun. H4 24
Meliau, Indon. D7 50
Meligalás, Grc. F4 28
Melilla, Sp. N. Afr. B4 64
Melimoyu, Cerro, vol., Chile H2 90
Melincué, Arg. F7 92
Melita, Mb., Can. E12 124
Melitopol', Ukr. E5 32
Melívoia, Grc. D5 28
Mellansel, Swe. E7 8
Mellen, Wi., U.S. E8 118
Mellerud, Swe. G5 8
Mellish Reef, at., Austl. C11 74
Mellit, Sudan E5 62
Mělník, Czech Rep. F10 16
Melo, Ur. F10 92
Melolo, Indon. H12 50
Melos see Mílos, i., Grc. G7 28
Melrhir, Chott, l., Alg. C6 64
Melrose, Austl. E4 74
Melrose, Austl. I6 76
Melrose, Mn., U.S. F4 118
Melrose, N.M., U.S. G5 128
Melrose, Wi., U.S. G8 118
Melsungen, Ger. E5 16
Meltaus, Fin. C11 8
Melton Mowbray, Eng., U.K. I12 12
Melun, Fr. F11 14
Melūr, India F4 53
Melvern, Ks., U.S. F2 120
Melvern Lake, res., Ks., U.S. F2 120
Melville, Sk., Can. D11 124
Melville, La., U.S. G7 122
Melville, Cape, c., Austl. B9 74
Melville Bugt, b., Grnld. B12 141
Melville Hall Airport, Dom. i6 105c
Melville Hills, hills, Can. B7 106
Melville Island, i., Austl. B6 74
Melville Island, i., Can. A17 140
Melville Peninsula, pen., Nu., Can. B14 106
Melvin, Ky., U.S. G3 114
Melvin, Tx., U.S. C8 130
Melyana, Alg. H13 20
Mélykút, Hung. C6 26
Mêmar Co, l., China A9 54
Memba, Moz. C7 68
Membalong, Indon. E5 50
Memboro, Indon. H11 50
Memel see Klaipėda, Lith. E3 10
Memel, S. Afr. E9 70
Mēmele (Nemunėlis), stm., Eur. D7 10
Memmingen, Ger. I5 16
Mempawah, Indon. C6 50
Memphis, Fl., U.S. I3 116
Memphis, Mi., U.S. B3 114
Memphis, Tn., U.S. B8 122
Memphis, Tx., U.S. G8 128
Memphrémagog, Lac (Memphremagog, Lake), l., N.A. E4 110
Memphremagog, Lake (Memphrémagog, Lac), l., N.A. E4 110
Memramcook, N.B., Can. D12 110
Mena, Ar., U.S. C4 122
Menado see Manado, Indon. E7 44
Ménaka, Mali F5 64
Menan, Id., U.S. G15 136
Menard, Tx., U.S. D8 130
Menasha, Wi., U.S. G10 118
Menate, Indon. D8 50
Mendawai, Indon. E8 50
Mendawai, stm., Indon. E8 50
Mende, Fr. E9 18
Mendebo, mts., Eth. F7 62
Mendenhall, Ms., U.S. F9 122
Mendī, Eth. F7 62
Mendi, Pap. N. Gui. b3 79a
Mendocino, Ca., U.S. D2 134
Mendocino, Cape, c., Ca., U.S. C1 134
Mendocino Fracture Zone, unds. E24 142
Mendon, Il., U.S. D6 120
Mendota, Ca., U.S. G5 134
Mendoza, Arg. F3 92
Mendoza, state, Arg. G3 92
Mendoza, stm., Arg. F3 92
Mene de Mauroa, Ven. B6 86
Mene Grande, Ven. C6 86
Menemen, Tur. E9 28
Menen, Bel. D12 14
Menfi, Italy G6 24
Mengban, China A5 48
Mengcheng, China E7 42
Mengellang, Palau f8 78b
Menggala, Indon. F4 50
Menggudai, China B2 42
Menghai, China B5 48
Mengjiawan, China B3 42
Mengla, China B5 48
Menglian, China A4 48
Mengxian, China D5 42
Mengyin, China D7 42
Mengzi, China A6 48
Menihek Lakes, l., Nf., Can. E17 106
Menin see Menen, Bel. D12 14
Menindee, Austl. I4 76
Menjuša, Russia B13 10
Menlo Park, Ca., U.S. F3 134
Menno, S.D., U.S. D15 126
Meno, Ok., U.S. E10 128
Menominee, Mi., U.S. C2 112
Menominee, stm., U.S. C2 112
Menomonee Falls, Wi., U.S. A9 120
Menomonie, Wi., U.S. G7 118
Menongue, Ang. C2 68
Menor, Mar, b., Spain G10 20
Menorca (Minorca), i., Spain D15 20
Mentasta Lake, Ak., U.S. D11 140
Mentawai, Kepulauan, is., Indon. E1 50
Mentawai, Selat, strt., Indon. D2 50
Menton, Fr. F13 18
Mentor, Oh., U.S. C4 114
Menyapa, Gunung, mtn., Indon. C9 50
Menzel Bourguiba, Tun. G3 24
Menzel Bou Zelfa, Tun. H4 24
Menzelinsk, Russia C8 32
Menzel Temime, Tun. H5 24
Menzies, Austl. E4 74
Menzies, Mount, mtn., Ant. C10 81
Meobbaai, b., Nmb. D2 70
Meoqui, Mex. A6 100
Meota, Sk., Can. A5 124
Meppel, Neth. B15 14
Meppen, Ger. D3 16
Meqerghane, Sebkha, pl., Alg. D5 64
Mequinenza, Embalse de, res., Spain C10 20
Mequon, Wi., U.S. E2 112
Merah, Indon. C10 50
Meramec, stm., Mo., U.S. F7 120
Meran see Merano, Italy D8 22
Merangin, stm., Indon. E3 50
Merano (Meran), Italy D8 22
Meratus, Pegunungan, mts., Indon. E9 50
Merauke, Indon. G11 44
Merbau, Indon. C3 50
Merbein, Austl. J4 76
Mercaderes, Col. G3 86
Mercāra, India E2 53
Merced, Ca., U.S. F5 134
Merced, stm., Ca., U.S. F5 134
Mercedario, Cerro, mtn., Arg. E2 92
Mercedes, Arg. D8 92
Mercedes, Arg. G8 92
Mercedes, Tx., U.S. H10 130
Mercedes, Ur. F8 92
Mercer, Mo., U.S. D4 120
Mercer, Pa., U.S. C5 114
Mercersburg, Pa., U.S. E7 114
Merchants Bay, b., Nu., Can. D13 141
Mercoal, Ab., Can. C13 138
Mercury, Nv., U.S. G10 134
Mercury Islands, is., N.Z. C6 80
Mercy, Cape, c., Nu., Can. E13 141
Mercy Bay, b., N.T., Can. B16 140
Meredith, Lake, res., Tx., U.S. F7 128
Meredosia, Il., U.S. E7 120
Mereeg, Som. D9 66
Méré Lava, i., Vanuatu j17 79d
Merevari, stm., Ven. E9 86
Merëža, Russia A19 10
Mergui, Mya. F4 48
Mergui Archipelago, is., Mya. G3 48
Meribah, Austl. J3 76
Mérida, Mex. B3 102
Mérida, Spain F4 20
Mérida, Ven. C6 86
Mérida, state, Ven. C6 86
Mérida, Cordillera de, mts., Ven. C6 86
Meridian, Ga., U.S. E4 116
Meridian, Ms., U.S. E10 122
Meridian, Tx., U.S. C10 130
Meridianville, Al., U.S. C12 122
Mérignac, Fr. E5 18
Merigold, Ms., U.S. D8 122
Merikarvia, Fin. F9 8
Merimbula, Austl. K7 76
Merín, Laguna (Mirim, Lagoa), b., S.A. F11 92
Merinda, Austl. B6 76
Merino, Co., U.S. G9 126
Merinos, Ur. F9 92
Merizo, Guam j9 78c
Merkinė, Lith. F7 10
Merkys, stm., Lith. F8 10
Merlin, On., Can. F7 112
Merlin, Or., U.S. H3 136
Merna, Ne., U.S. F13 126
Meron, Har (Meron, Mount), mtn., Isr. E6 58
Meron, Mount see Meron, Har, mtn., Isr. E6 58
Merouane, Chott, l., Alg. C6 64
Merredin, Austl. F3 74
Merrick, mtn., Scot., U.K. F8 12
Merrill, Ia., U.S. B1 120
Merrill, Mi., U.S. E5 112
Merrill, Or., U.S. A4 134
Merrillan, Wi., U.S. G8 118
Merrillville, In., U.S. G2 112
Merrimack, stm., U.S. H5 110
Merriman, Ne., U.S. E11 126
Merritt, B.C., Can. F10 138
Merritt Island, Fl., U.S. H5 116
Merriwa, Austl. I8 76
Mer Rouge, La., U.S. E7 122
Merrygoen, Austl. H7 76
Merryville, La., U.S. G5 122
Mersa Matruh, Egypt A5 62
Mersea Island, i., Eng., U.K. J13 12
Merseburg, Ger. E7 16
Mersey, stm., Austl. n13 77a
Mersey, stm., N.S., Can. F12 110
Mersing, Malay. K6 48
Mērsrags, Lat. C6 10
Merta, India E5 54
Merthyr Tydfil, Wales, U.K. J9 12
Mértola, Port. G3 20
Mertz Glacier Tongue, ice, Ant. B19 81
Méru, Fr. E11 14
Meru, Kenya D7 66
Meruoca, Braz. B5 88
Merweville, S. Afr. H5 70
Merzifon, Tur. A4 56
Merzig, Ger. G2 16
Mesa, Az., U.S. J5 132
Mesabi Range, hills, Mn., U.S. D6 118
Mesagne, Italy D11 24
Mesáras, Órmos, b., Grc. I7 28
Mesa Verde National Park, p.o.i., Co., U.S. F8 132
Mescalero, N.M., U.S. H3 128
Meščerino, Russia G20 10
Meschede, Ger. E4 16
Meščura, Russia E24 8
Mesewa see Massawa, Erit. D7 62
Mesgouez, Lac, l., Qc., Can. E16 106
Mesick, Mi., U.S. D4 112
Mesilla, N.M., U.S. K10 132
Meškuičiai, Lith. D6 10
Mesolóngi, Grc. E4 28
Mesopotamia, hist. reg., Asia C5 56
Mesquite, Tx., U.S. E2 122
Messalo, stm., Moz. C6 68
Messina, Italy F9 24
Messina, S. Afr. C9 70
Messina, Gulf of see Messiniakós Kólpos, b., Grc. G5 28
Messina, Stretto di, strt., Italy F9 24
Messíni, Grc. F4 28
Messíni, hist., Grc. F4 28
Messiniakós Kólpos, b., Grc. G5 28
Messix Peak, mtn., Ut., U.S. B4 132
Messkirch, Ger. H5 16
Messojaha, stm., Russia C4 34
Mesta (Néstos), stm., Eur. B6 28
Mestghanem, Alg. B4 64
Mestre, ngh., Italy E9 22
Mesuji, stm., Indon. E4 50
Meta, state, Col. F5 86
Meta, stm., S.A. D7 86
Métabetchouan, Qc., Can. B5 110
Métabetchouane, stm., Qc., Can. B4 110
Meta Incognita Peninsula, pen., Nu., Can. C17 106
Metairie, La., U.S. H8 122
Metaline Falls, Wa., U.S. B9 136
Metamora, Il., U.S. D8 120
Metán, Arg. B5 92
Metangula, Moz. C5 68
Metapán, El Sal. E3 102
Metaponto, hist., Italy D10 24
Metapontum see Metaponto, hist., Italy D10 24
Meteor Crater, crat., Az., U.S. H6 132
Metharaw, Mya. D4 48
Methow, Wa., U.S. B7 136
Methow, stm., Wa., U.S. B6 136
Methven, N.Z. F4 80
Metica, stm., Col. E5 86
Metiskow, Ab., Can. B3 124
Metlakatla, Ak., U.S. E13 140
Metlika, Slvn. E12 22
Meto, Bayou, stm., Ar., U.S. C7 122
Metropolis, Il., U.S. G9 120
Metropolitan, Mi., U.S. C2 112
Metter, Ga., U.S. D3 116
Mettuppālaiyam, India F3 53
Mettūr, India F3 53
Metz, Fr. E15 14
Metzingen, Ger. H5 16
Meu, stm., Fr. F7 14
Meulaboh, Indon. J2 48
Meureudu, Indon. J3 48
Meurthe, stm., Fr. F15 14
Meurthe-et-Moselle, state, Fr. F15 14
Meuse, state, Fr. E14 14
Meuse (Maas), stm., Eur. D14 14
Meuselwitz, Ger. E8 16
Mexiana, Ilha, i., Braz. C8 84
Mexicali, Mex. K10 134
Mexican Hat, Ut., U.S. F7 132
México see Ciudad de México, Mex. F9 100
Mexico, Me., U.S. F6 110
Mexico, Mo., U.S. E6 120
Mexico, N.Y., U.S. E13 112
México, state, Mex. F9 100
Mexico, ctry., N.A. C4 96
Mexico, Gulf of, b., N.A. B6 96
Mexico Basin, unds. F5 144
Mexico Bay, b., N.Y., U.S. E13 112
Mexico City see Ciudad de México, Mex. F9 100
Meycauayan, Phil. C3 52
Meydān Khvolah, Afg. B2 54
Meyersdale, Pa., U.S. E6 114
Meymaneh, Afg. B9 56
Meyronne, Sk., Can. E7 124
Meyungs, Palau g7 78b
Mëža (M'oža), stm., Eur. E14 10
Meẕada, Ḥorvot (Masada), hist., Isr. G6 58
Mezcala, Mex. G9 100
Mezcalapa, stm., Mex. G12 100
Meždurečensk, Russia D15 32
Meždurečenskij, Russia C10 32
Mèze, Fr. F9 18
Mezen', Russia D21 8
Mezen', stm., Russia D21 8
Mezenskaja guba, b., Russia C20 8
Mežica, Slvn. D11 22
Mezőberény, Hung. C8 26
Mezőcsát, Hung. B7 26

Name	Map Ref.	Page
Mezőkövesd, Hung.	B7	26
Mezőtúr, Hung.	B7	26
Mezquital, stm., Mex.	D6	100
Mfangano Island, i., Kenya	E6	66
Mgači, Russia	F17	34
M'Goun, Irhil, mtn., Mor.	C3	64
M'hai, B'nom, mtn., Viet.	G8	48
Mhasvād, India	C2	53
Mhow, India	G5	54
Mi, stm., China	H5	42
Mi, stm., China	C8	42
Mia, Oued, stm., Alg.	D5	64
Miahuatlán de Porfirio Díaz, Mex.	G10	100
Miajadas, Spain	E4	20
Miaméré, C.A.R.	C4	66
Miami, Mb., Can.	E15	124
Miami, Az., U.S.	J6	132
Miami, Fl., U.S.	K5	116
Miami, Ok., U.S.	H3	120
Miami, Tx., U.S.	F8	128
Miami Beach, Fl., U.S.	K5	116
Miami Canal, can., Fl., U.S.	J5	116
Miamisburg, Oh., U.S.	E1	114
Miami Springs, Fl., U.S.	K5	116
Miān Channūn, Pak.	C4	54
Mianchi, China	D4	42
Miandrivazo, Madag.	D8	68
Mianduhe, China	B9	36
Mīāneh, Iran	B6	56
Miang, Phu, mtn., Thai.	D5	48
Mianning, China	F5	36
Miānwāli, Pak.	B3	54
Mianxian, China	E2	42
Mianyang, China	F1	42
Mianzhu, China	E5	36
Miaodao Qundao, is., China	B9	42
Miaoli, Tai.	I9	42
Miao Ling, mts., China	H2	42
Miass, Russia	C10	32
Miass, stm., Russia	C10	32
Miastko, Pol.	B12	16
Micang Shan, mts., China	E2	42
Michalovce, Slov.	H17	16
Michaud, Point, c., N.S., Can.	E16	110
Micheal Peak, mtn., B.C., Can.	C4	138
Michel, B.C., Can.	G16	138
Miches, Dom. Rep.	C13	102
Michigan, N.D., U.S.	F15	124
Michigan, state, U.S.	C10	108
Michigan, stm., Co., U.S.	G6	126
Michigan, Lake, l., U.S.	E2	112
Michigan City, In., U.S.	G3	112
Michipicoten Island, i., On., Can.	F13	106
Michoacán, state, Mex.	F8	100
Micoud, St. Luc.	m7	105c
Micronesia, is., Oc.	B6	72
Micronesia, Federated States of, ctry., Oc.	C6	72
Mičurinsk, Russia	D6	32
Midai, Pulau, i., Indon.	B5	50
Midale, Sk., Can.	E10	124
Mid-Atlantic Ridge, unds.	F9	144
Middelburg, Neth.	C12	14
Middelburg, S. Afr.	G7	70
Middelburg, S. Afr.	D9	70
Middle, stm., B.C., Can.	B5	138
Middle, stm., Ia., U.S.	C3	120
Middle, stm., Mn., U.S.	C2	118
Middle Alkali Lake, l., Ca., U.S.	B5	134
Middle America Trench, unds.	H29	142
Middle Andaman, i., India	F7	46
Middleboro, Ma., U.S.	C15	114
Middlebourne, W.V., U.S.	E5	114
Middleburg, N.Y., U.S.	B11	114
Middleburg, Pa., U.S.	D8	114
Middlebury, Vt., U.S.	F3	110
Middle Caicos, i., T./C. Is.	B12	102
Middle Fabius, stm., Mo., U.S.	D5	120
Middlefield, Oh., U.S.	C4	114
Middlegate, Norf. I.	y25	78i
Middle Loup, stm., Ne., U.S.	F14	126
Middlemount, Austl.	D7	76
Middle Musquodoboit, N.S., Can.	E13	110
Middleport, Oh., U.S.	E3	114
Middle Raccoon, stm., Ia., U.S.	J4	118
Middlesboro, Ky., U.S.	H2	114
Middlesbrough, Eng., U.K.	G11	12
Middlesex, Belize	D3	102
Middle Stewiacke, N.S., Can.	E13	110
Middleton, N.S., Can.	F11	110
Middleton, Mi., U.S.	E5	112
Middleton, Wi., U.S.	A8	120
Middleton Island, i., Ak., U.S.	E10	140
Middleton Reef, at., Austl.	E11	74
Middletown, Ca., U.S.	E3	134
Middletown, Ct., U.S.	C13	114
Middletown, Il., U.S.	K9	118
Middletown, In., U.S.	H4	112
Middletown, Ky., U.S.	F12	120
Middletown, Md., U.S.	E8	114
Middletown, N.Y., U.S.	C11	114
Middletown, Oh., U.S.	E1	114
Middletown, Pa., U.S.	D9	114
Middletown, R.I., U.S.	C14	114
Middleville, Mi., U.S.	F4	112
Midgic, N.B., Can.	E12	110
Midi, Canal du, can., Fr.	F9	18
Midi de Bigorre, Pic du, mtn., Fr.	G5	18
Mid-Indian Basin, unds.	J10	142
Mid-Indian Ridge, unds.	L10	142
Midland, On., Can.	D9	112
Midland, Ca., U.S.	J2	132
Midland, Mi., U.S.	E5	112
Midland, S.D., U.S.	C11	126
Midland, Tx., U.S.	C5	130
Midlands, state, Zimb.	B10	70
Midleton, Ire.	J4	12
Midlothian, Tx., U.S.	B11	130
Midnapore, Ab., Can.	F16	138
Midongy Atsimo, Madag.	E8	68
Mid-Pacific Mountains, unds.	G19	142
Midsayap, Phil.	G5	52
Midville, Ga., U.S.	D3	116
Midway, B.C., Can.	G12	138
Midway, Al., U.S.	E13	122
Midway, Ky., U.S.	F13	120
Midway, Tx., U.S.	F3	122
Midway Islands, dep., Oc.	G22	30
Midway Park, N.C., U.S.	B8	116
Midwest City, Ok., U.S.	F11	128
Midyan, reg., Sau. Ar.	J6	58
Midžur (Midžor), mtn., Eur.	F9	26
Mie, Japan	G4	40
Mie, state, Japan	E9	40
Międzybórz, Pol.	E13	16
Międzylesie, Pol.	F12	16
Międzyrzec Podlaski, Pol.	D18	16
Międzyrzecz, Pol.	D11	16
Mielan, Fr.	F6	18
Mielec, Pol.	F17	16
Mier, Mex.	B9	100
Miercurea-Ciuc, Rom.	C12	26
Mieres, Spain	A5	20
Mieroszów, Pol.	F12	16
Mier y Noriega, Mex.	D8	100
Miesbach, Ger.	I7	16
Mī'ēso, Eth.	F8	62
Mieszkowice, Pol.	D10	16
Mifflinburg, Pa., U.S.	H12	112
Miguel Alemán, Presa, res., Mex.	F10	100
Miguel Alves, Braz.	C4	88
Miguel Auza, Mex.	C7	100
Miguel Calmon, Braz.	F5	88
Miguel Hidalgo, Presa, res., Mex.	B4	100
Miguelópolis, Braz.	K1	88
Miguel Riglos, Arg.	H6	92
Mihăești, Rom.	D12	26
Mihajlovka, Russia	D6	32
Mihajlovka, Russia	D14	32
Mihajlovka, Russia	C10	38
Mihajlovskij, Russia	F20	8
Mihalgazi, Tur.	C13	28
Mihanavičy, Bela.	G10	10
Mihara, Japan	E5	40
Mihara-yama, vol., Japan	E12	40
Mihninskaja, Russia	F21	8
Mikame, Japan	F5	40
Mikasa, Japan	C14	38
Mikaševičy, Bela.	H10	10
Mikhrot Timna'(King Solomon's Mines), hist., Isr.	I5	58
Mikindani, Tan.	G8	66
Mikkeli (Sankt Michel), Fin.	F12	8
Mikkeli, state, Fin.	F12	8
Mikołajki, Pol.	C17	16
Mikołów, Pol.	F14	16
Mikrá Préspa, Límni, l., Eur.	D15	24
Mikšino, Russia	C18	10
Mikulino, Russia	E14	10
Mikumi, Tan.	F7	66
Mikun', Russia	E23	8
Mikuni, Japan	C9	40
Miladummadulu Atoll, at., Mald.	h12	46a
Milagro, Arg.	E5	92
Milagro, Ec.	I2	86
Milagros, Phil.	D4	52
Milan see Milano, Italy	E6	22
Milan, Ga., U.S.	D2	116
Milan, In., U.S.	E12	120
Milan, Mi., U.S.	B2	114
Milan, Mn., U.S.	F3	118
Milan, Mo., U.S.	D4	120
Milan, N.M., U.S.	H8	132
Milang, Austl.	J2	76
Milange, Moz.	D6	68
Milano (Milan), Italy	E6	22
Milâs, Tur.	F10	28
Milavidy, Bela.	H8	10
Milazzo, Italy	F9	24
Milazzo, Golfo di, b., Italy	F9	24
Milbank, S.D., U.S.	F2	118
Milburn, Ok., U.S.	C2	122
Milden, Sk., Can.	C6	124
Mildmay, On., Can.	D8	112
Mildura, Austl.	J4	76
Mile, China	G5	36
Miles, Austl.	F8	76
Miles, Tx., U.S.	C7	130
Miles City, Mt., U.S.	A7	126
Milestone, Sk., Can.	E9	124
Milet, hist., Tur.	F10	28
Milford, De., U.S.	F10	114
Milford, Ia., U.S.	H3	118
Milford, Me., U.S.	F8	110
Milford, Ma., U.S.	B14	114
Milford, Mi., U.S.	B2	114
Milford, N.H., U.S.	B14	114
Milford, Pa., U.S.	C11	114
Milford, Ut., U.S.	E4	132
Milford Center, Oh., U.S.	D2	114
Milford Haven, Wales, U.K.	J7	12
Milford Lake, res., Ks., U.S.	B11	128
Milford Sound, strt., N.Z.	G2	80
Mili, at., Marsh. Is.	C8	72
Milian, stm., Malay.	A10	50
Milicz, Pol.	E13	16
Miljatino, Russia	F17	10
Milk, stm., N.A.	B6	108
Milk, North Fork (North Milk), stm., N.A.	B13	136
Mil'kovo, Russia	F20	34
Milk River, Ab., Can.	G18	138
Millard, Ne., U.S.	C1	120
Millau, Fr.	E9	18
Millboro, Va., U.S.	F6	114
Millbrook, N.Y., U.S.	C12	114
Mill City, Or., U.S.	F4	136
Millcreek, Pa., U.S.	B5	114
Millcreek, Ut., U.S.	C5	132
Mill Creek, W.V., U.S.	F5	114
Milledgeville, Ga., U.S.	C2	116
Milledgeville, Il., U.S.	C8	120
Mille Lacs, Lac des, l., On., Can.	C8	118
Mille Lacs Lake, l., Mn., U.S.	E5	118
Millen, Ga., U.S.	D4	116
Miller, Mo., U.S.	G4	120
Miller, S.D., U.S.	C14	126
Miller Mountain, mtn., Nv., U.S.	E7	134
Millerovo, Russia	E6	32
Millersburg, Ky., U.S.	F1	114
Millersburg, Mi., U.S.	C5	112
Millersburg, Oh., U.S.	D4	114
Millersport, Oh., U.S.	I7	112
Millerton, N.Y., U.S.	C12	114
Millet, Ab., Can.	C17	138
Millevaches, Plateau de, plat., Fr.	D7	18
Millicent, Austl.	K3	76
Milligan, Fl., U.S.	G12	122
Milligan, Ne., U.S.	G15	126
Millington, Mi., U.S.	E6	112
Millington, Tn., U.S.	B9	122
Millinocket, Me., U.S.	E8	110
Mill Island, i., Ant.	B15	81
Mill Island, i., Nu., Can.	C15	106
Millry, Al., U.S.	F10	122
Mills, Wy., U.S.	E6	126
Mills Creek, stm., Austl.	D4	76
Mills Lake, l., N.T., Can.	C7	106
Millstream, Austl.	D3	74
Milltown, Mt., U.S.	D13	136
Milltown, Wi., U.S.	F6	118
Milltown Malbay, Ire.	I3	12
Mill Valley, Ca., U.S.	F3	134
Millville, N.J., U.S.	E10	114
Millwood, Va., U.S.	E7	114
Millwood Lake, res., Ar., U.S.	D4	122
Milne Land, i., Grnld.	C20	141
Milnor, N.D., U.S.	A15	126
Milo, Ab., Can.	F18	138
Mílos, i., Grc.	G7	28
Miłosław, Pol.	D13	16
Milparinka, Austl.	G3	76
Milroy, In., U.S.	E12	120
Milroy, Pa., U.S.	D8	114
Miltenberg, Ger.	G5	16
Milton, On., Can.	E10	112
Milton, N.Z.	H4	80
Milton, Fl., U.S.	G11	122
Milton, Ia., U.S.	D5	120
Milton, Pa., U.S.	G13	112
Milton, Wi., U.S.	B9	120
Milton-Freewater, Or., U.S.	E8	136
Milton Keynes, Eng., U.K.	I12	12
Miltonvale, Ks., U.S.	B11	128
Miltou, Chad	E3	62
Miluo, stm., China	G5	42
Milwaukee, Wi., U.S.	E2	112
Milwaukee, stm., Wi., U.S.	H11	118
Milwaukie, Or., U.S.	E4	136
Mimbres, stm., N.M., U.S.	K9	132
Mimizan-les-Bains, Fr.	E4	18
Mimoň, Czech Rep.	F10	16
Mimoso do Sul, Braz.	K5	88
Mims, Fl., U.S.	H5	116
Min, stm., China	F5	36
Min, stm., China	I8	42
Mina, Mex.	H7	130
Mina, Nv., U.S.	E7	134
Mīnā' al-Aḥmadī, Kuw.	D6	56
Mīnāb, Iran	D8	56
Minahasa, pen., Indon.	E7	44
Minakuchi, Japan	E9	40
Minamata, Japan	G3	40
Minami-Alps-kokuritsu-kōen, p.o.i., Japan	D11	40
Minami-Tori-shima, i., Japan	G19	30
Minas, Cuba	B9	102
Minas, Indon.	C2	50
Minas, Ur.	G10	92
Minas Basin, b., N.S., Can.	E12	110
Minas de Barroterán, Mex.	B8	100
Minas de Corrales, Ur.	E10	92
Minas de Matahambre, Cuba	A5	102
Minas Gerais, state, Braz.	C8	90
Minas Novas, Braz.	I4	88
Minatare, Ne., U.S.	F9	126
Minatitlán, Mex.	F11	100
Minbu, Mya.	B2	48
Minbya, Mya.	B1	48
Minbyin, Mya.	C1	48
Mincio, stm., Italy	E7	22
Minco, Ok., U.S.	F10	128
Minčol, mtn., Slov.	G17	16
Mindanao, i., Phil.	G5	52
Mindanao, stm., Phil.	G5	52
Mindelheim, Ger.	H6	16
Mindelo, C.V.	k10	65a
Mindemoya, On., Can.	C7	112
Minden, On., Can.	D11	112
Minden, Ger.	D4	16
Minden, La., U.S.	E5	122
Minden, Ne., U.S.	G14	126
Minden, Nv., U.S.	E6	134
Minden City, Mi., U.S.	E7	112
Mindoro, i., Phil.	D3	52
Mindoro Strait, strt., Phil.	D3	52
Mine, Japan	E4	40
Mine Centre, On., Can.	C6	118
Minehead, Eng., U.K.	J9	12
Mineiros, Braz.	G7	84
Mineola, Tx., U.S.	E3	122
Mineral, Wa., U.S.	D4	136
Mineral Point, Wi., U.S.	B7	120
Mineral Springs, Ar., U.S.	D5	122
Mineral Wells, Tx., U.S.	B9	130
Minersville, Pa., U.S.	H13	112
Minerva, Oh., U.S.	D4	114
Minervino Murge, Italy	C9	24
Mineville, N.Y., U.S.	F3	110
Minfeng, China	A5	46
Minga, D.R.C.	G5	66
Mingäçevir, Azer.	A6	56
Mingāora, Pak.	C11	56
Mingary, Austl.	I3	76
Mingene, Austl.	E3	74
Mingin, Mya.	A2	48
Minglanilla, Spain	E9	20
Mingo Junction, Oh., U.S.	D5	114
Mingo Lake, l., Nu., Can.	C16	106
Mingshui, China	B10	36
Mingulay, i., Scot., U.K.	E5	12
Mingyuegou, China	C8	38
Minhang, China	F9	42
Minh Hai, Viet.	H7	48
Minhla, Mya.	B2	48
Minhla, Mya.	C2	48
Minho, hist. reg., Port.	C2	20
Minho (Miño), stm., Eur.	B2	20
Minićevo, Yugo.	F9	26
Minicoy Island, i., India	G3	46
Minigwal, Lake, l., Austl.	E4	74
Minija, stm., Lith.	E4	10
Minilya, Austl.	D2	74
Minilya, stm., Austl.	D2	74
Miniota, Mb., Can.	D12	124
Minitonas, Mb., Can.	B12	124
Minle, China	D5	36
Minna, Nig.	H6	64
Minneapolis, Ks., U.S.	B11	128
Minneapolis, Mn., U.S.	G5	118
Minnedosa, Mb., Can.	D13	124
Minneola, Ks., U.S.	D8	128
Minneota, Mn., U.S.	G2	118
Minnesota, state, U.S.	E4	118
Minnesota, stm., Mn., U.S.	G5	118
Minnesota Lake, Mn., U.S.	H5	118
Minnewanka, Lake, res., Ab., Can.	E15	138
Minnitaki Lake, l., On., Can.	B6	118
Mino, Japan	D9	40
Miño (Minho), stm., Eur.	B2	20
Minocqua, Wi., U.S.	F9	118
Minong, Wi., U.S.	E7	118
Minonk, Il., U.S.	D8	120
Minorca see Menorca, i., Spain	D15	20
Minot, N.D., U.S.	F12	124
Minqing, China	H8	42
Minquan, China	D6	42
Minquiers, Plateau des, is., Jersey	E6	14
Min Shan, mts., China	E5	36
Minsk, Bela.	G10	10
Minsk, state, Bela.	G10	10
Minskae uzvyšša, plat., Bela.	G10	10
Mińsk Mazowiecki, Pol.	D17	16
Minta, Cam.	D2	66
Minto, Mb., Can.	E13	124
Minto, Yk., Can.	C3	106
Minto, N.D., U.S.	C1	118
Minto, Lac, l., Qc., Can.	D16	106
Minto, Mount, mtn., Ant.	C22	81
Minto Inlet, b., N.T., Can.	A7	106
Minton, Sk., Can.	E9	124
Minturn, Co., U.S.	D10	132
Minûf, Egypt	H1	58
Minusinsk, Russia	D16	32
Minvoul, Gabon	D2	66
Minxian, China	E5	36
Minya see El-Minya, Egypt	J1	58
Minya el-Qamh, Egypt	H2	58
Mio, Mi., U.S.	D5	112
Miquan, China	F15	32
Mir, Bela.	G9	10
Mira, stm., Col.	G2	86
Mīrābād, Afg.	C9	56
Mirabella, Gulf of see Mirampéllou, Kólpos, b., Grc.	H8	28
Miracema do Tocantins, Braz.	E1	88
Mirador, Braz.	D3	88
Miradouro, Braz.	K4	88
Miraflores, Col.	E5	86
Miraflores, Col.	G5	86
Miraj, India	C2	53
Miramar, Arg.	I9	92
Miramar, Moz.	C12	70
Miramas, Fr.	F10	18
Miramichi Bay, b., N.B., Can.	C11	110
Mirampéllou, Kólpos, b., Grc.	H8	28
Mīrān, Pak.	C3	54
Miranda, Braz.	D5	90
Miranda, Col.	F3	86
Miranda, state, Ven.	B8	86
Miranda, stm., Braz.	D5	90
Miranda de Ebro, Spain	B7	20
Mirande, Fr.	F6	18
Mirando City, Tx., U.S.	G8	130
Mirandola, Italy	F8	22
Mira Táglio, Italy	E9	22
Miravalles, Volcán, vol., C.R.	G5	102
Miravete, Puerto de, p., Spain	E5	20
Mirbāṭ, Oman	F7	56
Mirecourt, Fr.	F14	14
Miri, Malay.	A9	50
Miria, Niger	G6	64
Miriam Vale, Austl.	E8	76
Mirim, Lagoa (Merín, Laguna), b., S.A.	F11	92
Miriñay, stm., Arg.	D9	92
Miritiparaná, stm., Col.	H6	86
Miriyama, Pap. N. Gui.	a3	79a
Mirnoe Ozero, Russia	C13	32
Mirny, sci., Ant.	B14	81
Mirnyj, Russia	D11	34
Mirnyy, sci., Ant.	B14	81
Miroslav, Czech Rep.	H12	16
Mirow, Ger.	C8	16
Mīrpur, Bngl.	G13	54
Mīrpur, Pak.	B4	54
Mīrpur Batoro, Pak.	F2	54
Mīrpur Khās, Pak.	F2	54
Mirror, Ab., Can.	D17	138
Miryang, Kor., S.	D1	40
Mirzāpur, India	F9	54
Misantla, Mex.	F10	100
Misawa, Japan	D14	38
Miscou Centre, N.B., Can.	C12	110
Miscou Island, i., N.B., Can.	C12	110
Miscou Point, c., N.B., Can.	B12	110
Mishan, China	B9	38
Mishawaka, In., U.S.	G3	112
Mishicot, Wi., U.S.	D2	112
Misima Island, i., Pap. N. Gui.	B10	74
Misiones, state, Arg.	C10	92
Misiones, state, Para.	C9	92
Misión Santa Rosa, Para.	D4	90
Misión San Vicente, Mex.	F4	98
Miskitos, Cayos, is., Nic.	E6	102
Miskolc, Hung.	A7	26
Mišnëvo, Russia	G19	10
Misool, Pulau, i., Indon.	F9	44
Miṣrātah, Libya	A3	62
Misr el-Bahrî (Lower Egypt), hist. reg., Egypt	G2	58
Misrikh, India	E8	54
Missinaibi, stm., On., Can.	E14	106
Missinaibi Lake, l., On., Can.	F14	106
Mission, B.C., Can.	G8	138
Mission, S.D., U.S.	D12	126
Mission, Tx., U.S.	H9	130
Mission Mountain, hill, Ok., U.S.	H3	120
Mission Viejo, Ca., U.S.	J8	134
Mississagi, stm., On., Can.	B6	112
Mississauga, On., Can.	E10	112
Mississinewa, stm., U.S.	H4	112
Mississippi, state, U.S.	D9	122
Mississippi, stm., On., Can.	C13	112
Mississippi, stm., U.S.	E9	108
Mississippi Lake, l., On., Can.	C13	112
Mississippi River Delta, La., U.S.	H9	122
Mississippi Sound, strt., U.S.	G10	122
Mississippi State, Ms., U.S.	D10	122
Missoula, Mt., U.S.	D12	136
Missouri, state, U.S.	F5	120
Missouri, stm., U.S.	D9	108
Missouri City, Tx., U.S.	H3	122
Mistake Creek, stm., Austl.	D6	76
Mistassibi, stm., Qc., Can.	A4	110
Mistassini, Qc., Can.	E16	106
Mistassini, Qc., Can.	B4	110
Mistassini, stm., Qc., Can.	B4	110
Mistassini, Lac, l., Qc., Can.	E16	106
Mistatim, Sk., Can.	B10	124
Mistelbach an der Zaya, Aus.	B13	22
Misterbianco, Italy	G9	24
Misti, Volcán, vol., Peru	G3	84
Misumi, Japan	E4	40
Mišutino, Russia	A19	10
Mita, Punta de, c., Mex.	E6	100
Mitchell, Austl.	F6	76
Mitchell, On., Can.	E8	112
Mitchell, In., U.S.	F11	120
Mitchell, Or., U.S.	F6	136
Mitchell, S.D., U.S.	D14	126
Mitchell, stm., Austl.	C8	74
Mitchell, stm., Austl.	K6	76
Mitchell, Mount, mtn., N.C., U.S.	I3	114
Mitchinamecus, stm., Qc., Can.	C2	110
Mitchinamecus, Réservoir, res., Qc., Can.	C1	110
Mît Ghamr, Egypt	H2	58
Mithapur, India	G2	54
Mithi, Pak.	F2	54
Mitidja, Plaine de la, pl., Alg.	H14	20
Mitiškovo, Russia	F16	10
Mitla, hist., Mex.	G10	100
Mito, Japan	C13	40
Mitsio, Nosy, i., Madag.	C8	68
Mitsukaidō, Japan	C13	40
Mitsuke, Japan	B11	40
Mittellandkanal, can., Ger.	D5	16
Mittenwald, Ger.	I7	16
Mittersill, Aus.	C9	22
Mittimatalik (Pond Inlet), Nu., Can.	A15	106
Mittweida, Ger.	E9	16
Mitú, Col.	G6	86
Mitumba, Monts, mts., D.R.C.	F5	66
Mitwaba, D.R.C.	F5	66
Mitzic, Gabon	D2	66
Miura, Japan	D12	40
Miura-hantō, pen., Japan	D12	40
Mixian, China	D5	42
Miyagi, state, Japan	A13	40
Miyake-jima, i., Japan	E12	40
Miyako, Japan	E14	38
Miyako-jima, i., Japan	G10	36
Miyakonojō, Japan	H4	40
Miyama, Japan	E9	40
Miyanojō, Japan	H3	40
Miyazaki, Japan	H4	40
Miyazaki, state, Japan	G4	40
Miyazu, Japan	D8	40
Miyoshi, Japan	E5	40
Miyun, China	A7	42
Miyun Shuiku, res., China	A7	42
Mīzan Teferī, Eth.	F7	62
Mizdah, Libya	A2	62
Mize, Ms., U.S.	F9	122
Mizen Head, c., Ire.	I6	12
Mizen Head, c., Ire.	J3	12
Mizhhir'ia, Ukr.	A10	26
Mizhi, China	C4	42
Mizil, Rom.	E13	26
Mizoram, state, India	G14	54
Mizpah Creek, stm., Mt., U.S.	A7	126
Mizque, Bol.	C3	90
Mizukaidō see Mitsukaidō, Japan	C13	40
Mizusawa, Japan	E14	38
Mjadzel, Bela.	F9	10
Mjakit, Russia	D19	34
Mjaksa, Russia	B21	10
Mjölby, Swe.	G6	8
Mjøsa, l., Nor.	F4	8
Mkalama, Tan.	E6	66
Mkhondvo, stm., Afr.	E10	70
Mkokotoni, Tan.	F7	66
Mkomazi, stm., S. Afr.	G10	70
Mkulwe, Tan.	F6	66
Mkuze, S. Afr.	E10	70
Mkuze, stm., S. Afr.	E11	70
Mkuze Game Reserve, S. Afr.	E11	70
Mladá Boleslav, Czech Rep.	F11	16
Mladenovac, Yugo.	E7	26
Mlava, stm., Yugo.	E8	26
Mława, Pol.	C16	16
Mljet, Otok, i., Cro.	H14	22
Mljet Nacionalni Park, p.o.i., Cro.	H14	22
Mmabatho, S. Afr.	D7	70
Mmadinare, Bots.	B8	70
Moa, stm., Afr.	H2	64
Moab, Ut., U.S.	E7	132
Moala, i., Fiji	q18	79e
Moama, Austl.	K5	76
Moamba, Moz.	D11	70
Moanda, Gabon	E2	66
Moar Lake, l., Can.	C18	124
Moate, Ire.	H5	12
Moba, D.R.C.	F5	66
Mobara, Japan	D13	40
Mobaye, C.A.R.	D4	66
Mobeetie, Tx., U.S.	F8	128
Moberly, Mo., U.S.	E5	120
Mobile, Al., U.S.	G10	122
Mobile, Az., U.S.	J4	132
Mobile, stm., Al., U.S.	G11	122
Mobile Bay, b., Al., U.S.	G10	122
Mobridge, S.D., U.S.	B12	126
Moca, Dom. Rep.	C12	102
Mocajuba, Braz.	B1	88
Mo Cay, Viet.	G8	48
Mocha see Al-Mukhā, Yemen	G5	56
Mochudi, Bots.	D8	70
Mocksville, N.C., U.S.	I5	114
Moclips, Wa., U.S.	C2	136
Môco, Morro de, mtn., Ang.	C2	68
Mocoa, Col.	G3	86
Mococa, Braz.	K2	88
Mocodoene, Moz.	C12	70
Mocoretá, Arg.	E8	92
Moctezuma, Mex.	G8	98
Moctezuma, stm., Mex.	G8	98
Moctezuma, stm., Mex.	E9	100
Mocuba, Moz.	D6	68
Modane, Fr.	D12	18
Modāsa, India	G4	54
Modder, stm., S. Afr.	F7	70
Módena, Italy	F7	22
Modeste, Mount, mtn., B.C., Can.	H6	138
Modesto, Ca., U.S.	F4	134
Modica, Italy	H8	24
Mödling, Aus.	B13	22
Modowi, Indon.	F9	44
Modra, Slov.	H13	16
Moe, Austl.	L6	76
Moeda, Braz.	K3	88
Moei (Thaungyin), stm., Asia	D3	48
Moema, Braz.	J3	88
Moengo, Sur.	B7	84
Moen-jo-Daro, hist., Pak.	D10	56
Moenkopi, Az., U.S.	G5	132
Moenkopi Wash, stm., Az., U.S.	G6	132
Moeris, Lake see Qârûn, Birket, l., Egypt	I1	58
Moeskroen see Mouscron, Bel.	D12	14
Moffat, Scot., U.K.	F9	12
Moga, India	C5	54
Mogadiscio see Muqdisho, Som.	D9	66
Mogadishu see Muqdisho, Som.	D9	66
Mogalakwena, stm., S. Afr.	C9	70
Mogami, stm., Japan	A13	40
Mogaung, Mya.	C8	46
Mogdy, Russia	F15	34
Mogilno, Pol.	D13	16
Mogincual, Moz.	D7	68
Mogoča, Russia	F12	34
Mogočin, Russia	C14	32
Mogogh, Sudan	F6	62
Mogok, Mya.	A3	48
Mogollon Rim, clf, Az., U.S.	I6	132
Mogor, Afg.	B1	54
Mogotes, Col.	D5	86
Mogotón, mtn., N.A.	F4	102
Moguer, Spain	G4	20
Mogzon, Russia	F11	34
Mohács, Hung.	C5	26
Mohall, N.D., U.S.	F12	124
Mohammed, Râs, c., Egypt	K5	58
Mohammedia, Mor.	C3	64
Mohania, India	F9	54
Mohawk, Mi., U.S.	D10	118
Mohawk, stm., N.Y., U.S.	B11	114
Mohe, China	F13	34
Mohéli see Mwali, i., Com.	C7	68
Mohnyin, Mya.	D8	46
Mohokare (Caledon), stm., Afr.	F8	70
Mohyliv-Podil's'kyi, Ukr.	A14	26
Moi, Nor.	G2	8
Moinești, Rom.	C13	26
Moira, stm., On., Can.	D12	112
Moiraba, Braz.	B1	88
Mo i Rana, Nor.	C5	8
Moiseevka, Russia	C13	32
Moisés Ville, Arg.	E7	92
Moisie, Qc., Can.	E17	106
Moisie, stm., Qc., Can.	E17	106
Moitaco, Ven.	C9	86
Mojácar, Spain	G9	20
Mojave, Ca., U.S.	H7	134
Mojave, stm., Ca., U.S.	H9	134
Mojave Desert, des., Ca., U.S.	D4	98
Mojero, stm., Russia	C9	34
Mojiguaçu, stm., Braz.	K2	88
Mojikit Lake, res., On., Can.	A10	118
Moji-Mirim, Braz.	L2	88
Mojo, Eth.	F7	62
Moju, Braz.	A1	88
Moju, stm., Braz.	D8	84
Mōka, Japan	C12	40
Mokāma, India	F10	54
Mokapu Peninsula, pen., Hi., U.S.	B4	78a
Mokau, stm., N.Z.	D6	80
Mokelumne, stm., Ca., U.S.	E5	134
Moknine, Tun.	B7	64
Mokochu, Khao, mtn., Thai.	E4	48
Mokokchūng, India	C7	46
Mokolo, Cam.	B2	66
Mokolo, stm., S. Afr.	C8	70
Mokpalin, Mya.	D3	48
Mokp'o, Kor., S.	G7	38
Mokša, stm., Russia	D6	32
Mokwa, Nig.	H5	64
Mol, Bel.	C14	14
Mola di Bari, Italy	C11	24
Molat, Otok, i., Cro.	F11	22
Moldary, Kaz.	D13	32
Moldau see Vltava, stm., Czech Rep.	F10	16
Moldavia, hist. reg., Rom.	C13	26
Molde, Nor.	E2	8
Moldova, ctry., Eur.	B15	26
Moldova, stm., Rom.	C13	26
Moldoveanu, Vârful, mtn., Rom.	D11	26
Môle, Cap du, c., Haiti	C11	102
Mole Creek, Austl.	n13	77a
Molega Lake, l., N.S., Can.	F12	110
Molène, Île de, i., Fr.	F3	14
Molepolole, Bots.	D7	70
Molėtai, Lith.	E8	10
Molfetta, Italy	C10	24
Molina, Chile	G2	92
Molina de Aragón, Spain	D9	20
Molina de Segura, Spain	F9	20
Moline, Il., U.S.	C7	120
Moline, Ks., U.S.	D12	128
Molino, Fl., U.S.	G11	122
Molino de Valdo de Piedras, Mex.	E3	130
Molinos, Arg.	B4	92
Molise, state, Italy	C8	24
Mollendo, Peru	G3	84
Mölln, Ger.	C6	16
Mölndal, Swe.	H4	8
Molodežnaja, sci., Ant.	B9	81
Molodogvardejskoe, Kaz.	D11	32
Mologa, stm., Russia	B19	10
Molokai, i., Hi., U.S.	B5	78a
Molokai Fracture Zone, unds.	G24	142
Molokovo, Russia	B19	10
Molong, Austl.	I7	76
Molopo, stm., Afr.	E5	70
Moloundou, Cam.	D3	66
Molson Lake, l., Mb., Can.	E11	106
Molu, Pulau, i., Indon.	G9	44
Moluccas see Maluku, is., Indon.	F8	44
Molucca Sea see Maluku, Laut, Indon.	F8	44
Molvoticy, Russia	C15	10
Moma, Moz.	D6	68
Moma, stm., Russia	C17	34
Mombaça, Braz.	C6	88
Mombasa, Kenya	E7	66
Mombetsu, Japan	B15	38
Momčilgrad, Blg.	H12	26
Momi, Fiji	p18	79e
Momotombo, Volcán, vol., Nic.	F4	102
Mompono, D.R.C.	D4	66
Mompós, Col.	C4	86
Momskij hrebet, mts., Russia	C18	34
Mon, state, Mya.	E3	48
Møn, i., Den.	I5	8
Mona, Ut., U.S.	D5	132
Mona, Isla de, i., P.R.	h14	96a
Mona, Punta, c., C.R.	H6	102
Monaca, Pa., U.S.	D5	114
Monach Islands, is., Scot., U.K.	D5	12
Monaco, Mon.	G4	22
Monaco, ctry., Eur.	F13	18
Monadnock Mountain, mtn., N.H., U.S.	B13	114
Monagas, state, Ven.	C10	86
Monaghan, Ire.	G6	12
Monaghan, state, Ire.	G6	12
Monahans, Tx., U.S.	C5	130
Monakino, Russia	C10	38
Mona Passage, strt., N.A.	C13	102
Monapo, Moz.	C7	68
Monarch, S.C., U.S.	B4	116
Monarch Mountain, mtn., B.C., Can.	E5	138
Monarch Pass, p., Co., U.S.	E10	132
Monashee Mountains, mts., B.C., Can.	F12	138
Monastir, Tun.	I4	24
Moncalieri, Italy	F4	22
Moncalvo, Italy	E5	22
Monção, Braz.	B3	88
Mončegorsk, Russia	B15	8
Mönchengladbach, Ger.	E2	16
Monchique, Port.	G2	20
Moncks Corner, S.C., U.S.	C5	116
Monclova, Mex.	B8	100
Moncton, N.B., Can.	D12	110
Monday, stm., Para.	B10	92
Mondego, stm., Port.	D3	20
Mondjamboli, D.R.C.	D4	66
Mondoubleau, Fr.	F9	14
Mondovi, Wi., U.S.	G7	118
Mondragone, Italy	C7	24
Monemvasía, Grc.	G6	28
Monessen, Pa., U.S.	D5	114
Monesterio, Spain	F4	20
Monett, Mo., U.S.	H4	120
Monette, Ar., U.S.	I7	120
Monfalcone, Italy	E10	22
Monferrato, hist. reg., Italy	F5	22
Monforte de Lemos, Spain	B3	20
Monga, D.R.C.	D4	66
Mongaguá, Braz.	B14	92
Mongalla, Sudan	F6	62
Mongers Lake, l., Austl.	E3	74
Monggon Qulu, China	B8	36
Möng Hai, Mya.	B4	48
Möng Hsat, Mya.	B4	48
Mongibello see Etna, Monte, vol., Italy	G8	24
Möng Küng, Mya.	B3	48
Möng Ma, Mya.	B4	48
Möng Nai, Mya.	B3	48
Mongo, Chad	E3	62
Mongol Altayn nuruu, mts., Asia	E16	32
Mongolia, ctry., Asia	E14	30
Mongonu, Nig.	G7	64
Möng Pai, Mya.	C3	48
Möng Pawn, Mya.	B3	48
Mongu, Zam.	D3	68
Möng Yai, Mya.	A4	48
Monico, Wi., U.S.	F9	118
Monida Pass, p., U.S.	F14	136
Monino, Russia	E21	10
Moniquirá, Col.	E5	86
Mõniste, Est.	H12	8
Monitor Valley, val., Nv., U.S.	E9	134
Mońki, Pol.	C18	16
Monkira, Austl.	E3	76
Monmouth, Wales, U.K.	J10	12
Monmouth, Or., U.S.	F3	136
Monmouth Mountain, mtn., B.C., Can.	E7	138
Mono, stm., Afr.	H5	64
Mono, Caño, stm., Col.	E7	86
Mono Island, i., Sol. Is.	d6	79b
Mono Lake, l., Ca., U.S.	E7	134
Monon, In., U.S.	H3	112
Monona, Ia., U.S.	H7	118
Monona, Wi., U.S.	A8	120
Monongahela, stm., U.S.	E6	114
Monopoli, Italy	D11	24
Monor, Hung.	B6	26
Monreal del Campo, Spain	D9	20
Monreale, Italy	F7	24
Monroe, La., U.S.	E6	122
Monroe, Mi., U.S.	C2	114
Monroe, N.Y., U.S.	C11	114
Monroe, N.C., U.S.	B5	116
Monroe, Or., U.S.	F3	136
Monroe, Ut., U.S.	E4	132
Monroe, Va., U.S.	G6	114
Monroe, Wa., U.S.	C4	136
Monroe, Wi., U.S.	B8	120
Monroe City, In., U.S.	F10	120
Monroe Lake, res., In., U.S.	E11	120
Monroeville, Al., U.S.	F11	122
Monroeville, In., U.S.	D1	114
Monroeville, Oh., U.S.	C3	114
Monroeville, Pa., U.S.	D6	114
Monrovia, Lib.	H2	64
Mons, Bel.	D12	14
Monsefú, Peru	E2	84
Monselice, Italy	E8	22
Monsenhor Hipólito, Braz.	D5	88
Monsenhor Tabosa, Braz.	C5	88
Mönsterås, Swe.	H7	8
Montabaur, Ger.	F3	16
Montagne, Neth. Ant.	p23	104g
Montagu, S. Afr.	H5	70
Montague, P.E., Can.	D14	110
Montague, Mi., U.S.	E3	112
Montague, Tx., U.S.	H11	128
Montague, Isla, i., Mex.	F5	98
Montague Island, i., Ak., U.S.	E10	140

I • 38 Mont-Muns

Name	Map Ref.	Page
Montagu Island, i., S. Geor.	K12	82
Montaigu, Fr.	H7	14
Montalbano Ionico, Italy	D10	24
Montalegre, Port.	C3	20
Montana, Blg.	F10	26
Montana, state, Blg.	F10	26
Montana, state, U.S.	B6	108
Montaña de Covadonga, Parque Nacional de la, p.o.i., Spain	A5	20
Montánchez, Spain	E4	20
Montanha, Braz.	J5	88
Montargis, Fr.	G11	14
Montauban, Fr.	E7	18
Montauk Point, c., N.Y., U.S.	C14	114
Montbard, Fr.	G13	14
Montbéliard, Fr.	G15	14
Mont Belvieu, Tx., U.S.	H3	122
Montblanc, Spain	C11	20
Montblanch see Montblanc, Spain	C11	20
Montbrison, Fr.	D9	18
Montbron, Fr.	D6	18
Montceau-les-Mines, Fr.	H13	14
Montclair, Ca., U.S.	I8	134
Mont-de-Marsan, Fr.	F5	18
Montdidier, Fr.	E11	14
Monte, Laguna del, l., Arg.	H6	92
Monteagudo, Bol.	C4	90
Monte Albán, hist., Mex.	G10	100
Monte Alegre, Braz.	D7	84
Monte Alegre de Goiás, Braz.	G2	88
Monte Alegre de Minas, Braz.	J1	88
Monte Alegre de Sergipe, Braz.	F7	88
Monte Azul, Braz.	H4	88
Montebello, Qc., Can.	C14	112
Montebello, P.R.	B2	104a
Montecarlo, Arg.	C10	92
Monte Carmelo, Braz.	J2	88
Monte Caseros, Arg.	E8	92
Montecassino, Abbazia di, Italy	C7	24
Montecatini Terme, Italy	G7	22
Montecito, Ca., U.S.	I6	134
Monte Comán, Arg.	G4	92
Monte Creek, B.C., Can.	F11	138
Monte Cristi, Dom. Rep.	C12	102
Monte Cristo, Bol.	B4	90
Montecristo, Isola di, i., Italy	H7	22
Monte do Carmo, Braz.	F1	88
Monte Escobedo, Mex.	D7	100
Montefalco, Italy	H9	22
Montefiascone, Italy	H8	22
Montego Bay, Jam.	i12	104d
Monteiro, Braz.	D7	88
Montejicar, Spain	G7	20
Montejinni, Austl.	C6	74
Montelíbano, Col.	C4	86
Montélimar, Fr.	E10	18
Monte Lindo, stm., Para.	A9	92
Montellano, Spain	H5	20
Montello, Nv., U.S.	B2	132
Montello, Wi., U.S.	H9	118
Monte Maíz, Arg.	F6	92
Montemayor, Meseta de, plat., Arg.	H3	90
Montemorelos, Mex.	C9	100
Montemor-o-Velho, Port.	D2	20
Montemuro, mtn., Port.	C2	20
Montenegro, Braz.	D12	92
Montenegro see Crna Gora, state, Yugo.	G6	26
Monte Pascoal, Parque Nacional de, p.o.i., Braz.	I5	88
Monte Patria, Chile	E2	92
Montepuez, Moz.	C6	68
Montepulciano, Italy	G8	22
Monte Quemado, Arg.	B6	92
Montereau-Faut-Yonne, Fr.	F11	14
Monterey, Ca., U.S.	G3	134
Monterey, Va., U.S.	F6	114
Monterey Bay, b., Ca., U.S.	G3	134
Montería, Col.	C3	86
Monteros, Arg.	C5	92
Monterotondo, Italy	H9	22
Monterrey, Mex.	C8	100
Montesano, Wa., U.S.	C3	136
Monte Sant'Angelo, Italy	I12	22
Monte Santu, Capo di, c., Italy	D3	24
Montes Claros, Braz.	I3	88
Montesilvano Marina, Italy	H11	22
Montevallo, Al., U.S.	D12	122
Montevarchi, Italy	G8	22
Montevideo, Mn., U.S.	G3	118
Montevideo, Ur.	G9	92
Monte Vista, Co., U.S.	D2	128
Montezuma, Ga., U.S.	D1	116
Montezuma, In., U.S.	I2	112
Montezuma, Ks., U.S.	D8	128
Montezuma Castle National Monument, p.o.i., Az., U.S.	I4	132
Montgenèvre, Col de, p., Fr.	E12	18
Montgomery, Al., U.S.	E12	122
Montgomery, La., U.S.	F6	122
Montgomery, Mn., U.S.	G5	118
Montgomery, Pa., U.S.	C8	114
Montgomery, Tx., U.S.	G3	122
Montgomery City, Mo., U.S.	E6	120
Montguyon, Fr.	D5	18
Monthey, Switz.	D3	22
Monticello, Ar., U.S.	D7	122
Monticello, Fl., U.S.	F2	116
Monticello, Il., U.S.	D9	120
Monticello, In., U.S.	H3	112
Monticello, Ky., U.S.	H13	120
Monticello, Mn., U.S.	F5	118
Monticello, Ms., U.S.	F8	122
Monticello, Mo., U.S.	D6	120
Monticello, N.Y., U.S.	C11	114
Monticello, Ut., U.S.	F7	132
Monticello, hist., Va., U.S.	G7	114
Montigny-le-Roi, Fr.	G14	14
Montigny-lès-Metz, Fr.	E15	14
Montijo, Pan.	I7	102
Montijo, Port.	F2	20
Montijo, Spain	F4	20
Montijo, Golfo de, b., Pan.	I7	102
Montilla, Spain	G6	20
Montivilliers, Fr.	E9	14
Mont-Joli, Qc., Can.	B8	110
Mont-Laurier, Qc., Can.	B14	112
Montluçon, Fr.	C8	18
Montmagny, Qc., Can.	D6	110
Montmédy, Fr.	E14	14
Montmorillon, Fr.	C6	18
Monto, Austl.	E8	76
Montoro, Spain	F6	20
Montour Falls, N.Y., U.S.	B9	114
Montpelier, Jam.	i13	104d
Montpelier, Id., U.S.	H15	136
Montpelier, In., U.S.	H4	112
Montpelier, Oh., U.S.	C1	114
Montpelier, Vt., U.S.	F4	110
Montpellier, Fr.	F9	18
Montréal, Qc., Can.	E3	110
Montreal, Wi., U.S.	E8	118
Montreal, stm., On., Can.	A10	112
Montreal Lake, l., Sk., Can.	E9	106
Montreuil-sur-Mer, Fr.	D10	14
Montreux, Switz.	D3	22
Montrose, Scot., U.K.	E10	12
Montrose, Co., U.S.	E9	132
Montrose, Mi., U.S.	E6	112
Montrose, Pa., U.S.	C9	114
Montrose, S.D., U.S.	D15	126
Montross, Va., U.S.	F9	114
Monts, Pointe des, c., Qc., Can.	A9	110
Mont-Saint-Michel, Qc., Can.	D1	110
Mont-Saint-Michel, Baie du, b., Fr.	F7	14
Mont-Saint-Michel, Le, Fr.	F7	14
Montserrat, dep., N.A.	h15	96a
Mont-Tremblant, Parc de récréation du, p.o.i., Qc., Can.	D2	110
Monument, Or., U.S.	F7	136
Monument Draw, stm., U.S.	B5	130
Monument Peak, mtn., Co., U.S.	D9	132
Monument Valley, val., U.S.	F6	132
Monviso, mtn., Italy	F4	22
Monyo, Mya.	C2	48
Monywa, Mya.	A2	48
Monza, Italy	E6	22
Monze, Zam.	D4	68
Monzen, Japan	B9	40
Monzón, Spain	C11	20
Mooi, stm., S. Afr.	F10	70
Moolawatana, Austl.	G2	76
Moon, Mountains of the see Ruwenzori, mts., Afr.	D6	66
Moonie, Austl.	F8	76
Moonie, stm., Austl.	G7	76
Moora, Austl.	F3	74
Moorcroft, Wy., U.S.	C8	126
Moore, Id., U.S.	G13	136
Moore, Ok., U.S.	F11	128
Moore, Tx., U.S.	E8	130
Moore, Lake, l., Austl.	E3	74
Moorea, i., Fr. Poly.	v20	78h
Moorefield, W.V., U.S.	E7	114
Moore Haven, Fl., U.S.	J4	116
Mooreland, Ok., U.S.	E9	128
Mooresville, N.C., U.S.	A5	116
Moorhead, Mn., U.S.	E2	118
Moorhead, Ms., U.S.	D8	122
Mooringsport, La., U.S.	E5	122
Moornanyah Lake, l., Austl.	I4	76
Moorreesburg, S. Afr.	H4	70
Moosburg an der Isar, Ger.	H7	16
Moosehead Lake, l., Me., U.S.	E7	110
Moose Island, i., Mb., Can.	C16	124
Moose Jaw, Sk., Can.	D8	124
Moose Jaw, stm., Sk., Can.	D8	124
Moose Lake, Mn., U.S.	E6	118
Moose Lake, l., Ab., Can.	B19	138
Mooselookmeguntic Lake, l., Me., U.S.	F5	110
Moose Mountain, mtn., Sk., Can.	E11	124
Moose Mountain Creek, stm., Sk., Can.	E11	124
Moose Pass, Ak., U.S.	D10	140
Moosomin, Sk., Can.	D12	124
Moosonee, On., Can.	E14	106
Mootwingee National Park, p.o.i., Austl.	H4	76
Mopane, S. Afr.	C9	70
Mopipi, Bots.	B7	70
Moppo see Mokp'o, Kor., S.	G7	38
Mopti, Mali	G4	64
Moquegua, Peru	G3	84
Mór, Hung.	B5	26
Mòr, Glen, val., Scot., U.K.	D8	12
Mora, Cam.	B2	66
Mora, Port.	F2	20
Mora, Swe.	F6	8
Mora, Mn., U.S.	F5	118
Mora, stm., N.M., U.S.	F4	128
Morač, stm., Bela.	H10	10
Morādābād, India	D7	54
Morada Nova, Braz.	C6	88
Morada Nova de Minas, Braz.	J3	88
Morąg, Pol.	C15	16
Moral de Calatrava, Spain	F7	20
Moraleda, Canal, strt., Chile	H2	90
Morales, Laguna de, b., Mex.	D10	100
Moramanga, Madag.	D8	68
Moran, Ks., U.S.	G2	120
Moran, Mi., U.S.	B5	112
Moran, Tx., U.S.	B8	130
Morant Bay, Jam.	j14	104d
Morant Cays, is., Jam.	D10	102
Morant Point, c., Jam.	j14	104d
Morar, Loch, l., Scot., U.K.	E7	12
Moratalla, Spain	F9	20
Moratuwa, Sri L.	H4	53
Morava, hist. reg., Czech Rep.	G13	16
Morava (March), stm., Eur.	H12	16
Moravia, N.Y., U.S.	B9	114
Moravské Budějovice, Czech Rep.	G11	16
Morawa, Austl.	E3	74
Morawhanna, Guy.	C12	86
Moray Firth, b., Scot., U.K.	D9	12
Morbi, India	G3	54
Morbihan, state, Fr.	G6	14
Morcenx, Fr.	E5	18
Morden, Mb., Can.	E15	124
Mordovia see Mordovija, state, Russia	D6	32
Mordovija, state, Russia	D6	32
Mordves, Russia	F21	10
Mordvinia see Mordovija, state, Russia	D6	32
Mordy, Pol.	D18	16
More, Ben, mtn., Scot., U.K.	E7	12
Moreau, stm., S.D., U.S.	B12	126
Moreau, North Fork, stm., S.D., U.S.	B9	126
Moreau, South Fork, stm., S.D., U.S.	B9	126
Moreau Peak, mtn., S.D., U.S.	B9	126
Moreauville, La., U.S.	F7	122
Morecambe, Eng., U.K.	G9	12
Morecambe Bay, b., Eng., U.K.	H9	12
Moree, Austl.	G7	76
Morehead, Ky., U.S.	F2	114
Morehead City, N.C., U.S.	B9	116
Moreland, Ga., U.S.	D14	122
Moreland, Ky., U.S.	G13	120
Morelia, Mex.	F8	100
Morell, P.E., Can.	D14	110
Morella, Austl.	D4	76
Morelos, Mex.	B5	100
Morelos, Mex.	I2	130
Morelos, state, Mex.	F9	100
Morena, India	E6	54
Morena, Sierra, mts., Spain	F5	20
Morenci, Az., U.S.	J7	132
Moreni, Rom.	D12	26
Moreno, Bahía, b., Chile	A2	92
Møre og Romsdal, state, Nor.	E2	8
Moresby Island, i., B.C., Can.	E4	106
Moreton, Austl.	B8	74
Moreton Island, i., Austl.	F9	76
Moreuil, Fr.	E11	14
Morez, Fr.	H14	14
Morgan, Mn., U.S.	G3	118
Morgan, Mt., U.S.	F6	124
Morgan, Tx., U.S.	B10	130
Morgan, Ut., U.S.	B5	132
Morgan City, Al., U.S.	C12	122
Morgan City, La., U.S.	H7	122
Morganfield, Ky., U.S.	G10	120
Morgan Hill, Ca., U.S.	F4	134
Morganito, Ven.	E8	86
Morganton, N.C., U.S.	I4	114
Morgantown, In., U.S.	E11	120
Morgantown, Ms., U.S.	F8	122
Morgantown, Ms., U.S.	F7	122
Morgantown, W.V., U.S.	E6	114
Morgenzon, S. Afr.	E9	70
Morghāb (Murgab), stm., Asia	B9	56
Moriah, Mount, mtn., Nv., U.S.	D2	132
Moriarty, N.M., U.S.	G2	128
Morice, stm., B.C., Can.	B4	138
Morice Lake, l., B.C., Can.	B3	138
Morichal Largo, stm., Ven.	C10	86
Moricsala rezervāts, Lat.	C5	10
Moriki, Nig.	G6	64
Morino, Russia	C13	10
Morinville, Ab., Can.	C17	138
Morioka, Japan	E14	38
Morīri, Tso, l., India	B6	54
Morisset, Austl.	I8	76
Morjakovskij Zaton, Russia	C14	32
Morkoka, stm., Russia	D11	34
Morlaix, Fr.	F5	14
Morley, Mi., U.S.	E4	112
Mormal', Bela.	H12	10
Mormugao, India	D1	53
Morne-à-l'Eau, Guad.	h5	105c
Morne du Vitet, hill, Guad.	B2	105a
Morne Trois Pitons National Park, p.o.i., Dom.	j6	105c
Morney, Austl.	E3	76
Morning Sun, Ia., U.S.	C6	120
Mornington, Austl.	L5	76
Mornington, Isla, i., Chile	I1	90
Mornington Island, i., Austl.	C7	74
Morobe, Pap. N. Gui.	b4	79a
Morocco, In., U.S.	H2	112
Morocco, ctry., Afr.	C3	64
Moro Creek, stm., Ar., U.S.	D6	122
Morogoro, Tan.	F7	66
Moro Gulf, b., Phil.	G4	52
Moroleón, Mex.	E8	100
Morombe, Madag.	E7	68
Morón, Arg.	G8	92
Morón, Cuba	A8	102
Mörön, Mong.	B5	36
Morón, Ven.	B7	86
Morona, stm., S.A.	I3	86
Morona Santiago, state, Ec.	I3	86
Morondava, Madag.	E7	68
Morón de Almazán, Spain	C8	20
Morón de la Frontera, Spain	G5	20
Moroni, Com.	C7	68
Moroni, Ut., U.S.	D5	132
Moron Us, stm., China	E3	36
Morošečnoe, Russia	E20	34
Morotai, i., Indon.	E8	44
Moroto, Ug.	D6	66
Moroto, mtn., Ug.	D6	66
Morovis, P.R.	B3	104a
Morozovsk, Russia	E6	32
Morpeth, Eng., U.K.	F11	12
Morrilton, Ar., U.S.	B6	122
Morrin, Ab., Can.	E18	138
Morrinhos, Braz.	B5	88
Morrinhos, Braz.	I1	88
Morrinsville, N.Z.	C6	80
Morris, Mb., Can.	E16	124
Morris, Il., U.S.	C9	120
Morris, Mn., U.S.	F2	118
Morrisburg, On., Can.	D14	112
Morris Jesup, Kap, c., Grnld.	A19	141
Morrison, Arg.	F6	92
Morrison, Il., U.S.	C8	120
Morrisonville, Il., U.S.	E8	120
Morristown, Az., U.S.	J4	132
Morristown, In., U.S.	E12	120
Morristown, S.D., U.S.	B11	126
Morristown, Tn., U.S.	H2	114
Morrisville, Pa., U.S.	H15	112
Morro, Punta, c., Mex.	C2	102
Morro Bay, Ca., U.S.	H5	134
Morro do Chapéu, Braz.	F5	88
Morros, Braz.	B3	88
Morrosquillo, Golfo de, b., Col.	C3	86
Morrow, La., U.S.	G6	122
Morrumbala, Moz.	D6	68
Morrumbene, Moz.	C12	70
Morse, La., U.S.	G6	122
Morse, Tx., U.S.	E7	128
Morsi, India	H6	54
Mörskom see Myrskylä, Fin.	F11	8
Morson, On., Can.	B4	118
Mortagne-sur-Sèvre, Fr.	H8	14
Mortara, Italy	E5	22
Morteau, Fr.	G15	14
Morteros, Arg.	E6	92
Mortes, stm., Braz.	F7	84
Mortlach, Sk., Can.	D7	124
Mortlock Islands, is., Micron.	C6	72
Morton, Il., U.S.	D8	120
Morton, Mn., U.S.	G4	118
Morton, Tx., U.S.	H6	128
Morton, Wa., U.S.	D4	136
Morton National Park, p.o.i., Austl.	J7	76
Morua, Vanuatu	k17	79d
Moruya, Austl.	J7	76
Morvan, mts., Fr.	G13	14
Morvant, Trin.	s12	105f
Morven, Austl.	F6	76
Morven, Ga., U.S.	F2	116
Morven, N.C., U.S.	B5	116
Morwell, Austl.	L6	76
Moryń, Pol.	D10	16
Moržovec, ostrov, i., Russia	C20	8
Mosal'sk, Russia	F17	10
Mosbach, Ger.	G5	16
Moscos Islands, is., Mya.	E3	48
Moscow see Moskva, Russia	E20	10
Moscow, Id., U.S.	D10	136
Moscow see Moskva, stm., Russia	E21	10
Mosel (Moselle), stm., Eur.	G2	16
Moselebe, stm., Bots.	D7	70
Moselle, Ms., U.S.	F9	122
Moselle, state, Fr.	F15	14
Moselle (Mosel), stm., Eur.	G2	16
Moses Lake, Wa., U.S.	C7	136
Moses Point, Ak., U.S.	D7	140
Moshaweng, stm., S. Afr.	E6	70
Mosheim, Tn., U.S.	H3	114
Moshi, Tan.	E7	66
Mosinee, Wi., U.S.	G9	118
Mosjøen, Nor.	D5	8
Moskalvo, Russia	F17	34
Moskenesøya, i., Nor.	C5	8
Moskovskaja oblast', co., Russia	D19	10
Moskovskaja vozvyšennost', plat., Russia	E19	10
Moskva (Moscow), Russia	E20	10
Moskva, stm., Russia	E21	10
Moskvy, kanal imeni, can., Russia	D20	10
Mosomane, Bots.	C8	70
Mosonmagyaróvár, Hung.	B4	26
Mosopa, Bots.	D7	70
Mosqueiro, Braz.	D8	84
Mosquera, Col.	F2	86
Mosquito Coast see Mosquitos, Costa de, hist. reg., Nic.	F6	102
Mosquitos, Costa de, hist. reg., Nic.	F6	102
Mosquitos, Golfo de los, b., Pan.	H7	102
Moss, Nor.	G4	8
Mossaka, Congo	E3	66
Mossbank, Sk., Can.	E7	124
Mossburn, N.Z.	G2	80
Mosselbaai (Mossel Bay), S. Afr.	I6	70
Mossel Bay see Mosselbaai, S. Afr.	I6	70
Mossleigh, Ab., Can.	F17	138
Mossman, Austl.	C9	74
Moss Mountain, mtn., Ar., U.S.	C6	122
Mossoró, Braz.	C7	88
Moss Point, Ms., U.S.	G10	122
Moss Vale, Austl.	J8	76
Mossy, stm., Mb., Can.	C13	124
Most, Czech Rep.	F9	16
Mostar, Bos.	F4	26
Mostardas, Braz.	E12	92
Møsting, Kap, c., Grnld.	E17	141
Mostovaja, Russia	D16	10
Mostyn, Malay.	A11	50
Mosul see Al-Mawṣil, Iraq	B5	56
Møsvatnet, l., Nor.	G2	8
Mot'a, Eth.	E7	62
Mota del Cuervo, Spain	E8	20
Mota del Marqués, Spain	C5	20
Motagua, stm., N.A.	E3	102
Motal', Bela.	H8	10
Motala, Swe.	G6	8
Mota Lava, i., Vanuatu	i16	79d
Motaze, Moz.	D11	70
Moteve, Cap, c., Fr. Poly.	s18	78g
Motherwell, Scot., U.K.	F9	12
Motihāri, India	E10	54
Motloutse, stm., Bots.	B9	70
Motopu, Fr. Poly.	s18	78g
Motozintla de Mendoza, Mex.	H12	100
Motril, Spain	H7	20
Motru, Rom.	E10	26
Mott, N.D., U.S.	A10	126
Motu, stm., N.Z.	C7	80
Motueka, N.Z.	E5	80
Motul de Felipe Carrillo Puerto, Mex.	B3	102
Motutapu, i., Cook Is.	a27	78j
Motygino, Russia	C17	32
Motyklejka, Russia	E18	34
Mouaskar, Alg.	B5	64
Mouchoir Passage, strt., N.A.	B12	102
Moudjéria, Maur.	F2	64
Moúdros, Grc.	D8	28
Mouila, Gabon	E2	66
Mould Bay, N.T., Can.	A16	140
Moule à Chique, Cap, c., St. Luc.	m7	105c
Moulins, Fr.	H12	14
Moulmein see Mawlamyine, Mya.	D3	48
Moulmeingyun, Mya.	D2	48
Moulouya, Oued, stm., Mor.	C4	64
Moulton, Al., U.S.	C11	122
Moulton, Ia., U.S.	D5	120
Moulton, Tx., U.S.	E10	130
Moultrie, Ga., U.S.	E2	116
Moultrie, Lake, res., S.C., U.S.	C5	116
Mouly, N. Cal.	m16	79d
Mounana, Gabon	E2	66
Mound City, Ks., U.S.	F3	120
Mound City, Mo., U.S.	D2	120
Mound City, S.D., U.S.	B12	126
Moundou, Chad	F3	62
Moundridge, Ks., U.S.	C11	128
Mounds, Ok., U.S.	B2	122
Moundsville, W.V., U.S.	E5	114
Moundville, Al., U.S.	E11	122
Mounlapamôk, Laos	E7	48
Mountain, Wi., U.S.	C1	112
Mountain, stm., N.T., Can.	C5	106
Mountainair, N.M., U.S.	G2	128
Mountainaire, Az., U.S.	H5	132
Mountain Brook, Al., U.S.	D12	122
Mountain City, Ga., U.S.	B2	116
Mountain City, Nv., U.S.	B1	132
Mountain Creek, Al., U.S.	E12	122
Mountain Grove, Mo., U.S.	G5	120
Mountain Home, Ar., U.S.	H5	120
Mountain Home, Id., U.S.	G11	136
Mountain Iron, Mn., U.S.	D6	118
Mountain Lake, Mn., U.S.	H3	118
Mountain Nile, stm., Afr.	F6	62
Mountain Park, Ab., Can.	D13	138
Mountain Pine, Ar., U.S.	C5	122
Mountain View, Ar., U.S.	I5	120
Mountain View, Ca., U.S.	F3	134
Mountain View, Ok., U.S.	F10	128
Mountain View, Wy., U.S.	E6	126
Mountain Village, Ak., U.S.	D7	140
Mountain Zebra National Park, p.o.i., S. Afr.	H7	70
Mount Airy, N.C., U.S.	H5	114
Mount Alida, S. Afr.	F10	70
Mount Angel, Or., U.S.	E4	136
Mount Aspiring National Park, p.o.i., N.Z.	G3	80
Mount Athos see Ágio Óros, state, Grc.	C7	28
Mount Ayliff, S. Afr.	G9	70
Mount Ayr, Ia., U.S.	D3	120
Mount Barker, Austl.	F3	74
Mount Barker, Austl.	J2	76
Mount Berry, Ga., U.S.	C13	122
Mount Buffalo National Park, p.o.i., Austl.	K5	76
Mount Calm, Tx., U.S.	C11	130
Mount Carmel, Il., U.S.	F10	120
Mount Carmel, Pa., U.S.	D9	114
Mount Carroll, Il., U.S.	B7	120
Mount Clemens, Mi., U.S.	B3	114
Mount Cook National Park, p.o.i., N.Z.	F4	80
Mount Dora, Fl., U.S.	H4	116
Mount Enterprise, Tx., U.S.	F4	122
Mount Field National Park, p.o.i., Austl.	o13	77a
Mount Forest, On., Can.	D9	112
Mount Frere, S. Afr.	G9	70
Mount Gambier, Austl.	K3	76
Mount Garnet, Austl.	A5	76
Mount Gay, W.V., U.S.	G3	114
Mount Hagen, Pap. N. Gui.	b3	79a
Mount Holly, N.C., U.S.	A4	116
Mount Holly Springs, Pa., U.S.	H12	112
Mount Hope, Austl.	F7	74
Mount Hope, Ks., U.S.	D11	128
Mount Horeb, Wi., U.S.	B8	120
Mount Ida, Ar., U.S.	C5	122
Mount Isa, Austl.	C2	76
Mount Jackson, Va., U.S.	F7	114
Mount Juliet, Tn., U.S.	H11	120
Mount Kaputar National Park, p.o.i., Austl.	H8	76
Mount Lebanon, Pa., U.S.	D6	114
Mount Lofty Ranges, mts., Austl.	I2	76
Mount Magnet, Austl.	E3	74
Mount Manara, Austl.	I4	76
Mount Margaret, Austl.	F4	76
Mount Morgan, Austl.	D8	76
Mount Morris, Il., U.S.	I9	118
Mount Morris, Mi., U.S.	E6	112
Mount Olive, Il., U.S.	E8	120
Mount Olive, Ms., U.S.	F9	122
Mount Olive, N.C., U.S.	A7	116
Mount Orab, Oh., U.S.	E2	114
Mount Perry, Austl.	E8	76
Mount Pleasant, On., Can.	E9	112
Mount Pleasant, Ia., U.S.	D6	120
Mount Pleasant, Mi., U.S.	E5	112
Mount Pleasant, Pa., U.S.	D6	114
Mount Pleasant, S.C., U.S.	D6	116
Mount Pleasant, Tn., U.S.	B11	122
Mount Pleasant, Tx., U.S.	D4	122
Mount Pleasant, Ut., U.S.	D5	132
Mount Pulaski, Il., U.S.	D8	120
Mount Rainier National Park, p.o.i., Wa., U.S.	D5	136
Mount Revelstoke National Park, p.o.i., B.C., Can.	E12	138
Mount Riddock, Austl.	D6	74
Mount Saint Helens National Volcanic Monument, p.o.i., Wa., U.S.	D5	136
Mount Selinda, Zimb.	B11	70
Mount Somers, N.Z.	F4	80
Mount Sterling, Il., U.S.	E7	120
Mount Sterling, Ky., U.S.	F2	114
Mount Sterling, Oh., U.S.	E2	114
Mount Uniacke, N.S., Can.	F12	110
Mount Union, Pa., U.S.	D8	114
Mount Vernon, Austl.	D3	74
Mount Vernon, Al., U.S.	F10	122
Mount Vernon, Ga., U.S.	D3	116
Mount Vernon, Il., U.S.	F8	120
Mount Vernon, Ia., U.S.	C6	120
Mount Vernon, Ky., U.S.	G1	114
Mount Vernon, Mo., U.S.	G4	120
Mount Vernon, Oh., U.S.	D3	114
Mount Vernon, Or., U.S.	F7	136
Mount Vernon, S.D., U.S.	D14	126
Mount Vernon, Wa., U.S.	B4	136
Mount Vernon, hist., Va., U.S.	F8	114
Mount William National Park, p.o.i., Austl.	n13	77a
Mount Willoughby, Austl.	E6	74
Mount Wolf, Pa., U.S.	H13	112
Moura, Braz.	H11	86
Moura, Port.	F3	20
Mourdi, Dépression du, depr., Chad	D4	62
Mourdiah, Mali	G3	64
Mourne Mountains, mts., N. Ire., U.K.	G6	12
Mouscron, Bel.	D12	14
Moussa 'Ali, mtn., Afr.	B8	66
Moussoro, Chad	E3	62
Moutier, Switz.	C4	22
Moutong, Indon.	E7	44
Mouzáki, Grc.	D4	28
Movenda, D.R.C.	D4	66
Moweaqua, Il., U.S.	E8	120
Moxotó, stm., Braz.	E7	88
Moyahua, Mex.	E7	100
Moyale, Kenya	D7	66
Moyamba, S.L.	H2	64
Moyen Atlas, mts., Mor.	C4	64
Moyeuvre-Grande, Fr.	E14	14
Moyie, B.C., Can.	G15	138
Moyie, stm., N.A.	H14	138
Moyo, Pulau, i., Indon.	H10	50
Moyobamba, Peru	E2	84
Moyu, China	A4	46
M'oža (Měža), stm., Eur.	E14	10
Možajsk, Russia	E18	10
Mozambique, ctry., Afr.	D5	68
Mozambique Channel, strt., Afr.	D7	68
Mozambique Plateau, unds.	M6	142
Mozdok, Russia	F6	32
Mozolevo, Russia	A16	10
Mpala, D.R.C.	F5	66
Mpanda, Tan.	F6	66
Mphoengs, Zimb.	B8	70
Mpika, Zam.	C5	68
Mporokoso, Zam.	B5	68
Mpui, Tan.	F6	66
Mpumalanga, state, S. Afr.	E9	70
Mpwapwa, Tan.	F7	66
Mqanduli, S. Afr.	G9	70
Mrągowo, Pol.	C17	16
Mrkonjić Grad, Bos.	E3	26
M'Saken, Tun.	I4	24
Mscislaŭ, Bela.	F14	10
Msciž, Bela.	F11	10
Msta, Russia	C17	10
Msta, stm., Russia	B15	10
Mszczonów, Pol.	E16	16
Mtama, Tan.	G7	66
Mtamvuna, stm., S. Afr.	G9	70
Mtwara, Tan.	G8	66
Mu, N. Cal.	m16	79d
Mu, stm., Mya.	A2	48
Mu, Cerro, mtn., S.A.	C5	86
Mu'a, Tonga	n14	78e
Mualang, Indon.	C7	50
Muanda, D.R.C.	F2	66
Muang Hay, Laos	B5	48
Muang Hôngsa, Laos	C5	48
Muang Hounxianghoung, Laos	B6	48
Muang Khammouan, Laos	D7	48
Muang Khao, Laos	C6	48
Muang Không, Laos	E7	48
Muang Khôngxédôn, Laos	E7	48
Muang La, Laos	B6	48
Muang Long, Laos	B5	48
Muang Ngoy, Laos	B6	48
Muang Nong, Laos	D8	48
Muang Ou Tai, Laos	A5	48
Muang Pak-Lay, Laos	C5	48
Muang Paktha, Laos	B5	48
Muang Pakxan, Laos	C6	48
Muang Phalan, Laos	D7	48
Muang Phônthong, Laos	E7	48
Muang Sam Sip, Thai.	E7	48
Muang Sing, Laos	B5	48
Muang Souvannakhili, Laos	E7	48
Muang Sung, Laos	B6	48
Muang Thatèng, Laos	E8	48
Muang Va, Laos	B6	48
Muang Vangviang, Laos	C6	48
Muang Xaignabouri, Laos	C5	48
Muang Xamtong, Laos	C6	48
Muang Xépôn, Laos	D7	48
Muang Yo, Laos	B5	48
Muar, Malay.	L6	48
Muar, stm., Malay.	K6	48
Muara, Bru.	A9	50
Muaraancalung, Indon.	C10	50
Muarabenangin, Indon.	D9	50
Muarabungo, Indon.	D2	50
Muaradua, Indon.	F4	50
Muaraenim, Indon.	E3	50
Muarajuloi, Indon.	D8	50
Muarakelingi, Indon.	E3	50
Muaralabuh, Indon.	D2	50
Muaralakitan, Indon.	E3	50
Muaralembu, Indon.	D2	50
Muarapangean, Indon.	B10	50
Muarapayang, Indon.	D9	50
Muarasabak, Indon.	D3	50
Muarasiberut, Indon.	D1	50
Muaratebo, Indon.	D3	50
Muarateladang, Indon.	E4	50
Muaratembesi, Indon.	D3	50
Muaratewe, Indon.	D9	50
Muaratunan, Indon.	D10	50
Mubārakpur, India	E9	54
Mubende, Ug.	D6	66
Mubi, Nig.	G7	64
Mubur, Pulau, i., Indon.	B4	50
Mucaitá, stm., Braz.	D4	88
Mucajaí, stm., Braz.	F11	86
Muchinga Escarpment, clf, Zam.	C4	68
Muchinga Mountains, mts., Zam.	C5	68
Muckadilla, Austl.	F7	76
Mučkas, Russia	D23	8
Mucojo, Moz.	C7	68
Muconda, Ang.	C3	68
Mucujê, Braz.	G5	88
Muçum, Braz.	D11	92
Mucuri, Braz.	J6	88
Mucuri, stm., Braz.	J6	88
Muda, stm., Malay.	J5	48
Mudan, stm., China	B10	36
Mudanjiang, China	B8	38
Mudanya, Tur.	C11	28
Mud Creek, stm., Ne., U.S.	F13	126
Mud Creek, stm., Tx., U.S.	E3	122
Muddus Nationalpark, p.o.i., Swe.	C9	8
Muddy, stm., Nv., U.S.	G2	132
Muddy Boggy Creek, stm., Ok., U.S.	C3	122
Muddy Creek, stm., Ut., U.S.	E6	132
Mudgee, Austl.	I7	76
Mudhol, India	C2	53
Mudjuga, Russia	E18	8
Mud Lake, l., Nv., U.S.	F8	134
Mudon, Mya.	D3	48
Mudurnu, Tur.	C14	28
Muelle de los Bueyes, Nic.	G5	102
Muenster, Tx., U.S.	H11	128
Muerto, Mar, l., Mex.	G11	100
Mufulira, Zam.	C4	68
Mufu Shan, mtn., China	G5	42
Mufu Shan, mts., China	G6	42
Mughal Sarāi, India	F9	54
Mugi, Japan	F7	40
Mu Gia, Deo, p., Asia	D7	48
Muğla, Tur.	F11	28
Muğla, state, Tur.	F11	28
Muḥammad Qawl, Sudan	C7	62
Muhanovo, Russia	D21	10
Muḥavec, stm., Bela.	H7	10
Muhino, Russia	F14	34
Mühlacker, Ger.	H4	16
Mühldorf am Inn, Ger.	H8	16
Mühlhausen, Ger.	E6	16
Muhlig-Hofmann Mountains, mts., Ant.	C5	81
Mühlviertel, reg., Aus.	B11	22
Muḥradah, Syria	C7	58
Muhu, i., Est.	G10	8
Muié, Ang.	C3	68
Mui Hopohoponga Point, c., Tonga	n14	78e
Muineachán see Monaghan, Ire.	G6	12
Muine Bheag, Ire.	I6	12
Muite, Moz.	C6	68
Muja, Russia	E12	34
Mujnak, Uzb.	F9	32
Mukah, Malay.	B8	50
Mukalla see Al-Mukallā, Yemen	G6	56
Mukatsjeve, Ukr.	A9	26
Mukāwir, hist., Jord.	G6	58
Mukdahan, Thai.	D7	48
Mukden see Shenyang, China	D5	38
Mukeriān, India	C5	54
Mukharram al-Fawqānī, Syria	D7	58
Mukilteo, Wa., U.S.	C4	136
Mukinbudin, Austl.	F3	74
Mukomuko, Indon.	E2	50
Mukry, Turkmen.	B10	56
Muktsar, India	C5	54
Mūl, India	A4	53
Mula, China	F5	36
Mula, Spain	F9	20
Mula, stm., India	B2	53
Mula, stm., India	B1	53
Mulaku Atoll, at., Mald.	i12	46a
Mulan, China	B10	36
Mulas, Punta de, c., Cuba	B10	102
Mulatos, Mex.	A4	100
Mulbāgal, India	E4	53
Mulberry, Ar., U.S.	B4	122
Mulberry, Fl., U.S.	I4	116
Mulberry Fork, stm., Al., U.S.	D12	122
Mulberry Mountain, mtn., Ar., U.S.	I5	120
Mulchatna, stm., Ak., U.S.	D8	140
Mulchén, Chile	H1	92
Mulde, stm., Ger.	E8	16
Muldoon, Tx., U.S.	E10	130
Muldraugh, Ky., U.S.	G12	120
Muldrow, Ok., U.S.	B4	122
Muleshoe, Tx., U.S.	G6	128
Mulgowie, Austl.	F9	76
Mulgrave, N.S., Can.	E15	110
Mulhacén, mtn., Spain	G7	20
Mulhall, Ok., U.S.	E11	128
Mulhouse, Fr.	G16	14
Muling, China	B9	38
Muling, China	B9	38
Muling, stm., China	B9	38
Mulinu'u, Cape, c., Samoa	g11	79c
Mūlki, India	E2	53
Mull, Island of, i., Scot., U.K.	E6	12
Mullengudgery, Austl.	H6	76
Muller, Pegunungan, mts., Indon.	C8	50
Mullet Peninsula, pen., Ire.	G2	12
Mullet Pond Bay, Neth. Ant.	A1	105a
Mullett Lake, l., Mi., U.S.	C5	112
Mullewa, Austl.	E3	74
Müllheim, Ger.	I3	16
Mullin, Tx., U.S.	C9	130
Mullingar, Ire.	H5	12
Mullins, S.C., U.S.	B6	116
Mulobezi, Zam.	D4	68
Mulongo, D.R.C.	F5	66
Mulshi Lake, res., India	B1	53
Multai, India	H7	54
Multān, Pak.	C3	54
Multé, Mex.	D2	102
Mulumbe, Monts, mts., D.R.C.	F5	66
Mulvane, Ks., U.S.	D11	128
Mumbai (Bombay), India	B1	53
Mumbwa, Zam.	D4	68
Mumen, China	E2	42
Mumeng, Pap. N. Gui.	b4	79a
Mumford, Tx., U.S.	G2	122
Mun, stm., Thai.	E7	48
Muna, stm., Russia	C13	34
Muna, Pulau, i., Indon.	F7	44
Muncar, Indon.	H9	50
Münchberg, Ger.	F7	16
München (Munich), Ger.	H7	16
Munchique, Cerro, mtn., Col.	F3	86
Munchique, Parque Nacional, p.o.i., Col.	F3	86
Muncie, In., U.S.	H4	112
Muncy, Pa., U.S.	C9	114
Mundare, Ab., Can.	C18	138
Munday, Tx., U.S.	H9	128
Mundelein, Il., U.S.	B9	120
Münden, Ger.	E5	16
Mundra, India	G2	54
Mundrabilla, Austl.	F5	74
Mundubbera, Austl.	E8	76
Munfordville, Ky., U.S.	G12	120
Mungallala Creek, stm., Austl.	F6	76
Mungana, Austl.	C8	74
Mungar Junction, Austl.	E9	76
Mungbere, D.R.C.	D5	66
Mungeli, India	G8	54
Munger, India	F11	54
Mungindi, Austl.	G7	76
Mungo, Ang.	C2	68
Mungo National Park, p.o.i., Austl.	I4	76
Munhango, Ang.	C2	68
Munich see München, Ger.	H7	16
Muniesa, Spain	C10	20
Munim, stm., Braz.	B3	88
Munising, Mi., U.S.	B3	112
Muniz Freire, Braz.	K5	88
Munku-Sardyk, gora, mtn., Asia	D17	32
Münsingen, Ger.	H5	16

Name — Map Ref. — Page

Neegro, Qooriga, b., Som. C10 66
Ñeembucú, state, Para. C8 92
Neenah, Wi., U.S. G10 118
Neepawa, Mb., Can. D14 124
Nefëdovo, Russia C12 32
Nefta, Tun. C6 64
Neftçala, Azer. B6 56
Neftejugansk, Russia B12 32
Nefza, Tun. H3 24
Negage, Ang. B2 68
Negara, Indon. H9 50
Negara, stm., Indon. E9 50
Negaunee, Mi., U.S. B2 112
Negēlē, Eth. F7 62
Negeribatin, Indon. F4 50
Negeri Sembilan, state, Malay. K6 48
Negev Desert see HaNegev, reg., Isr. H5 58
Negombo, Sri L. H4 53
Negra, Laguna, l., Ur. G11 92
Negreira, Spain B2 20
Nègres, Pointe des, c., Mart. k6 105c
Negrești-Oaș, Rom. B10 26
Negritos, Peru D1 84
Negro, stm., Arg. H4 90
Negro, stm., Braz. C13 92
Negro, stm., Col. E4 86
Negro, stm., Para. B9 92
Negro, stm., S.A. I11 86
Negro, stm., S.A. F9 92
Negros, i., Phil. F4 52
Nehalem, stm., Or., U.S. E3 136
Neharèlae, Bela. G9 10
Nehawka, Ne., U.S. D1 120
Nehbandān, Iran C8 56
Nehe see Nahe, China B9 36
Néhoué, Baie de, b., N. Cal. m14 79d
Neiba, Dom. Rep. C12 102
Neichiang see Neijiang, China G1 42
Neidpath, Sk., Can. D6 124
Neiges, Piton des, mtn., Reu. i10 69a
Neijiang, China G1 42
Neikiang see Neijiang, China G1 42
Neilburg, Sk., Can. B4 124
Neillsville, Wi., U.S. G8 118
Nei Monggol, state, China C7 36
Nei Mongol see Nei Monggol, state, China C7 36
Neiqiu, China C6 42
Neira, Col. E4 86
Neisse see Lausitzer Neisse, stm., Eur. F10 16
Neisse see Nysa Łużycka, stm., Eur. E10 16
Neiva, Col. F4 86
Neixiang, China E4 42
Neja, Russia G20 8
Nejapa de Madero, Mex. G11 100
Nejd see Najd, hist. reg., Sau. Ar. D5 56
Nejdek, Czech Rep. F8 16
Nek'emtē, Eth. F7 62
Nelichu, mtn., Sudan F6 62
Nelidovo, Russia D15 10
Neligh, Ne., U.S. E14 126
Neljaty, Russia E12 34
Nel'kan, Russia E16 34
Nellikuppam, India F4 53
Nellore, India D4 53
Nel'ma, Russia G16 34
Nelson, B.C., Can. G13 138
Nelson, N.Z. E5 80
Nelson, Ne., U.S. A10 128
Nelson, stm., Mb., Can. D12 106
Nelson, Cape, c., Austl. L3 76
Nelson, Estrecho, strt., Chile J2 90
Nelson Lakes National Park, p.o.i., N.Z. E5 80
Nelson's Dockyard, hist., Antig. f4 105b
Nelsonville, Oh., U.S. E3 114
Nelspoort, S. Afr. H6 70
Nelspruit, S. Afr. D10 70
Néma, Maur. F3 64
Nemadji, stm., U.S. E6 118
Neman, Russia E4 10
Neman (Nemunas), stm., Eur. E4 10
Nembe, Nig. I6 64
Nemenčinė, Lith. F8 10
Nemeriči, Russia G16 10
Nemours, Fr. F11 14
Nemunas (Neman), stm., Eur. E4 10
Nemunėlis (Mēmele), stm., Eur. D7 10
Nemuro, Japan C16 38
Nemuro Strait, strt., Asia C16 38
Nen, stm., China B9 36
Nenagh, Ire. I4 12
Nenana, Ak., U.S. D10 140
Nenana, stm., Ak., U.S. D10 140
Nendo, i., Sol. Is. E7 72
Nene, stm., Eng., U.K. I13 12
Neneckij avtonomnyj okrug, Russia C23 8
Nenets see Neneckij avtonomnyj okrug, Russia C23 8
Nenetsia see Neneckij avtonomnyj okrug, Russia C23 8
Nenggiri, stm., Malay. J5 48
Neodesha, Ks., U.S. G2 120
Neoga, Il., U.S. E9 120
Néo Karlovási, Grc. F9 28
Neola, Ut., U.S. C6 132
Neopit, Wi., U.S. G10 118
Neosho, Mo., U.S. H3 120
Neosho, stm., U.S. H2 120
Nepa, stm., Russia C19 32
Nepal, ctry., Asia E9 54
Nepālgañj, Nepal D8 54
Nepa Nagar, India H6 54
Nepeña, Peru E2 84
Nephin, mtn., Ire. G3 12
Nepisiguit, stm., N.B., Can. C10 110
Nepisiguit Bay, b., N.B., Can. C11 110
Neptune, N.J., U.S. D11 114
Neptune Beach, Fl., U.S. F4 116
Nérac, Fr. E6 18
Nerča, stm., Russia F12 34
Nerčinsk, Russia F12 34
Nerčinskij Zavod, Russia F12 34
Nerehta, Russia H19 8
Neretva, stm., Eur. G15 22
Neriquinha, Ang. D3 68
Neris (Vilija), stm., Eur. F6 10
Nerja, Spain H7 20
Nerjungri, Russia E13 34
Nerl', Russia C20 10
Nerl', stm., Russia D22 10
Nerópolis, Braz. I1 88
Nerussa, stm., Russia H16 10
Nerva, Spain G4 20
Nes, Neth. C1 16
Nesbyen, Nor. F3 8
Neščarda, vozero, l., Bela. E12 10
Neskaupstaður, Ice. k32 8a
Nesna, Nor. C5 8
Nespelem, Wa., U.S. B7 136
Ness, Loch, l., Scot., U.K. D8 12
Ness City, Ks., U.S. C8 128
Nesselrode, Mount, mtn., N.A. D4 106
Nesterkovo, Russia A13 10
Nestoïta, Ukr. B16 26
Netanya, Isr. F5 58
Netherdale, Austl. C7 76
Netherlands, ctry., Eur. B14 14
Netherlands Antilles, dep., N.A. i14 96a
Netherlands Guiana see Surinam, ctry., S.A. C6 84
Netrakona, Bngl. F13 54
Nettilling Fiord, b., Nu., Can. B17 106
Nettilling Lake, l., Nu., Can. B17 106
Nett Lake, l., Mn., U.S. C5 118
Nettuno, Italy C6 24
Neubrandenburg, Ger. C9 16
Neuburg an der Donau, Ger. H7 16
Neuchâtel, Switz. D3 22
Neuchâtel, Lac de, l., Switz. D3 22
Neudorf, Sk., Can. D11 124
Neuenburg see Neuchâtel, Switz. D3 22
Neuenhagen, Ger. D9 16
Neuerburg, Ger. F2 16
Neufchâteau, Fr. F14 14
Neufchâtel-en-Bray, Fr. E10 14
Neu-Isenburg, Ger. F4 16
Neumarkt in der Oberpfalz, Ger. G7 16
Neumünster, Ger. B6 16
Neun, stm., Laos C6 48
Neunkirchen, Aus. C13 22
Neuquén, Arg. G3 90
Neuquén, state, Arg. G2 90
Neuquén, stm., Arg. G3 90
Neurara, Chile B3 92
Neuruppin, Ger. D8 16
Neuse, stm., N.C., U.S. A8 116
Neusiedl am See, Aus. C13 22
Neuss, Ger. E2 16
Neustadt, Ger. F7 16
Neustadt an der Aisch, Ger. G6 16
Neustadt an der Weinstrasse, Ger. G3 16
Neustadt bei Coburg, Ger. F6 16
Neustadt in Holstein, Ger. B6 16
Neustrelitz, Ger. C9 16
Neutral Hills, hills, Ab., Can. B3 124
Neu-Ulm, Ger. H6 16
Neuvic, Fr. D8 18
Neuwied, Ger. F3 16
Neva, stm., Russia A13 10
Nevada, Ia., U.S. B4 120
Nevada, Mo., U.S. G3 120
Nevada, state, U.S. D4 108
Nevada, Sierra, mts., Spain G7 20
Nevada, Sierra, mts., Ca., U.S. F6 134
Nevada City, Ca., U.S. D4 134
Nevado, Cerro, mtn., Arg. G3 92
Nevado, Cerro, mtn., Col. E4 86
Nevado de Colima, Parque Nacional del, p.o.i., Mex. F7 100
Nevado de Toluca, Parque Nacional, p.o.i., Mex. F8 100
Neve, Serra da, mts., Ang. C1 68
Nevel', Russia D12 10
Nevel'sk, Russia G17 34
Nevel'skogo, proliv, strt., Russia F17 34
Never, Russia F13 34
Nevers, Fr. G12 14
Nevesinje, Bos. F5 26
Nevinnomyssk, Russia F6 32
Nevis, i., St. K./N. C2 105a
Nevis, Ben, mtn., Scot., U.K. E7 12
Nevis Peak, vol., St. K./N. C2 105a
Nevjansk, Russia C10 32
Nevşehir, Tur. B3 56
New, stm., Belize D3 102
New, stm., Guy. C6 84
New, stm., U.S. F4 114
New, stm., S.C., U.S. D4 116
Newala, Tan. G7 66
New Albany, In., U.S. F12 120
New Albany, Ms., U.S. C9 122
New Amsterdam, Guy. B6 84
New Angledool, Austl. G6 76
Newark, Ar., U.S. B7 122
Newark, De., U.S. E10 114
Newark, N.J., U.S. D11 114
Newark, N.Y., U.S. A8 114
Newark, Oh., U.S. D3 114
Newark Lake, l., Nv., U.S. D1 132
Newark-on-Trent, Eng., U.K. H12 12
Newark Valley, N.Y., U.S. B9 114
New Athens, Il., U.S. F8 120
New Augusta, Ms., U.S. F9 122
New Baden, Il., U.S. F8 120
New Bedford, Ma., U.S. C15 114
Newberg, Or., U.S. E4 136
New Berlin, Il., U.S. E7 120
New Berlin, N.Y., U.S. B10 114
New Berlin, Wi., U.S. F1 112
Newbern, Al., U.S. E11 122
New Bern, N.C., U.S. A8 116
Newbern, Tn., U.S. H8 120
Newberry, Fl., U.S. G3 116
Newberry, S.C., U.S. B4 116
Newberry National Volcanic Monument, p.o.i., Or., U.S. G5 136
New Bethlehem, Pa., U.S. D6 114
New Bloomfield, Pa., U.S. H12 112
New Boston, Oh., U.S. F3 114
New Boston, Tx., U.S. D4 122
New Braunfels, Tx., U.S. E9 130
New Britain, Ct., U.S. C13 114
New Britain, i., Pap. N. Gui. b5 79a
New Brockton, Al., U.S. F12 122
Newbrook, Ab., Can. B17 138
New Brunswick, N.J., U.S. D11 114
New Brunswick, state, Can. D10 110
Newburg, Mo., U.S. G6 120
Newburgh, In., U.S. G10 120
Newburgh, N.Y., U.S. C11 114
Newbury, Eng., U.K. J11 12
Newburyport, Ma., U.S. B15 114
New Caledonia, dep., Oc. F7 72
New Caledonia see Nouvelle-Calédonie, i., N. Cal. m15 79d
New Caledonia Basin, unds. L19 142
New Carlisle, Qc., Can. B11 110
New Carlisle, Oh., U.S. E2 114
New Castille see Castilla la Nueva, hist. reg., Spain E7 20
Newcastle, Austl. I8 76
Newcastle, N.B., Can. C11 110
Newcastle, St. K./N. C2 105a
Newcastle, S. Afr. E9 70
Newcastle, N. Ire., U.K. G7 12
New Castle, Co., U.S. D9 132
New Castle, De., U.S. E10 114
New Castle, In., U.S. I4 112
Newcastle, Ne., U.S. I2 118
Newcastle, Ok., U.S. F11 128
New Castle, Pa., U.S. D5 114
Newcastle, Tx., U.S. A9 130
New Castle, Va., U.S. G5 114
Newcastle, Wy., U.S. D8 126
Newcastle Bay, b., Austl. B8 74
Newcastle-under-Lyme, Eng., U.K. I10 12
Newcastle upon Tyne, Eng., U.K. G10 12
Newcastle Waters, Austl. C6 74
Newcastle West, Ire. I3 12
New City, N.Y., U.S. C11 114
Newcomerstown, Oh., U.S. D4 114
New Concord, Oh., U.S. D4 114
New Cumberland, W.V., U.S. D5 114
Newdegate, Austl. F3 74
New Delhi, India D6 54
New Denver, B.C., Can. F13 138
New Edinburg, Ar., U.S. D6 122
New Effington, S.D., U.S. F1 118
Newell, Ia., U.S. B2 120
Newell, W.V., U.S. D5 114
Newell, Lake, l., Ab., Can. F19 138
New Ellenton, S.C., U.S. C4 116
Newellton, La., U.S. E7 122
New England, N.D., U.S. A10 126
New England National Park, p.o.i., Austl. H9 76
Newfane, N.Y., U.S. E11 112
Newfane, Vt., U.S. A13 114
New Florence, Pa., U.S. D6 114
Newfound Gap, p., U.S. I2 114
Newfoundland, state, Can. j22 107a
Newfoundland, i., Nf., Can. j22 107a
Newfoundland Basin, unds. D9 144
New Franklin, Mo., U.S. E5 120
New Freedom, Pa., U.S. E9 114
New Galloway, Scot., U.K. F8 12
Newgate, B.C., Can. G15 138
New Georgia, i., Sol. Is. e7 79b
New Georgia Group, is., Sol. Is. d7 79b
New Georgia Sound, strt., Sol. Is. e8 79b
New Germany, N.S., Can. F12 110
New Glasgow, N.S., Can. E14 110
New Guinea, i. b3 79a
Newhalem, Wa., U.S. B5 136
New Hamburg, On., Can. E9 112
New Hampshire, state, U.S. G5 110
New Hampton, Ia., U.S. A5 120
New Hanover, S. Afr. F10 70
New Hanover, i., Pap. N. Gui. a4 79a
New Harmony, In., U.S. F10 120
New Hartford, Ia., U.S. I6 118
Newhaven, Eng., U.K. K13 12
New Haven, Ct., U.S. C13 114
New Haven, Il., U.S. G9 120
New Haven, Ky., U.S. G12 120
New Haven, Mo., U.S. F6 120
New Hazelton, B.C., Can. A3 138
New Hebrides see Vanuatu, ctry., Oc. k16 79d
New Hebrides, is., Vanuatu k16 79d
New Hebrides Trench, unds. L20 142
Newhebron, Ms., U.S. F9 122
New Holland, Oh., U.S. E2 114
New Holland, Pa., U.S. D9 114
New Holstein, Wi., U.S. E1 112
New Hope, Al., U.S. C12 122
New Iberia, La., U.S. G7 122
New Ireland, i., Pap. N. Gui. a5 79a
New Jersey, state, U.S. D11 114
New Johnsonville, Tn., U.S. H10 120
New Kensington, Pa., U.S. D6 114
New Kent, Va., U.S. G9 114
Newkirk, Ok., U.S. E11 128
New Kowloon see Xinjiulong, China J6 42
Newlands, Austl. C6 76
New Lexington, Oh., U.S. E3 114
New Lisbon, Wi., U.S. H8 118
New Liskeard, On., Can. F14 106
New Llano, La., U.S. F5 122
New London, Ct., U.S. C13 114
New London, Mo., U.S. E6 120
New London, N.H., U.S. G5 110
New London, Oh., U.S. C3 114
New London, Tx., U.S. E4 122
New London, Wi., U.S. G10 118
New Madrid, Mo., U.S. H8 120
Newman, Austl. D3 74
Newman, Ca., U.S. F4 134
Newman Grove, Ne., U.S. F15 126
Newmarket, On., Can. D10 112
Newmarket, Eng., U.K. I13 12
New Market, Al., U.S. C12 122
New Market, Ia., U.S. D3 120
Newmarket, N.H., U.S. G5 110
New Market, Va., U.S. F7 114
New Martinsville, W.V., U.S. E4 114
New Mexico, state, U.S. D9 98
New Milford, Ct., U.S. C12 114
New Milford, Pa., U.S. C10 114
Newnan, Ga., U.S. D14 122
New Norfolk, Austl. o13 77a
New Norway, Ab., Can. D18 138
New Orleans, La., U.S. G8 122
New Paris, Oh., U.S. I5 112
New Philadelphia, Oh., U.S. D4 114
New Pine Creek, Or., U.S. A5 134
New Plymouth, N.Z. D5 80
New Plymouth, Id., U.S. G10 136
Newport, Eng., U.K. K11 12
Newport, Wales, U.K. J10 12
Newport, Ar., U.S. B7 122
Newport, Ky., U.S. E1 114
Newport, Me., U.S. F7 110
Newport, N.H., U.S. G4 110
Newport, N.C., U.S. B8 116
Newport, Or., U.S. F2 136
Newport, Pa., U.S. D8 114
Newport, R.I., U.S. C14 114
Newport, Tn., U.S. I2 114
Newport, Vt., U.S. F4 110
Newport Beach, Ca., U.S. J7 134
Newport News, Va., U.S. G9 114
New Port Richey, Fl., U.S. H3 116
New Providence, i., Bah. C9 96
Newquay, Eng., U.K. K7 12
New Richland, Mn., U.S. H5 118
New Richmond, Qc., Can. B10 110
New Richmond, Wi., U.S. F6 118
New River, St. K./N. C2 105a
New Road, N.S., Can. F13 110
New Roads, La., U.S. G7 122
New Rochelle, N.Y., U.S. D12 114
New Ross, N.S., Can. F12 110
New Ross, Ire. I6 12
Newry, N. Ire., U.K. G6 12
Newry, S.C., U.S. B3 116
New Salem, N.D., U.S. A11 126
New Schwabenland, reg., Ant. C5 81
New Sharon, Ia., U.S. C5 120
New Siberian Islands see Novosibirskie ostrova, is., Russia A18 34
New Smyrna Beach, Fl., U.S. G5 116
New South Wales, state, Austl. I6 76
New Tazewell, Tn., U.S. H2 114
New Tecumseth, On., Can. D9 112
Newton, Ga., U.S. F14 122
Newton, Il., U.S. F9 120
Newton, Ia., U.S. C4 120
Newton, Ks., U.S. C11 128
Newton, Ma., U.S. B14 114
Newton, Ms., U.S. E9 122
Newton, N.J., U.S. C11 114
Newton, Tx., U.S. G5 122
Newton Falls, N.Y., U.S. F2 110
Newton Stewart, Scot., U.K. G8 12
New Town, N.D., U.S. F11 124
Newtownabbey, N. Ire., U.K. G6 12
Newtownards, N. Ire., U.K. G7 12
New Ulm, Mn., U.S. G4 118
New Ulm, Tx., U.S. H2 122
New Washington, Oh., U.S. D3 114
New Waterford, N.S., Can. D16 110
New Waverly, Tx., U.S. G3 122
New Westminster, B.C., Can. G8 138
New Whiteland, In., U.S. E11 120
New York, N.Y., U.S. D12 114
New York, state, U.S. C12 108
New York Mills, Mn., U.S. E3 118
New York State Barge Canal, can., N.Y., U.S. E12 112
New Zealand, ctry., Oc. D4 80
Neyrīz, Iran D7 56
Neyshābūr, Iran B8 56
Neyveli, India F4 53
Neyyāttinkara, India G3 53
Nezahualcóyotl, Presa, res., Mex. G12 100
Nezavertailovca, Mol. C16 26
Nezperce, Id., U.S. D10 136
Ngabang, Indon. C6 50
Ngabé, Congo E3 66
Ngambé, Cam. D2 66
Ngami, Lake, l., Bots. B6 70
Ngamiland, state, Bots. B6 70
Ngan-chouei see Anhui, state, China F7 42
Ngangla Ringco, l., China C9 54
Nganglong Kangri, mts., China B9 54
Ngangzê Co, l., China C11 54
Nganjuk, Indon. G7 50
Ngao, Thai. C5 48
Ngaoui, Mont, mtn., Afr. F3 62
Ngaoundéré, Cam. C2 66
Ngape, Mya. B2 48
Ngaputaw, Mya. D2 48
Ngara, Tan. E6 66
Ngatangiia, Cook Is. a27 78j
Ngatangiia Harbour, b., Cook Is. a27 78j
Ngawi, Indon. G7 50
Ngay Nua, Laos B5 48
Ngcheangel, is., Palau D9 44
Ngeaur, i., Palau D9 44
Ngereklmadel, Palau g7 78b
Ngerkeai, Palau g8 78b
Ngermetengel, Palau f7 78b
Ngeruktabel, i., Palau h7 78b
Ngetbong, Palau f8 78b
Nggatokae Island, i., Sol. Is. e8 79b
Nggela Pile, i., Sol. Is. e9 79b
Nghia Hanh, Viet. E9 48
Ngiap, stm., Laos C6 48
Ngidinga, D.R.C. F3 66
Ng'iro, mtn., Kenya D7 66
Ngiro, Ewaso, stm., Kenya D7 66
Ngo, Congo E3 66
Ngoko, stm., Afr. D3 66
Ngom, stm., China B8 46
Ngomeni, Ras, c., Kenya E8 66
Ngong, Kenya E7 66
Ngoring Hu, l., China E4 36
Ngounié, stm., Gabon E2 66
Ngouri, Chad E3 62
Nguigmi, Niger G7 64
Ngulu, at., Micron. C4 72
Ngum, stm., Laos C6 48
Nguna, Île, i., Vanuatu k17 79d
Nguru, Nig. G7 64
Nhacoongo, Moz. D12 70
Nhamundá, stm., Braz. D6 84
Nha Trang, Viet. F9 48
Nhill, Austl. K3 76
Nhoma, stm., Afr. D2 68
Niafounké, Mali F4 64
Niagara, Wi., U.S. C1 112
Niagara Falls, On., Can. E10 112
Niagara Falls, N.Y., U.S. A6 114
Niagara Falls, wtfl, N.A. E10 112
Niagara-on-the-Lake, On., Can. E10 112
Niagassola, Gui. G3 64
Niah, Malay. B8 50
Niamey, Niger G5 64
Niangara, D.R.C. D5 66
Niangay, Lac, l., Mali F4 64
Niangoloko, Burkina G4 64
Niangua, stm., Mo., U.S. G5 120
Nia-Nia, D.R.C. D5 66
Niantic, Il., U.S. E8 120
Nianyushan, China G7 42
Nianzishan, China B9 36
Niari, stm., Congo E2 66
Nias, Pulau, i., Indon. L3 48
Nicaragua, ctry., N.A. F5 102
Nicaragua, Lago de, l., Nic. G5 102
Nicaragua, Lake see Nicaragua, Lago de, l., Nic. G5 102
Nicastro, Italy F10 24
Nice, Fr. F13 18
Niceville, Fl., U.S. G12 122
Nichinan, Japan H4 40
Nicholas Channel (San Nicolás, Canal de), strt., N.A. G11 108
Nicholasville, Ky., U.S. G13 120
Nicholls, Ga., U.S. E3 116
Nicholl's Town, Bah. B9 96
Nicholson, Pa., U.S. C10 114
Nickel Centre, On., Can. B8 112
Nickerson, Ks., U.S. C10 128
Nicobar Islands, is., India G7 46
Nicola, B.C., Can. F10 138
Nicola, stm., B.C., Can. F9 138
Nicolae Bălcescu, Rom. B13 26
Nicolet, Qc., Can. D4 110
Nicolet, Lake, l., Mi., U.S. B5 112
Nicolet Sud-Ouest, stm., Qc., Can. E5 110
Nicollet, Mn., U.S. G4 118
Nicosia (Levkosía), Cyp. C4 58
Nicosia, Italy G8 24
Nicoya, Golfo de, b., C.R. H5 102
Nicoya, Península de, pen., C.R. H5 102
Nida, Lith. E3 10
Nida, stm., Pol. F16 16
Nidadavole, India C5 53
Nidzica, Pol. C16 16
Niebüll, Ger. B4 16
Niedere Tauern, mts., Aus. C10 22
Niederösterreich, state, Aus. B12 22
Niedersachsen, state, Ger. D4 16
Niekerkshoop, S. Afr. F6 70
Niemba, D.R.C. F5 66
Niemodlin, Pol. F13 16
Nienburg, Ger. D5 16
Niers, stm., Eur. C15 14
Niesky, Ger. E10 16
Nieszawa, Pol. D14 16
Nieu-Bethesda, S. Afr. G7 70
Nieuport see Nieuwpoort, Bel. C11 14
Nieuw Amsterdam, Sur. B6 84
Nieuw Nickerie, Sur. B6 84
Nieuwpoort, Bel. C11 14
Nieuwpoort, Neth. Ant. p22 104g
Nièvre, state, Fr. G12 14
Nifisha, Egypt H3 58
Niğde, Tur. H15 6
Niğde, state, Tur. A5 58
Nigei Island, i., B.C., Can. F3 138
Nigel, S. Afr. E9 70
Niger, ctry., Afr. F6 64
Niger, stm., Afr. H6 64
Niger Delta, Nig. I6 64
Nigeria, ctry., Afr. H6 64
Nightcaps, N.Z. G3 80
Nighthawk, Wa., U.S. B7 136
Nigríta, Grc. C6 28
Niheidât el-Sûd, Gebel el-, mtn., Egypt J3 58
Nihommatsu, Japan B13 40
Nihuil, Embalse del, res., Arg. G3 92
Niigata, Japan B11 40
Niigata, state, Japan B11 40
Niihama, Japan F6 40
Niihau, i., Hi., U.S. B1 78a
Nii-jima, i., Japan E12 40
Niitsu, Japan B12 40
Níjar, Spain H8 20
Nijmegen, Neth. C14 14
Nijvel see Nivelles, Bel. D13 14
Nikel', Russia B14 8
Nikki, Benin G5 64
Nikkō, Japan C12 40
Nikkō-kokuritsu-kōen, p.o.i., Japan B12 40
Nikolaevo, Russia B12 10
Nikolaevsk-na-Amure, Russia F17 34
Nikol'sk, Russia G21 8
Nikol'sk, Russia C6 32
Nikolski, Ak., U.S. F6 140
Nikol'skij, Russia F15 8
Nikol'skoe, Russia H19 10
Nikol'skoe, Russia E22 34
Nikopol', Ukr. E4 32
Nīkshahr, Iran D9 56
Nikšić, Yugo. G5 26
Nikumaroro, at., Kir. D9 72
Nikunau, i., Kir. D8 72
Nīl, Bahr el- see Nile, stm., Afr. B6 62
Nīl, Nahr an- see Nile, stm., Afr. D6 62
Nila, Pulau, i., Indon. G9 44
Nilakka, l., Fin. E12 8
Nile, stm., Afr. D6 62
Nile Delta, Egypt H1 58
Niles, Il., U.S. B10 120
Niles, Mi., U.S. G3 112
Niles, Oh., U.S. C5 114
Nīlgiri, India H11 54
Nilka, China F14 32
Nilsiä, Fin. E12 8
Nīmach, India F5 54
Nimba, Mount, mtn., Afr. H3 64
Nimbāhera, India F5 54
Nîmes, Fr. F10 18
Nimpkish Lake, l., B.C., Can. F3 138
Nimule, Sudan G6 62
Ninda, Ang. C3 68
Nindigully, Austl. G7 76
Nine Degree Channel, strt., India G3 46
Ninette, Mb., Can. E14 124
Ninetyeast Ridge, unds. K11 142
Ninety Mile Beach, cst., Austl. L6 76
Ninety Six, S.C., U.S. B3 116
Ninfas, Punta, c., Arg. H4 90
Ninga, Mb., Can. E14 124
Ning'an, China B8 38
Ningbo, China G9 42
Ningcheng, China D3 38
Ningde, China H8 42
Ningdu, China H6 42
Ningguo, China F8 42
Ninghai, China G9 42
Ning-hia see Ningxia, state, China D6 36
Ninghua, China H7 42
Ningi, Nig. G6 64
Ningjing Shan, mts., China F4 36
Ningming, China J2 42
Ningnan, China F5 36
Ningpo see Ningbo, China G9 42
Ningqiang, China E2 42
Ningshan, China E3 42
Ningsia see Yinchuan, China B2 42
Ningsia Hui see Ningxia, state, China D6 36
Ningsia Hui Autonomous Region see Ningxia, state, China D6 36
Ningwu, China B4 42
Ningxia, state, China D6 36
Ningxiang, China G5 42
Ningyuan, China I4 42
Ninh Binh, Viet. B7 48
Ninh Hoa, Viet. F9 48
Ninhue, Chile H1 92
Ninigo Group, is., Pap. N. Gui. a3 79a
Ninnescah, North Fork, stm., Ks., U.S. D10 128
Ninnescah, South Fork, stm., Ks., U.S. D10 128
Ninohe, Japan D14 38
Nioaque, Braz. D5 90
Niobrara, stm., U.S. E14 126
Nioghalvfjerdsfjorden, ice, Grnld. B22 141
Nioki, D.R.C. E3 66
Niono, Mali G3 64
Nioro, Mali F3 64
Niort, Fr. C5 18
Niota, Tn., U.S. B14 122
Nipāni, India C2 53
Nipawin, Sk., Can. E10 106
Nipe, Bahía de, b., Cuba B10 102
Nipigon, On., Can. B10 118
Nipigon, Lake, res., On., Can. B10 118
Nipigon Bay, b., On., Can. C10 118
Nipissing, Lake, l., On., Can. B10 112
Nipomo, Ca., U.S. H5 134
Niquelândia, Braz. H1 88
Niquero, Cuba B9 102
Niquivil, Arg. E3 92
Nīra, stm., India B2 53
Nirasaki, Japan D11 40
Nirgua, Ven. B7 86
Nirmal, India B4 53
Nirmāli, India E11 54
Niš, Yugo. F8 26
Nişāb, Yemen G6 56
Nišava, stm., Eur. F9 26
Niscemi, Italy G8 24
Nishio, Japan E10 40
Nishiwaki, Japan E7 40
Nisporeni, Mol. B15 26
Nisqually, stm., Wa., U.S. D4 136
Nisswa, Mn., U.S. E4 118
Nītaure, Lat. C8 10
Niterói, Braz. L4 88
Nith, stm., On., Can. E9 112
Nitinat Lake, l., B.C., Can. H6 138
Nitra, Slov. H14 16
Nitra, stm., Slov. H14 16
Nitro, W.V., U.S. F4 114
Niue, dep., Oc. E10 72
Niulakita, i., Tuvalu E8 72
Niut, Gunung, mtn., Indon. C6 50
Niutao, i., Tuvalu D8 72
Niutoushan, China B7 38
Niutou Shan, i., China G9 42
Niuzhuang, China A10 42
Nive, stm., Austl. E6 76
Nivelles, Bel. D13 14
Nivernais, hist. reg., Fr. G12 14
Niverville, Mb., Can. E16 124
Nixa, Mo., U.S. G4 120
Nixon, Nv., U.S. D6 134
Niža, Russia C20 8
Nizāmābād, India B4 53
Nizām Sāgar, res., India C3 53
Nižegorodskaja oblast', co., Russia H21 8
Nizip, Tur. A8 58
Nízke Tatry, Narodny Park, p.o.i., Slov. H15 16
Nižneangarsk, Russia E10 34
Nižnee Kujto, ozero, l., Russia D14 8
Nižneilimsk, Russia C18 32
Nižnekamsk, Russia C8 32
Nižnekamskoe vodohranilišče, res., Russia C8 32
Nižneudinsk, Russia D17 32
Nižnevartovsk, Russia B13 32
Nižnij Casučej, Russia F12 34
Nižnij Kuranah, Russia E14 34
Nižnij Novgorod (Gorki), Russia H21 8
Nižnij Pjandž, Taj. B10 56
Nižnij Tagil, Russia C10 32
Nižnjaja Peša, Russia C22 8
Nižnjaja Pojma, Russia C17 32
Nižnjaja Tavda, Russia C11 32
Nižnjaja Tunguska, stm., Russia B16 32
Nizza Monferrato, Italy F5 22
Njandoma, Russia F19 8
Njasviž, Bela. G9 10
Njazidja, i., Com. C7 68
Njesuthi, mtn., Afr. F9 70
Njombe, stm., Tan. F7 66
Njuhča, Russia E22 8
Njuja, Russia D12 34
Njuja, stm., Russia B20 32
Njuk, ozero, l., Russia D14 8
Njuksenica, Russia F21 8
Njurba, Russia D12 34
Njuvčim, Russia B8 32
Nkambe, Cam. C2 66
Nkawkaw, Ghana H4 64
Nkayi, Zimb. D4 68
Nkhata Bay, Mwi. C5 68
Nkhotakota, Mwi. C5 68
Nkomi, Lagune, l., Gabon E1 66
Nkongsamba, Cam. D2 66
Nkwalini, S. Afr. F10 70
Nmai, stm., Mya. C8 46
Noākhāli, Bngl. G13 54
Noatak, Ak., U.S. C7 140
Noatak, stm., Ak., U.S. C8 140
Nobeoka, Japan G4 40
Noble, Il., U.S. F9 120
Noblesville, In., U.S. H3 112
Noboribetsu, Japan C14 38
Nobres, Braz. F6 84
Nocatee, Fl., U.S. I4 116
Noce, stm., Italy D8 22
Nocera Inferiore, Italy D8 24
Nockatunga, Austl. F4 76
Nocona, Tx., U.S. H11 128
Nocupétaro, Mex. F8 100
Noetinger, Arg. F6 92
Nogales, Mex. F7 98
Nogales, Az., U.S. L5 132
Nogent-le-Rotrou, Fr. F9 14
Nogent-sur-Seine, Fr. F12 14
Noginsk, Russia E21 10
Nogliki, Russia F17 34
Nogoa, stm., Austl. E6 76
Nogoyá, Arg. F7 92
Nógrád, state, Hung. B6 26
Noguera Pallaresa, stm., Spain B12 20
Noguera Ribagorçana, stm., Spain B11 20
Nohar, India D5 54
Noia, Spain B2 20
Noir, Causse, plat., Fr. E9 18
Noir, Isla, i., Chile J2 90
Noire, stm., Qc., Can. B13 112
Noirmoutier, Île de, i., Fr. H6 14
Noirmoutier-en-l'Île, Fr. H6 14
Nojima-zaki, c., Japan E12 40
Nokha Mandi, India E4 54
Nokia, Fin. F10 8
Nokomis, Sk., Can. C8 124
Nokomis, Fl., U.S. I3 116
Nokomis, Il., U.S. E8 120
Nokou, Chad E2 62
Nokuku, Vanuatu j16 79d
Nola, C.A.R. D3 66
Nola, Italy D8 24
Nolichucky, stm., U.S. H2 114
Nolin, stm., Ky., U.S. G11 120
Nolin Lake, res., Ky., U.S. G11 120
Nolinsk, Russia C8 32
Nólsoy, i., Far. Is. n34 8b
Nombre de Dios, Pan. H8 102
Nome, Ak., U.S. D6 140
Nomozaki, Japan G2 40
Nomtsas, Nmb. D3 70
Nonacho Lake, l., N.T., Can. C8 106
Nonburg, Russia D24 8
Nondalton, Ak., U.S. D8 140
Nong'an, China B6 38
Nong Han, Thai. D6 48
Nong Khai, Thai. D6 48
Nongoma, S. Afr. E10 70
Nongpoh, India F13 54
Nongstoin, India F13 54
Nonoava, Mex. B5 100
Nonogasta, Arg. D4 92
Nonouti, at., Kir. D8 72
Nonsuch Bay, b., Antig. f4 105b
Nonthaburi, Thai. F5 48
Nooksack, Wa., U.S. B4 136
Noonkanbah, Austl. C4 74
Noordoostpolder, reg., Neth. B14 14
Noordpunt, c., Neth. Ant. p21 104g
Noordwijk aan Zee, Neth. B13 14
Noorvik, Ak., U.S. C7 140
Nootka Island, i., B.C., Can. G4 138
Nóqui, Ang. B1 68
Norah, is., Erit. D7 62
Nora Islands see Norah, is., Erit. D7 62
Noralee, B.C., Can. B4 138
Nora Springs, Ia., U.S. A5 120
Norcatur, Ks., U.S. B8 128
Norcia, Italy H10 22
Norcross, Ga., U.S. D14 122
Nord, Grnld. A22 141
Nord, state, Fr. D12 14
Nord, state, N. Cal. m15 79d
Nord, Canal du, can., Fr. D12 14
Nord, Canal du, can., Fr. E11 14
Nordaustlandet, i., Nor. B29 141
Nordborg, Den. A5 16
Nordegg, Ab., Can. D14 138
Nordegg, stm., Ab., Can. D15 138
Norden, Ger. C3 16
Nordenham, Ger. C4 16
Nordenšel'da, arhipelag, is., Russia A8 34
Nordenskjold Archipelago see Nordenšel'da, arhipelag, is., Russia A8 34
Norderstedt, Ger. C6 16
Nordfjord, b., Nor. F1 8
Nordfold, Nor. C6 8
Nordgrønland (Avanersuaq), state, Grnld. B15 141
Nordhausen, Ger. E6 16
Nordhorn, Ger. D2 16
Nordjylland, state, Den. H4 8
Nordkapp (North Cape), c., Nor. A11 8
Nordkinnhalvøya, pen., Nor. A12 8
Nordland, state, Nor. C6 8
Nördlingen, Ger. H6 16
Nordmaling, Swe. E8 8
Nordman, Id., U.S. B9 136
Nordostrundingen, c., Grnld. A23 141
Nord-Ostsee-Kanal (Kiel Canal), can., Ger. B5 16
Nordrhein-Westfalen, state, Ger. E4 16
Nordstrand, i., Ger. B4 16
Nord-Trøndelag, state, Nor. D5 8
Nordvik, Russia B11 34
Norfolk, Ne., U.S. E15 126
Norfolk, Va., U.S. H9 114
Norfolk Island, dep., Norf. I. x25 78i
Norfolk Island National Park, p.o.i., Norf. I. y25 78i
Norfolk Ridge, unds. L19 142
Norfork Lake, res., U.S. H5 120
Norikura-dake, vol., Japan C10 40
Noril'sk, Russia C6 34

O

Name | Map Ref. | Page

Oxford, N.Y., U.S. B10 114
Oxford, N.C., U.S. H7 114
Oxford, Oh., U.S. E13 120
Oxford, Pa., U.S. I14 112
Oxford, Wi., U.S. H9 118
Oxford Junction, Ia., U.S. J8 118
Oxford Lake, l., Mb., Can. E11 106
Oxford Peak, mtn., Id., U.S. H14 136
Oxkutzcab, Mex. B3 102
Oxley Downs, Austl. J4 76
Oxley Wild Rivers National Park, p.o.i., Austl. H8 76
Oxnard, Ca., U.S. I6 134
Oxus see Amu Darya, stm., Asia F10 32
Oya, stm., Malay. B8 50
Oyabe, Japan C9 40
Ōyama, Japan C12 40
Ōyano, Japan G3 40
Oyapok (Oiapoque), stm., S.A. C7 84
Oyem, Gabon D2 66
Oyen, Ab., Can. C3 124
Oyo, Nig. H5 64
Oyonnax, Fr. C11 18
Oyster Creek, mth., Tx., U.S. E12 130
Ozamis, Phil. F4 52
Ozark, Al., U.S. F13 122
Ozark, Ar., U.S. B5 122
Ozark, Mo., U.S. G4 120
Ozark Plateau, plat., U.S. H4 120
Ozarks, Lake of the, res., Mo., U.S. F5 120
Ózd, Hung. A7 26
Ožerele, Russia F21 10
Ozernovskij, Russia F20 34
Ozërnyj, Russia D10 32
Ozery, Russia F21 10
Ozette Lake, l., Wa., U.S. B2 136
Ozieri, Italy D2 24
Ozimek, Pol. F14 16
Ozinki, Russia D7 32
Ozorków, Pol. E15 16
Ōzu, Japan F5 40
Ozuluama, Mex. E9 100
Ozurgeti, Geor. F6 32

P

Paagoumène, N. Cal. m14 79d
Paama, state, Vanuatu k17 79d
Paama, i., Vanuatu k17 79d
Paamiut see Frederikshåb, Grnld. E15 141
Paarl, S. Afr. H4 70
Paauilo, Hi., U.S. C6 78a
Pabbay, i., Scot., U.K. D5 12
Pabbiring, Kepulauan, is., Indon. F11 50
Pabean, Indon. G9 50
Pabellón, Ensenada del, b., Mex. C4 100
Pabianice, Pol. E15 16
Pablo, Mt., U.S. C12 136
Pābna, Bngl. G12 54
Pabradė, Lith. F8 10
Pacaás Novos, Serra dos, mts., Braz. F5 84
Pacajus, Braz. C6 88
Pacasmayo, Peru E2 84
Pacatuba, Braz. C6 88
Pachino, Italy H9 24
Pachitea, stm., Peru E3 84
Pachmarhi, India G7 54
Pāchora, India H5 54
Pachuca de Soto, Mex. E9 100
Pacific, B.C., Can. B2 138
Pacific, Mo., U.S. F7 120
Pacifica, Ca., U.S. F3 134
Pacific-Antarctic Ridge, unds. P22 142
Pacific Grove, Ca., U.S. G3 134
Pacific Ocean F20 142
Pacific Ranges, mts., B.C., Can. E5 138
Pacific Rim National Park, p.o.i., B.C., Can. H5 138
Paciran, Indon. G8 50
Pacitan, Indon. H7 50
Pacora, Pan. C2 86
Pacov, Czech Rep. G11 16
Pacuí, stm., Braz. I3 88
Padada, Phil. G5 52
Padamo, stm., Ven. F9 86
Padampur, India H9 54
Padang, Indon. D6 50
Padang, Indon. G12 50
Padang, Indon. D2 50
Padang, Pulau, i., Indon. C3 50
Padang Endau, Malay. K6 48
Padangpanjang, Indon. D2 50
Padangsidempuan, Indon. C1 50
Padany, Russia E15 8
Padas, stm., Malay. A9 50
Padauari, stm., Braz. G9 86
Paddle, stm., Ab., Can. B16 138
Paddle Prairie, Ab., Can. D7 106
Paderborn, Ger. E4 16
Padjelanta Nationalpark, p.o.i., Swe. C7 8
Padloping Island, i., Nu., Can. D13 141
Padma see Ganges, stm., Asia G13 54
Pádova (Padua), Italy E8 22
Pādra, India G4 54
Padrauna, India E9 54
Padre Bernardo, Braz. H1 88
Padre Island, i., Tx., U.S. G10 130
Padre Island National Seashore, p.o.i., Tx., U.S. G10 130
Padre Paraíso, Braz. I5 88
Padstow, Eng., U.K. K8 12
Padua see Pádova, Italy E8 22
Paducah, Ky., U.S. G9 120
Paducah, Tx., U.S. G8 128
Paea, Fr. Poly. v21 78h
Paedun, Kor., S. D1 40
Paektu-san, mtn., Asia C10 36
Paestum, hist., Italy D8 24
Páez, stm., Col. F4 86
Pafúri, Moz. C10 70
Pag, Otok, i., Cro. F11 22
Pagadenbaru, Indon. G5 50
Pagadian, Phil. G4 52
Pagai Selatan, Pulau, i., Indon. E2 50
Pagai Utara, Pulau, i., Indon. E2 50
Pagan, Mya. B2 48
Pagan, i., N. Mar. Is. B5 72
Pagaralam, Indon. E3 50
Pagasitikós Kólpos, b., Grc. D5 28
Page, Az., U.S. G5 132
Page, N.D., U.S. G16 124
Pagėgiai, Lith. E4 10
Pagerdewa, Indon. E4 50
Paget, Mount, mtn., S. Geor. J9 90
Pagoda Peak, mtn., Co., U.S. C9 132
Pagoda Point, c., Mya. E2 48
Pagon, Bukit, mtn., Asia A9 50
Pago Pago, Am. Sam. h12 79c
Pagosa Springs, Co., U.S. F9 132
Paguate, N.M., U.S. H9 132
Pagudpud, Phil. A3 52
Pahača, Russia D22 34
Pahala, Hi., U.S. D6 78a
Pahang, state, Malay. K6 48
Pahang, stm., Malay. K6 48
Pahokee, Fl., U.S. J5 116
Pahost, Bela. G12 10
Pahrump, Nv., U.S. G10 134
Pai, Thai. C4 48
Pai, stm., Asia C3 48
Paico, Peru F3 84
Paide, Est. B8 10
Paige, Tx., U.S. D10 130
Paignton, Eng., U.K. K9 12
Paiguano, Chile E2 92
Päijänne, l., Fin. F11 8
Paikü Co, l., China D10 54
Pailolo Channel, strt., Hi., U.S. B5 78a
Paimpol, Fr. F5 14
Painan, Indon. D2 50
Painesdale, Mi., U.S. D10 118
Painesville, Oh., U.S. C4 114
Paint, stm., Mi., U.S. E10 118
Paint Creek, stm., Oh., U.S. E14 120
Painted Desert, des., Az., U.S. H5 132
Painted Rock Reservoir, res., Az., U.S. K3 132
Paintsville, Ky., U.S. G3 114
Paisley, Scot., U.K. F8 12
Paisley, Or., U.S. H6 136
Païta, N. Cal. n16 79d
Paita, Peru E1 84
Paitan, Telukan, b., Malay. G1 52
Paiton, Indon. G8 50
Pajala, Swe. C10 8
Paján, Ec. H1 86
Pajares, Puerto de, p., Spain B5 20
Pajaros Point, c., Br. Vir. Is. d9 104b
Pajęczno, Pol. E14 16
Pajer, gora, mtn., Russia C1 34
Pajeú, stm., Braz. E6 88
Paj-Hoj, hills, Russia A10 32
Paka, Malay. J6 48
Pākāla, India E4 53
Pakaraima Mountains, mts., S.A. E11 86
Pakashkan Lake, l., On., Can. B8 118
Pākaur, India F11 54
Pak Chong, Thai. E5 48
Pākhāl, l., India C5 53
Pákhna, Cyp. D3 58
Pakhoi see Beihai, China K3 42
Pakistan, ctry., Asia C2 46
Paklenica Nacionalni Park, p.o.i., Cro. F12 22
Pakokku, Mya. B2 48
Pakowki Lake, l., Ab., Can. E2 124
Pākpattan, Pak. C4 54
Pak Phanang, Thai. H5 48
Pak Phayun, Thai. I5 48
Pak Phraek, Thai. H5 48
Pakrac, Cro. E14 22
Pakruojis, Lith. E6 10
Paks, Hung. C5 26
Paktīā, state, Afg. B2 54
Paktīkā, state, Afg. B2 54
Pakwash Lake, l., On., Can. A5 118
Pakxé, Laos E7 48
Pala, Chad F2 62
Pala, Mya. F4 48
Palacios, Tx., U.S. F11 130
Palagruža, Otoci, is., Cro. H13 22
Palai, India G3 53
Palaiochóra, Grc. H6 28
Pālakodu, India C5 53
Palamós, Spain C14 20
Pālampur, India B6 54
Palamu National Park, p.o.i., India G10 54
Palamut, Tur. D10 28
Palana, Russia E20 34
Palanan Bay, b., Phil. B4 52
Palanga, Lith. E3 10
Palangkaraya, Indon. E8 50
Palani, India F3 53
Pālanpur, India F4 54
Palaoa Point, c., Hi., U.S. C4 78a
Palapye, Bots. C8 70
Pālār, stm., India E4 53
Palas de Rei, Spain B3 20
Palatka, Russia D19 34
Palatka, Fl., U.S. G4 116
Palau, Italy C3 24
Palau, ctry., Oc. g8 78b
Palau Islands, is., Palau D10 44
Palauk, Mya. F4 48
Palaw, Mya. F4 48
Palawan, i., Phil. F2 52
Palawan Passage, strt., Phil. F1 52
Palayan, Phil. C3 52
Pālayankottai, India G3 53
Palembang, Indon. E4 50
Palena, Italy I11 22
Palena, stm., S.A. H2 90
Palencia, Spain B6 20
Palencia, co., Spain B6 20
Palen Lake, l., Ca., U.S. J1 132
Palenque, Mex. G13 100
Palenque, hist., Mex. G12 100
Palermo, Col. F4 86
Palermo, Italy F7 24
Palermo, Ur. F10 92
Palestina, Mex. E6 130
Palestine, Ar., U.S. B7 122
Palestine, Il., U.S. E10 120
Palestine, Tx., U.S. F3 122
Palestine, hist. reg., Asia G6 58
Palestine, Lake, res., Tx., U.S. E3 122
Palestrina, Italy I9 22
Paletwa, Mya. D7 46
Pālghāt, India F3 53
Palgrave Point, c., Nmb. E1 68
Palhano, stm., Braz. C6 88
Pāli, India F4 54
Palikir, Micron. m11 78d
Palima, Indon. F12 50
Palinuro, Capo, c., Italy D9 24
Palisade, Ne., U.S. A7 128
Palisades, Id., U.S. G15 136
Palisades Reservoir, res., U.S. G15 136
Pālitāna, India H3 54
Palivere, Est. A6 10
Palizada, Mex. F12 100
Palk Bay, b., Asia G4 53
Palkino, Russia G20 8
Pālkonda, India B6 53
Pālkonda Range, mts., India D4 53
Palk Strait, strt., Asia G4 53
Pallastunturi, mtn., Fin. B11 8
Palliser, Cape, c., N.Z. E6 80
Palma, Braz. K4 88
Palma, Moz. C7 68
Palma, stm., Braz. G2 88
Palma, Badia de, b., Spain E13 20
Palmácia, Braz. C6 88
Palma del Río, Spain G5 20
Palma de Mallorca, Spain E13 20
Palma di Montechiaro, Italy G7 24
Palmar, stm., Ven. B6 86
Palmar, Lago Artificial del, res., Ur. F9 92
Palmar Camp, Belize D3 102
Palmarejo, P.R. B1 104a
Palmares, Braz. E8 88
Palmarito, Ven. D6 86
Palmarola, Isola, i., Italy D6 24
Palmas, Braz. F1 88
Palmas, Braz. C12 92
Palmas Bellas, Pan. H7 102
Palmas de Monte Alto, Braz. H4 88
Palma Soriano, Cuba B9 102
Palm Bay, Fl., U.S. H5 116
Palm Beach, Fl., U.S. J5 116
Palmdale, Ca., U.S. I7 134
Palm Desert, Ca., U.S. J9 134
Palmeira, Braz. B13 92
Palmeira das Missões, Braz. C11 92
Palmeira dos Índios, Braz. E7 88
Palmeiras, stm., Braz. F2 88
Palmeirinhas, Ponta das, c., Ang. B1 68
Palmelo, Braz. I1 88
Palmer, P.R. B4 104a
Palmer, Ak., U.S. D10 140
Palmer, Ma., U.S. B13 114
Palmer, Ne., U.S. F14 126
Palmer, Tn., U.S. B13 122
Palmer, sci., Ant. B34 81
Palmer Lake, Co., U.S. B3 128
Palmer Land, reg., Ant. C34 81
Palmerston, N.Z. G4 80
Palmerston, at., Cook Is. E10 72
Palmerston, Cape, c., Austl. C7 76
Palmerston North, N.Z. E6 80
Palmerton, Pa., U.S. D10 114
Palmetto, Ga., U.S. D14 122
Palmetto, La., U.S. G6 122
Palmetto Point, c., Antig. e4 105b
Palmi, Italy F9 24
Palmira, Col. F3 86
Palmira, Cuba A7 102
Palmira, Ec. I2 86
Palmitas, Ur. F9 92
Palm Springs, Ca., U.S. J9 134
Palmyra see Tudmur, Syria D9 58
Palmyra, Il., U.S. E7 120
Palmyra, Mo., U.S. E6 120
Palmyra, N.Y., U.S. A8 114
Palmyra, Va., U.S. G7 114
Palmyra, hist., Syria D9 58
Palmyra Atoll, at., Oc. C10 72
Palo Alto, Mex. H8 130
Palo Alto, Ca., U.S. F3 134
Palo Blanco, P.R. B2 104a
Palo Flechado Pass, p., N.M., U.S. E3 128
Paloh, Malay. B7 50
Paloich, Sudan E6 62
Palojoensuu, Fin. B10 8
Palomar Mountain, mtn., Ca., U.S. J9 134
Palomas, Mex. F4 130
Palo Pinto, Tx., U.S. B9 130
Palopo, Indon. E12 50
Palos, Cabo de, c., Spain G10 20
Palo Santo, Arg. B8 92
Palos Verdes Point, c., Ca., U.S. J7 134
Palouse, stm., U.S. D8 136
Palo Verde, Ca., U.S. J2 132
Palpa, Peru F2 84
Palpalá, Arg. B5 92
Palu, Indon. D11 50
Palu, Teluk, b., Indon. D11 50
Paluga, Russia D21 8
Palwal, India D6 54
Pama, Burkina G5 64
Pamanukan, Indon. G5 50
Pāmban Channel, strt., India G4 53
Pāmban Island, i., India G4 53
Pamekasan, Indon. G8 50
Pamenang, Indon. E3 50
Pameungpeuk, Indon. G5 50
Pamiers, Fr. F7 18
Pamir, mts., Asia B11 56
Pamlico Sound, strt., N.C., U.S. A10 116
Pampa, Tx., U.S. F8 128
Pampã, stm., Braz. I5 88
Pampa (Pampas), reg., Arg. G4 90
Pampa Almirón, Arg. C8 92
Pampa del Chañar, Arg. E3 92
Pampa del Indio, Arg. B7 92
Pampanga, stm., Phil. C3 52
Pampanua, Indon. F12 50
Pampas, Peru F3 84
Pampas, stm., Peru F3 84
Pampas see Pampa, reg., Arg. F4 90
Pamplico, S.C., U.S. B6 116
Pamplona, Col. D5 86
Pamplona, Spain B9 20
Pamukkale (Hierapolis), hist., Tur. F12 28
Pamukova, Tur. C13 28
Pana, Il., U.S. E8 120
Panabá, Mex. B3 102
Panabo, Phil. G5 52
Panacea, Fl., U.S. G14 122
Panadura, Sri L. H4 53
Panagjurište, Blg. G11 26
Panaitan, Pulau, i., Indon. G4 50
Panaji, India D1 53
Panamá, Pan. H8 102
Panama, Ok., U.S. B4 122
Panama, ctry., N.A. F9 96
Panamá, Bahía de, b., Pan. H8 102
Panamá, Canal de (Panama Canal), can., Pan. H8 102
Panamá, Golfo de, b., Pan. D2 86
Panama, Gulf of see Panamá, Golfo de, b., Pan. D2 86
Panama, Isthmus of see Panamá, Istmo de, isth., Pan. H8 102
Panamá, Istmo de (Panama, Isthmus of), isth., Pan. H8 102
Panama Basin, unds. H5 144
Panama Canal see Panamá, Canal de, can., Pan. H8 102
Panama City, Fl., U.S. G13 122
Panambi, Braz. D11 92
Panamint Range, mts., Ca., U.S. G8 134
Panamint Valley, val., Ca., U.S. G8 134
Panao, Peru E2 84
Panarea, Isola, i., Italy F9 24
Panaro, stm., Italy F8 22
Panay, i., Phil. E4 52
Panay Gulf, b., Phil. E4 52
Pančevo, Yugo. E7 26
Panciu, Rom. D14 26
Panda, Moz. D12 70
Pandaria, India G8 54
Pan de Azúcar, Ur. G10 92
Pandėlys, Lith. D8 10
Pāndharkawada, India A4 53
Pandharpur, India C2 53
Pāndhurna, India H7 54
Pando, Ur. G10 92
Panevėžys, Lith. E7 10
Panfilov, Kaz. F13 32
Pāng, stm., Mya. B4 48
Panga, D.R.C. D5 66
Pangala, Congo E2 66
Pangandaran, Indon. G6 50
Pangani, Tan. F7 66
Pangani, stm., Tan. E7 66
Pangburn, Ar., U.S. B7 122
Pangfou see Bengbu, China E7 42
Panghkam, Mya. D8 46
Pangi, D.R.C. E5 66
Pangkajene, Indon. F11 50
Pangkalanbrandan, Indon. J4 48
Pangkalanbuun, Indon. E7 50
Pangkalpinang, Indon. E5 50
Pango Aluquem, Ang. B1 68
Pangŏjin, Kor., S. D2 40
Pangong Tso, l., Asia B7 54
Panguiranan, Phil. D4 52
Panguitch, Ut., U.S. F4 132
Pangutaran, Phil. G3 52
Pangutaran Group, is., Phil. G3 52
Panhandle, Tx., U.S. F7 128
Paniau, mtn., Hi., U.S. B1 78a
Panié, Mont, mtn., N. Cal. m15 79d
Panīpāt, India D6 54
Panitan, Phil. E4 52
Panj (Pjandž), stm., Asia B11 56
Panjang, Indon. F4 50
Panjang, Selat, strt., Indon. C3 50
Pankshin, Nig. H6 64
Panlong (Lo), stm., Asia A7 48
P'anmunjŏm-ni, Kor., N. E7 38
Panna, India F8 54
Panna National Park, p.o.i., India F7 54
Pannawonica, Austl. D3 74
Pannirtuuq, Nu., Can. B17 106
Panola, U.S. E10 122
Páno Lévkara, Cyp. D4 58
Panopah, Indon. D7 50
Panorama, Braz. D6 90
Panovo, Russia C18 32
Panruti, India F4 53
Panshan, China D4 38
Pantanal, reg., S.A. C5 90
Pantanaw, Mya. D2 48
Pantar, Pulau, i., Indon. G7 44
Pantelleria, Isola di, i., Italy H6 24
Pantonlabu, Indon. J3 48
Pánuco, Mex. E10 100
Pánuco, stm., Mex. E9 100
Panxian, China F5 36
Panyam, Nig. H6 64
Panzós, Guat. E3 102
Pao, stm., Thai. D6 48
Pao, stm., Ven. C8 86
Pao, stm., Ven. C9 86
Paochi see Baoji, China D2 42
Paoki see Baoji, China D2 42
Paola, Italy E9 24
Paola, Ks., U.S. F3 120
Paoli, In., U.S. F11 120
Paopao, Fr. Poly. v20 78h
Paoting see Baoding, China B6 42
Paotou see Baotou, China A4 42
Paotow see Baotou, China A4 42
Pápa, Hung. B4 26
Papagaio, stm., Braz. I10 86
Papagaios, Braz. D3 88
Papagayo, Golfo de, b., C.R. G4 102
Papaikou, Hi., U.S. D6 78a
Papantla de Olarte, Mex. E10 100
Papara, Fr. Poly. v22 78h
Papa Stour, i., Scot., U.K. n18 12a
Papeari, Fr. Poly. w22 78h
Papeete, Fr. Poly. v21 78h
Papenburg, Ger. C3 16
Papetoai, Fr. Poly. v20 78h
Paphos see Néa Páfos, Cyp. D3 58
Papigochic, stm., Mex. G8 98
Papillion, Ne., U.S. C1 120
Paposo, Chile B2 92
Papua, Gulf of, b., Pap. N. Gui. D5 72
Papua New Guinea, ctry., Oc. D5 72
Papulovo, Russia F23 8
Papun, Mya. C3 48
Papunáua, stm., Col. G6 86
Papuri (Papurí), stm., S.A. G6 86
Papurí (Papuri), stm., S.A. G6 86
Pará, state, Braz. D7 84
Pará, stm., Braz. A1 88
Pará, stm., Braz. J3 88
Parabel', Russia C14 32
Paraburdoo, Austl. D3 74
Paracatu, Braz. I2 88
Paracatu, stm., Braz. I3 88
Paracel Islands see Xisha Qundao, is., China B5 50
Pārachinār, Pak. B3 54
Paracho de Verduzco, Mex. F7 100
Parachute, Co., U.S. D8 132
Paraćin, Yugo. F8 26
Paracuru, Braz. B6 88
Parada, Punta, c., Peru G2 84
Paradise, Ca., U.S. D4 134
Paradise, Mt., U.S. C12 136
Paradise, Nv., U.S. G1 132
Paradise Island, i., Bah. m18 104f
Paradise Valley, Az., U.S. J5 132
Paradise Valley, Nv., U.S. B8 134
Pāradwīp, India H11 54
Paragonah, Ut., U.S. F4 132
Paragould, Ar., U.S. H7 120
Paraguá, stm., Bol. B4 90
Paragua, stm., Ven. D10 86
Paraguaçu, stm., Braz. G6 88
Paraguai (Paraguay), stm., S.A. D5 90
Paraguaipoa, Ven. B6 86
Paraguaná, Península de, pen., Ven. A6 86
Paraguarí, Para. B9 92
Paraguarí, state, Para. C9 92
Paraguay, ctry., S.A. D5 90
Paraguay (Paraguai), stm., S.A. E5 90
Paraíba, state, Braz. D7 88
Paraíba do Sul, stm., Braz. K5 88
Paraibano, Braz. D3 88
Parainen, Fin. F9 8
Paraíso, Mex. F12 100
Paraiso, Pan. H8 102
Parakou, Benin H5 64
Paramakkudi, India G4 53
Paramaribo, Sur. B6 84
Parambu, Braz. D5 88
Paramillo, Parque Nacional, p.o.i., Col. D3 86
Paramirim, Braz. G4 88
Paramirim, stm., Braz. F4 88
Páramo de Masa, Puerto de, p., Spain B7 20
Paramušir, ostrov, i., Russia F20 34
Paramythiá, Grc. D3 28
Paran, Naḥal (Girafi, Wadi), stm. I5 58
Paraná, Arg. E7 92
Paranã, Braz. G1 88
Paraná, state, Braz. D6 90
Paranã, stm., Braz. G1 88
Paraná, stm., S.A. F5 90
Paranaguá, Braz. B13 92
Paranaguá, Baía de, b., Braz. B13 92
Paranaíba, Braz. C6 90
Paranaíba, stm., Braz. C6 90
Paranaidji, Braz. D2 88
Paranapanema, stm., Braz. D6 90
Paranapiacaba, Serra do, mts., Braz. B13 92
Paranavaí, Braz. D6 90
Parang, Phil. G5 52
Parang, Pulau, i., Indon. F7 50
Parângu Mare, Vârful, mtn., Rom. D10 26
Paranhos, Braz. A10 92
Paranoá, Lago do, res., Braz. H2 88
Paraopeba, Braz. J3 88
Parapetí, stm., Bol. C4 90
Parara, Indon. E12 50
Paratinga, Braz. G4 88
Paratoo, Austl. I2 76
Paray-le-Monial, Fr. C9 18
Pārbati, stm., India F6 54
Pārbatipur, Bngl. F12 54
Parbhani, India B3 53
Parchim, Ger. C7 16
Pardeeville, Wi., U.S. H9 118
Pārdi, India H4 54
Parding, China B12 54
Pardo, stm., Braz. K1 88
Pardo, stm., Braz. H6 88
Pardo, stm., Braz. L1 88
Pardo, stm., Braz. D6 90
Pardo, stm., Braz. D11 92
Pardubice, Czech Rep. F11 16
Paredón, Mex. C8 100
Parelhas, Braz. D7 88
Paren', Russia D21 34
Paren', stm., Russia D21 34
Parent, Qc., Can. C2 110
Parentis-en-Born, Fr. E4 18
Parepare, Indon. E11 50
Parera, Arg. G5 92
Parfenevo, Russia F20 8
Párga, Grc. D3 28
Parham, Antig. f4 105b
Paria, Gulf of, b. B10 86
Paria, Península de, pen., Ven. B10 86
Pariaguán, Ven. C9 86
Pariaman, Indon. D1 50
Paricutín, vol., Mex. F7 100
Parigi, Indon. D12 50
Parika, Guy. B6 84
Parikkala, Fin. F13 8
Parima, stm., Braz. F10 86
Parima, Serra (Parima, Sierra), mts., S.A. F9 86
Parima, Sierra (Parima, Serra), mts., S.A. F9 86
Parima Tapirapecó, Parque Nacional, p.o.i., Ven. F9 86
Parintins, Braz. D6 84
Paris, On., Can. E9 112
Paris, Fr. F11 14
Paris, Ar., U.S. B5 122
Paris, Il., U.S. I2 112
Paris, Ky., U.S. F1 114
Paris, Mo., U.S. E5 120
Paris, Tn., U.S. H9 120
Paris, Tx., U.S. D3 122
Parisienne, Ile, i., On., Can. B5 112
Parita, Bahía de, b., Pan. H7 102
Parit Buntar, Malay. J5 48
Parkano, Fin. E10 8
Park City, Mt., U.S. B3 126
Park City, Ut., U.S. C5 132
Parkdale, Or., U.S. E5 136
Parker, Az., U.S. I2 132
Parker, Co., U.S. B4 128
Parker, Fl., U.S. G13 122
Parker, Cape, c., Nu., Can. B10 141
Parker City, In., U.S. H4 112
Parker Dam, Ca., U.S. I2 132
Parker Dam, dam, U.S. I2 132
Parkersburg, Il., U.S. F9 120
Parkersburg, Ia., U.S. B5 120
Parkersburg, W.V., U.S. E4 114
Parkes, Austl. I7 76
Park Falls, Wi., U.S. F8 118
Park Forest, Il., U.S. G2 112
Parkhill, On., Can. E8 112
Parkland, Wa., U.S. C4 136
Park Range, mts., Co., U.S. C10 132
Park Rapids, Mn., U.S. E3 118
Parkrose, Or., U.S. E4 136
Park Rynie, S. Afr. G10 70
Parksley, Va., U.S. G10 114
Parkston, S.D., U.S. D14 126
Parksville, B.C., Can. G6 138
Parkville, Md., U.S. E9 114
Parkville, Mo., U.S. E3 120
Parla, Spain D7 20
Parlākimidi, India B7 53
Parli, India B3 53
Parma, Italy F7 22
Parma, Mo., U.S. H8 120
Parma, Oh., U.S. C4 114
Parnaguá, Braz. F3 88
Parnaíba, Braz. B5 88
Parnaíba, stm., Braz. B5 88
Parnaíbinha, stm., Braz. E2 88
Parnamirim, Braz. E6 88
Parnassós, mtn., Grc. E5 28
Párnitha, mtn., Grc. E6 28
Pärnu, Est. G11 8
Pärnu laht, b., Est. G11 8
Paro, Bhu. E12 54
Pārola, India H5 54
Paromaj, Russia F17 34
Paroo, stm., Austl. G5 76
Páros, i., Grc. F8 28
Parowan, Ut., U.S. F4 132
Parque Nacional da Chapada da Diamantina, p.o.i., Braz. G4 88
Parral, Chile H2 92
Parral, stm., Mex. B6 100
Parramatta, Austl. I8 76
Parras de la Fuente, Mex. C7 100
Parrish, Fl., U.S. I3 116
Parrsboro, N.S., Can. E12 110
Parry, Cape, c., N.T., Can. A6 106
Parry Bay, b., Nu., Can. B14 106
Parry Island, i., On., Can. C9 112
Parry Peninsula, pen., N.T., Can. B6 106
Parry Sound, On., Can. C9 112
Parsberg, Ger. G7 16
Parsęta, stm., Pol. B11 16
Parshall, N.D., U.S. G11 124
Paršino, Russia C20 32
Parsnip, stm., B.C., Can. A8 138
Parsons, Ks., U.S. G2 120
Parsons, Tn., U.S. B10 122
Pärsti, Est. B8 10
Partanna, Italy G6 24
Parthenay, Fr. H8 14
Partinico, Italy F7 24
Partizansk, Russia C10 38
Partizánske, Slov. H14 16
Paru, stm., Braz. D7 84
Parú, stm., Ven. E9 86
Paru de Oeste, stm., Braz. C6 84
Parūr, India F3 53
Pārvatīpuram, India B6 53
Paryang, China C9 54
Parys, S. Afr. E8 70
Pasadena, Ca., U.S. I7 134
Pasadena, Tx., U.S. H3 122
Pasaje, Ec. D2 84
Pa Sak, stm., Thai. E5 48
Paşaköy, N. Cyp. C4 58
Pasarbantal, Indon. E2 50
Pasawng, Mya. C3 48
Pascagoula, Ms., U.S. G10 122
Pascagoula, stm., Ms., U.S. G10 122
Paşcani, Rom. B13 26
Pasco, Wa., U.S. D7 136
Pascoag, R.I., U.S. C14 114
Pascua, Isla de (Easter Island) (Rapa Nui), i., Chile f30 78l
Pas-de-Calais, state, Fr. D11 14
Pasewalk, Ger. C10 16
Pasir Mas, Malay. J6 48
Pasirpengarayan, Indon. C2 50
Pasir Puteh, Malay. J6 48
Paškovo, Russia G15 34
Pasłęka, stm., Pol. C16 16
Pasley Bay, b., Nu., Can. A11 106
Pašman, Otok, i., Cro. G12 22
Pasmore, stm., Austl. H2 76
Pasni, Pak. D9 56
Paso de Indios, Arg. H3 90
Paso del Cerro, Ur. E9 92
Paso de los Libres, Arg. D9 92
Paso de los Toros, Ur. F9 92
Paso de Patria, Para. C8 92
Paso de San Antonio, Mex. E3 130
Paso Hondo, Mex. H13 100
Paso Robles, Ca., U.S. H5 134
Pašozero, Russia F16 8
Pasquia Hills, hills, Sk., Can. A11 124
Pasrūr, Pak. B5 54
Passadumkeag, Me., U.S. E8 110
Passadumkeag Mountain, hill, Me., U.S. E8 110
Passage Point, c., N.T., Can. B16 140
Passaic, N.J., U.S. H15 112
Passamaquoddy Bay, b., N.A. E10 110
Passau, Ger. H9 16
Passero, Capo, c., Italy H9 24
Passo Fundo, Braz. D11 92
Passo Real, Represa do, res., Braz. D11 92
Passos, Braz. K2 88
Pastavy, Bela. E9 10
Pastaza, state, Ec. H3 86
Pastaza, stm., S.A. D2 84
Pastillo, P.R. B3 104a
Pasto, Col. G3 86
Pastos Bons, Braz. D3 88
Pasuruan, Indon. G8 50
Pasvalys, Lith. D7 10
Pásztó, Hung. B6 26
Patacamaya, Bol. C3 90
Patadkal, hist., India C3 53
Patagonia, Az., U.S. L6 132
Patagonia, reg., Arg. I2 90
Pātan, India G3 54
Patchogue, N.Y., U.S. D13 114
Patea, N.Z. D6 80
Pategi, Nig. H6 64
Pate Island, i., Kenya E8 66
Patensie, S. Afr. H7 70
Paterna, Spain E10 20
Paternion, Aus. D10 22
Paternò, Italy G8 24
Paterson, N.J., U.S. D11 114
Pathānkot, India B5 54
Pathein, Mya. D2 48
Pathfinder Reservoir, res., Wy., U.S. E5 126
Pathiu, Thai. G4 48
Pathum Thani, Thai. E5 48
Pati, Indon. G7 50
Patía, Col. F3 86
Patía, stm., Col. F2 86
Patiāla, India C6 54
Patillas, P.R. B3 104a
Pati Point, c., Guam i10 78c
Pativilca, Peru F2 84
Pātkai Range, mts., Asia F4 36
Pat Mayse Lake, res., Tx., U.S. D3 122
Pátmos, i., Grc. F9 28
Patna, India F10 54
Patna, India H11 54
Patnāgarh, India H9 54
Patnanongan Island, i., Phil. C4 52
Pato Branco, Braz. C11 92
Patoka, Il., U.S. F8 120
Patoka, stm., In., U.S. F10 120
Patoka Lake, res., In., U.S. F11 120
Patomskoe nagor'e, plat., Russia E12 34
Patonga, Ug. D6 66
Patos, Braz. D7 88
Patos, stm., Arg. E3 92
Patos, Lagoa dos, b., Braz. E12 92
Patos de Minas, Braz. J2 88
Patquía, Arg. D4 92
Pátra, Grc. E4 28
Patrai, Gulf of see Patraïkós Kólpos, b., Grc. E4 28
Patraïkós Kólpos, b., Grc. E4 28
Patricio Lynch, Isla, i., Chile I1 90
Patrocínio, Braz. J2 88
Pattani, Thai. I5 48
Pattaya, Thai. F5 48
Patten, Me., U.S. D8 110
Patterson, Ca., U.S. F4 134
Patterson, Ga., U.S. E3 116
Patterson, Mount, mtn., Yk., Can. C4 106
Patti, Golfo di, b., Italy F9 24
Pattison, Ms., U.S. F8 122
Pattoki, Pak. C4 54
Pattonsburg, Mo., U.S. D3 120
Pattukkottai, India F4 53
Pattullo, Mount, mtn., B.C., Can. D5 106
Patuākhāli, Bngl. G13 54
Patuca, stm., Hond. E5 102
Pātūr, India H6 54
Patusi, Pap. N. Gui. a4 79a
Patuxent, stm., Md., U.S. F9 114
Pátzcuaro, Mex. F8 100
Pau, Fr. F5 18
Pau, Gave de, stm., Fr. F5 18
Pau Brasil, Braz. H6 88
Pau dos Ferros, Braz. D6 88
Pauh, Indon. E3 50
Pauini, stm., Braz. E4 84
Pauini, stm., Braz. H10 86
Pauk, Mya. B2 48
Pauksa Taung, mtn., Mya. C2 48
Paul, Id., U.S. H13 136
Paulding, Ms., U.S. E9 122
Paulicéia, Braz. D6 90
Paulina Peak, mtn., Or., U.S. G5 136
Pauline, Mount, mtn., Can. C11 138
Paulino Neves, Braz. B4 88
Paulistana, Braz. E5 88
Paulistas, Braz. J4 88
Paullina, Ia., U.S. B2 120
Paulo Afonso, Braz. E6 88
Paulo Afonso, Cachoeira de, wtfl, Braz. E6 88
Paulpietersburg, S. Afr. E10 70
Pauls Valley, Ok., U.S. G11 128
Paung, Mya. D3 48
Paungde, Mya. C2 48
Pauri, India C7 54
Paute, Ec. I2 86
Paute, stm., Ec. I2 86
Pauto, stm., Col. E6 86
Pavia, Italy E6 22
Pavilion, B.C., Can. F9 138
Pāvilosta, Lat. D4 10
Pavlikeni, Blg. F12 26
Pavlodar, Kaz. D13 32
Pavlof Volcano, vol., Ak., U.S. E7 140
Pavlovo, Russia I20 8
Pavlovsk, Russia A13 10
Pavlovsk, Russia D14 32
Pavlovskij Posad, Russia E21 10
Pavo, Ga., U.S. F2 116
Pavullo nel Frignano, Italy F7 22
Pavuvu Island, i., Sol. Is. e8 79b
Pawan, stm., Indon. D7 50
Pawhuska, Ok., U.S. E12 128
Pawn, stm., Mya. C3 48
Pawnee, Il., U.S. E8 120
Pawnee, Ok., U.S. A2 122
Pawnee, stm., Ks., U.S. C9 128
Pawnee Rock, Ks., U.S. C9 128
Pawni, India H7 54
Pawota, Mya. D3 48
Paw Paw, Il., U.S. C8 120
Paw Paw, Mi., U.S. F4 112
Pawtucket, R.I., U.S. C14 114
Paxoí, i., Grc. D3 28
Paxson, Ak., U.S. D10 140
Paxton, Ne., U.S. F11 126
Paya, Hond. E5 102
Payakumbuh, Indon. D2 50
Payamlı, Tur. A9 58
Payerne, Switz. D3 22
Payeti, Indon. H12 50
Payette, Id., U.S. F10 136
Payette, stm., Id., U.S. G10 136

I•44 Paye-Pine

Name	Map Ref.	Page
Payette, North Fork, stm., Id., U.S.	F11	136
Payette, South Fork, stm., Id., U.S.	F11	136
Payne, Oh., U.S.	C1	114
Payne, Lac, l., Can.	D16	106
Paynes Find, Austl.	E3	74
Paynton, Sk., Can.	A5	124
Paysandú, Ur.	F8	92
Payson, Az., U.S.	I5	132
Payson, Il., U.S.	E6	120
Payson, Ut., U.S.	C5	132
Payún, Cerro, mtn., Arg.	H3	92
Pazarbaşı Burnu, c., Tur.	B13	28
Pazarcık, Tur.	A8	58
Pazardžik, Blg.	G11	26
Pazaryeri, Tur.	D12	28
Paz de Ariporo, Col.	E6	86
Pčevža, Russia	A15	10
Pe, Mya.	F4	48
Pea, stm., U.S.	F12	122
Peabody, Ks., U.S.	C11	128
Peabody, Ma., U.S.	B14	114
Peace, stm., Can.	D8	106
Peace, stm., Fl., U.S.	I4	116
Peace River, Ab., Can.	D7	106
Peachland, B.C., Can.	G11	138
Peach Orchard, Ga., U.S.	C3	116
Peach Springs, Az., U.S.	H3	132
Peak District National Park, p.o.i., Eng., U.K.	H11	12
Peak Downs, Austl.	D7	76
Peak Hill, Austl.	E3	74
Peak Hill, Austl.	I7	76
Peäldoajvi, mtn., Fin.	B12	8
Peale, Mount, mtn., Ut., U.S.	E7	132
Pearisburg, Va., U.S.	G5	114
Pearl, Il., U.S.	E7	120
Pearl, Ms., U.S.	E8	122
Pearl, stm., U.S.	G9	122
Pearland, Tx., U.S.	H3	122
Pearl Harbor, b., Hi., U.S.	B3	78a
Pearl Peak, mtn., Nv., U.S.	C1	132
Pearl River, La., U.S.	G9	122
Pearson, Ga., U.S.	E3	116
Peary Land, reg., Grnld.	A18	141
Pease, stm., Tx., U.S.	G9	128
Pebane, Moz.	D6	68
Pebas, Peru	D3	84
Pebble Island, i., Falk. Is.	J5	90
Peć, Yugo.	G7	26
Pecan Gap, Tx., U.S.	D3	122
Peçanha, Braz.	J4	88
Peças, Ilha das, i., Braz.	B13	92
Pecatonica, Il., U.S.	B8	120
Pecatonica, stm., U.S.	B8	120
Pečenga, Russia	B14	8
Pechenizhyn, Ukr.	A11	26
Pechora see Pečora, stm., Russia	C25	8
Pechora Bay see Pečorskaja guba, b., Russia	A8	32
Pečora, Russia	A9	32
Pečora (Pechora), stm., Russia	A8	32
Pecoraro, Monte, mtn., Italy	F10	24
Pečorskaja guba, b., Russia	A8	32
Pečorskoe more, Russia	A8	32
Pečory, Russia	C10	10
Pecos, N.M., U.S.	F3	128
Pecos, Tx., U.S.	C4	130
Pecos, stm., U.S.	F12	98
Pecos National Monument, p.o.i., N.M., U.S.	F3	128
Pécs, Hung.	C5	26
Pedana, India	C5	53
Pedasí, Pan.	I7	102
Pedder, Lake, res., Austl.	o12	77a
Peddie, S. Afr.	H8	70
Pededze, stm., Eur.	C10	10
Pedernales, Dom. Rep.	C12	102
Pedernales, Ven.	C10	86
Pedernales, stm., Tx., U.S.	D9	130
Pedernales, Salar de, pl., Chile	C3	92
Pedra Azul, Braz.	I5	88
Pedra Branca, Braz.	C6	88
Pedra Lume, C.V.	k10	65a
Pedras de Fogo, Braz.	D8	88
Pedras Salgadas, Port.	C3	20
Pedraza, Col.	B4	86
Pedregal, Ven.	B6	86
Pedreiras, Braz.	C3	88
Pedriceña, Mex.	C6	100
Pedro, Point, c., Sri L.	G5	53
Pedro Afonso, Braz.	E1	88
Pedro Avelino, Braz.	C7	88
Pedro Cays, is., Jam.	D9	102
Pedro Gomes, Braz.	G7	84
Pedro II, Braz.	C5	88
Pedro II, Ilha, i., S.A.	G8	86
Pedro Juan Caballero, Para.	D5	90
Pedro Leopoldo, Braz.	J3	88
Pedro Osório, Braz.	E11	92
Pedro R. Fernández, Arg.	D8	92
Pedro Velho, Braz.	D8	88
Peebles, Scot., U.K.	F9	12
Peebles, Oh., U.S.	F2	114
Pee Dee, stm., U.S.	A6	116
Peekskill, N.Y., U.S.	C12	114
Peel, I. of Man	G8	12
Peel, stm., Can.	B4	106
Peel Point, c., N.T., Can.	B17	140
Peel Sound, strt., Nu., Can.	A11	106
Peene, stm., Ger.	C9	16
Peerless, Mt., U.S.	F8	124
Peesane, Sk., Can.	B10	124
Peetz, Co., U.S.	G9	126
Pegasus Bay, b., N.Z.	F5	80
Pegnitz, Ger.	G7	16
Pegu, stm., Mya.	D3	48
Pegu Yoma, mts., Mya.	C2	48
Pegyš, Russia	E24	8
Pehlivanköy, Tur.	B9	28
Pehuajó, Arg.	G7	92
Peian see Bei'an, China	B10	36
Peiching see Beijing, China	B7	42
Peihai see Beihai, China	K3	42
Peikang, Tai.	J9	42
Peine, Ger.	D6	16
Peine, Pointe à, c., Dom.	j6	105c
Peinnechaung, i., Mya.	I14	54
Peip'ing see Beijing, China	B7	42
Peipus, Lake, l., Eur.	B10	10
Peiraiás (Piraeus), Grc.	F6	28
Peissenberg, Ger.	I7	16
Peixe, Braz.	G1	88
Peixe, stm., Braz.	D6	90
Peixian, China	D7	42
Peixoto, Represa de, res., Braz.	K2	88
Pekalongan, Indon.	G6	50
Pekan, Malay.	K6	48
Pekanbaru, Indon.	C2	50
Pekin, Il., U.S.	D8	120
Pekin, In., U.S.	F11	120
Peking see Beijing, China	B7	42
Peklino, Russia	G16	10
Pekul'nej, hrebet, mts., Russia	C24	34
Pelabohan Klang, Malay.	K5	48
Pelabuhanratu, Indon.	G5	50
Pelagie, Isole, is., Italy	I6	24
Pelaihari, Indon.	E9	50
Pelat, Mont, mtn., Fr.	E12	18
Pełczyce, Pol.	C11	16
Peleduj, Russia	C20	32
Pelée, Montagne, vol., Mart.	k6	105c
Pelee, Point, c., On., Can.	G7	112
Pelee Island, i., On., Can.	G7	112
Pelega, Vârful, mtn., Rom.	D9	26
Peleliu see Beliliou, i., Palau	D9	44
Peleng, Pulau, i., Indon.	F7	44
Pelham, Al., U.S.	D12	122
Pelham, Ga., U.S.	E1	116
Pelhřimov, Czech Rep.	G11	16
Pelican, Ak., U.S.	E12	140
Pelican Bay, b., Mb., Can.	B13	124
Pelican Lake, Wi., U.S.	F9	118
Pelican Lake, l., Mb., Can.	E14	124
Pelican Lake, l., Mb., Can.	B13	124
Pelican Lake, l., Mn., U.S.	C5	118
Pelican Rapids, Mb., Can.	B13	124
Pelican Rapids, Mn., U.S.	E2	118
Pelister Nacionalni Park, p.o.i., Mac.	B4	28
Peljekaise Nationalpark see Pieljekaise Nationalpark, p.o.i., Swe.	C6	8
Pelješac, Poluotok, pen., Cro.	H14	22
Peljušnja, Russia	B15	10
Pella, Ia., U.S.	C5	120
Pélla, hist., Grc.	C5	28
Pell City, Al., U.S.	D12	122
Pellegrini, Arg.	H6	92
Pellegrini, Lago, l., Arg.	I4	92
Pello, Fin.	C11	8
Pellworm, i., Ger.	B4	16
Pelly, Sk., Can.	C12	124
Pelly, stm., Yk., Can.	C4	106
Pelly Bay, b., Nu., Can.	B12	106
Pelly Crossing, Yk., Can.	C3	106
Pelly Lake, l., Nu., Can.	B10	106
Pelly Mountains, mts., Yk., Can.	C4	106
Pelón de Ñado, mtn., Mex.	E9	100
Peloponnesus see Pelopónnisos, pen., Grc.	F5	28
Pelopónnisos, state, Grc.	F5	28
Pelopónnisos (Peloponnesus), pen., Grc.	F5	28
Pelotas, Braz.	E11	92
Pelotas, stm., Braz.	C12	92
Pelusium Bay see Tîna, Khalîg el-, b., Egypt	G3	58
Pemadumcook Lake, l., Me., U.S.	E7	110
Pemalang, Indon.	G6	50
Pemangkat, Indon.	C6	50
Pematangsiantar, Indon.	B1	50
Pemba, Moz.	C7	68
Pemba, Zam.	D4	68
Pemba, i., Tan.	F7	66
Pemberton, Austl.	F3	74
Pemberton, B.C., Can.	F8	138
Pembina, N.D., U.S.	C1	118
Pembina, stm., Ab., Can.	B16	138
Pembina, stm., N.A.	F16	124
Pembina Hills, hills, N.A.	E15	124
Pembroke, On., Can.	C12	112
Pembroke, Wales, U.K.	J7	12
Pembroke, Ga., U.S.	D4	116
Pembroke, Ky., U.S.	H10	120
Pembroke, Me., U.S.	F9	110
Pembroke, N.C., U.S.	B6	116
Pembroke, Cape, c., Nu., Can.	C14	106
Pembroke Pines, Fl., U.S.	K5	116
Pembrokeshire Coast National Park, p.o.i., Wales, U.K.	J7	12
Pembuang, Indon.	E7	50
Pembuang, stm., Indon.	D8	50
Pemigewasset, stm., N.H., U.S.	G5	110
Pemuco, Chile	H1	92
Penafiel, Port.	C2	20
Peñalara, Pico de, mtn., Spain	D6	20
Penalva, Braz.	B3	88
Penang see George Town, Malay.	J4	48
Peñaranda de Bracamonte, Spain	D5	20
Pen Argyl, Pa., U.S.	D10	114
Peñarroya-Pueblonuevo, Spain	F5	20
Peñas, Cabo de, c., Spain	A5	20
Penas, Golfo de, b., Chile	I2	90
Penasco, N.M., U.S.	E3	128
Pench National Park, p.o.i., India	H7	54
Pendembu, S.L.	H2	64
Pendembu, S.L.	H2	64
Pendências, Braz.	C7	88
Pendleton, In., U.S.	H4	112
Pendleton, Or., U.S.	E8	136
Pendleton, S.C., U.S.	B3	116
Pendolo, Indon.	E12	50
Pend Oreille, stm., N.A.	B9	136
Pend Oreille, Lake, l., Id., U.S.	B10	136
Pendžikent, Taj.	B10	56
Penebel, Indon.	H9	50
Penedo, Braz.	F7	88
Penetanguishene, On., Can.	D9	112
Peneus see Pineiós, stm., Grc.	D5	28
Penfield, Pa., U.S.	C7	114
Penganga, stm., India	H6	54
Penghu, China	I8	42
P'enghu Ch'üntao (Pescadores), is., Tai.	J8	42
P'enghu Shuitao, strt., Tai.	J8	42
Pengkou, China	I7	42
Penglai, China	C9	42
Pengpu see Bengbu, China	E7	42
Pengshui, China	G2	42
Pengwaluote Shan, mtn., China	B11	54
Pengxi, China	F1	42
Pengxian, China	E5	36
Pengze, China	G7	42
Penha, Braz.	C13	92
Penhsi see Benxi, China	D5	38
Penibética, Cordillera, mts., Spain	G8	20
Peniche, Port.	E1	20
Penicuik, Scot., U.K.	F9	12
Penida, Nusa, i., Indon.	H9	50
Peninsular Malaysia see Semenanjung Malaysia, hist. reg., Malay.	K6	48
Peníscola, Spain	D11	20
Penki see Benxi, China	D5	38
Pennant Station, Sk., Can.	D5	124
Penne, Italy	H10	22
Penneru, stm., India	D4	53
Penn Hills, Pa., U.S.	H10	112
Pennine Alps, mts., Eur.	C13	18
Pennines, mts., Eng., U.K.	G10	12
Pennington Gap, Va., U.S.	H2	114
Pennsboro, W.V., U.S.	E4	114
Pennsylvania, state, U.S.	C8	114
Penn Yan, N.Y., U.S.	B8	114
Penny Ice Cap, ice, Nu., Can.	B17	106
Penny Strait, strt., Nu., Can.	B6	141
Peno, Russia	D15	10
Penobscot, stm., Me., U.S.	F8	110
Penobscot, East Branch, stm., Me., U.S.	D8	110
Penobscot, West Branch, stm., Me., U.S.	D7	110
Penobscot Bay, b., Me., U.S.	F7	110
Penola, Austl.	K3	76
Peñón de Ifac see Penyal d'Ifac, misc. cult., Spain	F11	20
Penong, Austl.	F6	74
Penonomé, Pan.	H7	102
Penrhyn, at., Cook Is.	D11	72
Penrith, Austl.	I8	76
Penrith, Eng., U.K.	G10	12
Pensacola, Fl., U.S.	G11	122
Pensacola Bay, b., Fl., U.S.	G11	122
Pensacola Mountains, mts., Ant.	D36	81
Pense, Sk., Can.	D9	124
Pensilvania, Col.	E4	86
Pentagon Mountain, mtn., Mt., U.S.	C13	136
Pentecostes, Braz.	B6	88
Pentecost Island see Pentecôte, i., Vanuatu	j17	79d
Pentecôte, state, Vanuatu	j17	79d
Pentecôte (Pentecost Island), i., Vanuatu	j17	79d
Penticton, B.C., Can.	G11	138
Pentland, Austl.	C5	76
Pentland Firth, strt., Scot., U.K.	C9	12
Pentwater, Mi., U.S.	E3	112
Penuba, Indon.	D4	50
Peñuelas, P.R.	B2	104a
Penuguan, Indon.	E4	50
Penukonda, India	D3	53
Penyal d'Ifac, misc. cult., Spain	F11	20
Penza, Russia	D7	32
Penzance, Eng., U.K.	K7	12
Penzberg, Ger.	I7	16
Penžina, stm., Russia	D22	34
Penžinskaja guba, b., Russia	D21	34
Penžinskij hrebet, mts., Russia	D22	34
Peoples Creek, stm., Mt., U.S.	F5	124
People's Democratic Republic of Korea see Korea, North, ctry., Asia	D7	38
Peoria, Az., U.S.	J4	132
Peoria, Il., U.S.	D8	120
Peoria Heights, Il., U.S.	K9	118
Peotone, Il., U.S.	G2	112
Pepel, S.L.	H2	64
Pepin, Wi., U.S.	G6	118
Pepin, Lake, l., U.S.	G7	118
Peqin, Alb.	C13	24
Perabumulih, Indon.	E4	50
Perak, state, Malay.	J5	48
Perak, stm., Malay.	J5	48
Perak, Kuala, b., Malay.	J5	48
Perales de Alfambra, Spain	D9	20
Peralillo, Chile	G2	92
Peralta, N.M., U.S.	I10	132
Perambalur, India	F4	53
Percé, Qc., Can.	B12	110
Perchas, P.R.	B2	104a
Perche, Collines du, hills, Fr.	F9	14
Percival Lakes, l., Austl.	D4	74
Percy Isles, is., Austl.	C8	76
Perdida, stm., Braz.	E2	88
Perdido, stm., U.S.	G11	122
Perdido, Monte, mtn., Spain	B10	20
Perdizes, Braz.	J2	88
Perdue, Sk., Can.	B6	124
Perechyn, Ukr.	H18	16
Pereez'na, Russia	G22	8
Pereira, Col.	E4	86
Perelazy, Russia	G14	10
Peremyšl', Russia	F18	10
Pereslavl'-Zalesskij, Russia	D21	10
Pérez, Arg.	F7	92
Pergamino, Arg.	F7	92
Pergamum, hist., Tur.	D10	28
Pergine Valsugana, Italy	D8	22
Perham, Mn., U.S.	E3	118
Péribonka, Qc., Can.	B4	110
Péribonka, stm., Qc., Can.	B5	110
Péribonka, Lac, l., Qc., Can.	E16	106
Perico, Arg.	B5	92
Pericumã, stm., Braz.	B3	88
Peridot, Az., U.S.	J6	132
Perigiraja, Indon.	D3	50
Périgord, hist. reg., Fr.	D6	18
Périgueux, Fr.	D6	18
Perijá, Serranía de, mts., S.A.	C5	86
Perim see Barīm, i., Yemen	G5	56
Peri-Mirim, Braz.	B3	88
Perito Moreno, Arg.	I2	90
Peritoró, Braz.	C3	88
Periyār, stm., India	F3	53
Periyar Tiger Reserve, India	G3	53
Perkasie, Pa., U.S.	D10	114
Perkins, Ok., U.S.	A2	122
Perlas, Archipiélago de las, is., Pan.	H8	102
Perlas, Laguna de, b., Nic.	F6	102
Perleberg, Ger.	C7	16
Perlez, Yugo.	D7	26
Perlis, state, Malay.	I5	48
Perm', Russia	C9	32
Përmet, Alb.	D14	24
Pernambuco, state, Braz.	E6	88
Pernik, Blg.	G10	26
Péronne, Fr.	E11	14
Perote, Mex.	F10	100
Perow, B.C., Can.	B4	138
Perpignan, Fr.	G8	18
Perrault Falls, On., Can.	A5	118
Perrin, Tx., U.S.	A9	130
Perrine, Fl., U.S.	K5	116
Perris, Ca., U.S.	J8	134
Perro, Laguna del, l., N.M., U.S.	G3	128
Perro, Punta del, c., Spain	H4	20
Perros, Bahía de, strt., Cuba	A8	102
Perros-Guirec, Fr.	F5	14
Perry, Fl., U.S.	F2	116
Perry, Ia., U.S.	C3	120
Perry, Ks., U.S.	E2	120
Perry, Mi., U.S.	B1	114
Perry, Mo., U.S.	E6	120
Perry, N.Y., U.S.	B7	114
Perry, Kap, c., Grnld.	B11	141
Perry Lake, res., Ks., U.S.	E2	120
Perrysburg, Oh., U.S.	C2	114
Perry's Victory and International Peace Memorial, hist., Oh., U.S.	C2	114
Perrysville, Oh., U.S.	D3	114
Perryton, Tx., U.S.	E8	128
Perryville, Ak., U.S.	E8	140
Perryville, Ar., U.S.	B6	122
Perryville, Ky., U.S.	G12	120
Perseverancia, Bol.	B4	90
Persia, Ia., U.S.	C2	120
Persia see Iran, ctry., Asia	C7	56
Persian Gulf, b., Asia	D7	56
Perth, Austl.	F3	74
Perth, On., Can.	D13	112
Perth, Scot., U.K.	E9	12
Perth Amboy, N.J., U.S.	D11	114
Perth Basin, unds.	L13	142
Pertominsk, Russia	D18	8
Peru, Il., U.S.	C8	120
Peru, In., U.S.	H3	112
Peru, Ne., U.S.	D2	120
Peru, N.Y., U.S.	F3	110
Peru, ctry., S.A.	E2	84
Peru Basin, unds.	J5	144
Perućac, Jezero, res., Eur.	G16	22
Peru-Chile Trench, unds.	K6	144
Perugia, Italy	G9	22
Perugorría, Arg.	D8	92
Peruíbe, Braz.	B14	92
Perušić, Cro.	F12	22
Pervomais'k, Ukr.	A17	26
Pervomajsk, Russia	I20	8
Pervomajskij, Russia	F15	10
Pervoural'sk, Russia	C9	32
Pervyj Kuril'skij proliv, strt., Russia	F20	34
Pes', Russia	B17	10
Pesaro, Italy	G9	22
Pescadores see P'enghu Ch'üntao, is., Tai.	J8	42
Pescadores Channel see P'enghu Shuitao, strt., Tai.	J8	42
Pescara, Italy	H11	22
Pescara, stm., Italy	H11	22
Pescasseroli, Italy	C7	24
Pescia, Italy	G7	22
Pesé, Pan.	D1	86
Peshāwar, Pak.	B3	54
Peshkopi, Alb.	C14	24
Peshkopija see Peshkopi, Alb.	C14	24
Peshtigo, Wi., U.S.	C2	112
Peshtigo, stm., Wi., U.S.	F10	118
Peski, Bela.	G7	10
Pesočnoe, Russia	B22	10
Peso da Régua, Port.	C3	20
Pesquería, stm., Mex.	I8	130
Pessac, Fr.	E5	18
Pest, state, Hung.	B6	26
Peštera, Blg.	G11	26
Pestovo, Russia	B18	10
Pëstraja Dresva, Russia	D20	34
Petacalco, Bahía, b., Mex.	G7	100
Petaḥ Tiqwa, Isr.	F5	58
Petal, Ms., U.S.	F9	122
Petalcingo, Mex.	G12	100
Petalión, Kólpos, b., Grc.	F7	28
Petaluma, Ca., U.S.	E3	134
Petare, Ven.	B8	86
Petatlán, Mex.	G8	100
Petawawa, On., Can.	C12	112
Petén Itzá, Lago, l., Guat.	D2	102
Petenwell Lake, res., Wi., U.S.	G8	118
Peterborough, Austl.	I2	76
Peterborough, On., Can.	D11	112
Peterborough, Eng., U.K.	I12	12
Peterhead, Scot., U.K.	D11	12
Peter Island, i., Br. Vir. Is.	e8	104b
Peter Isøy, i., Ant.	B31	81
Peter Lake, l., Nu., Can.	C12	106
Peterlee, Eng., U.K.	G11	12
Peterman, Al., U.S.	F11	122
Peter Pond Lake, l., Sk., Can.	D9	106
Petersburg, Ak., U.S.	E13	140
Petersburg, Il., U.S.	K9	118
Petersburg, In., U.S.	F10	120
Petersburg, Tn., U.S.	B12	122
Petersburg, Tx., U.S.	H7	128
Petersburg, Va., U.S.	G8	114
Petersburg, W.V., U.S.	F6	114
Petersfield, Eng., U.K.	J12	12
Peterson, Ia., U.S.	B2	120
Peter the Great Bay see Petra Velikogo, zaliv, b., Russia	C9	38
Petilia Policastro, Italy	E10	24
Pétion-Ville, Haiti	C11	102
Petit-Bourg, Guad.	h5	105c
Petitcodiac, N.B., Can.	E11	110
Petite Rivière Noire, Piton de la, mtn., Mrts.	i10	69a
Petites-Anses, Guad.	i5	105c
Petit-Goâve, Haiti	C11	102
Petit Jean, stm., Ar., U.S.	B5	122
Petitot, stm., Can.	D6	106
Petit Piton, vol., St. Luc.	m6	105c
Petitsikapau Lake, l., Nf., Can.	E17	106
Petlād, India	G4	54
Peto, Mex.	B3	102
Petoskey, Mi., U.S.	C5	112
Petra see Al-Batrā', hist., Jord.	H6	58
Petra Velikogo, zaliv (Peter the Great Bay), b., Russia	C9	38
Petre, Point, c., On., Can.	E12	112
Petrič, Blg.	H10	26
Petrified Forest National Park, p.o.i., Az., U.S.	I7	132
Petrila, Rom.	D10	26
Petrinja, Cro.	E13	22
Petriščevo, Russia	E19	10
Petrodvorec, Russia	A12	10
Petrolândia, Braz.	E6	88
Petrólea, Col.	C5	86
Petrolia, Tx., U.S.	G10	128
Petrolina, Braz.	E5	88
Petrolina de Goiás, Braz.	I1	88
Petrona, Punta, c., P.R.	C3	104a
Petropavl see Petropavlovsk, Kaz.	D11	32
Petropavlovka, Russia	F10	34
Petropavlovsk, Kaz.	D11	32
Petropavlovsk-Kamčatskij, Russia	F20	34
Petrópolis, Braz.	L4	88
Petros, Tn., U.S.	H13	120
Petroşani, Rom.	D10	26
Petrovac, Yugo.	E8	26
Petrovsk, Russia	D6	32
Petrovskij, Russia	H18	8
Petrovsk-Zabajkal'skij, Russia	F10	34
Petrozavodsk, Russia	F15	8
Petrusburg, S. Afr.	F7	70
Petrusville, S. Afr.	G7	70
Petrykau, Bela.	H11	10
Pettus, Tx., U.S.	F10	130
Petuhovo, Russia	C11	32
Peuetsagoe, Gunung, vol., Indon.	J3	48
Peureulak, Indon.	J3	48
Peusangan, stm., Indon.	J3	48
Pevek, Russia	C23	34
Peza, stm., Russia	D23	8
Pezawa Taung, mtn., Mya.	C2	48
Pézenas, Fr.	F9	18
Pezinok, Slov.	H13	16
Pfarrkirchen, Ger.	H8	16
Pforzheim, Ger.	H4	16
Pfronten, Ger.	I6	16
Pfunds, Aus.	D7	22
Pfungstadt, Ger.	G4	16
Pha-an, Mya.	D3	48
Phagwāra, India	C5	54
Phalaborwa, S. Afr.	C10	70
Phalodi, India	E4	54
Phaltan, India	C2	53
Phan, Thai.	C4	48
Phanat Nikhom, Thai.	F5	48
Phangan, Ko, i., Thai.	H5	48
Phangnga, Thai.	H4	48
Phaniang, stm., Thai.	D6	48
Phanom Dongrak Range (Dângrêk, Chuŏr Phnum), mts., Asia	C3	44
Phan Rang, Viet.	G9	48
Phan Thiet, Viet.	G9	48
Phan Thong, Thai.	F5	48
Pharenda, India	E9	54
Pharr, Tx., U.S.	H9	130
Phat Diem, Viet.	B8	48
Phatthalung, Thai.	I5	48
Phayao, Thai.	C4	48
Phelps, N.Y., U.S.	B8	114
Phelps, Wi., U.S.	E9	118
Phelps Lake, l., N.C., U.S.	I9	114
Phenix City, Al., U.S.	E13	122
Phepane, stm., S. Afr.	E6	70
Phet Buri, stm., Thai.	F4	48
Phetchabun, Thai.	D5	48
Phetchabun, Thiu Khao, mts., Thai.	D5	48
Phetchaburi, Thai.	F4	48
Phibun Mangsahan, Thai.	E7	48
Phichai, Thai.	D5	48
Phichit, Thai.	D5	48
Philadelphia, Ms., U.S.	E9	122
Philadelphia, N.Y., U.S.	D14	112
Philadelphia, Pa., U.S.	E10	114
Phil Campbell, Al., U.S.	C11	122
Philip, S.D., U.S.	C11	126
Philippeville see Skikda, Alg.	B6	64
Philippeville, Bel.	D13	14
Philippi, W.V., U.S.	E5	114
Philippi see Fílippoi, hist., Grc.	B7	28
Philippi, Lake, l., Austl.	E2	76
Philippine Basin, unds.	H15	142
Philippines, ctry., Asia	C4	52
Philippine Sea	H15	142
Philippine Trench, unds.	I15	142
Philippolis, S. Afr.	G7	70
Philipsburg, Mt., U.S.	D13	136
Philipsburg, Pa., U.S.	D7	114
Philip Smith Mountains, mts., Ak., U.S.	C10	140
Philipstown, S. Afr.	G7	70
Phillaur, India	C5	54
Phillip Island, i., Austl.	L5	76
Phillips, Me., U.S.	F6	110
Phillips, Tx., U.S.	F7	128
Phillips, Wi., U.S.	F8	118
Phillipsburg, Ga., U.S.	E2	116
Phillipsburg, N.J., U.S.	D10	114
Philo, Il., U.S.	E9	120
Philo, Oh., U.S.	E4	114
Philpots Island, i., Nu., Can.	C10	141
Phimai, Thai.	E6	48
Phitsanulok, Thai.	D5	48
Phnom Penh see Phnum Pénh, Camb.	G7	48
Phnum Pénh (Phnom Penh), Camb.	G7	48
Phoenix, Az., U.S.	J4	132
Phoenix, N.Y., U.S.	E13	112
Phoenix, Or., U.S.	A3	134
Phoenix Islands, is., Kir.	D9	72
Phoenixville, Pa., U.S.	D10	114
Phofung (Sources, Mont-aux-), mtn., Afr.	F9	70
Phon, Thai.	E6	48
Phong, stm., Thai.	D6	48
Phôngsali, Laos	B6	48
Phon Phisai, Thai.	D6	48
Phra Chedi Sam Ong, p., Asia	E4	48
Phrae, Thai.	C5	48
Phra Nakhon Si Ayutthaya, Thai.	E5	48
Phran Kratai, Thai.	D4	48
Phrom Phiram, Thai.	D5	48
Phu Cat, Viet.	E9	48
Phuket, Thai.	I4	48
Phuket, Ko, i., Thai.	I4	48
Phu Ly, Viet.	B7	48
Phum Duang, stm., Thai.	H4	48
Phumĭ Bâ Khăm, Camb.	F8	48
Phumĭ Béng, Camb.	F7	48
Phumĭ Châmbák, Camb.	G7	48
Phumĭ Chhuk, Camb.	G7	48
Phumĭ Chruŏy Slĕng, Camb.	F8	48
Phumĭ Kâmpóng Srâlau, Camb.	E7	48
Phumĭ Kâmpóng Trâbêk, Camb.	F7	48
Phumĭ Kaôh Kért, Camb.	F7	48
Phumĭ Khpôb, Camb.	G7	48
Phumĭ Lvéa Kraôm, Camb.	F6	48
Phumĭ Narŭng, Camb.	F7	48
Phumĭ Prêk Kák, Camb.	F7	48
Phumĭ Puŏk Chăs, Camb.	F6	48
Phumĭ Sâmraông, Camb.	E6	48
Phumĭ Srê Kôkir, Camb.	F8	48
Phumĭ Tbêng, Camb.	F7	48
Phumĭ Thmâ Pôk, Camb.	F6	48
Phumĭ Tœk Choŭ, Camb.	F6	48
Phu My, Viet.	E9	48
Phuoc Long, Viet.	G8	48
Phuoc Long, Viet.	H7	48
Phu Pan National Park, p.o.i., Thai.	D6	48
Phu Quoc, Dao, i., Viet.	G6	48
Phu Tho, Viet.	B7	48
Phu Vang, Viet.	D8	48
Pi, stm., China	F7	42
Piaçabuçu, Braz.	F7	88
Piacenza, Italy	E6	22
Pialba, Austl.	E9	76
Piancó, Braz.	D7	88
Pianosa, Isola, i., Italy	H12	22
Pianosa, Isola, i., Italy	H6	22
Piapot, Sk., Can.	E4	124
Piaseczno, Pol.	D16	16
Piaski, Pol.	E18	16
Piatã, Braz.	G5	88
Piatra-Neamț, Rom.	B13	26
Piauí, state, Braz.	D4	88
Piauí, stm., Braz.	D4	88
Piauí, Morro do, mtn., Braz.	H2	88
Piave, stm., Italy	E9	22
Piaxtla, stm., Mex.	D5	100
Piazza Armerina, Italy	G8	24
Pibor Post, Sudan	F6	62
Pic, stm., On., Can.	B12	118
Picacho, Az., U.S.	K5	132
Picardie, hist. reg., Fr.	E11	14
Picardy see Picardie, hist. reg., Fr.	E11	14
Picayune, Ms., U.S.	G9	122
Pichanal, Arg.	D4	90
Picher, Ok., U.S.	H3	120
Pichilemu, Chile	G1	92
Pichimá, Col.	E3	86
Pichi Mahuida, Arg.	I5	92
Pichincha, state, Ec.	H2	86
Pichucalco, Mex.	G12	100
Pickardville, Ab., Can.	B16	138
Pickens, Ms., U.S.	E9	122
Pickens, S.C., U.S.	B3	116
Pickensville, Al., U.S.	D10	122
Pickerel Lake, l., Mb., Can.	B14	124
Pickering, Eng., U.K.	G12	12
Pickle Lake, On., Can.	E12	106
Pickstown, S.D., U.S.	D14	126
Pickton, Tx., U.S.	D3	122
Pickwick Lake, res., U.S.	B10	122
Pico, mtn., C.V.	I10	65a
Pico, i., Port.	C3	60
Pico da Neblina, Parque Nacional, p.o.i., Braz.	G9	86
Pico de Orizaba, Parque Nacional, p.o.i., Mex.	F10	100
Pico de Orizaba, Volcán (Citlaltépetl, Volcán), vol., Mex.	F10	100
Picos, Braz.	D5	88
Picquigny, Fr.	E11	14
Picton, On., Can.	D12	112
Picton, N.Z.	E6	80
Picton, Isla, i., Chile	K3	90
Pictou, N.S., Can.	E14	110
Pictou Island, i., N.S., Can.	E14	110
Picture Butte, Ab., Can.	G18	138
Pictured Rocks National Lakeshore, p.o.i., Mi., U.S.	B3	112
Picuí, Braz.	D7	88
Picún Leufú, Arg.	G3	90
Pidálion, Akrotírion, c., Cyp.	D5	58
Pidhorodna, Ukr.	A17	26
Pidurutalagala, mtn., Sri L.	H5	53
Piedecuesta, Col.	D5	86
Piedimonte Matese, Italy	C8	24
Piedmont, Al., U.S.	D13	122
Piedmont, Mo., U.S.	G7	120
Piedmont see Piemonte, state, Italy	F5	22
Piedra, stm., Co., U.S.	F9	132
Piedra, Cerro, mtn., Chile	H1	92
Piedra del Águila, Arg.	H3	90
Piedrafita, Puerto de, p., Spain	B3	20
Piedrahita, Spain	D5	20
Piedras, Punta, c., Arg.	G9	92
Piedras, Punta, c., Ven.	B11	86
Piedras Blancas, Arg.	E8	92
Piedras Negras, Guat.	D2	102
Piedras Negras, Mex.	A8	100
Pieksämäki, Fin.	E12	8
Pielinen, l., Fin.	E13	8
Pieljekaise Nationalpark, p.o.i., Swe.	C6	8
Piemonte, state, Italy	F5	22
Pienaarsrivier, S. Afr.	D8	70
Pieniężno, Pol.	B16	16
Pieniński Park Narodowy, p.o.i., Pol.	G16	16
Pienza, Italy	G8	22
Pierce, Co., U.S.	G8	126
Pierce, Id., U.S.	D11	136
Pierce City, Mo., U.S.	E14	128
Pierpont, S.D., U.S.	B15	126
Pierre, S.D., U.S.	C12	126
Pierre, Bayou, stm., La., U.S.	F5	122
Pierre, Bayou, stm., Ms., U.S.	E8	122
Pierre Part, La., U.S.	G7	122
Pierreville, Trin.	s13	105f
Pierz, Mn., U.S.	F4	118
Piešt'any, Slov.	H13	16
Pietarsaari, Fin.	E10	8
Pietermaritzburg, S. Afr.	F10	70
Pietersburg, S. Afr.	C9	70
Pietrasanta, Italy	F7	22
Piet Retief, S. Afr.	E10	70
Pietrosu, Vârful, mtn., Rom.	B12	26
Pigeon, Mi., U.S.	E6	112
Pigeon, stm., Mb., Can.	B17	124
Pigeon Forge, Tn., U.S.	I2	114
Pigeon Lake, l., Ab., Can.	C16	138
Pigeon Lake, l., On., Can.	D11	112
Piggs Peak, Swaz.	E10	70
Pigs, Bay of see Cochinos, Bahía de, b., Cuba	B7	102
Pigüé, Arg.	H6	92
Pihāri, India	E8	54
Pihlajavesi, l., Fin.	F13	8
Pihtipudas, Fin.	E11	8
Pijijiapan, Mex.	H12	100
Pikalëvo, Russia	A17	10
Pikangikum, On., Can.	E12	106
Pikes Peak, mtn., Co., U.S.	C3	128
Pikes Rocks, hill, Pa., U.S.	C6	114
Pikesville, Md., U.S.	E9	114
Piketberg, S. Afr.	H4	70
Piketon, Oh., U.S.	E2	114
Pikeville, Tn., U.S.	B13	122
Pikou, China	B10	42
Pikounda, Congo	D3	66
Piła, Pol.	C12	16
Piła, state, Pol.	C12	16
Pilanesberg Game Reserve, p.o.i., S. Afr.	D8	70
Pilão Arcado, Braz.	E4	88
Pilar, Arg.	E5	92
Pilar, Braz.	E8	88
Pilar, Para.	C8	92
Pilar de Goiás, Braz.	H1	88
Pilar do Sul, Braz.	A14	92
Pilares, Mex.	D3	130
Pilas Group, is., Phil.	G3	52
Pilawa, Pol.	D17	16
Pilcomayo, stm., S.A.	D4	90
Pilcomayo, Brazo Norte, stm., Para.	B8	92
Pilcomayo, Brazo Sur del, stm., S.A.	B8	92
Pilcomayo, Parque Nacional, p.o.i., Arg.	B8	92
Pilger, Ne., U.S.	E15	126
Pilgrim's Rest, S. Afr.	D10	70
Pili, Phil.	D4	52
Pīlībhīt, India	D7	54
Pilica, stm., Pol.	E16	16
Pilliga, Austl.	H7	76
Pilot, The, mtn., Austl.	K7	76
Pilot Butte, Sk., Can.	D9	124
Pilot Knob, Mo., U.S.	G7	120
Pilot Knob, mtn., Id., U.S.	E11	136
Pilot Mound, Mb., Can.	E15	124
Pilot Mountain, N.C., U.S.	H5	114
Pilot Peak, mtn., Nv., U.S.	E8	134
Pilot Peak, mtn., Wy., U.S.	F16	136
Pilot Rock, Or., U.S.	E8	136
Pilottown, La., U.S.	H9	122
Pilsen see Plzeň, Czech Rep.	G9	16
Pilu, stm., Mya.	B3	48
Pilzno, Pol.	G17	16
Pima, Az., U.S.	K7	132
Pimba, Austl.	F7	74
Pimenteira, Vereda, stm., Braz.	F4	88
Pimentel, Braz.	B3	88
Pinang, Pulau, i., Malay.	J4	48
Pınarbaşı, Tur.	B16	28
Pinar del Río, Cuba	A5	102
Pinarello, Fr.	H15	18
Pınarhisar, Tur.	B10	28
Pinas, Arg.	E5	92
Pinatubo, Mount, vol., Phil.	C3	52
Pincher Creek, Ab., Can.	G17	138
Pinchi Lake, l., B.C., Can.	B6	138
Pinckneyville, Il., U.S.	F8	120
Pinconning, Mi., U.S.	E5	112
Pindale, Mya.	B2	48
Pindamonhangaba, Braz.	L3	88
Pindaré, stm., Braz.	B3	88
Pindaré-Mirim, Braz.	B3	88
Pindi Gheb, Pak.	B4	54
Pindobaçu, Braz.	F5	88
Píndos Óros (Pindus Mountains), mts., Grc.	D4	28
Pindus Mountains see Píndos Óros, mts., Grc.	D4	28
Pindwāra, India	F4	54
Pine, stm., Mi., U.S.	E5	112
Pine Apple, Al., U.S.	F11	122
Pine Barrens, reg., N.J., U.S.	E11	114
Pine Bluff, Ar., U.S.	C7	122
Pine Bush, N.Y., U.S.	C11	114
Pine Castle, Fl., U.S.	H4	116
Pine City, Mn., U.S.	F6	118
Pine Creek, Austl.	B6	74
Pine Creek, stm., Nv., U.S.	C9	134
Pine Creek, stm., Pa., U.S.	C8	114
Pine Falls, Mb., Can.	D17	124
Pinega, Russia	D20	8
Pinega, stm., Russia	D20	8
Pine Grove, W.V., U.S.	E5	114
Pine Hill, Austl.	D6	76
Pine Hill, Al., U.S.	F11	122
Pine Hills, Fl., U.S.	H4	116
Pinehouse Lake, l., Sk., Can.	D9	106
Pinehurst, Ga., U.S.	D2	116
Pinehurst, Id., U.S.	E10	136
Pinehurst, N.C., U.S.	A6	116
Pinehurst Lake, l., Ab., Can.	B19	138
Pineiós (Peneus), stm., Grc.	D5	28
Pine Island, Mn., U.S.	G6	118
Pine Island, i., Fl., U.S.	J3	116
Pine Island Bay, b., Ant.	C30	81
Pinellas Park, Fl., U.S.	I3	116
Pine Mountain, mtn., Ca., U.S.	H4	134
Pine Pass, p., B.C., Can.	A8	138
Pine Point, N.T., Can.	C8	106
Pine Ridge, S.D., U.S.	D10	126
Pine River, Mb., Can.	C13	124
Pine River, Mn., U.S.	E4	118

Name	Map Ref.	Page
Pinerolo, Italy	F4	22
Piñeros, Isla, i., P.R.	B4	104a
Pines, Isle of see Juventud, Isla de la, i., Cuba	B6	102
Pines, Lake O' The, res., Tx., U.S.	E4	122
Pine Swamp Knob, mtn., W.V., U.S.	E6	114
Pinetop-Lakeside, Az., U.S.	I6	132
Pinetops, N.C., U.S.	I8	114
Pinetown, S. Afr.	F10	70
Pine Valley, val., Ut., U.S.	E3	132
Pineville, Ky., U.S.	H2	114
Pineville, La., U.S.	F6	122
Pineville, Mo., U.S.	H3	120
Pineville, W.V., U.S.	G4	114
Pinewood, S.C., U.S.	C5	116
Ping, stm., Thai.	E5	48
Ping'an, China	B5	38
Pingba, China	H2	42
Pingchang, China	F2	42
Pingding, China	C5	42
Pingdingshan, China	E5	42
Pingdu, China	C8	42
Pingelly, Austl.	F3	74
Pinghe, China	A6	48
Pinghu, China	F9	42
Pingjiang, China	G5	42
Pingle, China	I4	42
Pingli, China	E3	42
Pingliang, China	D2	42
Pingluo, China	B2	42
Pingnan, China	H8	42
Pingnan, China	J4	42
Pingquan, China	A8	42
Pingshi, China	I5	42
Pingtan, China	I8	42
Pingtan Dao, i., China	I8	42
P'ingtung, Tai.	J9	42
Pingwu, China	E5	36
Pingxiang, China	H5	42
Pingxiang, China	J2	42
Pingyang, China	H9	42
Pingyao, China	C5	42
Pingyi, China	D7	42
Pingyin, China	C7	42
Pingyuan, China	I6	42
Pinhão, Braz.	F7	88
Pinheiro, Braz.	B3	88
Pinheiros, Braz.	J5	88
Pinhel, Port.	D3	20
Pini, Pulau, i., Indon.	E2	44
Pinillos, Col.	C4	86
Pinjarra, Austl.	F3	74
Pinjug, Russia	F22	8
Pinkiang see Harbin, China	B7	38
Pink Mountain, B.C., Can.	D6	106
Pinnacle, mtn., Va., U.S.	E7	114
Pinnacle Buttes, mtn., Wy., U.S.	G17	136
Pinnacles National Monument, p.o.i., Ca., U.S.	G4	134
Pinnaroo, Austl.	J3	76
Pinneberg, Ger.	C5	16
Pinos, Mex.	D8	100
Pinos, Isla de see Juventud, Isla de la, i., Cuba	B6	102
Pinos, Mount, mtn., Ca., U.S.	I6	134
Pinos Puente, Spain	G7	20
Pinrang, Indon.	E11	50
Pins, Île des, i., N. Cal.	n16	79d
Pins, Pointe aux, c., On., Can.	F8	112
Pinsk, Bela.	H9	10
Pinsk Marshes see Pripet Marshes, reg., Eur.	H12	10
Pinson, Al., U.S.	D12	122
Pinta, Isla, i., Ec.	h11	84a
Pintada Arroyo, stm., N.M., U.S.	G3	128
Pintados, Chile	D3	90
Pintasan, Malay.	A10	50
Pinto Butte, mtn., Sk., Can.	E6	124
Pintoyacu, stm., Ec.	H3	86
Pin Valley National Park, p.o.i., India	C6	54
Pioche, Nv., U.S.	F2	132
Piombino, Italy	H7	22
Pioneer Mine, B.C., Can.	F8	138
Pionerskij, Russia	F3	10
Pionki, Pol.	E17	16
Piorini, stm., Braz.	D5	84
Piorini, Lago, l., Braz.	D5	84
Piotrków, state, Pol.	E15	16
Piotrków Trybunalski, Pol.	E15	16
Pio V. Corpuz, Phil.	E5	52
Piove di Sacco, Italy	E8	22
Pio XII, Braz.	B3	88
Pipanaco, Salar de, pl., Arg.	D4	92
Pīpār, India	E4	54
Piparia, India	G7	54
Pīpar Road, India	E4	54
Pipe Spring National Monument, p.o.i., Az., U.S.	G4	132
Pipestem Creek, stm., N.D., U.S.	G14	124
Pipestone, Mn., U.S.	H2	118
Pipestone, stm., On., Can.	E12	106
Pipestone Creek, stm., Can.	E12	124
Pipestone National Monument, p.o.i., Mn., U.S.	G2	118
Pipinas, Arg.	G9	92
Piplān, Pak.	B3	54
Pipmuacan, Réservoir, res., Qc., Can.	A6	110
Piqua, Oh., U.S.	D1	114
Piquet Carneiro, Braz.	C6	88
Piquiri, stm., Braz.	B11	92
Piracanjuba, Braz.	I1	88
Piracanjuba, stm., Braz.	I1	88
Piracicaba, Braz.	L2	88
Piracicaba, stm., Braz.	L1	88
Piracuruca, Braz.	B5	88
Pirae, Fr. Poly.	v21	78h
Piraeus see Peiraiás, Grc.	F6	28
Piraí do Sul, Braz.	B12	92
Piraju, Braz.	L1	88
Pirajuí, Braz.	L1	88
Piram Island, i., India	H4	54
Piran, Slvn.	E10	22
Pirané, Arg.	B8	92
Piranga, Braz.	K4	88
Piranhas, Braz.	G7	84
Piranhas, stm., Braz.	E1	88
Piranhas, stm., Braz.	C7	88
Piranji, stm., Braz.	C6	88
Pirapemas, Braz.	B3	88
Pirapora, Braz.	I3	88
Piraquara, Braz.	B13	92
Pirassununga, Braz.	K2	88
Pirata, Monte, hill, P.R.	B4	104a
Piratinga, stm., Braz.	H2	88
Piratini, Braz.	E11	92
Piratini, stm., Braz.	D10	92
Piratuba, Braz.	C11	92
Pires do Rio, Braz.	I1	88
Piriápolis, Ur.	G10	92
Pirin, Parki Narodowe, p.o.i., Blg.	H10	26
Piripiri, Braz.	C5	88
Píritu, Ven.	C7	86
Pirmasens, Ger.	G3	16
Pirna, Ger.	F9	16
Pirojpur, Bngl.	G12	54
Pirot, Yugo.	F9	26
Pirovano, Arg.	H7	92
Pirovskoe, Russia	C16	32
Pīr Panjāl Range, mts., Asia	B5	54
Pirtleville, Az., U.S.	L7	132
Pirttikylä, Fin.	E9	8
Piru, Indon.	F8	44
Pisa, Italy	G7	22
Pisagua, Chile	C2	90
Pisco, Peru	F2	84
Pișcolt, Rom.	B9	26
Písek, Czech Rep.	G10	16
Pishan, China	A4	46
Pishchanka, Ukr.	A15	26
Pisinemo, Az., U.S.	K4	132
Pismo Beach, Ca., U.S.	H5	134
Pisticci, Italy	D10	24
Pistoia, Italy	G7	22
Pisuerga, stm., Spain	C6	20
Pit, stm., Ca., U.S.	B4	134
Pit, North Fork, stm., Ca., U.S.	B5	134
Pita, Gui.	G2	64
Pitalito, Col.	G4	86
Pitanga, Braz.	B12	92
Pitangui, Braz.	J3	88
Pitcairn, dep., Pit.	c28	78k
Piteå, Swe.	D9	8
Piteälven, stm., Swe.	D8	8
Pitești, Rom.	E11	26
Pithapuram, India	C6	53
Pithiviers, Fr.	F11	14
Pithom, hist., Egypt	H2	58
Pithorāgarh, India	D8	54
Pitinga, stm., Braz.	H12	86
Pitiquito, Mex.	F6	98
Pitkjaranta, Russia	F14	8
Pitljar, Russia	C2	34
Pitomača, Cro.	D14	22
Pitrufquén, Chile	G2	90
Pitt Island, i., B.C., Can.	E5	106
Pitt Lake, l., B.C., Can.	G8	138
Pittsboro, N.C., U.S.	I6	114
Pittsburg, Ks., U.S.	G3	120
Pittsburg, Tx., U.S.	E4	122
Pittsburgh, Pa., U.S.	D6	114
Pittsfield, Il., U.S.	E7	120
Pittsfield, Me., U.S.	F7	110
Pittsfield, Ma., U.S.	B12	114
Pittsford, Mi., U.S.	C1	114
Pittston, Pa., U.S.	C10	114
Pittsview, Al., U.S.	E13	122
Pittsworth, Austl.	F8	76
Pituil, Arg.	D4	92
Pium, Braz.	F1	88
Piura, Peru	E1	84
Piute Peak, mtn., Ca., U.S.	H7	134
Pivan', Russia	F16	34
Pivdennyy Buh, stm., Ukr.	A17	26
Pizarro, Col.	E3	86
Pizzo, Italy	F10	24
Pjakupur, stm., Russia	B13	32
Pjalka, Russia	C19	8
Pjandž (Panj), stm., Asia	B11	56
Pjaozero, ozero, l., Russia	C14	8
Pjasina, stm., Russia	B6	34
Pjasino, ozero, l., Russia	B6	34
Pjasinskij zaliv, b., Russia	B5	34
Pjatigorsk, Russia	F6	32
Pjatovskij, Russia	F19	10
Pjažieva Sel'ga, Russia	F16	8
Placentia Bay, b., Nf., Can.	j23	107a
Placerville, Ca., U.S.	E5	134
Placetas, Cuba	A8	102
Plácido Rosas, Ur.	F11	92
Plai Mat, stm., Thai.	E6	48
Plain City, Ut., U.S.	B4	132
Plain Dealing, La., U.S.	E5	122
Plainfield, Ct., U.S.	C13	114
Plainfield, In., U.S.	I3	112
Plainfield, N.J., U.S.	D11	114
Plains, Ga., U.S.	E14	122
Plains, Ks., U.S.	D8	128
Plains, Mt., U.S.	C12	136
Plainview, Mn., U.S.	G6	118
Plainview, Ne., U.S.	E15	126
Plainview, Tx., U.S.	G7	128
Plainville, In., U.S.	F10	120
Plainwell, Mi., U.S.	F4	112
Plakhtiïvka, Ukr.	C16	26
Plamondon, Ab., Can.	B18	138
Plampang, Indon.	H10	50
Planá, Czech Rep.	G8	16
Plana, L'Illa, i., Spain	F10	20
Planada, Ca., U.S.	F5	134
Planalto, Braz.	C11	92
Planchón, Cerro del (El Planchón, Volcán), vol., S.A.	G2	92
Planeta Rica, Col.	C4	86
Plano, Il., U.S.	C9	120
Plano, Tx., U.S.	D2	122
Plantagenet, On., Can.	E2	110
Plantation, Fl., U.S.	J5	116
Plant City, Fl., U.S.	I3	116
Plantersville, Ms., U.S.	C10	122
Plantsite, Az., U.S.	J7	132
Plaquemine, La., U.S.	G7	122
Plasencia, Spain	D4	20
Plaster Rock, N.B., Can.	D9	110
Plasy, Czech Rep.	G9	16
Plata, Isla de la, i., Ec.	H1	86
Plata, Río de la, est., S.A.	G9	92
Plato, Col.	C4	86
Platte, stm., U.S.	E3	120
Platte, stm., Ne., U.S.	C7	108
Platte, Île, i., Sey.	k13	69b
Platte Center, Ne., U.S.	F15	126
Platte City, Mo., U.S.	E3	120
Platteville, Co., U.S.	A4	128
Platteville, Wi., U.S.	B7	120
Plattsburgh, N.Y., U.S.	F3	110
Plattsmouth, Ne., U.S.	D2	120
Plau, Ger.	C8	16
Plauen, Ger.	F8	16
Plav, Yugo.	G6	26
Plavsk, Russia	G20	10
Playa Azul, Mex.	G7	100
Playa de Fajardo, P.R.	B4	104a
Playa de Guayanilla, P.R.	B2	104a
Playa de Naguabo, P.R.	B4	104a
Playa de Ponce, P.R.	C2	104a
Playa Noriega, Laguna, l., Mex.	A3	100
Playa Vicente, Mex.	G11	100
Playgreen Lake, l., Mb., Can.	E11	106
Play Ku, Viet.	F8	48
Plaza, N.D., U.S.	F12	124
Pleasant, Mount, hill, N.B., Can.	E9	110
Pleasant Bay, N.S., Can.	D16	110
Pleasantdale, Sk., Can.	B9	124
Pleasant Grove, Ut., U.S.	C5	132
Pleasant Hill, Il., U.S.	E7	120
Pleasant Hill, La., U.S.	F5	122
Pleasant Hill, Mo., U.S.	F3	120
Pleasanton, Ks., U.S.	F3	120
Pleasanton, Tx., U.S.	F9	130
Pleasantville, N.J., U.S.	E11	114
Pleasantville, Pa., U.S.	C6	114
Pleaux, Fr.	D8	18
Plehanovo, Russia	F20	10
Plenty, Sk., Can.	C5	124
Plenty, Bay of, b., N.Z.	C7	80
Plentywood, Mt., U.S.	F9	124
Pleščeevo, ozero, l., Russia	D21	10
Pleseck, Russia	E19	8
Plessisville, Qc., Can.	D5	110
Pleszew, Pol.	E13	16
Plétipi, Lac, l., Qc., Can.	E16	106
Plettenbergbaai, S. Afr.	I6	70
Pleven, Blg.	F11	26
Plevna, Mt., U.S.	A8	126
Plitvička Jezera Nacionalni Park, p.o.i., Cro.	F12	22
Pljevlja, Yugo.	F6	26
Pljuskovo, Russia	H16	10
Pljussa, stm., Russia	A11	10
Płock, Pol.	D15	16
Płock, state, Pol.	D15	16
Ploërmel, Fr.	G6	14
Ploiești, Rom.	E12	26
Plomb du Cantal, mtn., Fr.	D8	18
Plomer, Point, c., Austl.	H9	76
Plön, Ger.	B6	16
Płońsk, Pol.	D16	16
Ploskoe, Russia	H21	10
Plotnica, Bela.	H9	10
Ploudalmézeau, Fr.	F4	14
Plovdiv, Blg.	G11	26
Plovdiv, state, Blg.	G11	26
Plumerville, Ar., U.S.	B6	122
Plummer, Id., U.S.	C9	136
Plumridge Lakes, l., Austl.	E5	74
Plumtree, Zimb.	B8	70
Plungė, Lith.	E4	10
Plutarco Elías Calles, Presa, res., Mex.	G8	98
Plymouth, Monts.	D3	105a
Plymouth, Eng., U.K.	K8	12
Plymouth, Ca., U.S.	E5	134
Plymouth, Il., U.S.	D6	120
Plymouth, Ma., U.S.	C15	114
Plymouth, Ne., U.S.	A11	128
Plymouth, N.H., U.S.	G5	110
Plymouth, N.C., U.S.	I9	114
Plymouth, Oh., U.S.	C3	114
Plymouth, Pa., U.S.	C10	114
Plzeň, Czech Rep.	G9	16
Pô, Burkina	G4	64
Po, stm., Italy	F8	22
Po, Foci del, mth., Italy	F9	22
Po, Mouths of the see Po, Foci del, mth., Italy	F9	22
Poarta Orientală, Pasul, p., Rom.	D9	26
Pobè, Benin	H5	64
Pobeda, gora, mtn., Russia	C18	34
Pobedino, Russia	G17	34
Pobedy, pik, mtn., Asia	F14	32
Poblado Cerro Gordo, P.R.	A3	104a
Poblado Jacaguas, P.R.	B2	104a
Poblado Medianía Alta, P.R.	B4	104a
Poblado Santana, P.R.	B2	104a
Pobra de Trives, Spain	B3	20
Pocahontas, Ar., U.S.	H6	120
Pocahontas, Ia., U.S.	B3	120
Poção, Braz.	E7	88
Pocatello, Id., U.S.	H14	136
Počep, Russia	H16	10
Počinok, Russia	D4	32
Pocitos, Salar, pl., Arg.	B4	92
Poço da Cruz, Açude, res., Braz.	E7	88
Poções, Braz.	H5	88
Pocola, Ok., U.S.	B4	122
Pocomoke City, Md., U.S.	F10	114
Poconé, Braz.	G6	84
Pocono Mountains, hills, Pa., U.S.	C10	114
Pocono Summit, Pa., U.S.	C10	114
Poço Redondo, Braz.	E7	88
Poços de Caldas, Braz.	K2	88
Pocrane, Braz.	J5	88
Podbereze, Russia	D13	10
Podborove, Russia	A18	10
Poddębice, Pol.	E14	16
Poddore, Russia	C13	10
Poděbrady, Czech Rep.	F11	16
Podgorica (Titograd), Yugo.	G6	26
Podjuga, Russia	F19	8
Podkamennaja Tunguska, Russia	B16	32
Podkamennaja Tunguska, stm., Russia	B16	32
Podlasie, reg., Pol.	D19	16
Podol'sk, Russia	E20	10
Podor, Sen.	F2	64
Podporože, Russia	F16	8
Podravina, reg., Cro.	E15	22
Podtësovo, Russia	C16	32
Podujevo, Yugo.	G8	26
Poel, i., Ger.	B7	16
Poelela, Lagoa, l., Moz.	D12	70
Pofadder, S. Afr.	F4	70
Pogar, Russia	H16	10
Poggibonsi, Italy	G8	22
Pogoanele, Rom.	E13	26
Pogoreloe Gorodišče, Russia	D17	10
Pogradec, Alb.	D14	24
Pogradeci see Pogradec, Alb.	D14	24
Pograničnyj, Russia	B9	38
P'ohang, Kor., S.	C2	40
Pohjanmaa, reg., Fin.	D11	8
Pohjois-Karjala, state, Fin.	E14	8
Pohnpei, i., Micron.	I11	78d
Pohri, India	F6	54
Pohvistnevo, Russia	D8	32
Pöide, Est.	B6	10
Poinsett, Cape, c., Ant.	B16	81
Poinsett, Lake, l., S.D., U.S.	C15	126
Point, Tx., U.S.	E3	122
Point Arena, Ca., U.S.	E2	134
Point Au Fer Island, i., La., U.S.	H7	122
Point Baker, Ak., U.S.	E13	140
Pointe-à-la-Garde, Qc., Can.	B10	110
Pointe a la Hache, La., U.S.	H9	122
Pointe-à-Pitre, Guad.	h5	105c
Pointe-à-Pitre-le Raizet, Aéroport de, Guad.	h5	105c
Pointe du Canonnier, c., Guad.	A1	105a
Point Edward, On., Can.	E7	112
Pointe-Noire, Congo	E2	66
Pointe-Noire, Guad.	h5	105c
Point Fortin, Trin.	s12	105f
Point Hope, Ak., U.S.	C6	140
Point Jupiter, c., St. Vin.	p11	105e
Point Lake, l., N.T., Can.	B8	106
Point Marion, Pa., U.S.	E5	114
Point Pelee National Park, p.o.i., On., Can.	G7	112
Point Pleasant, N.J., U.S.	D11	114
Point Reyes National Seashore, p.o.i., Ca., U.S.	E2	134
Point Roberts, Wa., U.S.	B3	136
Point Salines International Airport, Gren.	q10	105e
Point Sapin, N.B., Can.	D12	110
Poisson Blanc, Lac du, res., Qc., Can.	B14	112
Poissy, Fr.	F10	14
Poitiers, Fr.	H9	14
Poitou, hist. reg., Fr.	C5	18
Poivre Atoll, i., Sey.	k12	69b
Pojarkovo, Russia	G14	34
Pojoaque Valley, N.M., U.S.	F2	128
Pojuca, Braz.	G6	88
Pojuca, stm., Braz.	G6	88
Pokaran, India	E3	54
Pokataroo, Austl.	G7	76
Pokharā, Nepal	D10	54
Poko, D.R.C.	D5	66
Pokrovsk, Russia	D14	34
Pokrovskoe, Russia	H19	10
Pola, stm., Russia	C14	10
Polacca Wash, stm., Az., U.S.	H6	132
Polack, Bela.	E11	10
Pola de Lena, Spain	A5	20
Pola de Siero, Spain	A5	20
Poland, ctry., Eur.	D15	16
Polanów, Pol.	B12	16
Polatlı, Tur.	D15	28
Polcura, Chile	H2	92
Poldnevica, Russia	G22	8
Polebridge, Mt., U.S.	B12	136
Pol-e Khomrī, Afg.	B10	56
Polese see Pripet Marshes, reg., Eur.	H12	10
Polesine, reg., Italy	E8	22
Polewali, Indon.	E11	50
Polgár, Hung.	B8	26
Poli, Cam.	C2	66
Poli, China	D8	42
Policastro, Golfo di, b., Italy	E9	24
Police (Pölitz), Pol.	C10	16
Polička, Czech Rep.	G12	16
Polillo Island, i., Phil.	C3	52
Polillo Islands, is., Phil.	C4	52
Pólis, Cyp.	C3	58
Polist', stm., Russia	C14	10
Polistena, Italy	F10	24
Poljarnyj, Russia	B15	8
Poljarnyj, Russia	C24	34
Poljarnyj Ural, mts., Russia	A10	32
Polk, Ne., U.S.	F15	126
Polk, Pa., U.S.	C6	114
Pol'kino, Russia	B8	34
Pollāchi, India	F3	53
Pöllau, Aus.	C12	22
Pollino, Monte, mtn., Italy	E10	24
Pollock, La., U.S.	F6	122
Pollock, S.D., U.S.	B12	126
Polnovo-Seliger, Russia	C15	10
Polo, Il., U.S.	B8	120
Polomet', stm., Russia	C15	10
Polonnaruwa, Sri L.	H5	53
Polonnaruwa, hist., Sri L.	H5	53
Polotnjanyj, Russia	F19	10
Polotsk see Polack, Bela.	E11	10
Polski Trămbeš, Blg.	F12	26
Polson, Mt., U.S.	C12	136
Poltava, Ukr.	E4	32
Poltimore, Qc., Can.	C14	112
Põltsamaa, Est.	G12	8
Poluj, stm., Russia	A11	32
Polunočnoe, Russia	B10	32
Polur, India	E4	53
Polvijärvi, Fin.	E13	8
Políaigos, i., Grc.	G7	28
Polynesia, is., Oc.	J22	142
Polysajevo, Russia	F6	34
Pomarkku, Fin.	F9	8
Pombal, Braz.	D7	88
Pomerania, hist. reg., Eur.	C11	16
Pomeranian Bay, b., Eur.	B10	16
Pomerene, Az., U.S.	K6	132
Pomerode, Braz.	C13	92
Pomeroy, Ia., U.S.	B3	120
Pomeroy, Wa., U.S.	D9	136
Pomfret, S. Afr.	D6	70
Pomi, Rom.	B10	26
Pomme de Terre, stm., Mn., U.S.	F3	118
Pomme de Terre, stm., Mo., U.S.	G4	120
Pomme de Terre Lake, res., Mo., U.S.	G4	120
Pomona, Ca., U.S.	I8	134
Pomona, Ks., U.S.	F2	120
Pomona Lake, res., Ks., U.S.	F2	120
Pomorskij proliv, strt., Russia	B24	8
Pompano Beach, Fl., U.S.	J5	116
Pompei, hist., Italy	D8	24
Pompejevka, Russia	G15	34
Pompéu, Braz.	J3	88
Pomquet, N.S., Can.	E15	110
Ponass Lakes, l., Sk., Can.	B9	124
Ponazyrevo, Russia	G22	8
Ponca, Ne., U.S.	B1	120
Ponca City, Ok., U.S.	E11	128
Ponca Creek, stm., U.S.	E14	126
Ponce, P.R.	B2	104a
Ponce, Aeropuerto, P.R.	B2	104a
Ponce de Leon, Fl., U.S.	G12	122
Poncha Pass, p., Co., U.S.	C2	128
Pond Creek, Ok., U.S.	E11	128
Ponderay, Id., U.S.	B10	136
Pondicherry (Puduchcheri), India	F4	53
Pondicherry, state, India	E5	53
Pond Inlet see Mittimatalik, Nu., Can.	A15	106
Pond Inlet, b., Nu., Can.	A15	106
Pondosa, Ca., U.S.	B4	134
Ponente, Riviera di, cst., Italy	F5	22
Ponérihouen, N. Cal.	m15	79d
Ponferrada, Spain	B4	20
Pongolo, stm., S. Afr.	E10	70
Poniatowa, Pol.	E17	16
Ponizove, Russia	E14	10
Ponnaiyār, stm., India	E4	53
Ponnāni, India	F2	53
Ponnūru Nidubrolu, India	C5	53
Ponoj, Russia	C19	8
Ponoj, stm., Russia	C18	8
Ponoka, Ab., Can.	D17	138
Ponorogo, Indon.	G7	50
Pons, Fr.	D5	18
Ponta Delgada, Port.	C3	60
Ponta Grossa, Braz.	B12	92
Pontalina, Braz.	I1	88
Ponta Porã, Braz.	D5	90
Pontarlier, Fr.	H15	14
Pontas de Pedra, Braz.	D8	88
Pontassieve, Italy	G8	22
Pontchartrain, Lake, l., La., U.S.	G8	122
Pontchâteau, Fr.	G6	14
Pont-de-Vaux, Fr.	C10	18
Ponte Alta do Bom Jesus, Braz.	G2	88
Ponte-Caldelas, Spain	B2	20
Ponte de Lima, Port.	C2	20
Pontedera, Italy	G7	22
Pontedeume, Spain	A2	20
Ponte do Púngoè, Moz.	A12	70
Ponteix, Sk., Can.	E6	124
Ponte Nova, Braz.	K4	88
Ponte Serrada, Braz.	C12	92
Pontevedra, Spain	B2	20
Pontevedra, co., Spain	B2	20
Pontiac, Il., U.S.	D9	120
Pontiac, Mi., U.S.	B2	114
Pontianak, Indon.	C6	50
Pontine Islands see Ponziane, Isole, is., Italy	D6	24
Pontivy, Fr.	F5	14
Pontoise, Fr.	E11	14
Pontotoc, Ms., U.S.	C9	122
Pontotoc, Tx., U.S.	D9	130
Pontremoli, Italy	F6	22
Pontresina, Switz.	D6	22
Pont-Rouge, Qc., Can.	D5	110
Ponts, Spain	C12	20
Pont-sur-Yonne, Fr.	F12	14
Pontus Mountains see Doğu Karadeniz Dağları, mts., Tur.	A5	56
Pontypridd, Wales, U.K.	J9	12
Ponyri, Russia	H19	10
Ponziane, Isole (Pontine Islands), is., Italy	D6	24
Poole, Eng., U.K.	K11	12
Pooley Island, i., B.C., Can.	D2	138
Poolville, Tx., U.S.	B10	130
Pooncarie, Austl.	I4	76
Poopó, Bol.	C3	90
Poopó, Lago, l., Bol.	C3	90
Popayán, Col.	F3	86
Pope, Ms., U.S.	C8	122
Popești-Leordeni, Rom.	E13	26
Popham Bay, b., Nu., Can.	C17	106
Popigaj, Russia	B11	34
Popigaj, stm., Russia	B10	34
Popiltah Lake, l., Austl.	I3	76
Poplar, Mt., U.S.	F8	124
Poplar, stm., Can.	B16	124
Poplar, stm., N.A.	F8	124
Poplar, West Fork (West Poplar), stm., N.A.	F8	124
Poplar Bluff, Mo., U.S.	H7	120
Poplar Hill, On., Can.	E12	106
Poplar Point, Mb., Can.	D16	124
Poplarville, Ms., U.S.	G9	122
Popocatépetl, Volcán, vol., Mex.	F9	100
Popoh, Indon.	H7	50
Popokabaka, D.R.C.	F3	66
Popoli, Italy	H10	22
Popondetta, Pap. N. Gui.	b4	79a
Popovo, Blg.	F13	26
Poprad, Slov.	G16	16
Poprad, stm., Eur.	G16	16
Popricani, Rom.	B14	26
Pŏptong-ŭp, Kor., N.	E7	38
Poquoson, Va., U.S.	G9	114
Porangatu, Braz.	G1	88
Porbandar, India	H2	54
Porce, stm., Col.	D4	86
Porcher Island, i., B.C., Can.	E4	106
Porco, Bol.	C3	90
Porcos, stm., Braz.	G3	88
Porcuna, Spain	G6	20
Porcupine, stm., N.A.	B3	106
Pordenone, Italy	D9	22
Pordim, Blg.	F11	26
Poreče, Russia	E18	10
Poreče-Rybnoe, Russia	C22	10
Porhov, Russia	C12	10
Pori (Björneborg), Fin.	F9	8
Porjaguba, Russia	C15	8
Porlamar, Ven.	B10	86
Porog, Russia	E18	8
Poronajsk, Russia	G17	34
Poroshkove, Ukr.	H18	16
Porpoise Bay, b., Ant.	B17	81
Porrentruy, Switz.	C3	22
Porretta Terme, Italy	F7	22
Porsangen, b., Nor.	A11	8
Porsangerhalvøya, pen., Nor.	A11	8
Porsgrunn, Nor.	G3	8
Porsuk, stm., Tur.	D13	28
Portachuelo, Bol.	C4	90
Port Adelaide, Austl.	J2	76
Portadown, N. Ire., U.K.	G6	12
Portage, Mi., U.S.	F4	112
Portage, Ut., U.S.	B4	132
Portage Bay, b., Mb., Can.	C15	124
Portage Lake, l., Mi., U.S.	D10	118
Portage la Prairie, Mb., Can.	E15	124
Portageville, Mo., U.S.	H8	120
Portal, Ga., U.S.	D4	116
Portal, N.D., U.S.	F11	124
Port Alberni, B.C., Can.	G6	138
Portalegre, Port.	E3	20
Portalegre, state, Port.	E3	20
Portales, N.M., U.S.	G5	128
Port Alfred, S. Afr.	H8	70
Port Alice, B.C., Can.	F3	138
Port Allen, La., U.S.	G7	122
Port Alma, Austl.	D8	76
Port Angeles, Wa., U.S.	B3	136
Port Antonio, Jam.	i14	104d
Port Aransas, Tx., U.S.	G10	130
Portarlington, Ire.	H5	12
Port Arthur, Austl.	o13	77a
Port Arthur see Lüshun, China	E4	38
Port Arthur, Tx., U.S.	H4	122
Port Askaig, Scot., U.K.	F6	12
Port Augusta, Austl.	F7	74
Port au Port Peninsula, pen., Nf., Can.	B17	110
Port-au-Prince, Haiti	C11	102
Port-au-Prince, Baie de, b., Haiti	C11	102
Port Austin, Mi., U.S.	D6	112
Port Blair, India	F7	46
Port Borden, P.E., Can.	D13	110
Port Byron, Il., U.S.	J8	118
Port Canning, India	G12	54
Port-Cartier, Qc., Can.	E17	106
Port Chalmers, N.Z.	G4	80
Port Charlotte, Fl., U.S.	J3	116
Port Clinton, Oh., U.S.	C3	114
Port Clyde, Me., U.S.	G7	110
Port Colborne, On., Can.	F10	112
Port Coquitlam, B.C., Can.	G8	138
Port-de-Paix, Haiti	C11	102
Port Dickson, Malay.	K5	48
Porte Crayon, Mount, mtn., W.V., U.S.	F6	114
Port Edward see Weihai, China	C10	42
Port Edward, S. Afr.	G10	70
Port Edwards, Wi., U.S.	G9	118
Porteirinha, Braz.	H4	88
Portel, Braz.	D7	84
Port Elgin, N.B., Can.	D12	110
Port Elgin, On., Can.	D8	112
Port Elizabeth, S. Afr.	H7	70
Port-en-Bessin, Fr.	E8	14
Porter, Tx., U.S.	G3	122
Port Erin, I. of Man	G8	12
Porter Point, c., St. Vin.	o11	105e
Porterville, S. Afr.	H4	70
Porterville, Ca., U.S.	G7	134
Porterville, Ms., U.S.	E10	122
Portete, Bahía, b., Col.	A6	86
Port Fairy, Austl.	L4	76
Port Gamble, Wa., U.S.	C4	136
Port-Gentil, Gabon	E1	66
Port Gibson, Ms., U.S.	F8	122
Port Graham, Ak., U.S.	E9	140
Port-Harcourt, Nig.	I6	64
Port Hardy, B.C., Can.	F3	138
Port Hawkesbury, N.S., Can.	E15	110
Port Hedland, Austl.	D3	74
Port Heiden, Ak., U.S.	E8	140
Port Hill, P.E., Can.	D13	110
Porthmadog, Wales, U.K.	I8	12
Port Hood, N.S., Can.	D15	110
Port Hope, On., Can.	E11	112
Port Hope, Mi., U.S.	E7	112
Port Huron, Mi., U.S.	B3	114
Portimão, Port.	G2	20
Port Isabel, Tx., U.S.	H10	130
Port Jervis, N.Y., U.S.	C11	114
Port Kembla, Austl.	J8	76
Port Lairge see Waterford, Ire.	I5	12
Portland, Austl.	I7	76
Portland, Austl.	L3	76
Portland, Ar., U.S.	D7	122
Portland, In., U.S.	H5	112
Portland, Me., U.S.	G6	110
Portland, N.D., U.S.	G16	124
Portland, Or., U.S.	E4	136
Portland, Tn., U.S.	H11	120
Portland, Tx., U.S.	G10	130
Portland, Bill of, c., Eng., U.K.	K10	12
Portland, Cape, c., Austl.	n13	77a
Portland, Isle of, i., Eng., U.K.	K10	12
Portland Bay, b., Austl.	L3	76
Portland Bight, b., Jam.	j13	104d
Portland Point, c., Jam.	j13	104d
Portlaoise, Ire.	H5	12
Port Lavaca, Tx., U.S.	F11	130
Port Leyden, N.Y., U.S.	E14	112
Port Lincoln, Austl.	F7	74
Port Loko, S.L.	H2	64
Port-Louis, Guad.	h5	105c
Port Louis, Mrts.	h10	69a
Port-Lyautey see Kénitra, Mor.	C3	64
Port MacDonnell, Austl.	L3	76
Port Macquarie, Austl.	H9	76
Port Maria, Jam.	i14	104d
Port McNeill, B.C., Can.	F3	138
Port McNicoll, On., Can.	D10	112
Port Moller, Ak., U.S.	E7	140
Port Morant, Jam.	j14	104d
Portmore, Jam.	j13	104d
Port Moresby, Pap. N. Gui.	b4	79a
Port Morien, N.S., Can.	D17	110
Port Neches, Tx., U.S.	H4	122
Port Nelson, Mb., Can.	D12	106
Portneuf, stm., Qc., Can.	B7	110
Portneuf, stm., Id., U.S.	H14	136
Port Neville, B.C., Can.	F4	138
Port Nolloth, S. Afr.	F3	70
Port Norris, N.J., U.S.	E10	114
Porto, Port.	C2	20
Porto, state, Port.	C2	20
Porto Acre, Braz.	E4	84
Porto Alegre, Braz.	E12	92
Porto Alegre, S. Tom./P.	J6	64
Porto Amboim, Ang.	C1	68
Portobelo, Pan.	H8	102
Porto Calvo, Braz.	E8	88
Porto de Moz, Braz.	D7	84
Porto de Pedras, Braz.	E8	88
Porto dos Gaúchos, Braz.	F6	84
Porto Empedocle, Italy	G7	24
Porto Esperança, Braz.	C5	90
Porto Esperidião, Braz.	G6	84
Porto Feliz, Braz.	L2	88
Portoferraio, Italy	H7	22
Porto Ferreira, Braz.	K2	88
Port of Ness, Scot., U.K.	C6	12
Porto Franco, Braz.	D2	88
Port of Spain, Trin.	s12	105f
Portogruaro, Italy	E9	22
Portola, Ca., U.S.	D5	134
Portomaggiore, Italy	F8	22
Porto Mendes, Braz.	B10	92
Porto Murtinho, Braz.	D5	90
Porto Nacional, Braz.	F1	88
Porto-Novo, Benin	H5	64
Porto Novo, India	F4	53
Port Orange, Fl., U.S.	G5	116
Port Orchard, Wa., U.S.	C4	136
Port Orford, Or., U.S.	H2	136
Porto San Giorgio, Italy	G10	22
Porto Santana, Braz.	D7	84
Porto Santo, i., Port.	C1	64
Porto Santo Stefano, ngh., Italy	H7	22
Porto Seguro, Braz.	I6	88
Porto Tolle, Italy	F9	22
Porto Torres, Italy	D2	24
Porto União, Braz.	C12	92
Porto Válter, Braz.	E3	84
Porto-Vecchio, Fr.	H15	18
Porto Velho, Braz.	E5	84
Portoviejo, Ec.	H1	86
Port Patrick, Vanuatu	m17	79d
Port Perry, On., Can.	D11	112
Port Phillip Bay, b., Austl.	L5	76
Port Pirie, Austl.	F7	74
Portree, Scot., U.K.	D6	12
Port Renfrew, B.C., Can.	H6	138
Port Rowan, On., Can.	F9	112
Port Royal, Jam.	j14	104d
Port Royal, Pa., U.S.	D8	114
Port Royal, S.C., U.S.	D5	116
Port Said see Bûr Sa'îd, Egypt	G3	58
Port Saint Joe, Fl., U.S.	H13	122
Port Saint Johns, S. Afr.	G9	70
Port Saint Lucie, Fl., U.S.	I5	116
Port Sanilac, Mi., U.S.	E7	112
Port Saunders, Nf., Can.	i22	107a
Portsea, Austl.	L5	76
Portsmouth, Dom.	i6	105c
Portsmouth, Eng., U.K.	K11	12
Portsmouth, N.H., U.S.	G6	110
Portsmouth, Oh., U.S.	F2	114
Portsmouth, Va., U.S.	H9	114
Portsoy, Scot., U.K.	D10	12
Port Stanley, On., Can.	F8	112
Port Sudan see Būr Sūdān, Sudan	D7	62
Port Sulphur, La., U.S.	H9	122
Port Talbot, Wales, U.K.	J9	12
Porttipahdan tekojärvi, l., Fin.	B12	8
Port Townsend, Wa., U.S.	B4	136
Portugal, ctry., Eur.	D3	20
Portugalete, Spain	A7	20
Portuguesa, state, Ven.	C7	86
Portuguesa, stm., Ven.	C8	86
Portuguese Guinea see Guinea-Bissau, ctry., Afr.	G1	64
Port Vila, Vanuatu	k17	79d
Portville, N.Y., U.S.	B7	114
Port-Vladimir, Russia	B15	8
Port Wentworth, Ga., U.S.	D4	116
Port Wing, Wi., U.S.	E7	118
Porus, Jam.	i13	104d
Porvenir, Chile	J2	90
Porvoo, Fin.	F11	8
Porzuna, Spain	E6	20
Posadas, Arg.	C9	92
Posadas, Spain	G5	20
Posavina, val., Eur.	E14	22
Pošehon'e, Russia	B22	10
Poseidonos, Naós toy, hist., Grc.	F6	28
Posen, Mi., U.S.	C6	112
Poshan see Boshan, China	C7	42
Posio, Fin.	C12	8
Poso, Indon.	D12	50
Poso, Danau, l., Indon.	D12	50
Poso, Teluk, b., Indon.	D12	50
Pospeliha, Russia	D14	32
Posse, Braz.	H2	88
Possession Island, i., Nmb.	E2	70
Pössneck, Ger.	F7	16
Possum Kingdom Lake, res., Tx., U.S.	B9	130
Post, Tx., U.S.	A6	130
Posta de Jihuites, Mex.	I2	130
Postelle, Tn., U.S.	A1	116
Postmasburg, S. Afr.	F6	70
Postojna, Slvn.	E11	22
Postrervalle, Bol.	C4	90
Postville, Ia., U.S.	A6	120
Potaro, stm., Guy.	E12	86
Potaro-Siparuni, state, Guy.	E12	86
Potchefstroom, S. Afr.	E8	70
Poté, Braz.	I5	88
Poteau, Ok., U.S.	B4	122
Poteet, Tx., U.S.	E9	130
Potenza, Italy	D9	24
Potgietersrus, S. Afr.	D9	70
Poth, Tx., U.S.	E9	130
Potholes Reservoir, res., Wa., U.S.	D7	136
Poti, Geor.	F6	32
Poti, stm., Braz.	C4	88
Potiraguá, Braz.	H6	88
Potiskum, Nig.	G7	64
Potomac, Il., U.S.	H2	112
Potomac, stm., U.S.	F9	114
Potomac, North Fork South Branch, stm., U.S.	F6	114
Potomac, South Branch, stm., U.S.	E7	114
Potomac Heights, Md., U.S.	F8	114
Potosí, Bol.	C3	90
Potosi, Mo., U.S.	G7	120
Potrerillos, Chile	C3	92
Potro, Cerro del (El Potro, Cerro), mtn., S.A.	D3	92
Potsdam, Ger.	D9	16

Name	Map Ref.	Page
Potsdam, N.Y., U.S.	F2	110
Pott, Île, i., N. Cal.	I14	79d
Potter, Ne., U.S.	F9	126
Potterville, Mi., U.S.	B1	114
Potts Camp, Ms., U.S.	C9	122
Pottstown, Pa., U.S.	D10	114
Pottsville, Pa., U.S.	D9	114
Pouancé, Fr.	G7	14
Poughkeepsie, N.Y., U.S.	C11	114
Poulan, Ga., U.S.	E2	116
Poulsbo, Wa., U.S.	C4	136
Poultney, Vt., U.S.	G3	110
Poum, N. Cal.	m14	79d
Pouso Alegre, Braz.	L3	88
Poŭthĭsăt, Camb.	F6	48
Poŭthĭsăt, stm., Camb.	F6	48
Poutini see Westland National Park, p.o.i., N.Z.	F3	80
Poutrincourt, Lac, l., Qc., Can.	A2	110
Považská Bystrica, Slov.	G14	16
Povenec, Russia	E16	8
Póvoa de Varzim, Port.	C2	20
Povorino, Russia	D6	32
Povorotnyj, mys, c., Russia	C10	38
Povungnituk, Qc., Can.	C15	106
Povungnituk, stm., Qc., Can.	C15	106
Powassan, On., Can.	B10	112
Poway, Ca., U.S.	K9	134
Powder, stm., U.S.	A7	126
Powder, stm., Or., U.S.	F9	136
Powder, South Fork, stm., Wy., U.S.	D6	126
Powderly, Tx., U.S.	D3	122
Powder River Pass, p., Wy., U.S.	C5	126
Powell, Wy., U.S.	C4	126
Powell, stm., U.S.	H2	114
Powell, Lake, res., U.S.	F5	132
Powell Creek, stm., Austl.	E5	76
Powellhurst, Or., U.S.	E4	136
Powell Lake, l., B.C., Can.	F6	138
Powell River, B.C., Can.	G6	138
Powers, Mi., U.S.	C2	112
Powers, Or., U.S.	H2	136
Powers Lake, N.D., U.S.	F11	124
Powhatan, Va., U.S.	G7	114
Powhatan Point, Oh., U.S.	E4	114
Poxoréu, Braz.	G7	84
Poya, N. Cal.	m15	79d
Poyang Hu, l., China	G7	42
Poyen, Ar., U.S.	C6	122
Poygan, Lake, l., Wi., U.S.	G9	118
Požarevac, Yugo.	E8	26
Poza Rica de Hidalgo, Mex.	E10	100
Požega, Cro.	E14	22
Požega, Yugo.	F7	26
Poznań, Pol.	D12	16
Poznań, state, Pol.	D12	16
Pozoblanco, Spain	F6	20
Pozo-Cañada, Spain	F9	20
Pozo del Molle, Arg.	F6	92
Pozo del Tigre, Arg.	B7	92
Pozuelos, Ven.	B9	86
Pozzallo, Italy	H8	24
Pozzuoli, Italy	D8	24
Prachatice, Czech Rep.	G10	16
Prachin Buri, Thai.	E5	48
Prachuap Khiri Khan, Thai.	G4	48
Pradera, Col.	F3	86
Prado, Braz.	I6	88
Prados, Braz.	K3	88
Præstø, Den.	A8	16
Prague see Praha, Czech Rep.	F10	16
Prague, Ne., U.S.	F16	126
Prague, Ok., U.S.	B2	122
Praha (Prague), Czech Rep.	F10	16
Praha, state, Czech Rep.	F10	16
Praha, mtn., Czech Rep.	G9	16
Prahova, state, Rom.	D13	26
Prahova, stm., Rom.	E13	26
Praia, C.V.	I10	65a
Praia Grande, Braz.	D13	92
Prainha Nova, Braz.	E5	84
Prairie, Austl.	C5	76
Prairie, stm., Mi., U.S.	G4	112
Prairie City, Il., U.S.	D7	120
Prairie City, Ia., U.S.	C4	120
Prairie Creek, stm., Ne., U.S.	F15	126
Prairie Dog Creek, stm., Ks., U.S.	B8	128
Prairie du Chien, Wi., U.S.	A6	120
Prairie du Sac, Wi., U.S.	H9	118
Prairie River, Sk., Can.	B11	124
Prairies, Coteau des, hills, U.S.	C16	126
Prairies, Lake of the, res., Can.	C12	124
Prairie View, Tx., U.S.	G3	122
Prairie Village, Ks., U.S.	B14	128
Pran Buri, Thai.	F4	48
Pran Buri, stm., Thai.	F4	48
Prānhita, stm., India	B5	53
Praslin, i., Sey.	j13	69b
Prasonísi, Ákra, c., Grc.	H10	28
Praszka, Pol.	E14	16
Prata, Braz.	J1	88
Prata, stm., Braz.	J1	88
Prata, stm., Braz.	I2	88
Pratāpgarh, India	F5	54
Pratápolis, Braz.	K2	88
Pratas Island see Tungsha Tao, i., Tai.	K7	42
Prat de Llobregat see El Prat de Llobregat, Spain	C12	20
Prato, Italy	G8	22
Pratt, Ks., U.S.	D10	128
Prattville, Al., U.S.	E12	122
Pratudão, stm., Braz.	H3	88
Pravdinskij, Russia	D20	10
Pravia, Spain	A4	20
Praya, Indon.	H10	50
Preajba, Rom.	E12	26
Prečistoe, Russia	G19	8
Predeal, Rom.	D12	26
Preeceville, Sk., Can.	C11	124
Preetz, Ger.	B6	16
Pregolja, stm., Russia	F3	10
Pregonero, Ven.	D6	86
Preguiças, stm., Braz.	B4	88
Preila, Lith.	E4	10
Prěk Poŭthĭ, Camb.	G7	48
Prelate, Sk., Can.	D4	124
Premnitz, Ger.	D8	16
Premont, Tx., U.S.	G9	130
Premuda, Otok, i., Cro.	F11	22
Prenjasi see Prrenjas, Alb.	C14	24
Prentiss, Ms., U.S.	F9	122
Prenzlau, Ger.	C9	16
Preobraženie, Russia	C10	38
Preparis Island, i., Mya.	F7	46
Preparis North Channel, strt., Mya.	E7	46
Preparis South Channel, strt., Mya.	F7	46
Přerov, Czech Rep.	G13	16
Prescott, On., Can.	D14	112
Prescott, Az., U.S.	I4	132
Prescott, Ar., U.S.	D5	122
Prescott, Wi., U.S.	G6	118
Prescott Island, i., Nu., Can.	A11	106
Presidencia de la Plaza, Arg.	C7	92
Presidencia Roca, Arg.	C8	92
Presidencia Roque Sáenz Peña, Arg.	C7	92
Presidente Dutra, Braz.	C3	88
Presidente Epitácio, Braz.	D6	90
Presidente Hayes, state, Para.	B8	92
Presidente Prudente, Braz.	D6	90
Presidio, Tx., U.S.	E3	130
Presidio, stm., Mex.	D6	100
Presnogor'kovka, Kaz.	D11	32
Prešov, Slov.	H17	16
Prespa, Lake, l., Eur.	D14	24
Presque Isle, Me., U.S.	D8	110
Presque Isle, pen., Pa., U.S.	B5	114
Prestea, Ghana	H4	64
Preston, Eng., U.K.	H10	12
Preston, Id., U.S.	A5	132
Preston, Ia., U.S.	B7	120
Preston, Ks., U.S.	D10	128
Preston, Mn., U.S.	H6	118
Prestonsburg, Ky., U.S.	G3	114
Prestwick, Scot., U.K.	F8	12
Preto, stm., Braz.	I9	86
Preto, stm., Braz.	I2	88
Preto, stm., Braz.	F3	88
Preto, stm., Braz.	B4	88
Preto, stm., Braz.	G1	88
Preto, stm., Braz.	K1	88
Preto, stm., Braz.	L4	88
Preto do Igapó-açu, stm., Braz.	E5	84
Pretoria, S. Afr.	D9	70
Pretty Prairie, Ks., U.S.	D10	128
Préveza, Grc.	E3	28
Prey Lvéa, Camb.	G7	48
Prey Vêng, Camb.	G7	48
Pribilof Islands, is., Ak., U.S.	E5	140
Priboj, Yugo.	F6	26
Příbram, Czech Rep.	G10	16
Price, Ut., U.S.	D6	132
Price, stm., Ut., U.S.	D6	132
Price Island, i., B.C., Can.	D2	138
Prichard, Al., U.S.	G10	122
Prickly Pear Cays, is., Anguilla	A1	105a
Priddy, Tx., U.S.	C9	130
Priego de Córdoba, Spain	G6	20
Priekule, Lat.	D4	10
Priekule, Lith.	E4	10
Prieska, S. Afr.	F6	70
Priest, stm., Id., U.S.	B10	136
Priest Lake, res., Id., U.S.	B9	136
Priest River, Id., U.S.	B10	136
Prieta, Peña, mtn., Spain	A6	20
Prieto Diaz, Phil.	D5	52
Prievidza, Slov.	H14	16
Prijedor, Bos.	E3	26
Prilep, Mac.	B4	28
Priluki, Russia	A22	10
Primeira Cruz, Braz.	B4	88
Primera, Tx., U.S.	H10	130
Primero, stm., Arg.	E6	92
Primghar, Ia., U.S.	A2	120
Primorsk, Russia	F13	8
Primorskij, Russia	C9	38
Primorskij hrebet, mts., Russia	F10	34
Primo Tapia, Mex.	K8	134
Primrose Lake, l., Can.	E9	106
Prince Albert, Sk., Can.	A8	124
Prince Albert, S. Afr.	H6	70
Prince Albert Sound, strt., N.T., Can.	A7	106
Prince Alfred, Cape, c., N.T., Can.	B15	140
Prince Charles Island, i., Nu., Can.	B15	106
Prince Charles Mountains, mts., Ant.	C11	81
Prince Edward Island, state, Can.	D13	110
Prince Edward Island, i., P.E., Can.	F18	106
Prince Edward Island National Park, p.o.i., P.E., Can.	D13	110
Prince Frederick, Md., U.S.	F9	114
Prince George, B.C., Can.	C8	138
Prince George, Va., U.S.	G8	114
Prince Gustaf Adolf Sea, Can.	B4	141
Prince of Wales Island, i., Austl.	B8	74
Prince of Wales Island, i., Nu., Can.	A11	106
Prince of Wales Island, i., Ak., U.S.	E13	140
Prince of Wales Strait, strt., N.T., Can.	B15	140
Prince Olav Coast, cst., Ant.	B9	81
Prince Patrick Island, i., N.T., Can.	A16	140
Prince Regent Inlet, b., Nu., Can.	A12	106
Prince Rupert, B.C., Can.	E4	106
Prince Rupert Bluff Point, c., Dom.	i5	105c
Princes Islands see Kızıl Adalar, is., Tur.	C11	28
Princess Anne, Md., U.S.	F10	114
Princess Astrid Coast, cst., Ant.	C6	81
Princess Charlotte Bay, b., Austl.	B8	74
Princess Martha Coast, cst., Ant.	C4	81
Princess Ragnhild Coast, cst., Ant.	C7	81
Princess Royal Island, i., B.C., Can.	C1	138
Princes Town, Trin.	s12	105f
Princeton, B.C., Can.	G10	138
Princeton, Ca., U.S.	D3	134
Princeton, In., U.S.	F10	120
Princeton, Ky., U.S.	G9	120
Princeton, Me., U.S.	E9	110
Princeton, Mi., U.S.	B2	112
Princeton, N.J., U.S.	D11	114
Princeton, N.C., U.S.	A7	116
Princeton, W.V., U.S.	G4	114
Princeton, Wi., U.S.	H9	118
Princeville, Qc., Can.	D4	110
Princeville, Il., U.S.	D8	120
Prince William Sound, strt., Ak., U.S.	D10	140
Príncipe, i., S. Tom./P.	I6	64
Príncipe da Beira, Braz.	F5	84
Prineville, Or., U.S.	F6	136
Pringsewu, Indon.	F4	50
Prinses Margrietkanaal, can., Neth.	A14	14
Prins Karls Forland, i., Nor.	B27	141
Prinzapolka, stm., Nic.	F5	102
Priozërnyj, Kaz.	E14	32
Priozersk, Russia	F14	8
Pripet (Prypjac'), stm., Eur.	H10	10
Pripet Marshes, reg., Eur.	H12	10
Pripoljarnyj Ural, mts., Russia	A9	32
Priština, Yugo.	G8	26
Pritchett, Co., U.S.	D6	128
Pritzwalk, Ger.	C8	16
Privas, Fr.	E10	18
Priverno, Italy	C7	24
Privodino, Russia	F22	8
Prizren, Yugo.	G7	26
Prjaža, Russia	F15	8
Probolinggo, Indon.	G8	50
Probstzella, Ger.	F7	16
Procida, Isola di, i., Italy	D7	24
Procter, B.C., Can.	G13	138
Proctor, Mn., U.S.	E6	118
Proctor Lake, res., Tx., U.S.	C9	130
Proddatūr, India	D4	53
Proença-a-Nova, Port.	E2	20
Progreso, Mex.	B8	100
Progreso, Mex.	B3	102
Progreso, Mex.	K10	134
Progreso, Ur.	G9	92
Prohladnyj, Russia	F6	32
Project City, Ca., U.S.	C3	134
Prokopevsk, Russia	D15	32
Prokuplje, Yugo.	F8	26
Prokuševo, Russia	G16	8
Proletarskij, Russia	E20	10
Prome (Pyè), Mya.	C2	48
Pronja, stm., Bela.	G14	10
Pronja, stm., Russia	F21	10
Prony, Baie de, b., N. Cal.	n16	79d
Prophet, stm., B.C., Can.	D6	106
Prophetstown, Il., U.S.	C8	120
Propriá, Braz.	F7	88
Propriano, Fr.	H14	18
Proserpine, Austl.	C7	76
Prosna, stm., Pol.	E14	16
Prospect, Oh., U.S.	D2	114
Prosperidad, Phil.	F5	52
Prosser, Wa., U.S.	D7	136
Prostějov, Czech Rep.	G12	16
Prostki, Pol.	C18	16
Proston, Austl.	F8	76
Proszowice, Pol.	F16	16
Protection, Ks., U.S.	D9	128
Protem, S. Afr.	I5	70
Protva, stm., Russia	F20	10
Provadija, Blg.	F14	26
Prøven (Kangersuatsiaq), Grnld.	C14	141
Provence, hist. reg., Fr.	F12	18
Providence, Ky., U.S.	G10	120
Providence, R.I., U.S.	C14	114
Providence, Ut., U.S.	B5	132
Providence, Atoll de, i., Sey.	k12	69b
Providence, Cape, c., N.Z.	H2	80
Providencia, Mex.	G4	130
Providencia, Isla de, i., Col.	F7	102
Providenciales, i., T./C. Is.	B11	102
Providenija, Russia	D26	34
Provincetown, Ma., U.S.	B15	114
Provins, Fr.	F12	14
Provo, Ut., U.S.	C5	132
Provo, stm., Ut., U.S.	C5	132
Provost, Ab., Can.	B3	124
Prrenjas, Alb.	C14	24
Prudentópolis, Braz.	B12	92
Prudhoe Bay, Ak., U.S.	B10	140
Prudhoe Island, i., Austl.	C7	76
Prudnik, Pol.	F13	16
Pruszków, Pol.	D16	16
Prut, stm., Eur.	D15	26
Pružany, Bela.	H7	10
Prydz Bay, b., Ant.	B12	81
Pryluky, Ukr.	D4	32
Pryor, Ok., U.S.	H2	120
Przasnysz, Pol.	D16	16
Przedbórz, Pol.	E15	16
Przemyśl, Pol.	G18	16
Przemyśl, state, Pol.	F18	16
Przeworsk, Pol.	F18	16
Psachná, Grc.	E6	28
Pskov, Russia	C11	10
Pskov, Lake, l., Eur.	B11	10
Pskovskaja oblast', co., Russia	C11	10
Pszczyna, Pol.	G14	16
Ptarmigan, Cape, c., N.T., Can.	A7	106
Ptolemaís, Grc.	C4	28
Ptuj, Slvn.	D12	22
Puakatike, Volcán, vol., Chile	e30	78l
Puán, Arg.	H6	92
Pucallpa, Peru	E3	84
Pucará, Bol.	C4	90
Pučeveem, stm., Russia	C23	34
Pučež, Russia	H20	8
Pucheng, China	H8	42
Pucheng, China	D3	42
Púchov, Slov.	G14	16
Pučišća, Cro.	G13	22
Pudasjärvi, Fin.	D12	8
Pudož, Russia	F17	8
Puduari, stm., Braz.	I11	86
Puduchcheri see Pondicherry, India	F4	53
Pudukkottai, India	F4	53
Puebla, state, Mex.	F10	100
Puebla de Don Fadrique, Spain	G8	20
Puebla de Sanabria, Spain	B4	20
Puebla de Zaragoza, Mex.	F9	100
Pueblito, Mex.	E2	130
Pueblito de Ponce, P.R.	B1	104a
Pueblo, Co., U.S.	C4	128
Pueblonuevo, Col.	C4	86
Pueblo Nuevo, P.R.	B2	104a
Pueblo Nuevo, Ven.	B7	86
Pueblo Viejo, Laguna, l., Mex.	D10	100
Pueblo Yaqui, Mex.	B4	100
Puente-Caldelas see Ponte-Caldelas, Spain	B2	20
Puente del Arzobispo, Spain	E5	20
Puentedeume see Pontedeume, Spain	A2	20
Puente Genil, Spain	G6	20
Puerca, Punta, c., P.R.	B4	104a
Puerco, stm., U.S.	I7	132
Puerco, stm., N.M., U.S.	I10	132
Puerto Acosta, Bol.	C3	90
Puerto Adela, Para.	B10	92
Puerto Aisén, Chile	I2	90
Puerto Alegre, Bol.	B4	90
Puerto Ángel, Mex.	H10	100
Puerto Arista, Mex.	H11	100
Puerto Armuelles, Pan.	H6	102
Puerto Asís, Col.	G3	86
Puerto Ayacucho, Ven.	E8	86
Puerto Baquerizo Moreno, Ec.	i12	84a
Puerto Barrios, Guat.	E3	102
Puerto Bermúdez, Peru	F3	84
Puerto Berrío, Col.	D4	86
Puerto Bolívar, Col.	A5	86
Puerto Boyacá, Col.	E4	86
Puerto Cabello, Ven.	B7	86
Puerto Cabezas, Nic.	F6	102
Puerto Carreño, Col.	D8	86
Puerto Chicama, Peru	E2	84
Puerto Colombia, Col.	B4	86
Puerto Cortés, Hond.	E3	102
Puerto Cumarebo, Ven.	B7	86
Puerto Deseado, Arg.	I3	90
Puerto Escondido, Mex.	H10	100
Puerto Escondido, c., Ven.	p20	104g
Puerto Esperanza, Arg.	B10	92
Puerto Fonciere, Para.	D5	90
Puerto Francisco de Orellana, Ec.	H3	86
Puerto Heath, Bol.	B3	90
Puerto Iguazú, Arg.	B10	92
Puerto Ingeniero Ibáñez, Chile	I2	90
Puerto Inírida, Col.	F7	86
Puerto Juárez, Mex.	B4	102
Puerto la Cruz, Ven.	B9	86
Puerto Leguízamo, Col.	H4	86
Puerto Libertad, Mex.	G6	98
Puerto Limón, Col.	F5	86
Puerto Limón, C.R.	G6	102
Puertollano, Spain	F6	20
Puerto Lobos, Arg.	H4	90
Puerto López, Col.	E5	86
Puerto Madero, Mex.	H12	100
Puerto Madryn, Arg.	H3	90
Puerto Maldonado, Peru	F4	84
Puerto Montt, Chile	H2	90
Puerto Morelos, Mex.	B4	102
Puerto Natales, Chile	J2	90
Puerto Padre, Cuba	B9	102
Puerto Páez, Ven.	D8	86
Puerto Palmer, Pico, mtn., Mex.	G6	130
Puerto Peñasco, Mex.	F6	98
Puerto Pinasco, Para.	D5	90
Puerto Pirámides, Arg.	H4	90
Puerto Piray, Arg.	C10	92
Puerto Píritu, Ven.	B9	86
Puerto Plata, Dom. Rep.	C12	102
Puerto Princesa, Phil.	F2	52
Puerto Real, P.R.	B1	104a
Puerto Real, Spain	H4	20
Puerto Rico, Arg.	C10	92
Puerto Rico, Bol.	B3	90
Puerto Rico, Col.	G4	86
Puerto Rico, dep., N.A.	b3	104a
Puerto Rico Trench, unds.	G7	144
Puerto Rondón, Col.	D6	86
Puerto San José, Guat.	F2	102
Puerto San Julián, Arg.	I3	90
Puerto Santa Cruz, Arg.	J3	90
Puerto Sastre, Para.	D5	90
Puerto Suárez, Bol.	C5	90
Puerto Tejada, Col.	F3	86
Puerto Tolosa, Col.	H4	86
Puerto Umbría, Col.	G3	86
Puerto Vallarta, Mex.	E6	100
Puerto Varas, Chile	H2	90
Puerto Victoria, Arg.	C10	92
Puerto Viejo, C.R.	G5	102
Puerto Villamil, Ec.	i11	84a
Puerto Villamizar, Col.	C5	86
Puerto Wilches, Col.	D5	86
Puerto Ybapobó, Para.	D5	90
Pueyrredón, Lago (Cochrane, Lago), l., S.A.	I2	90
Pugačov, Russia	D7	32
Puget Sound, strt., Wa., U.S.	C4	136
Puglia, state, Italy	C10	24
Pugŏ-ri, Kor., N.	D9	38
Puhi-waero see South West Cape, c., N.Z.	H2	80
Puhja, Est.	B9	10
Puiești, Rom.	C14	26
Puigcerdá, Spain	B12	20
Puigmal d' Err (Puigmal), mtn., Eur.	G8	18
Pujiang, China	G8	42
Pujilí, Ec.	H2	86
Puka see Pukë, Alb.	B13	24
Pukaki, Lake, l., N.Z.	F3	80
Pukch'ŏng-ŭp, Kor., N.	D8	38
Pukë, Alb.	B13	24
Pukekohe, N.Z.	C6	80
Pukhrāyān, India	E7	54
Pukou, China	H8	42
Puksoozero, Russia	E19	8
Pula, Cro.	F10	22
Pula, Italy	F3	24
Pulacayo, Bol.	D3	90
Pulantien see Xinjin, China	B9	42
Pulap, at., Micron.	C5	72
Púlar, Cerro, vol., Chile	B3	92
Pulaski, N.Y., U.S.	E13	112
Pulaski, Tn., U.S.	B11	122
Pulaski, Va., U.S.	G5	114
Pulau, stm., Indon.	G10	44
Pulaukida, Indon.	E3	50
Pulau Pinang, state, Malay.	J5	48
Puławy, Pol.	E18	16
Pulgaon, India	H7	54
Puli, Tai.	J9	42
Pulicat, India	E5	53
Pulicat Lake, l., India	E4	53
Puliyangudi, India	G3	53
Pullman, Wa., U.S.	D9	136
Pulog, Mount, mtn., Phil.	B3	52
Pulon'ga, Russia	C18	8
Pułtusk, Pol.	D16	16
Puma Yumco, l., China	D13	54
Pumei, China	A7	48
Pumpkin Buttes, mtn., Wy., U.S.	D7	126
Pumpkin Creek, stm., Mt., U.S.	B7	126
Pumpkin Creek, stm., Ne., U.S.	F10	126
Puná, Isla, i., Ec.	I1	86
Punaauia, Fr. Poly.	v21	78h
Punakha, Bhu.	E12	54
Punan, Indon.	B10	50
Punata, Bol.	C3	90
Pūnch, India	B5	54
Punchaw, B.C., Can.	C7	138
Pune (Poona), India	B1	53
Punganūru, India	E4	53
P'ungsan-ŭp, Kor., N.	D7	38
Pungué, stm., Afr.	A12	70
Punia, D.R.C.	E5	66
Punilla, Sierra de la, mts., Arg.	D3	92
Punitaqui, Chile	E2	92
Punjab, state, India	C5	54
Punjab, state, Pak.	C4	54
Punnichy, Sk., Can.	C9	124
Puno, Peru	G3	84
Punta, Cerro de, mtn., P.R.	B2	104a
Punta Alta, Arg.	I6	92
Punta Arenas, Chile	J2	90
Punta Banda, Cabo, c., Mex.	L9	134
Punta Cardón, Ven.	B6	86
Punta Colnett, Mex.	F4	98
Punta de Agua Creek (Tramperos Creek), stm., U.S.	E5	128
Punta de Díaz, Chile	C2	92
Punta del Cobre, Chile	C2	92
Punta del Este, Ur.	G10	92
Punta Delgada, Arg.	H4	90
Punta de los Llanos, Arg.	E4	92
Punta de Piedras, Ven.	B9	86
Punta Gorda, Nic.	G6	102
Punta Gorda, Fl., U.S.	J3	116
Punta Gorda, Bahía de, b., Nic.	G6	102
Punta Negra, Salar de, pl., Chile	B3	92
Punta Prieta, Mex.	A1	100
Puntarenas, C.R.	G5	102
Punta Santiago, P.R.	B4	104a
Punto Fijo, Ven.	B6	86
Punung, Indon.	H7	50
Puper, Indon.	F9	44
Puppy's Point, c., Norf. I.	y24	78i
Puqi, China	G5	42
Puqian, China	L4	42
Puquio, Peru	F3	84
Pur, stm., Russia	A13	32
Puracé, Volcán, vol., Col.	F3	86
Pūranpur, India	D7	54
Purcell, Ok., U.S.	F11	128
Purcell Mountains, mts., N.A.	F14	138
Purcellville, Va., U.S.	E8	114
Purdy, Mo., U.S.	H3	120
Puré (Puruí), stm., S.A.	I6	86
Purgatoire, stm., Co., U.S.	D5	128
Puri, India	I10	54
Purificación, Col.	F4	86
Purificación, stm., Mex.	C9	100
Purísima, Mex.	E7	130
Purmerend, Neth.	B13	14
Pūrna, stm., India	H5	54
Pūrna, stm., India	H6	54
Pūrnia, India	F11	54
Puronga, Russia	F19	8
Puruí (Puré), stm., S.A.	I6	86
Puruliya, India	G11	54
Puruni, stm., Guy.	D12	86
Purús, stm., S.A.	E4	84
Puruvesi, l., Fin.	F13	8
Purvis, Ms., U.S.	F9	122
Purwakarta, Indon.	G5	50
Purwodadi, Indon.	G6	50
Purwodadi, Indon.	G7	50
Purwokerto, Indon.	G6	50
Purworejo, Indon.	G6	50
Pusa, Malay.	C7	50
Pusad, India	B3	53
Pusan (Fusan), Kor., S.	D2	40
Pusan-jikhalsi, state, Kor., S.	D2	40
Pusat Gayo, Pegunungan, mts., Indon.	J3	48
Pushkar, India	E5	54
Puškin, Russia	A13	10
Puškino, Russia	D20	10
Püspökladány, Hung.	B8	26
Püssi, Est.	A10	10
Pustozersk, Russia	C25	8
Putaendo, Chile	F2	92
Putao, Mya.	C8	46
Putian, China	G6	42
Putian, China	I8	42
Putignano, Italy	D10	24
Puting, Tanjung, c., Indon.	E7	50
Putla de Guerrero, Mex.	D5	96
Putnam, Ct., U.S.	C14	114
Putney, Ga., U.S.	E1	116
Putney, Vt., U.S.	B13	114
Putorana, plato, plat., Russia	C7	34
Puttalam, Sri L.	G4	53
Puttalam Lagoon, b., Sri L.	G4	53
Puttūr, India	E4	53
Putú, Chile	G1	92
Putumayo, state, Col.	G4	86
Putumayo (Içá), stm., S.A.	D3	84
Putuo, China	F10	42
Putussibau, Indon.	C8	50
Putyla, Ukr.	B12	26
Puula, l., Fin.	F12	8
Puurmani, Est.	B9	10
Puyallup, Wa., U.S.	C4	136
Puyang, China	D6	42
Puy-de-Dôme, state, Fr.	D9	18
Puymorens, Col de, p., Fr.	G7	18
Puyo, Ec.	H3	86
Pweto, D.R.C.	F5	66
Pwinbyu, Mya.	B2	48
Pyalo, Mya.	C2	48
Pyapon, Mya.	D2	48
Pyawbwe, Mya.	B3	48
Pyhäjärvi, l., Fin.	E11	8
Pyhäjärvi, l., Fin.	F9	8
Pyhäjoki, Fin.	D10	8
Pyhäjoki, stm., Fin.	D11	8
Pyhäselkä, l., Fin.	E13	8
Pyhätunturi, mtn., Fin.	C12	8
Pyinbongyi, Mya.	D3	48
Pyinmana, Mya.	C3	48
Pyin Oo Lwin see Maymyo, Mya.	A3	48
Pýlos, Grc.	G4	28
Pymatuning Reservoir, res., U.S.	C5	114
Pyŏktong-ŭp, Kor., N.	D6	38
P'yŏngch'ang, Kor., S.	B1	40
P'yonghae, Kor., S.	C2	40
P'yŏngt'aek, Kor., S.	F7	38
P'yŏngyang, Kor., N.	E6	38
Pyote, Tx., U.S.	C4	130
Pyramid Lake, l., Nv., U.S.	D6	134
Pyramid Peak, mtn., Wy., U.S.	G16	136
Pyrenees, mts., Eur.	G6	18
Pyrénées-Atlantiques, state, Fr.	F5	18
Pyrénées Occident, Parc National des, p.o.i., Fr.	G5	18
Pyrénées-Orientales, state, Fr.	G8	18
Pýrgos, Grc.	F4	28
Pytalovo, Russia	C10	10
Pyu, Mya.	C3	48
Pyūṭhān, Nepal	D9	54

Q

Name	Map Ref.	Page
Qaanaaq see Thule, Grnld.	B12	141
Qabbāsīn, Syria	B8	58
Qacentina (Constantine), Alg.	B6	64
Qā'en, Iran	C8	56
Qagan Moron, stm., China	C3	38
Qagan Nur, l., China	C7	36
Qahar Youyi Zhongqi, China	A5	42
Qaidam, stm., China	D4	36
Qaidam Pendi, bas., China	D3	36
Qalāt, Afg.	C10	56
Qal'at ash-Shaqīf (Beaufort Castle), hist., Leb.	E6	58
Qal'at Bīshah, Sau. Ar.	E5	56
Qal'at Ṣāliḥ, Iraq	C6	56
Qal'eh-ye Now, Afg.	C9	56
Qallābāt, Sudan	E7	62
Qalyûb, Egypt	H2	58
Qamani'tuaq (Baker Lake), Nu., Can.	C11	106
Qamar, Ghubbat al-, b., Yemen	F7	56
Qamdo, China	E4	36
Qamea, i., Fiji	p20	79e
Qamīnis, Libya	A3	62
Qānā, Leb.	E6	58
Qandahār, Afg.	C10	56
Qandala, Som.	B9	66
Qaqortoq see Julianehåb, Grnld.	E16	141
Qārah, Syria	D7	58
Qarazhal see Karažal, Kaz.	E12	32
Qardho, Som.	C9	66
Qarqan, stm., China	G15	32
Qârûn, Birket (Moeris, Lake), l., Egypt	I1	58
Qarwāw, Ra's, c., Oman	F8	56
Qasigiannguit see Christanshåb, Grnld.	D15	141
Qaṣr al-Azraq, hist., Jord.	G7	58
Qaṣr al-Kharānah, hist., Jord.	G7	58
Qaṣr al-Mushattá, hist., Jord.	G7	58
Qaṣr aṭ-Ṭūbah, hist., Jord.	G7	58
Qaṣr Ḍab'ah, hist., Jord.	G7	58
Qaṣr-e Shīrīn, Iran	C6	56
Qasr Farâfra, Egypt	B5	62
Qaṭanā, Syria	E6	58
Qatar, ctry., Asia	D7	56
Qatrani, Gebel, hill, Egypt	I1	58
Qattâra, Munkhafad el- (Qattara Depression), depr., Egypt	B5	62
Qattara Depression see Qattâra, Munkhafad el-, depr., Egypt	B5	62
Qaṭṭīnah, Buḥayrat, res., Syria	D7	58
Qausuittuq (Resolute), Nu., Can.	C7	141
Qāzigund, India	B5	54
Qazımämmäd, Azer.	B6	56
Qazvīn, Iran	B6	56
Qena, Egypt	B6	62
Qena, Wadi (Qinā, Wādī), stm., Egypt	K3	58
Qeqertarsuaq see Godhavn, Grnld.	D15	141
Qesari, Horbat (Caesarea), hist., Isr.	F5	58
Qeshm, Jazīreh-ye, i., Iran	D8	56
Qetura, Isr.	I5	58
Qezel Owzan, stm., Iran	B6	56
Qian, stm., China	J3	42
Qian'an, China	B6	38
Qian Gorlos, China	B6	38
Qianning, China	E5	36
Qianshan, China	F7	42
Qianwei, China	F5	36
Qianxi, China	H1	42
Qianyang, China	H3	42
Qiaolima, China	A8	54
Qiaowan, China	C4	36
Qidong, China	H5	42
Qiemo, China	G15	32
Qigong, China	F5	36
Qijiang, China	G2	42
Qila Saifullāh, Pak.	C2	54
Qilian Shan, mtn., China	D4	36
Qilian Shan, mts., China	D4	36
Qimen, China	G7	42
Qin, stm., China	D5	42
Qing, stm., China	F4	42
Qingcheng, China	C7	42
Qingchengzi, China	D5	38
Qingdao (Tsingtao), China	C9	42
Qingfeng, China	D6	42
Qinggang, China	B10	36
Qinghai, state, China	D4	36
Qinghai Hu, l., China	D5	36
Qingjiang, China	G6	42
Qingjiang, China	E8	42
Qinglong, China	F6	36
Qinglonggang, China	F9	42
Qingshen, China	F5	36
Qingshui, China	D4	36
Qingshui, China	D2	42
Qingshui, stm., China	H3	42
Qingshui, stm., China	C2	42
Qingtang, China	I5	42
Qingyang, China	B8	38
Qingyang, China	F7	42
Qingyang, China	C2	42
Qingyuan, China	C6	38
Qingyuan, China	J5	42
Qingyuan, China	H8	42
Qingyuan, China	I3	42
Qing Zang Gaoyuan (Tibet, Plateau of), plat., China	B6	46
Qingzhen, China	H2	42
Qinhuangdao, China	B8	42
Qin Ling, mts., China	E3	42
Qinshihuang Mausoleum (Terra Cotta Army), hist., China	D3	42
Qinshui, China	D5	42
Qinxian, China	C5	42
Qinyang, China	D5	42
Qinyuan, China	C5	42
Qinzhou, China	J3	42
Qionghai, China	L4	42
Qionglai, China	E5	36
Qionglaishan, mts., China	E5	36
Qiongzhong, China	L3	42
Qiongzhou Haixia, strt., China	K4	42
Qiqian, China	F13	34
Qiqihar, China	B9	36
Qira, China	A5	46
Qiryat Ata, Isr.	F6	58
Qiryat Gat, Isr.	G5	58
Qiryat Shemona, Isr.	E6	58
Qishn, Yemen	F7	56
Qitai, China	C2	36
Qitaihe, China	B11	36
Qitamu, China	B7	38
Qixia, China	C9	42
Qixian, China	D6	42
Qiyang, China	H4	42
Qizhou, China	F6	42
Qizil Jilga, China	A7	54
Qom, Iran	C7	56
Qomsheh, Iran	C7	56
Qonggyai, China	D13	54
Qôrnoq, Grnld.	E15	141
Qostanay see Kustanaj, Kaz.	D10	32
Qowowuyag (Chopu), mtn., Asia	D11	54
Qu, stm., China	F2	42
Qu, stm., China	G8	42
Quabbin Reservoir, res., Ma., U.S.	B13	114
Quadra Island, i., B.C., Can.	F5	138
Quadros, Lagoa dos, l., Braz.	D12	92
Quakenbrück, Ger.	D3	16
Qualicum Beach, B.C., Can.	G6	138
Quambatook, Austl.	J4	76
Quang Ngai, Viet.	E9	48
Quang Trach, Viet.	D8	48
Quantico, Va., U.S.	F8	114
Quanyang, China	C7	38
Quanzhou, China	I8	42
Qu'Appelle, Sk., Can.	D10	124
Qu'Appelle, stm., Can.	D12	124
Qu'Appelle Dam, dam, Sk., Can.	D7	124
Quaraí, Braz.	E9	92
Quaraí (Cuareim), stm., S.A.	E9	92
Quarles, Pegunungan, mts., Indon.	E11	50
Quarryville, Pa., U.S.	E9	114
Quartier d'Orléans, Guad.	A1	105a
Quartu Sant'Elena, Italy	E3	24
Quartz Lake, l., Nu., Can.	A14	106
Quartz Mountain, mtn., Or., U.S.	G4	136
Quartzsite, Az., U.S.	J2	132
Quba, Azer.	A6	56
Qūchān, Iran	B8	56
Quchijie, China	G4	42
Queanbeyan, Austl.	J7	76
Québec, Qc., Can.	D5	110
Québec, state, Can.	E16	106
Quebeck, Tn., U.S.	I12	120
Quebra-Anzol, stm., Braz.	J2	88
Quebracho, Ur.	E9	92
Quebrada Seca, P.R.	B4	104a
Quedal, Cabo, c., Chile	H2	90
Quedlinburg, Ger.	E7	16
Queen Charlotte Islands, is., B.C., Can.	E4	106
Queen Charlotte Sound, strt., B.C., Can.	E2	138
Queen Charlotte Strait, strt., B.C., Can.	F3	138
Queen City, Mo., U.S.	D5	120
Queen City, Tx., U.S.	D4	122
Queen Elizabeth Islands, is., Can.	B13	94
Queen Mary Coast, cst., Ant.	B14	81
Queen Maud Gulf, b., Nu., Can.	B10	106
Queen Maud Land, reg., Ant.	C4	81
Queen Maud Mountains, mts., Ant.	D23	81
Queenscliff, Austl.	L5	76
Queensland, state, Austl.	D8	74
Queensport, N.S., Can.	E15	110
Queenstown, Austl.	o12	77a
Queenstown, N.Z.	G3	80
Queenstown, S. Afr.	G8	70
Queguay Grande, stm., Ur.	F9	92
Queimada Nova, Braz.	E5	88
Queimadas, Braz.	F6	88
Queimados, Braz.	L4	88
Quela, Ang.	B2	68
Quelelevu, i., Fiji	p20	79e
Quelimane, Moz.	D6	68
Quelpart Island see Cheju-do, i., Kor., S.	H7	38
Quemado, Tx., U.S.	F7	130
Quemado, Punta de, c., Cuba	B10	102
Quemoy see Chinmen Tao, i., Tai.	I8	42
Quemú Quemú, Arg.	H6	92

Name Map Ref. Page

Quequén, Arg. I8 92
Querary, stm., Col. G6 86
Quercy, hist. reg., Fr. E7 18
Querétaro, Mex. E8 100
Querétaro, state, Mex. E8 100
Querobabi, Mex. F7 98
Quesada, C.R. E8 96
Quesada, Spain G7 20
Queshan, China E5 42
Quesnel, B.C., Can. C8 138
Quesnel, stm., B.C., Can. D8 138
Quesnel Lake, l., B.C., Can. D9 138
Que Son, Viet. E9 48
Questa, N.M., U.S. E3 128
Quetico Lake, l., On., Can. C7 118
Quetta, Pak. C10 56
Quetzaltenango, Guat. E2 102
Quevedo, Ec. H2 86
Quezon City, Phil. C3 52
Qufu, China D7 42
Quibala, Ang. C2 68
Quibdó, Col. E3 86
Quiberon, Fr. G5 14
Quíbor, Ven. C7 86
Quiculungo, Ang. B2 68
Quila, Mex. C5 100
Quilengues, Ang. C1 68
Quilimarí, Chile F2 92
Quillabamba, Peru F3 84
Quillacollo, Bol. C3 90
Quill Lake, Sk., Can. B9 124
Quillota, Chile F2 92
Quilon, India G3 53
Quilpie, Austl. F5 76
Quilpué, Chile F2 92
Quimarí, Alto de, mtn., Col. C3 86
Quimaria, Ang. B1 68
Quimby, Ia., U.S. B2 120
Quimilí, Arg. C6 92
Quimper (Kemper), Fr. F5 14
Quimperlé, Fr. G5 14
Quinault, stm., Wa., U.S. C3 136
Quince Mil, Peru F3 84
Quincy, Ca., U.S. D4 134
Quincy, Fl., U.S. G14 122
Quincy, Il., U.S. E6 120
Quincy, Ma., U.S. B14 114
Quincy, Wa., U.S. C7 136
Quindío, state, Col. E4 86
Quines, Arg. F5 92
Quinhagak, Ak., U.S. E7 140
Quinlan, Tx., U.S. E2 122
Quinn, stm., Nv., U.S. B7 134
Quintanar de la Orden, Spain E7 20
Quintana Roo, state, Mex. C3 102
Quinte, Bay of, b., On., Can. D12 112
Quinto, Spain C10 20
Quinto, stm., Arg. G5 92
Quinton, Ok., U.S. B3 122
Quipapá, Braz. E7 88
Quirauk Mountain, mtn., Md., U.S. E8 114
Quiriguá, hist., Guat. E3 102
Quirihue, Chile H1 92
Quirindi, Austl. H8 76
Quirinópolis, Braz. C6 90
Quiriquire, Ven. C10 86
Quiroga, Mex. F8 100
Quiros, Cap, c., Vanuatu j16 79d
Quissanga, Moz. C7 68
Quissico, Moz. D12 70
Quitaque, Tx., U.S. G7 128
Quitasueño, unds., Col. E7 102
Quitasueño, Banco see Quitasueño, unds., Col. E7 102
Quita Sueno Bank see Quitasueño, unds., Col. E7 102
Quiterajo, Moz. C7 68
Quitilipi, Arg. C7 92
Quitman, Ga., U.S. F2 116
Quitman, Tx., U.S. E3 122
Quito, Ec. H2 86
Quixadá, Braz. C6 88
Quixeramobim, Braz. C6 88
Qujiadian, China C5 38
Qujing, China F5 36
Qujiu, China J2 42
Qulin, Mo., U.S. H7 120
Qumarlêb, China E4 36
Qumrān, Khirbat, hist., W.B. G6 58
Quoich, stm., Nu., Can. C12 106
Quorn, Austl. F7 74
Quoxo, stm., Bots. C7 70
Qurdūd, Sudan E5 62
Qus, Egypt B6 62
Quseir, Egypt B6 62
Qutdligssat, Grnld. C15 141
Quthing, Leso. G8 70
Quweisna, Egypt H2 58
Quxian, China F2 42
Qüxü, China D13 54
Quyang, China B6 42
Quy Nhon, Viet. F9 48
Quyon, Qc., Can. C13 112
Quyquyó, Para. C9 92
Quzhou, China G8 42
Quzhou, China C6 42
Qyzylorda see Kzyl-Orda, Kaz. F11 32

R

Raab (Rába), stm., Eur. D12 22
Raalte, Neth. B15 14
Ra'ananna, Isr. F5 58
Raas, Pulau, i., Indon. G9 50
Raasay, i., Scot., U.K. D6 12
Raasiku, Est. A8 10
Rab, Otok, i., Cro. F11 22
Raba, Indon. H11 50
Rába (Raab), stm., Eur. D12 22
Rábade, Spain A3 20
Rabak, Sudan E6 62
Rabat, Malta I8 24
Rabat, Malta H8 24
Rabat, Mor. C3 64
Rabaul, Pap. N. Gui. a5 79a
Rabbit Creek, stm., S.D., U.S. B10 126
Rabbit Ears Pass, p., Co., U.S. C10 132
Rabi, i., Fiji p20 79e
Rābi', Ash-Shallāl ar- (Fourth Cataract), wtfl, Sudan D6 62
Rābigh, Sau. Ar. E4 56
Rabka, Pol. G15 16
Rabkavi Banhatti, India C2 53
Râbniţa, Mol. B16 26
Rabočeostrovsk, Russia D16 8
Rabwāh, Pak. C4 54
Rabyānah, Ramlat, des., Libya C4 62
Raccoon, stm., Ia., U.S. C4 120
Raccoon Creek, stm., Oh., U.S. E15 120
Race, Cape, c., Nf., Can. j23 107a
Race Point, c., Ma., U.S. B15 114
Rach Gia, Viet. G7 48
Rach Gia, Vinh, b., Viet. H7 48
Raciąż, Pol. D16 16
Racibórz, Pol. F14 16
Racine, Wi., U.S. F2 112
Radakovičy, Bela. F10 10
Rădăuţi, Rom. B12 26
Radcliff, Ky., U.S. G12 120
Radeberg, Ger. E9 16
Radebeul, Ger. E9 16
Radford, Va., U.S. G5 114
Rādhanpur, India G3 54
Rădineşti, Rom. E10 26
Radisson, Sk., Can. B6 124
Radium Hot Springs, B.C., Can. F14 138
Radnice, Czech Rep. G9 16
Radofinnikovo, Russia A13 10
Radom, Pol. E17 16
Radom, state, Pol. E16 16
Radomsko, Pol. E15 16
Radomyśl Wielki, Pol. F17 16
Radoviš, Mac. B5 28
Radstadt, Aus. C10 22
Radutino, Russia H17 10
Radviliškis, Lith. E6 10
Radville, Sk., Can. E9 124
Radymno, Pol. G18 16
Radzyń Chełmiński, Pol. C14 16
Rae, N.T., Can. C7 106
Rae, stm., Nu., Can. B7 106
Rãe Bareli, India E8 54
Raeford, N.C., U.S. B6 116
Rae Isthmus, isth., Nu., Can. B13 106
Rae Strait, strt., Nu., Can. B12 106
Rafaela, Arg. E7 92
Rafael Freyre, Cuba B10 102
Rafah, Gaza G5 58
Rafhā', Sau. Ar. D5 56
Rafsanjān, Iran C8 56
Raft, stm., U.S. H13 136
Raga, Sudan F5 62
Ragay Gulf, b., Phil. D4 52
Ragged Island, i., Bah. A10 102
Ragged Island Range, is., Bah. A10 102
Ragged Top Mountain, mtn., Wy., U.S. F7 126
Ragland, Al., U.S. D12 122
Raguva, Lith. E7 10
Rahačoŭ, Bela. G12 10
Rahad al-Bardī, Sudan E4 62
Rāhatgarh, India G7 54
Rahimatpur, India C1 53
Rahīm Ki Bāzār, Pak. F2 54
Rahīmyār Khān, Pak. D3 54
Rāīchūr, India C3 53
Raiganj, India F12 54
Raigarh, India H9 54
Rāikot, India C5 54
Railroad Valley, val., Nv., U.S. E10 134
Railton, Austl. n13 77a
Rainbow Bridge National Monument, p.o.i., Ut., U.S. F6 132
Rainbow Falls, wtfl, B.C., Can. D11 138
Rainelle, W.V., U.S. G5 114
Rainier, Mount, vol., Wa., U.S. D5 136
Rainy, stm., N.A. C4 118
Rainy Lake, l., N.A. C5 118
Rainy River, On., Can. C4 118
Raipur, India H8 54
Raipur Uplands, plat., India H9 54
Raisen, India G6 54
Raisin, stm., Mi., U.S. G6 112
Raivavae, i., Fr. Poly. F12 72
Rajabasa, Indon. F4 50
Rājahmundry, India C5 53
Rājaldesar, India E5 54
Rājampet, India D4 53
Rajang, stm., Malay. B7 50
Rājapālaiyam, India G3 53
Rājāpur, India C1 53
Rājasthān, state, India E4 54
Rājbāri, Bngl. G12 54
Rajčihinsk, Russia G14 34
Rāj Gāngpur, India G10 54
Rājgarh, India E6 54
Rājgarh, India G6 54
Rājgarh, India D5 54
Rajik, Indon. E4 50
Rājkot, India G3 54
Rāj Nāndgaon, India H8 54
Rājpipla, India H4 54
Rājpur, India G5 54
Rājpura, India C6 54
Rājshāhi, Bngl. F12 54
Rājshāhi, state, Bngl. F12 54
Rājula, India H3 54
Raka, stm., China D11 54
Rakamaz, Hung. A8 26
Rakaposhi, mtn., Pak. B11 56
Rakata, Pulau (Krakatoa), i., Indon. G4 50
Rakhine, state, Mya. C1 48
Rakhiv, Ukr. A11 26
Rakitnoe, Russia B11 36
Rakiura see Stewart Island, i., N.Z. H3 80
Rakoniewice, Pol. D12 16
Rakops, Bots. B7 70
Rakovník, Czech Rep. F9 16
Råkvåg see Råkvågen, Nor. E4 8
Råkvågen, Nor. E4 8
Rakvere, Est. G12 8
Raleigh, Ms., U.S. E9 122
Raleigh, N.C., U.S. I7 114
Ralik Chain, is., Marsh. Is. C7 72
Ralls, Tx., U.S. H7 128
Ralston, Pa., U.S. C9 114
Ramah, N.M., U.S. H8 132
Rām Allāh, W.B. G6 58
Rāmanagaram, India E3 53
Rāmanāthapuram, India G4 53
Rāmānuj Ganj, India G9 54
Ramat Gan, Isr. F5 58
Ramat HaSharon, Isr. F5 58
Ramatlabama, Bots. D7 70
Rambervillers, Fr. F15 14
Rambouillet, Fr. F10 14
Rambutyo Island, i., Pap. N. Gui. a4 79a
Rām Dās, India B5 54
Rāmdurg, India C2 53
Ramea, Nf., Can. j22 107a
Ramene, Russia F20 8
Ramenskoe, Russia E21 10
Rāmeswaram, India G4 53
Rāmgarh, Bngl. G13 54
Rāmgarh, India E5 54
Rāmgarh, India G10 54
Ram Head, c., V.I.U.S. e8 104b
Rāmhormoz, Iran C6 56
Ramírez, Mex. I10 130
Ramírez, Mex. G7 130
Ramla, Isr. G5 58
Ramlu, mtn., Afr. E8 62
Ramm, Jabal, mtn., Jord. I6 58
Rāmnagar, India F9 54
Rāmnagar, India D7 54
Râmnicu Sărat, Rom. D14 26
Râmnicu Vâlcea, Rom. D11 26
Ramona, Ca., U.S. J9 134
Ramona, S.D., U.S. C15 126
Ramos, Mex. D8 100
Ramos, stm., Mex. C6 100
Ramotswa, Bots. D7 70
Rampart, Ak., U.S. C9 140
Ramparts, stm., N.T., Can. B4 106
Rāmpur, India D7 54
Rāmpur, India C6 54
Rāmpura, India F5 54
Rāmpur Hāt, India F11 54
Ramree Island, i., Mya. C1 48
Ramseur, N.C., U.S. I6 114
Ramsey, I. of Man G8 12
Ramsey Lake, l., On., Can. A7 112
Ramsgate, Eng., U.K. J14 12
Ramshorn Peak, mtn., Mt., U.S. E15 136
Rāmtek, India H7 54
Rāmu, Bngl. H14 54
Ramu, stm., Pap. N. Gui. a3 79a
Ramville, Îlet, i., Mart. k7 105c
Ramygala, Lith. E7 10
Rānāghāt, India G12 54
Rana Kao, Volcán, vol., Chile f29 78l
Rāna Pratāp Sāgar, res., India F5 54
Ranau, Malay. H1 52
Ranau, Danau, l., Indon. F3 50
Ranburne, Al., U.S. D13 122
Rancagua, Chile G2 92
Rancah, Indon. G6 50
Rancevo, Russia D16 10
Rancharia, Braz. D6 90
Ranchería, stm., Col. B5 86
Ranchester, Wy., U.S. C5 126
Rānchi, India G10 54
Ranchillos, Arg. C5 92
Ranch Lake, l., Sk., Can. B9 124
Rancho Cordova, Ca., U.S. E4 134
Rancho Nuevo, Mex. H7 130
Ranchos, Arg. G8 92
Ranco, Lago, l., Chile H2 90
Randazzo, Italy G8 24
Randers, Den. H4 8
Randleman, N.C., U.S. I6 114
Randlett, Ok., U.S. G10 128
Randolph, Az., U.S. K5 132
Randolph, Me., U.S. F7 110
Randolph, Ne., U.S. E15 126
Randolph, N.Y., U.S. B7 114
Randolph, Ut., U.S. B5 132
Random Lake, Wi., U.S. E2 112
Randsfjorden, l., Nor. F3 8
Ranfurly, N.Z. G4 80
Rāngāmāti, Bngl. G13 54
Rangantemiang, Indon. D8 50
Rangas, Tanjung, c., Indon. E11 50
Rangasa, Tanjung, c., Indon. E11 50
Rangaunu Bay, b., N.Z. B5 80
Rangeley, Me., U.S. E6 110
Ranger, Tx., U.S. B9 130
Rangia, India E13 54
Rangitaiki, stm., N.Z. D7 80
Rangitata, stm., N.Z. F4 80
Rangitikei, stm., N.Z. D7 80
Rangkasbitung, Indon. G4 50
Rangoon see Yangon, Mya. D2 48
Rangoon, stm., Mya. D3 48
Rangpur, Bngl. F12 54
Rangpur, Pak. C3 54
Rangsang, Pulau, i., Indon. C3 50
Rānībennur, India D2 53
Rānīganj, India G11 54
Rānikhet, India D7 54
Rankamhaeng National Park, p.o.i., Thai. D4 48
Ranken, stm., Austl. D7 74
Ranken Store, Austl. C7 74
Rankin, Il., U.S. H2 112
Rankin, Tx., U.S. C6 130
Rankin Inlet see Kangiqsliniq, Nu., Can. C12 106
Rankins Springs, Austl. I6 76
Rann of Kutch see Kutch, Rann of, reg., Asia D2 46
Ranong, Thai. H4 48
Ranongga Island, i., Sol. Is. e7 79b
Ranot, Thai. I5 48
Ransiki, Indon. F9 44
Ransom, Ks., U.S. C8 128
Ranson, W.V., U.S. E8 114
Rantabe, Madag. D8 68
Rantaukampar, Indon. C2 50
Rantaupanjang, Indon. D2 50
Rantauprapat, Indon. B1 50
Rantekombola, Bulu, mtn., Indon. E12 50
Rantepao, Indon. E11 50
Rantoul, Il., U.S. D9 120
Raohe, China B11 36
Raoping, China J7 42
Raoul, Ga., U.S. B2 116
Raoul-Blanchard, Mont, mtn., Qc., Can. C6 110
Raoul Island, i., N.Z. F9 72
Rapa, i., Fr. Poly. F12 72
Rapallo, Italy F6 22
Rapang, Indon. E11 50
Rapa Nui see Pascua, Isla de, i., Chile f30 78l
Rāpar, India G3 54
Rapel, stm., Chile F2 92
Rapel, Embalse, res., Chile G2 92
Rapelli, Arg. C5 92
Raper, Cape, c., Nu., Can. B17 106
Rapidan, stm., Va., U.S. F7 114
Rapid City, Mb., Can. D13 124
Rapid City, S.D., U.S. C9 126
Rapid Creek, stm., S.D., U.S. D9 126
Rapide-Blanc, Qc., Can. C4 110
Rapid River, Mi., U.S. C2 112
Räpina, Est. G12 8
Rappahannock, stm., Va., U.S. G9 114
Rāpti, stm., Asia E9 54
Rapu Rapu Island, i., Phil. D5 52
Raraka, at., Fr. Poly. E12 72
Rarotonga, i., Cook Is. a26 78j
Rarotonga International Airport, Cook Is. a26 78j
Rasa, Punta, c., Arg. H9 92
Ra's al-Khaymah, U.A.E. D8 56
Ra's Ba'labakk, Leb. D7 58
Râşcani, Mol. B14 26
Rasčov, Mol. B15 26
Ras Dashen Terara, mtn., Eth. E7 62
Ras Dejen see Ras Dashen Terara, mtn., Eth. E7 62
Ras Djebel, Tun. G4 24
Raseiniai, Lith. E5 10
Râs el-Barr, Egypt G2 58
Rashād, Sudan E6 62
Rashid (Rosetta), Egypt G1 58
Rashid, Masabb (Rosetta Mouth), mth., Egypt G1 58
Rasht, Iran B6 56
Raška, Yugo. F7 26
Rās Koh, mtn., Pak. D10 56
Rasm al-Arwām, Sabkhat, l., Syria C8 58
Râşnov, Rom. D12 26
Rasra, India F9 54
Rasšua, ostrov, i., Russia G19 34
Rast, Rom. F10 26
Rastatt, Ger. H4 16
Rastede, Ger. C4 16
Rastenburg see Kętrzyn, Pol. B17 16
Rásttigáisá, mtn., Nor. A12 8
Ratak Chain, is., Marsh. Is. C8 72
Ratamka, Bela. G10 10
Ratangarh, India D5 54
Rat Buri, Thai. F4 48
Rāth, India F7 54
Rathbun Lake, res., Ia., U.S. D4 120
Rathdrum, Id., U.S. C9 136
Rathenow, Ger. D8 16
Rathkeale, Ire. I3 12
Rāth Luirc, Ire. I4 12
Rathwell, Mb., Can. E15 124
Rat Island, i., Ak., U.S. g22 140a
Rat Islands, is., Ak., U.S. g22 140a
Ratlām, India G5 54
Ratmanova, ostrov, i., Russia C27 34
Ratnāgiri, India C1 53
Ratnapura, Sri L. H5 53
Raton, N.M., U.S. E4 128
Raton Pass, p., N.M., U.S. E4 128
Rats, stm., Qc., Can. A4 110
Rattanaburi, Thai. E6 48
Rattaphum, Thai. I5 48
Rattlesnake, Mt., U.S. D13 136
Rattlesnake Creek, stm., Ks., U.S. D10 128
Ratz, Mount, mtn., B.C., Can. D4 106
Ratzeburg, Ger. C6 16
Rau, Indon. C2 50
Raub, Malay. K5 48
Rauch, Arg. H8 92
Raul Soares, Braz. K4 88
Rauma, Fin. F9 8
Rauma, stm., Nor. E2 8
Rauna, Lat. C8 10
Raung, Gunung, vol., Indon. H9 50
Raurkela, India G10 54
Răut, stm., Mol. B14 26
Ravalgaon, India H5 54
Ravanusa, Italy G7 24
Ravena, N.Y., U.S. B12 114
Ravenna, Italy F9 22
Ravenna, Ky., U.S. G2 114
Ravenna, Ne., U.S. F13 126
Ravenna, Oh., U.S. G8 112
Ravensburg, Ger. I5 16
Ravenscrag, Sk., Can. E4 124
Ravenshoe, Austl. A5 76
Ravensthorpe, Austl. F4 74
Ravenswood, W.V., U.S. F4 114
Rāvi, stm., Asia C4 54
Ravnina, Turkmen. B9 56
Rāwah, Iraq C5 56
Rawaki, at., Kir. D9 72
Rāwalpindi, Pak. B4 54
Rawas, stm., Indon. E3 50
Rawdon, Qc., Can. D3 110
Rawicz, Pol. E12 16
Rawlinna, Austl. F4 74
Rawlins, Wy., U.S. B9 132
Rawson, Arg. H4 90
Rawson, Arg. G7 92
Raxāul, India E10 54
Ray, Cape, c., Nf., Can. C17 110
Raya, Indon. C11 50
Raya, Bukit, mtn., Indon. D8 50
Rāyachoti, India D4 53
Rāyadurg, India D3 53
Rāyagarha, India B6 53
Ray Hubbard, Lake, res., Tx., U.S. E2 122
Raymond, Ab., Can. G18 138
Raymond, Il., U.S. E8 120
Raymond, Mn., U.S. F3 118
Raymond, Wa., U.S. D3 136
Raymond Terrace, Austl. I8 76
Raymondville, Tx., U.S. H10 130
Raymore, Sk., Can. C9 124
Rayne, La., U.S. G6 122
Rayones, Mex. C8 100
Rayong, Thai. F5 48
Rayside-Balfour, On., Can. B8 112
Raytown, Mo., U.S. E3 120
Rayville, La., U.S. E7 122
Raz, Pointe du, c., Fr. F4 14
Războieni, Rom. B13 26
Razdolinsk, Russia C17 32
Razeni, Mol. C15 26
Razgrad, Blg. F13 26
Razim, Lacul, l., Rom. E15 26
Rāznas ezers, l., Lat. D10 10
Razorback Mountain, mtn., B.C., Can. E6 138
Răzvani, Rom. E13 26
Ré, Île de, i., Fr. C4 18
Reading, Eng., U.K. J11 12
Reading, Mi., U.S. C1 114
Reading, Oh., U.S. E1 114
Reading, Pa., U.S. D9 114
Readlyn, Ia., U.S. B5 120
Readstown, Wi., U.S. H8 118
Real, stm., Braz. F6 88
Real, Cordillera, mts., S.A. G4 84
Real del Castillo, Mex. L9 134
Real del Padre, Arg. G4 92
Realicó, Arg. G5 92
Reardan, Wa., U.S. C8 136
Reata, Mex. B8 100
Reay, Scot., U.K. C9 12
Rebecca, Lake, l., Austl. F4 74
Rebiana Sand Sea see Rabyānah, Ramlat, des., Libya C4 62
Reboly, Russia E14 8
Rebouças, Braz. B12 92
Rebun-tō, i., Japan B14 38
Recanati, Italy G10 22
Recherche, Archipelago of the, is., Austl. F4 74
Recife, Braz. E8 88
Recinto, Chile H2 92
Recklinghausen, Ger. E2 16
Reconquista, Arg. D8 92
Recreio, Braz. K4 88
Recreo, Arg. D5 92
Rector, Ar., U.S. H7 120
Rečyca, Bela. H13 10
Recz, Pol. C11 16
Red (Hong, Song) (Yuan), stm., Asia D9 46
Red, stm., N.A. A2 118
Red, stm., U.S. E9 108
Red, stm., U.S. H10 120
Red, Elm Fork, stm., U.S. F8 128
Red, North Fork, stm., U.S. G9 128
Red, Prairie Dog Town Fork, stm., U.S. H7 122
Red, Salt Fork, stm., U.S. G9 128
Redang, Pulau, i., Malay. J6 48
Red Bank, N.J., U.S. D11 114
Red Bank, Tn., U.S. B13 122
Red Bay, Nf., Can. i22 107a
Red Bay, Al., U.S. C10 122
Redbay, Fl., U.S. G12 122
Redberry Lake, l., Sk., Can. B6 124
Red Bluff, Ca., U.S. C3 134
Red Bluff Reservoir, res., U.S. C4 130
Red Boiling Springs, Tn., U.S. H12 120
Red Canyon, val., S.D., U.S. D9 126
Redcar, Eng., U.K. G11 12
Red Cedar, stm., Mi., U.S. F5 112
Red Cedar Lake, l., On., Can. B9 112
Redcliff, Ab., Can. D3 124
Red Cliff, Co., U.S. D10 132
Redcliff see Red Cliff, Co., U.S. D10 132
Redcliffe, Austl. F9 76
Redcliffe, Mount, mtn., Austl. E4 74
Red Cliffs, Austl. J3 76
Red Cloud, Ne., U.S. A10 128
Red Creek, stm., Ms., U.S. G10 122
Red Deer, Ab., Can. D17 138
Red Deer, stm., Can. B12 124
Red Deer, stm., Can. F19 138
Red Deer Lake, l., Mb., Can. B12 124
Reddersburg, S. Afr. F8 70
Red Devil, Ak., U.S. D8 140
Redding, Ca., U.S. C3 134
Redditch, Eng., U.K. I10 12
Redenção, Braz. C6 88
Redfield, S.D., U.S. C14 126
Redford, Tx., U.S. E3 130
Redhead, Trin. s13 105f
Redja, stm., Russia C14 10
Redkey, In., U.S. H4 112
Redkino, Russia D19 10
Red Lake, On., Can. E12 106
Red Lake, l., On., Can. E12 106
Red Lake, l., Az., U.S. H2 132
Red Lake, stm., Mn., U.S. D2 118
Red Lake Falls, Mn., U.S. D2 118
Red Lake Road, On., Can. B5 118
Redlands, Ca., U.S. I8 134
Redlands, Co., U.S. D8 132
Red Level, Al., U.S. F12 122
Red Lion, Pa., U.S. E9 114
Red Lodge, Mt., U.S. B3 126
Redmond, Or., U.S. F5 136
Redmond, Ut., U.S. D5 132
Redmond, Wa., U.S. C4 136
Red Mountain, mtn., Mt., U.S. C14 136
Red Mountain Pass, p., Co., U.S. F9 132
Red Oak, Ia., U.S. D2 120
Redon, Fr. G6 14
Redonda, Isla, i., Ven. t12 105f
Redonda Islands, is., B.C., Can. F6 138
Redondela, Spain B2 20
Redondo, Port. F3 20
Redondo Beach, Ca., U.S. J7 134
Redoubt Volcano, vol., Ak., U.S. D9 140
Red Pass, B.C., Can. D11 138
Red Rock, B.C., Can. C8 138
Red Rock, On., Can. C10 118
Red Rock, stm., Mt., U.S. F14 136
Red Rock, Lake, res., Ia., U.S. C4 120
Redruth, Eng., U.K. K7 12
Red Sea C7 62
Redvers, Sk., Can. E12 124
Redwater, Ab., Can. C17 138
Redwater, stm., Mt., U.S. G8 124
Redwillow, stm., Can. A11 138
Red Willow Creek, stm., Ne., U.S. G12 126
Red Wing, Mn., U.S. G6 118
Redwood, stm., Mn., U.S. G3 118
Redwood Falls, Mn., U.S. G3 118
Redwood National Park, p.o.i., Ca., U.S. B1 134
Ree, Lough, l., Ire. H5 12
Reed City, Mi., U.S. E4 112
Reeder, N.D., U.S. A10 126
Reed Lake, l., Sk., Can. D6 124
Reedley, Ca., U.S. G6 134
Reedsburg, Wi., U.S. H8 118
Reedsville, Wi., U.S. D2 112
Reefton, N.Z. F4 80
Reelfoot Lake, l., Tn., U.S. H8 120
Rees, Ger. E2 16
Reese, Mi., U.S. E6 112
Reese, stm., Nv., U.S. C9 134
Reeseville, Wi., U.S. H10 118
Refuge Cove, B.C., Can. F6 138
Refugio, Tx., U.S. F10 130
Rega, stm., Pol. C11 16
Regência, Braz. J6 88
Regeneração, Braz. D4 88
Regensburg, Ger. H8 16
Regent, N.D., U.S. A10 126
Reggane, Alg. D5 64
Reggio di Calabria, Italy F9 24
Reggio nell'Emilia, Italy F7 22
Reghin, Rom. C11 26
Regina, Sk., Can. D9 124
Región Metropolitana, state, Chile F2 92
Registan see Rīgestān, reg., Afg. C9 56
Registro, Braz. B14 92
Regozero, Russia D14 8
Rehau, Ger. F7 16
Rehoboth, Nmb. C3 70
Rehoboth Beach, De., U.S. F10 114
Reḥovot, Isr. G5 58
Reichenbach, Ger. F8 16
Reidsville, Ga., U.S. D3 116
Reidsville, N.C., U.S. H6 114
Reigate, Eng., U.K. J12 12
Reihoku, Japan G2 40
Reims (Rheims), Fr. E12 14
Rein Anteriur (Vorderrhein), stm., Switz. D6 22
Reinbeck, Ia., U.S. B5 120
Reindeer Lake, l., Can. D10 106
Reinga, Cape, c., N.Z. B5 80
Reinosa, Spain A6 20
Reisa Nasjonalpark, p.o.i., Nor. B10 8
Reisterstown, Md., U.S. E9 114
Reitz, S. Afr. E9 70
Reliance, N.T., Can. C9 106
Remada, Tun. C7 64
Remagen, Ger. F3 16
Remanso, Braz. E4 88
Rembang, Indon. G7 50
Remedios, Col. D4 86
Remedios, Pan. H7 102
Remedios, Punta, c., El Sal. F2 102
Remer, Mn., U.S. D5 118
Remington, Va., U.S. F8 114
Rémire, Fr. Gu. C7 84
Remiremont, Fr. G15 14
Remoulins, Fr. F10 18
Rempang, Pulau, i., Indon. C4 50
Remscheid, Ger. E3 16
Remsen, Ia., U.S. B1 120
Remus, Mi., U.S. E4 112
Renaix see Ronse, Bel. D12 14
Renata, B.C., Can. G12 138
Renčeni, Lat. C8 10
Rende, Italy E10 24
Rendova Island, i., Sol. Is. e7 79b
Rendsburg, Ger. B5 16
Renfrew, On., Can. C13 112
Rengat, Indon. D3 50
Rengel, Indon. D5 50
Rengo, Chile G2 92
Reng Tlāng, mtn., Asia H14 54
Renheji, China F6 42
Renhuai, China H2 42
Reni, Ukr. D15 26
Renland, reg., Grnld. C20 141
Renmark, Austl. J3 76
Rennell, i., Sol. Is. f9 79b
Rennell, Islas, is., Chile J2 90
Rennell and Bellona, state, Sol. Is. f9 79b
Rennes, Fr. F7 14
Rennie, Mb., Can. E18 124
Reno, Nv., U.S. D6 134
Reno, stm., Italy F8 22
Reno Hill, mtn., Wy., U.S. E6 126
Renoster, stm., S. Afr. G5 70
Renous, N.B., Can. D11 110
Renovo, Pa., U.S. C8 114
Rensjön, Swe. B8 8
Rensselaer, In., U.S. H2 112
Rensselaer, N.Y., U.S. B12 114
Rentería, Spain A9 20
Renton, Wa., U.S. C4 136
Renville, Mn., U.S. G3 118
Renwick, Ia., U.S. B4 120
Reo, Indon. H12 50
Repetek, Turkmen. B9 56
Repton, Al., U.S. F11 122
Republic, Mi., U.S. B1 112
Republic, Mo., U.S. G4 120
Republic, Wa., U.S. B8 136
Republican, stm., U.S. B11 128
Republican, North Fork, stm., U.S. A6 128
Republican, South Fork, stm., U.S. B7 128
Republic of Korea see Korea, South, ctry., Asia G8 38
Repulse Bay see Naujaat, Nu., Can. B13 106
Repulse Bay, b., Austl. C7 76
Repvåg, Nor. A11 8
Requena, Spain E9 20
Reriutaba, Braz. C5 88
Reşadiye Yarımadası, pen., Tur. G10 28
Reschenpass (Resia, Passo di), p., Eur. C16 18
Reschenscheideck see Reschenpass, p., Eur. C16 18
Reschenscheideck see Resia, Passo di, p., Eur. C16 18
Resen, Mac. B4 28
Reserva, Braz. B12 92
Reserve, La., U.S. G8 122
Reserve, N.M., U.S. J8 132
Resia, Passo di (Reschenpass), p., Eur. C16 18
Resistencia, Arg. C8 92
Reşiţa, Rom. D8 26
Reško, Pol. C11 16
Resolute see Qausuittuq, Nu., Can. C7 141
Resolution Island, i., Nu., Can. E12 141
Resolution Island, i., N.Z. G2 80
Resplendor, Braz. J5 88
Restigouche, stm., Can. C9 110
Restinga Seca, Braz. D11 92
Reston, Mb., Can. E12 124
Retalhuleu, Guat. E2 102
Retamosa, Ur. F10 92
Retezat, Parcul Național, p.o.i., Rom. D9 26
Rethel, Fr. E13 14
Réthymno, Grc. H7 28
Rettihovka, Russia B10 38
Reunion, dep., Afr. I11 60
Reus, Spain C12 20
Reuss, stm., Switz. C5 22
Reuterstadt Stavenhagen, Ger. C8 16
Reutlingen, Ger. H5 16
Revda, Russia C16 8
Revelstoke, B.C., Can. F12 138
Revelstoke, Lake, res., B.C., Can. E12 138
Reventazón, Peru E1 84
Revilla del Campo, Spain B7 20
Revillagigedo, Islas, is., Mex. F2 100
Revillagigedo Island, i., Ak., U.S. E13 140
Revillagigedo Islands see Revillagigedo, Islas, is., Mex. F2 100
Revin, Fr. E13 14
Revolución, Mex. H2 130
Rewa, India F8 54
Rewāri, India D6 54
Rexburg, Id., U.S. G15 136
Rexford, Ks., U.S. B8 128
Rexford, Mt., U.S. B12 136
Rey, Isla del, i., Pan. H8 102
Rey, Laguna del, l., Mex. B7 100
Reyes, Bol. B3 90
Reyes, Point, c., Ca., U.S. F2 134
Reyhanlı, Tur. B7 58
Reykjanes Ridge, unds. C10 144
Reykjavík, Ice. k28 8a
Reyno, Ar., U.S. H7 120
Reynolds, Ga., U.S. D1 116
Reynolds, N.D., U.S. G16 124
Reynosa, Mex. B9 100
Rezé, Fr. G7 14
Rēzekne, Lat. D10 10
Rezina, Mol. B15 26
Rezovo, Blg. G15 26
Rezovska (Mutlu), stm., Eur. G14 26
Rhaetian Alps, mts., Eur. C15 18
Rhame, N.D., U.S. A9 126
Rheda-Wiedenbrück, Ger. E4 16
Rheims see Reims, Fr. E12 14
Rhein, Sk., Can. C11 124
Rhein see Rhine, stm., Eur. C15 14
Rheine, Ger. D3 16
Rheinland-Pfalz, state, Ger. G3 16
Rhine, Ga., U.S. E2 116
Rhine (Rhein) (Rhin), stm., Eur. C15 14
Rhinelander, Wi., U.S. F9 118
Rhineland-Palatinate see Rheinland-Pfalz, state, Ger. G3 16
Rhinns Point, c., Scot., U.K. F6 12
Rhir, Cap, c., Mor. C2 64
Rho, Italy E5 22
Rhode Island, state, U.S. C14 114
Rhode Island Sound, strt., U.S. C14 114
Rhodes see Ródos, Grc. G11 28
Rhodes see Ródos, i., Grc. G10 28
Rhodesia see Zimbabwe, ctry., Afr. D4 68
Rhodes Matopos National Park, p.o.i., Zimb. B8 70
Rhodes' Tomb, hist., Zimb. B9 70
Rhodope Mountains, mts., Eur. H11 26
Rhön, mts., Ger. F5 16
Rhondda, Wales, U.K. J9 12
Rhône, state, Fr. D10 18
Rhône, stm., Eur. E10 18
Rhyl, Wales, U.K. H9 12
Riachão, Braz. D2 88
Riachão do Jacuípe, Braz. F6 88
Riacho de Santana, Braz. G4 88
Riachos, Islas de los, is., Arg. H4 90
Riamkanan, Waduk, res., Indon. E9 50
Riaño, Spain A6 20
Riau, state, Indon. D2 50
Riau, Kepulauan, is., Indon. C4 50
Riaza, Spain C7 20
Ribadeo, Spain A3 20
Ribas do Rio Pardo, Braz. D6 90
Ribáuè, Moz. C6 68
Ribe, Den. I3 8
Ribe, state, Den. I3 8
Ribeira, Braz. B13 92
Ribeira do Pombal, Braz. F6 88
Ribeirão, Braz. E8 88
Ribeirão Preto, Braz. K1 88
Ribeirão Vermelho, Braz. K3 88
Ribeiro Gonçalves, Braz. D3 88
Riberalta, Bol. B3 90
Rib Lake, Wi., U.S. F8 118
Ribnica, Slvn. E11 22
Ribnitz-Damgarten, Ger. B8 16
Ribstone Creek, stm., Ab., Can. D19 138
Ricardo Flores Magón, Mex. F9 98
Riccione, Italy F9 22
Rice, Tx., U.S. E2 122
Rice Lake, l., On., Can. D11 112
Rice Lake, Wi., U.S. F7 118
Riceville, Ia., U.S. A5 120
Riceville, Tn., U.S. B14 122
Richan, On., Can. B6 118
Richard B. Russell Lake, res., U.S. B3 116
Richard Collinson Inlet, b., N.T., Can. B17 140
Richards, Tx., U.S. G3 122
Richards Bay, S. Afr. F11 70
Richards Bay, b., S. Afr. F11 70
Richards Island, i., N.T., Can. C13 140
Richardson, Tx., U.S. E2 122
Richardson, Wa., U.S. B4 136

Name / Map Ref. / Page

I•50 Salt-Sant

Name — Map Ref. — Page

Saltfjellet Svartisen Nasjonalpark, p.o.i., Nor. C6 8
Saltillo, Mex. C8 100
Saltillo, Tn., U.S. B10 122
Salt Lake City, Ut., U.S. C4 132
Salto, Arg. G7 92
Salto, Ur. E9 92
Salto del Guairá, Para. A10 92
Salto Grande, Embalse, res., S.A. E8 92
Salton City, Ca., U.S. J9 134
Salton Sea, l., Ca., U.S. J10 134
Salto Santiago, Represa de, res., Braz. B11 92
Saltspring Island, i., B.C., Can. H7 138
Saltville, Va., U.S. H4 114
Saluda, Va., U.S. G9 114
Saluda, stm., S.C., U.S. B4 116
Salûm, Egypt A5 62
Sālūmbar, India F5 54
Sālūr, India B6 53
Saluzzo, Italy F4 22
Salvador, Braz. G6 88
Salvador, El see El Salvador, ctry., N.A. F3 102
Salvador, Lake, l., La., U.S. H8 122
Salvatierra, Mex. E8 100
Salviac, Fr. E7 18
Salween (Nu) (Khong) (Thanlwin), stm., Asia E8 46
Salyan, Azer. B6 56
Salyān, Nepal D9 54
Salyer, Ca., U.S. C2 134
Salyersville, Ky., U.S. G2 114
Salzach, stm., Eur. B9 22
Salzburg, Aus. C10 22
Salzburg, state, Aus. C10 22
Salzgitter, Ger. D6 16
Salzkammergut, reg., Aus. C10 22
Salzwedel, Ger. D7 16
Samacá, Col. E5 86
Samacèvičy, Bela. G14 10
Samagaltaj, Russia D16 32
Samah, Libya B3 62
Samales Group, is., Phil. G3 52
Samalga Pass, strt., Ak., U.S. g25 140a
Samal Island, i., Phil. G5 52
Sāmalkot, India C6 53
Samâlût, Egypt J1 58
Samaná, Dom. Rep. C13 102
Samāna, India C5 54
Samaná, Bahía de, b., Dom. Rep. C13 102
Samaná, Cabo, c., Dom. Rep. C13 102
Samana Cay, i., Bah. A11 102
Samandağı, Tur. B6 58
Samaniego, Col. G3 86
Samaqua, stm., Qc., Can. A4 110
Samar, i., Phil. E5 52
Samara, Russia D8 32
Samara, stm., Russia D8 32
Samarai, Pap. N. Gui. c5 79a
Samaria, Id., U.S. A4 132
Samaria Gorge see Samariás, Farángi, val., Grc. H6 28
Samariapo, Ven. E8 86
Samariás, Farángi (Samaria Gorge), val., Grc. H6 28
Samarinda, Indon. D10 50
Samarka, Russia B10 38
Samarkand, Uzb. G11 32
Sāmarrā', Iraq C5 56
Samastīpur, India F10 54
Samaúna, Braz. E5 84
Samba Caju, Ang. B2 68
Sambaíba, Braz. D3 88
Sambalpur, India H9 54
Sambar, Tanjung, c., Indon. E7 50
Sambas, Indon. C6 50
Sambava, Madag. C9 68
Şambayat, Tur. A9 58
Sambhal, India D7 54
Sāmbhar, India E5 54
Sāmbhar Lake, l., India E5 54
Sambir, Ukr. G19 16
Sambit, Pulau, i., Indon. C11 50
Sambito, stm., Braz. D5 88
Samboja, Indon. D10 50
Sâmbor, Camb. F7 48
Samborombón, stm., Arg. G9 92
Samborombón, Bahía, b., Arg. G9 92
Sambre, stm., Eur. D12 14
Sambre à l'Oise, Canal de la, can., Fr. E12 14
Sambriāl, Pak. B5 54
Samch'ŏk, Kor., S. B2 40
Sam Chom, Khao, mtn., Thai. H4 48
Same, Tan. E7 66
Sam Ford Fiord, b., Nu., Can. A16 106
Samfya, Zam. C4 68
Samka, Mya. B3 48
Samnangjin, Kor., S. D1 40
Sam Ngao, Thai. D4 48
Samoa, ctry., Oc. g12 79c
Samoa Islands, is., Oc. h12 79c
Samo Alto, Chile E2 92
Samobor, Cro. E12 22
Samoded, Russia E19 8
Samokov, Blg. G10 26
Sámos, i., Grc. F9 28
Samoset, Fl., U.S. I3 116
Samosir, Pulau, i., Indon. B1 50
Samothrace see Samothráki, i., Grc. C8 28
Samothráki, Grc. C8 28
Samothráki (Samothrace), i., Grc. C8 28
Sampacho, Arg. F5 92
Sampanahan, Indon. E10 50
Sampang, Indon. G8 50
Sampit, Indon. E8 50
Sampit, stm., Indon. E8 50
Sampit, Teluk, b., Indon. E8 50
Sampwe, D.R.C. F5 66
Sam Rayburn Reservoir, res., Tx., U.S. F4 122
Samro, ozero, l., Russia B11 10
Sam Son, Viet. C7 48
Samsun, Tur. A4 56
Samsu-ŭp, Kor., N. D7 38
Samtown, La., U.S. F6 122
Samuhú, Arg. C7 92
Samui, Ko, i., Thai. H5 48
Samundri, Pak. C4 54
Samut Prakan, Thai. F5 48
Samut Sakhon, Thai. F5 48
Samut Songkhram, Thai. F5 48
San, Mali G3 64
San (Xan), stm., Asia F8 48
San, stm., China E8 42
San (Syan), stm., Eur. F18 16
Saña, Peru E2 84
Şan'ā', Yemen F5 56
Sana, stm., Bos. E3 26
Sanaa see Şan'ā', Yemen F5 56
Sanabu, Egypt K1 58
Sanaga, stm., Cam. D2 66
San Agustín, Arg. E5 92
San Agustín, Arg. I8 92
San Agustín, Mex. C1 130
San Agustin, Cape, c., Phil. G6 52
Sanak Islands, is., Ak., U.S. F7 140
San Alberto, Mex. G6 130
San Ambrosio, Isla, i., Chile H7 82
Sanana, Pulau, i., Indon. F8 44
Sānand, India G4 54
Sanandaj, Iran B6 56
San Andreas, Ca., U.S. E5 134
San Andrés, Col. F7 102
San Andrés, Isla de, i., Col. F7 102
San Andres Mountains, mts., N.M., U.S. H2 128
San Andrés Sajcabajá, Guat. E2 102
San Andrés Tuxtla, Mex. F11 100
San Andrés y Providencia, state, Col. F7 102
Sananduva, Braz. C12 92
San Angelo, Tx., U.S. C7 130
San Antero, Col. C4 86
San Antonio, Arg. D5 92
San Antonio, Chile F2 92
San Antonio, Col. F4 86
San Antonio, N.M., U.S. F2 128
San Antonio, N.M., U.S. J9 132
San Antonio, Tx., U.S. E9 130
San Antonio, Ur. E9 92
San Antonio, stm., Tx., U.S. F10 130
San Antonio, Cabo, pen., Arg. H9 92
San Antonio, Cabo de, c., Cuba B5 102
San Antonio, Lake, res., Ca., U.S. H4 134
San Antonio, Mount, mtn., Ca., U.S. I8 134
San Antonio, Punta, c., Mex. B3 100
San Antonio Abad see Sant Antoni de Portmany, Spain F12 20
San Antonio Bay, b., Tx., U.S. F11 130
San Antonio de Bravo, Mex. D3 130
San Antonio de La Paz see San Antonio, Arg. D5 92
San Antonio de los Baños, Cuba A6 102
San Antonio de los Cobres, Arg. B4 92
San Antonio del Táchira, Ven. D5 86
San Antonio de Tamanaco, Ven. C8 86
San Antonio el Grande, Mex. F2 130
San Antonio Mountain, mtn., N.M., U.S. E2 128
San Antonio Oeste, Arg. H4 90
Sanatorium, Ms., U.S. F9 122
San Augustine, Tx., U.S. F4 122
San Augustin Pass, p., N.M., U.S. K10 132
Sanāw, Yemen F7 56
Sanāwad, India G6 54
San Bartolomeo in Galdo, Italy C9 24
San Benedetto del Tronto, Italy H10 22
San Benedetto Po, Italy E7 22
San Benedicto, Isla, i., Mex. F3 100
San Benito, Tx., U.S. H10 130
San Benito, stm., Ca., U.S. G4 134
San Benito Mountain, mtn., Ca., U.S. G5 134
San Bernard, stm., Tx., U.S. E12 130
San Bernardino, Ca., U.S. I8 134
San Bernardino Mountains, mts., Ca., U.S. I9 134
San Bernardino Strait, strt., Phil. D5 52
San Bernardo, Chile F2 92
San Bernardo, Islas de, is., Col. C3 86
San Bernardo del Viento, Col. C3 86
Sanbe-yama, vol., Japan D5 40
San Blas, Mex. E6 100
San Blas, Mex. B4 100
San Blas, Cape, c., Fl., U.S. H13 122
San Blas, Golfo de, b., Pan. H8 102
San Blas, Serranía de, mts., Pan. H8 102
San Borja, Bol. B3 90
Sanborn, Ia., U.S. H3 118
Sanborn, N.D., U.S. H15 124
San Bruno, Ca., U.S. F3 134
San Buenaventura, Bol. B3 90
San Buenaventura, Mex. B8 100
San Buenaventura see Ventura, Ca., U.S. I6 134
San Carlos, Chile H2 92
San Carlos, Mex. C9 100
San Carlos, Mex. A8 100
San Carlos, Nic. G5 102
San Carlos, Phil. E4 52
San Carlos, Phil. C3 52
San Carlos, Az., U.S. J6 132
San Carlos, Ca., U.S. F3 134
San Carlos, Ur. G10 92
San Carlos, Ven. C7 86
San Carlos, stm., C.R. G5 102
San Carlos, stm., Ven. C7 86
San Carlos Centro, Arg. E7 92
San Carlos de Bariloche, Arg. H2 90
San Carlos de Bolívar, Arg. H7 92
San Carlos de Guaroa, Col. F5 86
San Carlos del Zulia, Ven. C5 86
San Carlos de Río Negro, Ven. G8 86
San Carlos Reservoir, res., Az., U.S. J6 132
San Cataldo, Italy G7 24
San Cayetano, Arg. I8 92
Sancha, stm., China H1 42
Sanchahe, China B7 38
Sanchenglong, China B4 38
San Ciro de Acosta, Mex. E9 100
San Clemente, Spain E8 20
San Clemente, Ca., U.S. J8 134
San Clemente Island, i., Ca., U.S. K7 134
San Cristóbal, Arg. E7 92
San Cristóbal, Dom. Rep. C12 102
San Cristóbal, Ven. D5 86
San Cristobal, i., Sol. Is. f9 79b
San Cristóbal, Bahía, b., Mex. B1 100
San Cristóbal, Isla, i., Ec. i12 84a
San Cristóbal, Volcán, vol., Nic. F4 102
San Cristóbal de las Casas, Mex. G12 100
Sancti Spíritus, Cuba A8 102
Sancy, Puy de, mtn., Fr. D8 18
Sand, Nor. G2 8
Sand, stm., Ab., Can. B19 138
Sand, stm., S. Afr. F8 70
Sand, stm., S. Afr. C9 70
Sandai, Indon. D7 50
Sandakan, Malay. H2 52
Sândăn, Camb. F8 48
Sandaré, Mali G2 64
Sand Arroyo, stm., U.S. D7 128
Sanday, i., Scot., U.K. B10 12
Sandefjord, Nor. G4 8
Sanderson, Tx., U.S. D5 130
Sandersville, Ga., U.S. D3 116
Sandersville, Ms., U.S. F9 122
Sand Fork, W.V., U.S. F5 114
Sand Hill, stm., Mn., U.S. D2 118
Sand Hills, hills, Ne., U.S. F11 126
Sāndi, India E8 54
Sandia, Peru F4 84
San Diego, Ca., U.S. K8 134
San Diego, Tx., U.S. G9 130
San Diego, Cabo, c., Arg. J3 90
San Diego Aqueduct, aq., Ca., U.S. J8 134
Sandıklı, Tur. E13 28
Sandīla, India E8 54
Sandilands Village, Bah. m18 104f
Sand Key, i., Fl., U.S. I3 116
Sand Lake, l., On., Can. A4 118
Sandnes, Nor. G1 8
Sandoa, D.R.C. F4 66
Sandomierz, Pol. F17 16
Sandoná, Col. G3 86
San Donà di Piave, Italy E9 22
Sandovo, Russia B19 10
Sandoway, Mya. C2 48
Sandown, Eng., U.K. K11 12
Sand Point, Ak., U.S. E7 140
Sandpoint, Id., U.S. B10 136
Sandringham, Austl. E2 76
Sandspit, B.C., Can. E4 106
Sand Springs, Ok., U.S. A2 122
Sand Springs, Tx., U.S. B6 130
Sandstone, Austl. E3 74
Sandstone, Mn., U.S. E5 118
Sandu Ao, b., China H8 42
Sandusky, Mi., U.S. E7 112
Sandusky, Oh., U.S. C3 114
Sandvika, Nor. G4 8
Sandviken, Swe. F7 8
Sandwich, Eng., U.K. J14 12
Sandwich Bay, b., Nmb. C2 70
Sandwick, B.C., Can. G5 138
Sandwīp Island, i., Bngl. G13 54
Sandy, Or., U.S. E4 136
Sandy, Ut., U.S. C5 132
Sandy Bay Mountain, mtn., Me., U.S. E6 110
Sandy Cape, c., Austl. E9 76
Sandy Cape, c., Austl. n12 77a
Sandy Creek, stm., Austl. I5 76
Sandy Hook, Ky., U.S. F2 114
Sandy Hook, spit, N.J., U.S. D12 114
Sandykači, Turkmen. B9 56
Sandy Lake, l., On., Can. E12 106
Sandy Point, c., Trin. r13 105f
Sandy Point Town, St. K./N. C2 105a
Sandy Springs, Ga., U.S. C1 116
Sandžak, reg., Yugo. F6 26
San Elizario, Tx., U.S. C1 130
San Enrique, Arg. G7 92
San Estanislao, Para. B9 92
San Esteban, Isla, i., Mex. A2 100
San Esteban de Gormaz, Spain C7 20
San Felipe, Chile F2 92
San Felipe, Col. G8 86
San Felipe, Mex. F5 98
San Felipe, Mex. E8 100
San Felipe, Ven. B7 86
San Felipe, Cayos de, is., Cuba B6 102
San Felipe Nuevo Mercurio, Mex. C7 100
San Felipe Pueblo, N.M., U.S. F2 128
San Felíu de Guixols see Sant Feliu de Guíxols, Spain C14 20
San Félix, Isla, i., Chile H6 82
San Fernando, Chile G2 92
San Fernando, Mex. C9 100
San Fernando, Mex. F6 130
San Fernando, Phil. B2 52
San Fernando, Phil. C3 52
San Fernando, Spain H4 20
San Fernando, Trin. s12 105f
San Fernando, Ca., U.S. I7 134
San Fernando de Apure, Ven. D8 86
San Fernando de Atabapo, Ven. E8 86
San Fernando del Valle de Catamarca, Arg. D4 92
Sånfjällets Nationalpark, p.o.i., Swe. E5 8
Sanford, Co., U.S. D2 128
Sanford, Fl., U.S. H4 116
Sanford, Me., U.S. G6 110
Sanford, N.C., U.S. A6 116
Sanford, Tx., U.S. F7 128
Sanford, stm., Austl. E3 74
Sanford, Mount, vol., Ak., U.S. D11 140
San Francisco, Arg. E6 92
San Francisco, El Sal. F3 102
San Francisco, Ca., U.S. F3 134
San Francisco, stm., Arg. B5 92
San Francisco, stm., U.S. J8 132
San Francisco, Paso de, p., S.A. C3 92
San Francisco Bay, b., Ca., U.S. F3 134
San Francisco Creek, stm., Tx., U.S. E5 130
San Francisco de Borja, Mex. B5 100
San Francisco de Horizonte, Mex. I4 130
San Francisco del Chañar, Arg. D5 92
San Francisco del Oro, Mex. B5 100
San Francisco del Rincón, Mex. E7 100
San Francisco de Macorís, Dom. Rep. C12 102
San Francisco de Mostazal, Chile F2 92
San Gabriel, Ec. G3 86
San Gabriel Chilac, Mex. F10 100
San Gabriel Mountains, mts., Ca., U.S. I8 134
Sangamankanda Point, c., Sri L. H5 53
Sangamner, India B1 53
Sangamon, stm., Il., U.S. D7 120
Sangar, Russia D14 34
Sangasanga-dalam, Indon. D10 50
San Gavino Monreale, Italy E2 24
Sangay, vol., Ec. I2 86
Sangay, Parque Nacional, p.o.i., Ec. H3 86
Sange, D.R.C. F5 66
Sangeang, Pulau, i., Indon. H11 50
Sanger, Ca., U.S. G6 134
Sanger, Tx., U.S. H11 128
Sângera, Mol. B15 26
Sangerhausen, Ger. E7 16
San Germán, P.R. B1 104a
Sangerville, Me., U.S. E7 110
Sanggan, stm., China A6 42
Sanggau, Indon. C7 50
Sangha, stm., Afr. E3 66
Sanghar, Pak. E2 54
Sangihe, Kepulauan, is., Indon. E7 44
Sangihe, Pulau, i., Indon. E8 44
San Gil, Col. D5 86
Sangilen, hrebet, mts., Russia D17 32
San Gimignano, Italy G7 22
San Giovanni in Fiore, Italy E10 24
San Giovanni in Persiceto, Italy F8 22
San Giovanni Rotondo, Italy C9 24
San Giovanni Valdarno, Italy G8 22
Sangiyn Dalay nuur, l., Mong. B4 36
Sangju, Kor., S. F8 38
Sangkapura, Indon. F8 50
Sângkê, stm., Camb. F6 48
Sangkulirang, Indon. C10 50
Sāngli, India C2 53
Sangmélima, Cam. D2 66
Sāngole, India C2 53
Sangolquí, Ec. H2 86
San Gorgonio Mountain, mtn., Ca., U.S. I9 134
San Gottardo, Passo del, p., Switz. D5 22
Sangre de Cristo Mountains, mts., U.S. E3 128
San Gregorio, Arg. G6 92
Sangre Grande, Trin. s12 105f
Sangro, stm., Italy H11 22
Sangrūr, India C5 54
Sangsang, China D11 54
Sangue, stm., Braz. F6 84
Sangutane, stm., Moz. C11 70
Sangya, China C13 54
San Hipólito, Punta, c., Mex. B1 100
Sanhu, China H6 42
Sânhûr, Egypt I1 58
Sanibel Island, i., Fl., U.S. J3 116
San Ignacio, Arg. C10 92
San Ignacio, Mex. D8 100
San Ignacio, Mex. B2 100
San Ignacio, Para. C9 92
San Ignacio, Isla, i., Mex. C4 100
San Ignacio, Laguna, b., Mex. B2 100
San Ignacio de Moxo, Bol. B3 90
San Ignacio de Velasco, Bol. C4 90
San Isidro, Arg. D5 92
San Isidro, Arg. G8 92
San Isidro del General, C.R. H5 102
San Jacinto, Col. C4 86
San Jacinto, Ca., U.S. J9 134
San Jacinto Peak, mtn., Ca., U.S. J9 134
San Jaime, Arg. E8 92
San Javier, Arg. C10 92
San Javier, Arg. E8 92
San Javier, Bol. C4 90
San Javier, Chile G2 92
San Javier, Mex. H8 130
San Javier, Ur. F8 92
San Javier, stm., Arg. E8 92
Sanjay National Park, p.o.i., India G8 54
San Jerónimo, Guat. E2 102
Sanjiang, China I3 42
Sanjō, Japan B11 40
San Joaquín, Bol. B4 90
San Joaquín, stm., Bol. B4 90
San Joaquin, stm., Ca., U.S. E4 134
San Joaquín de Omaguas, Peru D3 84
San Joaquin Valley, val., Ca., U.S. G5 134
San Jorge, Arg. E6 92
San Jorge, stm., Col. C4 86
San Jorge, Bahía de, b., Mex. F6 98
San Jorge, Golfo, b., Arg. I3 90
San Jorge Island, i., Sol. Is. e8 79b
San José, C.R. H5 102
San José, Mex. F7 130
San Jose, Phil. E3 52
San Jose, Ca., U.S. F4 134
San Jose, Il., U.S. D8 120
San Jose, N.M., U.S. F3 128
San José, Ven. q19 104g
San Jose, stm., N.M., U.S. I9 132
San José, Cerro, mtn., Mex. H2 130
San José, Isla, i., Mex. C3 100
San José, Isla, i., Pan. H8 102
San José, Laguna, b., P.R. B3 104a
San José de Bácum, Mex. B3 100
San José de Batuc, Mex. A3 100
San José de Chiquitos, Bol. C4 90
San José de Feliciano, Arg. E8 92
San José de Guanipa, Ven. C9 86
San José de Jáchal, Arg. E3 92
San José de la Popa, Mex. H7 130
San José de las Lajas, Cuba A6 102
San José del Cabo, Mex. D4 100
San José del Guaviare, Col. F5 86
San José de Mayo, Ur. G9 92
San José de Ocuné, Col. E6 86
San José de Tiznados, Ven. C8 86
San Jose Island, i., Tx., U.S. G11 130
San Juan, Arg. E3 92
San Juan, Mex. E3 130
San Juan, P.R. B3 104a
San Juan, state, Arg. E3 92
San Juan, stm., Arg. F4 92
San Juan, stm., Col. E3 86
San Juan, stm., Mex. H8 130
San Juan, stm., N.A. G5 102
San Juan, stm., U.S. F6 132
San Juan, stm., Ven. B10 86
San Juan, Cabezas de, c., P.R. B4 104a
San Juan, Cabo, c., Arg. J4 90
San Juan Basin, bas., N.M., U.S. G8 132
San Juan Bautista, Mex. H6 130
San Juan Bautista, Para. C9 92
San Juan Bautista see Sant Joan de Labritja, Spain E12 20
San Juan Bautista, Ca., U.S. G4 134
San Juan Creek, stm., Ca., U.S. H5 134
San Juan de Colón, Ven. C5 86
San Juan de Guadalupe, Mex. C7 100
San Juan de la Maguana, Dom. Rep. C12 102
San Juan del Norte, Nic. G6 102
San Juan de los Cayos, Ven. B7 86
San Juan de los Morros, Ven. C8 86
San Juan del Río, Mex. C6 100
San Juan del Río, Mex. E8 100
San Juan del Sur, Nic. G4 102
San Juan de Micay, stm., Col. F3 86
San Juan de Payara, Ven. D8 86
San Juan de Sabinas, Mex. G6 130
San Juanico, Mex. B2 100
San Juan Islands, is., Wa., U.S. B3 136
San Juanito, Isla, i., Mex. E5 100
San Juan Mountains, mts., Co., U.S. C9 98
San Juan Nepomuceno, Col. C4 86
San Juan Nepomuceno, Para. C9 92
San Justo, Arg. E7 92
Sankarani, stm., Afr. G3 64
Sankeshwar, India C2 53
Sankh, stm., India G10 54
Sankheda, India G4 54
Sankosh, stm., Asia E13 54
Sankt Anton am Arlberg, Aus. C7 22
Sankt Gallen, Switz. C6 22
Sankt Goarshausen, Ger. F3 16
Sankt Ingbert, Ger. G3 16
Sankt Michel see Mikkeli, Fin. F12 8
Sankt Moritz, Switz. D6 22
Sankt-Peterburg (Saint Petersburg), Russia A13 10
Sankt Peter-Ording, Ger. B4 16
Sankt Pölten, Aus. B12 22
Sankt Veit an der Glan, Aus. D11 22
Sankt-Vith see Saint-Vith, Bel. D14 14
Sankt Wendel, Ger. G3 16
Sankuru, stm., D.R.C. E4 66
San Lázaro, Cabo, c., Mex. C2 100
San Leandro, Ca., U.S. F3 134
San Leonardo, Mex. G3 130
Şanlıurfa (Urfa), Tur. A9 58
Şanlıurfa, state, Tur. A9 58
San Lorenzo, Arg. D8 92
San Lorenzo, Arg. F7 92
San Lorenzo, Bol. D4 90
San Lorenzo, Ec. G2 86
San Lorenzo, Mex. C7 100
San Lorenzo, P.R. B4 104a
San Lorenzo, stm., Mex. C5 100
San Lorenzo, Cabo, c., Ec. H1 86
San Lorenzo, Isla, i., Mex. A2 100
San Lorenzo, Monte (Cochrane, Cerro), mtn., S.A. I2 90
San Lorenzo de la Parrilla, Spain E8 20
Sanlúcar de Barrameda, Spain H4 20
San Lucas, Bol. D3 90
San Lucas, Mex. D3 100
San Lucas, Cabo, c., Mex. D4 100
San Luis, Arg. F4 92
San Luis, Cuba B10 102
San Luis, Guat. D3 102
San Luis, Co., U.S. D3 128
San Luis, Ven. B7 86
San Luis, state, Arg. F5 92
San Luís, Laguna, l., Bol. B4 90
San Luis, Sierra de, mts., Arg. F5 92
San Luis Creek, stm., Co., U.S. C3 128
San Luis de la Paz, Mex. E8 100
San Luis Gonzaga, Mex. C3 100
San Luis Gonzaga, Bahía, b., Mex. G5 98
San Luis Jilotepeque, Guat. E3 102
San Luis Obispo, Ca., U.S. H5 134
San Luis Potosí, Mex. D8 100
San Luis Potosí, state, Mex. D8 100
San Luis Reservoir, res., Ca., U.S. F4 134
San Luis Río Colorado, Mex. E5 98
San Luis Valley, val., Co., U.S. D3 128
San Manuel, Arg. H8 92
San Manuel, Az., U.S. K6 132
San Marcial, stm., Mex. A3 100
San Marcos, Col. C4 86
San Marcos, Mex. G9 100
San Marcos, Tx., U.S. E9 130
San Marcos, Isla, i., Mex. B2 100
San Marino, S. Mar. G9 22
San Marino, ctry., Eur. G9 22
San Martín, Arg. D5 92
San Martín, Arg. F3 92
San Martín, Col. F5 86
San Martín, stm., Bol. B4 90
San Martin, sci., Ant. B34 81
San Martín, Lago (O'Higgins, Lago), l., S.A. I2 90
San Martín de los Andes, Arg. H2 90
San Martino di Castrozza, ngh., Italy D8 22
San Mateo, Mex. G1 130
San Mateo see Sant Mateu del Maestrat, Spain D10 20
San Mateo, Ca., U.S. F3 134
San Mateo, Fl., U.S. G4 116
San Mateo, N.M., U.S. H9 132
San Matías, Bol. C5 90
San Matías, Golfo, b., Arg. H4 90
Sanmen, China G9 42
Sanmenhsia see Sanmenxia, China D4 42
Sanmenxia, China D4 42
San Miguel, Ec. H2 86
San Miguel, El Sal. F3 102
San Miguel, Mex. A8 100
San Miguel, Pan. H8 102
San Miguel, stm., Bol. B4 90
San Miguel, stm., S.A. G3 86
San Miguel, stm., Co., U.S. E8 132
San Miguel, Golfo de, b., Pan. H8 102
San Miguel de Allende, Mex. E8 100
San Miguel de Cruces, Mex. C6 100
San Miguel del Monte, Arg. G8 92
San Miguel de Salcedo, Ec. H2 86
San Miguel de Tucumán, Arg. C4 92
San Miguel Island, i., Ca., U.S. I5 134
Sanming, China H7 42
San Miniato, Italy G7 22
Sannār, Sudan E6 62
Sannicandro Garganico, Italy I12 22
San Nicolás, Peru G2 84
San Nicolas, Phil. A3 52
San Nicolás de los Arroyos, Arg. F7 92
San Nicolás de los Garza, Mex. C8 100
San Nicolas Island, i., Ca., U.S. J6 134
Sânnicolau Mare, Rom. C7 26
Sannieshof, S. Afr. E7 70
Sannikova, proliv, strt., Russia B16 34
Sano, Japan C12 40
Sanok, Pol. G18 16
Sânon, stm., Fr. F15 14
San Pablo, Phil. C3 52
San Pablo Bay, b., Ca., U.S. E3 134
San Pasqual, Punta, c., Mex. C3 100
San Pedro, Arg. B5 92
San Pedro, Arg. C5 92
San Pedro, Arg. F8 92
San Pedro, Chile F2 92
San Pedro, Col. C4 86
San-Pédro, C. Iv. I3 64
San Pedro, Neth. Ant. A1 105a
San Pedro, state, Para. B9 92
San Pedro, stm., Mex. F8 98
San Pedro, stm., Mex. G2 130
San Pedro, stm., N.A. D2 102
San Pedro, stm., N.A. K6 132
San Pedro, Punta, c., Chile B2 92
San Pedro, Volcán, vol., Chile D3 90
San Pedro Carchá, Guat. E2 102
San Pedro de Jujuy see San Pedro, Arg. B5 92
San Pedro de las Colonias, Mex. C7 100
San Pedro del Gallo, Mex. C6 100
San Pedro del Paraná, Para. C9 92
San Pedro de Macorís, Dom. Rep. C13 102
San Pedro de Ycuamandiyú, Para. B9 92
San Pedro Peaks, mtn., N.M., U.S. G10 132
San Pedro Sula, Hond. E3 102
San Pedro Tabasco, Mex. D2 102
San Pellegrino Terme, Italy E6 22
San Pietro, Isola di, i., Italy E2 24
San Pitch, stm., Ut., U.S. D5 132
Sanquhar, Scot., U.K. F9 12
Sanquianga, Parque Nacional, p.o.i., Col. F2 86
San Quintín, Cabo, c., Mex. F4 98
San Rafael, Arg. G3 92
San Rafael, Chile G2 92
San Rafael, Mex. C8 100
San Rafael, Ca., U.S. E3 134
San Rafael, N.M., U.S. H8 132
San Rafael, Ven. B6 86
San Rafael, stm., Mex. F5 98
San Rafael, stm., Ut., U.S. E6 132
San Rafael del Norte, Nic. F4 102
San Rafael Swell, plat., Ut., U.S. E6 132
San Ramón, Arg. C5 92
San Ramón, Bol. B4 90
San Ramón de la Nueva Orán, Arg. D4 90
San Remo, Italy G4 22
San Rodrigo, stm., Mex. F6 130
San Roque, Arg. D8 92
San Roque, Punta, c., Mex. B1 100
San Saba, Tx., U.S. C9 130
San Saba, stm., Tx., U.S. C9 130
San Salvador, Arg. E8 92
San Salvador, El Sal. F3 102
San Salvador, i., Bah. C10 96
San Salvador de Jujuy, Arg. A5 92
Sansanné-Mango, Togo G5 64
San Sebastián, P.R. B1 104a
San Sebastián see Donostia, Spain A9 20
San Sebastián, Bahía, b., Arg. J3 90
Sansepolcro, Italy G9 22
San Severo, Italy I12 22
Sansha, China H9 42
San Simon, Az., U.S. K7 132
San Simon, stm., Az., U.S. K7 132
San Simon Wash, stm., Az., U.S. K4 132
Sanski Most, Bos. E3 26
San Solano, Arg. E4 92
Sans-Souci, hist., Haiti C11 102
Santa, stm., Peru E2 84
Santa Adélia, Braz. K1 88
Santa Amalia, Spain E4 20
Santa Ana, Bol. B3 90
Santa Ana, Ec. H1 86
Santa Ana, El Sal. E3 102
Santa Ana, Mex. F7 98
Santa Ana, Mex. C8 100
Santa Ana, Ca., U.S. J8 134
Santa Ana, Ven. C9 86
Santa Ana del Alto Beni, Bol. C3 90
Santa Anna, Tx., U.S. C8 130
Santa Bárbara, Chile H2 92
Santa Barbara, Col. E4 86
Santa Bárbara, Hond. E3 102
Santa Bárbara, Mex. B6 100
Santa Barbara, Ca., U.S. I6 134
Santa Bárbara, Ven. D6 86
Santa Barbara Channel, strt., Ca., U.S. I6 134
Santa Barbara Island, i., Ca., U.S. J7 134
Santa Catalina, Gulf of, b., Ca., U.S. J7 134
Santa Catalina, Isla, i., Mex. C3 100
Santa Catalina Island, i., Ca., U.S. J7 134
Santa Catarina, Mex. C8 100
Santa Catarina, Mex. L10 134
Santa Catarina, state, Braz. C12 92
Santa Catarina, Ilha de, i., Braz. C13 92
Santa Cecília, Braz. C12 92
Santa Clara, Col. I7 86
Santa Clara, Cuba A7 102
Santa Clara, Ca., U.S. F3 134
Santa Clara, Ut., U.S. F3 132
Santa Clara, stm., Ca., U.S. I7 134
Santa Clarita, Ca., U.S. I7 134
Santa Clotilde, Peru D3 84
Santa Coloma de Farners, Spain C13 20
Santa Coloma de Farnés see Santa Coloma de Farners, Spain C13 20
Santa Comba, Spain A2 20
Santa Cruz, Braz. J5 88
Santa Cruz, Braz. D8 88
Santa Cruz, C.R. G5 102
Santa Cruz, Phil. C2 52
Santa Cruz, Phil. D4 52
Santa Cruz, Phil. C3 52
Santa Cruz, Ca., U.S. G3 134
Santa Cruz, state, Arg. I2 90
Santa Cruz, stm., Arg. J3 90
Santa Cruz, stm., N.A. J4 132
Santa Cruz, Isla, i., Ec. i11 84a
Santa Cruz Cabrália, Braz. I6 88
Santa Cruz de la Sierra, Bol. C4 90
Santa Cruz del Quiché, Guat. E2 102
Santa Cruz del Sur, Cuba B9 102
Santa Cruz de Mudela, Spain F7 20
Santa Cruz do Capibaribe, Braz. D7 88
Santa Cruz do Piauí, Braz. D5 88
Santa Cruz do Rio Pardo, Braz. L1 88
Santa Cruz do Sul, Braz. D11 92
Santa Cruz Island, i., Ca., U.S. J6 134
Santa Cruz Islands, is., Sol. Is. E7 72
Santa Elena, Arg. E8 92
Santa Elena, Ec. I1 86
Santa Elena, Mex. B7 100
Santa Elena, Bahía de, b., Ec. H1 86
Santa Elena, Cabo, c., C.R. G4 102
Santa Eufemia, Spain F6 20
Santa Eulalia, Spain D9 20
Santa Eulalia del Río see Santa Eulària del Riu, Spain E12 20
Santa Eulària del Riu, Spain E12 20
Santa Fe, Arg. E7 92
Santa Fe, Spain G7 20
Santa Fe, N.M., U.S. F3 128
Santa Fe, state, Arg. D7 92
Santa Fe, stm., Fl., U.S. G3 116
Santa Fe Baldy, mtn., N.M., U.S. F3 128
Santa Fe de Bogotá, Col. E4 86
Santa Fe de Minas, Braz. I3 88
Santa Fé do Sul, Braz. D6 90
Santa Filomena, Braz. E3 88
Sant'Agata di Militello, Italy F8 24
Santa Gertrudis, Mex. G2 130
Santa Helena, Braz. B3 88
Santa Helena de Goiás, Braz. G7 84
Santai, China F1 42
Santa Inês, Braz. G5 88
Santa Inés, Bahía, b., Mex. B3 100
Santa Inés, Isla, i., Chile J2 90
Santa Isabel, Arg. H4 92
Santa Isabel, P.R. C3 104a
Santa Isabel, i., Sol. Is. e8 79b
Santa Isabel, stm., Mex. F1 130
Santa Isabel, Pico de, mtn., Eq. Gui. I6 64
Santa Isabel Creek, stm., Tx., U.S. G8 130
Santa Juliana, Braz. J2 88
Santal, Baie du, b., N. Cal. m16 79d
Santa Lucía, Arg. D8 92
Santa Lucía, Ur. G9 92
Santa Lucia Range, mts., Ca., U.S. G4 134
Santaluz, Braz. F6 88
Santa Luzia, Braz. D7 88
Santa Magdalena, Arg. G6 92
Santa Magdalena, Isla, i., Mex. C2 100
Santa Margarita, Ca., U.S. H5 134
Santa Margarita, Isla, i., Mex. C2 100
Santa Margherita Ligure, Italy F6 22
Santa María, Arg. C4 92
Santa Maria, Braz. D10 92
Santa María, Mex. F6 130
Santa Maria, Ca., U.S. I5 134

Name	Map Ref.	Page

Name	Map Ref.	Page
Shoal, stm., Fl., U.S.	G12	122
Shoal Creek, stm., U.S.	H3	120
Shoal Creek, stm., Mo., U.S.	E4	120
Shoalhaven, stm., Austl.	J8	76
Shoal Lake, l., Can.	B3	118
Shoals, In., U.S.	F11	120
Shoalwater Bay, b., Austl.	D8	76
Shōbara, Japan	E6	40
Shōdo-shima, i., Japan	E7	40
Sholingnur, India	E4	53
Shorāpur, India	C3	53
Shoreacres, B.C., Can.	G13	138
Shorewood, Wi., U.S.	E2	112
Shorkot, Pak.	C3	54
Shortland Island, i., Sol. Is.	d6	79b
Shortland Islands, is., Sol. Is.	d6	79b
Shoshone, Id., U.S.	H12	136
Shoshone, stm., Wy., U.S.	C4	126
Shoshone, South Fork, stm., Wy., U.S.	G17	136
Shoshone Lake, l., Wy., U.S.	F15	136
Shoshone Mountains, mts., Nv., U.S.	E8	134
Shoshone Peak, mtn., Nv., U.S.	G9	134
Shoshone Range, mts., Nv., U.S.	C9	134
Shoshong, Bots.	C8	70
Shostka, Ukr.	D4	32
Shouchang, China	G8	42
Shouguang, China	C8	42
Shouning, China	H8	42
Shouxian, China	E7	42
Shouyang, China	C5	42
Show Low, Az., U.S.	I6	132
Shqipëria see Albania, ctry., Eur.	C14	24
Shreve, Oh., U.S.	D4	114
Shreveport, La., U.S.	E5	122
Shrewsbury, Eng., U.K.	I10	12
Shri Dūngargarh, India	D4	54
Shri Mohangarh, India	E3	54
Shū see Šu, Kaz.	F12	32
Shū see Ču, stm., Asia	F11	32
Shu, stm., China	D8	42
Shuajingsi, China	B9	46
Shuangcheng, China	B7	38
Shuangfeng, China	H5	42
Shuanggou, China	E5	42
Shuanggou, China	D7	42
Shuangji, stm., China	D5	42
Shuangjiang, China	G4	36
Shuangliao, China	C5	38
Shuangpai, China	I4	42
Shuangshutai, China	C4	38
Shuangyang, China	C6	38
Shuangyashan, China	B11	36
Shubrâ el-Kheima, Egypt	H1	58
Shubuta, Ms., U.S.	F10	122
Shucheng, China	F7	42
Shuibatang, China	G2	42
Shuiji, China	H8	42
Shuijingtang, China	G2	42
Shuikoushan, China	H5	42
Shuitou, China	I8	42
Shuiye, China	C5	42
Shujāābād, Pak.	D3	54
Shujālpur, India	G6	54
Shuksan, Mount, mtn., Wa., U.S.	B5	136
Shulan, China	B7	38
Shulaps Peak, mtn., B.C., Can.	F8	138
Shule, China	B12	56
Shule, stm., China	C4	36
Shumagin Islands, is., Ak., U.S.	F7	140
Shunchang, China	H7	42
Shunde, China	J5	42
Shungnak, Ak., U.S.	C8	140
Shunyi, China	A7	42
Shuqualak, Ms., U.S.	E10	122
Shurkhua, Mya.	A1	48
Shurugwi, Zimb.	D5	68
Shūshtar, Iran	C6	56
Shuswap, stm., B.C., Can.	F12	138
Shuswap Lake, l., B.C., Can.	F11	138
Shuwak, Sudan	E7	62
Shuyak Island, i., Ak., U.S.	E9	140
Shuyang, China	D8	42
Shwangliao see Liaoyuan, China	C6	38
Shwebo, Mya.	A2	48
Shwegun, Mya.	D3	48
Shwegyin, Mya.	D3	48
Shymkent see Šymkent, Kaz.	F11	32
Shyok, India	A7	54
Shyok, stm., Asia	B4	46
Si, stm., China	D7	42
Sia, Indon.	G9	44
Siāhān Range, mts., Pak.	D9	56
Siak, stm., Indon.	C2	50
Siak Sri Indrapura, Indon.	C3	50
Siālkot, Pak.	B5	54
Siam see Thailand, ctry., Asia	E5	48
Siam, Gulf of see Thailand, Gulf of, b., Asia	G5	48
Sian see Xi'an, China	D3	42
Siangtan see Xiangtan, China	H5	42
Sianów, Pol.	B12	16
Siantan, Pulau, i., Indon.	B4	50
Siapa, stm., Ven.	G9	86
Siargao Island, i., Phil.	F6	52
Siasconset, Ma., U.S.	C15	114
Siasi, Phil.	H3	52
Siasi Island, i., Phil.	H3	52
Siaškotan, ostrov, i., Russia	G19	34
Siau, Pulau, i., Indon.	E7	44
Šiauliai, Lith.	E6	10
Sibaj, Russia	D9	32
Sibayi, Lake, l., S. Afr.	E11	70
Šibenik, Cro.	G12	22
Siberia see Sibir', reg., Russia	C12	34
Siberut, Pulau, i., Indon.	D1	50
Sibi, Pak.	D10	56
Sibigo, Indon.	K2	48
Sibir', reg., Russia	C12	34
Sibircevo, Russia	B10	38
Sibirjakova, ostrov, i., Russia	B4	34
Sibiti, Congo	E2	66
Sibiu, Rom.	D11	26
Sibiu, state, Rom.	D11	26
Sibley, Ia., U.S.	H3	118
Sibley, La., U.S.	E5	122
Sibley, Ms., U.S.	F7	122
Sibley Peninsula, pen., On., Can.	C10	118
Sibolga, Indon.	C1	50
Sibsāgar, India	C7	46
Sibu, Malay.	B7	50
Sibuguey Bay, b., Phil.	G4	52
Sibut, C.A.R.	C3	66
Sibutu Island, i., Phil.	H2	52
Sibutu Passage, strt., Asia	H2	52
Sibuyan Island, i., Phil.	D4	52
Sibuyan Sea, Phil.	D4	52
Sicapoo, Mount, mtn., Phil.	B3	52
Siccus, stm., Austl.	H2	76
Sichang see Xichang, China	F5	36
Si Chon, Thai.	H4	48
Sichuan, state, China	E5	36
Sichuan Pendi, bas., China	F1	42
Sichuanzhai, China	A5	48
Sicilia, state, Italy	F8	24
Sicilia (Sicily), i., Italy	G7	24
Sicily see Sicilia, state, Italy	F8	24
Sicily see Sicilia, i., Italy	G7	24
Sicily, Strait of, strt.	G5	24
Sicily Island, La., U.S.	F7	122
Sicuani, Peru	F3	84
Sidareja, Indon.	G6	50
Sidas, Indon.	C6	50
Siddhapur, India	G4	54
Siddipet, India	B4	53
Sidéradougou, Burkina	G4	64
Siderno, Italy	F10	24
Siderópolis, Braz.	D13	92
Síderos, Ákra, c., Grc.	H9	28
Sidhauli, India	E8	54
Sidhi, India	F8	54
Sîdi Barrâni, Egypt	A5	62
Sidi bel Abbès, Alg.	B4	64
Sidi-Ifni, Mor.	D2	64
Siding Spring Mountain, mtn., Austl.	H7	76
Sidirókastro, Grc.	B6	28
Sidi Sâlim, Egypt	G1	58
Sidlaghatta, India	E3	53
Sidley, Mount, mtn., Ant.	C28	81
Sidmouth, Eng., U.K.	K9	12
Sidnaw, Mi., U.S.	E10	118
Sidney, B.C., Can.	H7	138
Sidney, Il., U.S.	D9	120
Sidney, Mt., U.S.	G9	124
Sidney, Ne., U.S.	F10	126
Sidney, N.Y., U.S.	B10	114
Sidney, Oh., U.S.	D1	114
Sidney Lanier, Lake, res., Ga., U.S.	B2	116
Sidon see Ṣaydā, Leb.	E6	58
Sidon, Ms., U.S.	D8	122
Sidorovsk, Russia	A14	32
Sidra, Gulf of see Surt, Khalīj, b., Libya	A3	62
Sidrolândia, Braz.	D6	90
Siedlce, Pol.	D18	16
Siedlce, state, Pol.	D17	16
Siegburg, Ger.	F3	16
Siegen, Ger.	F4	16
Siemianowice Śląskie, Pol.	F15	16
Siĕmpang, Camb.	E8	48
Siĕmréab, Camb.	F6	48
Siena, Italy	G8	22
Sienyang see Xianyang, China	D3	42
Sieradz, Pol.	E14	16
Sieradz, state, Pol.	E14	16
Sieraków, Pol.	D12	16
Sierpc, Pol.	D15	16
Sierra Blanca, Tx., U.S.	C2	130
Sierra Blanca Peak, mtn., N.M., U.S.	H3	128
Sierra Chica, Arg.	H7	92
Sierra Colorada, Arg.	H3	90
Sierra Gorda, Chile	D3	90
Sierra Leone, ctry., Afr.	H2	64
Sierra Mojada, Mex.	G4	130
Sierra Nevada see Nevada, Sierra, mts., Ca., U.S.	F6	134
Sierra Nevada, Parque Nacional, p.o.i., Ven.	C6	86
Sierra Vista, Az., U.S.	L6	132
Sierre, Switz.	D4	22
Siesta Key, Fl., U.S.	I3	116
Sífnos, i., Grc.	F7	28
Sifón Villanueva, Mex.	G7	130
Sig, Russia	D16	8
Sigatoka, Fiji	q18	79e
Sigep, Indon.	D1	50
Sighetu Marmației, Rom.	B10	26
Sighișoara, Rom.	C11	26
Siglan, Russia	E19	34
Sigli, Indon.	J2	48
Siglufjörður, Ice.	j30	8a
Sigmaringen, Ger.	H5	16
Signal Mountain, Tn., U.S.	B13	122
Signal Mountain, mtn., Vt., U.S.	F4	110
Signy, sci., Ant.	B36	81
Sigourney, Ia., U.S.	C5	120
Sigsig, Ec.	D2	84
Siguanea, Ensenada de la, b., Cuba	B6	102
Siguatepeque, Hond.	E3	102
Sigüenza, Spain	C8	20
Siguiri, Gui.	G3	64
Sigulda, Lat.	C7	10
Sigurd, Ut., U.S.	E5	132
Siguri Falls, wtfl, Tan.	F7	66
Sihabuhabu, Dolok, mtn., Indon.	B1	50
Sihanoukville see Kâmpóng Saôm, Camb.	G6	48
Sihor, India	H3	54
Sihorā, India	G8	54
Sihote-Alin', mts., Russia	E17	30
Sihtovo, Russia	E15	10
Sihui, China	J5	42
Siirt, Tur.	B5	56
Sija, Russia	E19	8
Sijunjung, Indon.	D2	50
Sikandarābād, India	D6	54
Sikanni Chief, stm., B.C., Can.	D6	106
Sikao, Thai.	I4	48
Sīkar, India	E5	54
Sikasso, Mali	G3	64
Sikeston, Mo., U.S.	H8	120
Sikhote-Alin Mountains see Sihote-Alin', mts., Russia	E17	30
Sikiang see Xi, stm., China	J5	42
Siking see Xi'an, China	D3	42
Síkinos, i., Grc.	G8	28
Sikkim, state, India	E12	54
Sikonge, Tan.	F6	66
Sikotan, ostrov (Shikotan-tō), i., Russia	C17	38
Siktjah, Russia	B13	34
Sikuati, Malay.	G1	52
Sikyón, hist., Grc.	F5	28
Sil, stm., Spain	B3	20
Šila, Russia	E7	34
Šilalė, Lith.	E5	10
Silao, Mex.	E8	100
Silas, Al., U.S.	F10	122
Silaut, Indon.	E2	50
Silay, Phil.	E4	52
Silchar, India	F14	54
Şile, Tur.	B12	28
Siler City, N.C., U.S.	I6	114
Sileru, stm., India	C5	53
Silesia, hist. reg., Eur.	F13	16
Siletyteniz, ozero, l., Kaz.	D12	32
Siletz, Or., U.S.	F3	136
Siletz, stm., Or., U.S.	F3	136
Silgadhī, Nepal	D8	54
Silghāt, India	E14	54
Silhouette, i., Sey.	j13	69b
Siliana, Tun.	H3	24
Siliana, Oued, stm., Tun.	I3	24
Silifke, Tur.	B4	58
Siling Co, l., China	C12	54
Silistra, Blg.	E14	26
Silivri, Tur.	B11	28
Siljan, l., Swe.	F6	8
Šilka, Russia	F12	34
Šilka, stm., Russia	F12	34
Silkeborg, Den.	H3	8
Sillamäe, Est.	A10	10
Sillem Island, i., Nu., Can.	A16	106
Sillian, Aus.	D9	22
Sillon de Talbert, pen., Fr.	F5	14
Šiloviči, Russia	E15	10
Silsbee, Tx., U.S.	G4	122
Silton, Sk., Can.	D9	124
Siluas, Indon.	C6	50
Šilutė, Lith.	E4	10
Silvânia, Braz.	I1	88
Silvassa, India	H4	54
Silver, Tx., U.S.	B7	130
Silver Bank Passage, strt., N.A.	B12	102
Silver Bell, Az., U.S.	K5	132
Silver City, N.M., U.S.	K8	132
Silver City, N.C., U.S.	B6	116
Silver Creek, Ms., U.S.	F9	122
Silver Creek, Ne., U.S.	F15	126
Silver Creek, stm., Az., U.S.	I6	132
Silver Creek, stm., Or., U.S.	G7	136
Silverdale, Wa., U.S.	C4	136
Silver Lake, Ks., U.S.	E2	120
Silver Lake, Mn., U.S.	G4	118
Silver Lake, Wi., U.S.	F1	112
Silver Lake, l., Or., U.S.	G7	136
Silver Lake, l., Or., U.S.	G5	136
Silver Spring, Md., U.S.	E8	114
Silver Star Mountain, mtn., Wa., U.S.	B6	136
Silverthrone Mountain, vol., B.C., Can.	E4	138
Silverton, Austl.	H3	76
Silverton, B.C., Can.	G13	138
Silverton, Co., U.S.	F9	132
Silverton, Tx., U.S.	G7	128
Silvi, Italy	H11	22
Silvia, Col.	F3	86
Silvies, stm., Or., U.S.	G7	136
Šimanovsk, Russia	F14	34
Simao, China	A5	48
Simão Dias, Braz.	F6	88
Simav, Tur.	D11	28
Simav, stm., Tur.	C11	28
Simbach, Ger.	H8	16
Simbo Island, i., Sol. Is.	e7	79b
Simcoe, On., Can.	F9	112
Simcoe, Lake, l., On., Can.	D10	112
Simdega, India	G10	54
Simeria, Rom.	D10	26
Simeulue, Pulau, i., Indon.	K2	48
Simferopol', Ukr.	G15	6
Simikoṭ, Nepal	C8	54
Similkameen, stm., N.A.	G10	138
Simití, Col.	D4	86
Simi Valley, Ca., U.S.	I7	134
Simizu see Shimizu, Japan	D11	40
Simla, Co., U.S.	B4	128
Simmern, Ger.	G3	16
Simmie, Sk., Can.	E5	124
Simms, Mt., U.S.	C15	136
Simnas, Lith.	F6	10
Simoca, Arg.	C5	92
Simões, Braz.	D5	88
Simojärvi, l., Fin.	C12	8
Simojovel, Mex.	G12	100
Simon, Lac, l., Qc., Can.	E1	110
Simonette, stm., Ab., Can.	A12	138
Simonoseki see Shimonoseki, Japan	F3	40
Simonstad see Simon's Town, S. Afr.	I4	70
Simon's Town, S. Afr.	I4	70
Simoom Sound, B.C., Can.	F4	138
Simpang, Indon.	D3	50
Simpang-kiri, stm., Indon.	K3	48
Simplon Pass, p., Switz.	D4	22
Simpson Desert, des., Austl.	D7	74
Simpson Island, i., On., Can.	C11	118
Simpson Peninsula, pen., Nu., Can.	B13	106
Simpson Strait, strt., Nu., Can.	B11	106
Simpsonville, S.C., U.S.	B3	116
Simrishamn, Swe.	I6	8
Simsonbaai, Neth. Ant.	A1	105a
Simunjan, Malay.	C7	50
Simušir, ostrov, i., Russia	G19	34
Sīna, stm., India	B2	53
Sinabang, Indon.	K3	48
Sinabung, Gunung, vol., Indon.	K4	48
Sinai (Sinai Peninsula), pen., Egypt	J4	58
Sinai, Mount see Mûsa, Gebel, mtn., Egypt	J5	58
Sinai, Mount, vol., Gren.	q10	105e
Sinaia, Rom.	D12	26
Sinai Peninsula see Sinai, pen., Egypt	J4	58
Sinajana, Guam	j10	78c
Sinaloa, state, Mex.	C5	100
Sinaloa, stm., Mex.	C5	100
Sinamaica, Ven.	B6	86
Sinan, China	H3	42
Sinanpaşa, Tur.	E13	28
Sīnāwin, Libya	A2	62
Sincan, Tur.	D15	28
Sincé, Col.	B2	84
Sincelejo, Col.	C4	86
Sinch'ang-ŭp, Kor., N.	D8	38
Sin-ch'on, Kor., N.	E6	38
Sinclair, Wy., U.S.	B9	132
Sinclair, Lake, res., Ga., U.S.	C2	116
Sinclair Mills, B.C., Can.	B9	138
Sind, state, Pak.	F2	54
Sind, stm., India	F7	54
Sindañgan, Phil.	F4	52
Sindangbarang, Indon.	G5	50
Sindara, Gabon	E2	66
Sindari, India	F3	54
Sindelfingen, Ger.	H4	16
Sindhnūr, India	D3	53
Sindhulī Māḍhi, Nepal	E10	54
Sindingale, Mya.	C2	48
Sindor, Russia	B8	32
Sines, Port.	G2	20
Sinfra, C. Iv.	H3	64
Singalamwe, Nmb.	D3	68
Singapore, Sing.	C3	50
Singapore, ctry., Asia	L6	48
Singapore, Strait of, strt., Asia	C4	50
Singaraja, Indon.	H9	50
Sing Buri, Thai.	E5	48
Singen, Ger.	I4	16
Singida, Tan.	E6	66
Singitic Gulf see Agíou Órous, Kólpos, b., Grc.	C6	28
Singkaling Hkāmti, Mya.	C8	46
Singkang, Indon.	F11	50
Singkawang, Indon.	C6	50
Singkep, Pulau, i., Indon.	D4	50
Singkil, Indon.	K3	48
Singkuang, Indon.	C1	50
Singleton, Austl.	I8	76
Singleton, Mount, mtn., Austl.	E3	74
Singuédeze (Shingwidzi), stm., Afr.	C10	70
Sining see Xining, China	D5	36
Sinj, Cro.	G13	22
Sinjah, Sudan	E6	62
Sinjai, Indon.	F12	50
Sinjaja, stm., Eur.	D11	10
Sinjaja, stm., Russia	D14	34
Sinjuga, Russia	E12	34
Sinkāt, Sudan	D7	62
Sinkiang see Xinjiang, state, China	A5	46
Sinnamahoning, Pa., U.S.	C7	114
Sinnamary, Fr. Gu.	B7	84
Sinnar, India	B2	53
Sinnûris, Egypt	I1	58
Sinnyŏng, Kor., S.	C1	40
Sinoie, Lacul, l., Rom.	E15	26
Sinop, Tur.	A4	56
Sinsheim, Ger.	G4	16
Sinsiang see Xinxiang, China	D5	42
Sinskoe, Russia	D14	34
Sintang, Indon.	C7	50
Sint Christoffelberg, hill, Neth. Ant.	p21	104g
Sint Eustatius, i., Neth. Ant.	B1	105a
Sint Helenabaai, b., S. Afr.	H3	70
Sint Kruis, Neth. Ant.	p21	104g
Sint Maarten (Saint-Martin), i., N.A.	A1	105a
Sint Nicolaas, Aruba	p20	104g
Sint-Niklaas, Bel.	C12	14
Sintra, Port.	F1	20
Sint-Truiden, Bel.	D14	14
Sinú, stm., Col.	C4	86
Sinŭiju, Kor., N.	D6	38
Sió, stm., Hung.	C5	26
Siocon, Phil.	G4	52
Siófok, Hung.	C5	26
Sion, Switz.	D4	22
Siorapaluk, Grnld.	B12	141
Sioux Center, Ia., U.S.	H2	118
Sioux City, Ia., U.S.	B1	120
Sioux Falls, S.D., U.S.	H2	118
Sioux Lookout, On., Can.	A6	118
Sioux Narrows, On., Can.	B4	118
Sioux Rapids, Ia., U.S.	B2	120
Sipalay, Phil.	F4	52
Šipan, Otok, i., Cro.	H14	22
Sipapo, stm., Ven.	E8	86
Siparia, Trin.	s12	105f
Šipčenski Prohod (Shipka Pass), p., Blg.	G12	26
Šipicyno, Russia	F22	8
Siping, China	C6	38
Sipiwesk Lake, l., Mb., Can.	D11	106
Siple, Mount, mtn., Ant.	C28	81
Siple Island, i., Ant.	C28	81
Si Prachan, Thai.	E4	48
Sipsey, stm., Al., U.S.	D10	122
Šipunskij, mys, c., Russia	F21	34
Sipura, Pulau, i., Indon.	E1	50
Siqueira Campos, Braz.	A12	92
Siquia, stm., Nic.	F5	102
Siquijor, Phil.	F4	52
Siquijor Island, i., Phil.	F4	52
Siquirres, C.R.	G6	102
Şīra, India	E3	53
Šira, Russia	D16	32
Sira, stm., Nor.	G2	8
Si Racha, Thai.	F5	48
Siracusa, Italy	G9	24
Sirāhā, Nepal	E11	54
Sirājganj, Bngl.	F12	54
Şīr Banī Yās, i., U.A.E.	E7	56
Sirdar, B.C., Can.	G14	138
Sir Douglas, Mount, mtn., Can.	F15	138
Sir Edward Pellew Group, is., Austl.	C7	74
Siret, Rom.	B12	26
Siret (Seret), stm., Eur.	A12	26
Sirḥān, Wādī as-, val., Sau. Ar.	H8	58
Sirik, Tanjong, c., Malay.	B7	50
Sirikit Reservoir, res., Thai.	D5	48
Sirino, Monte, mtn., Italy	D9	24
Sir James MacBrien, Mount, mtn., N.T., Can.	C4	106
Sīrjān, Iran	D8	56
Sirkeli, Tur.	C15	28
Sirocina, Bela.	E12	10
Şirohi, India	F4	54
Širokovo, Russia	C17	32
Sironj, India	F6	54
Sırpsındığı, Tur.	B9	28
Sīrrī, Jazīreh-ye, i., Iran	D7	56
Sirsa, India	D5	54
Sir Sandford, Mount, mtn., B.C., Can.	E13	138
Sirsi, India	D2	53
Sirsilla, India	B4	53
Sirte, Gulf of see Surt, Khalīj, b., Libya	A3	62
Sir Timothy's Hill, hill, St. K./N.	C2	105a
Şirupa, stm., Mex.	G8	98
Širvintos, Lith.	E7	10
Sir Wilfrid Laurier, Mount, mtn., B.C., Can.	D11	138
Sisaba, mtn., Tan.	F6	66
Sisak, Cro.	E13	22
Si Sa Ket, Thai.	E7	48
Sishen, S. Afr.	E6	70
Sishilijie, China	G7	42
Sishui, China	D7	42
Sisib Lake, l., Mb., Can.	B14	124
Sisimiut see Holsteinsborg, Grnld.	D15	141
Siskiyou Pass, p., Or., U.S.	A3	134
Sisseton, S.D., U.S.	F1	118
Sīstān, reg., Asia	C9	56
Sister Bay, Wi., U.S.	C2	112
Sisteron, Fr.	E11	18
Sisters, Or., U.S.	F5	136
Sistersville, W.V., U.S.	E5	114
Sit', stm., Russia	B20	10
Sītāmarhi, India	E10	54
Sītāpur, India	E8	54
Siteia, Grc.	H9	28
Siteki, Swaz.	E10	70
Si Thep, hist., Thai.	E5	48
Sithoniá, pen., Grc.	C6	28
Sitidgi Lake, l., N.T., Can.	B4	106
Sítio d'Abadia, Braz.	H2	88
Sitka, Ak., U.S.	E12	140
Sitkalidak Island, i., Ak., U.S.	E9	140
Sittard, Neth.	C14	14
Sitten see Sion, Switz.	D4	22
Sittoung, stm., Mya.	C3	48
Sittwe, Mya.	D7	46
Siuri, India	G11	54
Siuslaw, stm., Or., U.S.	G3	136
Sivaganga, India	G4	53
Sivakāsi, India	G3	53
Sivaki, Russia	F14	34
Sivas, Tur.	B4	56
Ševeluč, vulkan, vol., Russia	E21	34
Siverek, Tur.	B4	56
Siverskij, Russia	A12	10
Sivrihisar, Tur.	D14	28
Siwa, Egypt	B5	62
Siwalik Range, mts., India	C6	54
Siwān, India	E10	54
Sixian, China	E7	42
Sixth Cataract see Sablūkah, Shallāl as-, wtfl, Sudan	D6	62
Siyang, China	E8	42
Sizuoka see Shizuoka, Japan	E11	40
Sjælland, i., Den.	I4	8
Sjalec, Bela.	G13	10
Sjamža, Russia	F19	8
Sjarheevičy, Bela.	G10	10
Sjas', stm., Russia	A15	10
Sjas'stroj, Russia	F15	8
Sjenica, Yugo.	F7	26
Sjuzikozero, Russia	F17	8
Skærfjorden, b., Grnld.	B22	141
Skaftafell Nasjonalpark, p.o.i., Ice.	k31	8a
Skagafjörður, b., Ice.	j31	8a
Skagen, Den.	H4	8
Skagerrak, strt., Eur.	H3	8
Skagit, stm., N.A.	H8	138
Skagway, Ak., U.S.	E12	140
Skaistkalne, Lat.	D7	10
Skalbmierz, Pol.	F16	16
Skalino, Russia	G18	8
Skalistyj Golec, gora, mtn., Russia	E12	34
Skalka, l., Swe.	C8	8
Skåne, state, Swe.	H5	8
Skārdu, Pak.	B12	56
Skarszewy, Pol.	B14	16
Skarżysko-Kamienna, Pol.	E16	16
Skaudvilė, Lith.	E5	10
Skawina, Pol.	F15	16
Skeena, stm., B.C., Can.	B1	138
Skeena Crossing, B.C., Can.	A3	138
Skeena Mountains, mts., B.C., Can.	D5	106
Skegness, Eng., U.K.	H13	12
Skei, Nor.	F2	8
Skeleton Coast, cst., Nmb.	B1	70
Skellefteå, Swe.	D9	8
Skellefteälven, stm., Swe.	D8	8
Skellytown, Tx., U.S.	F7	128
Skerryvore, r., Scot., U.K.	E5	12
Ski, Nor.	G4	8
Skiatook, Ok., U.S.	H1	120
Skibbereen, Ire.	J3	12
Skidal', Bela.	G7	10
Skiddaw, mtn., Eng., U.K.	G9	12
Skidmore, Tx., U.S.	F10	130
Skien, Nor.	G3	8
Skierniewice, Pol.	E16	16
Skierniewice, state, Pol.	D16	16
Skikda, Alg.	B6	64
Skilak Lake, l., Ak., U.S.	D9	140
Skillet Fork, stm., Il., U.S.	F9	120
Skinnastaðir, Ice.	j31	8a
Skipton, Austl.	K4	76
Skipton, Eng., U.K.	H10	12
Skive, Den.	H3	8
Skjálfandafljót, stm., Ice.	k31	8a
Šklad, Russia	B13	34
Šklou, Bela.	F13	10
Škofja Loka, Slvn.	D11	22
Skoganvarre, Nor.	B11	8
Skoganvarri see Skoganvarre, Nor.	B11	8
Skokie, Il., U.S.	F2	112
Skón, Camb.	F7	48
Skópelos, i., Grc.	D6	28
Skopin, Russia	D5	32
Skopje, Mac.	A4	28
Skoplje see Skopje, Mac.	A4	28
Skórcz, Pol.	C14	16
Skövde, Swe.	G5	8
Skowhegan, Me., U.S.	F7	110
Skownan, Mb., Can.	C14	124
Skriplivka, Russia	C13	10
Skrudaliena, Lat.	E9	10
Skudeneshavn, Nor.	G1	8
Skukuza, S. Afr.	D10	70
Skull Valley, Az., U.S.	I4	132
Skuna, can., Ms., U.S.	D9	122
Skunk, stm., Ia., U.S.	D6	120
Skuodas, Lith.	D4	10
Skuratovskij, Russia	F20	10
Skwierzyna, Pol.	D11	16
Skye, Island of, i., Scot., U.K.	D6	12
Skyland, N.C., U.S.	A3	116
Skyring, Península, pen., Chile	I1	90
Skyring, Seno, strt., Chile	J2	90
Skýros, i., Grc.	E7	28
Slabada, Bela.	G11	10
Slagelse, Den.	I4	8
Slagnäs, Swe.	D8	8
Slamet, Gunung, vol., Indon.	G6	50
Slancy, Russia	A11	10
Slaney, stm., Ire.	H6	12
Slănic, Rom.	D12	26
Slano, Cro.	H14	22
Slaný, Czech Rep.	F10	16
Slater, Ia., U.S.	C4	120
Slater, Mo., U.S.	E4	120
Slatina, Cro.	E14	22
Slatina, Rom.	E11	26
Slaughter, La., U.S.	G7	122
Slaunae, Bela.	F12	10
Slautnoe, Russia	D22	34
Slave, stm., Can.	C8	106
Slave Coast, cst., Afr.	H5	64
Slave Lake, Ab., Can.	A16	138
Slavgorod, Russia	D13	32
Slavjanka, Russia	C9	38
Slavjansk-na-Kubani, Russia	E5	32
Slavkoviči, Russia	C12	10
Slavonia see Slavonija, hist. reg., Cro.	E14	22
Slavonija, hist. reg., Cro.	E14	22
Slavonski Brod, Cro.	E15	22
Slavsk, Russia	E4	10
Sławno, Pol.	B12	16
Slayton, Mn., U.S.	G3	118
Sleaford, Eng., U.K.	H12	12
Sledge, Ms., U.S.	C8	122
Sledzjuki, Bela.	G13	10
Sleeper Islands, is., Nu., Can.	D14	106
Sleeping Bear Dunes National Lakeshore, p.o.i., Mi., U.S.	D3	112
Sleepy Eye, Mn., U.S.	G4	118
Ślesin, Pol.	D14	16
Slidell, La., U.S.	G9	122
Slide Mountain, mtn., N.Y., U.S.	B11	114
Sliema, Malta	I8	24
Slievekimalta, mtn., Ire.	I4	12
Sligeach see Sligo, Ire.	G4	12
Sligo, Ire.	G4	12
Sligo, Pa., U.S.	C6	114
Sligo, state, Ire.	G4	12
Sligo Bay, b., Ire.	G4	12
Slinger, Wi., U.S.	H10	118
Šlino, ozero, l., Russia	C16	10
Slippery Rock, Pa., U.S.	C5	114
Šlissel'burg, Russia	A13	10
Slīteres Rezervāts, Lat.	C5	10
Sliven, Blg.	G13	26
Sljudjanka, Russia	D18	32
Sloan, Nv., U.S.	H1	132
Slobidka, Ukr.	B16	26
Slobodskoj, Russia	C8	32
Slobozia, Mol.	C16	26
Slobozia, Rom.	E14	26
Slobozia, Rom.	F12	26
Slocan, B.C., Can.	G13	138
Slocan Lake, l., B.C., Can.	G13	138
Slocomb, Al., U.S.	F13	122
Słomniki, Pol.	F15	16
Slonim, Bela.	G8	10
Slough, Eng., U.K.	J12	12
Slovakia, ctry., Eur.	H14	16
Slovenia, ctry., Eur.	E11	22
Slovenija see Slovenia, ctry., Eur.	E11	22
Slovenské rudohorie, mts., Slov.	H15	16
Slov'ians'k, Ukr.	E5	32
Slovinka, Russia	G20	8
Słowiński Park Narodowy, p.o.i., Pol.	B13	16
Słubice, Pol.	D10	16
Sluč, stm., Bela.	H10	10
Sluck, Bela.	G10	10
Šluknov, Czech Rep.	E10	16
Słupca, Pol.	D13	16
Słupia, stm., Pol.	B13	16
Słupsk (Stolp), Pol.	B13	16
Słupsk, state, Pol.	B13	16
Slutsk see Sluck, Bela.	G10	10
Smålandsfarvandet, b., Den.	I4	8
Smalininkai, Lith.	E5	10
Smaljavičy, Bela.	F10	10
Smallwood Reservoir, res., Nf., Can.	E18	106
Smalouka, Bela.	E13	10
Smarhon', Bela.	F9	10
Smederevo, Yugo.	E7	26
Smeralda, Costa, cst., Italy	C3	24
Smethport, Pa., U.S.	C7	114
Smidovič, Russia	G15	34
Šmidta, poluostrov, pen., Russia	F17	34
Śmigiel, Pol.	D12	16
Smila, Ukr.	E4	32
Smiley, Sk., Can.	C4	124
Smiley, Tx., U.S.	E10	130
Smiltene, Lat.	C8	10
Smith, Ab., Can.	A16	138
Smith, stm., U.S.	H5	114
Smith, stm., Ca., U.S.	B2	134
Smith, stm., Mt., U.S.	C15	136
Smith, stm., Or., U.S.	G2	136
Smith Arm, b., N.T., Can.	B6	106
Smith Bay, b., Nu., Can.	B10	141
Smith Bay, b., Ak., U.S.	B9	140
Smith Canyon, val., Co., U.S.	D5	128
Smithers, B.C., Can.	B3	138
Smithfield, S. Afr.	G8	70
Smithfield, N.C., U.S.	A7	116
Smithfield, Va., U.S.	G9	114
Smith Island see Sumisu-jima, i., Japan	E13	36
Smith Island, i., N.C., U.S.	C8	116
Smithland, Ky., U.S.	G9	120
Smith Mountain Lake, res., Va., U.S.	G6	114
Smith Point, c., N.S., Can.	E13	110
Smith River, Ca., U.S.	B1	134
Smiths, Al., U.S.	E13	122
Smiths Falls, On., Can.	D13	112
Smiths Grove, Ky., U.S.	G11	120
Smithton, Austl.	n12	77a
Smithville, Ga., U.S.	E1	116
Smithville, Ms., U.S.	C10	122
Smithville, Tn., U.S.	I12	120
Smithville, Tx., U.S.	D10	130
Smithville Lake, res., Mo., U.S.	E3	120
Smoke Creek Desert, des., Nv., U.S.	C6	134
Smokey, Cape, c., N.S., Can.	D16	110
Smoky, stm., Ab., Can.	A12	138
Smoky Cape, c., Austl.	H9	76
Smoky Dome, mtn., Id., U.S.	G12	136
Smoky Hill, stm., U.S.	B12	128
Smoky Hill, North Fork, stm., U.S.	B7	128
Smoky Lake, Ab., Can.	B18	138
Smøla, i., Nor.	E2	8
Smolensk, Russia	F15	10
Smolenskaja-Moskovskaja vozvyšennost', plat., Eur.	F16	10
Smolenskaja oblast', co., Russia	F15	10
Smoljan, Blg.	H11	26
Smoot, Wy., U.S.	H16	136
Smoothrock Lake, l., On., Can.	A9	118
Smorodovka, Russia	C12	10
Smyrna see İzmir, Tur.	E10	28
Smyrna, De., U.S.	E10	114
Smyrna, Ga., U.S.	D14	122
Smyrna, Tn., U.S.	I11	120
Smythe, Mount, mtn., B.C., Can.	D6	106
Snæfell, mtn., Ice.	k32	8a
Snaefell, mtn., I. of Man	G8	12
Snæfellness, pen., Ice.	k28	8a
Snag, Yk., Can.	C3	106
Snake, stm., Yk., Can.	B4	106
Snake, stm., U.S.	D8	136
Snake, stm., Mn., U.S.	E5	118
Snake, stm., Ne., U.S.	E11	126
Snake Creek, stm., S.D., U.S.	B14	126
Snake River Plain, pl., Id., U.S.	G13	136
Snake Valley, val., U.S.	D3	132
Snares Islands, is., N.Z.	H2	80
Snåsavatnet, l., Nor.	D4	8
Sneads, Fl., U.S.	G13	122
Sneedville, Tn., U.S.	H2	114
Sneek, Neth.	A14	14
Sněžka, mtn., Czech Rep.	F11	16
Śniardwy, Jezioro, l., Pol.	C17	16
Sniatyn, Ukr.	A12	26
Snina, Slov.	G18	16
Snipe Lake, l., Ab., Can.	A14	138
Snjadin, Bela.	H11	10
Snøhetta, mtn., Nor.	E3	8
Snohomish, Wa., U.S.	C4	136
Snoqualmie Pass, p., Wa., U.S.	C5	136
Snøtinden, mtn., Nor.	C5	8
Snov, stm., Eur.	H15	10
Snover, Mi., U.S.	E7	112
Snowbird Lake, l., N.T., Can.	C10	106
Snowdon, mtn., Wales, U.K.	H8	12
Snowdonia National Park, p.o.i., Wales, U.K.	I8	12
Snowflake, Az., U.S.	I6	132
Snow Hill, Md., U.S.	F10	114
Snow Hill, N.C., U.S.	A8	116
Snow Lake, Mb., Can.	E10	106
Snowmass Mountain, mtn., Co., U.S.	D9	132
Snow Mountain, mtn., Ca., U.S.	D3	134
Snowtown, Austl.	I2	76
Snowy, stm., Austl.	K7	76
Snowy Mountain, mtn., N.Y., U.S.	G2	110
Snowy Mountains, mts., Austl.	K7	76
Snowy River National Park, p.o.i., Austl.	K6	76
Snuŏl, Camb.	F8	48
Snyder, Ok., U.S.	G10	128
Snyder, Tx., U.S.	B7	130
Soacha, Col.	E4	86
Soalala, Madag.	D8	68
Soap Lake, Wa., U.S.	C7	136
Soavinandriana, Madag.	D8	68
Sobaek-sanmaek, mts., Kor., S.	C1	40
Soběslav, Czech Rep.	G10	16
Sobinka, Russia	I19	8
Sobradinho, Braz.	D11	92
Sobradinho, Represa de, res., Braz.	E5	88
Sobral, Braz.	B5	88
Sobrance, Slov.	H18	16
Sobrarbe, hist. reg., Spain	B10	20
Sochaczew, Pol.	D16	16
Soch'e see Shache, China	B12	56
Soči, Russia	F5	32
Société, Archipel de la (Society Islands), is., Fr. Poly.	E11	72
Society Hill, S.C., U.S.	B6	116
Society Islands see Société, Archipel de la, is., Fr. Poly.	E11	72
Soco, stm., Dom. Rep.	C13	102
Socompa, Paso (Socompa, Portezuelo de), p., S.A.	B3	92
Socompa, Portezuelo de (Socompa, Paso), p., S.A.	B3	92
Soconusco, Sierra de see Madre de Chiapas, Sierra, mts., N.A.	G12	100
Socorro, Col.	D5	86
Socorro, N.M., U.S.	I10	132
Socorro, Tx., U.S.	C1	130
Socorro, Isla, i., Mex.	F3	100
Socotra see Suquṭrā, i., Yemen	G7	56
Soc Trang, Viet.	H8	48
Socuéllamos, Spain	E8	20

Name	Map Ref.	Page
Stevenson Entrance, strt., Ak., U.S.	E9	140
Stevens Pass, p., Wa., U.S.	C5	136
Stevens Peak, mtn., Id., U.S.	C11	136
Stevens Point, Wi., U.S.	G9	118
Stevensville, Mi., U.S.	F3	112
Stevensville, Mt., U.S.	D12	136
Stewardson, Il., U.S.	E9	120
Stewart, B.C., Can.	D4	106
Stewart, stm., Yk., Can.	C3	106
Stewart, Isla, i., Chile	J2	90
Stewart Island, i., N.Z.	H3	80
Stewartstown, Pa., U.S.	E9	114
Stewartsville, Mo., U.S.	E3	120
Stewart Valley, Sk., Can.	D6	124
Stewartville, Mn., U.S.	H6	118
Stewiacke, N.S., Can.	E13	110
Steyr, Aus.	B11	22
Steytlerville, S. Afr.	H7	70
Stickney, S.D., U.S.	D14	126
Stiene, Lat.	C7	10
Stif, Alg.	B6	64
Stigler, Ok., U.S.	B3	122
Stih, hora, mtn., Ukr.	A10	26
Stikine, stm., N.A.	D4	106
Stikine Ranges, mts., B.C., Can.	D4	106
Stilbaai, S. Afr.	I5	70
Stilfontein, S. Afr.	E8	70
Stillhouse Hollow Lake, res., Tx., U.S.	D10	130
Stillwater, B.C., Can.	G6	138
Stillwater, Mn., U.S.	F6	118
Stillwater, Ok., U.S.	A1	122
Stillwell, Ok., U.S.	I3	120
Stînca-Costești, Lacul, res., Eur.	B14	26
Stine Mountain, mtn., Mt., U.S.	E13	136
Stinking Water Creek, stm., Ne., U.S.	G11	126
Stinnett, Tx., U.S.	F7	128
Štip, Mac.	B5	28
Stirling, Austl.	F3	74
Stirling, On., Can.	D12	112
Stirling, Scot., U.K.	E8	12
Stirling City, Ca., U.S.	D4	134
Stirrat, W.V., U.S.	G15	120
Stjernøya, i., Nor.	A9	8
Stobi, hist., Mac.	B4	28
Stockach, Ger.	I5	16
Stockbridge, Ga., U.S.	C1	116
Stockbridge, Mi., U.S.	B1	114
Stockdale, Tx., U.S.	E9	130
Stockerau, Aus.	B13	22
Stockholm, Swe.	G8	8
Stockholm, Me., U.S.	C8	110
Stockholm, state, Swe.	G8	8
Stockport, Eng., U.K.	H10	12
Stockton, Al., U.S.	G11	122
Stockton, Ca., U.S.	F4	134
Stockton, Il., U.S.	B8	120
Stockton, Ks., U.S.	B9	128
Stockton, Mo., U.S.	G4	120
Stockton-on-Tees, Eng., U.K.	G11	12
Stockton Plateau, plat., Tx., U.S.	D5	130
Stockton Reservoir, res., Mo., U.S.	G4	120
Stockton Springs, Me., U.S.	F8	110
Stoczek Łukowski, Pol.	D18	16
Stœng Trĕng, Camb.	F8	48
Stoffberg, S. Afr.	D9	70
Stojba, Russia	F15	34
Stoke-on-Trent, Eng., U.K.	I11	12
Stokes Point, c., Austl.	n11	77a
Stolberg, Ger.	F2	16
Stolbovo, Russia	H17	10
Stolbovoj, ostrov, i., Russia	B16	34
Stoneboro, Pa., U.S.	C5	114
Stone Harbor, N.J., U.S.	E11	114
Stonehaven, Scot., U.K.	E10	12
Stonehenge, Austl.	E4	76
Stonehenge, hist., Eng., U.K.	J11	12
Stone Mountain, Ga., U.S.	C1	116
Stone Mountain, mtn., Vt., U.S.	F5	110
Stoner, B.C., Can.	C8	138
Stoneville, N.C., U.S.	H6	114
Stonewall, Mb., Can.	D16	124
Stonewall, Ms., U.S.	E10	122
Stonewall, Ok., U.S.	C2	122
Stoney Creek, On., Can.	E10	112
Stonington, Il., U.S.	E8	120
Stonington, Me., U.S.	F8	110
Stony Creek, stm., Ca., U.S.	D3	134
Stony Lake, l., Mb., Can.	D11	106
Stony Lake, l., On., Can.	D11	112
Stony Plain, Ab., Can.	C16	138
Stony Point, N.C., U.S.	I4	114
Stony Rapids, Sk., Can.	D9	106
Stony River, Ak., U.S.	D8	140
Stopnica, Pol.	F16	16
Stora Lulevatten, l., Swe.	C8	8
Storavan, l., Swe.	D8	8
Stord, i., Nor.	G1	8
Storebælt, strt., Den.	I4	8
Store Koldewey, i., Grnld.	B22	141
Støren, Nor.	E4	8
Store Sotra, i., Nor.	F1	8
Storkerson Bay, b., N.T., Can.	B14	140
Storkerson Peninsula, pen., Nu., Can.	A9	106
Storlien, Swe.	E5	8
Storm Bay, b., Austl.	o13	77a
Storm Lake, Ia., U.S.	B2	120
Stornoway, Scot., U.K.	C6	12
Storozhynets', Ukr.	A12	26
Storrs, Ct., U.S.	C13	114
Storsjøen, l., Nor.	F4	8
Storsjön, l., Swe.	E5	8
Storstrøm, state, Den.	I5	8
Storthoaks, Sk., Can.	E12	124
Storuman, Swe.	D7	8
Storuman, l., Swe.	D6	8
Storvindeln, l., Swe.	D7	8
Storvreta, Swe.	F7	8
Story City, Ia., U.S.	B4	120
Stosch, Isla, i., Chile	I1	90
Stoŭbcy, Bela.	G9	10
Stoughton, Sk., Can.	E10	124
Stoughton, Ma., U.S.	B14	114
Stoughton, Wi., U.S.	B8	120
Stoŭng, stm., Camb.	F7	48
Stow, Oh., U.S.	C4	114
Stowe, Vt., U.S.	F4	110
Stowell, Tx., U.S.	H4	122
Stowmarket, Eng., U.K.	I14	12
Stoyoma Mountain, mtn., B.C., Can.	G9	138
Stradella, Italy	E6	22
Stradzečy, Bela.	I6	10
Strahan, Austl.	o12	77a
Strakonice, Czech Rep.	G9	16
Stralsund, Ger.	B9	16
Strand, S. Afr.	I4	70
Stranraer, Scot., U.K.	G8	12
Strasbourg, Sk., Can.	C9	124
Strasbourg, Fr.	F16	14
Strasburg, Ger.	C9	16
Strasburg, N.D., U.S.	A12	126
Strasburg, Oh., U.S.	D4	114
Strasburg, Pa., U.S.	E9	114
Strășeni, Mol.	B15	26
Stratford, On., Can.	E8	112
Stratford, N.Z.	D6	80
Stratford, Ca., U.S.	G6	134
Stratford, Ct., U.S.	C12	114
Stratford, Ia., U.S.	B4	120
Stratford, Ok., U.S.	C2	122
Stratford, Wi., U.S.	G8	118
Stratford-upon-Avon, Eng., U.K.	I11	12
Strathalbyn, Austl.	J2	76
Strathclair, Mb., Can.	D13	124
Strathgordon, Austl.	o12	77a
Strathlorne, N.S., Can.	D15	110
Strathmore, Ab., Can.	E17	138
Strathmore, val., Scot., U.K.	E9	12
Strathroy, On., Can.	F8	112
Strathy Point, c., Scot., U.K.	C8	12
Stratton, Co., U.S.	B6	128
Stratton, Me., U.S.	E6	110
Stratton, Ne., U.S.	A7	128
Straubing, Ger.	H8	16
Strausberg, Ger.	D9	16
Strawberry, stm., Ar., U.S.	H6	120
Strawberry, stm., Ut., U.S.	C6	132
Strawberry Mountain, mtn., Or., U.S.	F8	136
Strawberry Reservoir, res., Ut., U.S.	C5	132
Strawn, Tx., U.S.	B9	130
Strážnice, Czech Rep.	H13	16
Streaky Bay, b., Austl.	F6	74
Streatham, B.C., Can.	C4	138
Streator, Il., U.S.	C9	120
Středočeský, state, Czech Rep.	G10	16
Stredoslovenský Kraj, state, Slov.	H15	16
Streeter, N.D., U.S.	A13	126
Streetsboro, Oh., U.S.	C4	114
Streetsville, On., Can.	E10	112
Strehaia, Rom.	E10	26
Strelka-Čunja, Russia	B18	32
Strel'na, stm., Russia	C18	8
Strel'skaja, Russia	G22	8
Strenči, Lat.	C8	10
Strèšyn, Bela.	H13	10
Strickland, stm., Pap. N. Gui.	b3	79a
Strimon, Gulf of see Strymonikós Kólpos, b., Grc.	C6	28
Strjama, stm., Blg.	G11	26
Stroeder, Arg.	H4	90
Strofádes, is., Grc.	F3	28
Stromboli, Isola, i., Italy	F9	24
Strome, Ab., Can.	D18	138
Stromeferry, Scot., U.K.	D7	12
Stromsburg, Ne., U.S.	F15	126
Strömstad, Swe.	G4	8
Strömsund, Swe.	E6	8
Strong City, Ks., U.S.	C12	128
Stronghurst, Il., U.S.	D7	120
Stronsay, i., Scot., U.K.	B10	12
Stropkov, Slov.	G17	16
Stroud, Austl.	I8	76
Stroud, Eng., U.K.	J10	12
Stroud, Ok., U.S.	B2	122
Stroudsburg, Pa., U.S.	D10	114
Struga, Mac.	B3	28
Struma, stm., Eur.	H10	26
Strumble Head, c., Wales, U.K.	I7	12
Strumica, Mac.	B5	28
Strunino, Russia	D21	10
Struthers, Oh., U.S.	C5	114
Stryi, stm., Ukr.	H19	16
Stryker, Mt., U.S.	B12	136
Stryker, Oh., U.S.	G5	112
Stryków, Pol.	E15	16
Strymonikós Kólpos (Strimon, Gulf of), b., Grc.	C6	28
Strzegom, Pol.	F12	16
Strzelce Krajeńskie, Pol.	D11	16
Strzelce Opolskie, Pol.	F14	16
Strzelecki Creek, stm., Austl.	G3	76
Strzelecki Desert, des., Austl.	F3	76
Strzelecki National Park, p.o.i., Austl.	n13	77a
Strzelin, Pol.	F12	16
Strzyżów, Pol.	G17	16
Stuart, Fl., U.S.	I5	116
Stuart, Ia., U.S.	C3	120
Stuart, Va., U.S.	H5	114
Stuart, stm., B.C., Can.	B7	138
Stuart Island, i., Ak., U.S.	D7	140
Stuart Lake, l., B.C., Can.	B5	138
Stuarts Draft, Va., U.S.	G6	114
Studen Kladenec, Jazovir, res., Blg.	H12	26
Stuie, B.C., Can.	D4	138
Stupino, Russia	F20	10
Stura di Demonte, stm., Italy	F4	22
Sturge Island, i., Ant.	B21	81
Sturgeon, stm., On., Can.	B9	112
Sturgeon, stm., Mi., U.S.	E10	118
Sturgeon Bay, Wi., U.S.	D2	112
Sturgeon Bay, b., Mb., Can.	B15	124
Sturgeon Falls, On., Can.	B10	112
Sturgeon Lake, l., Ab., Can.	A13	138
Sturgeon Lake, l., On., Can.	D11	112
Sturgeon Lake, l., On., Can.	A7	118
Sturgis, Sk., Can.	C11	124
Sturgis, Ky., U.S.	G10	120
Sturgis, Mi., U.S.	G4	112
Sturgis, S.D., U.S.	C9	126
Štúrovo, Slov.	I14	16
Sturt, Mount, mtn., Austl.	G3	76
Sturtevant, Wi., U.S.	F2	112
Sturt National Park, p.o.i., Austl.	G3	76
Sturt Stony Desert, des., Austl.	G3	76
Stutterheim, S. Afr.	H8	70
Stuttgart, Ger.	H5	16
Stuttgart, Ar., U.S.	C7	122
Stylís, Grc.	E5	28
Styr, stm., Eur.	H9	10
Styria see Steiermark, state, Aus.	C11	22
Šu, Kaz.	F12	32
Suaçuí Grande, stm., Braz.	J4	88
Suai, Malay.	B8	50
Suaita, Col.	D5	86
Suapure, stm., Ven.	D8	86
Suaqui Grande, Mex.	A4	100
Subah, Indon.	G6	50
Subang, Indon.	G5	50
Subansiri, stm., Asia	D14	54
Šubarkuduk, Kaz.	E9	32
Subarnarekha, stm., India	G11	54
Sūbāṭ, stm., Sudan	F6	62
Subate, Lat.	D8	10
Subei, China	D3	36
Subeita see Shivta, Ḥorvot, hist., Isr.	H5	58
Subiaco, Italy	I10	22
Sublette, Ks., U.S.	D8	128
Sublett Range, mts., Id., U.S.	H14	136
Subotica, Yugo.	C6	26
Sucarnoochee, stm., U.S.	E10	122
Succotah, hist., Egypt	H3	58
Suceava, Rom.	B13	26
Suceava, state, Rom.	B12	26
Suchań, Pol.	C11	16
Suchou see Suzhou, China	F9	42
Süchow see Xuzhou, China	D7	42
Sucio, stm., Col.	D3	86
Sucre, Bol.	C3	90
Sucre, Col.	C4	86
Sucre, state, Col.	C4	86
Sucre, state, Ven.	B10	86
Sucuaro, Col.	E7	86
Sucumbíos, state, Ec.	H3	86
Sucuriju, Braz.	C8	84
Sucuriú, stm., Braz.	C6	90
Sud, state, N. Cal.	m16	79d
Sud, Canal du, strt., Haiti	C11	102
Suda, Russia	A20	10
Suda, stm., Russia	A20	10
Sudan, Tx., U.S.	G6	128
Sudan, ctry., Afr.	E5	62
Sudan, reg., Afr.	E4	62
Sudbišči, Russia	H20	10
Sudbury, On., Can.	B8	112
Sudbury, Eng., U.K.	I13	12
Sudd see As-Sudd, reg., Sudan	F6	62
Sudetes, mts., Eur.	F11	16
Sudogda, Russia	H19	8
Sudomskaja vozvyšennost', plat., Russia	C12	10
Sudost', stm., Eur.	H16	10
Südtirol see Trentino-Alto Adige, state, Italy	D8	22
Suđuroy, i., Far. Is.	n34	8b
Sue, stm., Sudan	F5	62
Sueca, Spain	E10	20
Suez see El-Suweis, Egypt	I3	58
Suez, Gulf of see Suweis, Khalîg el-, b., Egypt	J4	58
Suez Canal see Suweis, Qanâ el-, can., Egypt	H3	58
Suffield, Ab., Can.	D2	124
Suffolk, Va., U.S.	H9	114
Sufu see Kashi, China	B12	56
Sugar City, Id., U.S.	G15	136
Sugar Hill, Ga., U.S.	B1	116
Sugar Island, i., Mi., U.S.	B5	112
Sugar Land, Tx., U.S.	H3	122
Sugarloaf, hill, Oh., U.S.	C4	114
Sugarloaf Mountain, mtn., Me., U.S.	E6	110
Sugarloaf Point, c., Austl.	I9	76
Suğla Gölü, l., Tur.	F14	28
Sugoj, stm., Russia	D20	34
Sugut, stm., Malay.	G1	52
Suhag, Egypt	B6	62
Suhai Hu, l., China	G16	32
Suhana, Russia	C12	34
Ṣuḥār, Oman	E8	56
Sühbaatar, Mong.	A6	36
Suhindol, Blg.	F12	26
Suhiniči, Russia	F18	10
Suhl, Ger.	F6	16
Suhodol'skij, Russia	G21	10
Suhona, stm., Russia	F22	8
Suhoverkovo, Russia	D18	10
Suhumi, Geor.	F6	32
Şuhut, Tur.	E13	28
Suiá-Miçu, stm., Braz.	F7	84
Suichuan, China	H6	42
Suide, China	C4	42
Suifu see Yibin, China	F5	36
Suihua, China	B10	36
Suijiang, China	F5	36
Suileng, China	B10	36
Suining, China	E7	42
Suining, China	F1	42
Suipacha, Arg.	G8	92
Suiping, China	E5	42
Suippes, Fr.	E13	14
Suir, stm., Ire.	I5	12
Suixi, China	E7	42
Suiyang, China	B9	38
Suiyang, China	H2	42
Suiyangdian, China	E5	42
Suizhong, China	A9	42
Suizhou, China	F5	42
Šuja, Russia	H19	8
Šuja, stm., Russia	E15	8
Sujāngarh, India	E5	54
Sujāwal, Pak.	F2	54
Sukabumi, Indon.	G5	50
Sukadana, Indon.	D6	50
Sukadana, Indon.	F4	50
Sukadana, Teluk, b., Indon.	D6	50
Sukagawa, Japan	B13	40
Sukamara, Indon.	E7	50
Sukaraja, Indon.	E7	50
Sukau, Malay.	A11	50
Sukhothai, Thai.	D4	48
Sukhumi see Suhumi, Geor.	F6	32
Sukkertoppen (Maniitsoq), Grnld.	D15	141
Sukkozero, Russia	E14	8
Sukkur, Pak.	E2	54
Sukoharjo, Indon.	G7	50
Sukromlja, Russia	D17	10
Sukses, Nmb.	B3	70
Sukumo, Japan	G5	40
Sukunka, stm., B.C., Can.	A9	138
Sul, Baía, b., Braz.	C13	92
Sula, i., Nor.	F1	8
Sula, stm., Russia	C23	8
Sula, Kepulauan (Sula Islands), is., Indon.	F8	44
Sulaimān Range, mts., Pak.	C3	54
Sula Islands see Sula, Kepulauan, is., Indon.	F8	44
Sulawesi (Celebes), i., Indon.	F7	44
Sulawesi Selatan, state, Indon.	E11	50
Sulawesi Tengah, state, Indon.	D12	50
Sulawesi Tenggara, state, Indon.	E12	50
Sulaymān, Birak (Solomon's Pools), hist., W.B.	G5	58
Sulcis, reg., Italy	E2	24
Sulechów, Pol.	D11	16
Sulęcin, Pol.	D11	16
Sulejówek, Pol.	D17	16
Sulen, Mount, mtn., Pap. N. Gui.	a3	79a
Sulina, Rom.	D16	26
Sulina, Braţul, stm., Rom.	D16	26
Sulingen, Ger.	D4	16
Sulitelma, mtn., Eur.	C7	8
Sullana, Peru	D1	84
Sulligent, Al., U.S.	D10	122
Sullivan, Il., U.S.	E9	120
Sullivan, In., U.S.	E10	120
Sullivan Lake, l., Ab., Can.	E18	138
Sulmona, Italy	H10	22
Sulphur, La., U.S.	G5	122
Sulphur, Ok., U.S.	C2	122
Sulphur, stm., U.S.	D5	122
Sulphur Springs, Tx., U.S.	D3	122
Sulphur Springs Draw, stm., U.S.	H6	128
Sulphur Springs Valley, val., Az., U.S.	L7	132
Sultan, Wa., U.S.	C5	136
Sultan Alonto, Lake, l., Phil.	G5	52
Sultandağı, Tur.	E14	28
Sultanhisar, Tur.	F11	28
Sultan Kudarat, Phil.	G4	52
Sultānpur, India	E8	54
Sulu Archipelago, is., Phil.	H3	52
Sulu Chi, l., China	C11	54
Sulūq, Libya	A4	62
Sulu Sea, Asia	F2	52
Sulzbach-Rosenberg, Ger.	G7	16
Šum, Russia	A14	10
Šumadija, reg., Yugo.	E7	26
Sumangat, Tanjong, c., Malay.	G1	52
Sumatera (Sumatra), i., Indon.	E3	44
Sumatera Barat, state, Indon.	D2	50
Sumatera Selatan, state, Indon.	E4	50
Sumatera Utara, state, Indon.	K4	48
Sumatra see Sumatera, i., Indon.	E3	44
Sumba, Far. Is.	n34	8b
Sumba, i., Indon.	H11	50
Sumba, Selat, strt., Indon.	H11	50
Sumbawa, i., Indon.	H10	50
Sumbawa Besar, Indon.	H10	50
Sumbawanga, Tan.	F6	66
Sumbe, Ang.	C1	68
Sumburgh Head, c., Scot., U.K.	o18	12a
Sumé, Braz.	D7	88
Sumedang, Indon.	G5	50
Sümeg, Hung.	B4	26
Šumen, Blg.	F13	26
Sumenep, Indon.	G8	50
Šumerlja, Russia	C7	32
Sumisu-jima (Smith Island), i., Japan	E13	36
Šumjači, Russia	G15	10
Summerfield, Fl., U.S.	G3	116
Summerfield, N.C., U.S.	H6	114
Summer Lake, l., Or., U.S.	H6	136
Summerland, B.C., Can.	G11	138
Summerside, P.E., Can.	D13	110
Summersville, Mo., U.S.	G6	120
Summerton, S.C., U.S.	C5	116
Summerville, Ga., U.S.	C13	122
Summerville, S.C., U.S.	C5	116
Summit, S.D., U.S.	F1	118
Summit Lake, B.C., Can.	B8	138
Summit Mountain, mtn., Nv., U.S.	D9	134
Sumner, Ia., U.S.	B5	120
Sumner, Ms., U.S.	D8	122
Sumner, Wa., U.S.	C4	136
Sumoto, Japan	E7	40
Sumpangbinangae, Indon.	F11	50
Šumperk, Czech Rep.	G13	16
Sumpiuh, Indon.	G6	50
Sumqayıt, Azer.	A6	56
Šumšu, ostrov, i., Russia	F20	34
Sumter, S.C., U.S.	C5	116
Sumusta el-Waqf, Egypt	J1	58
Sumy, Ukr.	D4	32
Sumzom, China	F4	36
Sun, stm., Mt., U.S.	C14	136
Sunāmganj, Bngl.	F13	54
Sunbright, Tn., U.S.	H13	120
Sunburst, Mt., U.S.	B14	136
Sunbury, Austl.	K5	76
Sunbury, Oh., U.S.	D3	114
Sunbury, Pa., U.S.	D9	114
Sunchales, Arg.	E7	92
Suncho Corral, Arg.	C6	92
Sunch'ŏn, Kor., S.	G7	38
Sunch'ŏn-ŭp, Kor., N.	E6	38
Sun City, Az., U.S.	J4	132
Suncook, N.H., U.S.	G5	110
Sunda, Selat (Sunda Strait), strt., Indon.	G4	50
Sundance, Wy., U.S.	C8	126
Sundarbans, reg., Asia	H12	54
Sundargarh, India	G9	54
Sunda Shelf, unds.	I13	142
Sunda Strait see Sunda, Selat, strt., Indon.	G4	50
Sundays, stm., S. Afr.	H7	70
Sunde, Nor.	G1	8
Sunderland, Eng., U.K.	G11	12
Sundown, Tx., U.S.	H6	128
Sundridge, On., Can.	C10	112
Sundsvall, Swe.	E7	8
Sunflower, Ms., U.S.	D8	122
Sunflower, Mount, mtn., Ks., U.S.	B7	128
Sungaianyar, Indon.	E10	50
Sungaibuntu, Indon.	F5	50
Sungaidareh, Indon.	D2	50
Sungaiguntung, Indon.	C3	50
Sungai Kolok, Thai.	I5	48
Sungailangsat, Indon.	D2	50
Sungailimau, Indon.	D1	50
Sungaipenuh, Indon.	E2	50
Sungai Petani, Malay.	J5	48
Sungaipinang, Indon.	D8	50
Sungairotan, Indon.	E4	50
Sungaiselan, Indon.	E5	50
Sungari see Songhua, stm., China	B11	36
Sungari Reservoir see Songhua Hu, res., China	C7	38
Sungchiang see Songjiang, China	F9	42
Sungguminasa, Indon.	F11	50
Sungsang, Indon.	E4	50
Sunland Park, N.M., U.S.	L10	132
Sunne, Swe.	G5	8
Sunnynook, Ab., Can.	E19	138
Sunnyside, Ut., U.S.	D6	132
Sunnyside, Wa., U.S.	D7	136
Sunnyslope, Ab., Can.	E17	138
Sunnyvale, Ca., U.S.	F3	134
Sun Prairie, Wi., U.S.	A8	120
Sunrise, Fl., U.S.	J5	116
Sunrise, Wy., U.S.	E8	126
Sunrise Manor, Nv., U.S.	G1	132
Sunset, La., U.S.	G6	122
Sunset, Tx., U.S.	H11	128
Sunset Country, reg., Austl.	J3	76
Sunset Crater National Monument, p.o.i., Az., U.S.	H5	132
Sunshine, Austl.	K5	76
Suntar, Russia	D12	34
Suntar-Hajata, hrebet, mts., Russia	D17	34
Sun Valley, Id., U.S.	G12	136
Sunwu, China	B10	36
Sunwui see Jiangmen, China	J5	42
Sunyani, Ghana	H4	64
Suojarvi, Russia	E15	8
Suomussalmi, Fin.	D13	8
Suō-nada, Japan	F4	40
Suordah, Russia	C15	34
Supamo, stm., Ven.	D10	86
Supaul, India	E11	54
Superí see La Merced, Arg.	D5	92
Superior, Az., U.S.	J5	132
Superior, Mt., U.S.	C12	136
Superior, Wi., U.S.	E6	118
Superior, Wy., U.S.	B7	132
Superior, Laguna, b., Mex.	G11	100
Superior, Lake, l., N.A.	B10	108
Supetar, Cro.	G13	22
Suphan Buri, Thai.	E4	48
Suphan Buri, stm., Thai.	E5	48
Suponevo, Russia	G17	10
Supung Reservoir, res., Asia	D6	38
Suqian, China	E8	42
Sūq Suwayq, Sau. Ar.	E4	56
Suquṭrā (Socotra), i., Yemen	G7	56
Ṣūr (Tyre), Leb.	E6	58
Ṣūr, Oman	E8	56
Sur, Point, c., Ca., U.S.	G4	134
Sura, stm., Russia	C7	32
Surabaya, Indon.	G8	50
Surakarta, Indon.	G7	50
Ṣūrān, Syria	C7	58
Šurany, Slov.	H14	16
Surat, Austl.	F7	76
Sūrat, India	H4	54
Sūratgarh, India	D4	54
Surat Thani, Thai.	H4	48
Suraž, Bela.	E13	10
Suraž, Russia	G15	10
Surendranagar, India	G3	54
Surf City, N.J., U.S.	E11	114
Surfers Paradise, Austl.	G9	76
Surgères, Fr.	C5	18
Surgoinsville, Tn., U.S.	H3	114
Surgut, Russia	B12	32
Suriāpet, India	C4	53
Surigao, Phil.	F5	52
Surin, Thai.	E6	48
Surinam, ctry., S.A.	C6	84
Suring, Wi., U.S.	D1	112
Surprise Valley, val., U.S.	B5	134
Surrency, Ga., U.S.	E3	116
Surrey, N.D., U.S.	F12	124
Surry, Va., U.S.	G9	114
Sursee, Switz.	C5	22
Surt, Libya	A3	62
Surt, Khalīj (Sidra, Gulf of), b., Libya	A3	62
Surtanāhu, Pak.	E2	54
Surtsey, i., Ice.	I29	8a
Suru, Pap. N. Gui.	b3	79a
Sürüç, Tur.	A9	58
Suruga-wan, b., Japan	E11	40
Surulangun, Indon.	E3	50
Surumu, stm., Braz.	F11	86
Šuryškary, Russia	A10	32
Susa, Italy	E4	22
Sušac, Otok, i., Cro.	H13	22
Sūsah, Libya	A4	62
Susaki, Japan	F6	40
Susanino, Russia	G19	8
Susanino, Russia	F17	34
Susanville, Ca., U.S.	C5	134
Šušenskoe, Russia	D16	32
Susitna, stm., Ak., U.S.	D9	140
Susleni, Mol.	B15	26
Susoh, Indon.	K3	48
Susong, China	F7	42
Suspiro del Moro, Puerto, p., Spain	G7	20
Susquehanna, Pa., U.S.	C10	114
Susquehanna, stm., U.S.	E9	114
Susquehanna, West Branch, stm., Pa., U.S.	C8	114
Susques, Arg.	D3	90
Sussex, N.B., Can.	E11	110
Sussex, N.J., U.S.	C11	114
Sussex, Va., U.S.	H8	114
Susuman, Russia	D18	34
Susurluk, Tur.	D11	28
Susuzmüsellim, Tur.	B9	28
Šušvė, stm., Lith.	E6	10
Sutak, India	B6	54
Sutherland, S. Afr.	H5	70
Sutherland, Ia., U.S.	A2	120
Sutherlin, Or., U.S.	G3	136
Sutjeska Nacionalni Park, p.o.i., Bos.	F5	26
Sutlej (Langqên) (Satluj), stm., Asia	D3	54
Sutter, Ca., U.S.	D4	134
Sutter Buttes, mtn., Ca., U.S.	D4	134
Sutter Creek, Ca., U.S.	E5	134
Sutton, Ak., U.S.	D10	140
Sutton, W.V., U.S.	F5	114
Sutton, Monts see Green Mountains, mts., N.A.	G4	110
Sutton in Ashfield, Eng., U.K.	H11	12
Sutton West, On., Can.	D10	112
Suttor, stm., Austl.	C6	76
Sutwik Island, i., Ak., U.S.	E8	140
Suure-Jaani, Est.	B8	10
Suur Munamägi, hill, Est.	C9	10
Suur Pakri, i., Est.	A6	10
Suva, Fiji	q19	79e
Suvadiva Atoll, at., Mald.	i12	46a
Suvarlı, Tur.	A8	58
Suvasvesi, l., Fin.	E12	8
Suvorov, Russia	F19	10
Suwa, Japan	C11	40
Suwałki, Pol.	B18	16
Suwałki, state, Pol.	C18	16
Suwannaphum, Thai.	E6	48
Suwannee, stm., U.S.	G2	116
Suwanose-jima, i., Japan	k19	39a
Suwarrow, at., Cook Is.	E10	72
Suweis, Khalîg el- (Suez, Gulf of), b., Egypt	J4	58
Suweis, Qanâ el- (Suez Canal), can., Egypt	H3	58
Suwŏn, Kor., S.	F7	38
Suzak, Kaz.	F11	32
Suzaka, Japan	C11	40
Suzdal', Russia	H19	8
Suzhou, China	F9	42
Suzhou, China	E7	42
Suzigou, China	A10	42
Suzuka, Japan	E9	40
Suzuka-sammyaku, mts., Japan	D9	40
Suzu-misaki, c., Japan	B10	40
Suzun, Russia	D14	32
Suzzara, Italy	F7	22
Svalbard, dep., Eur.	B6	30
Svaliava, Ukr.	A10	26
Svapa, stm., Russia	H18	10
Svappavaara, Swe.	C9	8
Svärdsjö, Swe.	F6	8
Svartenhuk, pen., Grnld.	C15	141
Svartisen, ice, Nor.	C5	8
Svataj, Russia	C19	34
Svay Riĕng, Camb.	G7	48
Svėdasai, Lith.	E8	10
Svegssjön, l., Swe.	E5	8
Švėkšna, Lith.	E4	10
Svelvik, Nor.	G4	8
Švenčionėliai, Lith.	E8	10
Švenčionys, Lith.	E9	10
Svendborg, Den.	A6	16
Šventoji, Lith.	D3	10
Šventoji, stm., Lith.	E7	10
Sverdlovsk see Ekaterinburg, Russia	C10	32
Sverdrup, ostrov, i., Russia	B4	34
Sverdrup Channel, strt., Nu., Can.	A6	141
Sverdrup Islands, is., Nu., Can.	B5	141
Sveti Nikole, Mac.	B4	28
Svetlahorsk, Bela.	H12	10
Svetlaja, Russia	B12	36
Svetlogorsk, Russia	F2	10
Svetlograd, Russia	E6	32
Svetlyj, Russia	F3	10
Svetlyj, Russia	D10	32
Svetlyj, Russia	E12	34
Svetogorsk, Russia	F13	8
Svetozarevo, Yugo.	F8	26
Svidník, Slov.	G17	16
Svilengrad, Blg.	H13	26
Svínoy, i., Far. Is.	m34	8b
Svir, Bela.	F9	10
Svir', stm., Russia	F16	8
Svirica, Russia	F15	8
Svirsk, Russia	D18	32
Svislač, stm., Bela.	G11	10
Svištov, Blg.	F12	26
Svit, Slov.	G16	16
Svitavy, Czech Rep.	G12	16
Svjacilavičy, Bela.	H14	10
Svjatoj Nos, mys, c., Russia	B18	8
Svjatoj Nos, mys, c., Russia	B17	34
Svobodnyj, Russia	F14	34
Svolvær, Nor.	B6	8
Svratka, stm., Czech Rep.	G12	16
Swabia see Schwaben, hist. reg., Ger.	H5	16
Swain Reefs, rf., Austl.	C9	76
Swainsboro, Ga., U.S.	D3	116
Swains Island, at., Am. Sam.	E9	72
Swakop, stm., Nmb.	C2	70
Swakopmund, Nmb.	C2	70
Swale, stm., Eng., U.K.	G11	12
Swan, stm., Can.	B13	124
Swan, stm., Ab., Can.	A15	138
Swan, stm., Mt., U.S.	C13	136
Swanage, Eng., U.K.	K11	12
Swanee see Suwannee, stm., U.S.	G2	116
Swan Hill, Austl.	J4	76
Swan Hills, Ab., Can.	B15	138
Swan Islands see Santanilla, Islas, is., Hond.	D6	102
Swan Lake, Mb., Can.	E15	124
Swan Lake, l., Mb., Can.	B13	124
Swan Lake, l., Mn., U.S.	G4	118
Swannanoa, N.C., U.S.	I3	114
Swan Peak, mtn., Mt., U.S.	C13	136
Swanquarter, N.C., U.S.	A9	116
Swan Range, mts., Mt., U.S.	C13	136
Swan Reach, Austl.	J2	76
Swan River, Mb., Can.	B12	124
Swansboro, N.C., U.S.	B8	116
Swansea, Austl.	o13	77a
Swansea, Wales, U.K.	J8	12
Swanton, Vt., U.S.	F3	110
Swanville, Mn., U.S.	F4	118
Swart-Mfolozi, stm., S. Afr.	F10	70
Swartz Creek, Mi., U.S.	F6	112
Swarzędz, Pol.	D13	16
Swāt, stm., Pak.	A3	54
Swatow see Shantou, China	J7	42
Swaziland, ctry., Afr.	E10	70
Sweden, ctry., Eur.	E6	8
Swedish Knoll, mtn., Ut., U.S.	D5	132
Swedru, Ghana	H4	64
Sweeny, Tx., U.S.	E12	130
Sweet Briar, Va., U.S.	G6	114
Sweetgrass, Mt., U.S.	A15	136
Sweet Grass Hills, hills, Mt., U.S.	B15	136
Sweet Home, Tx., U.S.	E10	130
Sweet Springs, Mo., U.S.	F4	120
Sweetwater, Tn., U.S.	A1	116
Sweetwater, Tx., U.S.	B7	130
Sweetwater, stm., Wy., U.S.	E5	126
Swellendam, S. Afr.	H5	70
Świdnica, Pol.	F12	16
Świdnik, Pol.	E18	16
Świdwin, Pol.	C11	16
Świebodzice, Pol.	F12	16
Świebodzin, Pol.	D11	16
Świecie, Pol.	C14	16
Świerzawa, Pol.	E11	16
Świętokrzyski Park Narodowy, p.o.i., Pol.	F16	16
Swift Current, Sk., Can.	D6	124
Swift Current Creek, stm., Sk., Can.	D6	124
Swinburne, Cape, c., Nu., Can.	A11	106
Swindle Island, i., B.C., Can.	D2	138
Swindon, Eng., U.K.	J11	12
Swinford, Ire.	H4	12
Świnoujście (Swinemünde), Pol.	C9	16
Switzerland, ctry., Eur.	C14	18
Swords, Ire.	H6	12
Syalah, Russia	C13	34
Syan (San), stm., Eur.	F18	16
Sycamore, Ga., U.S.	E2	116
Sycamore, Il., U.S.	C9	120
Sycamore, Oh., U.S.	D2	114
Syčovka, Russia	E17	10
Sydenham, stm., On., Can.	F7	112
Sydney, Austl.	I8	76
Sydney, N.S., Can.	D16	110
Sydney Bay, b., Norf. I.	y25	78i
Sydney Lake, l., On., Can.	A4	118
Sydney Mines, N.S., Can.	D16	110
Syičy, Bela.	H12	10
Syke, Ger.	D4	16
Sykesville, Pa., U.S.	C7	114
Syktyvkar, Russia	B8	32
Sylacauga, Al., U.S.	D12	122
Sylhet, Bngl.	F13	54
Syloga, Russia	E20	8
Sylt, i., Ger.	B4	16
Sylva, N.C., U.S.	A2	116
Sylvan Grove, Ks., U.S.	C10	128
Sylvania, Ga., U.S.	D4	116
Sylvania, Oh., U.S.	C2	114
Sylvan Lake, Ab., Can.	D16	138
Sylvan Lake, l., Ab., Can.	D16	138
Sylvan Pass, p., Wy., U.S.	F16	136
Sylvester, Ga., U.S.	E2	116
Sylvester, Tx., U.S.	B7	130
Sym, Russia	B15	32
Syme see Sými, i., Grc.	G10	28
Sými, i., Grc.	G10	28
Šymkent, Kaz.	F11	32
Synevir, Ukr.	A10	26
Syowa, sci., Ant.	C9	81
Syracuse, In., U.S.	G4	112
Syracuse, Ks., U.S.	C7	128
Syracuse, Ne., U.S.	D1	120
Syracuse, N.Y., U.S.	A9	114
Syrdarja, Uzb.	A10	56
Syr Darya (Syrdar'ja), stm., Asia	F11	32
Syria, ctry., Asia	B4	56
Syriam, Mya.	D3	48
Syrian Desert (Shām, Bādiyat ash-), des., Asia	C4	56
Sýrna, i., Grc.	G9	28
Sýros, i., Grc.	F7	28
Sysmä, Fin.	F11	8
Sysola, stm., Russia	B8	32
Syt'kovo, Russia	D16	10
Syväri, l., Fin.	E13	8
Syzran', Russia	D7	32
Szabolcs-Szatmár-Bereg, state, Hung.	A9	26
Szamos (Someș), stm., Eur.	B9	26
Szamotuły, Pol.	D12	16
Szarvas, Hung.	C7	26
Szczawnica, Pol.	G16	16
Szczecin (Stettin), Pol.	C10	16
Szczecin, state, Pol.	C11	16
Szczecinek, Pol.	C12	16
Szczuczyn, Pol.	C18	16
Szczytno, Pol.	C17	16
Szechwan see Sichuan, state, China	E5	36
Szechwan Basin see Sichuan Pendi, bas., China	F1	42
Szeged, Hung.	C7	26
Szeghalom, Hung.	B8	26
Székesfehérvár, Hung.	B5	26
Szekszárd, Hung.	C5	26
Szentendre, Hung.	B5	26
Szentes, Hung.	C7	26
Szeping see Siping, China	C6	38
Szerencs, Hung.	A8	26
Szob, Hung.	B5	26
Szolnok, Hung.	B7	26
Szombathely, Hung.	B3	26
Szprotawa, Pol.	E11	16
Szubin, Pol.	C13	16
Szypliszki, Pol.	B19	16

T

Name	Map Ref.	Page
Taal, Lake, l., Phil.	D3	52
Tábara, Spain	C5	20
Tabar Islands, is., Pap. N. Gui.	a5	79a
Tabarka, Tun.	H2	24
Tabasco, state, Mex.	D6	96
Tabelbala, Alg.	D4	64
Taber, Ab., Can.	G18	138
Tabernes de Valldigna see Tavernes de la Valldigna, Spain	E10	20
Tabira, Braz.	D7	88
Tablas de Daimiel, Parque Nacional de las, p.o.i., Spain	E7	20
Tablas Island, i., Phil.	D4	52

Name — Map Ref. — Page

Tehuantepec, Istmo de, isth., Mex. G11 100
Teignmouth, Eng., U.K. K9 12
Teixeira, Braz. D7 88
Teixeira Pinto, Gui.-B. G1 64
Tejakula, Indon. H9 50
Tejkovo, Russia H19 8
Tejon Pass, p., Ca., U.S. I7 134
Tejupilco de Hidalgo, Mex. F8 100
Tekamah, Ne., U.S. C1 120
Tekapo, Lake, l., N.Z. F4 80
Tekax, Mex. B3 102
Teke, Tur. B12 28
Teke Burnu, c., Tur. E9 28
Tekeli, Kaz. F13 32
Tekezē (Satīt), stm., Afr. E7 62
Tekirdağ, Tur. C10 28
Tekirdağ, state, Tur. B10 28
Tekkali, India B7 53
Tekoa, Wa., U.S. C9 136
Tekonsha, Mi., U.S. B1 114
Te Kuiti, N.Z. D6 80
Tel, stm., India A6 53
Tela, Hond. E4 102
Telaopengsha Shan, mtn., China C11 54
Telavi, Geor. F7 32
Tel Aviv-Jaffa see Tel Aviv-Yafo, Isr. F5 58
Tel Aviv-Yafo, Isr. F5 58
Telč, Czech Rep. G11 16
Teleckoe, ozero, l., Russia D15 32
Telefomin, Pap. N. Gui. b3 79a
Telegraph Creek, B.C., Can. D4 106
Telêmaco Borba, Braz. B12 92
Telemark, state, Nor. G3 8
Telembí, stm., Col. G2 86
Telén, Arg. H5 92
Telen, stm., Indon. C10 50
Teleneşti, Mol. B15 26
Teleno, mtn., Spain B4 20
Teleorman, state, Rom. E12 26
Teleorman, stm., Rom. E12 26
Telescope Point, c., Gren. q10 105e
Telese, Italy C8 24
Telford, Eng., U.K. I10 12
Télimélé, Gui. G2 64
Telire, stm., C.R. H6 102
Teljo, Jabal, mtn., Sudan E5 62
Telkwa, B.C., Can. B3 138
Tell Basta, hist., Egypt H2 58
Tell City, In., U.S. G11 120
Tell El-Amarna, hist., Egypt K1 58
Tellel Rub, hist., Egypt H2 58
Teller, Ak., U.S. C6 140
Tellicherry, India F2 53
Tellier, Arg. I3 90
Tello, Col. F4 86
Telluride, Co., U.S. F9 132
Tel Megiddo, hist., Isr. F6 58
Telmen nuur, l., Mong. B4 36
Teloloapan, Mex. F8 100
Telos see Tílos, i., Grc. G10 28
Telsen, Arg. H3 90
Telšiai, Lith. E5 10
Teltow, Ger. D9 16
Telukbayur, Indon. D2 50
Telukbayur, Indon. B10 50
Telukdalem, Indon. L3 48
Teluk Intan, Malay. K5 48
Tema, Ghana H5 64
Temagami, Lake, l., On., Can. A9 112
Temaju, Pulau, i., Indon. C6 50
Te Manga, mtn., Cook Is. a26 78j
Temangga, Indon. C7 50
Tematangi, at., Fr. Poly. F12 72
Temax, Mex. B3 102
Tembeling, stm., Malay. J6 48
Tembenči, stm., Russia A17 32
Tembesi, stm., Indon. D3 50
Tembilahan, Indon. D3 50
Temblador, Ven. C10 86
Temblor Range, mts., Ca., U.S. H6 134
Teme, stm., Eng., U.K. I10 12
Temecula, Ca., U.S. J8 134
Temelli, Tur. D15 28
Temengor, Tasik, res., Malay. J5 48
Temetiu, mtn., Fr. Poly. s18 78g
Temir, Kaz. E9 32
Temirtau, Kaz. D12 32
Témiscaming, Qc., Can. B10 112
Témiscamingue, Lac (Timiskaming, Lake), res., Can. B10 112
Témiscouata, Lac, l., Qc., Can. C7 110
Tëmkino, Russia E17 10
Temora, Austl. J6 76
Temosachic, Mex. A5 100
Tempe, Az., U.S. J5 132
Tempe, Danau, l., Indon. F12 50
Tempino, Indon. D3 50
Tempio Pausania, Italy D2 24
Temple, Tx., U.S. C10 130
Templi, Valle dei, hist., Italy G7 24
Templin, Ger. C9 16
Tempoal, stm., Mex. E9 100
Tempoal de Sánchez, Mex. E9 100
Tempy, Russia D20 10
Temuco, Chile G2 90
Temwen, i., Micron. m12 78d
Tena, Ec. H3 86
Tenabo, Mex. B2 102
Tenaha, Tx., U.S. F4 122
Tena Kourou, mtn., Burkina G4 64
Tenāli, India C5 53
Tenasserim, Mya. F4 48
Tendaho, Eth. E8 62
Tende, Col de, p., Eur. E13 18
Ten Degree Channel, strt., India G7 46
Tendō, Japan A13 40
Ténenkou, Mali G3 64
Ténéré, des., Niger F7 64
Ténès, Alg. H12 20
Ténès, Cap, c., Alg. H12 20
Teng, stm., Mya. B3 48
Tengah, Kepulauan, is., Indon. G10 50
Tengchong, China G4 36
Tenggara, Nusa (Lesser Sunda Islands), is., Indon. G6 44
Tenggara Celebes see Sulawesi Tenggara, state, Indon. E12 50
Tenggarong, Indon. D10 50
Tengger Shamo, des., China D5 36
Tenghilan, Malay. G1 52
Tengiz, ozero, l., Kaz. D11 32
Tengréla, C. Iv. G3 64
Tengtiao (Na), stm., Asia A6 48
Tengxian, China J4 42
Tengxian, China D7 42
Tenkāsi, India G3 53
Tenke, D.R.C. G5 66
Tenkeli, Russia B17 34
Tenkiller Ferry Lake, res., Ok., U.S. B4 122
Tenkodogo, Burkina G4 64
Tennant Creek, Austl. C6 74
Tennessee, state, U.S. D10 108
Tennessee, stm., U.S. A11 122
Tennille, Ga., U.S. D3 116
Teno, Chile G2 92
Teno (Tana), stm., Eur. B12 8
Tenom, Malay. A9 50
Tenos see Tínos, Grc. F8 28
Tenos see Tínos, i., Grc. F8 28
Tenosique, Mex. D2 102
Tenryū, Japan E10 40
Tenryū, stm., Japan E10 40
Tensas, stm., La., U.S. F7 122
Tensed, Id., U.S. C10 136
Ten Sleep, Wy., U.S. C5 126
Tenterfield, Austl. G8 76
Ten Thousand Islands, is., Fl., U.S. K4 116
Tentolomatinan, Gunung, mtn., Indon. E7 44
Teocaltiche, Mex. E7 100
Teodelina, Arg. G7 92
Teófilo Otoni, Braz. I5 88
Teo Lakes, l., Sk., Can. C4 124
Teotihuacán, hist., Mex. F9 100
Tepa, Indon. G8 44
Tepalcatepec, Mex. F7 100
Tepebaşı, Tur. B3 58
Tepehuanes, Mex. C6 100
Tepehuanes, stm., Mex. C6 100
Tepeji de Ocampo, Mex. F9 100
Tepelenë, Alb. D13 24
Tepic, Mex. E6 100
Teplice, Czech Rep. F9 16
Tepoca, Bahía de, b., Mex. F6 98
Tepoca, Punta, c., Mex. G6 98
Ter, stm., Spain B14 20
Téra, Niger G5 64
Tera, stm., Spain C4 20
Teradomari, Japan B11 40
Teraina, i., Kir. C11 72
Teramo, Italy H10 22
Terbuny, Russia H21 10
Terceira, i., Port. C3 60
Tercero, stm., Arg. F6 92
Terdal, India C2 53
Terek, stm., Russia G18 6
Terempa, Indon. B5 50
Terengganu, state, Malay. J6 48
Terengganu, stm., Malay. J6 48
Terenos, Braz. D6 90
Teresina, Braz. C4 88
Teresópolis, Braz. L4 88
Terespol, Pol. D19 16
Terevaka, Cerro, mtn., Chile e29 78l
Tergüün Bogd uul, mtn., Mong. C5 36
Teriang, stm., Malay. K6 48
Teriberka, Russia B16 8
Terihi, i., Fr. Poly. t19 78g
Terlingua, Tx., U.S. E4 130
Terlingua Creek, stm., Tx., U.S. E4 130
Termas del Arapey, Ur. E9 92
Termas de Río Hondo, Arg. C5 92
Termez, Uzb. B10 56
Termini Imerese, Italy G7 24
Termini Imerese, Golfo di, b., Italy F7 24
Terminillo, Monte, mtn., Italy H9 22
Términos, Laguna de, b., Mex. C2 102
Termoli, Italy H11 22
Termonde see Dendermonde, Bel. C12 14
Ternej, Russia B12 38
Terneuzen, Neth. C12 14
Terni, Italy H9 22
Ternitz, Aus. C12 22
Ternopil', Ukr. F14 6
Terpenija, mys, c., Russia G17 34
Terpenija, zaliv, b., Russia G17 34
Terra Alta, W.V., U.S. E6 114
Terra Bella, Ca., U.S. H6 134
Terrace, B.C., Can. B2 138
Terracina, Italy C7 24
Terra Cotta Army (Qinshihuang Mausoleum), hist., China D3 42
Terral, Ok., U.S. H11 128
Terralba, Italy E2 24
Terra Santa, Braz. D6 84
Terrassa, Spain C13 20
Terrebonne Bay, b., La., U.S. H8 122
Terre-de-Bas, Guad. i5 105c
Terre-de-Haut, Guad. i5 105c
Terre-de-Haut, i., Guad. i5 105c
Terre Haute, In., U.S. E10 120
Terrell, Tx., U.S. E2 122
Terre-Neuve see Newfoundland, state, Can. B17 110
Territoire du Yukon see Yukon, state, Can. B3 106
Territoires du Nord-Ouest see Northwest Territories, state, Can. C6 106
Terry, Ms., U.S. E8 122
Terry, Mt., U.S. A7 126
Terschelling, i., Neth. A14 14
Terskej-Alatau, hrebet, mts., Kyrg. F13 32
Teruel, Col. F4 86
Teruel, Spain D9 20
Teruel, co., Spain D10 20
Terujak, Indon. J3 48
Tervola, Fin. C11 8
Terzaghi Dam, dam, B.C., Can. F8 138
Tes, stm., Asia D16 32
Tescott, Ks., U.S. B11 128
Teseney, Erit. D7 62
Teshekpuk Lake, l., Ak., U.S. B9 140
Teshio, Japan B14 38
Teshio, stm., Japan B15 38
Teslin, Yk., Can. C4 106
Teslin, stm., Can. C4 106
Teslin Lake, l., Can. C4 106
Tësovo, Russia E17 10
Tësovo-Netyl'skij, Russia B13 10
Tësovskij, Russia B13 10
Tessalit, Mali E5 64
Tessaoua, Niger G6 64
Testa, Capo, c., Italy C3 24
Testour, Tun. H3 24
Tetachuck Lake, res., B.C., Can. C4 138
Tete, Moz. D5 68
Tête Jaune Cache, B.C., Can. D11 138
Tetepare Island, i., Sol. Is. e7 79b
Teterow, Ger. C8 16
Tetica, mtn., Spain G8 20
Teton, Id., U.S. G15 136
Teton, stm., Id., U.S. G15 136
Teton, stm., Mt., U.S. C15 136
Tetonia, Id., U.S. G15 136
Teton Range, mts., Wy., U.S. G16 136
Tetouan, Mor. B4 64
Tetovo, Mac. A4 28
Tetufera, Mont, mtn., Fr. Poly. v22 78h
Teuco, stm., Arg. D4 90
Teulada, Italy F2 24
Teulada, Capo, c., Italy F2 24
Teulon, Mb., Can. D16 124
Teutoburger Wald, hills, Ger. D4 16
Teuva, Fin. E9 8
Tevere (Tiber), stm., Italy H9 22
Teverya, Isr. F6 58
Te Waewae Bay, b., N.Z. H2 80
Tewah, Indon. D8 50
Tewantin-Noosa, Austl. F9 76
Tewkesbury, Eng., U.K. I11 12
Texada Island, i., B.C., Can. G6 138
Texana, Lake, res., Tx., U.S. F11 130
Texarkana, Ar., U.S. D4 122
Texarkana, Tx., U.S. D4 122
Texas, Austl. G8 76
Texas, state, U.S. E8 108
Texas City, Tx., U.S. H4 122
Texel, i., Neth. A13 14
Texhoma, Ok., U.S. E7 128
Texico, N.M., U.S. G5 128
Texoma, Lake, res., U.S. H11 128
Teyateyaneng, Leso. F8 70
Teywarah, Afg. C9 56
Teziutlán, Mex. F10 100
Tezpur, India E14 54
Tezzeron Lake, l., B.C., Can. B6 138
Tha, stm., Laos B5 48
Tha-anne, stm., Nu., Can. C11 106
Thabana-Ntlenyana, mtn., Leso. F9 70
Thabaung, Mya. D2 48
Thabazimbi, S. Afr. D8 70
Thabyu, Mya. E4 48
Thagyettaw, Mya. F3 48
Thai Binh, Viet. B8 48
Thailand, ctry., Asia E5 48
Thailand, Gulf of, b., Asia G5 48
Thai Nguyen, Viet. B7 48
Thak, Pak. C3 54
Thal, Pak. B3 54
Thala, Tun. I2 24
Thal Desert, des., Pak. C3 54
Thalfang, Ger. G2 16
Tha Li, Thai. D5 48
Thalia, Tx., U.S. H9 128
Thālith, Ash-Shallāl ath- (Third Cataract), wtfl, Sudan D6 62
Thalwil, Switz. C5 22
Thames, N.Z. C6 80
Thames, stm., On., Can. F8 112
Thames, stm., Eng., U.K. J13 12
Thames, Firth of, b., N.Z. C6 80
Thamesford, On., Can. E8 112
Thamesville, On., Can. F7 112
Thāna, India B1 53
Thandaung, Mya. C3 48
Thangoo, Austl. C4 74
Thangool, Austl. E8 76
Thanh Hoa, Viet. C7 48
Thanh Pho Ho Chi Minh (Saigon), Viet. G8 48
Thanjāvūr, India F4 53
Thann, Fr. B12 18
Thap Than, stm., Thai. E6 48
Tharabwin West, Mya. F4 48
Tharād, India F3 54
Thar Desert (Great Indian Desert), des., Asia D3 54
Thargomindah, Austl. F5 76
Tharrawaddy, Mya. D2 48
Tha Sala, Thai. H4 48
Thásos, Grc. C7 28
Thásos, i., Grc. C7 28
Thásos, hist., Grc. C7 28
Thaton, Mya. D3 48
Tha Tum, Thai. E6 48
Thau, Bassin de, l., Fr. F9 18
Thaungyin (Moei), stm., Asia D3 48
Thaya (Dyje), stm., Eur. H12 16
Thayawthadangyi Kyun, i., Mya. F3 48
Thayer, Ks., U.S. G2 120
Thayer, Mo., U.S. H6 120
Thayetchaung, Mya. F4 48
Thayetmyo, Mya. C2 48
Thazi, Mya. B3 48
Thebes see Thíva, Grc. E6 28
The Bottom, Neth. Ant. B1 105a
The Cheviot, mtn., Eng., U.K. F10 12
The Dalles, Or., U.S. E5 136
Thedford, Ne., U.S. E12 126
The Father see Ulawun, Mount, vol., Pap. N. Gui. b5 79a
The Fens, reg., Eng., U.K. I12 12
The Fishing Lakes, l., Sk., Can. D10 124
The Granites, hill, Austl. D6 74
The Hague see 's-Gravenhage, Neth. B12 14
The Heads, c., Or., U.S. H2 136
Theinkun, Mya. G4 48
The Lakes National Park, p.o.i., Austl. L6 76
The Little Minch, strt., Scot., U.K. D6 12
Thelon, stm., Can. C11 106
The Lynd, Austl. B5 76
The Minch, strt., Scot., U.K. D6 12
Thenia, Alg. H14 20
Theodore, Austl. E8 76
Theodore, Sk., Can. C10 124
Theodore, Al., U.S. G10 122
Theodore Roosevelt National Park North Unit, p.o.i., N.D., U.S. G10 124
Theodore Roosevelt National Park South Unit, p.o.i., N.D., U.S. G10 124
The Pas, Mb., Can. E10 106
Thepha, Thai. I5 48
The Pinnacle, hill, Mo., U.S. E6 120
The Rand see Witwatersrand, mts., S. Afr. D8 70
Theresa Creek, stm., Austl. D6 76
The Rhins, pen., Scot., U.K. G7 12
Thermaïkós Kólpos (Salonika, Gulf of), b., Grc. C6 28
Thermopolis, Wy., U.S. D4 126
Thermopylae see Thermopýles, hist., Grc. E5 28
Thermopýles (Thermopylae), hist., Grc. E5 28
The Rock, Austl. J6 76
The Rockies, mtn., Wa., U.S. D4 136
The Rope, clf, Pit. c28 78k
Thesiger Bay, b., N.T., Can. B15 140
The Slot see New Georgia Sound, strt., Sol. Is. e8 79b
Thessalía, state, Grc. D5 28
Thessalía, hist. reg., Grc. D5 28
Thessalon, On., Can. B6 112
Thessaloníki (Salonika), Grc. C6 28
Thessaly see Thessalía, hist. reg., Grc. D5 28
Thetford, Eng., U.K. I13 12
Thetford Mines, Qc., Can. D5 110
Theunissen, S. Afr. F8 70
The Valley, Anguilla A1 105a
The Village, Ok., U.S. F11 128
The Wash, b., Eng., U.K. I13 12
The Weald, reg., Eng., U.K. J13 12
Thibodaux, La., U.S. H8 122
Thief Lake, l., Mn., U.S. C3 118
Thief River Falls, Mn., U.S. C2 118
Thiene, Italy E8 22
Thiers, Fr. D9 18
Thiès, Sen. G1 64
Thika, Kenya E7 66
Thimphu, Bhu. E12 54
Thingvallavatn, l., Ice. k29 8a
Thingvellir, Ice. k29 8a
Thingvellir Nasjonalpark, p.o.i., Ice. k29 8a
Thio, N. Cal. m16 79d
Thionville, Fr. E15 14
Thíra, Grc. G8 28
Thíra (Santoríni), i., Grc. G8 28
Third Cataract see Thālith, Ash-Shallāl ath-, wtfl, Sudan D6 62
Thiruvananthapuram see Trivandrum, India G3 53
Thiruvārūr, India F4 53
Thistilfjörður, b., Ice. j32 8a
Thíva, Grc. E6 28
Thiviers, Fr. D6 18
Thjórsá, stm., Ice. k30 8a
Thohoyandou, S. Afr. C10 70
Thoi Binh, Viet. H7 48
Thomas, Ok., U.S. F10 128
Thomas, W.V., U.S. E6 114
Thomaston, Al., U.S. E11 122
Thomaston, Ga., U.S. D1 116
Thomaston, Me., U.S. F7 110
Thomasville, Ga., U.S. F2 116
Thomasville, N.C., U.S. I5 114
Thompson, Mb., Can. D11 106
Thompson, Ia., U.S. H5 118
Thompson, N.D., U.S. D1 118
Thompson, stm., B.C., Can. F9 138
Thompson, stm., U.S. E4 120
Thompson Falls, Mt., U.S. C11 136
Thompson Peak, mtn., Ca., U.S. B3 134
Thomsen, stm., N.T., Can. B16 140
Thomson, Ga., U.S. C3 116
Thomson, Il., U.S. C7 120
Thomson, stm., Austl. E4 76
Thongwa, Mya. D3 48
Thonon-les-Bains, Fr. C12 18
Thonotosassa, Fl., U.S. H3 116
Thonze, Mya. D2 48
Thorhild, Ab., Can. B17 138
Thórisvatn, l., Ice. k30 8a
Thorlákshöfn, Ice. l29 8a
Thornaby-on-Tees, Eng., U.K. G11 12
Thornbury, On., Can. D9 112
Thorndale, Tx., U.S. D10 130
Thornton, Co., U.S. B4 128
Thornton, Tx., U.S. F2 122
Thorntonville, Tx., U.S. C4 130
Thorp, Wi., U.S. G8 118
Thorsby, Ab., Can. C16 138
Thorshavn see Tórshavn, Far. Is. n34 8b
Thórshöfn, Ice. j32 8a
Thouars, Fr. H8 14
Thoune see Thun, Switz. D4 22
Thousand Lake Mountain, mtn., Ut., U.S. E5 132
Thousand Oaks, Ca., U.S. I7 134
Thousand Ships Bay, b., Sol. Is. e8 79b
Thousand Springs Creek, stm., U.S. B2 132
Thrace, hist. reg., Eur. H13 26
Thrakikó Pélagos, Grc. C8 28
Three Forks, Mt., U.S. E15 136
Three Gorges Dam, dam, China F4 42
Three Hills, Ab., Can. E17 138
Three Hummock Island, i., Austl. n12 77a
Three Kings Islands, is., N.Z. B5 80
Three Mile Plains, N.S., Can. F12 110
Three Points, Cape, c., Ghana I4 64
Three Rivers, Mi., U.S. G4 112
Three Rivers, Tx., U.S. F9 130
Three Sisters, mtn., Or., U.S. F5 136
Three Sisters Islands, is., Sol. Is. f10 79b
Three Springs, Austl. E3 74
Thrissur see Trichūr, India F3 53
Throssel, Lake, l., Austl. E4 74
Thu, Cu Lao, i., Viet. G9 48
Thuan Chau, Viet. B6 48
Thu Dau Mot, Viet. G8 48
Thuin, Bel. D13 14
Thule (Qaanaaq), Grnld. B12 141
Thun, Switz. D4 22
Thun Chang, Thai. C5 48
Thunder Bay, On., Can. C9 118
Thunder Bay, b., On., Can. C9 118
Thunderbird, Lake, res., Ok., U.S. F11 128
Thunderbolt, Ga., U.S. D4 116
Thunder Butte Creek, stm., S.D., U.S. B10 126
Thunder Creek, stm., Sk., Can. D7 124
Thuner See, l., Switz. D4 22
Thung Salaeng Luang National Park, p.o.i., Thai. D5 48
Thung Wa, Thai. I4 48
Thüringen, state, Ger. F7 16
Thüringer Wald, mts., Ger. F6 16
Thuringia see Thüringen, state, Ger. F7 16
Thurles, Ire. I5 12
Thurmont, Md., U.S. E8 114
Thursday Island, Austl. B8 74
Thurso, Scot., U.K. C9 12
Thurston Island, i., Ant. C31 81
Thusis, Switz. D6 22
Thylungra, Austl. F4 76
Thyolo, Mwi. D5 68
Thysville see Mbanza-Ngungu, D.R.C. F3 66
Tiachiv, Ukr. A10 26
Tianchang, China E8 42
Tiandeng, China J2 42
Tiandong, China J2 42
Tian'e, China I2 42
Tiangang, China C7 38
Tianguá, Braz. B5 88
Tianjin (Tientsin), China B7 42
Tianjin, state, China B7 42
Tianjun, China D4 36
Tianlin, China I2 42
Tian Ling, mtn., China B8 38
Tianmen, China F5 42
Tianqiaoling, China C8 38
Tianshifu, China D6 38
Tianshui, China D1 42
Tiantai, China G9 42
Tiantang, China J4 42
Tianwangsi, China F8 42
Tianyang, China J2 42
Tianzhen, China A6 42
Tianzhu, China D5 36
Tianzhu, China H3 42
Tiarei, Fr. Poly. v22 78h
Tiaro, Austl. E9 76
Tiassalé, C. Iv. H4 64
Ti'avea, Samoa g12 79c
Tibaji, stm., Braz. A12 92
Tibal-og, Phil. G5 52
Tibasti, Sarīr, des., Libya C3 62
Tibati, Cam. C2 66
Tibbie, Al., U.S. F10 122
Tiber see Tevere, stm., Italy H9 22
Tiberias, Lake see Kinneret, Yam, l., Isr. F6 58
Tibesti, mts., Afr. C3 62
Tibet see Xizang, state, China B5 46
Tibet, Plateau of see Qing Zang Gaoyuan, plat., China B6 46
Tiblawan, Phil. G6 52
Tibnīn, Leb. E6 58
Tibooburra, Austl. G4 76
Tiburón, Cabo, c. C3 86
Tiburón, Isla, i., Mex. G6 98
Tiča, Jazovir, res., Blg. F13 26
Ticao Island, i., Phil. D4 52
Tîchît, Maur. F3 64
Ticino, stm., Eur. D14 18
Tickfaw, stm., U.S. G8 122
Ticonderoga, N.Y., U.S. G3 110
Ticul, Mex. B3 102
Tidioute, Pa., U.S. C6 114
Tidiquin, Jbel, mtn., Mor. C4 64
Tidjikja, Maur. F2 64
Tiébissou, C. Iv. H3 64
T'iehling see Tieling, China C5 38
Tiel, Neth. C14 14
Tieli, China B10 36
Tieling, China C5 38
Tielt, Bel. C12 14
Tiémé, C. Iv. H3 64
T'ienching see Tianjin, China B7 42
Tien Giang see Mekong, stm., Asia F9 46
Tien Shan, mts., Asia F13 32
T'ienshui see Tianshui, China D1 42
Tientsin see Tianjin, China B7 42
Tientsin see Tianjin, state, China B7 42
Tien Yen, Viet. B8 48
Tie Plant, Ms., U.S. D9 122
Tierp, Swe. F7 8
Tierra Amarilla, Chile C2 92
Tierra Blanca, Mex. F10 100
Tierra Blanca, Mex. G3 130
Tierra Blanca Creek, stm., U.S. G6 128
Tierra de Campos, reg., Spain C5 20
Tierra del Fuego, Arg. J3 90
Tierra del Fuego, i., S.A. J3 90
Tiétar, stm., Spain E5 20
Tietê, Braz. L2 88
Tietê, stm., Braz. D6 90
Tiéti, N. Cal. m15 79d
Tiffany Mountain, mtn., Wa., U.S. B7 136
Tiffin, Oh., U.S. C2 114
Tifton, Ga., U.S. E2 116
Tiga, Île, i., N. Cal. m16 79d
Tigalda Island, i., Ak., U.S. F7 140
Tigapuluh, Pegunungan, mts., Indon. D3 50
Tighina, Mol. C16 26
Tigil', Russia E20 34
Tignall, Ga., U.S. C3 116
Tignish, P.E., Can. D12 110
Tigoda, stm., Russia A14 10
Tigre, Col. F7 86
Tigre, stm., Peru D2 84
Tigre, stm., Ven. C10 86
Tigris (Dicle) (Dijlah), stm., Asia C5 56
Tiguentourine, Alg. D6 64
Tihany, hist., Hung. C4 26
Tihert, Alg. B5 64
Tihon, Russia G22 8
Tihookeanskij, Russia C10 38
Tihoreck, Russia E6 32
Tihua see Ürümqi, China C2 36
Tihuatlán, Mex. E10 100
Tihvin, Russia A16 10
Tijuana, Mex. K8 134
Tijuana, stm., N.A. K9 134
Tijucas, Braz. C13 92
Tijucas do Sul, Braz. B13 92
Tijuco, stm., Braz. J1 88
Tikal, hist., Guat. D3 102
Tikal, Parque Nacional, p.o.i., Guat. D3 102
Tikrīt, Iraq C5 56
Tikša, Russia D15 8
Tikšeozero, ozero, l., Russia C14 8
Tiksi, Russia B14 34
Tiladummati Atoll, at., Mald. h12 46a
Tilburg, Neth. C14 14
Tilbury, On., Can. F7 112
Tilcha, Austl. G3 76
Tilden, Il., U.S. F8 120
Tilden, Ne., U.S. E15 126
Tilden, Tx., U.S. F9 130
Tilhar, India D7 54
Tilimsen, Alg. C4 64
Tilin, Mya. B2 48
Tillabéri, Niger G5 64
Tilley, Ab., Can. F19 138
Tillia, Niger F5 64
Tillmans Corner, Al., U.S. G10 122
Tillson, N.Y., U.S. C11 114
Tillsonburg, On., Can. F9 112
Tílos, i., Grc. G10 28
Tilpa, Austl. H5 76
Tilton, N.H., U.S. G5 110
Tiltonsville, Oh., U.S. D5 114
Tima, Egypt L2 58
Timaná, Col. G3 86
Timanskij krjaž, hills, Russia B8 32
Timaru, N.Z. G4 80
Timbalier Bay, b., La., U.S. H8 122
Timbaúba, Braz. D8 88
Timbavati Game Reserve, S. Afr. D10 70
Timbedgha, Maur. F3 64
Timber Lake, S.D., U.S. B11 126
Timbiras, Braz. C4 88
Timbó, Braz. C13 92
Timbo, Lib. H3 64
Timbuktu see Tombouctou, Mali F4 64
Timétrine, Mali F4 64
Timétrine, mts., Mali F4 64
Timimoun, Alg. D5 64
Timirist, Râs, c., Maur. F1 64
Timirjazevo, Russia E4 10
Timiș, state, Rom. D8 26
Timiș (Tamiš), stm., Eur. D7 26
Timiskaming, Lake (Témiscamingue, Lac), res., Can. B10 112
Timișoara, Rom. D8 26
Timmendorfer Strand, Ger. B7 16
Timmins, On., Can. F14 106
Timmonsville, S.C., U.S. B6 116
Timms Hill, mtn., Wi., U.S. F8 118
Timna' see Mikhrot Timna', hist., Isr. I5 58
Timok, stm., Eur. E9 26
Timon, Braz. C4 88
Timor, i., Asia G8 44
Timor Sea K15 142
Timošino, Russia H21 8
Timotes, Ven. C6 86
Timpanogos Cave National Monument, p.o.i., Ut., U.S. C5 132
Timpton, stm., Russia E14 34
Timšer, Russia B9 32
Tims Ford Lake, res., Tn., U.S. B12 122
Tina, stm., S. Afr. G9 70
Tîna, Khalîg el- (Pelusium Bay), b., Egypt G3 58
Tinaca Point, c., Phil. H5 52
Tinambung, Indon. E11 50
Tinapagee, Austl. G5 76
Tinaquillo, Ven. C7 86
Tindivanam, India E4 53
Tindouf, Alg. D3 64
Tineba, Pegunungan, mts., Indon. D12 50
Tineg, stm., Phil. B3 52
Ting, stm., China I7 42
Tinggi, Pulau, i., Malay. K7 48
Tingha, Austl. G8 76
Tinghert, Ḥamādat (Tinghert, Plateau du), plat., Afr. D7 64
Tinghert, Plateau du (Tinghert, Ḥamādat), plat., Afr. D6 64
Tinghsien see Dingxian, China B6 42
Tinglev, Den. B5 16
Tingo María, Peru E2 84
Tingri, China D11 54
Tingri see Dinggyê, China D11 54
Tinguiririca, Volcán, vol., Chile G2 92
Tinharé, Ilha de, i., Braz. G6 88
Tinh Bien, Viet. G7 48
Tinian, i., N. Mar. Is. B5 72
Tinjar, stm., Malay. B9 50
Tínos, Grc. F8 28
Tínos, i., Grc. F8 28
Tinsley, Ms., U.S. E8 122
Tinsukia, India C8 46
Tintagel, B.C., Can. B5 138
Tintina, Arg. C6 92
Tintinara, Austl. J3 76
Tio, Erit. E8 62
Tiobrad Árann see Tipperary, Ire. I4 12
Tioga, N.D., U.S. F11 124
Tiojala, Fin. F10 8
Tioman, Pulau, i., Malay. K7 48
Tionesta, Pa., U.S. C6 114
Tipasa, Alg. H13 20
Tipitapa, Nic. F4 102
Tippecanoe, stm., In., U.S. H3 112
Tipperary, Ire. I4 12
Tipperary, state, Ire. I5 12
Tipton, Ca., U.S. G6 134
Tipton, Ia., U.S. C6 120
Tipton, Mo., U.S. F5 120
Tipton, Ok., U.S. G9 128
Tipton, Mount, mtn., Az., U.S. H2 132
Tiptonville, Tn., U.S. H8 120
Tip Top Mountain, mtn., On., Can. F13 106
Tiptūr, India E3 53
Tiputini, stm., Ec. H4 86
Tira, Isr. F5 58
Tīrān, i., Sau. Ar. K5 58
Tiran, Strait of, strt. K5 58
Tirana see Tiranë, Alb. C13 24
Tiranë, Alb. C13 24
Tirano, Italy D7 22
Tiraspol, Mol. C16 26
Tire, Tur. E10 28
Tiree, i., Scot., U.K. E6 12
Tirich Mīr, mtn., Pak. B11 56
Tirna, stm., India B3 53
Tirodi, India H7 54
Tirol, state, Aus. C8 22
Tiros, Braz. J3 88
Tirso, stm., Italy E2 24
Tīrthahalli, India E2 53
Tiruchchirāppalli, India F4 53
Tiruchengodu, India F3 53
Tirukkalukkunram, India E5 53
Tirukkovilūr, India F4 53
Tiruliai, Lith. E6 10
Tirunelveli, India G3 53
Tirupati, India E4 53
Tiruppattūr, India E4 53
Tiruppur, India F3 53
Tirūr, India F2 53
Tirutturaippūndi, India F4 53
Tiruvalla, India G3 53
Tiruvannāmalai, India E4 53
Tirūvottiyūr, India E5 53
Tiruvur, India C5 53
Tisa (Tisza) (Tysa), stm., Eur. D7 26
Tisaiyanvilai, India G3 53
Tisdale, Sk., Can. B9 124
Tishomingo, Ok., U.S. C2 122
Tisīyah, Syria F7 58
Tiskilwa, Il., U.S. C8 120
Tisovec, Slov. H15 16
Tīsta, stm., Asia F12 54
Tisza (Tisa) (Tysa), stm., Eur. C7 26
Tiszaföldvár, Hung. C7 26
Tiszaújváros, Hung. B7 26
Tiszavasvári, Hung. A8 26
Titaf, Alg. D4 64
Tit-Ary, Russia B14 34
Titicaca, Lake, l., S.A. G4 84
Titilāgarh, India H9 54
Titonka, Ia., U.S. H4 118
Titov Veles, Mac. B4 28
Titran, Nor. E2 8
Tittabawassee, stm., Mi., U.S. E5 112
Tittmoning, Ger. H8 16
Titule, D.R.C. D5 66
Titusville, Fl., U.S. H5 116
Titusville, Pa., U.S. C6 114
Tiuni, India C6 54
Tivaouane, Sen. F1 64
Tiverton, Eng., U.K. K9 12
Tivoli, Italy I9 22
Tivoli, Tx., U.S. F11 130
Tiyās, Syria D8 58
Tizimín, Mex. B3 102
Tizi-Ouzou, Alg. B5 64
Tizmant el-Zawâya, Egypt I1 58
Tiznados, stm., Ven. C8 86
Tiznit, Mor. D3 64
Tjörn, i., Swe. G4 8
Tjukalinsk, Russia C12 32
Tjul'gan, Russia D9 32
Tjumen', Russia C10 32
Tjung, stm., Russia D13 34
Tjuva-Guba, Russia B15 8
Tlacotalpan, Mex. F11 100
Tlacotepec, Mex. G9 100
Tlahualilo de Zaragoza, Mex. B7 100
Tlalnepantla, Mex. F9 100
Tlaltenango de Sánchez Román, Mex. E7 100
Tlapaneco, stm., Mex. G9 100
Tlaquepaque, Mex. E7 100
Tlaxcala, state, Mex. F9 100
Tlaxcala de Xicohténcatl, Mex. F9 100
Tłuszcz, Pol. D17 16
Tmassah, Libya B3 62
Tnâot, stm., Camb. G7 48
Toa Alta, P.R. B3 104a
Toa Baja, P.R. B3 104a
Toachi, stm., Ec. H2 86
Toahayana, Mex. B5 100
Toamasina, Madag. D8 68
Toba, Japan E9 40
Toba, Danau, l., Indon. K4 48
Tobago, i., Trin. r13 105f
Toba Inlet, b., B.C., Can. F6 138
Toba Kākar Range, mts., Pak. C10 56
Tobarra, Spain F9 20
Tobas, Arg. D6 92
Toba Tek Singh, Pak. C4 54
Tobejuba, Isla, i., Ven. C11 86
Tobermorey, Austl. D7 74
Tobermory, On., Can. C8 112
Tobermory, Scot., U.K. E6 12
Tobias, Ne., U.S. G15 126
Tobias Barreto, Braz. F6 88
Tobin, Mount, mtn., Nv., U.S. C8 134
Tobique, stm., N.B., Can. C9 110
Toboali, Indon. E5 50
Tobol, Kaz. D10 32
Tobol, stm., Asia C11 32
Toboli, Indon. D12 50
Tobol'sk, Russia C11 32
Toboso, Phil. E4 52
Tobruk see Ṭubruq, Libya A4 62
Tobseda, Russia B25 8
Tobyhanna, Pa., U.S. C10 114
Tobyš, stm., Russia C24 8
Tocantínia, Braz. E1 88
Tocantinópolis, Braz. D2 88
Tocantins, state, Braz. F8 84
Tocantins, stm., Braz. D8 84

I•58 Toca-Tume

Name | Map Ref. | Page

Tocantins, stm., Braz. F1 88
Tocantinzinho, stm., Braz. H1 88
Tochcha Lake, l., B.C., Can. B5 138
Tochigi, Japan C12 40
Tochigi, state, Japan C12 40
Tochio, Japan B12 40
Toco, Trin. s13 105f
Tocoa, Hond. E5 102
Toconao, Chile D3 90
Tocopilla, Chile D2 90
Tocuco, stm., Ven. C5 86
Tocumwal, Austl. J5 76
Tocuyo, stm., Ven. B7 86
Tocuyo de la Costa, Ven. B7 86
Toda Rāisingh, India E5 54
Todi, Italy H9 22
Todos os Santos, Baia de, b., Braz. G6 88
Todos Santos, Bol. C3 90
Todos Santos, Mex. D3 100
Todos Santos, Bahía de, b., Mex. L8 134
Tofino, B.C., Can. G5 138
Toga, i., Vanuatu i16 79d
Togi, Japan B9 40
Togiak, Ak., U.S. E7 140
Togian, Kepulauan, is., Indon. F7 44
Togo, ctry., Afr. H5 64
Togtoh, China A4 42
Togučin, Russia C14 32
Togur, Russia C14 32
Togwotee Pass, p., Wy., U.S. G15 136
Tōhaku, Japan D6 40
Tohiea, Mont, mtn., Fr. Poly. v20 78h
Tohopekaliga, Lake, l., Fl., U.S. H4 116
Tohtamyš, Taj. B11 56
Toi-misaki, c., Japan H4 40
Toiyabe Range, mts., Nv., U.S. D8 134
Tōjō, Japan E6 40
Tojtepa, Uzb. F11 32
Tok, Ak., U.S. D11 140
Tokachi, stm., Japan C15 38
Tokachi-dake, vol., Japan C15 38
Tokaj, Hung. A8 26
Tōkamachi, Japan B11 40
Tokara-kaikyō, strt., Japan j19 39a
Tokara-rettō, is., Japan k19 39a
Tokat, Tur. A4 56
Tŏkchŏk-kundo, is., Kor., S. F6 38
Tokelau, dep., Oc. D9 72
Tokko, Russia D12 34
Tokma, Russia C19 32
Tokmak, Kyrg. F13 32
Tokoro, stm., Japan C15 38
Tokoroa, N.Z. D6 80
Tok-to, is., Asia B4 40
Toktogul, Kyrg. F12 32
Tokuno-shima, i., Japan I19 39a
Tokur, Russia F15 34
Tokushima, Japan E7 40
Tokushima, state, Japan F7 40
Tokuyama, Japan E4 40
Tokwe, stm., Zimb. B10 70
Tōkyō, Japan D12 40
Tōkyō, state, Japan D12 40
Tokyo Bay see Tōkyō-wan, b., Japan D12 40
Tōkyō-daigaku-uchūkūkan-kenkyūsho, sci., Japan H4 40
Tōkyō-wan, b., Japan D12 40
Tôlañaro, Madag. F8 68
Tolbo, Mong. B3 36
Toledo, Braz. B11 92
Toledo, Col. D5 86
Toledo, Phil. E4 52
Toledo, Spain E6 20
Toledo, Il., U.S. E9 120
Toledo, Oh., U.S. C2 114
Toledo, Or., U.S. F3 136
Toledo, co., Spain E6 20
Toledo, Montes de, mts., Spain E6 20
Toledo Bend Reservoir, res., U.S. F4 122
Tolentino, Italy G10 22
Toli, China B1 36
Toliara, Madag. E7 68
Tolima, state, Col. E4 86
Tolima, Nevado del, vol., Col. E4 86
Tolitoli, Indon. C12 50
Toljatti, Russia D7 32
Tol'ka, Russia B14 32
Tolleson, Az., U.S. J4 132
Tolloche, Arg. B6 92
Tolmači, Russia C18 10
Tolmezzo, Italy D10 22
Tolmin, Slvn. D10 22
Tolna, state, Hung. C5 26
Tolo, Teluk, b., Indon. F7 44
Tolosa, Spain A8 20
Tolstoj, mys, c., Russia E20 34
Tolti, Pak. A6 54
Tolú, Col. C4 86
Toluca, Il., U.S. D8 120
Toluca, Nevado de, vol., Mex. F9 100
Toluca de Lerdo, Mex. F9 100
Tolybaj, Kaz. D10 32
Tom', stm., Russia C14 32
Tomah, Wi., U.S. H8 118
Tomahawk, Wi., U.S. F9 118
Tomakomai, Japan C14 38
Tomanivi, mtn., Fiji p19 79e
Tomar, Port. E2 20
Tomari, Russia G17 34
Tomás Gomensoro, Ur. E9 92
Tomasine, stm., Qc., Can. B13 112
Tomaszów Lubelski, Pol. F19 16
Tomaszów Mazowiecki, Pol. E15 16
Tombador, Serra do, plat., Braz. F6 84
Tomball, Tx., U.S. G3 122
Tombigbee, stm., U.S. F10 122
Tombos, Braz. K5 88
Tombouctou (Timbuktu), Mali F4 64
Tombstone, Az., U.S. L6 132
Tombstone Mountain, mtn., Yk., Can. C3 106
Tombua, Ang. D1 68
Tom Burke, S. Afr. C9 70
Tomé, Chile H1 92
Tomé-Açu, Braz. B1 88
Tomelilla, Swe. I5 8
Tomelloso, Spain E8 20
Tomichi Creek, stm., Co., U.S. C2 128
Tomini, Indon. C12 50
Tomini, Teluk, b., Indon. F7 44
Tomioka, Japan C11 40
Tommot, Russia E14 34
Tomo, stm., Col. E7 86
Tompkins, Sk., Can. D5 124
Tompkinsville, Ky., U.S. H12 120
Tompo, Indon. C12 50
Tom Price, Austl. D3 74
Tomptokan, Russia E15 34
Tomsk, Russia C15 32
Toms River, N.J., U.S. E11 114
Tonalá, Mex. G12 100
Tonami, Japan C9 40
Tonantins, Braz. I7 86
Tonantins, stm., Braz. I7 86
Tonasket, Wa., U.S. B7 136
Tonawanda, N.Y., U.S. B6 114
Tonbo, Mya. C2 48
Tonbridge, Eng., U.K. J13 12
Tondano, Indon. E8 44
Tønder, Den. B4 16
Tondi, India G4 53
Tone, stm., Japan D13 40
Tonekābon, Iran B7 56
Tonga, ctry., Oc. E9 72
Tongaat, S. Afr. F10 70
Tong'an, China I7 42
Tonganoxie, Ks., U.S. E2 120
Tonga Ridge, unds. K21 142
Tongariro National Park, p.o.i., N.Z. D6 80
Tongatapu, state, Tonga o14 78e
Tongatapu, i., Tonga n13 78e
Tonga Trench, unds. L21 142
Tongbai, China E5 42
Tongbai Shan, mts., China E5 42
Tongbei, China B10 36
Tongcheng, China F7 42
Tongchuan, China D3 42
Tongde, China D5 36
Tongeren, Bel. D14 14
Tongguan, China G5 42
Tongguan, China D3 42
Tonghai, China G5 36
Tonghe, China B10 36
Tonghua, China D6 38
Tongjiang, China B11 36
Tongjiang, China F2 42
Tongjosŏn-man, b., Kor., N. E7 38
Tongliang, China G1 42
Tongliao, China C4 38
Tongling, China F7 42
Tongling, China J3 42
Tonglu, China G8 42
Tongnae, Kor., S. D2 40
Tongnan, China F1 42
Tongo, Austl. H4 76
Tongoa, i., Vanuatu k17 79d
Tongoy, Chile E2 92
Tongren, China D5 36
Tongren, China H3 42
Tongres see Tongeren, Bel. D14 14
Tongsa Dzong, Bhu. E13 54
Tongtian, stm., China E4 36
Tongue, Scot., U.K. C8 12
Tongue, stm., U.S. A7 126
Tongue of the Ocean, unds. C9 96
Tongwei, China D1 42
Tongxian, China B7 42
Tongxin, China C1 42
Tongxu, China D6 42
Tongyu, China B5 38
Tongzi, China G2 42
Tonj, Sudan F5 62
Tonk, India E5 54
Tonkawa, Ok., U.S. E11 128
Tonkin see Bac Phan, hist. reg., Viet. A7 48
Tonkin, Gulf of, b., Asia C8 48
Tônlé Sab, Bœng, l., Camb. F6 48
Tonle Sap see Tônlé Sab, Bœng, l., Camb. F6 48
Tonneins, Fr. E6 18
Tonopah, Nv., U.S. E8 134
Tonoshō, Japan E7 40
Tonosí, Pan. D1 86
Tonotha, Bots. B8 70
Tons, stm., India F8 54
Tønsberg, Nor. G4 8
Tonstad, Nor. G2 8
Tonto Creek, stm., Az., U.S. I5 132
Tonto National Monument, p.o.i., Az., U.S. J5 132
Toodyay, Austl. F3 74
Tooele, Ut., U.S. C4 132
Toogoolawah, Austl. F9 76
Toomsboro, Ga., U.S. D2 116
Toora-Hem, Russia D17 32
Toowoomba, Austl. F8 76
Topeka, Ks., U.S. E2 120
Top Hill, hill, Gren. q11 105e
Topia, Mex. C5 100
Topki, Russia C15 32
Topko, gora, mtn., Russia E16 34
Topley, B.C., Can. B4 138
Toplița, Rom. C12 26
Topocalma, Punta, c., Chile G1 92
Topol'čany, Slov. H14 16
Topolobampo, Mex. C4 100
Topolovățu Mare, Rom. D8 26
Toporok, Russia B16 10
Topozero, ozero, l., Russia D14 8
Toppenish, Wa., U.S. D6 136
Topsa, Russia E20 8
Top Springs, Austl. C6 74
Tor, Eth. F6 62
Torbalı, Tur. E10 28
Torbat-e Heydarīyeh, Iran B8 56
Torbat-e Jām, Iran B9 56
Torbrook, N.S., Can. F12 110
Torch Lake, l., Mi., U.S. C4 112
Tordesillas, Spain C5 20
Töre, Swe. C10 8
Torgau, Ger. E8 16
Torhout, Bel. C12 14
Toribulu, Indon. D11 50
Torino (Turin), Italy E4 22
Torit, Sudan G6 62
Tormes, stm., Spain C5 20
Torna, Russia B20 8
Torna, mtn., India B1 53
Torneälven (Tornionjoki), stm., Eur. C10 8
Torneträsk, l., Swe. B8 8
Torngat Mountains, mts., Can. F13 141
Tornillo, Tx., U.S. C1 130
Tornionjoki (Torneälven), stm., Eur. C10 8
Tornquist, Arg. I6 92
Toro, Spain C5 20
Toro, mtn., Mex. F6 100
Toro, Lago del, l., Chile J2 90
Toro, Punta, c., Chile F1 92
Törökszentmiklós, Hung. B7 26
Torom, Russia F16 34
Toronto, On., Can. E10 112
Toronto, Ks., U.S. G1 120
Toronto, S.D., U.S. G2 118
Toropec, Russia D14 10
Tororo, Ug. D6 66
Toros Dağları (Taurus Mountains), mts., Tur. A3 58
Torosozero, Russia E18 8
Toroume, hill, Cook Is. b26 78j
Torquay, Sk., Can. E10 124
Torquay (Torbay), Eng., U.K. K9 12
Torrance, Ca., U.S. J7 134
Torrão, Port. F2 20
Torreblanca, Spain D11 20
Torre del Greco, Italy D8 24
Torredonjimeno, Spain G6 20
Torrejoncillo, Spain E4 20
Torrejón de Ardoz, Spain D7 20
Torrejón-Tiétar, Embalse de, res., Spain E5 20
Torrelavega, Spain A6 20
Torremolinos, Spain H6 20
Torrens, Lake, l., Austl. F7 74
Torrens Creek, Austl. C5 76
Torrens Creek, stm., Austl. D5 76
Torrent, Arg. D9 92
Torrent, Spain E10 20
Torrente see Torrent, Spain E10 20
Torrenueva, Spain F7 20
Torreón, Mex. C7 100
Torre Pellice, Italy F4 22
Torreperojil, Spain F7 20
Torres, Braz. D13 92
Torres, Îles, is., Vanuatu i16 79d
Torres Islands see Torres, Îles, is., Vanuatu i16 79d
Torres Strait, strt., Oc. b3 79a
Torres Vedras, Port. E1 20
Torrevella, Spain G10 20
Torrevieja see Torrevella, Spain G10 20
Torridon, Scot., U.K. D7 12
Torrijos, Spain D6 20
Torrington, Ct., U.S. C12 114
Torrington, Wy., U.S. E8 126
Torröjen, l., Swe. E5 8
Torsa (Amo), stm., Asia E12 54
Torsby, Swe. F5 8
Tórshavn (Thorshavn), Far. Is. n34 8b
Tortola, i., Br. Vir. Is. e8 104b
Tórtolas, Cerro de las (Las Tórtolas, Cerro), mtn., S.A. D2 92
Tortona, Italy F5 22
Tortorici, Italy F8 24
Tortosa, Spain D11 20
Tortosa, Cap de, c., Spain D11 20
Tortue, Île de la, i., Haiti B11 102
Tortuga Island see Tortue, Île de la, i., Haiti B11 102
Tortuguero, Laguna, b., P.R. B2 104a
Toruń, Pol. C14 16
Toruń, state, Pol. C15 16
Torup, Swe. H5 8
Toržok, Russia C17 10
Torzym, Pol. D11 16
Tosa, Japan F6 40
Tosa-shimizu, Japan G5 40
Tosa-wan, b., Japan F6 40
Tosca, S. Afr. D6 70
Toscana, state, Italy G8 22
Toses, Collada de, p., Spain B12 20
Tosno, Russia A13 10
Toson Hu, l., China D4 36
Tosontsengel, Mong. B4 36
Tostado, Arg. D7 92
Tõstamaa, Est. G10 8
Tosu, Japan F3 40
Totana, Spain G9 20
Toteng, Bots. B6 70
Totiyas, Som. D8 66
Tot'ma, Russia F20 8
Totness, Sur. B6 84
Totoya, i., Fiji q20 79e
Tottenham, Austl. I6 76
Tottenham, On., Can. D10 112
Tottori, Japan D7 40
Tottori, state, Japan D6 40
Touba, C. Iv. H3 64
Toubkal, Jebel, mtn., Mor. C3 64
Touchet, stm., Wa., U.S. D8 136
Touchwood Lake, l., Ab., Can. B19 138
Toudao, stm., China C7 38
Touggourt, Alg. C6 64
Touho, N. Cal. m15 79d
Toul, Fr. F14 14
Touliu, Tai. J9 42
Toulon, Fr. F11 18
Toulon-sur-Arroux, Fr. H13 14
Toulouse, Fr. F7 18
Toumodi, C. Iv. H3 64
Tounassine, Hamada, des., Alg. D3 64
Toungo, Nig. H7 64
Toungoo, Mya. C3 48
Touraine, hist. reg., Fr. G9 14
Tourcoing, Fr. D11 14
Touriñan, Cabo, c., Spain A1 20
Tournai, Bel. D12 14
Tournon, Fr. D10 18
Tournus, Fr. H13 14
Touros, Braz. C8 88
Tours, Fr. G9 14
Toussidé, Pic, vol., Chad C3 62
Touws, stm., S. Afr. H5 70
Toužim, Czech Rep. F9 16
Tovar, Ven. C6 86
Tovarkovskij, Russia G21 10
Tovuz, Azer. A6 56
Tow, Tx., U.S. D9 130
Towada, Japan D14 38
Towanda, Ks., U.S. D12 128
Towanda, Pa., U.S. C9 114
Tower, Mn., U.S. D6 118
Tower City, Pa., U.S. D9 114
Tower Hill, Austl. D5 76
Tower Hill, Il., U.S. E9 120
Towerhill Creek, stm., Austl. C5 76
Towla, Mount, mtn., Zimb. B9 70
Town and Country, Wa., U.S. C9 136
Town Hill, hill, Ber. k16 104e
Townsend, Mt., U.S. D15 136
Townshend Island, i., Austl. D8 76
Townsville, Austl. B6 76
Towson, Md., U.S. E9 114
Towuti, Danau, l., Indon. F7 44
Toyah, Tx., U.S. C4 130
Toyah Creek, stm., Tx., U.S. D4 130
Toyama, Japan C10 40
Toyama, state, Japan C10 40
Toyama-wan, b., Japan C10 40
Tōyo, Japan F6 40
Tōyō, Japan F7 40
Toyohashi, Japan E10 40
Toyokawa, Japan E10 40
Toyonaka, Japan E8 40
Toyooka, Japan D7 40
Toyosaka, Japan B12 40
Toyota, Japan D10 40
Toyoura, Japan E3 40
Tozeur, Tun. C6 64
Trabzon, Tur. A4 56
Tracadie, N.B., Can. C12 110
Tracy, Qc., Can. E3 110
Tracy, Ca., U.S. F4 134
Tracy City, Tn., U.S. B13 122
Tradewater, stm., Ky., U.S. G10 120
Traer, Ia., U.S. B5 120
Trafalgar, Cabo, c., Spain H4 20
Traíd, Spain D9 20
Tráighlí see Tralee, Ire. I3 12
Traiguén, Chile I1 92
Trail, B.C., Can. G13 138
Traill Ø, i., Grnld. C21 141
Traipu, Braz. E7 88
Traíra (Taraira), stm., S.A. H7 86
Trairi, Braz. B6 88
Trakai, Lith. F7 10
Tralee, Ire. I3 12
Trá Lí see Tralee, Ire. I3 12
Trammel, Va., U.S. G3 114
Tramperos Creek (Punta de Agua Creek), stm., U.S. E5 128
Tramping Lake, l., Sk., Can. B5 124
Tra My, Viet. E9 48
Trăn, Blg. G9 26
Tranås, Swe. G6 8
Trancas, Arg. C5 92
Tranco de Beas, Embalse de, res., Spain F8 20
Trang, Thai. I4 48
Trangan, Pulau, i., Indon. G9 44
Trang Dinh, Viet. A8 48
Trani, Italy C10 24
Tran Ninh see Xiangkhoang, Plateau de, plat., Laos C6 48
Tranqueras, Ur. E9 92
Transantarctic Mountains, mts., Ant. D30 81
Transkei, hist. reg., S. Afr. G8 70
Transylvania, hist. reg., Rom. C10 26
Transylvanian Alps see Carpații Meridionali, mts., Rom. D11 26
Trapani, Italy F6 24
Trapper Peak, mtn., Mt., U.S. E12 136
Traralgon, Austl. L6 76
Trârza, reg., Maur. F1 64
Trasimeno, Lago, l., Italy G9 22
Trás-os-Montes, hist. reg., Port. C3 20
Trat, Thai. F6 48
Traun, Aus. B11 22
Traun, stm., Aus. B11 22
Traunstein, Ger. I8 16
Travellers Lake, l., Austl. I4 76
Traverse, Lake, res., U.S. F2 118
Traverse City, Mi., U.S. D4 112
Tra Vinh, Viet. H8 48
Travis, Lake, l., Tx., U.S. D10 130
Travnik, Bos. E4 26
Trayning, Austl. F3 74
Trbovlje, Slvn. D12 22
Třebíč, Czech Rep. G11 16
Trebinje, Bos. G5 26
Trebišov, Slov. H17 16
Treblinka, Pol. D18 16
Trece Martires, Phil. C3 52
Tregosse Islets, is., Austl. A8 76
Tregubovo, Russia B14 10
Treinta y Tres, Ur. F10 92
Trélazé, Fr. G8 14
Trelew, Arg. H3 90
Trelleborg, Swe. I5 8
Tremadog Bay, b., Wales, U.K. I8 12
Tremblant, Mont, mtn., Qc., Can. D2 110
Trembleur Lake, l., B.C., Can. B5 138
Tremiti, Isole, is., Italy H12 22
Tremont, Il., U.S. K9 118
Tremonton, Ut., U.S. B4 132
Tremp, Spain B11 20
Trempealeau, Wi., U.S. G7 118
Trenche, stm., Qc., Can. B4 110
Trenčín, Slov. H14 16
Trenel, Arg. G5 92
Trêng, Camb. F6 48
Trenggalek, Indon. H7 50
Trenque Lauquen, Arg. G6 92
Trent, stm., On., Can. D12 112
Trent, stm., Eng., U.K. H12 12
Trente et Un Milles, Lac des, l., Qc., Can. B13 112
Trentino-Alto Adige, state, Italy D8 22
Trento (Trent), Italy D7 22
Trenton, N.S., Can. E14 110
Trenton, On., Can. D12 112
Trenton, Fl., U.S. G3 116
Trenton, Ga., U.S. C13 122
Trenton, Mo., U.S. D4 120
Trenton, Ne., U.S. A8 128
Trenton, N.J., U.S. D11 114
Trenton, N.C., U.S. A8 116
Trentwood, Wa., U.S. C9 136
Trepassey, Nf., Can. j23 107a
Tres Algarrobos, Arg. G6 92
Tres Arroyos, Arg. I7 92
Três Corações, Braz. K3 88
Três Coroas, Braz. D12 92
Três de Maio, Braz. C10 92
Tres Esquinas, Col. G4 86
Três Lagoas, Braz. D6 90
Tres Lagos, Arg. I2 90
Tres Lomas, Arg. H6 92
Três Marias, Braz. J3 88
Tres Marías, Islas, is., Mex. E5 100
Três Marias, Represa de, res., Braz. J3 88
Tres Montes, Península, pen., Chile I1 90
Tres Montosas, mtn., N.M., U.S. I9 132
Tres Palos, Laguna, l., Mex. G9 100
Três Passos, Braz. C11 92
Tres Picos, Cerro, mtn., Arg. I6 92
Três Pontas, Braz. K3 88
Tres Puntas, Cabo, c., Arg. I3 90
Três Rios, Braz. L4 88
Tres Vírgenes, Volcán de las, vol., Mex. B2 100
Tres Zapotes, hist., Mex. F11 100
Tretten, Nor. F4 8
Treuchtlingen, Ger. H6 16
Treuenbrietzen, Ger. D8 16
Treviglio, Italy E6 22
Treviso, Italy E9 22
Trevorton, Pa., U.S. D9 114
Trgovište, Yugo. G9 26
Triabunna, Austl. o13 77a
Triberg, Ger. H4 16
Tribugá, Ensenada de, b., Col. E3 86
Tribune, Sk., Can. E10 124
Tribune, Ks., U.S. C7 128
Tricarico, Italy D10 24
Tricase, Italy E12 24
Trichonída, Límni, l., Grc. E4 28
Trichūr, India F3 53
Tri County Supply Canal, can., Ne., U.S. G12 126
Trida, Austl. I5 76
Trident Peak, mtn., Nv., U.S. B7 134
Trier, Ger. G2 16
Trieste (Trst), Italy E10 22
Trieste, Gulf of, b., Eur. E10 22
Triglav, mtn., Slvn. D10 22
Triglavski narodni park, p.o.i., Slvn. D10 22
Trigueros, Spain G4 20
Tríkala, Grc. D4 28
Trikora, Puncak, mtn., Indon. F10 44
Trilby, Fl., U.S. H3 116
Triman, Pak. D2 54
Trincheras, Mex. F7 98
Trincomalee, Sri L. G5 53
Trindade, Braz. I1 88
Trindade, i., Braz. H12 82
Třinec, Czech Rep. G14 16
Trinidad, Bol. B3 90
Trinidad, Col. E6 86
Trinidad, Cuba B8 102
Trinidad, Co., U.S. D4 128
Trinidad, Tx., U.S. E2 122
Trinidad, Ur. F9 92
Trinidad, i., Trin. s13 105f
Trinidad, Isla, i., Arg. I7 92
Trinidad and Tobago, ctry., N.A. s13 105f
Trinity, Tx., U.S. G3 122
Trinity, stm., Ca., U.S. C2 134
Trinity, stm., Tx., U.S. D13 130
Trinity, Elm Fork, stm., Tx., U.S. H11 128
Trinity, South Fork, stm., Ca., U.S. C2 134
Trinity, West Fork, stm., Tx., U.S. H11 128
Trinity Bay, b., Nf., Can. j23 107a
Trinity Bay, b., Tx., U.S. H4 122
Trinity Islands, is., Ak., U.S. E9 140
Trinity Peak, mtn., Nv., U.S. C7 134
Trinity Site, hist., N.M., U.S. H2 128
Trino, Italy E5 22
Tripa, stm., Indon. J3 48
Trípoli, Grc. F5 28
Tripoli see Țarābulus, Leb. D6 58
Tripoli see Țarābulus, Libya A2 62
Tripoli, Ia., U.S. I6 118
Tripolis, hist., Tur. F12 28
Tripp, S.D., U.S. D15 126
Tripura, state, India G13 54
Tristan da Cunha Group, is., St. Hel. J4 60
Tristao, Îles, is., Gui. G2 64
Triste, Spain B10 20
Triste, Golfo, b., Ven. B7 86
Tri Ton, Viet. G7 48
Triumph, La., U.S. H9 122
Trivandrum, India G3 53
Trnava, Slov. H13 16
Trobriand Islands, is., Pap. N. Gui. b5 79a
Trogir, Cro. G13 22
Troia, Italy C9 24
Troick, Russia D10 32
Troickoe, Russia D15 32
Troickoe, Russia G16 34
Troicko-Pečorsk, Russia B9 32
Troina, Italy G8 24
Troisdorf, Ger. F2 16
Trois-Pistoles, Qc., Can. B7 110
Trois Pitons, Morne, vol., Dom. j6 105c
Trois-Rivières, Qc., Can. D4 110
Trois-Rivières, Guad. i5 105c
Trojan, Blg. G11 26
Trojanova Tabla, hist., Yugo. E9 26
Trollhättan, Swe. G5 8
Trombetas, stm., Braz. C6 84
Troms, state, Nor. B8 8
Tromsø, Nor. B8 8
Trona, Ca., U.S. H8 134
Tronador, Cerro, mtn., S.A. H2 90
Trondheim, Nor. E4 8
Trondheimsfjorden, b., Nor. E4 8
Troödos, Cyp. D3 58
Troodos Mountains, mts., Cyp. D3 58
Troon, Scot., U.K. F8 12
Trophy Mountain, vol., B.C., Can. E11 138
Tropic, Ut., U.S. F4 132
Tropojë, Alb. B14 24
Troškūnai, Lith. E7 10
Trosna, Russia H18 10
Trotuș, stm., Rom. C13 26
Troup, Tx., U.S. E3 122
Trout, La., U.S. F6 122
Trout, stm., N.T., Can. C6 106
Trout Creek, Mi., U.S. E9 118
Trout Creek Pass, p., Co., U.S. C3 128
Trout Lake, l., N.T., Can. C6 106
Trout Lake, l., On., Can. E12 106
Troutville, Va., U.S. G6 114
Trouville-sur-Mer, Fr. E9 14
Trowbridge, Eng., U.K. J10 12
Troy, Al., U.S. F13 122
Troy, Id., U.S. D10 136
Troy, Mo., U.S. F7 120
Troy, N.H., U.S. B13 114
Troy, N.Y., U.S. B12 114
Troy, N.C., U.S. A6 116
Troy, Oh., U.S. D1 114
Troy, Pa., U.S. C9 114
Troy, Tn., U.S. H8 120
Troy, Tx., U.S. C10 130
Troy see Truva, hist., Tur. D9 28
Troyes, Fr. F13 14
Troy Peak, mtn., Nv., U.S. E1 132
Trst see Trieste, Italy E10 22
Trstená, Slov. G15 16
Truax, Sk., Can. E8 124
Trubč'evsk, Russia H16 10
Truchas, N.M., U.S. E3 128
Truchas Peak, mtn., N.M., U.S. E3 128
Trucial States see United Arab Emirates, ctry., Asia E7 56
Truckee, Ca., U.S. D5 134
Truckee, stm., U.S. D6 134
Trud, Russia C16 10
Trujillo, Col. E3 86
Trujillo, Hond. E4 102
Trujillo, Peru E2 84
Trujillo, Spain E5 20
Trujillo, Ven. C6 86
Trujillo, state, Ven. C6 86
Trujillo Alto, P.R. B4 104a
Truk Islands see Chuuk, is., Micron. C6 72
Truman, Mn., U.S. H4 118
Trumann, Ar., U.S. B8 122
Trumansburg, N.Y., U.S. B9 114
Trumbull, Ct., U.S. C12 114
Trumbull, Mount, mtn., Az., U.S. G3 132
Trundle, Austl. I6 76
Trung Phan (Annam), hist. reg., Viet. D8 48
Truro, N.S., Can. E13 110
Truro, Eng., U.K. K7 12
Trusan, stm., Malay. A9 50
Truscott, Tx., U.S. H9 128
Trușeni, Mol. B15 26
Truth or Consequences, N.M., U.S. J9 132
Trutnov, Czech Rep. F11 16
Truva (Troy), hist., Tur. D9 28
Truxton Wash, stm., Az., U.S. H3 132
Truyère, stm., Fr. E8 18
Tryduby, Ukr. A17 26
Tryon, Ne., U.S. F12 126
Tryon, N.C., U.S. A3 116
Trzcianka, Pol. C12 16
Trzciel, Pol. D11 16
Trzebiatów, Pol. B11 16
Trzebinia, Pol. F15 16
Trzebnica, Pol. E13 16
Tsagaannuur, Mong. E15 32
Tsaidam Basin see Qaidam Pendi, bas., China D3 36
Tsala Apopka Lake, l., Fl., U.S. H3 116
Tsamkong see Zhanjiang, China K4 42
Ts'anghsien see Cangzhou, China B7 42
T'sangwu see Wuzhou, China J4 42
Tsaratanana, Madag. D8 68
Tsaratanana, mts., Madag. C8 68
Tsau, Bots. E3 68
Tsavo, Kenya E7 66
Tsaydaychuz Peak, mtn., B.C., Can. C4 138
Tsebrykove, Ukr. B17 26
Tses, Nmb. D4 70
Tsetserleg, Mong. B5 36
Tsévié, Togo H5 64
Tshabong, Bots. D6 70
Tshane, Bots. D5 70
Tshela, D.R.C. E2 66
Tshidilamolomo, S. Afr. D7 70
Tshikapa, D.R.C. F4 66
Tshofa, D.R.C. F5 66
Tshuapa, stm., D.R.C. E4 66
Tshumbe (Chiumbe), stm., Afr. B3 68
Tsiafajavona, vol., Madag. D8 68
Tsiigehtchic, N.T., Can. B4 106
Tsimlyansk Reservoir see Cimljanskoe vodohranilišče, res., Russia E6 32
Tsinan see Jinan, China C7 42
Tsineng, S. Afr. E6 70
Tsinghai see Qinghai, state, China D4 36
Tsingkiang see Qingjiang, China E8 42
Tsingtao see Qingdao, China C9 42
Tsingyuan see Baoding, China B6 42
Ts'in-hai see Qinghai, state, China D4 36
Tsining see Jining, China D7 42
Tsinling Shan see Qin Ling, mts., China E3 42
Tsintsabis, Nmb. D2 68
Tsiombe, Madag. F8 68
Tsipa see Cipa, stm., Russia F11 34
Tsiribihina, stm., Madag. D7 68
Tsiroanomandidy, Madag. D8 68
Tsitsihar see Qiqihar, China B9 36
Tsna see Cna, stm., Russia D6 32
Tsomo, stm., S. Afr. H8 70
Tsomog, Mong. B6 36
Tsu, Japan E9 40
Tsubame, Japan B11 40
Tsuchiura, Japan C13 40
Tsugaru-kaikyō, strt., Japan D14 38
Tsukumi, Japan F4 40
Tsukushi-sanchi, mts., Japan F3 40
Tsumeb, Nmb. D2 68
Tsumkwe, Nmb. D3 68
Tsuni see Zunyi, China H2 42
Tsuruga, Japan D9 40
Tsurugi-san, mtn., Japan F7 40
Tsuruoka, Japan A12 40
Tsushima, is., Japan E2 40
Tsushima-kaikyō (Eastern Channel), strt., Japan F2 40
Tsuyama, Japan D7 40
Tswaane, Bots. C6 70
Ttruchchendūr, India G4 53
Tua, D.R.C. E3 66
Tua, stm., Port. C3 20
Tua, Tanjung, c., Indon. F4 50
Tua Chua, Viet. B6 48
Tual, Indon. G9 44
Tuam, Ire. H4 12
Tuamotu, Îles, is., Fr. Poly. E12 72
Tuamotu Archipelago see Tuamotu, Îles, is., Fr. Poly. E12 72
Tuamotu Ridge, unds. K24 142
Tuanan, Indon. E9 50
Tuangku, Pulau, i., Indon. K3 48
Tuapse, Russia F5 32
Tuasivi, Cape, c., Samoa g11 79c
Tuba, Russia C18 32
Tuba, stm., Russia D16 32
Tubac, Az., U.S. L5 132
Tuban, Indon. G8 50
Tubarão, Braz. D13 92
Ṭūbās, W.B. F6 58
Tübingen, Ger. H4 16
Ṭubruq, Libya A4 62
Tubuai, i., Fr. Poly. F12 72
Tucacas, Ven. B7 86
Tucano, Braz. F6 88
Tucheng, China G2 42
Tuchów, Pol. G17 16
Tuckerman, Ar., U.S. B7 122
Tuckerton, N.J., U.S. E11 114
Tučkovo, Russia E19 10
Tucson, Az., U.S. K5 132
Tucumán, state, Arg. C5 92
Tucumcari, N.M., U.S. F5 128
Tucunuco, Arg. E3 92
Tucupido, Ven. C9 86
Tucupita, Ven. C11 86
Tucuruí, Braz. D8 84
Tucuruí, Represa de, res., Braz. D8 84
Tudela, Phil. F4 52
Tudela, Spain B9 20
Tudmur (Palmyra), Syria D9 58
Tufānganj, India E12 54
Tufi, Pap. N. Gui. b4 79a
Tugela, stm., S. Afr. F10 70
Tug Fork, stm., U.S. G3 114
Tuggerah Lake, b., Austl. I8 76
Tuguegarao City, Phil. B3 52
Tugur, Russia F16 34
Tuhai, stm., China C7 42
Tuhuangba, China F3 42
Tui, Spain B2 20
Tuibo, China C7 38
Tuira, stm., Pan. D3 86
Tujmazy, Russia D8 32
Tukangbesi, Kepulauan, is., Indon. G7 44
Tukituki, stm., N.Z. D7 80
Tukosméra, Mont, mtn., Vanuatu I17 79d
Tūkrah, Libya A4 62
Tuktoyaktuk, N.T., Can. B4 106
Tukums, Lat. D6 10
Tukuringra, hrebet, mts., Russia F14 34
Tukuyu, Tan. F6 66
Tula, Mex. D9 100
Tula, Russia F20 10
Tulach Mhór see Tullamore, Ire. H5 12
Tulaghi, Sol. Is. e8 79b
Tulancingo, Mex. E9 100
Tulangbawang, stm., Indon. F4 50
Tulare, Ca., U.S. G6 134
Tulare, S.D., U.S. C14 126
Tulare Lake Bed, reg., Ca., U.S. G6 134
Tulare Lake Canal, can., Ca., U.S. G6 134
Tularosa, N.M., U.S. H2 128
Tularosa Valley, bas., N.M., U.S. E9 98
Tulbagh, S. Afr. H4 70
Tulcán, Ec. G3 86
Tulcea, Rom. D15 26
Tulcea, state, Rom. D15 26
Tulelake, Ca., U.S. B4 134
Tule Lake, l., Ca., U.S. B4 134
Tulemalu Lake, l., Nu., Can. C11 106
Tule Valley, val., Ut., U.S. D3 132
Tuli, Zimb. B9 70
Tuliszków, Pol. D14 16
Tulita, N.T., Can. C5 106
Ṭūlkarm, W.B. F6 58
Tullahoma, Tn., U.S. B12 122
Tullamore, Ire. H5 12
Tulle, Fr. D7 18
Tullibigeal, Austl. I6 76
Tulln, Aus. B13 22
Tullos, La., U.S. F6 122
Tullus, Sudan E4 62
Tully, Austl. A5 76
Tulsa, Ok., U.S. H2 120
Tulsequah, B.C., Can. D4 106
Tul'skaja oblast', co., Russia G20 10
Tuluá, Col. E3 86
Tulum, Mex. B4 102
Tulum, hist., Mex. B4 102
Tulun, Russia D18 32
Tulungagung, Indon. H7 50
Tulungselapan, Indon. E4 50
Tuma, stm., Nic. F5 102
Tumacacori National Historical Park, p.o.i., Az., U.S. L5 132
Tumaco, Col. G2 86
Tumaco, Rada de, b., Col. G2 86
Tuman-gang (Tumen), stm., Asia C8 38
Tumanskij, Russia D24 34
Tumany, Russia D20 34
Tumbarumba, Austl. J6 76
Tumbes, Peru D1 84
Tumbes, Punta, c., Chile H1 92
Tumbler Ridge, B.C., Can. A10 138
Tumen, China C8 38
Tumen (Tuman-gang), stm., Asia C8 38
Tumeremo, Ven. D11 86

I•60 Vaca-Vina

Name — Map Ref. — Page

Vacaria, stm., Braz. I4 88
Vacaville, Ca., U.S. E4 134
Vaccarès, Étang de, l., Fr. F10 18
Vache, Île à, i., Haiti C11 102
Vad, Russia I21 8
Vadakara see Badagara, India F2 53
Vădeni, Rom. D14 26
Vadnagar, India G4 54
Vado, N.M., U.S. K10 132
Vadodara (Baroda), India G4 54
Vado Ligure, Italy F5 22
Vadsø, Nor. A13 8
Vaduz, Liech. C6 22
Vaga, stm., Russia F20 8
Vågåmo, Nor. F3 8
Vágar, i., Far. Is. m34 8b
Vaghena Island, i., Sol. Is. d7 79b
Vah, stm., Russia B13 32
Váh, stm., Slov. H13 16
Vahsel, Cape, c., S. Geor. J9 90
Vaiden, Ms., U.S. D9 122
Vaigai, stm., India G4 53
Vaigat, strt., Grnld. C15 141
Vaijāpur, India B2 53
Vaikam, India G3 53
Väike-Maarja, Est. A9 10
Vail, Co., U.S. D10 132
Vail, Ia., U.S. B2 120
Vaimali, Vanuatu k17 79d
Vaippār, stm., India G4 53
Vaison-la-Romaine, Fr. E11 18
Vaitahu, Fr. Poly. s18 78g
Vākhān, hist. reg., Afg. B11 56
Valaam, Russia F14 8
Valadeces, Mex. H9 130
Valandovo, Mac. B5 28
Valašské Meziříčí, Czech Rep. G13 16
Valatie, N.Y., U.S. B12 114
Vâlcea, state, Rom. E11 26
Vălčedrăm, Blg. F10 26
Valcheta, Arg. H3 90
Valdagno, Italy E8 22
Valdai Hills see Valdajskaja vozvyšennost', hills, Russia C15 10
Valdaj, Russia E16 8
Valdaj, Russia B16 10
Valdajskaja vozvyšennost' (Valdai Hills), hills, Russia C15 10
Valdarno, val., Italy G8 22
Val-de-Cães, Braz. A1 88
Valdecañas, Embalse de, res., Spain E5 20
Valdemarsvik, Swe. G7 8
Valdepeñas, Spain F7 20
Valderaduey, stm., Spain C5 20
Valdés, Península, pen., Arg. H4 90
Val-des-Bois, Qc., Can. C14 112
Valdez, Ak., U.S. D10 140
Valdivia, Chile G2 90
Valdivia, Col. D4 86
Valdobbiadene, Italy E8 22
Val-d'Oise, state, Fr. E10 14
Val-d'Or, Qc., Can. F15 106
Valdosta, Ga., U.S. F2 116
Valdoviño see Aviño, Spain A2 20
Vale, Or., U.S. G9 136
Valemount, B.C., Can. D11 138
Valença, Braz. L4 88
Valença, Braz. G6 88
Valença, Port. B2 20
Valença do Piauí, Braz. D4 88
Valence, Fr. E10 18
Valencia, Phil. F5 52
València, Spain E10 20
Valencia, Ven. B7 86
València, state, Spain E10 20
València, co., Spain E10 20
València, Golf de, b., Spain E10 20
Valencia, Golfo de see València, Golf de, b., Spain E10 20
Valencia, Gulf of see València, Golf de, b., Spain E10 20
Valencia, Lago de, l., Ven. B8 86
Valencia de Alcántara, Spain E3 20
Valencia de Don Juan, Spain B5 20
Valencia Island, i., Ire. J2 12
Valenciennes, Fr. D12 14
Valente, Braz. F6 88
Valentin, Russia C11 38
Valentine, Ne., U.S. E12 126
Valentine, Tx., U.S. D3 130
Valenza, Italy F5 22
Valera, Ven. C6 86
Valga, Est. H12 8
Valiente, Península, pen., Pan. H7 102
Valili, mtn., Fiji p19 79e
Valjevo, Yugo. E6 26
Valkeakoski, Fin. F11 8
Valkenswaard, Neth. C14 14
Valkininkas, Lith. F7 10
Valladares, Mex. H7 130
Valladolid, Mex. B3 102
Valladolid, Spain C6 20
Valladolid, co., Spain C6 20
Vall de Uxó see La Vall d'Uixó, Spain E10 20
Valle, Lat. D7 10
Vallecillo, Mex. H7 130
Valle d'Aosta, state, Italy E4 22
Valle de Allende, Mex. H2 130
Valle de la Pascua, Ven. C8 86
Valle del Cauca, state, Col. F3 86
Valle del Rosario, Mex. G1 130
Valle de Olivos, Mex. B5 100
Valle de Santiago, Mex. E8 100
Valledupar, Col. B5 86
Vallée d'Aoste see Valle d'Aosta, state, Italy E4 22
Valle Edén, Ur. E9 92
Vallegrande, Bol. C4 90
Valle Hermoso, Mex. C10 100
Vallejo, Ca., U.S. E3 134
Vallenar, Chile D2 92
Valle Redondo, Mex. K9 134
Valletta, Malta I8 24
Valley, Al., U.S. E13 122
Valley, Ne., U.S. C1 120
Valley, Wa., U.S. B9 136
Valley, stm., Mb., Can. C13 124
Valley Bend, W.V., U.S. F6 114
Valley City, N.D., U.S. H16 124
Valley East, On., Can. B8 112
Valley Falls, Ks., U.S. E2 120
Valley Farms, Az., U.S. K5 132
Valley Head, Al., U.S. C13 122
Valley Mills, Tx., U.S. C10 130
Valley of the Kings, hist., Egypt B6 62
Valley Springs, S.D., U.S. H2 118
Valley Station, Ky., U.S. F12 120
Valleyview, Ab., Can. A13 138
Valley View, Tx., U.S. H11 128
Vallimanca, Arroyo, stm., Arg. H7 92
Vallorbe, Switz. D3 22
Valls, Spain C12 20
Valmeyer, Il., U.S. F7 120
Valmiera, Lat. C8 10
Valoria la Buena, Spain C6 20
Valožyn, Bela. F9 10
Vālpārai, India F3 53
Valparaíso, Chile F2 92
Valparaíso, Mex. D7 100
Valparaiso, Fl., U.S. G12 122
Valparaiso, In., U.S. G2 112
Valparaiso, Ne., U.S. F16 126
Valparaíso, state, Chile F2 92
Valréas, Fr. E10 18
Vals, stm., S. Afr. E8 70
Vals, Tanjung, c., Indon. G10 44
Valsbaai see False Bay, b., S. Afr. I4 70
Valtimo, Fin. E13 8
Valujki, Russia D5 32
Valverde del Camino, Spain G4 20
Valyncy, Bela. E11 10
Vamori Wash, stm., Az., U.S. L5 132
Van, Tur. B5 56
Van, Lake see Van Gölü, l., Tur. B5 56
Vanadzor, Arm. A5 56
Vanajavesi, l., Fin. F10 8
Van Alstyne, Tx., U.S. D2 122
Vananda, B.C., Can. G6 138
Vanavara, Russia B18 32
Van Bruyssel, Qc., Can. C4 110
Van Buren, Ar., U.S. B4 122
Van Buren, Me., U.S. C8 110
Vanceboro, Me., U.S. E9 110
Vanceburg, Ky., U.S. F2 114
Vancouver, B.C., Can. G7 138
Vancouver, Wa., U.S. E4 136
Vancouver Island, i., B.C., Can. G4 138
Vancouver Island Ranges, mts., B.C., Can. G5 138
Vandalia, Il., U.S. F8 120
Vandalia, Mo., U.S. E6 120
Vandalia, Oh., U.S. E1 114
Vandavāsi, India E4 53
Vanderbijlpark, S. Afr. E8 70
Vanderbilt, Tx., U.S. F11 130
Vanderhoof, B.C., Can. B6 138
Vanderkloof Dam, res., S. Afr. F7 70
Vanderlin Island, i., Austl. C7 74
Vandervoort, Ar., U.S. C4 122
Van Diemen Gulf, b., Austl. B6 74
Vandry, Qc., Can. C3 110
Vandžiogala, Lith. E6 10
Vanegas, Mex. D8 100
Vänern, l., Swe. G5 8
Vänersborg, Swe. G5 8
Vangaindrano, Madag. E8 68
Van Gölü, l., Tur. B5 56
Vangunu Island, i., Sol. Is. e8 79b
Van Horn, Tx., U.S. C3 130
Van Horne, Ia., U.S. B5 120
Vanier, On., Can. C14 112
Vanikolo, i., Sol. Is. E7 72
Vanimo, Pap. N. Gui. a3 79a
Vanino, Russia G17 34
Vānīvilāsa Sāgara, res., India E3 53
Vāniyambādi, India E4 53
Vankarem, Russia C25 34
Vankleek Hill, On., Can. E2 110
Van Lear, Ky., U.S. G3 114
Vanna, i., Nor. A8 8
Vännäs, Swe. E8 8
Vanndale, Ar., U.S. B8 122
Vannes, Fr. G6 14
Van Ninh, Viet. F9 48
Van Phong, Vung, b., Viet. F9 48
Van Phong Bay see Van Phong, Vung, b., Viet. F9 48
Van Reenen, S. Afr. F9 70
Van Rees, Pegunungan, mts., Indon. F10 44
Vanrhynsdorp, S. Afr. G4 70
Vansant, Va., U.S. G3 114
Vansittart Island, i., Nu., Can. B14 106
Vanskoe, Russia B19 10
Vanthali, India H3 54
Vanua Balavu, i., Fiji p20 79e
Vanua Lava, i., Vanuatu i16 79d
Vanua Levu, i., Fiji p19 79e
Vanuatu (New Hebrides), ctry., Oc. k16 79d
Van Wert, Oh., U.S. D1 114
Van Wyksdorp, S. Afr. H5 70
Van Zylsrus, S. Afr. E6 70
Vao, N. Cal. n16 79d
Var, state, Fr. F12 18
Var, stm., Fr. F13 18
Varada, stm., India D2 53
Varallo, Italy E5 22
Vārānasi (Benares), India F9 54
Varandej, Russia A9 32
Varangerfjorden, b., Nor. A14 8
Varangerhalvøya, pen., Nor. A13 8
Varano, Lago di, l., Italy I12 22
Varaždin, Cro. D13 22
Varazze, Italy F5 22
Varberg, Swe. H5 8
Vardak, state, Afg. A2 54
Vardar (Axiós), stm., Eur. B5 28
Varde, Den. I3 8
Vardø, Nor. A14 8
Varel, Ger. C4 16
Varela, Arg. G4 92
Varėna, Lith. F7 10
Varennes-sur-Allier, Fr. C9 18
Varese, Italy E5 22
Vârfurile, Rom. C9 26
Vargem, Riacho da, stm., Braz. E6 88
Vargem Grande, Braz. B3 88
Varginha, Braz. K3 88
Varkallai, India G3 53
Varkaus, Fin. E12 8
Värmeln, l., Swe. G5 8
Värmland, state, Swe. G5 8
Varna, Blg. F14 26
Varna, Russia D10 32
Varna, state, Blg. F14 26
Värnamo, Swe. H6 8
Varniai, Lith. E5 10
Varnjany, Bela. F9 10
Varnsdorf, Czech Rep. F10 16
Varnville, S.C., U.S. D4 116
Várpalota, Hung. B5 26
Värska, Est. C10 10
Varvarin, Yugo. F8 26
Várzea, stm., Braz. C11 92
Várzea Alegre, Braz. D6 88
Várzea da Palma, Braz. I3 88
Várzea Grande, Braz. G6 84
Varzino, Russia B17 8
Vas, state, Hung. B3 26
Vasa see Vaasa, Fin. E9 8
Vasa see Vaasa, state, Fin. E10 8
Vasai, India E3 46
Vasalemma, Est. A7 10
Vasco, País see Euskal Herriko, state, Spain A8 20
Vashkivtsi, Ukr. A12 26
Vashkivtsi, Ukr. A14 26
Vashon Island, i., Wa., U.S. C4 136
Vasilevičy, Bela. H12 10
Vasilevskij Moh, Russia C18 10
Vasiliká, Grc. C6 28
Vasjugan, stm., Russia C13 32
Vaška, stm., Russia D21 8
Vaskelovo, Russia F14 8
Vaslui, Rom. C14 26
Vaslui, state, Rom. C14 26
Vass, N.C., U.S. A6 116
Vassar, Mi., U.S. E6 112
Västerås, Swe. G7 8
Västerbotten, state, Swe. D8 8
Västernorrland, state, Swe. E7 8
Västervik, Swe. H7 8
Västmanland, state, Swe. G7 8
Vasto, Italy H11 22
Västra Götaland, state, Swe. G4 8
Vasvár, Hung. B3 26
Vatan, Fr. G10 14
Vatican see Vatican City, ctry., Eur. I9 22
Vatican City, ctry., Eur. I9 22
Vaticano, Capo, c., Italy F9 24
Vatnajökull, ice, Ice. k31 8a
Vatomandry, Madag. D8 68
Vatra Dornei, Rom. B12 26
Vättern, l., Swe. G6 8
Vatu-i-ra Channel, strt., Fiji p19 79e
Vatukoula, Fiji p18 79e
Vauclin, Montagne du, mtn., Mart. k7 105c
Vaucluse, state, Fr. F11 18
Vaucouleurs, Fr. F14 14
Vaughan, On., Can. E10 112
Vaughn, N.M., U.S. G3 128
Vaukavysk, Bela. G7 10
Vaupés, state, Col. G6 86
Vaupés (Uaupés), stm., S.A. G7 86
Vava'u, i., Tonga E9 72
Vavoua, C. Iv. H3 64
Vavuniya, Sri L. G5 53
Växjö, Swe. H6 8
Vaza-barris, stm., Braz. E6 88
Vazante, Braz. J2 88
Vazuza, stm., Russia E17 10
Vazuzskoe vodohranilišče, res., Russia E16 10
Veazie, Me., U.S. F8 110
Veblen, S.D., U.S. B15 126
Vecht (Vechte), stm., Eur. B15 14
Vechta, Ger. D4 16
Vechte (Vecht), stm., Eur. B15 14
Vecpiebalga, Lat. C8 10
Vecsés, Hung. B6 26
Veddige, Swe. H4 8
Vedea, stm., Rom. F12 26
Vedia, Arg. G7 92
Vednoe, Russia C19 10
Veedersburg, In., U.S. H2 112
Veendam, Neth. A15 14
Veenendaal, Neth. C14 14
Vega, i., Nor. D4 8
Vega Alta, P.R. B3 104a
Vega Baja, P.R. B3 104a
Vegreville, Ab., Can. C18 138
Veguita, N.M., U.S. I10 132
Veinticinco de Mayo, Arg. G7 92
Veiros, Braz. D7 84
Veisiejai, Lith. F6 10
Vejle, Den. I3 8
Vejle, state, Den. I3 8
Vela Luka, Cro. H13 22
Velas, Cabo, c., C.R. G4 102
Velázquez, Ur. G10 92
Velden, Ger. H8 16
Veleka, stm. G14 26
Veleuščina, Bela. F11 10
Vélez, Col. D5 86
Vélez-Málaga, Spain H6 20
Vel'gija, Russia B17 10
Velhas, stm., Braz. I3 88
Velikaja, stm., Russia C11 10
Velikaja, stm., Russia D23 34
Velikaja Kema, Russia B12 38
Velika Morava, stm., Yugo. E8 26
Velikie Luki, Russia D13 10
Velikij Ustjug, Russia F21 8
Veliki Vitorog, mtn., Bos. E4 26
Velikoe, Russia G17 8
Velikoe, ozero, l., Russia C19 10
Velikonda Hills, hills, India D4 53
Veliko Tărnovo, Blg. F12 26
Velikovisočnoe, Russia C25 8
Veli Lošinj, Cro. F11 22
Vélingara, Sen. G2 64
Veliž, Russia E14 10
Vel'ké Kapušany, Slov. H18 16
Velké Meziříčí, Czech Rep. G12 16
Vella Gulf, strt., Sol. Is. d7 79b
Vella Lavella, i., Sol. Is. d7 79b
Vellār, stm., India F4 53
Velletri, Italy I9 22
Vellore, India E4 53
Velma, Ok., U.S. G11 128
Vel'sk, Russia F20 8
Velten, Ger. D9 16
Velva, N.D., U.S. F13 124
Velyka Mykhailivka, Ukr. B16 26
Velykodolyns'ke, Ukr. C17 26
Velykoplos'ke, Ukr. C16 26
Velykyi Bychkiv, Ukr. B11 26
Velykyj Kuialnyk, stm., Ukr. B17 26
Venadillo, Col. E4 86
Venado Tuerto, Arg. F6 92
Venafro, Italy C8 24
Venâncio Aires, Braz. D11 92
Vence, Fr. F13 18
Venda, hist. reg., S. Afr. C10 70
Vendas Novas, Port. F2 20
Vendée, state, Fr. C4 18
Vendéen, Bocage, reg., Fr. C4 18
Vendôme, Fr. G10 14
Vendrell see El Vendrell, Spain C12 20
Veneta, Laguna, b., Italy E9 22
Venetie, Ak., U.S. C10 140
Veneto, state, Italy E8 22
Venev, Russia F21 10
Venézia (Venice), Italy E9 22
Venezuela, ctry., S.A. B4 84
Venezuela, Golfo de, b., S.A. A3 84
Venezuela, Gulf of see Venezuela, Golfo de, b., S.A. A3 84
Venezuelan Basin, unds. G7 144
Vengerovo, Russia C13 32
Vengurla, India D1 53
Veniaminof, Mount, vol., Ak., U.S. E8 140
Venice see Venézia, Italy E9 22
Venice, Fl., U.S. I3 116
Venice, La., U.S. H9 122
Venice, Gulf of, b., Eur. E9 22
Vénissieux, Fr. D10 18
Venkatagiri, India E4 53
Venlo, Neth. C15 14
Venosa, Italy D9 24
Venoste, Alpi (Ötztaler Alpen), mts., Eur. D7 22
Venray, Neth. C15 14
Venta, stm., Eur. C4 10
Ventanas, Ec. H2 86
Ventersdorp, S. Afr. E8 70
Venterstad, S. Afr. G7 70
Ventimiglia, Italy G4 22
Ventotene, Isola, i., Italy D7 24
Ventspils, Lat. C4 10
Ventuari, stm., Ven. E8 86
Ventura, Ca., U.S. I6 134
Venturia, N.D., U.S. B13 126
Venustiano Carranza, Mex. G12 100
Venustiano Carranza, Presa, res., Mex. B8 100
Vera, Arg. D7 92
Vera, Spain G9 20
Vera, Cape, c., Nu., Can. B8 141
Veracruz, Mex. F10 100
Veracruz, state, Mex. F10 100
Veranópolis, Braz. D12 92
Verāval, India H3 54
Verbania, Italy E5 22
Verbano see Maggiore, Lago, l., Eur. C14 18
Verbeek, Pegunungan, mts., Indon. E12 50
Verbilki, Russia D20 10
Vercelli, Italy E5 22
Vercors, reg., Fr. E11 18
Verde, stm., Braz. F6 84
Verde, stm., Braz. F4 88
Verde, stm., Braz. J1 88
Verde, stm., Braz. H1 88
Verde, stm., Braz. D4 90
Verde, stm., Mex. E7 100
Verde, stm., Az., U.S. J5 132
Verde, Cape, c., Bah. A10 102
Verde Grande, stm., Braz. H4 88
Verden, Ger. D5 16
Verden, Ok., U.S. F10 128
Verde Pequeno, stm., Braz. H4 88
Verdi, Nv., U.S. D5 134
Verdigre, Ne., U.S. E14 126
Verdigris, stm., U.S. E13 128
Verdon, stm., Fr. F12 18
Verdun, Qc., Can. E3 110
Verdun-sur-Garonne, Fr. F7 18
Verdun-sur-Meuse, Fr. E14 14
Vereeniging, S. Afr. E9 70
Veregin, Sk., Can. C11 124
Vereja, Russia E19 10
Vereščagino, Russia B15 32
Vergemont Creek, stm., Austl. D4 76
Vergennes, Vt., U.S. F3 110
Verhnedneprovskij, Russia E16 10
Verhneimbatsk, Russia B15 32
Verhnemulomskoe vodohranilišče, res., Russia B14 8
Verhneural'sk, Russia D9 32
Verhneviljujsk, Russia D13 34
Verhnij Baskunčak, Russia E7 32
Verhnij Most, Russia C11 10
Verhnij Ufalej, Russia C10 32
Verhnjaja Amga, Russia E14 34
Verhnjaja Angara, stm., Russia E11 34
Verhnjaja Inta, Russia A10 32
Verhnjaja Salda, Russia C10 32
Verhnjaja Tajmyra, stm., Russia B8 34
Verhnjaja Tojma, Russia E21 8
Verhojansk, Russia C15 34
Verhojanskij hrebet (Verkhoyansk Mountains), mts., Russia C14 34
Verhopuja, Russia F19 8
Verhove, Russia H20 10
Verigin see Veregin, Sk., Can. C11 124
Verín, Spain C3 20
Veríssimo, Braz. J1 88
Verkhovyna, Ukr. A11 26
Verkhoyansk Mountains see Verhojanskij hrebet, mts., Russia C14 34
Vermelho, stm., Braz. E2 88
Vermilion, Oh., U.S. C3 114
Vermilion, stm., Ab., Can. C19 138
Vermilion, stm., On., Can. B8 112
Vermilion, stm., Mn., U.S. C6 118
Vermilion Bay, b., La., U.S. H6 122
Vermilion Lake, l., On., Can. A6 118
Vermilion Lake, l., Mn., U.S. D5 118
Vermilion Pass, p., Can. E14 138
Vermillion, S.D., U.S. E16 126
Vermillion, stm., S.D., U.S. E15 126
Vermillion, East Fork, stm., S.D., U.S. D15 126
Vermillon, stm., Qc., Can. C3 110
Vermont, Il., U.S. D7 120
Vermont, state, U.S. F4 110
Vernal, Ut., U.S. C7 132
Verndale, Mn., U.S. E3 118
Verneuil, Fr. F9 14
Vernon, B.C., Can. F11 138
Vernon, Fr. E10 14
Vernon, Al., U.S. D10 122
Vernon, Ct., U.S. C13 114
Vernon, In., U.S. F12 120
Vernon, Tx., U.S. G9 128
Vernon, Ut., U.S. C4 132
Vernonia, Or., U.S. E3 136
Vernon Lake, res., La., U.S. F5 122
Vernon River, P.E., Can. D13 110
Vero Beach, Fl., U.S. I5 116
Véroia, Grc. C5 28
Verona, On., Can. D13 112
Verona, Italy E8 22
Verona, Ms., U.S. C10 122
Verónica, Arg. G9 92
Versailles, Fr. F11 14
Versailles, Il., U.S. E7 120
Versailles, Ky., U.S. F13 120
Versailles, Mo., U.S. F5 120
Versailles, Oh., U.S. D1 114
Veršino-Darasunskij, Russia F12 34
Veršino-Šahtaminskij, Russia F12 34
Vertedero, P.R. B3 104a
Vertientes, Cuba B8 102
Verulam, S. Afr. F10 70
Verviers, Bel. D14 14
Verwoerd Reservoir see Gariep Dam, res., S. Afr. G7 70
Vescovato, Fr. G15 18
Veselí nad Lužnicí, Czech Rep. G10 16
Vesëlyj Jar, Russia C11 38
Vesole, Monte, mtn., Italy D9 24
Vesoul, Fr. G15 14
Vespasiano, Braz. J4 88
Vesta, C.R. H6 102
Vest-Agder, state, Nor. G2 8
Vestavia Hills, Al., U.S. D12 122
Vesterålen, is., Nor. B6 8
Vestfjorden, b., Nor. C5 8
Vestfold, state, Nor. G4 8
Vestgrønland (Kitaa), state, Grnld. D16 141
Vestmannaeyjar, Ice. I29 8a
Vestsjælland, state, Den. I4 8
Vestvågøya, i., Nor. B5 8
Vesuvio (Vesuvius), vol., Italy D8 24
Vesuvius see Vesuvio, vol., Italy D8 24
Veszprém, Hung. B4 26
Veszprém, state, Hung. B4 26
Vésztő, Hung. C8 26
Vet, stm., S. Afr. F8 70
Vetapālem, India D5 53
Vetju, Russia E24 8
Vetlanda, Swe. H6 8
Vetluga, Russia H21 8
Vetluga, stm., Russia C7 32
Vetlužskij, Russia G21 8
Vetlužskij, Russia H21 8
Vetrișoaia, Rom. C15 26
Vetschau, Ger. E9 16
Veurne, Bel. C11 14
Vevey, Switz. D3 22
Veynes, Fr. E11 18
Vézère, stm., Fr. D7 18
Viacha, Bol. C3 90
Viadana, Italy F7 22
Viale, Arg. E8 92
Viamão, Braz. E12 92
Viamonte, Arg. F6 92
Vian, Ok., U.S. B4 122
Viana, Braz. B3 88
Viana do Bolo, Spain B3 20
Viana do Castelo, Port. C1 20
Viana do Castelo, state, Port. C2 20
Viangchan (Vientiane), Laos D6 48
Viareggio, Italy G7 22
Vibank, Sk., Can. D10 124
Viborg, Den. H3 8
Viborg, S.D., U.S. D15 126
Viborg, state, Den. H3 8
Vibo Valentia, Italy F10 24
Vic, Spain C13 20
Vícam, Mex. B3 100
Vicebsk, Bela. E13 10
Vicebsk, state, Bela. E11 10
Vicente Guerrero, Mex. D6 100
Vicente Guerrero, Presa, res., Mex. D9 100
Vicenza, Italy E8 22
Viceroy, Sk., Can. E8 124
Vich see Vic, Spain C13 20
Vichada, state, Col. E7 86
Vichada, stm., Col. E7 86
Vichadero, Ur. E10 92
Vichra, stm., Eur. F14 10
Vichuquén, Chile G1 92
Vichy, Fr. C9 18
Vici, Ok., U.S. E9 128
Vicksburg, Ms., U.S. E8 122
Viçosa, Braz. K4 88
Viçosa do Ceará, Braz. B5 88
Vic-sur-Cère, Fr. E8 18
Victor, Id., U.S. G15 136
Victor, Ia., U.S. C5 120
Victor, Mt., U.S. D12 136
Victor Harbor, Austl. J2 76
Victoria, Arg. F7 92
Victoria, B.C., Can. H7 138
Victoria, P.E., Can. D13 110
Victoria, Chile I1 92
Victoria see Labuan, Malay. A9 50
Victoria see Rabat, Malta H8 24
Victoria, Sey. j13 69b
Victoria, Ks., U.S. C9 128
Victoria, Tx., U.S. F11 130
Victoria, Va., U.S. G7 114
Victoria, state, Austl. K4 76
Victoria, stm., Austl. C6 74
Victoria, Chutes see Victoria Falls, wtfl, Afr. D4 68
Victoria, Lake, l., Afr. E6 66
Victoria, Lake, l., Austl. I3 76
Victoria, Mount, mtn., Mya. B1 48
Victoria, Mount, mtn., Pap. N. Gui. b4 79a
Victoria Falls, wtfl, Afr. D4 68
Victoria Fjord, b., Grnld. A16 141
Victoria Harbour, On., Can. D10 112
Victoria Island, i., Can. A8 106
Victoria Land, reg., Ant. C20 81
Victoria Nile, stm., Afr. D6 66
Victoria Peak, mtn., Belize D3 102
Victoria Peak, mtn., B.C., Can. F4 138
Victoria River Downs, Austl. C6 74
Victorias, Phil. E4 52
Victoria Strait, strt., Nu., Can. B10 106
Victoriaville, Qc., Can. D4 110
Victoria West, S. Afr. G6 70
Victorica, Arg. H5 92
Victorino, Ven. F8 86
Victorville, Ca., U.S. I8 134
Vičuga, Russia H19 8
Vicuña, Chile E2 92
Vicuña Mackenna, Arg. F5 92
Vidalia, Ga., U.S. D3 116
Vidalia, La., U.S. F7 122
Vidal Ramos, Braz. C13 92
Videira, Braz. C12 92
Vidigueira, Port. F3 20
Vidin, Blg. E9 26
Vidisha, India G6 54
Vidor, Tx., U.S. G4 122
Viđoy, i., Far. Is. m34 8b
Vidra, Rom. E13 26
Vidsel, Swe. D9 8
Vidzeme, hist. reg., Lat. C8 10
Viechtach, Ger. G8 16
Viedma, Arg. H4 90
Viedma, Lago, l., Arg. I2 90
Vieille Case, Dom. i6 105c
Viejo, Cerro, mtn., Peru D2 84
Viella, Spain B11 20
Vienna see Wien, Aus. B13 22
Vienna, Ga., U.S. D2 116
Vienna, Il., U.S. G9 120
Vienna, Mo., U.S. F5 120
Vienna, W.V., U.S. E4 114
Vienna see Wien, state, Aus. B13 22
Vienna Woods see Wienerwald, mts., Aus. B13 22
Vienne, Fr. D10 18
Vienne, state, Fr. C6 18
Vienne, stm., Fr. C6 18
Vientiane see Viangchan, Laos D6 48
Vieques, P.R. B5 104a
Vieques, Aeropuerto, P.R. B5 104a
Vieques, Isla de, i., P.R. B5 104a
Vieremä, Fin. E12 8
Vierwaldstätter See (Lucerne, Lake of), l., Switz. D5 22
Vierzon, Fr. G11 14
Viesca, Mex. C7 100
Vieste, Italy I13 22
Vietnam, ctry., Asia E9 48
Viet Tri, Viet. B7 48
Vieux-Fort, Qc., Can. i22 107a
Vieux Fort, St. Luc. m7 105c
Vieux-Fort, Pointe du, c., Guad. i5 105c
Vieux-Habitants, Guad. h5 105c
Vievis, Lith. F7 10
Vigala, Est. B7 10
Vigan, Phil. B3 52
Vigevano, Italy E5 22
Vigie Airport, St. Luc. l6 105c
Vignola, Italy F7 22
Vigo, Spain B2 20
Vigo, Ría de, est., Spain B1 20
Vihāri, Pak. D4 54
Vihorevka, Russia C18 32
Vihowa, Pak. C3 54
Vihren, mtn., Blg. H10 26
Viinijärvi, Fin. E13 8
Viivikonna, Est. A10 10
Vijāpur, India G4 54
Vijayawāda, India C5 53
Vikārābād, India C3 53
Viking, Ab., Can. C19 138
Vikna, Nor. D4 8
Vikna, i., Nor. D4 8
Vikramasingapuram, India G3 53
Vikulovo, Russia C12 32
Vila da Ribeira Brava, C.V. k10 65a
Vila de Sena, Moz. D5 68
Vila do Bispo, Port. G1 20
Vila do Conde, Port. C2 20
Vila Fontes, Moz. D6 68
Vilafranca del Panadés see Vilafranca del Penedès, Spain C12 20
Vilafranca del Penedès, Spain C12 20
Vila Franca de Xira, Port. F2 20
Vila Gamito, Moz. C5 68
Vilagarcía de Arousa, Spain B1 20
Vilaine, stm., Fr. G7 14
Vilaka, Lat. C10 10
Vilalba, Spain A3 20
Vilanandro, Tanjona, c., Madag. D7 68
Vilāni, Lat. D9 10
Vilankulo, Moz. B12 70
Vila Nova de Famalicão, Port. C2 20
Vila Nova de Gaia, Port. C2 20
Vilanova i la Geltrú, Spain C12 20
Vila Real, Port. C3 20
Vila-Real, Spain E10 20
Vila Real, state, Port. C3 20
Vila Velha, Braz. K5 88
Vila Verde, Port. C2 20
Vilcabamba, Cordillera de, mts., Peru F3 84
Vilejka, Bela. F9 10
Vilelas, Arg. C6 92
Vilhelmina, Swe. D7 8
Vilhena, Braz. F5 84
Vilija (Neris), stm., Eur. F6 10
Viljandi, Est. G11 8
Viljuj, stm., Russia D13 34
Viljujsk, Russia D13 34
Viljujskoe vodohranilišče, res., Russia B20 32
Vilkaviškis, Lith. F6 10
Vil'kickogo, ostrov, i., Russia A19 34
Vil'kickogo, proliv, strt., Russia A9 34
Vilkija, Lith. E6 10
Villa Abecia, Bol. D3 90
Villa Ana, Arg. D8 92
Villa Ángela, Arg. C7 92
Villa Atamisqui, Arg. D6 92
Villa Bella, Bol. B3 90
Villa Berthet, Arg. C7 92
Villablino, Spain B4 20
Villa Bruzual, Ven. C7 86
Villa Cañás, Arg. G7 92
Villacañas, Spain E7 20
Villa Carlos Paz, Arg. E5 92
Villacarrillo, Spain F7 20
Villacastín, Spain D6 20
Villach, Aus. D10 22
Villacidro, Italy E2 24
Villa Clara, Arg. E8 92
Villa Concepción del Tío, Arg. E6 92
Villa Constitución, Arg. F7 92
Villa de Arista, Mex. D8 100
Villa de Cos, Mex. D7 100
Villa de Cura, Ven. B8 86
Villa del Carmen, Arg. F5 92
Villa del Río, Spain G6 20
Villa del Rosario, Arg. E8 92
Villa del Rosario, Arg. E6 92
Villa del Rosario, Ven. B5 86
Villa de Soto, Arg. E5 92
Villadiego, Spain B7 20
Villa Dolores, Arg. E5 92
Villa Flores, Mex. G12 100
Villa Florida, Para. C9 92
Villafranca de los Barros, Spain F4 20
Villafranca di Verona, Italy E7 22
Villagarcía de Arosa see Vilagarcía de Arousa, Spain B1 20
Village see The Village, Ok., U.S. F11 128
Villa General Roca, Arg. F4 92
Villa Gesell, Arg. H9 92
Villagrán, Mex. C9 100
Villa Grove, Il., U.S. E9 120
Villaguay, Arg. E8 92
Villa Guerrero, Mex. F9 100
Villa Hayes, Para. B9 92
Villahermosa, Mex. G12 100
Villa Hidalgo, Mex. H3 130
Villa Huidobro, Arg. G5 92
Villa Insurgentes, Mex. C3 100
Villa Iris, Arg. I6 92
Villajoyosa see La Vila Joiosa, Spain F10 20
Villa Juárez, Mex. B3 100
Villa Krause, Arg. E3 92
Villalba, P.R. B3 104a
Villalba see Vilalba, Spain A3 20
Villaldama, Mex. B8 100
Villalon, Phil. E5 52
Villalonga, Arg. G4 90
Villalpando, Spain C5 20
Villa Mainero, Mex. C9 100
Villa María, Arg. F6 92
Villamartín, Spain H5 20
Villa Mazán, Arg. D4 92
Villa Media Agua, Arg. E3 92
Villa Mercedes, Arg. F5 92
Villa Montes, Bol. D4 90
Villa Nueva, Arg. F6 92
Villanueva, Col. B5 86
Villanueva, N.M., U.S. F3 128
Villanueva de Córdoba, Spain F6 20
Villanueva de la Serena, Spain F5 20
Villanueva de la Sierra, Spain D4 20
Villanueva de los Infantes, Spain F8 20
Villanueva del Río y Minas, Spain G4 20
Villanueva y Geltrú see Vilanova i la Geltrú, Spain C12 20
Villa Ocampo, Arg. D8 92
Villa Ocampo, Mex. H2 130
Villa Oliva, Para. B8 92
Villa Pérez, P.R. B2 104a
Villapinzón, Col. E5 86
Villarcayo, Spain B7 20
Villa Regina, Arg. G3 90
Villa Reynolds, Arg. F5 92
Villa Rica, Ga., U.S. D14 122
Villarreal see Vila-Real, Spain E10 20
Villarrica, Para. B9 92
Villarrobledo, Spain E8 20
Villarrubia de los Ojos, Spain E7 20
Villas, N.J., U.S. E10 114
Villa San Giovanni, Italy F9 24
Villa Santa Rita de Catuna, Arg. E4 92
Villasayas, Spain C8 20
Villa Serrano, Bol. C4 90
Villasis, Phil. C3 52
Villa Unión, Arg. D3 92
Villa Unión, Arg. D6 92
Villa Unión, Mex. D5 100
Villa Valeria, Arg. G5 92
Villavicencio, Col. E5 86
Villaviciosa de Córdoba, Spain F5 20
Villazón, Bol. D3 90
Villefranche-de-Rouergue, Fr. E8 18
Villefranche-sur-Saône, Fr. C10 18
Villena, Spain F10 20
Villeneuve-sur-Lot, Fr. E6 18
Villeneuve-sur-Yonne, Fr. F12 14
Ville Platte, La., U.S. G6 122
Villers-Cotterêts, Fr. E12 14
Villerupt, Fr. E14 14
Villeta, Col. E4 86
Villeurbanne, Fr. D10 18
Villiers, S. Afr. E9 70
Villingen-Schwenningen, Ger. H4 16
Villisca, Ia., U.S. D3 120
Villmanstrand see Lappeenranta, Fin. F12 8
Vilnius, Lith. F8 10
Vilsbiburg, Ger. H8 16
Vil'shanka, Ukr. A17 26
Vilshofen, Ger. H9 16
Viluppuram, India E4 53
Vilvoorde, Bel. D13 14
Vilvorde see Vilvoorde, Bel. D13 14
Vimmerby, Swe. H6 8
Vimperk, Czech Rep. G9 16
Vina, Ca., U.S. D3 134
Vina, stm., Cam. C2 66
Viña del Mar, Chile F2 92
Vinalhaven, Me., U.S. F8 110
Vinalhaven Island, i., Me., U.S. F8 110
Vinaròs, Spain D11 20

Name   Map   Page
         Ref.